# NEW CTHULHU 2:
# MORE RECENT WEIRD

# NEW CTHULHU 2: MORE RECENT WEIRD

Edited by Paula Guran

PRIME BOOKS

NEW CTHULHU 2: MORE RECENT WEIRD

Copyright © 2015 by Paula Guran.

Cover art by Nikita Veprikov.
Cover design by Jason Gurley.

Prime Books
www.prime-books.com
Germantown, MD

For more information, contact Prime Books:
prime@prime-books.com

Print ISBN: 978-1-60701-450-8
Ebook ISBN: 978-1-60701-459-1

Printed in Canada

*In Memory of Michael Shea,*
*1946-2014.*
*Shine on.*

# • Contents •

# · INTRODUCTION 2.0 ·

Not even five years ago I wrote the introduction for *New Cthulhu: The Recent Weird*, an anthology that showcased some of the best "New Lovecraftian" short fiction of the first decade of the twenty-first century. Now we're back with a sequel of equally excellent "recent weird" published from 2010 through 2014. (Although this is only a sampling. My Year's Best Dark Fantasy and Horror series covering the same period, for just one example, reprints a dozen or so New Lovecraftian stories by some of the authors included here and others.)

I'll recap some of that earlier introduction here, but also provide some newer opinion toward the end. (The earlier introduction can be found at paulaguran.com/new-cthulhu-intro.)

It took close to seventy years for Howard Phillip Lovecraft's fiction to be deemed respectable. His influence on horror, fantasy, and science fiction may have been established decades ago, but his place in the literary canon had no conformtion until 2005 when The Library of America series recognized his significance with *H. P. Lovecraft: Tales*, edited by Peter Straub. And, even thus "canonized," his respectability is still being debated.

During his life Lovecraft did "not expect to become a serious competitor" of his "favorite weird authors." After his death in 1937 he was usually dismissed, outside of genre and often within, as nothing more than a pulp fictionist who wrote outdated florid prose.

Respectable or not, Lovecraft's fiction and the fictional universe he established have provided inspiration not only for writers, but for creators of film, television, music, graphic arts, comics, manga, gaming, and theatre as well. And it continues to do so. Even if you've never read a word of H. P. Lovecraft's fiction, you have been introduced to his imagination without realizing its origin.

Born in 1890, Howard Phillips Lovecraft was little known to the general public while alive and never saw a book of his work professionally published. Brilliant and eccentric, he was also decidedly odd.

His father, probably a victim of untreated syphilis, went mad before his son reached age three. The elder Lovecraft died in an insane asylum in 1898. (It is highly doubtful that HPL was aware of his father's disease.) Young Howard was raised by his mother; two of her sisters; and his maternal grandfather, a successful Providence, Rhode Island, businessman. His controlling mother smothered him with maternal affection while also inflecting devastating emotional cruelty.

Sickly (probably due more to psychological factors more than physical ailments) and precocious, Lovecraft read the *Arabian Nights* and *Grimm's Fairy Tales* at an early age, then developed an intense interest in ancient Greece and Rome. His grandfather often entertained him with tales in the gothic mode. HPL started writing around age six or seven.

Lovecraft started school in 1889, but attended erratically due to his supposed ill health. After his grandfather's death in 1904, the family—already financially challenged—was even less well off. Lovecraft and his mother moved to a far less comfortable domicile and the adolescent Howard no longer had access to his grandfather's extensive library. He attended a public high school, but a physical and mental breakdown kept him from graduating.

He became reclusive, rarely venturing out during the day. At night, he walked the streets of Providence, drinking in its atmosphere.

He read, studied astronomy, and, in his early twenties, began writing poetry, essays, short stories, and eventually longer works. He also began reading Jules Verne, H. G. Wells, and pulp magazines like *The Argosy*, *The Cavalier*, and *All-Story Magazine*.

Lovecraft became involved in amateur writing and publishing, a salvation of sorts. HPL himself wrote: "In 1914, when the kindly hand of amateurdom was first extended to me, I was as close to the state of vegetation as any animal well can be . . . "

His story, "The Alchemist" (written in 1908 when he was 18), was published in *United Amateur* in 1916. Other stories soon appeared in other amateur publications.

Lovecraft's mother suffered a nervous breakdown in 1919 and was admitted to the same hospital in which her husband had died. Her death, in 1921, was the result of a bungled gall bladder operation.

"Dagon" was published in the October 1923 issue of *Weird Tales*, which became a regular market for his stories. He also began what became his prolific letter-writing with a continuously broadening group of correspondents.

Shortly thereafter, Lovecraft met Sonia Haft Greene—a Russian Jew seven years his senior—at a writers convention. They married in 1924. As *The Encyclopedia of Fantasy*, edited by John Clute and John Grant, puts it, " . . . the marriage lasted only until 1926, breaking up largely because HPL disliked sex; the fact that she was Jewish and he was prone to anti-Semitic rants cannot have helped." After two years of married life in New York City (which he abhorred and where he became an even more intolerant racist) he returned to his beloved Providence.

In the next decade, he traveled widely around the eastern seaboard, wrote what is considered to be his finest fiction, and continued his immense— estimated at 100,000 letters—correspondence through which he often nurtured young writers.

Lovecraft's literary significance today can be at least partially credited to this network with other contemporary writers. Letter writing was the "social media" of his time, and he was a master of it. Although he seldom met those who became members of the "Lovecraft Circle" in person, he knew them well—just as, these days, we have friends we know only through email or Facebook.

H. P. Lovecraft was probably the first author to create what we would now term an open-source fictional universe that any writer could make use of. Other authors, with Lovecraft's blessing, began superficially referencing his dabblers in the arcane, mentioning his unhallowed imaginary New England towns and their strange citizens, writing of cosmic horror, alluding to his godlike ancient extraterrestrials with strange names, and citing his fictional forbidden books of the occult (primarily the *Necronomicon* of the mad Arab Abdul Alhazred): the Lovecraft Mythos—or, rather, anti-mythology—was born.

There were certainly "better" writers of science fiction and fantasy of roughly the same era—like Algernon Blackwood, Clark Ashton Smith, Fritz Leiber, and Olaf Stapledon—whose work may be influential, but is now mostly ignored by the general public. Lovecraft's survival, current popularity, and the subgenre of "Lovecraftian fiction" is due in great part to his willingness to share his creations. His concepts were interesting, attracted other writers, and ultimately other artists.

Lovecraft's universe was fluid: the "Great Old Ones" and other elements merely serving his theme of the irrelevance of humanity to the cosmic horrors that exist in the universe. As S. T. Joshi wrote: "Lovecraft's imaginary cosmogony was never a static system but rather a sort of aesthetic construct that remained ever adaptable to its creator's developing personality and altering interests . . . there was never a rigid system that might be posthumously appropriated . . . the essence of the mythos lies not in a pantheon of imaginary deities nor in a cobwebby collection of forgotten tomes, but rather in a certain convincing cosmic attitude."

Lovecraft never used the term "Cthulhu Mythos" himself. (HPL was known to refer to his "mythos" as the *Arkham Cycle*—named for the main fictional town in his world—or, flippantly, as *Yog-Sothothery*—after Yog-Sothoth, a cosmic entity of his invention made only of "congeries of iridescent globes.") The term "Cthulhu Mythos" was probably invented by August Derleth or Clark Ashton Smith after HPL's death in 1937. They and others also added their own flourishes and inventions to the mythology, sometimes muddling things with non-Lovecraftian concepts and attempts at categorization. Derleth misused Lovecraft's name to promote his own work, and tried to change HPL's universe into one that included hope and a struggle between good and evil. This accommodated Derleth's Christian world view, but was at odds with Lovecraft's depiction of a bleak, amoral universe. However, to his credit, Derleth—with Donald Wandrei—also founded Arkham House expressly to publish Lovecraft's work and to bring it to the attention of the public. Without it, Lovecraft may never have had a legacy.

Authors like Robert Bloch (now best known as the author of *Psycho*), Robert E. Howard (creator of Conan the Barbarian), and younger writers such as Henry Kuttner, Fritz Leiber, and Ramsey Campbell all romped within the Lovecraftian milieu and added elements to it. Later writers with no direct connection to HPL joined in as well.

Not all of Lovecraft's work falls within the boundaries we now identify as "Lovecraftian," but his best works were atmospheric tales that, to quote Stefan Dziemianowicz, "strove to express a horror rooted in humanity's limited understanding of the universe and humankind's arrogant overconfidence in its significance in the cosmic scheme."

Lovecraft felt such stories conveyed "the fundamental premise that common human laws and interests and emotions have no validity or significance in the cosmos-at-large."

HPL's fiction also differed fundamentally from earlier supernatural fiction. In his introduction to *At the Mountains of Madness: The Definitive Edition*, China Miéville points out: "Traditionally genre horror is concerned with the irruption of dreadful forces into a comforting status quo—one which the protagonist scrambles to preserve. By contrast, Lovecraft's horror is not one of intrusion but of realization. The world has always been implacably bleak; the horror lies in us acknowledging the fact."

We also must acknowledge how H. P. Lovecraft's personal beliefs tie in to his work. Lovecraft—as evidenced in his fiction, poetry, essays, and letters—was racist, xenophobic, and anti-Semitic. He may not have hated women (misogyny), but he does seem to have feared them (gynophobia). His abhorrence of sexuality and physicality went beyond the Puritanical. In fact, ol' Howard Phillip seemed to be afraid of a lot of things.

Although not a new discussion, HPL's racism has lately become a topic of discourse in the fantasy writing and publishing community. In 2011 Nnedi Okorafor realized her World Fantasy Award for Best Novel—a statuette of H. P. Lovecraft's unattractive head—honored a man who was deeply racist. As a Nigerian-American and the first black author to be recognized in the novel category, Okorafor was more than a little conflicted and posted about it on her blog.

She also quoted correspondance with China Miéville, another World Fantasy Award winner on the subject:

Yes, indeed, the depth and viciousness of Lovecraft's racism is known to me . . . It goes further, in my opinion, than "merely" being a racist—I follow Michel Houellebecq (in this and in no other arena!) [Note: Houellebecq is the author of *H. P. Lovecraft: Against the World, Against Life*, Believer Books, 2005] in thinking that Lovecraft's oeuvre, his work itself, is inspired by and deeply structured with race hatred. As Houellebecq said, it is racism itself that raises in Lovecraft a "poetic trance." He was a bilious anti-Semite (though one who married a Jew, because, if you please, he granted that she was "assimilated"), and if you read stories like "The Horror at Red

Hook," the bile you will see towards people of color, of all kinds (with particular sneering contempt for African-Americans unless they were suitably Polite and therefore were patricianly granted the soubriquet "Negro") and the mixed communities of New York and, above all . . . "miscegenation" are extended and toxic."

Surprisingly, some Lovecraft scholars and fans deny the author's racism or brush it aside as "typical" for a man of his time. Yes, Lovecraft lived an age when racism was more overt and racial segregation was the law, but Lovecraft's prejudice seems, at the very least, somewhat more pronounced than many of his contemporaries. More importantly, it is part of Lovecraft's fiction.

Miscegenation, racial impurity, ethnic xenophia, "mental, moral and physical degeneration" due to inbreeding, interbreeding with non-human creatures . . . these were all integral to the fiction Lovecraft produced. Yes, we must consider the context: Lovecraft lived during what was probably the nadir of race relations and height of white supremacy in the U.S. But whether these were prevalent views of his day is beside the point: H. P. Lovecraft *chose* to make them "horrors" in his fiction.

Just because we recognize H. P. Lovecraft's racism does not mean we must deny his influence or reject his work. We might even understand it better if we acknowledge it.

We can be cognizant of and discuss Lovecraft's prejudices, even condemn him for them. But many authors are doing a great deal more. They are taking inspiration from H. P. Lovecraft and using it to write stories that often intentionally subvert his bigotry.

S. T. Joshi, considering what is meant by a "Lovecraftian" story, wrote in the introduction to his anthology *Black Wings II: New Tales of Lovecraftian Horror*:

> What is now needed is a more searching, penetrating infusion of Lovecraftian elements that can work seamlessly with the author's own style and outlook. . . . it becomes vital for both writers and readers to understand the essence of the Lovecraftian universe, and the literary tools he used to convey his aesthetic and philosophical principles. . . . [Lovecraft] continually grappled with the central questions of philosophy and sought to suggest answers to them by means of horror fiction. What is our place in the cosmos? Does a god

or gods exist? What is the ultimate fate of the human species? These and other "big" questions are perennially addressed in Lovecraft's fiction, and in a manner that conveys his "cosmic" sensibility—a sensibility that keenly etches humankind's transience and fragility in a boundless universe that lacks a guiding purpose or direction. At the same time, Lovecraft's intense devotion to his native soil made him something of a regionalist who vivified the history and topography of Providence, Rhode Island, and all of New England, establishing a foundation of unassailable reality from which his cosmic speculations could take wing.

Just as Lovecraft loved New England and used it in his fiction, he hated and feared people who were not of his own race and that attitude was also part of his work.

Although subversion of Lovecraft's beliefs is not a theme of this anthology, it contains short stories, novelettes, and novellas that—for example—consider the fictional containment of the citizens of Innsmouth in light of Guantanamo Bay or the Japanese-American internment camps of World War Two, recognize Lovecraft himself as a killer of dreams, feature gay couples confronting the unknown, see pollution as the source and sustenance of a dark goddess, present sexualized transformations, soar into spacefaring horror, dive into virtual dread . . .

And, of course, the proverbial *more*.

Paula Guran
2 January 2015
National Science Fiction Day

*[Note: The excerpts at the beginning of each story are simply my way of introducing them. (In the cases of Marc Laidlaw and John Shirley, they had already prefaced their stories with the quotations here.) The symbol found on the title page and at the end of each story is an "Elder Sign," a symbol Lovecraft drew in a 1930 letter to Clark Ashton Smith. Apparently, if you are protected by an Elder Sign, the Deep Ones cannot harm you.]*

*During the winter of 1927–28 officials of the Federal government made a strange and secret investigation of certain conditions in the ancient Massachusetts seaport of Innsmouth. . . . news-followers. . . wondered at the prodigious number of arrests, the abnormally large force of men used in making them, and the secrecy surrounding the disposal of the prisoners. No trials, or even definite charges, were reported; nor were any of the captives seen thereafter in the regular gaols of the nation. There were vague statements about disease and concentration camps, and later about dispersal in various naval and military prisons, but nothing positive ever developed.*

*"The Shadow Over Innsmouth" · H. P. Lovecraft (1936)*

## • THE SAME DEEP WATERS AS YOU •
### Brian Hodge

They were down to the last leg of the trip, miles of iron-gray ocean skimming three hundred feet below the helicopter, and she was regretting ever having said yes. The rocky coastline of northern Washington slid out from beneath them and there they were, suspended over a sea as forbidding as the day itself. If they crashed, the water would claim them for its own long before anyone could find them.

Kerry had never warmed to the sea—now less than ever.

Had saying no even been an option? *The Department of Homeland Security would like to enlist your help as a consultant*, was what the pitch boiled down to, and the pair who'd come to her door yesterday looked genetically incapable of processing the word no. They couldn't tell her what. They couldn't tell her where. They could only tell her to dress warm. Better be ready for rain, too.

The sole scenario Kerry could think of was that someone wanted her insights into a more intuitive way to train dogs, maybe. Or something a little more out there, something to do with birds, dolphins, apes, horses . . . a plan that some questionable genius had devised to exploit some animal ability that they wanted to know how to tap. She'd been less compelled by the appeal to patriotism than simply wanting to make whatever they were doing go as well as possible for the animals.

But this? No one could ever have imagined this.

The island began to waver into view through the film of rain that streaked and jittered along the window, a triangular patch of uninviting rocks and evergreens and secrecy. They were down there.

Since before her parents were born, they'd always been down there.

It had begun before dawn: an uncomfortably silent car ride from her ranch to the airport in Missoula, a flight across Montana and Washington, touchdown at Sea-Tac, and the helicopter the rest of the way. Just before this final leg of the journey was the point they took her phone from her and searched her bag. Straight off the plane and fresh on the tarmac, bypassing the terminal entirely, Kerry was turned over to a man who introduced himself as Colonel Daniel Escovedo and said he was in charge of the facility they were going to.

"You'll be dealing exclusively with me from now on," he told her. His brown scalp was speckled with rain. If his hair were any shorter, you wouldn't have been able to say he had hair at all. "Are you having fun yet?"

"Not really, no." So far, this had been like agreeing to her own kidnapping.

They were strapped in and back in the air in minutes, just the two of them in the passenger cabin, knee-to-knee in facing seats.

"There's been a lot of haggling about how much to tell you," Escovedo said as she watched the ground fall away again. "Anyone who gets involved with this, in any capacity, they're working on a need-to-know basis. If it's not relevant to the job they're doing, then they just don't know. Or what they think they know isn't necessarily the truth, but it's enough to satisfy them."

Kerry studied him as he spoke. He was older than she first thought, maybe in his mid-fifties, with a decade and a half on her, but he had the lightly lined face of someone who didn't smile much. He would still be a terror in his seventies. You could just tell.

"What ultimately got decided for you is full disclosure. Which is to say, you'll know as much as I do. You're not going to know what you're looking for, or whether or not it's relevant, if you've got no context for it. But here's the first thing you need to wrap your head around: What you're going to see, most of the last fifteen presidents haven't been aware of."

She felt a plunge in her stomach as distinct as if their altitude had plummeted. "How is that possible? If he's the commander-in-chief, doesn't he . . . ?"

Escovedo shook his head. "Need-to-know. There are security levels above the office of president. Politicians come and go. Career military and intelligence, we stick around."

"And I'm none of the above."

It was quickly getting frightening, this inner circle business. If she'd ever thought she would feel privileged, privy to something so hidden, now she knew better. There really were things you didn't want to know, because the privilege came with too much of a cost.

"Sometimes exceptions have to made," he said, then didn't even blink at the next part. "And I really wish there was a nicer way to tell you this, but if you divulge any of what you see, you'll want to think very hard about that first. Do that, and it's going to ruin your life. First, nobody's going to believe you anyway. All it will do is make you a laughingstock. Before long, you'll lose your TV show. You'll lose credibility in what a lot of people see as a fringe field anyway. Beyond that . . . do I even need to go beyond that?"

*Tabby*—that was her first thought. Only thought, really. They would try to see that Tabitha was taken from her. The custody fight three years ago had been bruising enough, Mason doing his about-face on what he'd once found so beguiling about her, now trying to use it as a weapon, to make her seem unfit, unstable. *She talks to animals, your honor. She thinks they talk back.*

"I'm just the messenger," Colonel Escovedo said. "Okay?"

She wished she were better at conversations like this. Conversations in general. Oh, to not be intimidated by this. Oh, to look him in the eye and leave no doubt that he'd have to do better than that to scare her. To have just the right words to make him feel smaller, like the bully he was.

"I'm assuming you've heard of Guantanamo Bay in Cuba? What it's for?"

"Yes," she said in a hush. Okay, this was the ultimate threat. Say the wrong thing and she'd disappear from Montana, or Los Angeles, and reappear there, in the prison where there was no timetable for getting out. Just her and 160-odd suspected terrorists.

His eyes crinkled, almost a smile. "Try not to look so horrified. The threat part, that ended before I mentioned Gitmo."

Had it been that obvious? How nice she could amuse him this fine, rainy day.

"Where we're going is an older version of Guantanamo Bay," Escovedo went on.

"It's the home of the most long-term enemy combatants ever held in U.S. custody."

"How long is long-term?"

"They've been detained since 1928."

She had to let that sink in. And was beyond guessing what she could bring to the table. Animals, that was her thing, it had always been her thing. Not P.O.W.s, least of all those whose capture dated back to the decade after the First World War.

"Are you sure you have the right person?" she asked.

"Kerry Larimer. Star of *The Animal Whisperer*, a modest but consistent hit on the Discovery Channel, currently shooting its fourth season. Which you got after gaining a reputation as a behavioral specialist for rich people's exotic pets. You *look* like her."

"Okay, then." Surrender. They knew who they wanted. "How many prisoners?" From that long ago, it was a wonder there were any left at all.

"Sixty-three."

Everything about this kept slithering out of her grasp. "They'd be over a hundred years old by now. What possible danger could they pose? How could anyone justify—"

The colonel raised a hand. "It sounds appalling, I agree. But what you need to understand from this point forward is that, regardless of how or when they were born, it's doubtful that they're still human."

He pulled an iPad from his valise and handed it over, and here, finally, was the tipping point when the world forever changed. One photo, that was all it took. There were more—she must've flipped through a dozen—but really, the first one had been enough. Of course it wasn't human. It was a travesty of human. All the others were just evolutionary insult upon injury.

"What you see there is what you get," he said. "Have you ever heard of a town in Massachusetts called Innsmouth?"

Kerry shook her head. "I don't think so."

"No reason you should've. It's a little pisshole seaport whose best days were already behind it by the time of the Civil War. In the winter of 1927-28, there was a series of raids there, jointly conducted by the FBI and U.S. Army, with naval support. Officially—remember, this was during Prohibition—it was to shut down bootlegging operations bringing whiskey down the coast from Canada. The truth . . . " He took back the iPad from her nerveless fingers. "Nothing explains the truth better than seeing it with your own eyes."

"You can't talk to them. That's what this is about, isn't it?" she said. "You can't communicate with them, and you think I can."

Escovedo smiled, and until now, she didn't think he had it in him. "It must be true about you, then. You're psychic after all."

"Is it that they can't talk, or won't?"

"That's never been satisfactorily determined," he said. "The ones who still looked more or less human when they were taken prisoner, they could, and did. But they didn't stay that way. Human, I mean. That's the way this mutation works." He tapped the iPad. "What you saw there is the result of decades of change. Most of them were brought in like that already. The rest eventually got there. And the changes go more than skin deep. Their throats are different now. On the inside. Maybe this keeps them from speaking in a way that you and I would find intelligible, or maybe it doesn't but they're really consistent about pretending it does, because they're all on the same page. They do communicate with each other, that's a given. They've been recorded extensively doing that, and the sounds have been analyzed to exhaustion, and the consensus is that these sounds have their own syntax. The same way bird songs do. Just not as nice to listen to."

"If they've been under your roof all this time, they've spent almost a century away from whatever culture they had where they came from. All that would be gone now, wouldn't it? The world's changed so much since then they wouldn't even recognize it," she said. "You're not doing science. You're doing national security. What I don't understand is why it's so important to communicate with them after all this time."

"All those changes you're talking about, that stops at the seashore. Drop them in the ocean and they'd feel right at home." He zipped the iPad back into his valise. "Whatever they might've had to say in 1928, that doesn't matter. Or '48, or '88. It's what we need to know *now* that's created a sense of urgency."

• • •

Once the helicopter had set down on the island, Kerry hadn't even left the cabin before thinking she'd never been to a more miserable place in her life. Rocky and rain-lashed, miles off the mainland, it was buffeted by winds that snapped from one direction and then another, so that the pines that grew here didn't know which way to go, twisted until they seemed to lean and leer with ill intent.

"It's not always like this," Escovedo assured her. "Sometimes there's sleet, too."

It was the size of a large shopping plaza, a skewed triangular shape, with a helipad and boat dock on one point, and a scattering of outbuildings clustered along another, including what she assumed were offices and barracks for those unfortunate enough to have been assigned to duty here, everything laced together by a network of roads and pathways.

It was dominated, though, by a hulking brick monstrosity that looked exactly like what it was—a vintage relic of a prison—although it could pass for other things, too: an old factory or power plant, or, more likely, a wartime fortress, a leftover outpost from an era when the west coast feared the Japanese fleet. It had been built in 1942, Escovedo told her. No one would have questioned the need for it at the time, and since then, people were simply used to it, if they even knew it was there. Boaters might be curious, but the shoreline was studded at intervals with signs, and she imagined that whatever they said was enough to repel the inquisitive—that, and the triple rows of fencing crowned with loops of razor wire.

Inside her rain slicker, Kerry yanked the hood's drawstring tight and leaned into the needles of rain. October—it was only October. Imagine this place in January. Of course it didn't bother the colonel one bit. They were halfway along the path to the outbuildings when she turned to him and tugged the edge of her hood aside.

"I'm not psychic," she told him. "You called me that in the helicopter. That's not how I look at what I do."

"Noted," he said, noncommittal and unconcerned.

"I'm serious. If you're going to bring me out here, to this place, it's important to me that you understand what I do, and aren't snickering about it behind my back."

"You're here, aren't you? Obviously somebody high up the chain of command has faith in you."

That gave her pause to consider. This wouldn't have been a lark on their part. Bringing in a civilian on something most presidents hadn't known about would never have been done on a hunch—see if this works, and if it doesn't, no harm done. She would've been vetted, extensively, and she wondered how they'd done it. Coming up with pretenses to interview past clients, perhaps, or people who'd appeared on *The Animal Whisperer*, to ascertain that they really were the just-folks they were purported to be, and that it wasn't scripted; that she genuinely had done for them what she was supposed to.

"What about you, though? Have you seen the show?"

"I got forwarded the season one DVDs. I watched the first couple episodes." He grew more thoughtful, less official. "The polar bear at the Cleveland Zoo, that was interesting. That's fifteen hundred pounds of apex predator you're dealing with. And you went in there without so much as a stick of wood between you and it. Just because it was having OCD issues? That takes either a big pair of balls or a serious case of stupid. And I don't think you're stupid."

"That's a start, I guess," she said. "Is that particular episode why I'm here? You figured since I did that, I wouldn't spook easily with these prisoners of yours?"

"I imagine it was factored in." The gravel that lined the path crunched underfoot for several paces before he spoke again. "If you don't think of yourself as psychic, what is it, then? How *does* it work?"

"I don't really know." Kerry had always dreaded the question, because she'd never been good at answering it. "It's been there as far back as I can remember, and I've gotten better at it, but I think that's just through the doing. It's a sense as much as anything. But not like sight or smell or taste. I compare it to balance. Can you explain how your sense of balance works?"

He cut her a sideways glance, betraying nothing, but she saw he didn't have a clue. "Mine? You're on a need-to-know basis here, remember."

Very good. Very dry. Escovedo was probably more fun than he let on.

"Right," she said. "Everybody else's, then. Most people have no idea. It's so intrinsic they take it for granted. A few may know it has to do with the inner ear. And a few of them, that it's centered in the vestibular apparatus, those three tiny loops full of fluid. One for up, one for down, one for forward and backward. But you don't need to know any of that to walk like we are now and not fall over. Well . . . that's what the animal thing is like for me. It's there, but I don't know the mechanism behind it."

He mused this over for several paces. "So that's your way of dodging the question?"

Kerry grinned at the ground. "It usually works."

"It's a good smokescreen. Really, though."

"Really? It's . . . " She drew the word out, a soft hiss while gathering her thoughts. "A combination of things. It's like receiving emotions, feelings, sensory impressions, mental imagery, either still or with motion. Any or all. Sometimes it's not even that, it's just . . . pure knowing, is the best way I know to phrase it."

"Pure knowing?" He sounded skeptical.

"Have you been in combat?"

"Yes."

"Then even if you haven't experienced it yourself, I'd be surprised if you haven't seen it or heard about it in people you trust—a strong sense that you should be very careful in that building, or approaching that next rise. They can't point to anything concrete to explain why. They just know. And they're often right."

Escovedo nodded. "Put in that context, it makes sense."

"Plus, for what it's worth, they ran a functional MRI on me, just for fun. That's on the season two DVD bonuses. Apparently the language center of my brain is very highly developed. Ninety-eighth percentile, something like that. So maybe that has something to do with it."

"Interesting," Escovedo said, and nothing more, so she decided to quit while she was ahead.

The path curved and split before them, and though they weren't taking the left- hand branch to the prison, still, the closer they drew to it, darkened by rain and contemptuous of the wind, the greater the edifice seemed to loom over everything else on the island. It was like something grown from the sea, an iceberg of brick, with the worst of it hidden from view. When the wind blew just right, it carried with it a smell of fish, generations of them, as if left to spoil and never cleaned up.

Kerry stared past it, to the sea surging all the way to the horizon. This was an island only if you looked at it from out there. Simple, then: *Don't ever go out there.*

She'd never had a problem with swimming pools. You could see through those. Lakes, oceans, rivers . . . these were something entirely different. These were *dark* waters, full of secrets and unintended tombs. Shipwrecks, sunken airplanes, houses at the bottom of flooded valleys . . . they were sepulchers of dread, trapped in another world where they so plainly did not belong.

Not unlike the way she was feeling this very moment.

As she looked around Colonel Escovedo's office in the administrative building, it seemed almost as much a cell as anything they could have over at the prison. It was without windows, so the lighting was all artificial, fluorescent and unflattering. It aged him, and she didn't want to think what it had to be doing to her own appearance. In one corner, a dehumidifier chugged away, but the air still felt heavy and damp. Day in, day out, it must have been like working in a mine.

"Here's the situation. Why now," he said. "Their behavior over there, it's been pretty much unchanged ever since they were moved to this installation. With one exception. Late summer, 1997, for about a month. I wasn't here then, but according to the records, it was like . . . " He paused, groping for the right words. "A hive mind. Like they were a single organism. They spent most of their time aligned to a precise angle to the southwest. The commanding officer at the time mentioned in his reports that it was like they were waiting for something. Inhumanly patient, just waiting. Then, eventually, they stopped and everything went back to normal."

"Until now?" she said.

"Nine days ago. They're doing it again."

"Did anybody figure out what was special about that month?"

"We think so. It took years, though. Three years before some analyst made the connection, and even then, you know, it's still a lucky accident. Maybe you've heard how it is with these agencies, they don't talk to each other, don't share notes. You've got a key here, and a lock on the other side of the world, and nobody in the middle who knows enough to put the two together. It's better now than it used to be, but it took the 9/11 attacks to get them to even *think* about correlating intel better."

"So what happened that summer?"

"Just listen," he said, and spun in his chair to the hardware behind him.

She'd been wondering about that anyway. Considering how functional his office was, it seemed not merely excessive, but out of character, that Escovedo would have an array of what looked to be high-end audio-video components, all feeding into a pair of three-way speakers and a subwoofer. He dialed in a sound file on the LCD of one of the rack modules, then thumbed the play button.

At first it was soothing, a muted drone both airy and deep, a lonely noise that some movie's sound designer might have used to suggest the desolation of outer space. But no, this wasn't about space. It had to be the sea, this all led back to the sea. It was the sound of deep waters, the black depths where sunlight never reached.

Then came a new sound, deeper than deep, a slow eruption digging its way free of the drone, climbing in pitch, rising, rising, then plummeting back to leave her once more with the sound of the void. After moments of anticipation, it happened again, like a roar from an abyss, and prickled the fine hairs on the back of her neck—a primal response, but then, what was more primal than the ocean and the threats beneath its waves?

*This* was why she'd never liked the sea. This never knowing what was there, until it was upon you.

"Heard enough?" Escovedo asked, and seemed amused at her mute nod. "*That* happened. Their hive mind behavior coincided with that."

"What *was* it?"

"That's the big question. It was recorded several times during the summer of 1997, then never again. Since 1960, we've had the oceans bugged for sound, basically. We've got them full of microphones that we put there to listen for Soviet submarines, when we thought it was a possibility we'd be going to war with them. They're down hundreds of feet, along an ocean layer called the sound channel. For sound conductivity, it's the Goldilocks zone—it's just right. After the Cold War was over, these mic networks were decommissioned from military use and turned over for scientific research. Whales, seismic events, underwater volcanoes, that sort of thing. Most of it, it's instantly identifiable. The people whose job it is to listen to what the mics pick up, 99.99 percent of the time they know exactly what they've got because the sounds conform to signature patterns, and they're just so familiar.

"But every so often they get one they can't identify. It doesn't fit any known pattern. So they give it a cute name and it stays a mystery. This one, they called it the 'Bloop.' Makes it sound like a kid farting in the bathtub, doesn't it?"

She pointed at the speakers. "An awfully big kid and an awfully big tub."

"Now you're getting ahead of me. The Bloop's point of origin was calculated to be in the South Pacific . . . maybe not coincidentally, not far from Polynesia, which is generally conceded as the place of origin for what eventually came to be known in Massachusetts as 'the Innsmouth look.' Some outside influence was brought home from Polynesia in the 1800s during a series of trading expeditions by a sea captain named Obed Marsh."

"Are you talking about a disease, or a genetic abnormality?"

Escovedo slapped one hand onto a sheaf of bound papers lying on one side of his desk. "You can be the judge of that. I've got a summary here for you to look over, before you get started tomorrow. It'll give you more background on the town and its history. The whole thing's a knotted-up tangle of fact and rumor and local legend and god knows what all, but it's not my job to sort out what's what. I've got enough on my plate sticking with facts, and the fact is, I'm in charge of keeping sixty-three of these proto-human monstrosities hidden from the world, and I know they're cued into something anomalous, but I don't know what. The other fact is, the last time they acted like this was fifteen years ago, while those mics were picking up one of the loudest sounds ever recorded on the planet."

"How loud was it?"

"Every time that sound went off, it wasn't just a local event. It was picked up over a span of five thousand kilometers."

The thought made her head swim. Something with that much power behind it . . . there could be nothing good about it. Something that loud was the sound of death, of cataclysm and extinction events. It was the sound of an asteroid strike, of a volcano not just erupting, but vaporizing a land mass—Krakatoa, the island of Thera. She imagined standing here, past the northwestern edge of the continental U.S., and hearing something happen in New York. Okay, sound traveled better in water than in air, but still— *three thousand miles.*

"Despite that," Escovedo said, "the analysts say it most closely matches a profile of something alive."

"A whale?" There couldn't be anything bigger, not for millions of years.

The colonel shook his head. "Keep going. Somebody who briefed me on this compared it to a blue whale plugged in and running through the amplifier stacks at every show Metallica has ever played, all at once. She also said that what they captured probably wasn't even the whole sound. That it's likely that a lot of frequencies and details got naturally filtered out along the way."

"Whatever it was . . . there have to be theories."

"Sure. Just nothing that fits with all the known pieces."

"Is the sound occurring again?"

"No. We don't know what they're cueing in on this time."

He pointed at the prison. Even though he couldn't see it, because there were no windows, and now she wondered if he didn't prefer it that way. Block it out with walls, and maybe for a few minutes at a time he could pretend he was somewhere else, assigned to some other duty.

"But *they* do," he said. "Those abominations over there know. We just need to find the key to getting them to tell us."

She was billeted in what Colonel Escovedo called the guest barracks, the only visitor in a building that could accommodate eight in privacy, sixteen if they doubled up. Visitors, Kerry figured, would be a rare occurrence here, and the place felt that way, little lived-in and not much used. The rain had strengthened closer to evening and beat hard on the low roof, a lonely sound that built from room to vacant room.

When she heard the deep thump of the helicopter rotors pick up, then recede into the sky—having waited, apparently, until it was clear she would be staying—she felt unaccountably abandoned, stranded with no way off this outpost that lay beyond not just the rim of civilization, but beyond the frontiers of even her expanded sense of life, of humans and animals and what passed between them.

Every now and then she heard someone outside, crunching past on foot or on an all-terrain four-wheeler. If she looked, they were reduced to dark, indistinct smears wavering in the water that sluiced down the windows. She had the run of most of the island if she wanted, although that was mainly just a license to get soaked under the sky. The buildings were forbidden, other than her quarters and the admin office, and, of course, the prison, as long as she was being escorted. And, apart for the colonel, she was apparently expected to pretend to be the invisible woman. She and the duty personnel were off-limits to each other. She wasn't to speak to them, and they were under orders not to speak with her.

They didn't know the truth—it was the only explanation that made sense. They didn't know, because they didn't need to. They'd been fed a cover story. Maybe they believed they were guarding the maddened survivors of a disease, a genetic mutation, an industrial accident or something that had fallen from space and that did terrible things to DNA. Maybe they'd all been fed a different lie, so that if they got together to compare notes they wouldn't know which to believe.

For that matter, she wasn't sure she did either.

First things first, though: She set up a framed photo of Tabitha on a table out in the barracks' common room, shot over the summer when they'd gone horseback riding in the Sawtooth Range. Her daughter's sixth birthday. Rarely was a picture snapped in which Tabby wasn't beaming, giddy with life, but this was one of them, her little face rapt with focus. Still in the saddle, she was leaning forward, hugging the mare's neck, her braided hair a blond stripe along the chestnut hide, and it looked for all the world as if the two of them were sharing a secret.

The photo would be her beacon, her lighthouse shining from home.

She fixed a mug of hot cocoa in the kitchenette, then settled into one of the chairs with the summary report that Escovedo had sent with her.

Except for its cold, matter-of-fact tone, it read like bizarre fiction. If she hadn't seen the photos, she wouldn't have believed it: a series of raids in an isolated Massachusetts seaport that swept up more than two hundred residents, most of whose appearances exhibited combinations of human, ichthyoid, and amphibian traits. The Innsmouth look had been well-known to the neighboring towns for at least two generations—"an unsavory haven of inbreeding and circus folk," according to a derisive comment culled from an Ipswich newspaper of the era—but even then, Innsmouth had been careful to put forward the best face it possibly could. Which meant, in most cases, residents still on the low side of middle-age . . . at least when it came to the families that had a few decades' worth of roots in the town, rather than its more recent newcomers.

With age came change so drastic that the affected people gradually lost all resemblance to who they'd been as children and young adults, eventually reaching the point that they let themselves be seen only by each other, taking care to hide from public view in a warren of dilapidated homes, warehouses, and limestone caverns that honeycombed the area.

One page of the report displayed a sequence of photos of what was ostensibly the same person, identified as Giles Shapleigh, eighteen years old when detained in 1928. He'd been a handsome kid in the first photo, and if he had nothing to smile about when it was taken, you could at least see the potential for a roguish, cockeyed grin. By his twenty-fifth year, he'd visibly aged, his hair receded and thinning, and after seven years of captivity he had the sullen look of a convict. By thirty, he was bald as a cue ball, and his skull had seemed to narrow. By thirty-five, his jowls had widened enough to render his neck almost nonexistent, giving him a bullet-headed appearance that she found all the more unnerving for his dead-eyed stare.

By the time he was sixty, with astronauts not long on the moon, there was nothing left to connect Giles Shapleigh with who or what he'd been, neither his identity nor his species. Still, though, his transformation wasn't yet complete.

He was merely catching up to his friends, neighbors, and relatives. By the time of those Prohibition-era raids, most of the others had been this way for years—decades, some of them. Although they aged, they didn't seem to weaken and, while they could be killed, if merely left to themselves, they most certainly didn't die.

They could languish, though. As those first years went on, with the Innsmouth prisoners scattered throughout a handful of remote quarantine facilities across New England, it became obvious that they didn't do well in the kind of environment reserved for normal prisoners: barred cells, bright lights, exercise yards . . . *dryness*. Some of them developed a skin condition that resembled powdery mildew, a white, dusty crust that spread across them in patches. There was a genuine fear that, whatever it was, it might jump from captives to captors, and prove more virulent in wholly human hosts, although this never happened.

Thus it was decided: They didn't need a standard prison so much as they needed their own zoo. That they got it was something she found strangely heartening. What was missing from the report, presumably because she had no need to know, was *why*.

While she didn't want to admit it, Kerry had no illusions—the expedient thing would've been to kill them off. No one would have known, and undoubtedly there would've been those who found it an easy order to carry out. It was wartime, and if war proved anything, it proved how simple it was to dehumanize people even when they looked just like you. This was 1942, and this was already happening on an industrial scale across Europe. These people from Innsmouth would have had few advocates. To merely look at them was to feel revulsion, to sense a challenge to everything you thought you knew about the world, about what could and couldn't be. Most people would look at them and think they deserved to die. They were an insult to existence, to cherished beliefs.

Yet they lived. They'd outlived the men who'd rounded them up, and their first jailers, and most of their jailers since. They'd outlived everyone who'd opted to keep them a secret down through the generations . . . yet for what?

Perhaps morality *had* factored into the decision to keep them alive, but she doubted morality had weighed heaviest. Maybe, paradoxically, it had been done out of fear. They may have rounded up over two hundred of Innsmouth's strangest, but many more had escaped—by most accounts, fleeing into the harbor, then the ocean beyond. To exterminate these captives because they were unnatural would be to throw away the greatest resource they might possess in case they ever faced these beings again, under worse circumstances.

Full disclosure, Escovedo had promised. She would know as much as he did. But when she finished the report along with the cocoa, she had no faith whatsoever that she was on par with the colonel, or that even he'd been told the half of it himself.

How much did a man need to know, really, to be a glorified prison warden?

Questions nagged, starting with the numbers. She slung on her coat and headed back out into the rain, even colder now, as it needled down from a dusk descending on the island like a dark gray blanket. She found the colonel still in his office, and supposed by now he was used to people dripping on his floor.

"What happened to the rest of them?" she asked. "Your report says there were over two hundred to start with. And that this place was built to house up to three hundred. So I guess somebody thought more might turn up.

But you're down to sixty-three. And they don't die of natural causes. So what happened to the others?"

"What does it matter? For your purposes, I mean. What you're here to do."

"Did you know that animals understand the idea of extermination? Wolves do. Dogs at the pound do. Cattle do, once they get to the slaughterhouse pens. They may not be able to articulate it, but they pick up on it. From miles away, sometimes, they can pick up on it." She felt a chilly drop of water slither down her forehead. "I don't know about fish or reptiles. But whatever humanity may still exist in these prisoners of yours, I wouldn't be surprised if it's left them just as sensitive to the concept of extermination, or worse."

He looked at her blankly, waiting for more. He didn't get it.

"For all I know, you're sending me in there as the latest interrogator who wants to find out the best way to commit genocide on the rest of their kind. *That's* why it matters. Is that how they're going to see me?"

Escovedo looked at her for a long time, his gaze fixated on her, not moving, just studying her increasing unease as she tried to divine what he was thinking. If he was angry, or disappointed, or considering sending her home before she'd even set foot in the prison. He stared so long she had no idea which it could be, until she realized that the stare *was* the point.

"They've got these eyes," he said. "They don't blink. They've got no white part to them anymore, so you don't know where they're looking, exactly. It's more like looking into a mirror than another eye. A mirror that makes you want to look away. So . . . how they'll *see* you?" he said, with a quick shake of his head and a hopeless snort of a laugh. "I have no idea *what* they see."

She wondered how long he'd been in this command. If he would ever get used to the presence of such an alien enemy. If any of them did, his predecessors, back to the beginning. That much she could see.

"Like I said, I stick with facts," he said. "I can tell you this much: When you've got a discovery like *them*, you have to expect that every so often another one or two of them are going to disappear into the system."

"The system," she said. "What does that mean?"

"You were right, we don't do science here. But they do in other places," he told her. "You can't be naïve enough to think research means spending the day watching them crawl around and writing down what they had for lunch."

Naïve? No. Kerry supposed she had suspected before she'd even slogged over here to ask. Just to make sure. You didn't have to be naïve to hope for better.

She carried the answer into dreams that night, where it became excruciatingly obvious that, while the Innsmouth prisoners may have lost the ability to speak in any known language, when properly motivated, they could still shriek.

Morning traded the rain for fog, lots of it, a chilly cloud that had settled over the island before dawn. There was no more sky and sea, no more distance, just whatever lay a few feet in front of her, and endless gray beyond. Without the gravel pathways, she was afraid she might've lost her bearings, maybe wander to the edge of the island. Tangle herself in razor wire, and hang there and die before anyone noticed.

She could feel it now, the channels open and her deepest intuition rising: This was the worst place she'd ever been, and she couldn't tell which side bore the greater blame.

With breakfast in her belly and coffee in hand, she met Escovedo at his office, so he could escort her to the corner of the island where the prison stood facing west, looking out over the sea. There would be no more land until Asia. Immense, made of brick so saturated with wet air that its walls looked slimed, the prison emerged from the mist like a sunken ship.

What would it be like, she wondered, to enter a place and not come out for seventy years? What would that do to one's mind? Were they even sane now? Or did they merely view this as a brief interruption in their lives? Unless they were murdered outright—a possibility—their lifespans were indefinite. Maybe they knew that time was their ally. Time would kill their captors, generation by generation, while they went on. Time would bring down every wall. All terrestrial life might go extinct, while they went on.

As long as they could make it those last few dozen yards to the sea.

"Have any of them ever escaped from here?" she asked.

"No."

"Don't you find that odd? I do. Hasn't most every prison had at least one escape over seventy years?"

"Not this one. It doesn't run like a regular prison. The inmates don't work. There's no kitchen, no laundry trucks, no freedom to tunnel. They don't get visitors. We just spend all day looking at each other." He paused in the arched, inset doorway, his finger on the call button that would summon the guards inside to open up. "If you want my unfiltered opinion, those of us who pulled this duty are the real prisoners."

Inside, it was all gates and checkpoints, the drab institutional hallways saturated with a lingering smell of fish. *Them*, she was smelling *them*. Like people who spent their workdays around death and decay, the soldiers here would carry it home in their pores. You had to pity them that. They would be smelling it after a year of showers, whether it was there or not.

Stairs, finally, a series of flights that seemed to follow the curvature of some central core. It deposited them near the top of the building, on an observation deck. Every vantage point around the retaining wall, particularly a trio of guard posts, overlooked an enormous pit, like an abandoned rock quarry. Flat terraces and rounded pillows of stone rose here and there out of a pool of murky seawater. Along the walls, rough stairways led up to three tiers of rooms, cells without bars.

This wasn't a prison where the inmates would need to be protected from each other. They were all on the same side down there, prisoners of an undeclared war.

Above the pit, the roof was louvered, so apparently, although closed now, it could be opened. They could see the sky. They would have air and rain. Sunshine, if that still meant anything to them.

The water, she'd learned from last night's briefing paper, was no stagnant pool. It was continually refreshed, with drains along the bottom and grated pipes midway up the walls that periodically spewed a gusher like a tidal surge. Decades of this had streaked the walls with darker stains, each like a ragged brush stroke straight down from the rusty grate to the foaming surface of their makeshift sea.

Fish even lived in it, and why not? The prisoners had to eat.

Not at the moment, though. They lined the rocks in groups, as many as would fit on any given surface, sitting, squatting, facing the unseen ocean in eerily perfect alignment to one another.

"What do you make of it?" he asked.

Kerry thought of fish she'd watched in commercial aquariums, in nature documentaries, fish swimming in their thousands, singularly directed, and then, in an instantaneous response to some stimulus, changing directions in perfect unison. "I would say they're schooling."

From where they'd entered the observation deck, she could see only their backs, and began to circle the retaining wall for a better view.

Their basic shapes looked human, but the details were all wrong. Their skin ranged from dusky gray to light green, with pale bellies—dappled sometimes, an effect like sunlight through water—and rubbery looking even from here, as though it would be slick as a wetsuit to the touch, at least the areas that hadn't gone hard and scaly. Some wore the remnants of clothing, although she doubted anything would hold up long in the water and rocks, while others chose to go entirely without. They were finned and they were spiny, no two quite the same, and their hands webbed between the fingers, their feet ridiculously outsized. Their smooth heads were uncommonly narrow, all of them, but still more human than not. Their faces, though, were ghastly. These were faces for another world, with thick-lipped mouths made to gulp water, and eyes to peer through the murky gloom of the deep. Their noses were all but gone, just vestigial nubs now, flattened and slitted. The females' breasts had been similarly subsumed, down to little more than hard bumps.

She clutched the top of the wall until her fingernails began to bend. Not even photographs could truly prepare you for seeing them in the flesh.

*I wish I'd never known,* she thought. *I can never be the same again.*

"You want to just pick one at random, see where it goes?" Escovedo asked.

"How do you see this working? We haven't talked about that," she said. "What, you pull one of them out and put us in a room together, each of us on either side of a table?"

"Do you have any better ideas?"

"It seems so artificial. The environment of an interrogation room, I mean. I need them open, if that makes sense. Their minds, open. A room like that, it's like you're doing everything you can to close them off from the start."

"Well, I'm not sending you in down there into the middle of all sixty-three of them, if that's what you're getting at. I have no idea how they'd react, and there's no way I could guarantee your safety."

She glanced at the guard posts, only now registering why they were so perfectly triangulated. Nothing was out of reach of their rifles.

"And you don't want to set up a situation where you'd have to open fire on the group, right?"

"It would be counterproductive."

"Then you pick one," she said. "You know them better than I do."

If the Innsmouth prisoners still had a sense of patriarchy, then Escovedo must have decided to start her at the top of their pecking order.

The one they brought her was named Barnabas Marsh, if he even had a use anymore for a name that none of his kind could speak. Maybe names only served the convenience of their captors now, although if any name still carried weight, it would be the name of Marsh. Barnabas was the grandson of Obed Marsh, the ship's captain who, as village legend held, had sailed to strange places above the sea and below it, and brought back both the DNA and partnerships that had altered the course of Innsmouth's history.

Barnabas had been old even when taken prisoner, and by human terms he was now beyond ancient. She tried not to think of him as monstrous, but no other word wanted to settle on him, on any of them. Marsh, though, she found all the more monstrous for the fact that she could see in him the puffed-up, barrel-chested bearing of a once-domineering man who'd never forgotten who and what he had been.

Behind the wattles of his expanded neck, gills rippled with indignation. The thick lips, wider than any human mouth she'd ever seen, stretched downward at each corner in a permanent, magisterial sneer.

He waddled when he walked, as if no longer made for the land, and when the two guards in suits of body armor deposited him in the room, he looked her up and down, then shuffled in as if resigned to tolerating her until this interruption was over. He stopped long enough to give the table and chairs in the center of the room a scornful glance, then continued to the corner, where he slid to the floor with a shoulder on each wall, the angle where they met giving room for his sharp-spined back.

She took the floor as well.

"I believe you can understand me. Every word," Kerry said. "You either can't or won't speak the way you did for the first decades of your life, but I can't think of any reason why you shouldn't still understand me. And that puts you way ahead of all the rest of God's creatures I've managed to communicate with."

He looked at her with his bulging dark eyes, and Escovedo had been right. It was a disconcertingly inhuman gaze, not even mammalian. It wasn't anthropomorphizing to say that mammals—dogs, cats, even a plethora of wilder beasts—had often looked at her with a kind of warmth. But *this*, these eyes . . . they were cold, with a remote scrutiny that she sensed regarded her as lesser in every way.

The room's air, cool to begin with, seemed to chill even more as her skin crawled with an urge to put distance between them. Could he sense that she feared him? Maybe he took this as a given. That he could be dangerous was obvious—the closer you looked, the more he seemed covered with sharp points, none more lethal than the tips of his stubby fingers. But she had to trust the prison staff to ensure her safety. While there was no guard in here to make the energy worse than it was already, they were being watched on a closed-circuit camera. If Marsh threatened her, the room would be flooded with a gas that would put them both out in seconds. She'd wake up with a headache, and Marsh would wake up back in the pit.

And nothing would be accomplished.

"I say God's creatures because I don't know how else to think of you," she said. "I know how *they* think of you. They think you're all aberrations. Unnatural. Not that I'm telling you anything you probably haven't already overheard from them every day for more than eighty years."

And did that catch his interest, even a little? If the subtle tilt of his head meant anything, maybe it did.

"But if you exist, entire families of you, colonies of you, then you can't be an aberration. You're within the realm of nature's possibilities."

Until this moment, she'd had no idea what she would say to him. With animals, she was accustomed to speaking without much concern for what exactly she said. It was more how she said it. Like very young children, animals cued in on tone, not language. They nearly always seemed to favor a higher-pitched voice. They responded to touch.

None of which was going to work here.

But Barnabas Marsh was a presence, and a powerful one, radiant with a sense of age. She kept speaking to him, seeking a way through the gulf between them, the same as she always did. No matter what the species, there always seemed to be a way, always something to which she could attune—an image, a sound, a taste, some heightened sense that overwhelmed her and, once she regained her equilibrium, let her use it as the key in the door that would open the way for more.

She spoke to him of the sea, the most obvious thing, because no matter what the differences between them, they had that much in common. It flowed in each of them, water and salt, and they'd both come from it; he was just closer to returning, was all. Soon she felt the pull of tides, the tug of currents, the cold wet draw of gravity luring down, down, down to greater depths, then the equipoise of pressure, and where once it might've crushed, now it comforted, a cold cocoon that was both a blanket and a world, tingling along her skin with news coming from a thousand leagues in every direction—

And with a start she realized that the sea hadn't been her idea at all.

She'd only followed where he led. Whether Marsh meant to or not.

Kerry looked him in his cold, inhuman eyes, not knowing quite what lay behind them, until she began to get a sense that the sea was *all* that lay behind them. The sea was all he thought of, all he wanted, all that mattered, a yearning so focused that she truly doubted she could slip past it to ferret out what was so special about *now*. What they all sensed happening *now*, just as they had fifteen years ago.

It was all one and the same, of course, bound inextricably together, but first they had to reclaim the sea.

And so it went the rest of the day, with one after another of this sad parade of prisoners, until she'd seen nearly twenty of them. Nothing that she would've dared call progress, just inklings of impressions, snippets of sensations, none of it coalescing into a meaningful whole, and all of it subsumed beneath a churning ache to return to the sea.

It was their defense against her, and she doubted they even knew it.

Whatever was different about her, whatever had enabled her to whisper with creatures that she and the rest of the world found more appealing, it wasn't made to penetrate a human-born despair that had hardened over most of a century.

There was little light remaining in the day when she left the prison in defeat, and little enough to begin with. It was now a colorless world of approaching darkness. She walked a straight line, sense of direction lost in the clammy mist that clung to her as surely as the permeating smell of the prisoners. She knew she had to come to the island's edge eventually, and if she saw another human being before tomorrow, it would be too soon.

Escovedo found her anyway, and she had to assume he'd been following all along. Just letting her get some time and distance before, what, her debriefing? Kerry stood facing the water as it slopped against a shoreline of rocks the size of piled skulls, her hand clutching the inner fence. By now it seemed that the island was less a prison than a concentration camp.

"For what it's worth," the colonel said, "I didn't expect it to go well the first day."

"What makes you think a second day is going to go any better?"

"Rapport?" He lifted a thermos, uncapped it, and it steamed in the air. "But rapport takes time."

"Time." She rattled the fence. "Will I even be leaving here?"

"I hope that's a joke." He poured into the thermos cup without asking and gave it to her. "Here. The cold can sneak up on you out like this."

She sipped at the cup, coffee, not the best she'd ever had but far from the worst. It warmed her, though, and that was a plus. "Let me ask you something. Have they ever bred? Either here or wherever they were held before? Have *any* of them bred?"

"No. Why do you ask?"

"It's something I was picking up on from a few of them. The urge. You know it when you feel it. Across species, it's a great common denominator."

"I don't know what to tell you, other than that they haven't."

"Don't you find that odd?"

"I find the whole situation odd."

"What I mean is, even pandas in captivity manage to get pregnant once in a while."

"I've just never really thought about it."

"You regard them as prisoners, you *have* to, I get that. And the females don't look all that different from the males. But suppose they looked more like normal men and women. What would you expect if you had a prison with a mixed-gender population that had unrestricted access to each other?"

"I get your point, but . . . " He wasn't stonewalling, she could tell. He genuinely had never considered this. Because he'd never had to. "Wouldn't it be that they're too old?"

"I thought it was already established that once they get like this, age is no longer a factor. But even if it was, Giles Shapleigh wasn't too old when they first grabbed him. He was eighteen. Out of more than two hundred, he can't have been the only young one. You remember what the urge was like when you were eighteen?"

Escovedo grunted a laugh. "Every chance I get."

"Only he's never acted on it. None of them have."

"A fact that I can't say distresses me."

"It's just . . . " she said, then shut up. She had her answer. They'd never bred. Wanted to, maybe felt driven to, but hadn't. Perhaps captivity affected their fertility, or short-circuited the urge from becoming action.

Or maybe it was just an incredible act of discipline. They had to realize what would happen to their offspring. They would never be allowed to keep them, raise them. Their children would face a future of tests and vivisection. Even monstrosities would want better for their babies.

"I have an observation to make," Kerry said. "It's not going to go any better tomorrow, or the day after that. Not if you want me to keep doing it like today. It's like they have this shell around them." She tipped the coffee to her lips and eyed him over the rim, and he was impossible to read. "Should I go on?"

"I'm listening."

"You're right, rapport takes time. But it takes more than that. Your prisoners may have something beyond human senses, but they still have human intellects. More or less. It feels overlaid with something else, and it's not anything good, but fundamentally they haven't stopped being human, and they need to be dealt with that way. Not like they're entirely animals."

She stopped a moment to gauge him, and saw that she at least hadn't lost him. Although she'd not proposed anything yet.

"If they *looked* more human to you, don't you think the way you'd be trying to establish rapport would be to treat them more like human beings?" she said. "I read the news. I watch TV. I've heard the arguments about torture. For and against. I know what they are. The main thing I took away is that when you consult the people who've been good at getting reliable information from prisoners, they'll tell you they did it by being humane. Which includes letting the prisoner have something he wants, or loves. There was a captured German officer in World War Two who loved chess. He opened up after his interrogator started playing chess with him. That's all it took."

"I don't think these things are going to be interested in board games."

"No. But there's something every one of them wants," she said. "There's something they love more than anything else in the world."

*And why does it have to be the same thing I dread?*

When she told him how they might be able to use that to their advantage, she expected Escovedo to say no, out of the question. Instead, he thought it over for all of five seconds and said yes.

"I don't like it, but we need to fast-track this," he said. "We don't just eyeball their alignment in the pit, you know. We measure it with a laser. That's how we know how precisely oriented they are. And since last night they've shifted. Whatever they're cued in on has moved north."

The next morning, dawn came as dawn should, the sky clear and the fog blown away and the sun an actual presence over the horizon. After two days of being scarcely able to see fifty feet in front of her, it seemed as if she could see forever. There was something joyously liberating in it. After just two days.

So what was it going to feel like for Barnabas Marsh to experience the ocean for the first time in more than eighty years? The true sea, not the simulation of it siphoned off and pumped into the pit. Restrained by a makeshift leash, yes, three riflemen ready to shoot from the shore, that too, three more ready to shoot from the parapet of the prison . . . but it would still be the sea.

That it would be Marsh they would try this with was inevitable. It might not be safe and they might get only one chance at this. He was cunning, she had to assume, but he was the oldest by far, and a direct descendant of the man who'd brought this destiny to Innsmouth in the first place. He would have the deepest reservoir of knowledge.

And, maybe, the arrogance to want to share it, and gloat.

Kerry was waiting by the shallows when they brought him down, at one end of a long chain whose other end was padlocked to the frame of a four-wheel all-terrain cycle that puttered along behind him—he might have been able to throw men off balance in a tug-of-war, but not this.

Although he had plenty of slack, Marsh paused a few yards from the water's edge, stopping to stare out at the shimmering expanse of sea. The rest of them might have seen mistrust in his hesitation, or savoring the moment, but neither of these felt right. *Reacquainting*, she thought. *That's it.*

He trudged forward then, trailing chain, and as he neared the water, he cast a curious look at her, standing there in a slick blue wetsuit they'd outfitted her with, face-mask and snorkel in her hand. It gave him pause again, and in whatever bit of Marsh that was still human, she saw that he understood, realized who was responsible for this.

Gratitude, though, was not part of his nature. Once in the water, he vanished in moments, marked only by the clattering of his chain along the rocks.

She'd thought it wise to allow Marsh several minutes alone, just himself and the sea. They were midway through it when Escovedo joined her at the water's edge.

"You sure you're up for this?" he said. "It's obvious how much you don't like the idea, even if it was yours."

She glanced over at Marsh's chain, now still. "I don't like to see anything captive when it has the capacity to lament its conditions."

"That's not what I mean. If you think you've been keeping it under wraps that you've got a problem with water, you haven't. I could spot it two days ago, soon as we left the mainland behind."

She grinned down at her flippers, sheepish. Busted. "Don't worry. I'll deal."

"But you still know how to snorkel . . . ?"

"How else are you going to get over a phobia?" She laughed, needing to, and it helped. "It went great in the heated indoor pool."

She fitted the mask over her face and popped in the snorkel's mouthpiece, and went in after Marsh. Calves, knees . . . every step forward was an effort, so she thought of Tabby. *The sooner I get results, the quicker I'll get home.* Thighs, waist . . . then she was in Marsh's world, unnerved by the fear that she would find him waiting for her, tooth and claw, ready to rip through her in a final act of defiance.

But he was nowhere near her. She floated facedown, kicking lightly and visually tracking the chain down the slope of the shoreline, until she saw it disappear over a drop-off into a well that was several feet deeper. *There he is.* She hovered in place, staring down at Marsh as he luxuriated in the water. Ecstatic—there was no other word for him. Twisting, turning, undulating, the chain only a minor impediment, he would shoot up near the surface, then turn and plunge back to the bottom, rolling in the murk he stirred up, doing it again, again, again. His joyous abandon was like a child's.

He saw her and stilled, floating midway between surface and sand, a sight from a nightmare, worse than a shark because even in this world he was so utterly alien.

And it was never going to get any less unnerving. She sucked in a deep breath through the snorkel, then plunged downward, keeping a bit of distance between them as she swam to the bottom.

Two minutes and then some—that was how long she could hold her breath.

Kerry homed in on a loose rock that looked heavy enough to counter her buoyancy, then checked the dive compass strapped to her wrist like an oversized watch. She wrestled the wave-smoothed stone into her lap and sat cross-legged on the bottom, matching as precisely as she could the latest of the southwesterly alignments that had so captivated Marsh and the other sixty-two of them. Sitting on the seabed with the Pacific alive around her, muffled in her ears and receding into a blue-green haze, as she half expected something even worse than Marsh to come swimming straight at her out of the void.

Somewhere above and behind her, he was watching.

She stayed down until her lungs began to ache, then pushed free of the stone and rose to the surface, where she purged the snorkel with a gust of spent air, then flipped to return to the seabed. Closer this time, mere feet between her and Marsh as she settled again, no longer needing the compass—she found her bearing naturally, and time began to slow, and so did her heartbeat in spite of the fear, then the fear was gone, washed away in the currents that tugged at her like temptations.

Up again, down again, and it felt as if she were staying below longer each time, her capacity for breath expanding to fill the need, until she was all but on the outside of herself looking in, marveling at this creature she'd become, amphibious, neither of the land nor the water, yet belonging to both. She lived in a bubble of breath in an infinite now, lungs satiated, awareness creeping forward along this trajectory she was aligned with, as if it were a cable that spanned the seas, and if she could only follow it, she would learn the secrets it withheld from all but the initiated—

And he was there, Barnabas Marsh a looming presence drifting alongside her. If there was anything to read in his cold face, his unplumbed eyes, it was curiosity. She had become something he'd never seen before, something between his enemies and his people, and changing by the moment.

She peered at him, nothing between them now but the thin plastic window of her mask and a few nourishing inches of water.

*What is it that's out there?* she asked. *Tell me. I want to know. I want to understand.*

It was true—she did. She would wonder even if she hadn't been asked to. She would wonder every day for the rest of her life. Her existence would be marred by not knowing.

*Tell me what it is that lies beyond . . .*

She saw it then, a thought like a whisper become an echo, as it began to build on itself, the occlusions between worlds parting in swirls of ink and oceans. And there was so *much* of it, this was something that couldn't be— who could build such a thing, and who would dream of finding it *here*, at depths that might crush a submarine—then she realized that all she was seeing was one wall, one mighty wall, built of blocks the size of boxcars, a feat that couldn't be equaled even on land. She knew without seeing the whole that it spanned miles, that if this tiny prison island could sink into it, it would be lost forever, an insignificant patch of pebbles and mud to what lived there—

And she was wholly herself again, with a desperate need to breathe.

Kerry wrestled the rock off her lap for the last time, kicking for a surface as far away as the sun. As she shot past Barnabas Marsh she was gripped by a terror that he would seize her ankle to pull her back down.

But she knew she could fight that, so what he did was worse somehow, nothing she knew that he *could* do, and maybe none of these unsuspecting men on the island did either. It was what sound could be if sound were needles, a piercing skirl that ripped through her like an electric shock and clapped her ears as sharply as a pressure wave. She spun in the water, not knowing up from down, and when she stabilized and saw Marsh nearby, she realized he wasn't even directing this at her. She was just a bystander who got in the way. Instead, he was facing out to sea, the greater sea, unleashing this sound into the abyss.

She floundered to the surface and broke through, graceless and gasping, and heard Colonel Escovedo shout a command, and in the next instant heard the roar of an engine as the four-wheeler went racing up the rock-strewn slope of the island's western edge. The chain snapped taut, and moments later Marsh burst from the shallows in a spray of surf and foam, dragged twisting up onto the beach. Someone fired a shot, and someone else another, and of course no one heard her calling from nearly a hundred feet out, treading water now, and they were all shooting, so none of them heard her cry out that they had the wrong idea. But bullets first, questions later, she supposed.

His blood was still red. She had to admit, she'd wondered.

It took the rest of the morning before she was ready to be debriefed, and Escovedo let her have it, didn't press for too much, too soon. She needed to be warm again, needed to get past the shock of seeing Barnabas Marsh shot to pieces on the beach. Repellent though he was, she'd still linked with him in her way, whispered back and forth, and he'd been alive one minute, among the oldest living beings on the earth, then dead the next.

She ached from the sound he'd made, as if every muscle and organ inside her had been snapped like a rubber band. Her head throbbed with the assault on her ears.

In the colonel's office, finally, behind closed doors, Kerry told him of the colossal ruins somewhere far beneath the sea.

"Does any of that even make sense?" she asked. "It doesn't to me. It felt real enough at the time, but now . . . it has to have been a dream of his. Or maybe Marsh was insane. How could anyone have even known if he was?"

Behind his desk, Escovedo didn't move for the longest time, leaning on his elbows and frowning at his interlaced hands. Had he heard her at all? Finally he unlocked one of the drawers and withdrew a folder; shook out some photos, then put one back and slid the rest across to her. Eight in all.

"What you saw," he said. "Did it look anything like this?"

She put them in rows, four over four, like puzzle pieces, seeing how they might fit together. And she needed them all at once, to bludgeon herself into accepting the reality of it: stretches of walls, suggestions of towers, some standing, some collapsed, all fitted together from blocks of greenish stone that could have been shaped by both hammers and razors. Everything was restricted to what spotlights could reach, limned by a cobalt haze that faded into inky blackness. Here, too, were windows and gateways and wide, irregular terraces that might have been stairs, only for nothing that walked on human feet. There was no sense of scale, nothing to measure it by, but she'd sensed it once today already, and it had the feeling of enormity and measureless age.

It was the stuff of nightmares, out of place and out of time, waiting in the cold, wet dark.

"They've been enhanced because of the low-light conditions and the distance," Escovedo said. "It's like the shots of the Titanic. The only light down that far is what you can send on a submersible. Except the Navy's lost every single one they've sent down there. They just go offline. These pictures . . . they're from the one that lasted the longest."

She looked up again. The folder they'd come from was gone. "You held one back. I can't see it?"

He shook his head. "Need to know."

"It shows something that different from the others?"

Nothing. He was as much a block of stone as the walls.

"Something living?" She remembered his description of the sound heard across three thousand miles of ocean: *The analysts say it most closely matches a profile of something alive.* "Is that it?"

"I won't tell you you're right." He appeared to be choosing his words with care. "But if that's what you'd picked up on out there with Marsh, then maybe we'd have a chance to talk about photo number nine."

She wanted to know. Needed to know as badly as she'd needed to breathe this morning, waking up to herself too far under the surface of the sea.

"What about the rest of them? We can keep trying."

He shook his head no. "We've come to the end of this experiment. I've already arranged for your transportation back home tomorrow."

Just like that. It felt as if she were being fired. She hadn't even delivered. She'd not told them anything they didn't already know about. She'd only confirmed it. What had made that unearthly noise, what the Innsmouth prisoners were waiting for—that's what they were really after.

"We're only just getting started. You can't rush something like this. There are sixty-two more of them over there, one of them is sure to—"

He cut her off with a slash of his hand. "Sixty-two of them who are in an uproar now. They didn't see what happened to Marsh, but they've got the general idea."

"Then maybe you shouldn't have been so quick to order his execution."

"That was for you. I thought we were protecting you." He held up his hands then, appeasement, time-out. "I appreciate your willingness to continue. I do. But even if they were still in what passes for a good mood with them, we've still reached an impasse here. You can't get through to them on our turf, and I can't risk sending you back out with another of them onto theirs. It doesn't matter that Marsh didn't actually attack you. I can't risk another of them doing what he did to make me think he had."

"I don't follow you." It had been uncomfortable, yes, and she had no desire to experience it again, but it was hardly fatal.

"I've been doing a lot of thinking about what that sound he made meant," Escovedo said. "What I keep coming back to is that he was sending a distress call."

She wished she could've left the island sooner. That the moment the colonel told her they were finished, he'd already had the helicopter waiting. However late they got her home again, surely by now she would be in her own bed, holding her daughter close because she needed her even more than Tabby needed her.

Awake part of the time and a toss-up the rest, asleep but dreaming she was still trying to get there. Caught between midnight and dawn, the weather turning for the worse again, the crack and boom of thunder like artillery, with bullets of rain strafing the roof.

She had to be sleeping some of the time, though, and dreaming of something other than insomnia. She knew perfectly well she was in a bed, but there were times in the night when it felt as if she were still below, deeper than she'd gone this morning, in the cold of the depths far beyond the reach of the sun, drifting beside leviathan walls lit by a phosphorescence whose source she couldn't pin down. The walls themselves were tricky to navigate, like being on the outside of a maze, yet still lost within it, finding herself turning strange corners that seemed to jut outward, only to find that they turned in. She was going to drown down here, swamped by a sudden thrashing panic over her air tank going empty, only to realize . . .

She'd never strapped on one to begin with.

She belonged here, in this place that was everything that made her recoil.

*Marsh*, she thought, once she could tell ceiling from sea. Although he was dead, Marsh was still with her, in an overlapping echo of whispers. Dead, but still dreaming.

When she woke for good, though, it was as abruptly as could be, jolted by the sound of a siren so loud it promised nothing less than a cataclysm. It rose and fell like the howling of a feral god. She supposed soldiers knew how to react, but she wasn't one of them. Every instinct told her to hug the mattress and melt beneath the covers and hope it all went away.

But that was a strategy for people prone to dying in their beds.

She was dressed and out the door in two minutes, and though she had to squint against the cold sting of the rain, she looked immediately to the prison. Everything on the island, alive or motorized, seemed to be moving in that direction, and for a moment she wondered if she should too—safety in numbers, and what if something was *driving* them that way, from the east end?

But the searchlights along the parapet told a different story, three beams stabbing out over the open water, shafts of brilliant white shimmering with rain and sweeping to and fro against the black of night. *A distress call*, Escovedo had said—had it been answered? Was the island under attack, an invasion by Innsmouth's cousins who'd come swarming onto the beach? No, that didn't seem right either. The spotlights were not aimed down, but out. Straight out.

She stood rooted to the spot, pelted by rain, lashed by wind, frozen with dread that something terrible was on its way. The island had never felt so small. Even the prison looked tiny now, a vulnerable citadel standing alone against the three co-conspirators of ocean, night, and sky.

Ahead of the roving spotlights, the rain was a curtain separating the island from the sea, then it parted, silently at first, the prow of a ship spearing into view, emerging from the blackness as though born from it. No lights, no one visible on board, not even any engine noise that she could hear—just a dead ship propelled by the night or something in it. The sound came next, a tortured grinding of steel across rock so loud it made the siren seem weak and thin. The ship's prow heaved higher as it was driven up onto the island, the rest of it coming into view, the body of the shark behind the cone of its snout.

And she'd thought the thunder was loud. When the freighter plowed into the prison the ground shuddered beneath her, the building cracking apart as though riven by an axe, one of the spotlights tumbling down along with an avalanche of bricks and masonry before winking out for good. She watched men struggle, watched men fall, and at last the ship's momentum was spent. For a breathless moment it was perfectly still. Then, with another grinding protest of metal on stone, the ship began to list, like twisting a knife after sticking it in. The entire right side of the prison buckled and collapsed outward, and with it went the siren and another of the searchlights. The last of the lights reeled upward, aimed back at the building's own roofline.

Only now could she hear men shouting, only now could she hear the gunfire.

Only now could she hear men scream.

And still the ground seemed to shudder beneath her feet.

It seemed as if that should've been the end of it, accident and aftermath, but soon more of the prison began to fall, as if deliberately wrenched apart. She saw another cascade of bricks tumble to the left, light now flickering and spilling from within the prison on both sides.

Something rose into view from the other side, thick as the trunk of the tallest oak that had ever grown, but flexible, glistening in the searing light. It wrapped around another section of wall and pulled it down as easily as peeling wood from rotten wood. She thought it some kind of serpent at first, until, through the wreckage of the building, she saw the suggestion of more, coiling and uncoiling, and a body—or head—behind those.

And still the ground seemed to shudder beneath her feet.

It was nothing seismic—she understood that now. She recalled being in the majestic company of elephants once, and how the ground sometimes quivered in their vicinity as they called to one another from miles away, booming out frequencies so deep they were below the threshold of human hearing, a rumble that only their own kind could decipher.

*This was the beast's voice.*

And if they heard it in New York, in Barrow, Alaska, and in the Sea of Cortez, she would not have been surprised.

It filled her, reverberating through rock and earth, up past her shoes, juddering the soles of her feet, radiating through her bones and every fiber of muscle, every cell of fat, until her vision scrambled and she feared every organ would liquefy. At last it rose into the range of her feeble ears, a groan that a glacier might make. As the sound climbed higher she clapped both hands over her ears, and if she could have turtled her head into her body she would've done that too, as its voice became a roar became a bellow became a blaring onslaught like the trumpets of Judgment Day, a fanfare to split the sky for the coming of God.

Instead, *this* was what had arrived, this vast and monstrous entity, some inhuman travesty's idea of a deity. She saw it now for what it was to these loathsome creatures from Innsmouth—the god they prayed to, the Mecca that they faced—but then something whispered inside, and she wondered if she was wrong. As immense and terrifying as this thing was, what if it presaged more, and was only preparing the way, the John the Baptist for something even worse.

Shaking, she sunk to her knees, hoping only that she might pass beneath its notice as the last sixty-two prisoners from Innsmouth climbed up and over the top of the prison's ruins, and reclaimed their place in the sea.

To be honest, she had to admit to herself that the very idea of Innsmouth, and what had happened here in generations past, fascinated her as much as it appalled her.

Grow up and grow older in a world of interstate highways, cable TV, satellite surveillance, the Internet, and cameras in your pocket, and it was easy to forget how remote a place could once be, even on the continental U.S., and not all that long ago, all things considered. It was easy to forget how you might live a lifetime having no idea what was going on in a community just ten miles away, because you never had any need to go there, or much desire, either, since you'd always heard they were an unfriendly lot who didn't welcome strangers, and preferred to keep to themselves.

Innsmouth was no longer as isolated as it once was, but it still had the feeling of remoteness, of being adrift in time, a place where businesses struggled to take root, then quietly died back into vacant storefronts. It seemed to dwell under a shadow that would forever keep outsiders from finding a reason to go there, or stay long if they had.

Unlike herself. She'd been here close to a month, since two days after Christmas, and still didn't know when she would leave.

She got the sense that, for many of the town's residents, making strangers feel unwelcome was a tradition they felt honor-bound to uphold. Their greetings were taciturn, if extended at all, and they watched as if she were a shoplifter, even when crossing the street, or strolling the riverwalk along the Manuxet in the middle of the day. But her money was good, and there was no shortage of houses to rent—although her criteria were stricter than most—and a divorced mother with a six-year-old daughter could surely pose no threat.

None of them seemed to recognize her from television, although would they let on if they did? She recognized none of them, either, nothing in anyone's face or feet that hinted at the old, reviled Innsmouth look. They no longer seemed to have anything to hide here, but maybe the instinct that they did went so far back that they knew no other way.

Although what to make of that one storefront on Eliot Street, in what passed for the heart of the town? The stenciled lettering—charmingly antiquated and quaint—on the plate glass window identified the place as The Innsmouth Society for Preservation and Restoration.

It seemed never to be open.

Yet it never seemed neglected.

Invariably, whenever she peered through the window Kerry would see that someone had been there since the last time she'd looked, but it always felt as if she'd missed them by five minutes or so. She would strain for a better look at the framed photos on the walls, tintypes and sepia tones, glimpses of bygone days that seemed to be someone's idea of something worth bringing back.

Or perhaps their idea of a homecoming.

It was January in New England, and most days so cold it redefined the word bitter, but she didn't miss a single one, climbing seven flights of stairs to take up her vigil for as long as she could endure it. The house was an old Victorian on Lafayette Street, four proud stories tall, peaked and gabled to within an inch of its moldering life. The only thing she cared about was that its roof had an iron-railed widow's walk with an unobstructed view of the decrepit harbor and the breakwater and, another mile out to sea, the humpbacked spine of rock called Devil Reef.

As was the custom during the height of the Age of Sail, the widow's walk had been built around the house's main chimney. Build a roaring fire down below, and the radiant bricks would keep her warm enough for a couple of hours at a time, even when the sky spit snow at her, while she brought the binoculars to her eyes every so often to check if there was anything new to see out there.

"I'm bored." This from Tabitha, nearly every day. *Booorrrrred*, the way she said it. "There's nothing to do here."

"I know, sweetie," Kerry would answer. "Just a little longer."

"When are they coming?" Tabby would ask.

"Soon," she would answer. "Pretty soon."

But in truth, she couldn't say. Their journey was a long one. Would they risk traversing the locks and dams of the Panama Canal? Or would they take the safer route, around Argentina's Cape Horn, where they would exchange Pacific for Atlantic, south for north, then head home, at long last home.

She knew only that they were on their way, more certain of this than any sane person had a right to be. The assurance was there whenever the world grew still and silent, more than a thought . . . a whisper that had never left, as if not all of Barnabas Marsh had died, the greater part of him subsumed into the hive mind of the rest of his kind. To taunt? To punish? To gloat? In the weeks after their island prison fell, there was no place she could go where its taint couldn't follow. Not Montana, not Los Angeles, not New Orleans, for the episode of *The Animal Whisperer* they'd tried to film before putting it on hiatus.

She swam with them in sleep. She awoke retching with the taste of coldest blood in her mouth. Her belly skimmed through mud and silt in quiet moments; her shoulders and flanks brushed through shivery forests of weeds; her fingers tricked her into thinking that her daughter's precious cheek felt cool and slimy. The dark of night could bring on the sense of a dizzying plunge to the blackest depths of ocean trenches.

Where else was left for her to go but here, to Innsmouth, the place that time seemed to be trying hard to forget.

And the more days she kept watch from the widow's walk, the longer at a time she could do it, even while the fire below dwindled to embers, and so the more it seemed that her blood must've been going cold in her veins.

"I don't like it here," Tabby would say. "You never used to yell in your sleep until we came here."

How could she even answer that? No one could live like this for long.

"Why can't I go stay with Daddy?" Tabby would ask. *Daddeeeee*, the way she said it.

It really would've been complete then, wouldn't it? The humiliation, the surrender. The admission: *I can't handle it anymore, I just want it to stop, I want them to make it stop*. It still mattered, that her daughter's father had once fallen in love with her when he thought he'd been charmed by some half-wild creature who talked to animals, and then once he had her, tried to drive them from her life because he realized he hated to share. He would never possess all of her.

*You got as much as I could give*, she would tell him, as if he too could hear her whisper. *And now they won't let go of the rest*.

"Tell me another story about them," Tabby would beg, and so she would, a new chapter of the saga growing between them about kingdoms under the sea where people lived forever, and rode fish and giant seahorses, and how they had defenders as tall as the sky who came boiling up from the waters to send their enemies running.

Tabby seemed to like it.

When she asked if there were pictures, Kerry knew better, and didn't show her the ones she had, didn't even acknowledge their existence. The ones taken from Colonel Escovedo's office while the rains drenched the wreckage, after she'd helped the few survivors that she could, the others dead or past noticing what she might take from the office of their commanding officer, whom nobody could locate anyway.

The first eight photos Tabby would've found boring. As for the ninth, Kerry wasn't sure she could explain to a six-year-old what exactly it showed, or even to herself. Wasn't sure she could make a solid case for what was the mouth and what was the eye, much less explain why such a thing was allowed to exist.

One of them, at least, should sleep well while they were here. Came the day, at last, in early February, when her binoculars revealed more than the tranquil pool of the harbor, the snow and ice crusted atop the breakwater, the sullen chop of the winter-blown sea. Against the slate-colored water, they were small, moving splotches the color of algae. They flipped like seals, rolled like otters. They crawled onto the ragged dark stone of Devil Reef, where they seemed to survey the kingdom they'd once known, all that had changed about it and all that hadn't.

And then they did worse.

Even if something was natural, she realized, you could still call it a perversity.

Was it preference? Was it celebration? Or was it blind obedience to an instinct they didn't even have the capacity to question? Not that it mattered. Here they were, finally, little different from salmon now, come back to their headwaters to breed, indulging an urge eighty-some years strong.

It was only a six-block walk to the harbor, and she had the two of them there in fifteen minutes. This side of Water Street, the wharves and warehouses were deserted, desolate, frosted with frozen spray and groaning with every gust of wind that came snapping in over the water.

She wrenched open the wide wooden door to one of the smaller buildings, the same as she'd been doing every other day or so, the entire time they'd been here, first to find an abandoned rowboat, and then to make sure it was still there. She dragged it down to the water's edge, plowing a furrow in a crust of old snow, and once it was in the shallows, swung Tabby into it, then hopped in after. She slipped the oars into the rusty oarlocks, and they were off.

"Mama . . . ?" Tabitha said after they'd pushed past the breakwater and cleared the mouth of the harbor for open sea. "Are you crying?"

In rougher waters now, the boat heaved beneath them. Snow swirled in from the depths overhead and clung to her cheeks, eyelashes, hair, and refused to melt. She was that cold. She was *always* that cold.

"Maybe a little," Kerry said.

"How come?"

"It's just the wind. It stings my eyes."

She pulled at the oars, aiming for the black line of the reef. Even if no one else might've, even if she could no longer see them, as they hid within the waves, she heard them sing a song of jubilation, a song of wrath and hunger. Their voices were the sound of a thousand waking nightmares.

To pass the time, she told Tabby a story, grafting it to all the other tales she'd told about kingdoms under the sea where people lived forever, and rode whales and danced with dolphins, and how they may not have been very pleasant to look at, but that's what made them love the beautiful little girl from above the waves, and welcome her as their princess.

Tabby seemed to like it.

Ahead, at the reef, they began to rise from the water and clamber up the rock again, spiny and scaled, finned and fearless. Others began to swim out to meet the boat. Of course they recognized her, and she them. She'd sat with nearly a third of them, trying trying trying to break through from the wrong side of the shore.

While they must have schemed like fiends to drag her deep into theirs.

*I bring you this gift*, she would tell them, if only she could make herself heard over their jeering in her head. *Now could you please just set me free?*

*[T]he titles of those books told him much. They were the black, forbidden things which most sane people have never even heard of, or have heard of only in furtive, timorous whispers; the banned and dreaded repositories of equivocal secrets and immemorial formulae which have trickled down the stream of time from the days of man's youth, and the dim, fabulous days before man was.*

*"The Haunter of the Dark" · H. P. Lovecraft (1936)*

## · MYSTERIUM TREMENDUM ·
### Laird Barron

### 1.

We bought supplies for our road trip at an obscure general goods store in Seattle—a multi-generational emporium where you could purchase anything from space age tents to snowshoes once worn by Antarctic explorers. That's where we came across the guidebook.

Glenn found it on a low shelf in the rear of the shop, wedged between antique souvenir license plates and an out of print *Jenkins' Field Guide to Birds of Puget Sound*. Fate is a strange and wondrous force—the aisles were dim and narrow and a large, elderly couple in muumuus was browsing the very shelf and it was time for us to go, but as I opened my mouth to suggest we head for the bar down the street, one of them, the man I think, bumped a rack of postcards and several items splatted on the floor. The man didn't glance back as he walked away.

Glenn despised that sort of rudeness, although he contented himself to mutter and replace the fallen cards. So we poked at the shelves and there *it* was. He brushed off the cover, gave it a look then passed it around to Victor, Dane, and myself. The book shone in the dusty gloom of that aisle, and it radiated an aura of antiquity and otherworldliness, like a blackened bone unearthed from the Burgess Shale. The book was pocket-sized and bound in dark leather. An embossment of a broken red ring was the only cover art. Its interior pages were of thin, brown paper crammed with articles and essays and route directions typed in a small, blurry font that gave you a migraine if you stared at it too long. The table of contents divided Washington State into regions and documented, in exhaustive detail, areas of interest to the prospective tourist. A series of appendices provided illustrations and reproductions of hand-drawn maps. The original copyright was 1909, and this seventh edition had been printed in 1986. On the title page: attributed to *Divers Hands* and no publisher; entitled *Moderor de Caliginis*.

"*Moderor de Caliginis!*" Victor said in a flawless imitation of Bruce Campbell in *Army of Darkness*. He punctuated each syllable with a stabbing flourish—a magician conjuring a rabbit, or vanishing his nubile assistant.

Dane tilted his head so his temple touched Victor's. "But what does it mean?" he said in the stentorian tone of a 1950s broadcaster reporting a saucer landing. He'd done a bit of radio in college.

"I flunked Latin," Glenn said, running his thumb across the book's spine. His expression was peculiar.

The proprietor didn't know anything either. He pawed through a stack of manifests without locating an entry or price for the book. He sold it to Glenn for five dollars. We took it home (along with two of the fancy tents) and I stuck it in the top drawer of my nightstand. Those crinkly, musty pages, their water stains and blemishes, fascinated me. The book smelled as if it had been fished from a stagnant well and left to dry on a rock. Its ambiguous pedigree and nebulous diction hinted at mysteries and wonders. I was the one who translated the title. *Moderor de Caliginis* means *The Black Guide*. Or close enough.

2.

I'd lived with Glenn for five years in a hilly Magnolia neighborhood. Our house was a brick two story built in the 1930s and lovingly restored by the previous owner. The street was quiet and crowded by huge, spreading magnolias. There was a sheer stone staircase walkup from the curb and a good-sized yard bordered by a wrought iron fence and dense shrubbery. Glenn was junior partner at a software development firm that hadn't quite been obliterated by the dot-com implosion. His office was a nook across from the kitchen with a view of the garden and moldering greenhouse. I wrote articles for the culture sections of several newspapers and did freelance appraisals for galleries and estates. Glenn got a kick out of showing my column photo around—I wore my hair shaggy, with thick sideburns and a thicker mustache, and everybody thought I looked like a 1970s pimp or an undercover cop. I moonlighted as an instructor at a dojo in the University district. We taught little old ladies to poke muggers and rapists in the eyes with car keys and hat pins. Good times.

Dane and Victor flew in from Denver for the long-planned and plotted journey through the hills and dales of our fair state. The plan included them spending a week or so doing the tourist bit in town before we lit out into the wilds. I knew the fellows through Glenn who'd attended college with them. Dane managed telecommunications and advertising for the Denver Broncos. A rugged blond with a flattened nose and cauliflower ears from amateur boxing matches and tavern brawls. His partner Victor was stocky and bald and decidedly non-violent. He'd inherited a small fortune from his parents and devoted his time to editing an online poetry journal of repute. The journal was once mentioned by then U.S. poet laureate Billy Collins in his weekly column. Victor was a Charles Simic and Mark Strand man and I liked him from the start. Glenn referred to them as Ebony and Ivory on account of Victor's resemblance to a young Stevie Wonder and Dane's being as white as a bar of soap.

We threw a party and invited a few friends from Glenn's company and some writer and photographer colleagues of mine. Glenn barbequed steak on the back porch. I mixed a bunch of Margaritas in pitchers and after dinner we sat around drinking as the sky darkened and the stars came out.

The big news was Dane and Victor had gotten hitched in California before Proposition Eight overturned the Ninth Circuit Court of Appeals. This was a year and a half gone by, so their visit was part vacation and part honeymoon. I confess to a flash of jealousy at the matching rings, the wallet of sepia tone wedding photos and the sea of family and friends in those photos. The permanence of their relationship galled me and I loathed myself for it. Glenn hadn't proposed and I was too stubborn, too afraid of rejection to propose to him. I slipped away while everybody was laughing about the wedding high jinks.

Glenn sauntered in as I was rinsing the dishes and put his arm around me and kissed my cheek. He was tall and lanky and had to lean over to do it. I'd drunk four or five Margaritas in the meantime and my eyes were watery and doubtless red. He was oblivious, not that I held it against him. Glenn could be tender and thoughtful and wasn't so much indifferent as clueless. Despite his interest in classical music, literature and art, a possibly less wholesome, but no less cerebral, fascination with the esoteric and the occult, he didn't like to think very deeply about certain things. His father was dead; a career railroad man, second generation Irish, he dropped in his traces from a heart attack when Glenn was fifteen. Glenn's parents had known he was gay since grade school and they accepted him. Everything came easy. He cheerfully took what we had for granted as he took everything else for granted. The guy read books and worked with strings of code, for Christ's sake. Truly a miracle he possessed any social graces whatsoever.

As for me, my father had been a white boy from the Bronx who served thirty years in the Army, the last decade of it as a colonel. My mother was a former Brazilian teen queen bathing beauty who married Dad to get the hell out of her hometown. Dad passed away in his sleep from an overdose of sleeping pills a few weeks before I met Glenn. I sometimes wondered if it'd been accidental, or closer to the protagonist's opt-out in that famous little novel by Graham Greene. Mom pretended I'd court a fine young lady one day soon and sire a brood of kids. My three brothers were scattered across the world. The eldest kept in touch from India. Otherwise, I received birthday cards, the odd phone call or email, and that was that. Glenn kissed me again—hard and on the mouth, and he tasted sweetly of booze. I wiped my eyes and grinned and let it ago like I always did.

Gnats and mosquitoes descended. The guests retreated to the living room. Glenn put on music and began serving another round of drinks from the wet bar. I fetched *Moderor de Caliginis* and took it to my office. An examination of the book revealed phone numbers and mailing addresses amidst the other text, although considering the edition's publishing date, I assumed most were dead ends. In tiny print on the copyright page was a line that read SUBMISSIONS with a P.O. box address in Walla Walla.

Meanwhile, the party was in full gear. Between songs, raucous laughter floated to me. My CDs—Glenn preferred classical music; Beethoven, Chopin, Gershwin, Sibelius. That wouldn't do at our casual get-togethers. Somebody sang along to the choruses of Neil Sedaka, Miles Davis, and Linda Ronstadt, a step behind and off-key. Daulton, our grizzled tomcat, jumped onto the easy chair near my desk and went to sleep. Old Daulton was a comforting soul.

I hunched over my computer monitor and ran searches of key phrases from the book. A guy in Germany claimed there were numerous versions of *The Black Guide*—he'd acquired editions for regions in France, Spain, Portugal, and South Africa. A college student in Pullman wrote of a friend of a friend who'd used the book to explore caves in Yakima. That struck me as odd—I wasn't familiar with any notable caves in Washington. Another man, an anthropologist named Berman, explained that several of the entries provided contact information for practitioners of the occult. During the late 1990s he'd visited some of these persons and joined them in séances, divinations, and fertility rituals. He was currently a professor at Central Washington University. On a lark, I sent him an email, noting I'd inherited a copy of the guide.

The most interesting item I retrieved during my three lonely hours at the keyboard was the journal of an individual from Ellensburg who went by the handle of Rose. Rose started her journal in April, 2007. There were three entries—the first talked about not really wanting a journal at all, but keeping one on the advice of her therapist. The second was a twenty-five hundred word essay on her travels abroad and eventually finding *The Black Guide* at a gift shop in Ellensburg. Apparently Rose had sought the book for several years and was elated. The guide contained a listing of secret attractions, hidden places, and persons "in the know" regarding matters esoteric and arcane. In the final entry, she mentioned packing for a trip with three friends to the "tomb" on the Olympic Peninsula and would make a full report on her return. The journal hadn't been updated since June, 2007. Nonetheless, I left an anonymous message inquiring after her status. This satisfied me in a perverse way—it felt as if I'd thrown her a lifeline.

I signed off around three a.m. Glenn was already in bed and snoring. I lay beside him and stared at the pale reflection of streetlights on the ceiling. Who was Rose? Young, pretty, wounded. Or, maybe not. The kind of girl who took pictures of herself in period costumes. Pale, thick mascara, in her rhinestone purse a deck of tarot cards she'd inherited from an older woman, a long lost sweetheart. Rose was a girl with many friends and lovers, yet who was usually alone. I pressed *The Black Guide* against the breast of my pajamas and wondered where she was at that moment. I dreamed of her that night, but in the morning all I remembered was flying above an endless forest and the rocky bluff of a small mountain, and into a cave that swallowed me whole.

## 3.

"C'mon. Tell Willem a Tommy story," Glenn wore a loopy smirk. He'd done one too many shots of Cuervo.

"Oh, yes!" Victor pounded his empty glass on the table.

"Okay, okay. Here's one about Thomas-san," Dane said. His hair was tousled, his cheeks were flushed. He eyed me with an intensity that indicated such a story symbolized a great confidence, that I was on the verge of admittance to the inner circle.

This was in the early evening after hiking up and down Queen Anne Hill since breakfast, peeking into shops, trying the innumerable bistros and pubs on for size, and yelling raucous comments at the construction boys ripping apart the sidewalk in front of the Phoenician Theatre. Now we were just off campus at a corner booth in a dimly lighted hole in the wall called The Angry Norseman. We'd drunk with the vigor of sailors on shore leave the entire day and were almost sober again. A gaggle of college students in University of Washington sweatshirts congregated at the bar and overflowed the tables. It was getting rowdy.

"Who the hell is Tommy?" I said.

"A short, stubby guy who took six years to graduate," Glenn said. Older than us. Balding, but he had this Michael Bolton thing going on. Hair down to his bum. Managed a pizza parlor."

"Mean sonofabitch," Dane said. "He'd get drunked up and pick fights with the frat boys. One of 'em whacked him in the head with a golf club. Just pissed him off."

"I remember that." Glenn chuckled and licked the salt from his wrist. He downed his tequila. His eyes were bright. "Cops locked him in the tank overnight and slapped him with disorderly conduct."

"A real loveable asshole," Dane said.

Glenn said, "He got killed waterskiing a couple years ago. First time out, too. Strapped on a pair of skis and got his neck broken fifteen minutes later. Tried to jump a ramp. Dunno who the hell was driving. All their fault, y'know."

"Holy shit," I said.

Glenn patted my hand and shrugged. "Whole thing was moronic. Sorta fit, though. He was gonna go out from a rotten liver, a motorcycle accident, or a prison fight. That's just how it was with the crazy fool."

"Wait, that's—" Victor closed his mouth.

Dane said, "Anyway. This isn't really a Tommy story per se. We had this other buddy named Max. Ol' Maximus was a real cocksman and he was cozy with this little rich girl who was going to an all girl school on the other end of town. A real honey."

"Hear, hear," Glenn raised his glass. "Glittery green eye-shadow, Catholic schoolgirl skirts and thigh-high lace-up boots. Ruff!"

"Right, right. Becky Rimmer."

"You're kidding," I said.

"Her name *was* Rimmer. Kinda unfortunate. Her folks were out of town and she invited Max over for the weekend, and me, Glenn, Thomas and Vicky latched on. Becky didn't like it much, but what the hell was she gonna do? So we arrive at the house—and man, it's posh. A gaming room with a kickass sound system and a stocked bar. We were in seventh heaven. She laid down the ground rules—be careful with the new pool table and hands off Daddy's scotch. No problem! Max promised.

"Becky disappears with Max for some nooky. First thing—Tommy, who's already high as a kite, decides to shoot some pool. He misses the cue ball and digs a three inch groove in the felt."

"And the booze?" I said.

Dane pantomimed guzzling from a bottle. "Heh, Thomas had her old man's supply of Dewar's in his guts in short order. Pretty quick, Tommy gets bored and decides to check on Becky and Max who've locked themselves in Daddy's den and are making like wild animals. Tommy gets some tools from the garage and the next thing we know, he's standing on a stool and drilling a hole in the door to make a peephole. Laughing like a lunatic, sawdust piling on his shoes."

Victor said, "Me and Dane dragged him away from the door and gave him some more booze. Things are going okay until there's a crash from the den and Max starts hollering. Turns out, he was banging the girl on a glass coffee table and at the height of the rumpy pumpy it shattered and she dropped through. They were going at it doggy-style, so she sliced her arms and knees. Nothing serious, but it looked awful. Blood and jizz everywhere."

"Yeah," Dane said. "A scene from one of Takashi Miike's films. Naturally, we took her to the hospital. The docs gave her some sutures and bandaged her head to toe. Many awkward questions were asked. Max drives her home and the rest of us split. Mom and Dad get back early. Becky's lying in bed trying to think of a story when she hears her mom in the study go, 'Oh. My. God. What is this *filth*—?' And, as Mommy dearest comes through the door waving her daughter's soiled undergarments, from downstairs her dad bellows, 'WHO THE HELL DRANK MY DEWAR'S?' "

I laughed so hard my side ached. "What did she do?"

"Girl was a soap opera junkie. She squinted and said in a pitiful whisper, 'Mommy? Mommy? Is that you?' "

Glenn bought us another round. Conversation turned to the impending trip. Victor unfolded a sheet of paper and showed us notes he'd made in heavy pencil. On the itinerary was a day hike on Mount Vernon, a tour of the Tacoma Museum of Glass, a leisurely day in the state capital of Olympia, then a blank slate. There'd definitely be a night or two camping on the Peninsula; *where* was yet to be settled. Victor said, "That leaves us some days to check out the sights. Maybe visit Port Angeles?"

After much noncommittal mumbling from the three of them, I took *The Black Guide* from my pocket and thumbed through the section on the Olympic Peninsula. "The Lavender Festival in Sequim is coming up. Port Angeles is close by, and Lake Crescent. Glenn and I stayed at the lodge a few years ago. Gorgeous scenery."

"Absolutely," Glenn said. Victor said, "I hear it's spooky. The Lady of the Lake murders . . . "

"Oh, that was ages ago," I said, albeit it made me uneasy that I'd recently read a passage in the guide documenting the scandalous tale. Too many coincidences were accumulating for my taste.

Dane took the guide and turned it toward the dim lamp hanging above our table. He grinned. "Vicky, look at this!" Victor leaned in and scanned the page. Dane said, "This thing is a kick in the pants. Says there's a hotel in Centralia where they hold séances once a month. And a . . . dolmen up a trail on Mystery Mountain."

"See," I said. "we should put Sequim on the calendar. Go visit this dolmen after we see how the lavender jelly gets made."

"What's that, anyhow?" Dane said.

"A prehistoric tomb," Glenn said. "There aren't any dolmen in this state. Maybe I'm wrong, but it sounds fishy." He spent an inordinate amount of time cruising Wikipedia. "Up a trail, eh?"

"About seventeen or eighteen miles up a crappy road, more like. The Kalamov Dolmen and Cavern. There are some campsites. It's on the edge of a preserve." Victor stroked his goatee.

Dane said, "This is a seriously cool idea. I gotta see it. I gotta." He poked Victor in the ribs and laughed. "C'mon, baby. This sounds awesome, don't it?"

Victor agreed that it indeed sounded awesome. Glenn promised to arrange for a bed and breakfast in Sequim and to make a few calls regarding the mysterious dolmen. If nothing else, the park seemed as decent a place as any to camp for a night or two. The guide mentioned trout in the mountain streams. I wasn't much for the sport, but Glenn and Dane had dabbled in fly fishing.

Once I got the guide back, I studied the entry on the Kalamov Dolmen and its attendant notes in the appendix, which included references to celestial phases and *occultation rites.* I didn't know what any of that stuff meant. Nonetheless, we'd have lively anecdotes for future vacation slide shows and a story to tell, I was certain.

4.

Glenn and I frequently made love the first year we were together. Not so much later. We were perpetually exhausted because of project deadlines, hostile takeovers at the workplace and, of late, the ever shrinking newspaper circulation. Glenn had climbed the ladder by dint of overtime and weekends; I still received more commissions than I could shake a stick at. Familiarity took its toll as well.

Once Dane and Victor arrived, Glenn tried to fuck me every night. That hurt my feelings. I knew he was jealous of Victor—Victor was a flirt and he came on to me in a not too serious way. Glenn laughed it off, however, when the lights dimmed. . . . He was also a territorial sonofabitch and it aroused him that they were screwing like rabbits down the hall. I tried not to let it bother me too much, although I drew the line at him groping me while dead drunk. That night, after we piled into a cab and finally made it home from the Angry Norseman, I smacked his hands away as he kept grabbing at my zipper. He persisted. I lurched downstairs and crashed on the couch, a maneuver I hadn't resorted to since our last real argument the year prior.

There was a special on the History Channel. A crack team of geologists and a film crew were mucking about Spain, exploring caverns and whatnot. My eyelids drooped. I slowly emerged from a doze to hear a man discussing holy rites among the Klallam tribes and other ancient peoples of the Pacific Northwest. He described burial mounds along the Klallam River and the locations of megaliths and dolmens throughout Western Washington. I was confused, second-guessing Glenn's assertions that no ancient megaliths or dolmen existed in our state, but the narrator continued: *Of particular interest is the Kalamov Cavern site near Mystery Mountain National Park. The Kalamov Dolmen, named after Dr. Boris Kalamov, who discovered it in 1849, is remarkable in its size and antiquity. A relic of the Neolithic Age . . . 3000 B.C. Perhaps older. A word of caution is in order. There is a dangerous . . .* The monologue faded and someone wailed in pain.

I lifted my head and the room was full of blue, unfocused light. The television screen skipped, and ghostly figures shifted between bars of static. Soundless because I'd hit the mute button prior to nodding off. Every channel was full of snow and shadow, except for the ones with the black bar saying NO SIGNAL. Unsettled without knowing precisely why, I rubbed my eyes and went to the window. The neighborhood was blanketed in darkness but for a scattering of porch lights. The cityscape was hidden by the canopy of the trees. I hugged myself against an inexplicable chill as I attempted to recall the odd commentary of the dream.

Turning, I saw a man sitting in the armchair in the corner near the pine shelf that housed a meager selection of my books. A burst of light from the TV screen revealed this wasn't Glenn or our guests. I was woozily drunk— the topknot, the surly, piggish features, the short, bulky frame, was precisely how I'd envisioned the inimitable Tommy of college lore. He reclined, mostly concealed in shadow, but I saw he was naked, one thick leg folded across the other to artfully cover his manhood. His flesh was very pale; the flesh of a creature who'd dwelt in a sunless grotto for ages. He raised a finger to his lips. "I've just come to talk," he said, imparting menace with the over enunciation of each syllable, hinting that on any other day I'd experience something other than conversation. "Scream, and our buddy

Glenn is going to come running. He'll trip over Vicky's jacket on the top step and roll down the stairs. It'll be a mess, trust me."

I wiped drool from the corner of my mouth. The horrible vision of Glenn falling, shattering his spine, kept me from yelling. I said, "You're him."

"Call me Tom."

"Tom. Can't be."

"Didn't say I *was* Tom. I said, *call* me Tom. Got any hooch? That's a rhetorical question, by the way."

I shuffled to the kitchen and immediately noticed the cellar door ajar by several inches. The way down was via a narrow wooden staircase missing its railing. The cellar itself was small and cramped and mildewed and we never used it. I took a bottle of Stoli from the cupboard. I poured two tall water glasses a finger below the rims and carried them to the living room. In the back of my mind I'd hoped this would break the spell, that I'd snap out of this somnambulant state and find the visitor had evaporated. He hadn't. Tom accepted the glass and drank half of it in one long gulp. I sat on the couch, elbows on my knees, clasping my own drink with both shaky hands. "Why you? I don't get it. Why you and not my granny? Or my dad?" He shrugged. I said, "It's because of that story tonight."

"Real double-breasted asshole, wasn't I?" he said, and laughed. "Your granny and your old man don't have anything to say to you, I guess. You're making assumptions about where I come from, anyway. This ain't like that. See wings on me? Horns?"

"Maybe *An American Werewolf in London* made a bigger impression on me than I thought. Next time we meet your face will be a melted pizza."

"Loved that fucking movie. Damn, that nurse was hot. For months I got a boner every time I heard a shower running."

"She didn't do much for me."

"I suppose not."

"What's going on here?"

"I could use a smog. Drinking and smoking go hand and hand. My old man was Black Irish. Like Glenn's. We Black Irish smoke and drink and beat our wives." Tommy laughed, grating and nasty.

"Glenn quit," I said. "I don't smoke, either. Sorry."

Tom stared at me through the dark. His eyes glistened in the blue radiance of the TV, brightening, dimming, disappearing with each flicker of the screen. There was a hateful weight in that stare. "Dane smokes," he said.

"So, go ask *him* for a *smog*," I said.

He laughed again. "You wouldn't like what happens."

I had another vision, a confused, menacing premonition that sickened me even though I couldn't see anything but weird, jerky movement in the shadows, and a smash close-up of Dane's eyes growing too wide. I walked into the kitchen and rummaged in a drawer until I found a pack of Kools that had been squished under the silverware tray since forever. I lighted a cigarette on the burner, returned to Tom and handed it over. He said, "Tastes shitty like a cigarette should." I had set my glass on the arm of the couch. I drank the rest of the vodka while Tom smoked. A sulfurous stench filled the room. "You play with Ouija boards when you was a kid, Willem?"

I nodded. "Sure, in high school. I bought one—Parker Brothers."

"Hell, all you need is a piece of construction paper and a glass. They work. Ouija boards. Other things too. Like that book you've been dicking with. It completes a circuit."

I snapped my fingers. "I knew it. The book."

"Right on, Ace. The book. *The Black Guide.* You been fucking around with it, haven't you?"

"If by fucking around with it, you mean reading it, then yeah. I have."

"C'mon, those drawings in the back—you didn't copy some of them? Maybe scribbled a few of those weird doodads that look like hieroglyphics onto scratch paper. Tried to sound out some of those gobbledygook Latin phrases. You're a nerd. Course you did."

He was right. I'd copied a diagram of a solar eclipse and its related alchemical symbols into my moleskin journal with the heavy enamel pen my younger brother bought me back when we were still talking. I'd also made dozens of curlicue doodles of the broken circle on the cover. There was something ominously compelling about that ring—it struck a chord on what I could only describe as an atavistic level. It spoke to my inner hominid and the hominid screeched and capered its distress. "What if I did? Did I do something wrong?" My voice was flat and metallic in my ears. I sounded strident and absurd.

He said, "Remember the Golden Rules. Action equals reaction. The

Crack that runs through everything stares into you. Big fish eats little fish. Night's agents watch you, ape."

"Yeah? Why are you here? Why are you warning me and not your chums. Their idea to use the book for sight-seeing, not mine."

"I'm not here to warn anybody. I'm here to give you a good ol' mindfucking, among other things. Think you found the book by accident? There are no accidents around here. Time is a ring. Everything and everyone gets squished under the wheel."

"I don't understand."

"Then you, my friend, are an idiot. And friend, keep going the way you're going and maybe a friend will slice your heart from your chest and take a bite out of it like a Washington's Best in the name of The First Power. That's how friends are."

"This an *idiotic* imaginary conversation," I said. There wasn't anything imaginary, however, about the searing alcohol in my burps, or the fact my head was wobbling, nor the flutter-flutter of my heart. "Shoo, fly, shoo."

Tom didn't answer. The cherry of his cigarette dulled and blackened. A split second before his shape merged with the darkness, it changed. The room became cold. A woman said, *There are frightful things.* I couldn't tell where the whisper originated. I finally gathered the courage to switch on the lamp and I was alone.

Sleep was impossible. I made a cup of coffee and crept into my office and ran a search on the Kalamov Cavern, the Kalamov Dolmen, and Dr. Kalamov himself. There wasn't a record of a dolmen of any kind in Washington. Boris Kalamov turned out to be no doctor at all, but a rather smarmy nineteenth century charlatan who faked his academic credentials in order to bolster extraordinary claims made in his series of faux scholarly books regarding naturalism and the occult. The good doctor's fraudulent escapades came to a sad end thanks to French justice—he was convicted of some cryptic act of pagan barbarism and confined to a Parisian asylum for the remainder of his years. As to whether any of Dr. Kalamov's treatises mentioned a cavern or dolmen on the Olympic Peninsula, I'd likely never know as all were long out of print. However, Mystery Mountain National Park was indeed where *The Black Guide* indicated, and open for business until mid-October.

• • •

Glenn scrambled eggs for breakfast. He didn't comment on my absence from bed. I spent enough late nights at the computer he scarcely noticed anymore. He was hung over—all of us were. Pale sunlight streamed through the window and illuminated our chalky faces as we sat at the kitchen table and sipped orange juice and picked at scrambled eggs. The whiteness of Glenn's cheeks, the raccoon-dark circles of his blank eyes, startled me. My own hands shone, for a moment, gnarled and black-veined, as if from tremendous age. I gulped a whole glass of juice, coughing a bit, and when I looked again I saw it was only an illusion. I'd seen it before, watching Glenn sleep with the light illuminating him in such a way that his future self, the wrinkled senior citizen, was forecast.

5.

Glenn's Land Rover was a rattletrap sky-blue hulk. He'd driven the rig exactly four times since purchasing it at an estate sale in Wenatchee some years prior. Normally, we tooled around in his Saab or rode the bus. The Land Rover had bench seats wide enough to host a football team, a huge cargo bed, and smelled of mold, rust, and cigarette smoke.

"Hurray," Victor said when Glenn backed it out of the garage. "Let's get this safari started!"

September was unseasonably warm. The Land Rover lacked modern amenities including a CD player and air conditioning. I sat in back with the window rolled down. Everybody wore off-the-rack Hawaiian shirts (a gag dreamed up by Dane) and sunglasses—designer shades for my companions; for me, a cheapo set I'd gotten at an airport gift shop. I also strapped on a pair of steel-toed boots as I usually did when away from home. One never knew when one might need to stomp a mugger or other nefarious type. Victor wore a digital camera on a strap around his neck. While drinking one night, he'd confided parlaying his access (through Dane's position) to the Broncos' sideline into almost twenty-five hundred close-up pictures of the cheerleaders in action. He was toying with the notion of auctioning the album on the underground channels of the internet. I thought there were already plenty of candid cheerleader shots floating around the internet; then what did I know?

The voyage started well—Victor even pronounced a soothsaying to that effect: "Sun and moon augur a favorable and erotically charged escapade!"

I said goodbye to the cat—a neighbor would pop in and feed him every day—and locked the doors.

The hiking trip to Mount Vernon was a relaxed affair as none of us were hardcore outdoorsmen. We had a picnic in the foothills and returned to the lodge well before dark, where we played pinochle with some other tourists, and drank beer until it was time to turn in for the night. Glenn and I got into bed. He typed on his computer while I labored over *The Essential Victor Hugo*—the Blackmore translation. My problem was less with Hugo than the nagging urge to dig *The Black Guide* from my suitcase and have another go at the procession of peculiar diagrams in the appendices and to attempt to tease more meaning from the cryptic entries and footnotes.

I'd told Glenn about my encounter with Tom, careful to frame it as a weird dream. Glenn frowned and asked for more details. He was intrigued by the occult, fascinated to learn of the secret lives of the famous artists I studied. His interest in such matters waxed stronger than mine—alas, his patience for wading through baroque texts wasn't equal to the task. Upon listening to the tale of Tom's apparition, he'd muttered, "What does it mean?" He was too calm, obviously throttling a much more visceral reaction. Whether this deeper emotion was one of sympathy for my strange encounter, or worry that my screws were loose, I couldn't tell. And I'd said, "I was drunk. It didn't mean anything," while thinking otherwise. Tom indeed referred to cigarettes as "smogs," a fact I'd been unaware, and thus a detail that lent creepy and disturbing authenticity to the encounter. Dream or not, I hadn't cracked the book for three days. I imagined it burning a hole in the case, a chunk of meteorite throbbing with sinister energy.

The next day we spent a few hours at the Tacoma Museum of Glass, then soldiered on to Olympia for a desultory afternoon of wandering the streets and poking around the cafes and boutiques. While my companions were sipping ice coffees, I stepped into a used bookstore and investigated the regional history and travel sections. I got into a conversation with the clerk on duty, a bored ex-librarian who stirred to life when I showed her the guide. She adjusted her glasses and made ticking noises with her tongue as she flipped pages. "I've heard of these. Farmer's Almanacs for pagans."

The ex-librarian was tall and thin and wore cat's-eye glasses with pearly frames. Her hair was black and straight and her hands were bigger than Dane's. She asked where I'd gotten the book and seemed disappointed that

I couldn't remember the name of the store in Seattle. I asked her what she made of the appendices, directing her to the drawings and arcane symbols.

"Well, I'm sure I can't say." She shut the book with one hand in the resounding manner they must teach in Librarian School. She smiled obliquely. "Perhaps you should visit one of the individuals listed in *Moderor de Caliginis.* Such a person could doubtless tell you a few things."

Long shadows lay across the buildings when I rejoined everyone at the sidewalk table. My ice coffee had melted to a cup of slush. I envisioned the ex librarian's hair swept in a raven's wing over her bony shoulder, her simple blouse and Capri pants transformed into an elegant evening dress some vamp in a Hammer film might toss on for a wild night at the castle. Her smile smoldered in my imagination. Clammy and unnerved, I suggested we repair to the hotel and change for dinner.

The Flintlock Hotel (est. 1895) was a brick and plaster building set back from Capitol Boulevard between a floral shop and an antique furniture store. The boulevard was lined with trees, and a mini U.S. flag rustled on every light pole between downtown and the Tumwater Bridge. Glenn had rented the McKinley Quarters. This was on the third floor, overlooking the street; a cozy number with a sitting room, bedroom, and two baths. There were all kinds of frontier photographs in frames and the place smelled like roses and Douglas fir. Dane and Victor got the Monroe Suite down the hall. Same décor, same layout, but a view of the alley.

I told Glenn I had a migraine. Concerned, he volunteered to cancel our dinner plans and stay in to watch over me. I was having none of that—what I needed was a couple of hours rest, then, I'd join him and the boys for drinks and dancing at one of the clubs. He ordered warm milk and aspirin from room service and waited with me like a perfect dear until it arrived. He watched me take the aspirin and drink the milk. He felt my forehead then left with his jacket slung over his shoulder.

I waited five minutes, then dialed the anthropologist at his office. We'd arranged to talk a couple of days beforehand. Dr. Berman answered on the second ring. "Look, this guide. It's special." His voice was rough. I pictured him: alone in the wing of large, decrepit campus museum, a disheveled academic wearing a tweed jacket and thick glasses, slouched in a chair at a desk cluttered with papers and a skull paperweight. His office was lighted by a single lamp. He was smoking a cigarette, a cheap bottle of whiskey in arm's reach. "Say, any notes in the margins? Pages eighty through one-ten. That'd be the chapters on the Juniper Dunes, Olympia, the Mima Mounds . . . "

"Yeah," I said. "So that was you. I can't read your handwriting."

"Neither can I." His chair creaked in the background. I got the impression he was pouring from his bottle and congratulated myself on being so damned clever.

I said, "Why'd you get rid of the book?"

"I didn't. My assistant accidentally put it in a box of materials the department donated to the University of Washington. It was some months before I discovered the mistake. The university had no record of its arrival. If I may ask, where did you find it?" I told him. He said, "Odd. Well, perhaps I could inveigle you to return it to me. To be honest, it might fetch a considerable sum on the collector market. Likely more than I can afford."

"I'm not interested in money. Sure, I'll send it back—after our vacation. Where did *you* come across the book?"

"In the foothills of the Cascades. I was backpacking with friends. They knew of this cabin near an abandoned mine. Supposedly a trapper dwelt there in the 1940s. The place was remarkably intact, albeit vermin-infested. The book lay at the bottom of a rusty footlocker, buried beneath newspaper clippings and magazines. Passing strange. A hiker must've hidden it. I often ponder the scenario that led to such an act." While he talked, I reflected that anthropologists and their ilk came by their reputations as tomb robbers honestly. He got cagey when I inquired after his experiences with the pagans mentioned in the book. "Ah, all I can say is some farmers here and there cleave to ancient customs. More country folk look to the sun, the moon, and the stars for succor than you might think. The nature spirits and the old gods. They don't advertise, what with Western culture and Christianity's persecution of such traditions." This latter comment struck an unpleasant chord.

I said, "The good folk don't advertise, except in the little black book. You mean cults. Satanists?"

"Those too, I suppose. I don't know firsthand, but to my knowledge I never met any."

"My boyfriend tells me Washington State is a hotbed of Satanic worship," I said. "By the way. Have you visited the Kalamov Dolmen?"

"The what?"

"Page, um, seventy-two. The Kalamov Dolmen on Mystery Mountain."

There was a long pause. "I don't recall reading that entry. A dolmen? Hard to believe I'd miss something so important. Well, the guide has a peculiar . . . effect. The type is so tiny." He hesitated and the bottle and glass clinked again. "This may sound, nutty, but be careful. As I said, I met decent folk on the main. User-generated content has its perils. There exists a certain potential for mischief on behalf of whomever anonymously recommends an attraction or service. Look sharp."

"Sure, Doc." We said goodbye, then I blurted, "Oh, wait. I meant to ask—you happen to meet any of the folks who've owned the book? There's a girl in your area . . . Rose. That's her online persona." I gave him the rundown of Rose's journal entries.

"Hm. Doesn't ring any bells," Dr. Berman said. "She found the book in Ellensburg? I taught there for a decade. I wonder if she was one of my students. A striking coincidence if so. Please, keep in touch."

We said goodbye again, for real.

Tree branches scraped the window. A streetlamp illuminated the edges of the leaves. I checked my watch. The good doctor had seemed in a hurry to end the conversation. Maybe he knew more about the anonymous journalist than he admitted. I unzipped my suitcase and lifted *Moderor de Caliginis* in its swaddling cloth from amid my socks and underwear. I unwrapped the guide and set it on the table. "Boy, you do get around," I said. A shiny black beetle, easily the size of my thumbnail, crawled from the lumpy pages. It scuttled across the tabletop and fell to the carpet, shriveled in death.

## 6.

I went downstairs to the lounge and started a tab with a double vodka on the rocks. The place was small and half full of patrons, yet full of mirrors, thus it appeared busy. Behind the bar there was a big photograph of three loggers standing in the sawn wedge of a redwood. The trio had short hair and handlebar mustaches. Two of them leaned on double-headed axes. The third logger stood a Swede saw on end so it rested against his shoulder. The men wore dirty long johns and suspenders. I finished my drink and the bartender set me up with another without my asking.

A guy in a cream-colored suit sweated on the crescent dais under blue and gold lights, and crooned a Marty Robbins ballad about the life of a twentieth-century drifter. I loved Marty Robbins, but I always hated that song. "Hey there, stud." Victor squeezed my arm as he slid in next to me. He wore a cardigan that smelled of smoke and aftershave. The bartender brought him something pink with an umbrella floating in the middle.

"Where are the other Musketeers?" I said.

Victor toyed with the umbrella. "Athos and Porthos are flirting with a bevy of cute tourista chicks at the Brotherhood Tavern down the street. Totally yanking the poor girls' chains. Too hilarious for me. I bailed."

I laughed. "How cute are they?"

He shrugged, sipped his drink and smiled back. "Not at all, really. Dane's hammered. I told him if he gets drunk and obnoxious I'm Audi 5000. Let Glenn drag his worthless carcass back to the hotel."

I said, "Hear, hear," and drained my vodka. I crunched the ice and watched the door. The lobby was dim and the doorway hung in space, a black rectangle.

The singer finished his set with "Cool Water" and "Big Iron." He made his way from the dais and slumped farther down the bar. His toupee was bad and he'd pancaked his makeup far too heavily. His face seemed familiar, but I couldn't place it. Victor asked the bartender to put his drinks on our bill. The singer raised his glass and grinned at us and I saw that his dentures were as cheap and awful as everything else. "Poor bastard," I said, and went to work on my third double. I still smelled the acrid odor of the Kools I'd given the phantom visitor of a few nights prior. The memory of the scent made me ill. It also made me crave a cigarette. "I've got an odd question."

"Ya, okay. Shoot."

"That friend of yours who passed away. Tom. He into anything, I dunno, for want of a better term—weird? Such as fortune telling, magic . . . anything of that nature?"

Victor gave me a long, wondering look. He shook his head and laughed. "Oh, hells yeah. Didn't Glenn ever tell you? Man, we all got into that shit. Tarot cards, mainly. But, I really dug cultural anthropology. Those dudes get into spooky situations. And the poets of yore. Yeats and company. Can't read the classical poets without coming across funky ideas. Anyhow, the whole point of college is to experiment. Did I ever!"

"Anything heavy?"

"Like black magic? Voodoo? We joked around, but no, nothing heavy.

Tommy was extra flakey. Dane and I tried astral projection with him and this Deadhead girl. Lawanda. Tommy kept cutting up until we quit and Dane went and scored some weed to keep him quiet. What about you? Are you a true believer?"

"I'm a theorist. Thing is, I've been studying that guide book we got in Seattle."

"I seen that, girlfriend. A hoax, I'm sure. I bet you anything it's a novelty gag. Somebody printed a couple dozen of them, like pamphlets, and scattered them to the winds." I considered enumerating the reasons his theory didn't hold water. The book materials were too expensive to suggest a joke, its articles and essays were too complex. I refrained because my tongue was getting thick from the booze and also because I wanted him to be correct. He said, "What's Tommy got to do with the book?"

"Not a damned thing. Popped into my head for some reason. You didn't care for Tom much, huh?"

"He was cruel to me. Dane and Glenn were his boys. None of us called him Tom, by the way. In fact, saying it aloud gives me chills. His father called him Tom. Used to beat his ass, or something. Dude was touchy about that. He's in my dreams a lot since the accident."

"That's understandable. You should get some grief counseling if you haven't."

Victor rubbed his bald head and gave me another look. "But I didn't like him."

I said, "Doesn't matter. He's part of your life. In those dreams—what's he want?"

"He doesn't want anything. He moves in the background like a ghost. That makes total sense, though. The irony! I'm at a party with Dane. The party's in a posh Malibu house, one of those places that hangs over a cliff, and the host is my second grade teacher, except he's actually a cinematographer or a screenwriter named Rick or Dick. He's got a star on the boulevard. I mingle with all sorts of people I've known. Weird combinations of grade school classmates and high school sweethearts, janitors, the chick who used to pour coffee at an all-night diner on the corner, a guy who dealt weed from the back of his El Camino when I lived in North Portland, some hookers who hung out near my friend's apartment, and famous dead people—Ginsberg and Kerouac; Johnny Cash and Natalie Wood. Lee Van fucking Cleef. Then

I'll spot Tommy in a corner or on the deck, maybe lurking behind some bushes. Sometimes he's watching me and I'll try to go talk with him. He disappears before I get there." Victor's diamond ring sparked like fire.

I knew he was lying because of how he leaned away from me. Not wholesale lying; some of it was true. The ice had disappeared. I signaled for another drink. My lips were numb; always a bad sign. My forehead was cold and that meant I was afraid. I thought about Tom and the beetle and the pentagram in Appendix B of *Moderor de Caliginis.* I thought about the rough pentagram I'd carved into my desk with a penknife. I'd done it without thinking and covered it with the keyboard afterward, ashamed. This double shot didn't last long either.

"How'd he die? Really."

"Waterskiing."

"Come on, man."

Victor glanced toward the door before signaling the bartender. "I need another one." He waited until a fresh drink was in hand to continue. "Look, I wanted to let you in on this the other night. We invented the water skiing story. *Dane* invented the story. I think he and Glenn have convinced themselves that's what actually happened. Ah, Dane's gonna wring my neck. We agreed to let it be. Tommy fell into a sinkhole. We'd camped in the hills—a couple of miles from here, in fact—and were hiking some trail. A lot of it blurs, you know? Traumatic stress syndrome, or whatever. One minute Tommy was behind me, the next he was gone. The hole wasn't much. I doubt he ever even saw it. Rescue teams came the next day, but the thing was too deep and too unstable. The proverbial bottomless pit. They didn't recover the body. I admit, me and Dane and Glenn freaked. After we finally got our shit together, we didn't talk about it at all. First time somebody asked, Dane smiled and told them the skiing whopper. Couldn't believe my ears. I didn't argue, though. I went along with it. Except, when Glenn was telling you . . . frankly, that shocked the hell out of me. You two are serious. You're serious, aren't you?"

"That's the most horrible thing I've ever heard," I said.

Victor nodded. "Pretty awful. Thomas didn't suffer, at least. Poor bastard."

"You didn't see him fall?" I don't know why it occurred to me to ask.

"He fell. No other explanation. I doubt the guy slipped into the bushes and faked his own death. Living in Maui under an assumed name . . . nah."

"I'm kinda puzzled why you guys still want to go camping after an experience like that. Me, I'd burn my hiking boots and backpack in a nice bonfire."

"Don't be silly. We've gone camping a half dozen times at least. Honestly, I see it your way. Dane and Glenn—those two are macho, macho, macho. What happened to Tommy just made them more bullheaded and foolhardy. Dane wants to go tramping the Indonesian backwoods next year, or the year after. Please, God, no. Snakes, spiders, diseases. I might take a pass."

"Uh-huh, and he'll wind up hitting on some eighteen-year-old stud muffin islander and blame it on the booze and loneliness."

"Ha, yeah. He'd actually blame it on me, if he cheated. Which he wouldn't. He's well aware I carry a switchblade."

"You carry a switchblade?"

"In my sock. Not that I'd use it. I'm too pretty to fight. Although, if D. decided to fuck around, I might make an exception for his balls."

I'd had enough. My body was Jell-O. Victor and I leaned on one another as we walked out of the bar and into the elevator. He gave me a sloppy goodnight kiss that landed on my ear as we parted ways. I crawled under the covers and slept, but not before I spent a few unhappy moments envisioning Tommy lying in subterranean darkness, his legs shattered. He screamed and screamed for help that wouldn't arrive. I said, *"Yes, for the love of God."*

## 7.

Sequim (pronounced *skwim* by the locals) was lovely that summer. The town rested near the Dungeness River at the heart of a shallow basin of the Dungeness-Sequim Valley and not far from the bay. Fields of lavender and poppies and tulips dominated the countryside. There were farms and mills and old, dusty roads that wound between wooden fences and stands of oak and birch and poplar trees. Raymond Carver wrote a poem about Sequim. I'd never read that one.

Our merry band rolled into town after dark and, since Sequim was the kind of place that locked its doors at sundown, we proceeded directly to the bed and breakfast—a cute two-story farmhouse—where Glenn had rented our rooms. The proprietors were an elderly couple named Leland and Portia Teller. Mrs. Teller fixed us a nice dinner despite our being three hours late. Baked salmon, steamed carrots, sourdough bread, and ice cream and black coffee for dessert. After dinner, we sat on the front porch in a collection of rockers and a swing, and smoked cigarettes. Glenn shared one with Dane. They reclined on the swing and giggled like teenagers. The night was muggy and overcast. Lights were off all over town except for the neon flicker of a bar several blocks down and across a the parking lot of a community baseball diamond.

It was a good thing I hadn't been drinking because watching Glenn casually indulge in a habit we'd mutually conquered at great physical and mental anguish ignited a slow burn in my chest. Were I drunk and vulnerable, God knows what I'd have done—wept, cursed him, slapped him, walked away into the night and disappeared. A half dozen times I opened my mouth to say something sharp and ill-tempered. I mastered the impulse. I knew how Glenn would react if I confronted him. He'd laugh and play it as a joke. Then we wouldn't talk for the rest of the trip.

I bit my tongue and moved to the opposite end of the porch and counted lights. Small towns disquieted me with their clannishness, their secretiveness, how everybody interacted as an extended, dirt-beneath-the-fingernails-family, how they scurried into their modernized huts as the sun set. A city boy was always a stranger, no matter how much money he spent, or how much he smiled. Being gay and from the wicked metropolis wasn't a winning combination with country folk.

Later, tucked as near the edge of the bed as possible, I studied the cover of *The Black Guide,* entranced by the broken ring. What was the significance? Its thickness, the suggestion of whorls, brought to mind images of the Ouroboros, the serpent eating its tail. This wasn't the Ouroboros. This was more worm-like, leech-like, and it disturbed me that it wasn't eating its tail. The jaws, the proboscis, the shearing appendage, was free to devour other, weaker delicacies.

8.

The next day marked the opening celebrations of the lavender festival, an event that included a downtown farmers market and fair, and a bus tour of the seven major lavender farms in the area. None of us were lavender aficionados, yet we'd all enjoyed the film *Perfume: The Story of a Murderer*, while Victor and I had also read the novel by Süskind.

There were two buses ready to ferry us around the area. I was grateful for the tinted windows and air conditioning as the temperature had already climbed into the nineties by eleven a.m. The sun hung low and blazed hellishly, but, secure in our plush seats behind dim glass, we laughed. Glenn surprised me by holding my hand. The bus was crowded with senior citizens and a smattering of sunburned couples and their raucous children. Nobody paid us any mind, nor did I think they would; however, his lack of customary reserve took me off guard. I accepted his overture as further rapprochement for hurting my feelings by smoking with Dane. Obviously he wished to appease my jealousy by jumping at the idea of the farm tour.

The tour was organized in the manner of a wine-tasting. We spent the long, insufferably hot day visiting restaurants and observing demonstrations of lavender's multifarious uses in the culinary arts. The traveling show wound down late in the afternoon and we loaded into the Land Rover and sped off in search of booze. The Sarcobatus Tavern was closest, and not too crowded despite the numerous tourists wandering the streets.

A half-dozen college-aged guys occupied a table near the bar. Clean-shaven, muscular, decked in regulation fraternity field attire—baseball caps, sweaters, cargo pants, and athletic shoes. There were a lot of empty bottles on the table. Clearly out of their element and heat-maddened, a couple of the kids gave us hard, bleary stares. "Damn it," I said.

"What?" Glenn said, although he apparently noticed them too because he squeezed my elbow, then stepped away from me. Dane actually said hello to the group in a loud, gregarious tone. A burly kid wearing a Washington State University Cougars cap said something unfriendly and his friends clapped and jeered. Dane winked and flipped the double bird to each of them ("—and you, and you, and you, and you too, cutie pie!") with exaggerated gusto, and while the college boys fumed and sulked, he ordered a round of beers that we carried to the opposite corner of the tavern near a pinball machine with its cord pulled out of the wall.

"Great Scott," Glenn said a few moments after picking up a stray newspaper and scanning the headlines. It still amazed me that my lover seldom actually swore by means of shit, or asshole, or that hoary crowd-pleaser, fuck. No, with Glenn it was always hell, damn, holy cow, and Great Scott, and, on special occasions, jeepers and Zounds. I wasn't fully privy to the origin of this eccentricity, except to note it had to do with a fondness of Golden Age comics and an aversion to his father's egregious addiction to cursing which I gather had been a subject of lifelong embarrassment. "Ten shot dead at a cantina in Ciudad Juarez. Two guys in motorcycle helmets ran in and opened fire with submachine guns. No leads. Police suspect it's connected to drugs . . ."

We all snorted derisive laughter at his humor. Dane said, "Man, I really liked vacationing in Mexico. No way, Jose. That isn't any place for a gringo these days."

"It's not any place for *Mexicans*," Glenn said. "Eleven thousand people killed since 2006 via drug violence. I think you might be safer signing up for Iraq."

"Nonsense—Cancun is safe as houses, as the Brits say," Victor said. "Um, sure, of course Cancun is safe," Glenn said, "but Cancun isn't Mexico. It's an American college resort. Home away from home of damn fool tourists and yon Neanderthals."

"The hell you say!"

"Cancun's *technically* Mexico, just not the *real* Mexico."

"What about Cabo?"

"Fake Mexico."

"I wanna Corona," Dane said. "Hey, barkeep, four Coronas. A ripe lemon wedge this time, for the love of Baby Jesus. Now, friends, let us weep for poor old May-he-co."

We drank our beers and decided the hour had come to mosey out of town. I went into the restroom and pissed and when I returned only three of the frat brothers were still hanging around the tavern. Music from outside throbbed through the window glass. I found everybody else in the parking lot, a fist-fight already in progress. Dane was on one knee, pressed against the wheel well of a truck tricked out with oversized tires and radio antenna. The truck's headlights were on, its door was open and radio speakers boomed "Four Kicks" by The Kings of Leon. Cougars-cap and two of the other guys stood in a semicircle and were punching him in the head. His scalp and nose ran with blood. Darkness was inches away and his blood flowed black in the neon lighting.

I lunged and Glenn caught my arm. "Don't get in his way, baby." Dane bellowed and surged to his feet, scattering his opponents. He slapped Cougars-cap on the ear. While the kid held his ear and shrieked, Dane snatched the antenna off the truck and began whipping all three of them.

He grinned through a mask of gore, cocking his forearm behind his neck and then slashing in an elegant diamond pattern. The dying sun limned him in gold. He was a Viking god exacting retribution on his foes. The hair on my arms prickled and I gaped in awe. Then Glenn yelled and I turned and partially blocked a golf club swung at my head. The other three frat boys had followed us—Glenn rolled around on the ground with the guy who'd tackled him. Another went after Victor, who adroitly fled behind the Land Rover. I had a moment to admire the lightness of his step. The golf club made a *thwock!* as it struck my upraised arm. The pain cranked a rotor in my brain and turned operation over to the lizard. I laughed with rage and joy and impending lunacy.

I caught the golf club as my attacker—a J. Crew pretty boy—readied for another crack at me, and wrenched him off balance. I punched him in the balls. He vomited and slumped on all fours and I grabbed his hair and kneed him in the jaw, twice, with enthusiasm. His nose and jaw squished nicely. He crawled away spewing blood and teeth as he shrieked. The other punk sat astride Glenn's chest and they were choking one another. I drove the toe of my steel-toed boot into the frat boy's kidney and he recoiled like a worm zapped by an electrode. He went purple almost instantly as his throat shut, paralyzed. Glenn rolled him over and proceeded to smash his face. The notion that someone might actually die in the fracas flickered through my mind, but my will to put the brakes on melted fast as the ultraviolence swept me along.

Pivoting again, I saw Victor had scooted up onto the windshield of the Land Rover, kicking wildly. His opponent belly-flopped across the hood, intent on clambering atop him. I grabbed the kid's ankles and jerked him backward, dragged him over the jaggedy hood ornament, hoisting his legs as in a game of wheelbarrow so his face slid down the grille, clunked off the bumper and slammed into the asphalt. I dropped his legs. He didn't move as blood seeped in a puddle around his head. A shadow passed through my peripheral vision. Dane seized one of the poor bastards by the crotch and neck and gorilla-pressed him overhead. I'd not seen anything like that in my entire life, but there it was, Dane raising him in a Frazetta pose from the cover of a Conan novel. Dane tossed him against the side of the truck. The frat boy bounced and landed on his shoulder and neck and Dane methodically lined up and drop-kicked him in the ribs. Like me, Dane wore heavy-duty boots, although his didn't have any metal reinforcement. It still sounded like an axe whacking into a log. Magnificent.

The bartender stood in the doorway of the tavern. I waved at her and the kid whose jaw I'd certainly broken chucked a loose piece of concrete at me and it caromed off my temple. I was still flattened on the ground trying to shake free of the red haze as Cougar-cap wrapped himself around Dane's leg and bit him in the thigh. Somebody's boot thumped my left butt cheek. Victor came swooping in and snatched up the concrete chunk and hurled it, chasing away whomever was trying to punt my ass up around my shoulders. He helped me to my feet, and in the nick of time—Glenn went to the Land Rover and rummaged around under the front seat. He came around with a shiny, tiny automatic. Me and Victor got hold of him and I took the pistol away and stuck it in my pocket. Meanwhile, Dane elbowed poor Cougar-cap (the cap had flown off long since) on the crown of his skull until the frat boy stopped gnawing his leg and curled into a fetal position. The rest—the ones still ambulatory—had fled at the appearance of the gun.

"Jesus jumping Christ!" Victor said. "We gotta bail before the heat gets here and guns us down like dogs!"

"Shit, where'd you get the piece? Do you even have a permit?" I said to Glenn.

His eyes were wild. "That time those gang-bangers cornered us on the bus in Rainier," he said. "I went to a pawn shop the next day."

I said, "Oh, for the love of . . . nothing happened. They were just screwing with us." It scared and hurt me he'd gone to such an extreme and then successfully kept a secret for this long. The bus incident was two years gone and I'd not suspected it affected him so deeply. This trip was proving to be painfully educational.

He looked away. "Not going to ever take chances again. Say what you like."

I wanted to grab his collar and shake some sense into him. Things were moving too fast, my emotional equilibrium, my sense of security in our private little world together, was sliding from under my feet.

"So long, fuckers!" Dane said, vaunting as Achilles had after wreaking havoc among his foes before the walls of Troy. He stomped Cougar-cap's splayed hand.

We piled into the truck. I shouldn't have been driving with what was a probable concussion and all the blood dripping into my eyes, but nobody else volunteered. I smoked rubber.

## 9.

I pulled into a Rite Aid and killed the engine. Victor was the only one of us who didn't look as if somebody had dumped a bucket of pig's blood over his head. He ran in and bought bandages, dental floss, cotton balls, Ibuprofen, medicinal alcohol, and two cases of Natty Ice.

Dane draped a towel over his face and it turned red. "Now this takes me back to the good ol' days," he said. His voice sounded nasally because his nose was smashed to a pulp.

"We should get to an emergency room," Glenn said. His eye was blackened and he'd ruined his shirt on the asphalt. Otherwise, he'd escaped the battle relatively unscathed.

He checked my scalp. The bleeding had mostly stopped. My left arm was swollen and purple from where the golf club had caught me. Sharp pains radiated from my instep. I figured it got stepped on in the confusion. "No hospital," I said. "If the cops are looking for us, we'll get nailed. Dane, I hope to God you didn't pay with a credit card back there."

"What? No, man, I paid cash. I always pay cash if I think there's gonna be a rumble."

"You thought there was going to be a fight?"

"Actually, I *knew* there'd be one. I decided to beat the hell out of those punks the minute we walked in. They rubbed me the wrong way."

"That lady bartender probably got our plates anyhow," Victor said. He cracked beers and handed them around. "Oh, man. Warm Natty sucks. Might as well gimme a can of watery cream corn," Dane said.

"Guess if you're going to keep tangling with gangs of frat boys half your age you'd best cultivate a taste for creamed food in general, eh?" I said.

He hissed in pain. "Yep, yep. Busted tooth. One of those assholes knocked it loose and I just swallowed the damn thing. Ha, Glenn tell you about the bikers we thrashed at a Willie Nelson concert? That's why I've got so much gold in my grill."

"Willie Nelson?"

"Everybody loves Willie," Glenn said. "Vicky, are you serious? You going to stitch the Danester's scalp with dental floss?"

Victor poured a capful of alcohol across a needle. "I can do it. Willem says no hospital. I am confident Hagar the Horrible is with Willem on this one—right sweetie?"

"Right," Dane said in his rusty, honking voice. "Besides, we still got some camping to do. That park is what, an hour from here? Let's make ourselves scarce in case Johnny Law comes round."

Glenn said, "Look, boys. I'm not exactly high on roughing it in the boonies at the moment. I think we should get back to Seattle and soak away our misery in the hot tub. Willem?"

The adrenaline hadn't completely worn off, nor the rush from the sense of admiration I'd received from my comrades. I wasn't about to let Dane out-tough me. "I'm game for the park. Another case of beer and some ice for the cooler and we're good to go."

Glenn took my face in his hands. He said in a whisper, "You look like you got hit in the head with a rock, my dear."

"Is that what it was?" I said.

He kissed my nose. "You are such a Billy badass."

"Yee-haw!" I cheered sotto voce.

Victor finished stitching Dane's lacerated scalp. He washed his hands in the alcohol, then returned to the store for bags of ice and more beer.

I drove east from Sequim along the Old Mystery Mountain Highway, a two-lane blacktop in major decline. It carried us up from the valley floor into big timber along the flank of Mystery Mountain. I dodged potholes while keeping an eye on the rearview mirror for police flashers. Occasionally, deer froze in the sweep of the headlights, eyes glittering from the brush and ferns at the road's edge. I'd expected heavy July traffic, but there weren't any other cars in sight.

Glenn said, "Jeepers, kinda creepy through here, isn't it?"

"Yeah, Fred," Victor said. "You should paint the pimp-mobile green and slap a flower on the door."

"Don't forget to recruit a hot, clueless Catholic school dropout and a not-so-hot dyke," Dane said.

But Glenn was right—the woods were spooky. Mist thickened and clung to the bushes. Cold air rushed across my feet. I turned on the heater. Glenn explained that this road once served as the main access for several towns. A railroad line ran parallel, lost somewhere in the dark. A lot of timber was hacked down in the days of yore, although from my vantage the wilderness had recovered and then some.

Glenn unfolded a road atlas and studied it by flashlight. Victor told the story about the couple driving through woods—*just like these!*—while a radio broadcast reports the escape of inmates from a local asylum. Of course the car breaks down and the boyfriend leaves his girl locked up while he goes for help and all through the night she hears noises. She cowers on the floorboard as someone tries the door handles. The wind rises and branches scrape the roof. She wakes in broad daylight to the police rapping on the window. Upon exiting the car she glances back and witnesses her boyfriend hanging upside down from a tree limb, his bloody fingernails scratching the roof as his corpse sways in the breeze . . .

"No asylums in these parts," I said. "On the other hand, there might be ghouls and goblins. The Klallam spoke of demons that dwelt among the trees and in the earth. The white pioneers sure came to believe some of the tales." I'd read about this and other eerie factoids in the guide. Victor pressed another beer into my hand. Even though I didn't dare lift my gaze from the twisting road, I felt my companions' attention focused on me. This convinced me Victor wasn't kidding when he said they were all way into the supernatural during college. Were circumstances otherwise I would've changed the subject, but I felt like a piece of meat tenderized by a mallet; the fight had drained from me, replaced by the fatalistic urge to confess or pontificate, which was an indicator I'd breached my alcohol threshold.

To distract myself from the excruciating pain in my foot, arm, and skull, I dredged up my research from the pages of *The Black Guide* and explained how, according to local legends, diabolical spirits lurked in fissures and caverns of the mountains and the rivers and lakes and assumed the guise of loved ones, or beautiful strangers, and lured hunters and fishermen to their doom. There was even a tale of the Slango logging camp that vanished during the 1920s. The spirits seized unwary men and dragged them into the depths and feasted upon them, or worse. Victor wondered what "worse" meant. I assumed worse meant torture or transformation. The demons might lobotomize their victims and change them into something inhuman. As it was a cautionary branch of native mythology, it was doubtless left vague as storytellers couldn't hope to match whatever horrors were conjured by the imaginations of their audiences. "Maybe the monsters enslave the ones they don't eat," Victor said in a half-serious manner. I flashed to dead Tom lying in an unmarked tomb and wondered if Victor was sharing that unwholesome thought. I drained my beer and gestured for another.

"Now I really, really want to go camping," Glenn said. "The turn should be on the right. Another three miles or so."

Victor screamed and I almost swerved the Land Rover into the ditch. Considering the size of the trees, we would've likely been squashed like a can of soup under a steamroller. Glenn and Dane yelled at Victor for almost making them pee their pants. I didn't say anything; I glimpsed his expression in the rearview. His eyes were shiny as quarters in Glenn's flashlight beam.

"Dude, what was that?" Dane said. "Willem almost hit a deer? Spider climb into your shorts? What?"

"Sorry, guys. I looked back to the storage compartment and something moved."

"WTF? One of those native American bogeymen of Willem's? It have red eyes?"

"Yeah. Bright red as the Devil. That's why I yelled."

"You didn't yell, you screamed."

"Because a black form moved in the back of the truck and its eyes glowed. Course I screamed. Diabolical Disney cartoon shit going down, I'm giving a shout-out. Just Glenn's coat, though. Headlight's reflected off the mile marker must've lit up the tape on the sleeves."

"Glad that's solved and we aren't parked inside one of these ginormous cedars."

I almost pulled over and asked Glenn to drive. Victor's cry had shaken me and the mist was screwing with my vision, because as I considered Victor's explanation, shadows slipped among the shrubbery a few yards ahead. Smaller than deer, and lower to the ground. I counted three of these jittery, fast-moving shapes before they melted into the greater darkness. Coyotes? Dogs? My febrile imagination powered by dopamine, a fistful of Ibuprofen, and God knew how many beers? The heavy, ponderous vehicle seemed fragile now, and I imagined how it must appear from above—a lonely speck trundling through an immense forest. Mild vertigo hit me, and the vehicle swayed just enough to cause an intake of breath from Glenn. I clamped my jaw and rallied.

Thick branches obscured the Mystery Mountain Campground signpost, but I saw it in time and braked hard and swung into a gravel lane. I proceeded a hundred yards to the darkened ranger shack. A carved wooden sign read CAMPGROUND FULL. A few lights glimmered through the trees. A Winnebago was the closest vehicle. Its occupants, a family of four dressed in identical bright orange shirts, clustered around a meager fire roasting hotdogs. "Argh—we forgot the bloody marshmallows," Victor said.

"Maybe it's for the best there's no room at the inn," Glenn said. "The rangers might be on the lookout for us too." Victor said, "Aw, who cares. What now?"

The road forked: the paved section veered to the right and into the campground. The leftward path was unpaved and led into the boonies. If *The Black Guide* was accurate, this was the southern terminus of a logging road network that crisscrossed the mountains. The Kalamov Dolmen lay at the end of a footpath a few miles ahead. I said, "Two-thirds of a tank. I say we cruise up the trail and find a place to bivouac." The others agreed and I eased the rig along the washboard lane. It climbed and climbed. Brush closed in tight and lashed the windows.

A hillside rose steeply to my left. The hillside was covered in uprooted trees and rocks and boulders. A few of the rocks had tumbled loose and lay scattered in the path. I picked my way through them; some were the size of bowling balls. Victor and Glenn warned me to hug the left-hand side of the road as they were looking at a precipitous drop. I glanced over at the tops of trees below us, a phantom picket floating in an abyss. Erosion and debris narrowed the lane until the Land Rover had perhaps a foot to spare between its wheels and the cliff. I halted and shut off the engine and engaged the parking brake. I asked Victor to get my rucksack from behind his seat and hand me the humidor in the belly pouch.

"Oh, snap," Victor said. "Honduran?"

"Nicaraguan," I said. "Be a love and snip one for me. Glenn, that bottle of Scotch still in the glove box?" He knew better than to say a word. He rummaged through the compartment, retrieved the quarter bottle of Laphroaig, and popped the cap. I had a slug of whisky, then accepted the cigar from Victor and got it burning with Victor's lighter. The sweet, harsh taste filled my mouth and lungs, sent a rush of energy through me. I exhaled and watched the smoke curl against the windshield. Nobody spoke. The only sound was the tick of cooling metal and Dane's wet breathing. "I saved these for a special occasion. A wedding, a funeral, a conjugal visit. But, hell . . . no better time for Scotch and cigars than right before you roll your rusted-out Land Rover over a two-hundred foot cliff. You boys help yourselves." Glenn and Victor lighted cigars.

Dane said no thanks and held the towel to his face again. He said, "You up to this, Willem?"

Glenn said, "He's got it handled. He drove transports in the Army."

"Oh. I didn't realize you'd been in the military," Dane said. "Thanks a lot, Glenn."

Glenn shrugged. "He doesn't like to spread it around. So I don't."

"Hell, man. Thanks for all you guys do." Dane roused himself and leaned over and patted my shoulder. "Were you in Iraq?"

"Yugoslavia. They stationed me in Kosovo for a year. And no, I didn't shoot anybody. I drove transports." We sat like that for a while. Finally, I drained the Scotch and threw the bottle on the floorboard at Glenn's feet. I turned the key and pegged it.

## 10.

Eventually the grade leveled and swung away from the cliff. I parked in the middle of the road near a stand of fir trees. We pitched the tent by headlight beam, unrolled our sleeping bags, and collapsed.

"Wait," Glenn said. "We need to make a bargain." He sounded strange, but it'd been a strange day. My heart beat faster. Dane and Victor kept quiet and that chilled me somehow, lending weight to the word *bargain*. These guys knew from bargains, didn't they? Glenn said, "Look, after what happened in town . . . maybe we'll get lucky and nobody will press charges. But, wow, Dane. You might've ruined a couple of those guys."

"I hope I smashed their guts out."

"Be serious." The edge in Glenn's voice surprised me. I wished I could see his face. "I'm not asking for anything heavy. Let's just promise to see this through, okay? Will, I'm so proud of you. We were going to tuck our tails and go yipping home. Thanks for showing grit. The plan was to camp out a couple of nights and see the dolmen. That's what we should do. Tommy would approve." The mention of dead Tom gave me the creeps and it reminded me how hurt I was that Glenn still hadn't confided the truth to me. Mostly, though, it gave me the creeps. Dane and Victor muttered acquiescence to Glenn's rather nebulous charge and we did the hand over hand thing, like a sports team. It was all awkward and phony, yet deadly serious in a Boy Scout way, and I squirmed and went along.

Right before we fell asleep, I pulled him close and murmured, "We're going to talk about the gun when we get home." He kissed me and put his cheek against my chest.

I dreamt horror show dreams and woke panicked, Glenn mumbling into my ear, sunlight blazing through the mesh of the tent flap. I crawled outside and vomited. My skull felt as if a football team had taken turns stomping it with cleats. I couldn't make a fist with my left hand. From wrist to elbow, my arm was puffed like a black and purple sausage. The possibility I might have a hairline fracture further soured my mood.

"Man alive, I thought a bear was ralphing in the blueberry bushes," Dane said. His face resembled a bowl of mashed potatoes with the skins still on. He hunched on a log near the cold fire pit. The end of the log was charred to a point. I started to laugh and puked again. I worried my nausea might be due to a cerebral hematoma rather than a hangover, but it was pointless to follow that line of thought. Until I could find a loop, intersection, or wide spot in the road, we were committed to this rustic interlude of the vacation. No way was I man enough to back the truck down to the campground.

Glenn and Victor emerged from the lair. Glenn didn't look nearly as bad as Dane, but his black eye was impressive and he limped and complained about pissing blood. Dane told him pissing blood was a rite of passage (then corrected it as "pissage" to some effect). I broke out the propane camp stove and boiled water for coffee and instant oatmeal. Dane poured two fingers of Schnapps from his hip flask over his oatmeal and I almost barfed again. He grinned at us, and I saw that yes, indeed, he'd lost a tooth during the skirmish. His lip was fat and blistered and Victor tenderly dabbed it with a napkin as they huddled together and shared a mug of coffee.

Glenn spread the Triple-A roadmap of Washington State on the ground and weighed down the corners with rocks. "We're in *this* general vicinity." He poked the map with a dead stick. "Unfortunately, the area is represented as a green blob. No roads, nothing. Green blobbiness, and more green blobbiness. Willem?"

I fetched *The Black Guide* and opened it to the relevant entry which was accompanied by a rude sketch not unlike the Hollywood-popularized treasure maps, and cryptic directions such as—*Left at ravine* and *Keep north of Devil Tower. 'Ware crevasse. Leech.* "The dolmen is about twelve miles yonder. I propose we pull stakes and ease along a bit. Got to find a spot to turn this beast around." I indicated the Land Rover.

"Good grief," Glenn said. "I didn't realize how far seventeen miles was when we were sitting around the bar back in Seattle."

Dane said, "I'm with Willem—let's see what's over the next hill, so to speak. As for that dolmen, the more I think on it, the more I think we've been had. There aren't any goddamned dolmens in this part of the world. I ought a know, Erik the Red being kin and such."

"This whole expedition is your idea!" Victor swatted his shoulder. "There better be a 'dolmen' or I'm kicking your ass back down this mountain."

"Yo, man. Don't get so excited. I said dolmen, not Dolemite."

Breaking camp proved twice the job as setting it up because everyone was hurting from the previous evening's brutality—we hobbled like old men and it was noon before we got packed and moving. Glenn took over at the wheel while I navigated. With my arm injury, I couldn't be trusted to keep the rig out of the ditch. The road continued along the mountainside, wending its way through a series of valleys. Our path intersected a handful of decrepit logging roads. There were occasional fields where forest had been leveled to stumps and roots, but nothing more recent than a decade or two.

"Who comes out here if not loggers?" Victor said.

I said, "Mountain bikers. Hikers. Dope growers. Game wardens and surveyors. The state keeps tabs, I'm sure. The timber companies will be back with chainsaws buzzing sooner or later."

"Think anybody owns land, a house? Y'know, regular people."

The Land Rover hit a pothole and I almost flew through the windshield. "Nah," I said. "Imagine what this will be like when it rains in September. A man would need mules to get around."

The ravines were steep and rugged with exposed rock and descended into cool, fuzzy shadows that never quite melted even during this, the hottest span of summer. Ridgelines hemmed the winding road, topped by evergreens and redwoods. Rabbits shot across our path. Far below in the vast crease of the landscape was the highway and civilization, obscured by a shifting blue haze. A hawk glided in the breeze.

As the afternoon light reddened near the horizon, we arrived at a

T-intersection. There was a convenient site bracketed by several trees and a picturesque scatter of boulders, a couple the approximate height and girth of the Land Rover, and it reminded me of a scene from a Western film where the cowboys sit around a cozy fire in the badlands, eating beans and drinking coffee from tin cups. If the guide was to be trusted, a semi-hidden footpath to the dolmen lay about a quarter of a mile down the southerly wending road. From there the anonymous author claimed it to be an hour's hike to the dolmen itself.

Once the tent was pitched we took stock of our supplies and determined that between trail mix, canned hash, chili, and fruit cocktail, three five gallon jerrycans of water, and a case of beer, the situation was golden for another night, and possibly two, should the next day's expedition prove too exhausting. Dane and Glenn took a hatchet into the woods and chopped several armloads of firewood while Victor dug a shallow pit and lined it with stones. I munched aspirin and supervised. Glenn had made me a sling from a shirt. I wore it to be on the safe side, and because it reduced the pain in my arm to the category of a toothache.

Night crept over the wilderness and the temperature cooled rapidly. Dane lighted a roaring bonfire and boiled a pot of chili and we washed that down with the better part of the case of beer. After supper, Glenn unpacked a teapot and mugs and fixed us instant cocoa. We sipped cocoa while Victor played a harmonica he'd bought in Seattle for the occasion.

"Dear God, not the harmonica," Dane said, and spat a gob of blood into the fire. His nose was definitely broken. He'd crunched it back into joint himself, much to my horror—at which Glenn and Victor snickered and mocked my squeamishness. Evidently, they'd seen this show many a time during their debauched college adventures.

Glenn fiddled with the transistor radio until he dialed in a grainy, but reasonably clear signal—a canned programming station playing big band music from the 1930s and '40s. Victor rolled his eyes and tossed the harmonica through the open window of the truck. He rolled a couple of joints and we passed them around. Talk turned to the macabre and I entertained them with Baba Yaga legends I'd heard around similar campfires while stationed in Eastern Europe; then Glenn and Dane discussed their favorite horror movies, most of which I knew by heart, and I nodded off, lulled by their easy laughter, the warmth of the fire.

Victor said something about "doorways" and I snapped awake, but missed the rest as he and the others were speaking softly. He said, "It's only a coincidence."

Dane said, "Come on, dude. Don't even start down that road—"

I cleared my throat. "What road?"

Victor said, "The road not taken, of course. I need to shake hands with the governor—ta, ta, my lovelies!" He rose and walked into the shadows.

"That's a wrap—I'm for bed," Glenn said and he kissed me and headed for the tent.

Dane stared into the flames and the red light bathed his ravaged face, and he glanced at me as if about to speak. He smiled a sad, tortuous smile, and followed Glenn.

Victor returned, zipping his fly.

"C'mere, pull up a rock." I patted the log I was sitting on.

He settled next to me, his posture stiff as a plank. Soon, Dane's snores drifted from the tent and Victor's shoulders relaxed. He tossed some dead leaves and twigs onto the fire, and said quietly, "What's on your mind, Will, old bean?" He was high as a kite.

"Not much. The book. Weird, weird thing happened to me before we left on the trip." I told him, as I had Glenn, about Tom's visitation, except I didn't pull any punches.

As I spoke, Victor's expression became increasingly unhappy. He fumbled in his pocket for a pack of cigarettes and lighted one with apparent difficulty. He offered me a drag. I declined and said, "Glenn didn't tell you, huh? I sort of figured he would've."

"This explains a lot. No wonder he's treated me like I'm loony tunes for . . . He prefers to pretend we weren't a pack of superstitious nerds in college. Dane follows his lead. It's a survival tool. The front office in Denver sucks—they don't even know he's gay. And the hoodoo aspect—that shit ain't cool now that we're grownups. Getting your face punched like a speed bag is trendy; crystal meditation and *The Golden Bough* reading circle is for wackos. I mention anything along those lines, Dane gives me the stink eye and Glen changes subjects like he's a senator putting the moves on the press corps. Why are we talking about it?"

"Because I can tell you want to. You aren't the kind of guy to keep deep, dark secrets."

"The thing with Tommy isn't really a deep, dark secret. A minor scandal. I had a bed-wetter type dream about him the other night. Neither of the other bozos dream about him, which seems unfair. But whatever, man. I couldn't stand him and you didn't even know him, yet we're the schleps who've got him on the brain."

"Seems rather simple to me," I said. "He's obviously haunting you from beyond the grave. You stole Dane away, then he got killed in a tragic manner that trapped his soul on the material plane."

"Oh, yeah? He didn't care for Dane like that. Well, fuck, maybe he did. Tommy loved to hump and he didn't seem too picky regarding with whom. What's he messing with you for?"

"He's not messing with either of us. I was checking your credulity."

"You got me, Tex. I'm a credulous motherfucker these days. Our boys are goddamned credulous too, if you could get them to cop to it. You're a devious one. Funny, you and Glenn getting together. He's such a rube."

I chuckled. "Yeah, yeah, Glenn is as pure as the driven snow. Plus, unlike us his family was damned progressive. A well-adjusted man's one of my turn-ons."

"That's the attraction?"

"He reads. He can be a devil. I like that a whole lot."

"He's hot and makes a heap of money."

"Goodness, Vicky, you're a real bitch when you want." I didn't mean anything by that, however. His bluntness was sweet in its own way.

The fire burned low. Victor stood and stretched. "I was raised Pentecostal. Got any idea what that's like? I saw a few things you wouldn't believe. My daddy was a snake-handlin', babblin' in tongues psycho-sonofabitch, let me tell you what. I've no problem with the plausibility of the fundamentally implausible after witnessing my daddy and two uncles cast 'demons' from my cousin one sultry, backwoods night. I can't say I'm religious, but I surely do believe we aren't alone on this mortal coil. There are frightful things lurking in the shadows."

I remembered the woman's voice whispering in the dark—*There are frightful things*. I got goosebumps.

He said, "Something else I didn't mention when I told you about the dreams I had of Tommy. I think I pushed it down into my subconscious. Whenever I first see him, for a split second he's somebody else. He covers his face with his hands, as if he's rubbing his eyes, or sobbing, and when he looks up, it's him, smiling this evil little smile. Once in a while, he ducks his head and pantomimes pulling on a ski mask. Same thing—it's him again. The act bothers the fuck outta me. Anyway. Goodnight."

Shadows from the dying fire capered against the trunks of the trees and the boulders nearby. The goosebumps returned and I recognized the nauseated thrill in my stomach as a reaction to being watched. This sense of being observed was powerful and I became conscious again of our frailty, the dim patch of light, the flimsy shelter of the tent, our insignificance. I massaged my aching forearm. Farther out, branches crashed and grew still.

A few minutes passed as I listened to the night. Weariness overcame my nerves. I decided to make for the tent and as I rose, a large, dark shape emerged from the brush and moved onto the road about seventy feet away. There was sufficient starlight to discern its bulky outline, a patch of thicker blackness against the blurry backdrop, but not enough to identify individual features. It had to be a bear, and so I'm sure my brain gave it a bearlike shape. Bears didn't particularly frighten me—I'd gone hunting on occasion as a teen and hiked plenty since. Bears, cougars, moose; critters could be reliably expected to live and left live. This encounter, however, alarmed me. Had the cooking smells drawn it in? Glenn's gun lay snug in my pocket since the brawl, but that didn't comfort me—it was a .25 automatic with no stopping power; more likely to infuriate a bear than kill it.

The animal stood in the center of the road and there was no mistaking it was staring at me. Then another shape appeared near the first and that caused my balls to tighten. The animal rose directly from the road, as if the shadows had coalesced into solid form, and as it materialized I noted that even obscured by darkness, it didn't resemble any bear I'd ever seen. The beast was too lean, too angular; the neck and forelegs were abnormally long, and its skull lopsided and cumbersome. I pulled the automatic and chambered a round. I considered calling to my companions, but hesitated because of the impression this entire situation was balanced on the edge of some terrible consequence and any precipitous action on my part would initiate the chain reaction.

*There are terrible things.*

A cloud rolled across the stars and as the darkness thickened, the animals moved in an unnatural, sideways fashion, an undulation at odds with their bulk, and vanished. Symbols of warning conjured from night mist and shadows; ill omens dispensed, they drained back into the earth. I half-crouched, gun in my fist, until my legs cramped. A scream echoed far off from one of the hidden gulches, and I almost blew a hole in my foot. It took me a long while to convince myself it had been the cry of a bear or a wildcat and not a human—not something inhuman, either.

By then it was dawn.

<h2 style="text-align:center">11.</h2>

During breakfast I relayed my encounter with the mystery animals, floating the idea that perhaps we should skip the hike.

"Wow, a couple of bears outside? Why didn't you get us up? I would've loved to see that." Victor seemed truly disappointed while Dane and Glenn dismissed my concerns that we might run afoul of them during the day.

Dane said, "We'll just let Vicky run his yapper while we walk. Bears will hear that a mile away and beat it for the hills."

"Gonna be hotter than the hobs of Hades," Glenn said after shrugging on his backpack.

"What the hell are hobs?" Dane said.

"Hubs, farm boy," Glenn said. "Don't neglect your canteens, fellow campers. Put on some sunscreen. Bring extra socks."

"How far we going? The Andes?"

"It's a surprise. Let's move out."

I took the lead, *Moderor de Caliginis* in hand. The sky shone a hard, brilliant blue and I already sweated from the rising heat. Fortunately, half the road lay in shadow and we kept to that. I felt rather absurd trudging along like a pith helmeted explorer in a black and white pulp film, novelty almanac map clutched in a death grip—Dane and Glenn even carried the requisite hatchets and machetes.

Despite my morbid curiosity, it would've relieved me if the book had proved inaccurate, if we'd tromped for an hour or two until my comrades grew hot and irritable and voted to call it a trip and bolt for civilization. The beating I'd received in Sequim had taken its toll and I just wanted to face the music, to deal with any legal repercussions of the battle royal and then soak in the hot tub for a month.

But, there it was behind a screen of bushes and rocks—the path, little more than a deer trail, angled away from the road and climbed through a ravine overgrown with brush and ferns. There weren't any trail markers, nor recent footprints. We picked our way over mossy stones and deadfalls, pausing frequently to sip from our canteens and for Dane and Victor to share a cigarette. Victor unlimbered his camera and snapped numerous pictures. Walking was slightly difficult with the sling throwing off my balance. Glenn stayed close, taking my elbow whenever I stumbled.

We pressed onward and upward, past a dozen points where the game trail forked and I would've lost the way if not for the landmarks detailed in the guide entry and by the subtle blazes the author had slashed into the bark of trees along the way. I whistled under my breath. My companions were silent but for the occasional grunt or curse. A similar hush had fallen over the woods.

We rounded a bend and came to a spot where the trail forked yet again, except this time both paths were wider and recently trod by boots. He spotted the ruins a second before I did and just after Dane wondered aloud if we'd gotten lost and pegged me in the back with a pinecone. "Everybody, hold on!"

Glenn kept his voice low and pointed along the secondary path where it passed through a notch in the trees. I swept the area with binoculars. There was a clearing beyond the screen of trees, and piles of burned logs, like a palisade had ignited into an inferno. Further in, discrete piles of charcoal debris glittered with bits of melted glass. This appeared to be the old ruins of an encampment, or a village. I could imagine a mob of men in tri-corner hats loitering about, priming their muskets.

"This is weird," Victor said. "You guys think this is weird?" I said, "In my opinion this qualifies as weird. Also highly unsettling."

"Unsettling?" Dane said. Victor said, "Well duh. Don't know about you, but I'm picking up a creepy vibe. I dare you to walk down there and see if anybody's around."

"There's nothing left," Dane said. Victor said, "That path didn't make itself. *Somebody* uses it. Like I said, walk your sweet little butt down there and take a gander."

"Not a chance," Dane said and briefly mimed plucking strings as he hummed "Dueling Banjos."

Glenn took the binoculars and walked uphill to get a better vantage. He slowly lowered the glasses and held them toward me. "Will . . . " I joined him and scanned where he pointed. Offset from the main ruins, a canted stone tower rose four or so stories. The tower was scorched and blackened and draped in moss and creepers, on a slight rise and surrounded by the remnants of a fieldstone wall. Window slots were bricked over and it was surmounted by a crenellated parapet. "Anything about this in the guide?" he said. I told him about the *Devil Tower* notation. "I thought the entry referred to a rock formation, or dead tree. Not a real live fucking tower."

"Something strange about that thing," Dane said.

"Besides the fact it's the completely wrong continent and time period for a medieval piece of architecture, and that said architecture is sitting on the side of the mountain in the Pacific Northwest, miles from any human habitation?" Victor said.

Dane said, "Yeah, besides that. I've seen it before—in a book or a movie. Fucked if I remember, though. I mean, it looks like it should be on the moor, Boris Karloff working the front door when the dumbass travelers stop for the night."

"How much farther?" Glenn said.

I consulted the book. "Close."

He said, "Unless you guys want to hunt for souvenirs in the burn piles, let's mosey." None of us liked the ruins enough to hang around and we continued walking.

Fifteen minutes later, we arrived at our destination. The trail wound under the arch of a toppled dead log, and ended in a large hollow partially ringed by firs and hemlocks. The hollow was a shadowy-green amphitheatre that smelled of moist, decayed leaves and musty earth. Directly ahead, reared the dolmen—two squat pillars of rock supporting a third, enormous slab. I was amazed by its cyclopean dimensions. The dolmen was seated near the slope of the hill and blanketed with moss, and at its base: ferns and patches of devil's club. It woke in me a profound unease that was momentarily overshadowed by my awe that the structure actually existed.

None of us spoke at first; we stood close together and took in our surroundings. Glenn squeezed my wrist and pressed his hip against mine. Victor hadn't taken a single picture, demonstrably cowed upon encountering something so far beyond his reckoning and Dane's mouth actually hung open. I whispered into Glenn's ear, "The History Channel isn't quite the same, is it?" He smiled and pecked my cheek. That broke the tension and, after shucking their packs, the others began exploring the hollow. My uneasiness remained, a burr that I couldn't work loose. I checked the book again—the author hadn't written much about the site proper, nor documented any revelations about its history or importance besides the astronomical diagrams in the appendix. I stowed the guide and tried to set aside my misgivings as well.

The moss that bearded the dolmen was also thick upon the ground that it sucked at my boots as it sucked at the voices of my friends and the daylight itself. I thought of lying in a sticky web, of drowsing in the heart of a cocoon. The pain in my arm spiked and I shook off the sudden lassitude. We approached within a few feet of the tomb and stared into the opening. This made me queasy, like peering over the lip of a pit. This was a stylized maw, the mossy path its unfurled tongue.

"This isn't right," Glenn said. Victor and Dane flanked us, so our group stood before the structure in a semicircle.

"A hoax?" I said without conviction, thinking of the artificial Stonehenge modern entrepreneurs had erected in Eastern Washington as a tourist attraction.

"I don't think so," Glenn said. "But, I've seen a few of these in France. They don't look like this at all. The pile of rocks is close. That other stuff, I dunno." The stones were covered in runes and glyphs. Time had eroded deep grooves and incisions into shallow, blurred lines of demarcation. Lichen and horrid white fungi filled the crevices and spread in festering keloids.

Dane forged ahead and boldly slashed at some of the creepers, revealing more carvings. Fat, misshapen puffball mushrooms nested in beds among the creepers and his machete hacked across some and they disintegrated in clouds of red smoke. I joined him at the threshold and shined the beam of my flashlight through the swirling motes of mushroom dust, illuminating a chamber eight feet wide and twenty feet deep. Stray fingers of reddish sunlight came through small gaps. Vines had penetrated inside and lay in slimy, rotten loops and wallows along the edges of the foundation. My hair brushed against the slick threshold and beetles and pill bugs recoiled from our intrusion. Just inside, the chamber vaulted to a height of fifteen feet and was decorated with multitudes of fantastical carvings of symbols and creatures and stylized visages of the kind likely dreamt by Neanderthals. The far end of the chamber dug into the mountain; a wall of shale and granite sundered by long-past seismic violence into a vertical crack, its plates and ridges splattered rust orange by alkaline water oozing from rock.

The floor was composed of dirt and sunken flagstones, and at its center, a low mound of crumbling granite that was an an oblong basin, the opposite rim worked into the likeness of a massive, bloated humanoid. The statue was worn smooth and darkened by grime with only vague hollows for its eyes and mouth in a skull too proportionally small for its torso.

I clicked off the flashlight and allowed my eyes to adjust to the crimson gloom.

"Okay, I'm thunderstruck," Glenn said.

"Gob smacked!" Victor said, his jovial tone strained. He shot a rapid series of pictures that promptly ruined my night vision with the succession of strobe flashes. The glyphs crawled and the primeval visages yawned and leered.

Dane must've seen it as well. "Stash that goddamned camera or I'm going to ram it where the sun don't shine!"

Victor frowned and snapped the lens cap in place and in the midst of my visceral reaction to our circumstances, I wondered if this exchange was a window into their souls, and how much did Glenn know about *that*. I watched Glenn as he examined the idol and the pool. I felt a brief, searing contempt for his gawky frame, his mincing steps and too-skinny ass. I hung my head, ashamed, and also confused that something so petty and domestic would impinge upon the bizarre scene. For the hundredth time I considered the possibility my meninges were filling with blood like plastic sacks.

Up close, the basin was larger than I'd estimated, and rudely chiseled, as if it were simply a hollowed-out rock. Small square-ish recesses were spaced at intervals around the rim, each encrusted with lichen and moss so they resembled mouths. Cold, green water dripped from the ceiling and filled the basin, its surface webbed with algae scum and fir needles and leaves. The attendant figurehead loomed, imposing bulk precariously inclined forward, giving the illusion that it gazed at us. I glanced at my companions, their faces eerily lighted by the reflection of the water.

. . . A horrible idea took root—that these men masked in blood, eyes gleaming with febrile intensity, had conned me, maneuvered me to this remote and profane location. They were magicians, descendants of the Salamanca

Seven, necromancers of the secret grotto, Satan's disciples, who planned to slice my throat and conduct a black magic ritual to commune with their dear dead Tom, perhaps to raise him like Lazarus. Everything Glenn ever told me was a half-truth, a mockery—Tom hadn't been the black sheep sidekick, oh no!, but rather the darksome leader, a sorcerer who'd initiated each of them into the foul cabal. Any moment now, Dane or my sweet beloved Glenn would reach into his pocket and draw the hunting knife sharpened just for my jugular, Victor's coil of rope would truss me, and then . . .

Glenn touched my arm and I choked back a cry and everybody flinched. Their fear and concern appeared genuine. I allowed Glenn to comfort me, smiled weakly at his solicitous questions.

Victor said, "Boys, what now? I feel like calling CNN, the secretary of the interior. Somebody."

Glenn rubbed his jaw. "Vicky, it's in the book, so apparently people are aware of this place. There's a burned-down village back thataway. That explorer, Pavlov, Magalov, whoever, named it after himself. People surely know."

"Just because it's in the book doesn't mean jackshit. How come there's no public record? I bet you my left nut this site isn't even on the government radar. Question is, why? How is that possible?"

I said, "An even better question is, do we want to screw around with the ineffable?"

Victor sighed. "Oh, come on. You got the heebie-jeebies over some primitive art?"

"Take a closer look at the demon faces," Dane said. "This is forces of darkness shit. Hardcore Iron Maiden album cover material." He snorted and spat a lump of gory snot into the water. For moment, we stood in shocked silence.

"If you want to flee, dears, say the word." Victor laid the sarcasm on too thick to fool anybody. "Let's march back to the land of beer, pizza, and long, hot showers." He drew a cigarette and leaned against the basin to steady himself. The snick of his lighter, the bloom of flame, shifted the universe off its axis. He shuddered and dropped the lighter and stepped back far enough that I glimpsed a shivering cord the diameter of a blue ribbon leech extended from beneath the lip of the basin and plunged into the junction of his inner thigh and groin.

Greasy bubbles surfaced from the depths of the stagnant water, and burst, their odor more foul than the effluvium of the dead vines liquefying along the walls, and the scum dissolved to reveal a surface as clear as glass. The trough was a divining pool and the water a lens magnifying the slothful splay of the farthest cosmos where its gases and storms of dust lay like a veil upon the Outer Dark. A thumbnail-sized alabaster planetoid blazed beneath the ruptured skein of leaves and algae, a membranous cloud rising.

The cloud seethed and darkened, became black as a thunderhead. It keened—chains dragging against iron, a theremin dialed to eleven, a hypersonic shriek that somehow originated and emanated from inside my brain rather than an external source. Whispers drifted from the abyss, unsynchronized, unintelligible, yet conveying malevolent and obscene lust that radiated across the vast wastes of deep space. The cloud peeled, bloomed, and a hundred thousand miles long tendril uncoiled, a proboscis telescoping from the central mass, and the whispers amplified in a burst of static. I went cold, warmth and energy drained from my body with such abruptness and violence, I staggered.

Glenn shouted and jerked my shoulder, and we tripped over each other. I saw Dane scrambling toward the entrance, and Victor frozen before the idol, face illuminated in the lurid radiance. His expression contorted and he gripped his skull in both hands, fingernails digging. The slimy cord drew taut and released from the muscle of his leg with a wet pop, left a bleeding circle in the fabric of his pants. Another of these appendages partially spooled from the niche nearest me, writhing blindly as it sought to connect with warm meat.

The howl intensified. My vision distorted into streaks of white, resolving to the flickering vacuum of space where I floated near the rim of the Earth, and the moon slid as a black disk across the face of the sun.

12.

Glenn cuffed and shook me awake. His cheeks were wet with tears. "You weren't moving," he said. I sat up and looked around. The unearthly light had faded to a dull glow, but I could make out some details of the chamber. Victor stood beside the idol, his back to us. He caressed the statue's rotund belly, palm flat the way a man touches his wife's stomach, feeling for the baby's kick. Dane was nowhere to be seen.

I said, "Vicky? Vicky, you okay?" It required great effort to form the words.

Victor slowly turned. Something was wrong with his face. Dried gore caked his forehead and temples. He grinned ghoulishly. "You should've seen what I saw. This isn't a tomb . . . it's . . . " He laughed and it gurgled in his throat. "They'll be here soon, my sweets."

Victor's certitude, the lunacy in his expression, his tone, frightened me. "Glenn, we've got to get out of here." I pushed away his arm and rose. "Vicky, come on. Let's find your husband."

"Where's Dane going? He won't leave me here, nor you, his best buddies. However, if he doesn't come to his senses, if he's run screaming for the hills, I'll visit him soon enough. I'll drag him home to the dark."

"Vicky—" Glenn said.

Victor mocked him. "Glenn! Be still, be at peace. They love you. You'll see, you'll see. Everything will change; you'll be remade, turned inside out. We won't need our skin, our teeth, our bones." He licked his thumb and casually gouged his chest an inch above the nipple. Blood flowed, coursed over his rooting thumb and across the knuckles of his fist.

Glenn screamed. I glanced at the ground near my feet, hoping for a loose rock with which to brain Victor. Victor ripped loose a flap of skin and let it hang, revealing muscle. "We won't need this, friends. Every quivering nerve, every sinew will be laid bare." He leaned over and reached for the switchblade taped to his ankle.

"Oh, shit," I said.

Glenn said shrilly, "What's that?" There was movement in the fissure. A figure manifested as a pale smudge against the background. It was naked and its skin glistened a pallid white like the soft meat of a grub. Its features were hidden by the gloom, and I was glad of that. Victor raised his arms and uttered a glottal exclamation.

The Man (it *was* a man, wasn't it?) crept forward to the very edge of the crevice, and hesitated there, apparently loath to emerge into the feeble light despite its palpable yearning do so. Whether man or woman I couldn't actually determine as its wattles and pleats disguised its sex, but the figure's size and proportions were so large I couldn't imagine it being a woman. The weight of its hunger and lust echoed the empathic blast I'd received from the black cloud, and my mind itched as this damp, corpulent apparition whispered to me, tried to insinuate its thoughts into mine via a psychic frequency.

I beheld again the cloud, a dank cosmic mold seeping from galaxy to galaxy, a system of hollow planets and a brown dwarf star nested within its coils and cockles. Sunless seas of warm ichor sloshed with the gravitational spin of those hollow, lightless worlds, spoiled yolks within eggshells. Hosts of darksome inhabitants squirmed and joined in terrible communion. I felt unclean, violated in bearing witness to their coupling.

Beyond the entrance of the dolmen and the encircling trees, the sun burned cool and red. Soon it would be dusk . . . and then, and then . . .

"Vicky! For the love of God, get over here." Victor ignored me and shuffled toward the figure, and the figure's luminous flesh darkened with a spreading, cancerous stain, like a piece of paper charring in a flame, or a sheet soaked in blood, and it reached, extending a hideously long arm. Its spindly fingers tapered to filthy, sharp points. Those fingers crooked, beckoning languidly. What did it promise Victor, with its whispers and wheedles?

I moved without thinking, for if I'd stopped to think I would've sprinted after Dane, who'd obviously exercised common sense in beating a retreat. I tackled Victor and slung him to the ground. The impact sent shocks through my wounded arm and I almost fainted again, but I hung tough and pinned him. Stunned, he resisted ineffectually, flopped like a worm until I freed the pistol from my pocket and smacked him in the forehead with the butt. That worked just like the movies—his eyes rolled back and he went limp. Glenn came running and we grabbed Victor beneath the arms and dragged him from the chamber. The figure in the crevice laughed, a hyena drowning or a lunatic with a sliced throat.

The flight down the trail toward camp was harrowing. We bound Victor's hands with his own belt, and made a tourniquet to staunch the bleeding from his leg as it refused to clot, and half-carried him as he raved and shrieked—I finally pistol-whipped him again and he was quiet after that. The entire way, I glanced over my shoulder fully expecting the dreadful presence to overtake us. Hysteria galvanized me into forty minutes of superhuman exertion— had Glenn not been there, I'm sure I could've easily hoisted Victor onto my shoulders and made like a track star.

Dane jumped from the bushes near the main road and Glenn nearly lopped his head with a hatchet. Dane had run to the camp before his panic subsided and he'd mustered the courage to double back and find us. His shame was soon replaced by horror at Victor's condition, which neither I nor Glenn could fully explain. I convinced Dane there wasn't time to talk lest someone or something had followed us from the dolmen. So, the three of us lugged Victor to camp, loaded into the Land Rover and got the hell off Mystery Mountain.

13.

I put the pedal to the metal and Glenn made the calls as we hurtled down the logging road in the dark. The authorities were waiting at the campgrounds. Victor recovered from his stupor as they strapped him to a gurney. He cursed and snarled and thrashed until the paramedics tranquilized him. Dane, Glenn, and I were escorted to the local sheriff's office where the uniforms asked a lot of questions.

The smartest move would've been to fudge the details. That's the movies, though. None of us were coherent enough to concoct a cover story to logically explain the hole in Victor's leg, or the monster, or the bad acid trip phantasmagoria of the pool. We just spilled the tale, drew an X on a topographical map and invited the Sheriff and his boys to go see for themselves. It didn't help our credibility that the cops found Victor's weed stash and several hundred empty beer cans in the truck.

Ultimately, they let us walk. The fight at the tavern wasn't mentioned, despite our mashed faces and missing teeth, which surprised the hell out of me. Victor's wound was presumed an accident; the investigators decided he harpooned himself on a branch while we were drunkenly wandering the mountainside. Personally, I preferred that version as well—the reality was too frightening. Victor's deranged state was obviously a hysterical reaction to the near death incident. Our statements were taken and we were shown the door. Once the cops put two and two together that the four of us were queer, they couldn't end the conversation fast enough. Someone would be in touch, thank you for your cooperation, etcetera, etcetera.

Dane went to stay with Victor at Harborview Hospital while Glenn and I returned home. Neither of us was in any shape to linger by Victor's bedside. I'd tried to talk Dane into crashing at the house, to no avail—he hadn't even acknowledged the offer. His face was blank and prematurely lined. I'd seen refugees from shelled villages wearing the exact same look. In his own way, he was as removed from reality as Victor.

Glenn fared a little better—he was a wreck too, but we had each other. I dreaded his reaction when the shock dissipated and the magnitude of the tragedy sank in. He'd lost one friend, possibly forever, and the jury was out on the other. God help me, a bit of my heart savored the notion I finally had him all to myself. Another, even more bitter and shriveled bit slightly gloated over the fact it was finally his turn to suffer. I'd done all the crying in our relationship.

Daulton meowed when we came in and turned on the lights and circled our ankles. The house, our comfy furniture and family pictures, all of it, seemed artificial, props from someone else's life. I showered for the first time in several days, spent an hour with my forehead pressed against the stall tiles. I saw the wound in Victor's leg, his mouth chanting soundlessly, saw the stars thicken into a stream that poured into that black hole. The black hole, the black cloud, was limned in red and it made me think of the broken circle on the cover of *Moderor de Caliginis*. These images were not exact, not perfectly symmetrical, yet the hot water cascading over my back no longer thawed me. My teeth chattered.

I wrapped myself in one of the luxuriously thick towels we'd gotten for a mutual anniversary gift and shuffled into the hall and found Glenn on hands and knees, his ear pressed to the vent. "What the hell?" I said.

He gestured awkwardly over his shoulder for quiet. After a few moments he rose and dusted his pajamas with a half dozen brisk pats. "I thought the TV was on downstairs. It's not. Must've been sound traveling along the pipes from the neighbors, or I dunno. Let's hit the rack, huh?"

I lay in bed, chilled and shaking, Glenn a dead lump next to me. The accent lamp in the hall gave a warm, albeit fragile yellow light. Without shifting to face me like he normally would've, Glenn said, "Tommy fell into a hole in the woods. That's how he really died."

I said, "Yeah. Vicky told me. You fucker."

Glenn still didn't move. I couldn't recall him ever being so still. He said, "I figured that's why you've been so bent. Then you know why we kept quiet."

"No, I don't."

The light flickered and now Glenn's head turned. "True. You don't. I apologize. I should've come clean long ago. Tommy was so deep into black magic it blew my mind when I finally caught on. He always sneered at the lightweight stuff me and Dane fooled with. I really believed he was just a redneck who made good. Then we hit some extra heavy duty acid one night and he bared his soul. We were on spring break and spending a weekend in the Mojave with some of the guys and he got to rambling. His parents were basically illiterate, but he had well-to-do relatives on his mom's side. Scholars. He lived a few summers with them and they turned him on to very, very dark occultism. Tommy intimated he'd taken part in a human sacrifice. He lied to impress me, I'm sure."

*I* wasn't sure. "What did they do? The relatives."

"His uncle was a professor. World traveler who went native. Hear Tommy tell it, the old dude was a connoisseur of the black arts, but specialized in blood rituals and necromancy. Tommy said the man could . . . Conjure things. Doctor Faustus style."

"I might've laughed at that the other day," I said. The lamp flickered again and shadows raced across the wall. Glenn said, "Tommy showed me some moldy manuscript pages he carried in his pocket. They were wrinkled and obviously torn from a book. The words were written in Latin—he actually read Latin! He wouldn't say what they meant, but he consulted them later when we went on our trip into the Black Hills near Olympia. Looking back, I get the feeling maybe he had his own *Black Guide*."

"It could've been a possum stew recipe from his grandma's cookbook," I said. "The motherfucker didn't come visit me in the night. I dreamed that when I was rocked off my ass. The guide, well there's a coincidence. I'm not going to buy a conspiracy theory about how dead Tom made sure we found it at ye old knickknack shop. I sure as fuck ain't going to worry my pretty head over what we saw on the mountain. I'm sorry for Vicky and Dane. We're okay, though and I say let sleeping dogs lie." I breathed heavily and stared at the hall lamp so hard my eyes hurt, despising my fearfulness.

"Ignoring those sleeping dogs is what got us here. Tommy talked and talked that enchanted evening, had a scary expression as he watched me. His eyes were so strange. I got paranoid thinking he wasn't really high, that this was a test. Or a trap. I remember him saying there was 'sure as God made little green apples' life out there. He pointed at the stars. Cold night in the desert and those stars were right on top of us in their billions. He wanted to meet them, except he was afraid. His uncle warned him the only thing an advanced species would want from us would be our meat and bones."

Glenn didn't say anything for a while. He rubbed my arm, which still ached fiercely. Finally, he said, "Everything returned to normal after the Mojave trip—he didn't mention our chat, didn't seem to recall letting me in on his secret life. A few months later it was summer vacation and we were knocking around Seattle. I came home to visit my folks and the others tagged along. Tommy put together an overnight hike and away we went. I saw him fall into the hole as we were walking way up in the hills along a well-beaten path. Mountain bikers used it a lot, even though it's a remote spot. Dane and Victor were joking around and I glanced over my shoulder exactly as he fell. I didn't tell those two what I saw. I made a show of yelling for him until Dane found the sinkhole. Course we called in the troops. I'm sure Vicky told you what happened next. Cops, Fish and Wildlife, everybody we could think of. No luck. That pit just dropped into the center of the Earth and it was impossible to help him. To this day nobody but me is completely sure that's where Tommy disappeared—it just makes the most sense. Him tripping into a bottomless pit is awful, yeah. Not as awful as other possibilities, though."

The lamp clicked off and on three times and I raised myself against the headboard and clutched the coverlet to my chin. I lost interest in finally getting to the bottom of Tommy's death and the weird conspiracy to sanitize its circumstances. "Holy shit—Glenn, please stop. I've got a bad feeling." I had a sense of impending doom, in fact. I could easily envision a colossal meteor descending from on high and smashing the house to bits. Daulton fluffed into a ball of bristling fur and scooted under the bed where he hissed and growled.

Glenn kept rubbing my arm and the light flickered again and again, and the filament ticked like a rattler. "I never told the guys what I really saw that day. Tommy didn't fall. He was snatched by a hand . . . not a hand that belonged to any regular person I've seen. An arm, fish-belly white, shot up and caught his belt and yanked him in . . . and the hand had . . . claws. He didn't even scream. He didn't make a peep. It happened so fast I thought it couldn't be real. I dreamed it like you dreamed Tommy was in the living room after the party."

"I can't believe this shit," I said. What had Tommy expected to find in the Black Hills? Another ancient ruin hidden from all but the initiated and the doomed? I was getting colder. I wanted to ask Glenn if he still loved Tommy. Nothing he said would've mattered and so I comforted myself with smoldering resentment.

"When we were in the dolmen, did you get a look at that guy's face?" he said.

"The dude in the crevice? That freaky inbred motherfucker who got separated from all his Ozarks kin? No."

"I did," Glenn said. "It was *him*."

The light went off and stayed off.

14.

I woke with dry mouth. Glenn's covers were thrown back and his side of the sheets were cool. I listened to the creaks of the house. The power was out. Glenn laughed, downstairs. He said something unintelligible. In my semi-conscious state, I assumed he'd called the power company and was sharing a joke with the poor sap manning the phone center.

Fuzzy-headed, I put on my robe and negotiated the hall and the stairs. A bit of starlight and the tip of the crescent moon gleamed through the windows. Glenn had lighted a candle in the kitchen and it led me through the haunted woods to the doorway. It was only a single candle, a fat one I'd bought at a bookstore for my office but stuck in a kitchen drawer for emergencies instead, and so the room remained mostly in gloom.

She slouched at the opposite end of the dining table. She was naked and lush and repellently white. Her hair was long and thick and black. Her hands rested on the table, and her fingers and cracked, sharp nails were far too long and thin. *Moderor de Caliginis* lay open before her. She lazily riffled pages and smiled at me. I couldn't see her teeth.

Glenn stood to her left in the breakfast nook, the toes of his slippers in the light, his shape otherwise indistinct. He waited mutely.

"Who are you?" I said to her, although I already knew. The covetous way she handled the guide made it clear.

"Three guesses," she said in a perfectly normal, good-humored tone.

"Rose, I presume," I said, voice cracking and ruining my attempt at bravado. "How kind of you to drop in." The gun was in my coat in the living room. I thought I might make it if I ran and if I didn't trip over anything.

"How kind of *you* to open your home. Thank you for the lovely note. Yes, I had a fabulous visit to the Peninsula—and points beyond. That saying, *a nice place to visit . . .* Well, I liked it so much, I decided to naturalize."

"Glenn," I said. I was exhausted. It came over me in a wave—the seasick feeling of giving way too much blood at the nurse's station. I resisted a sudden compulsion to collapse into a chair and lay my head on the table. My fingers and toes tingled. I gripped the door frame for balance. "Glenn," I tried again, weak, hopeless. Glenn said nothing.

"He's not for you. He belongs to Tommy," Rose said. "He belongs to us. We love him. You were never part of their inner circle, were you, Willem? Second best for Glenn. His vanilla life after graduation into the real world of jobs, bills, routine sex. No thrills, not like college." She closed the book and traced the broken ring on its cover. "Alas, nice guys do indeed finish last. I, however, believe in second chances and do-overs. Would you like a do-over, Willem? You'll need to decide whether to come along with us and see the sights. Or not. You are more than welcome to join the fun. Goodness knows, I hope you do. Tommy does too."

The cellar door had swung open while I was distracted. Rose stood and took Glenn's hand. They passed over the threshold. He turned and stared at me. Behind him was infinite blackness. Her arms, pale as death, emerged from that blackness and draped his shoulders. She caressed him. She whispered in his ear, and in mine.

The pull was ineluctable; I released the door frame and crossed the room in slow, tottering steps like a man wading into high tide. The universe whirled and roared. I came within kissing distance of my love and looked deep into his dull, wet eyes, gazed into the bottomless pit. His face was inert but for the eyes. Maybe that was really him waiting somewhere down there in the dark.

"Oh, honey," I said, and stepped back and shut the door.

## 15.

I sold the house and moved across the country. For nearly a decade, I've lived on a farm in Kingston, New York with an artist who welds bed frames and puts them on display in galleries. We share the property with a couple of nanny goats, some chickens, two dogs, and Daulton II. I write my culture essays, although Burt makes enough neither of us needs a real job.

Repairing the fences in the field, patching the shed roof, and making the odd repairs around the house keep me occupied, keep me from chewing my nails. Nothing can help me as I lie awake at night, unfortunately. That's when I do the real damage to myself. Against my better judgment I mailed *The Black Guide* to Professor Berman, though I cursed him for a fool during our last email exchange.

Victor's confined to an asylum and his doctor contacts me on occasion, hoping I'll reveal what "massive trauma" befell his patient to precipitate his catastrophic break from reality. From what I gather, Victor keeps journals— dozens of them. He's got a yen for astronomy and physics and at least one scientist thinks he's a savant. Dane disappeared three years after our fateful trip and hasn't resurfaced. His credit cards and bank accounts remain untouched. The cops asked me about this, too. I really don't know, and I don't want to, either.

Burt raised his eyebrows when I bought the .12 gauge shotgun a few months back and parked it by my side of the bed. I told him it was for varmints and he accepted that. There are cougars and bears and coyotes lurking in the nearby forest. He hasn't a clue that when he's away on his infrequent art show trips, I sit in our homey kitchen by the light of a kerosene lamp with the gun on the table and watch the small door leading into the cellar. The door is bolted, not that I'm convinced it matters. It began a few weeks ago and only happens when Burt's out of town. He's not a part of this, thank God for small favors—that's why they bide their time, of course. The dogs used to lie at my feet and whine. Lately, the normally loyal pair won't come into the room after dark, and I don't blame them.

Burt's in the city for the weekend. He's mixing with the royalty and pining for home, has said as much in no less than a half dozen phone messages. I sit here in the gathered gloom, with a bottle of scotch, a glass, and a loaded gun. Really, it's pointless. I sip scotch and wait for the soft, insistent knocks against the cellar door, for Glenn to whisper that he loves me. Guilt and loneliness have worked like acid on my insides. God help me, but more and more, I'm tempted to rack the slide and eject the shells, send them spinning across the floor. I'm tempted to leave the deadbolt unlocked. Then see what happens next.

*Only a very rare affliction, of course, could bring about such vast and radical anatomical changes in a single individual after maturity—changes involving osseous factors as basic as the shape of the skull—but then, even this aspect was no more baffling and unheard-of than the visible features of the malady as a whole.*

*"The Shadow Over Innsmouth" · H. P. Lovecraft (1936)*

## · THE TRANSITION OF ELIZABETH HASKINGS ·
### Caitlín R. Kiernan

Elizabeth Haskings inherited the old house on Water Street from her grandfather. It would have passed to her mother, but she'd gone away to Oregon when Elizabeth was six years old, leaving her daughter with the old man. She'd said she would come back, but she never did, and after a while the letters stopped coming, and then the postcards stopped coming, too. And now Elizabeth Haskings is twenty-nine, and she has no idea whether her mother is alive or dead. It's not something she thinks about very often. But she does understand *why* her mother left, that it was fear of the broad, tea-colored water of the Ipswich River, flowing lazily down to the salt marshes and the Atlantic. Flowing down to Little Neck and the deep channel between the mainland and Plum Island, finally emptying into the ocean hardly a quarter of a mile north of Essex Bay. Elizabeth understands it was the ruins surrounding the bay, there at the mouth of the Manuxet River—labeled the Castle Neck River on more recent maps, maps drawn up after the late 1920s. She's never blamed her mother for running like that. But here, in Ipswich, she has the house and her job at the library, and in Oregon—or *wherever* she might have run—she'd have nothing at all. Here she has roots, even if they're roots she does her best not to dwell on.

But this is only history, the brief annals of a young woman's life. Relevant, certainly, but only as prologue. What happened in the town that once ringed Essex Bay, the strange seaport town that abruptly died one winter eighty-four years ago, where her grandfather lived as a boy.

It's a Saturday night in June, and on most Saturday nights Elizabeth Haskings entertains what she quaintly thinks of as her "gentleman caller." She enjoys saying, "Tonight, I will be visited by my gentleman caller." Even though Michael's gay. They work together at archives at the Ipswich Public Library, though, sometimes, he switches over to circulation. Anyway, he knows about Elizabeth's game, and usually he brings her a small bouquet of flowers of one sort of another—calla lilies, Peruvian lilies, yellow roses fringed with red, black-eyed Susans—and she carefully arranges them in one of her several vases while he cooks her dinner. She feels bad that Michael is always the one who cooks, but, truthfully, Elizabeth isn't a very good cook, and tends to eat from the microwave most nights.

They might watch a DVD afterwards, or play Scrabble, or just sit at the wide dinner table she also inherited from her grandfather and talk. About work or books or classical music, something Michael knew much more about than she did. Truth is, he often makes her feel inadequate, but she's never said so. She loves him, and it's not a simple, Platonic love, so she's always kept it a secret, allowed their "dates" to seem like nothing more than a ritual between friends who seem to have more in common with one another than with most anyone else they know in the little New England town (whether that's true or not). Sometimes, she lies in bed, thinking about him lying beside her, instead of thinking about all the things she works so hard *not* thinking about: the river, the sea, her lost mother, the gray, weathered boards and stone foundations where there was once a dingy town, etcetera and etcetera. It's her secret, and she'll never tell him.

Though Michael knows the most terrible secret that she'll ever have, and she's fairly sure that his knowing it has kept her sane for the five years they've known one another. In an odd way, it doesn't seem fair, the same way his always cooking doesn't seem fair. No, much worse than that. But him knowing this awful thing about her, and her never telling him how she feels. Still, Elizabeth assures herself, telling him that would only ruin their friendship. A bird in the hand being worth two in the bush, and in this instance it really is better not to have one's cake and eat it, too.

They don't always play board games after dinner, or watch movies, or talk. Because there are nights that his just *knowing* her secret isn't enough. There are nights it weighs so much Elizabeth imagines it might crush her flat, like the pressure at the bottom of the deep sea. Those nights, after dinner, they go upstairs to her bedroom, and he runs a porcelain bowl of water from the bathtub faucet. He adds salt to it while she undresses before the tall mirror affixed to one wall, taller than her by a foot, and framed with ornately carved walnut. She pretends that it's only carved with acanthus leaves and cherubs. It's easier that way. It doesn't embarrass her for Michael to see her nude, not even with the disfigurements of her secret uncovered and plainly visible to him. After all, that's why he's returned from the bathroom with the bowl of salty water and a yellow sponge (he leaves the tap running). That's why they've come upstairs, because she can't always be the only one to look at herself.

"It's bad tonight?" he asks.

She doesn't answer straightaway. She's never been one to complain if she can avoid complaining, and it's bad enough that he knows. She doesn't also want to seem weak. After a minute or half a minute she answers, "It's been worse." That's the truth, even if it's also a way evading his question.

"Betsy, just tell me when you're ready." He always calls her Betsy, never Elizabeth. She's never called him Mike, though.

"I'm ready," she says, leaning her neck to the left or to the right, exposing the pale skin below the ridge of her chin. *But I'm not ready at all. I'm never ready, am I?*

"Okay, then. I'll be as gentle as I can."

He's always as gentle as anyone could be.

"You've never hurt me, Michael. Not even once."

But she has no doubt he can see the discomfort in her eyes when the washcloth touches her skin. She tries hard not to flinch, but, usually, she flinches regardless.

"Was that too hard?"

"No. I'm fine. I'm okay," she tells him, so he continues administering the salt water to her throat, dabbing carefully, and Elizabeth Haskings tries to concentrate on his fingertips, whenever they happen to brush against her. It never takes very long for the three red slits on each side of her throat to appear, and not much longer for them to open. They never open very far, not until later on. Just enough that she can see the barn-red gills behind the stiff, crescent-shaped flaps of skin that weren't there only moments before. That never are there until the salt water. Here, she always loses her breath for a few seconds, and the flaps spasm, opening and closing, and she has to gasp several times to find a balance between the air being draw in through her nostrils and mouth, and the air flowing across the feathery red gill filaments. Sometimes her legs go weak, but Michael has never let her fall.

"Breathe," he whispers. "Don't panic. Take it slow and easy, Betsy. Just breathe." The dizziness passes, the dark blotches that swim before her eyes, and she doesn't need him to support her any longer. She stares at herself in the mirror, and by now her eyes have gone black. No irises, no pupils, no sclera. Just inky black where her hazel-green eyes used to be.

"I'm right here," he says.

He doesn't have to tell her that again. He's always there, behind her or at her side.

Unconsciously, she tries to blink her eyes, but all trace of her lids have vanished, and she can only stare at those black, blank eyes. Later, when they begin to smart, Michael will have the eye drops at the ready.

"It's getting harder," she says. He doesn't reply, because she says this almost every time. *All his replies have been used up*, Elizabeth thinks. *No matter how much he might want to calm me or offer surcease, he's already said it all a dozen times over.*

Instead, he asks, "Keep going?"

She nods.

"We don't have to, you know."

"Yes we do. It's bad if we do. It's worse if we don't. It hurts more if we don't." Of course, Michael knows this perfectly well, and there's the briefest impatience that she has to remind him. Not anger, no, but an unmistakable flash of impatience, there and gone in the stingy space of a single heartbeat.

He dips the sponge into the saltwater again, not bothering to squeeze it out, because the more the better. The more, the easier. Water runs down his arm and drips to the hardwood floor. Before they're finished, there will be a puddle about her bare feet and his shoes, too. Michael gingerly swabs both her hands with the sponge, and at once the vestigial webbing between her fingers, common to all men and women, begins to expand, pushing the digits farther away from one another.

Elizabeth watches, biting her lip against the discomfort, and watches. It doesn't horrify her the same way that the appearance of the gills and the change to her eyes does, but it's much more painful. Not nearly so much as the greater portion of her metamorphosis to come, but enough she does bite her lip (careful not to draw blood). Within five minutes, the webbing has grown enough that it's attached at the uppermost joint between each finger, and is at least twice as thick as usual. And the texture of the skin on the backs of her hands and her palms is becoming smoother and faintly iridescent, more transparent, and gradually taking on the faintest tinge of turquoise. She used to think of the color as *celeste opaco*, because the Italian sounded prettier. But now she settles for *turquoise*. Not as lyrical, no, but it's not opaque, and turquoise is somehow more honest. Monsters should be honest. Before half an hour has passed, most of her skin will have taken on variations of the same hue.

"Yesterday," she says, "during nay lunch break, when I said I needed to go to the bank, I didn't."

There are a few seconds of quiet before he asks, "Where did you go, Elizabeth?"

"Choate Bridge," she answers. "I just stood there a while, watching the river." It's the oldest stone-arch bridge anywhere in Massachusetts, built in 1764. There are two granite archways through which the river flows on its easterly course.

"Did it make you feel any better?"

"It made me want to swim. The river always makes me want to swim, Michael. You know that."

"Yeah, Betsy. I know."

She wants to add, *Please don't ask me questions you already know the answers to*, but she doesn't. It would be rude. He means well, and she's never rude if she can help it. Especially not to Michael.

All evidence of her fingernails has completely vanished.

"It terrified me. It always fucking terrifies me."

"Maybe one day it won't. Maybe one day you'll be able to look at the water without being frightened."

"Maybe," she whispers, hoping it isn't true. Pretty sure what'll happen if she ever stops being afraid of the river and the sea. *I can't drown. I can't ever drown. How does a woman who can't drown fear the water?*

*There are things in the water. Things that* can *hurt me. And places I never want to see awake.*

Now he's running the sponge down her back, beginning at the nape of her neck and ending at the cleft between her buttocks. This time, the pain is bad enough she wants to double over, wants to go down on her knees and vomit. But that would be weak, and she won't be weak. Michael used to bring her pills to dull the pain, but she stopped taking them almost a year ago because she didn't like the fogginess they brought, the way they caused her to feel detached from herself, as though these transformations were happening to someone else.

*Monsters should be honest.*

At once, the neural processes of her vertebrae begin to broaden and elongate. She's made herself learn a lot about anatomy: human, anuran, chondrichthian, osteichthian, et al. Anything and everything that seems relevant to what happens to her on these nights. *The devil you know*, as her grandfather used to say. So, Elizabeth Haskings knows that the processes will grow the longest between her third and seventh thoracic vertebrae, and between her last lumbar, sacrals, and coccygeals (though less so than in the thoracic region), greatly accenting both the natural lumbar and curve of her back.

Musculature responds accordingly. She knows the Latin names of all those muscles, and if there were less pain, she could recite them for Michael. She imagines herself laughing like a madwoman and reciting the names of the shifting, straining tendons. In the end, there won't quite be fins, *sensu stricto*. Almost, but not quite.

*Aren't I a madwoman? How can I possibly still be sane?*

"Betsy, you don't have to be so strong," he tells her, and she hates the pity in his voice. "I know you think you do, but you don't. Certainly not in front of me." She takes the yellow sponge from him, her hands shaking so badly she spills most of the saltwater remaining in the bowl, but still manages to get the sponge sopping wet. Her gums have begun to ache, and she smiles at herself before wringing out the sponge with both her webbed hands so that the water runs down her belly and between her legs. In the mirror, she sees Michael turn away.

She drops the sponge to the floor at her feet (she doesn't have to look to know her toes have begun to fuse one to the next), and gazes into her pitchy eyes until she's sure the adjustments to her genitals are finished. When she does look down at herself, there's a taut, flat place where the low mound of the mons pubis was, and the labia majora, labia minora, and clitoris— all the intricacies of her sex—have been reduced to the vertical slit of an oviduct where her vagina was moments before. On either side of the slit are tiny, triangular pelvic fins, no more than an inch high and three inches long.

"We should hurry now, Betsy," Michael says. He's right, of course. She has to reach the bathtub full of warm salty water while she can still walk. Once or twice before she's waited to long, and he's had to carry her, and that humiliation was almost worse than all the rest combined. In the tub, she curls almost fetal, and the flaps in front of Elizabeth's gills open and close, pumping in and out again, extracting all the oxygen she'll need until sunrise. Michael will stay with her, guarding her, as he always does.

She can sleep without lids to shield her black eyes, and, when she sleeps, she dreams of the river flowing down to the mined seaport, to Essex Bay, and then out into the Atlantic due south of Plum island. She dreams of the craggy spine of Devil Reef rising a few feet above the waves and of those who crawl out *onto* the reef most nights to bask beneath the moon. Those like her. And, worst of all, she dreams of the abyss beyond the reef, and towers and halls of the city there, a city that has stood for eighty thousand years and will stand for eighty thousand more. On these nights, changed and slumbering, Elizabeth Haskings can't lie to herself and pretend that her mother fled to Oregon, or even that her grandfather lies in his grave in Highland Cemetery. On these nights, she isn't afraid of anything.

*The sciences, each straining in its own direction, have hitherto harmed us little; but some day the piecing together of dissociated knowledge will open up such terrifying vistas of reality, and of our frightful position therein, that we shall either go mad from the revelation or flee from the light into the peace and safety of a new dark age.*

*"The Call of Cthulhu" · H. P. Lovecraft (1928)*

# · BLOOM ·
## John Langan

"Is that—do you see—"

Already, Rick was braking, reaching for the hazards. Connie turned from the passenger-side window at whose streaky surface she had spent the last half hour staring. Eyes on something ahead, her husband was easing the steering wheel left, toward the meridian. Following the line of his gaze, she saw, next to the guardrail about ten yards in front of them, a smallish red and white container. "What?" she said. "The cooler?"

"It's not a cooler," Rick said, bringing the Forrester to a stop. His voice was still sharp with the edge of their argument.

"What do you—" She understood before she could complete her question. "Jesus—is that a—"

"A cooler," Rick said, "albeit of a different sort."

The car was in neutral, the parking brake on, Rick's door open in the time it took her to arrive at her next sentence. "What's it doing here?"

"I have no idea," he said, and stepped out of the car. She leaned forward, watching him trot to the red and white plastic box with the red cross on it. It resembled nothing so much as the undersized cooler in which she and her roommates had stored their wine coolers during undergrad: the same peaked top that would slide back when you pressed the buttons on either side of it. Rick circled around it once clockwise, once counterclockwise, and squatted on his haunches beside it. He was wearing denim shorts and the faded green Mickey Mouse T-shirt that he refused to allow Connie to claim for the rag drawer, even though it had been washed so many times it was practically translucent. (It was the outfit he chose whenever they went to visit his father.) He appeared to be reading something on the lid. He stood, turning his head to squint up and down this stretch of the Thruway, empty in both directions. He blew out his breath and ran his hand through his hair—the way he did when he was pretending to debate a question he'd already decided—then bent, put his hands on the cooler, and picked it up. Apparently, it was lighter than he'd anticipated, because it practically leapt into the air. Almost race-walking, he carried the container towards the car.

Connie half expected him to hand it to her. Instead, he continued past her to the trunk. She tilted the rearview mirror to see him balancing the cooler against his hip and unlocking the trunk. When he thunked the lid down, his hands were empty.

The answer was so obvious she didn't want to ask the question; nonetheless, once Rick was back behind the wheel, drawing his seatbelt across, she said, "What exactly are you doing?"

Without looking at her, he said, "We can't just leave it there."

"If the cell phone were charged, we could call 911."

"Connie—"

"I'm just saying. You wanted to know why that kind of stuff was so important, well, here you are."

"You—" He glanced over his shoulder to make sure the highway was clear. As he accelerated onto it, he said, "You know what? You're right. If I'd charged the cell phone last night like you asked me to, we could dial 911 and have a state trooper take this off our hands. That's absolutely true. Since the phone is dead, however, we need another plan. We're about forty, forty-five minutes from the house. I say we get home as quickly as we can and start calling around the local hospitals. Maybe this is for someone in one of them. In any event, I'm sure they'll know who to call to find out where this is supposed to go."

"Do they even do transplants in Wiltwyck?"

"I don't know. Maybe. I think Penrose might."

"We could stop at the next state trooper barracks."

"The nearest one is our exit, up 209. We're as quick going to the house."

"You're sure there's something in there?"

"I didn't look, but when I lifted it, I heard ice moving inside."

"It didn't look that heavy."

"It wasn't. But I don't know how much a heart, or a kidney, would weigh. Not too much, I think."

"I don't know, I just—" She glanced over her shoulder. "I mean, Jesus, how does something like that wind up in the middle of the Thruway? How does that happen?"

Rick shrugged. "They don't always hire the most professional guys to transport these things. Maybe someone's tail flap was down, or they swerved to avoid a deer in the road and the cooler went tumbling out."

"Surely not."

"Well, if you knew the answer to the question—"

For a second, their argument threatened to tighten its coils around them again. Connie said, "What about the lid? I thought you were reading something on it."

"There's a sticker on top that looks as if it had some kind of information, but the writing's all blurred. Must have been that storm a little while ago."

"So it's been sitting here at least that long."

"Seems likely. Maybe that was what happened—maybe the truck skidded and that caused the cooler to come loose."

"Wouldn't you stop and go back for something like that? Someone's life could be on the line."

"Could be the driver never noticed, was too busy trying to keep himself from crashing into the guardrail."

The scenario sounded plausible enough—assuming, that is, you accepted Rick's assertion about underqualified drivers employed to convey freshly harvested organs from donor to recipient. Which was, now that Connie thought about it, sufficiently venal and depressing likely to be the truth. "What if it's supposed to be heading north, to Albany?"

"There's probably still enough time, even if whoever it is has to drive back the way we came."

"Maybe they could fly it wherever it needs to go. Doesn't Penrose do that?"

"I think so."

Already, she was buying into Rick's plan. Would it make that much difference to call the hospitals from their house instead of the police station? Equipped with a fully charged cell phone, they could have been rushing whatever was packed in the cooler's ice to the surgical team who at this moment must be in the midst of preparations to receive it. Connie could picture herself and Rick striding into the Emergency Room at Wiltwyck, the cooler under Rick's arm, a green-garbed surgeon waiting with gloves outstretched. With the cell inert, though, home might be their next best option. Based on her experiences with them at an embarrassing number of stops for speeding, the Wiltwyck troopers would require more time than whoever was waiting for this cooler's contents could spare for her and Rick to make clear to them the gravity of the situation.

*That's not true*, she thought. *You know that isn't true. You're just pissed because that guy wouldn't agree to plead down to ten miles an hour over the speed limit.* She was justifying Rick's plan, shoring up his ambition to be part of the story—an important part, the random, passing stranger who turns out to be crucial to yanking someone at death's very doorway back from that black rectangle. Because . . . because it was exciting to feel yourself caught up in a narrative like this, one that offered you the opportunity to be part of something bigger than yourself.

Rick had the speedometer to the other side of eighty-five. Connie reached her left hand across and squeezed his leg, lightly.

He did not remove his hands from the wheel.

Hour hours later, they were staring at the cooler sitting on the kitchen table. Its surface was pebbled plastic; Connie wondered if that contributed in any way to keeping its contents chilled. The red cross stenciled on its lid was faded, a shade lighter than the bottom half of the cooler, and beginning to flake off. The symbol didn't look like your typical red cross. This design was narrow at the join, the sides of each arm curving outwards on their way to its end—the four of which were rounded, like the edges of a quartet of axes. Connie had seen this style of cross, or one close to it, before: Alexa, the first girl with whom she'd shared an apartment, and who had been more Catholic than the Pope, had counted a cross in this style among her religious jewelry. A Maltese cross? Cross of Malta? Something like that, although Connie remembered her old roommate's cross ornamented with additional designs—little pictures, she thought; of what, she couldn't recall. To be honest, this version of the cross seemed less a religious icon and more the image of something else—an abstract flower, perhaps, or an elaborate keyhole. For a moment, the four red lines opening out resembled nothing so much as the pupil of some oversized, alien eye, but that was ridiculous.

What it meant that the cooler resting on the blond wood of their kitchen table bore this emblem, she could not say. Did the Red Cross have subdivisions, local branches, and might this be one of their symbols? She'd never heard of such a thing, but she was a manager at Target; this was hardly her area of expertise.

Rick said, "Maybe it's a Mob thing."

"What?" Connie looked across the table at him, slouched back in his chair, arms folded over his chest.

"I said, maybe it's a Mob thing."

"What do you mean?"

He straightened. "Maybe it's part of someone who, you know, messed with the Mob. Or someone they had a contract on."

"Like what—a finger?"

"Finger, hand—proof that the job was done."

"Seriously?"

He shrugged.

"It's a possibility."

"I don't know."

"You don't know what?"

"I don't know—I mean, the Mob? Transporting—what? Severed body parts in medical coolers? Wasn't that a movie?"

"Was it?"

"Yes—we saw it together. It was on TNT or TBS or something. Joe Pesci was in it. Remember: he's a hit man and he's got these heads in a duffle bag—"

*"Eight Heads in a Duffel Bag."*

"That's it!"

"So there was a movie. What does that prove?"

"It's just—"

"Or maybe it's some kind of black market thing, a kidney for sale to the highest bidder, no questions asked."

"Isn't that an urban legend?"

"Where do you think these things come from?"

"I—"

"Look—all I'm saying is, we've exhausted the legitimate avenues, so it makes sense to consider other possibilities."

Connie took a breath. "Granted. But we don't even know what's inside the cooler—if there's anything in it."

"You're the one who said we shouldn't open it."

"I know. It's—if there's something in it, then we need to be careful about not contaminating it."

"Are you listening to yourself? We don't know if there's anything in the cooler, so we shouldn't be too concerned about it, but we shouldn't open it, in case there is something in there. What are we supposed to do?"

Before she could answer, Rick pushed himself up from his chair and stalked to the refrigerator, the bottles in whose door rattled as he yanked it open. Connie bit the remark ready to leap off her tongue. Instead, she stood and leaned over to have another look at the square sticker on the cooler's lid. There were no identifying names on the label, no hospital or transport service logos, no barcode, even, which, in the age of global computer tracking, struck her as stranger than the absence of a corporate ID. There were only four or five lines of smeared black ink, unintelligible except for one word that she and Rick had agreed read "Howard" and another that he guessed was "orchid" but of which Connie could identify no more than the initial "o." Now, as her gaze roamed over the ink blurred into swirls and loops, she had the impression that the words which had been written on this sticker hadn't been English, the letters hadn't been any she would have recognized. Some quality of the patterns into which the writing had been distorted suggested an alphabet utterly unfamiliar, which might smear into a configuration resembling "Howard" or "orchid" by the merest coincidence.

*God, you're worse than Rick.* She resumed her seat as he returned from the fridge, an open bottle of Magic Hat in hand. Not that she wanted a drink, exactly, but his failure to ask her if she did sent Connie on her own mission to the fridge. They were out of hard cider, dammit. She had intended to stop at Hannaford for a quick shop on the way home, then the cooler had appeared and obscured all other concerns. They were almost out of milk, too, and butter. She selected a Magic Hat for herself and swung the door shut.

Rick had set his beer on the table and was standing with his back to her, bent forward slightly, his arms out, his hands on the cooler.

"Rick?" Connie said. "What are you doing?"

"Is that a trick question?"

"Very funny," she said, crossing the kitchen to him. He was staring at the cooler as if he could will its contents visible. He said, "We have to open it."

"But if there's something inside it—"

"I know, I know. I can't see any other choice. We called Wiltwyck, and they didn't know anything about it. Neither did Penrose or Albany Med or Westchester Med. The transport services they gave us the numbers for weren't missing any shipments—the one said they aren't even using coolers like this anymore. The cops were useless. Hell, that guy at the sheriff's thought it was probably just someone's cooler. Maybe there'll be some kind of information inside that'll tell us where this is supposed to go."

"What if it's a Mob thing?"

"Do you really believe that?"

"No, but I could be wrong, in which case, what would we do?"

"Get rid of it as quickly as possible. Burn it. I don't think there's any way it could be traced to us."

To her surprise, Connie said, "All right. Go ahead."

Rick didn't ask if she were sure. He pressed in the catches on the lid and slid it back. As Connie inclined toward it, he drew the cooler toward them. It scraped against the table; its contents shifted with a sound like gravel rasping. Connie had been anticipating a strong odor washing out of the cooler's interior, raw meat full of blood; instead, there was the faintest blue hint of air long-chilled and another, even fainter trace of iodine. Rick's arm was blocking her view; she nudged him. "What is it?"

"I don't know."

"Let me see."

He shifted to the right. The cooler was full of ice, chips of it heaped in shining piles around, around—

She registered the color first, the dark purple of a ripe eggplant, shot through with veins of lighter purple—blue, she thought, some shade of blue. It was maybe as wide as a small dinner plate, thicker at the center than at its scalloped circumference. At five—no, six spots around its margin, the surface puckered, the color around each spot shading into a rich rose. The texture of the thing was striated, almost coarse.

"What the fuck?"

"I know—right?"

"Rick—what is this?"

"A placenta?"

"That is not a placenta."

"Like you've seen one."

"As a matter of fact, I have. There was a show on Lifetime—I can't remember what it was called, but it was about women giving birth, in living color, no detail spared. I saw plenty of placentas, and trust me, that is not a placenta."

"Okay, it's not a placenta. So what is it?"

"I—is it even human?"

"You're saying what? That it's an animal?"

"I don't know—some kind of jellyfish?"

"Looks too solid, doesn't it? Besides, wouldn't you store a jellyfish in water?"

"I guess."

Rick started to reach into the cooler. Connie grabbed his wrist. "Jesus! What are you doing?"

"I thought I'd take it out so we could have a better look at it." He tugged his hand free.

"You don't know what it is."

"I'm pretty sure it isn't someone's kidney."

"Granted, but you can't just—it could be dangerous, toxic."

"Really."

"There are animals whose skin is poisonous. Haven't you heard of Poison Dart Frogs?"

"Oh." He lowered his hand. "Fair enough." He stepped away from the cooler. "Sweetie—what is this?"

"Well, I'm pretty sure we can say what it isn't. I doubt there's anyone whose life depends on receiving this, and I'm pretty sure it wasn't attached to any Mob informer. Nor was it feeding a fetus nutrients for nine months. That leaves us with—I don't have the faintest idea. Some kind of animal."

"I don't know."

Connie shrugged. "The world's a big place. There are all kinds of crazy things living at the bottom of the ocean. Or it could be from someplace else—deep underground. Maybe it's a new discovery that was being transported to a museum."

Rick grunted. "Okay. Let's assume this was on its way to an eager research scientist. What's our next move?"

"Another round of phone calls, I guess."

"You want to start on that, and I'll get dinner going?"

She wasn't hungry, but she said, "Sure."

Rick reached for the cooler. "Relax," he said as she tensed, ready to seize his arms. Steadying the cooler with his left hand, he closed it with the right. The lid snicked shut.

No surprise: she dreamed about the thing in the cooler. She was in Rick's father's room at the nursing home (even asleep, she was unable to think of him as "Gary" or "Mr. Wilson," let alone "Dad"). Rick's father was in the green vinyl recliner by the window, his face tilted up to the sunlight pouring over him in a way that reminded Connie of a large plant feeding on light. The green Jets sweatsuit he was wearing underscored the resemblance. His eyes were closed, his lips moving in the constant murmur that had marked the Alzheimer's overwhelming the last of his personality. In the flood of brightness, he looked younger than fifty-eight, as if he might be Rick's young uncle, and not the father not old enough for the disease that had consumed him with the relentless patience of a python easing itself around its prey.

Connie was standing with her back to the room's hefty dresser, the top of which was heaped with orchids, their petals eggplant and rose. The air was full of the briny smell of seaweed baking on the beach, which she knew was the flowers' scent.

Although she hadn't noticed him enter the room, Rick was kneeling in front of his father, his hands held up and out as if offering the man a gift. His palms cupped the thing from the cooler. Its edges overflowed his hands. In the dense sunlight, the thing was even darker, more rather than less visible. If the scene in front of her were a photograph, the thing was a dab of black paint rising off its surface.

"Here," Rick said to his father. "I brought it for you." When his father did not respond, Rick said, "Dad."

The man opened his eyes and tilted his head in his son's direction. Connie didn't think he saw what Rick was offering him. He croaked, "Bloom."

"Beautiful," Rick said.

His father's eyes narrowed, and his face swung toward Connie. He was weeping, tears coursing down his cheeks like lines of fire in the sunlight. "Bloom," he said.

Almost before she knew she was awake, she was sitting up in bed. Although she was certain it must be far into the night, one of those hours you only saw when the phone rang to announce some family tragedy, the digital clock insisted it was two minutes after midnight. She had been asleep for an hour. She turned to Rick and found his side of the bed empty.

There was no reason for her heart to start pounding. Rick stayed up late all the time, watching *Nightline* or *Charlie Rose*. For the seven years Connie had known him, he had been a light sleeper, prone to insomnia, a tendency that had worsened with his father's unexpected and sudden decline. She had sought him out enough times in the beginning of their relationship to be sure that there was no cause for her to leave the bed. She would find him on the couch, bathed in the TV's glow, a bag of microwave popcorn open on his lap. So prepared was she for him to be there that, when she reached the bottom of the stairs and discovered the living room dark, something like panic straightened her spine. "Rick?" she said. "Honey?"

Of course he was in the kitchen. She glimpsed him out of the corner of her eye the same instant he said, "I'm in here." By the streetlight filtering through the window, she saw him seated at the kitchen table, wearing a white T-shirt and boxers, his arms on the table, his hands on the keyboard of his father's laptop, which was open and on. The cooler, which he had pushed back to make room for the computer, appeared to be closed. (She wasn't sure why that detail made her heart slow.) She walked down the hallway to him, saying, "Couldn't sleep, huh?"

"Nah." His eyes did not leave the computer screen. "You're like this every time we visit your Dad."

"Am I? I guess so."

She rubbed his back. "You're doing all you can for him. It's a good place."

"Yeah."

On the laptop's screen, a reddish sphere hung against a backdrop of stars. Connie recognized the painting from the NASA website, and the next picture Rick brought up, of a rough plane spread out under a starry sky, at the center of which a cluster of cartoonishly fat arrows identified a handful of the dots of light as the sun and planets of solar system. A third image showed eight green circles arranged concentrically around a bright point, all of it inside one end of an enormous red ellipse.

The screen after that was a photo of a massive stone monument, a rectangular block stood on its short end, another block laid across its top to form a T-shape. The front of the tall stone was carved with a thick line that descended from high on the right to almost the bottom of the left, where it curved back right again; in the curve, a representation of a four-legged animal Connie could not identify crouched. The image that followed was another painting, this one of a trio of circular structures set in the lee of a broad hill, the diameter of each defined by a thick wall, the interior stood with T-shaped monoliths like the one on the previous screen.

Rick sped through the next dozen screens, long rows of equations more complex than any Connie had encountered in her college math class, half of each line composed of symbols she thought were Greek but wasn't sure. When he came to what appeared to be a list of questions, Rick stopped. Connie could read the first line: *Twelve thousand year orbit coincides with construction of Gobekli Tepe: built in advance of, or in response to, seeding?*

Oh God, Connie thought. She said, "You want to come to bed?"

"I will. You go ahead."

"I don't want you sitting up half the night feeling guilty."

He paused, then said, "It isn't guilt."

"Oh? What is it?"

He shook his head. "I had a dream."

Her mouth went dry. "Oh?"

He nodded. "I was sitting here with my Dad. We were both wearing tuxedoes, and the table had been set for some kind of elaborate meal: white linen tablecloth, candelabra, china plates, the works. It was early in the morning—at least, I think it was, because the windows were pouring light into the room. The plates, the cutlery, the glasses—everything was shining, it was so bright. For a long time, it felt like, we sat there—here—and then I noticed Dad was holding his fork and knife and was using them to cut something on his plate. It was this," he nodded at the cooler, "this thing. He was having a rough time. He couldn't grip the cutlery right; it was as if he'd forgotten how to hold them. His knife kept slipping, scraping on the plate. The thing was tough; he really had to saw at it. It was making this noise, this high-pitched sound that was kind of like a violin. It was bleeding, or leaking, black syrupy stuff that was all over the plate, the knife, splattering the tablecloth, Dad's shirt. Finally, he got a piece of the thing loose and raised it to his mouth. Only, his lips were still trembling, you know, doing that silent mumble, and he couldn't maneuver the fork past them. The piece flopped on the table. He frowned, speared it with his fork again, and made another try. No luck. The third time, the piece hit the edge of the table and bounced off. That was it. He dropped the cutlery, grabbed the thing on his plate with both hands, and brought it up. His face was so eager. He licked his lips and took a huge bite. He had to clamp down hard, pull the rest away. There was a ripping noise. The thing's blood was all over his lips, his teeth, his tongue; his mouth looked like a black hole."

Connie waited for him to continue. When he didn't, she said, "And?"

"That was it. I woke up and came down here. There was nothing on TV, so I thought I'd get out Dad's laptop and . . . It's like a connection to him, to how he used to be, you know? I mean, I know he was already pretty bad when he was working on this stuff, but at least he was there."

"Huh." Connie considered relating her own dream, decided instead to ask, "What do you think your dream means?"

"I don't know. I dream about my Dad a lot, but this . . . "

"Do you—"

"What if it's from another planet?"

"What?"

"Maybe the dream's a message."

"I don't—"

"That would explain why there's no record of it, anywhere, why none of the museums knows anything about it."

"That doesn't make any sense," Connie said. "If this thing were some kind of alien, you'd expect it'd be all over the news."

"Maybe it's dangerous—or they aren't sure if it's dangerous."

"So they pack it into a cooler?"

"They're trying to fly under the radar."

"I don't know—that's so low, it's underground."

"Or . . . what if a couple of guys found it—somewhere, they were out hunting or fishing or something—and they decided to take it with them in the cooler they'd brought for their beers?"

"Then why the red cross on the cooler? What about the sticker?"

"Coincidence—they just happened to take that cooler."

"I could—look, even if that is the case, if a couple of hunters came upon this thing, I don't know, fresh from its meteorite, and emptied out their oddly decorated cooler so they could be famous as the first guys to encounter E.T., how does that help us know what to do?"

"We could call NASA."

"What? Would they send out the Men in Black?"

"I'm serious!" Rick almost shouted. "This is serious! Jesus! We could be—we have—why can't you take this seriously?" He turned to glare at her as he spoke.

"Rick—"

"Don't 'Rick' me."

Connie inhaled. "Honey—it's late. We're tired. Let's not do this, okay? Not now. I'm sorry if I'm not taking this seriously. It's been a long day. Whatever it is, the thing in the cooler'll keep until we get some sleep. If you want, we can call NASA first thing in the morning. Really—I swear."

"I—" She readied herself for the next phase of his outburst, then, "You're right," Rick said. "You're right. It has been a long day, hasn't it?"

"Very. I can't believe you aren't exhausted."

"I am—believe me, I'm dead on my feet. It's just, this thing—"

"I understand—honest, I do. Why don't you come up to bed? Maybe once you lie down—"

"All right. You go up. I just need a minute more."

"For what?" she wanted to ask but didn't, opting instead to drape her arms over his shoulders and press her cheek against his neck. "Love you," she said into his skin.

"Love you, too."

Her heart, settled after its earlier gallop, broke into a trot again as she padded down the hall to the stairs. The sight of Rick, once more staring at the computer screen, did nothing to calm it, nor did her lowering herself onto the bed, drawing the covers up. If anything, the thoroughbred under her ribs charged faster. She gazed at the bedroom ceiling, feeling the mattress resound with her pulse. Was she having a panic attack? *Don't think about it*, she told herself. *Concentrate on something else.*

Rick. What else was there beside him at the table, his fingers resting on the keyboard's sides, sifting through his father's last, bizarre project? Not the most reassuring behavior; although it was true: each monthly pilgrimage to his father left him unsettled for the rest of that day, sometimes the next. No matter how many times she told him that his dad was in the best place, that the home provided him a quality of care they couldn't have (not to mention, his father's insurance covered it in full), and no matter how many times Rick answered, "You're right; you're absolutely right," she knew that he didn't accept her reasoning, her reassurance. In the past, thinking that anger might help him to articulate his obvious guilt, she had tried to pick a fight with him, stir him to argument, but he had headed the opposite direction, descended into himself for the remainder of the weekend. She had suggested they visit his dad more often, offered to rearrange her work schedule so that they could go up twice a month, even three times. What good was being store manager, she'd said, if you couldn't use it to your advantage? Albany wasn't that far, and there were supposed to be good restaurants there; they could make a day of it, spend time with his father and have some time for themselves, too.

No, no, Rick had said. It wasn't fair for her to have to rework the schedule (arriving at which she'd compared to the circus act where the clown spins the plates on the ends of all the poles he's holding while balancing his unicycle on the highwire). It wasn't as if his dad would know the difference, anyway.

*He might not*, Connie had said, *but you will.*

It was no good, though; Rick's mind had been made up before their conversation had started. He had never admitted it, but Connie was sure he was still traumatized by his father's last months of—you couldn't call it lucidity, exactly, since what he would call to yell at Rick about was pretty insane. Gary Wilson had been an astronomer, his most recent work an intensive study of the dwarf planets discovered beyond Neptune in the first decade of the twenty-first century: Eris, Sedna, and Orcus were the names she remembered. From what she understood, his research on the surface conditions on these bodies was cutting-edge stuff; he had been involved in the planning for a probe to explore some of them. Plenty of times, she and Rick had arrived at his apartment to take him to dinner, only to find him seated at his desk, staring at his computer monitor, at a painting of one or the other of the dwarf planets. At those moments, he had seemed a million miles away, further, as far as one of the spheres he studied. Hindsight's clarity made it obvious he was experiencing the early effects of Alzheimer's, but the spells had always broken the moment Rick shook him and said, "Dad, it's us," and it had been easier to accept her father-in-law's assurance that he had merely been daydreaming.

Not until his behavior became more erratic did it dawn on them that Rick's father might not be well. His attention had been focused on one dwarf planet, Sedna, for months. Connie had sat beside him at the Plaza diner as he flipped over his mat and drew an asterisk in the center of it which he surrounded with a swirl of concentric circles, all of which he placed at one end of a great oval. "This is Sedna's orbit," he had said, jabbing his pen at the oval. "Twelve thousand years, give or take a few hundred. Over the next couple of centuries, it will be as close to us as it's been during the whole of recorded history. The last time it was this near, well . . . ."

"What?" Rick had said.

"You'll see," his father had declared.

They hadn't, though, not directly. One of Rick's father's friends at the state university had phoned after a presentation during which the extent of Gary Wilson's breakdown had become manifest. Connie had heard the lecture, herself, in person, on the phone, and in a long, rambling voicemail. She considered herself reasonably well-educated in a hold-your-own-at-Trivial-Pursuit kind of way, but Rick's father's discussion strained her comprehension. Almost thirteen thousand years ago, a comet had burst over the Great Lakes—yes, that was a controversial claim, but how else to explain the high levels of iridium, the nano-diamonds? The glaciers were already in retreat, you see; it was the right time, if you could measure time in centuries—millennia. This was when the Clovis disappeared—wiped out, or assimilated in some way, it was hard to say. You wouldn't think a stone point much of a threat, but you'd be surprised. The drawings at Lascaux—well, never mind them. It's what happens at Gobekli Tepe that's important. Those curves on the stones—has anyone thought of mapping them onto Sedna's orbit? The results—as for the shape of the monuments, those giant T's, why, they're perches, for the messengers.

And so on. The thing was, while Rick's father was propounding this lunatic hodgepodge of invention, he sounded as reasonable, as kindly, as he ever had. Perhaps that was because she hadn't challenged him in the way that Rick did, tell him that his ideas were crazy, he was flushing his career down the toilet. Confronted by his son's strenuous disbelief, Gary flushed with anger, was overtaken by storms of rage more intense than any she had witnessed in the seven years she had known him. He would stalk from their house and demand that Connie drive him home, then, once home, he would call and harangue Rick for another hour, sometimes two, until Rick reached his boiling point and hung up on him.

The end, when it came, had come quickly: she had been amazed at the speed with which Rick's father had been convinced to accept early retirement and a place in an assisted living facility. There had been a brief period of days, not even a full week, during which he had returned to something like his old self. He had signed all the papers necessary to effect his departure from the college and his relocation to Morrison Hills. He had spoken to Rick and Connie calmly, with barely a mention of Sedna's impending return. Two days after he settled into his new, undersized room, Gary had suffered a catastrophic event somewhere in his brain that the doctors refused to call a stroke, saying the MRI results were all wrong for that. (Frankly, they seemed mystified by what had happened to him during the night.) Whatever its name, the occurrence had left him a few steps up from catatonic, intermittently responsive and usually in ways that made no sense. There was talk of further study, of sub-specialists being brought in, possible trips to hospitals in other states, but nothing, as yet, had come to pass. Connie doubted any of it would. There were more than enough residents of the facility who could and did vocalize their complaints, and less than enough staff to spare on a man whose tongue was so much dead weight.

Harrowing as Rick's father's decline had been, she supposed she should be grateful that it had not stretched out longer than it had. From talking with staff at Morrison, she knew that it could take years for a parent's worsened condition to convince them/their family that something had to be done. At the same time, though, Rick had been ambivalent about his father entering assisted living. There was enough room in the house for him: he could have stayed in the downstairs bedroom and had his own bathroom. But neither of them was available for—or, to be honest, up for—the task of caring for him. Rick's consent to his father's move had been conditional; he had insisted and Connie had agreed that they would re-evaluate the situation in six months. Their contract had been rendered null and void by Gary's collapse, which had left him in need of a level of care far beyond that for which either of them was equipped. However irrational the sentiment might be, Connie knew that Rick took his father's crash as a rebuke from the universe for having agreed to send him away in the first place.

Connie didn't realize she had crossed over into sleep again until she noticed that the bedroom's ceiling and walls had vanished, replaced by a night sky brimming with stars. Her bed was sitting on a vast plane, dimly lit by the stars' collective radiance. Its dark red expanse was stippled and ridged, riven by channels; she had the impression of dense mud. That and cold: although she could not feel it on her skin, she sensed that wherever this was was so cold it should have frozen her in place, her blood crystallized, her organs chunks of ice.

To her left, a figure was progressing slowly across the plane. It was difficult to be sure, but it looked like a man, dressed in black. Every few steps, he would pause and study the ground in front of him, occasionally crouching and poking it with one hand. Connie watched him for what might have been a long time. Her bed, she noticed, was strewn with orchids, their petals eggplant and rose. At last, she drew back the blanket, lowered herself onto the red mud, and set out toward him.

She had expected the mud to be ice-brittle, but while it was firm under her feet, it was also the slightest bit spongy. She wasn't sure how this could be. A glance over her shoulder showed the bed and its cargo of flowers unmoved. While she was still far away from him, she saw that the man ahead of her was wearing a tuxedo, and that he was Rick's father. She was not surprised by either of these facts.

In contrast to her previous dream of him, Gary Wilson stood tall, alert. He was following a series of depressions in the plane's surface, each a concave dip of about a foot, maybe six feet from the one behind it. At the bottom of the depressions, something dark shone through the red mud. When he bent to prod one, he licked his finger clean afterwards. Connie could feel his awareness of her long before she drew near, but he waited until she was standing beside him to say, "Well?"

"Where is this?"

"Oh, come now," he said, disappointment bending his voice. "You know the answer to that already."

She did. "Sedna."

He nodded. "The nursery."

"For those?" She pointed at the depression before him. "Of course."

"What are they?"

"Embryos." The surface of his cheek shifted. "I don't understand."

"Over here." He turned to his left and crossed to another row of depressions. Beside the closest was a small red and white container—a cooler, its top slid open. To either side, the depressions were attended by thermoses, lunchboxes, larger coolers, even a small refrigerator. Rick's father knelt at a dip and reached his hand down into the mud, working his fingers in a circle around whatever lay half-buried in it. Once it was freed, he raised it, using his free hand to brush the worst of the mud from it. "This," he said, holding out to Connie a copy of the thing she and Rick had found on the Thruway. Its surface was darker than the spaces between the stars overhead.

"That's an embryo?" she said.

"Closest word." Bending to the open cooler, he gently deposited the thing inside it. His hands free, he clicked the cooler's lid shut. "Someone will be by for this, shortly," he said, raising his fingers to his tongue.

"I don't—" Connie started, and there was an explosion of wings, or what might have been wings, a fury of black flapping. She put up her hands to defend herself, and the wings were gone, the cooler with them. "What . . . ?"

"You have to prepare the ground, first," Rick's father said, "fertilize it, you could say. A little more time would have been nice, but Tunguska was long enough ago. To tell the truth, if we'd had to proceed earlier, it wouldn't have mattered." He stepped to the next hole and its attendant thermos and repeated his excavation. As he was jiggling the thing into the thermos, Connie said, "But—why?"

"Oh, that's . . . " Rick's father gestured at the thermos's side, where the strange cross with the slender join and rounded arms was stenciled. "You know."

"No, I don't."

Gary Wilson shrugged. His face slid with the movement, up, then down, the flesh riding on the bone. The hairs on Connie's neck, her arms, stood rigid. She did not want to accompany him as he turned left again and headed for a deep slice in the mud, but she could not think what else to do. Behind her, there was a chaos of flapping, and silence.

The fissure in the mud ran in both directions as far as she could see. It was probably narrow enough for her to jump across. She was less sure of its depth, rendered uncertain by dimness. At or near the bottom, something rose, not high enough for her to distinguish it, but sufficiently near for her to register a great mass. "Too cold out here," Rick's father said. "Makes them sluggish. Inhibits their"—he waved his hands—"development. Confines it." There were more of whatever-it-was down there. Some quality of their movement made Connie grateful she couldn't see any more of them.

"Funny," Rick's father said. "They need this place for infancy, your place for maturity. Never known another breed with such extreme requirements."

"What are they?"

"I guess you would call them . . . gods? Is that right? *Orchidaceae deus*? They bloom."

"What?"

"Bloom."

There was a small deck at the back of the house, little more than a half-dozen planks of unfinished wood raised on as many thick posts, bordered by an unsteady railing, at the top of a flight of uneven stairs. A door led from the deck into the house's laundry room, whose location on the second floor had impressed Connie as one of the reasons to rent the place two years ago, when her promotion to manager had allowed sufficient money to leave their basement apartment and its buffet of molds behind. On mornings when she didn't have to open the store, and Rick hadn't worked too late the night before, they would carry their mugs of coffee out here. She liked to stand straight, her mug cradled in her hands, while Rick preferred to take his chances leaning on the rail. Sometimes they spoke, but mostly they were quiet, listening to the birds performing their various morning songs, watching the squirrels chase one another across the high branches of the trees whose roots knitted together the small rise behind the house.

A freak early frost had whited the deck and stairs. Once the sun was streaming through the trunks of the oaks and maples stationed on the rise, the frost would steam off, but at the moment dawn was a red hint amidst the dark trees. *Red sky at morning*, Connie thought.

She was seated at the top of the deck stairs, wrapped in the green and white knitted blanket she'd grabbed when she'd left the laundry room hours ago. The bottle of Stolichnaya cradled in her arms was almost empty, despite which, she felt as sober as she ever had. More than sober—her senses were operating past peak capacity. The grooves in the bark of the oaks on the rise were deep gullies flanked by vertical ridges. The air eddying over her skin was dense with moisture. The odor of the soil in which the trees clutched their roots was the brittle-paper smell of dead leaves crumbling mixed with the damp thickness of dirt. It was as if she were under a brilliant white light, one that allowed her no refuge, but that also permitted her to view her surroundings with unprecedented clarity.

She had emerged from her dream of Rick's father to silence, to a stillness so profound the sound of her breathing thundered in her ears. Rick's side of the bed was still cold. Except for a second strange dream on the same night, there had been no reason for Connie to do anything other than return to sleep. Her dream, however, had seemed sufficient cause for her to rouse herself and (once more) set out downstairs in search of Rick. In the quiet that had draped the house, the creaks of the stairs under her feet had been horror-movie loud.

She had not been sure what she would find downstairs, and had walked past the front parlor before her brain had caught up to what it had noticed from the corner of her eye and sent her several steps back. The small room they called the front parlor, whose bay window overlooked the front porch, had been dark. Not just nighttime dark (which, with the streetlight outside, wasn't really that dark), but complete and utter blackness. This hadn't been the lack of light so much as the overwhelming presence of its opposite, a dense inkiness that had filled the room like water in a tank. Connie had reached out her hand to touch it, only to stop with her fingers a hair's-breadth away from it, when the prospect of touching it had struck her as a less than good idea. Lowering her hand, she had retreated along the hall to the dining room.

Before the dining room, though, she had paused at the basement door, open wide and allowing a thick, briny stench up from its depths. The smell of seaweed and assorted sea-life baking on the beach, the odor had been oddly familiar, despite her inability to place it. She had reached around the doorway for the light switch, flipped it on, and poked her head through the doorway. Around the foot of the stairs, she had seen something she could not immediately identify. There had been no way she was venturing all the way into the basement; already, the night had taken too strange a turn for her to want to put herself into so ominous, if clichéd, a location. But she had been curious enough to descend the first couple of stairs and crouch to look through the railings.

When she had, Connie had seen a profusion of flowers, orchids, their petals eggplant and rose. They had covered the concrete floor so completely she could not see it. A few feet closer to them, the tidal smell was stronger, almost a taste. The orchids were motionless, yet she had had the impression that she had caught them on the verge of movement. She had wanted to think, *I'm dreaming; this is part of that last dream*, but the reek of salt and rot had been too real. She had stood and backed upstairs.

Mercifully, the dining room had been unchanged, its table, chairs, and china cabinet highlighted by the streetlight's orange glow. Unchanged, that is, except for the absence of the cooler from the table, and why had she been so certain that, wherever the container was, its lid was open, its contents gone? Rick's father's laptop had remained where her husband had set it up, its screen dark. Connie had pressed the power button, and the rectangle had brightened with the image of one of the T-shaped stone monuments, its transverse section carved with what appeared to be three birds processing down from upper left to lower right, their path taking them over the prone form of what might have been a man—though if it was, the head was missing. The upright block was carved with a boar, its tusks disproportionately large.

Thinking Rick might have decided to sleep in the guestroom, she had crossed to the doorway to the long room along the back of the house, the large space for which they had yet to arrive at a use. To the right, the room had wavered, as if she had been looking at it through running water. One moment, it had bulged toward her; the next, it had telescoped away. In the midst of that uncertainty, she had seen . . . she couldn't say what. It was as if that part of the house had been a screen against which something enormous had been pushing and pulling, its form visible only through the distortions it caused in the screen. The sight had hurt her eyes, her brain, to behold; she had been not so much frightened as sickened, nauseated. No doubt, she should have fled the house, taken the car keys from the hook at the front door and driven as far from here as the gas in the tank would take her.

Rick, though: she couldn't leave him here with all this. Dropping her gaze to her feet, she had stepped into the back room, flattening herself against the wall to her left. A glance had showed nothing between her and the door to the guest room, and she had slid along the wall to it as quickly as her legs would carry her. A heavy lump of dread, for Rick, alone down here as whatever this was had happened, had weighed deep below her stomach. At the threshold to the guest room, she had tried to speak, found her voice caught in her throat. She had coughed, said, "Rick? Honey?" the words striking the silence in the air like a mallet clanging off a gong; she had flinched at their loudness.

Connie had not been expecting Rick to step out of the guest room as if he had been waiting there for her. With a shriek, she had leapt back. He had raised his hands, no doubt to reassure her, but even in the dim light she could see they were discolored, streaked with what looked like tar, as was his mouth, his jaw. He had stepped toward her, and Connie had retreated another step. "Honey," he had said, but the endearment had sounded wrong, warped, as if his tongue had forgotten how to shape his words.

"Rick," she had said, "what—what happened?"

His lips had peeled back, but whatever he had wanted to say, it would not come out.

"The house—you're—"

"It's . . . okay. He showed me . . . Dad."

"Your father? What did he show you?"

Rick had not lowered his hands; he gestured with them to his mouth.

"Oh, Christ. You—you didn't."

Yes, he did, Rick had nodded.

"Are you insane? Do you have any idea what—? You don't know what that thing was! You probably poisoned yourself . . . "

"Fine," Rick had said. "I'm . . . fine. Better. More."

"What?"

"Dad showed me."

Whatever the cooler's contents, she had been afraid the effects of consuming it were already in full swing, the damage already done. Yet despite the compromise in his speech, Rick's eyes had burned with intelligence. Sweeping his hands around him, he had said, "All . . . the same. Part of—" He had uttered a guttural sound she could not decipher, but that had hurt her ears to hear.

"Rick," she had said, "we have to leave—we have to get you to a doctor. Come on." She had started toward the doorway to the dining room, wondering whether Wiltwyck would be equipped for whatever toxin he had ingested. The other stuff, the darkness, the orchids, the corner, could wait until Rick had been seen by a doctor.

"No." The force of his refusal had halted Connie where she was. "See."

"What—" She had turned to him and seen . . . she could not say what. Hours later, her nerves calmed if not soothed by the vodka that had washed down her throat, she could not make sense of the sight that had greeted her. When she tried to replay it, she saw Rick, then saw his face, his chest, burst open, pushed aside by the orchids thrusting their eggplant and rose petals out of him. The orchids, Rick, wavered, as if she were looking at them through a waterfall, and then erupted into a cloud of darkness that coalesced into Rick's outline. Connie had the sense that that was only an approximation of what she actually had witnessed, and not an especially accurate one, at that. As well say she had seen all four things simultaneously, like a photograph overexposed multiple times, or that she had seen the cross from the top of the cooler, hanging in the air.

She had responded with a headlong flight that had carried her upstairs to the laundry room. Of course, it had been a stupid destination, one she was not sure why she had chosen, except perhaps that the side and front doors had lain too close to one of the zones of weirdness that had overtaken the house. The bottle of Stolichnaya had been waiting next to the door to the deck, no doubt a refugee from their most recent party. She could not think of a reason not to open it and gulp a fiery mouthful of its contents; although she couldn't think of much of anything. She had been, call it aware of the quiet, the silence pervading the house, which had settled against her skin and become intolerable, until she had grabbed a blanket from the cupboard and let herself out onto the deck. There, she had wrapped herself in the blanket and seated herself at the top of the deck stairs.

Tempting to say she had been in shock, but shock wasn't close: shock was a small town she had left in the rearview mirror a thousand miles ago. This was the big city, metropolis of a sensation like awe or ecstasy, a wrenching of the self that rendered such questions as how she was going to help Rick, how they were going to escape from this, immaterial. From where she was sitting, she could look down on their Subaru, parked maybe fifteen feet from the foot of the stairs. There was an emergency key under an overturned flowerpot in the garage. These facts were neighborhoods separated by hundreds of blocks, connected by a route too byzantine for her understanding to take in. She had stayed where she was as the constellations wheeled above her, the sky lightened from blue-bordering-on-black to dark blue. Her breath plumed from her lips; she pulled the blanket tighter and nursed the vodka as, through a process too subtle for her to observe, frost spread over the deck, the stairs.

When the eastern sky was a blue so pale it was almost white, she had noticed a figure standing at the bottom of the stairs. For a moment, she had mistaken it for Rick, had half stood at the prospect, and then she had recognized Rick's father. He'd been dressed in the same tuxedo he'd worn in her second dream of him, the knees of his trousers and the cuffs of his shirt and jacket crusted with red mud. His presence prompted her to speech. "You," she had said, resuming her seat. "Are you Rick's dad, or what?"

"Yes."

"Great. Can you tell me what's happened to my husband?"

"He's taken the seed into himself."

"The thing from the cooler."

"He blooms."

"I don't—" She'd shaken her head. "Why . . . why? Why him? Why this?"

Rick's father had shrugged, and she had done her best not to notice if his face had shifted with the movement.

She had sighed. "What now?"

"He will want a consort."

"He what?"

"His consort."

She would not have judged herself capable of the laughter that had burst from her. "You have got to be fucking kidding me."

"The process is underway."

"I don't think so."

"Look at your bottle."

"This?" She had held up the vodka. "It's alcohol."

"Yes. He thought that might help."

"What do you—" Something, some glint of streetlight refracting on the bottle's glass, had caused her to bring it to her eyes, tilting it so that the liquor sloshed up one side. In the orange light shimmering in it, Connie had seen tiny black flakes floating, dozens, hundreds of them. "Oh, no. No way. No."

"It will take longer this way, but he thought you would need the time."

" 'He'? You mean Rick? Rick did this?"

"To bring you to him, to what he is."

"Bring me—"

"To bloom."

"This is— No. No." She had wanted to hurl the bottle at Rick's father, but had been unable to release her grip on it. "Not Rick. No."

He had not argued the point; instead, before the last denial had left her mouth, the space where he'd stood had been empty.

That had been . . . not that long ago, she thought. Time enough for the horizon to flush, for her to feel herself departing the city of awe to which the night's sights had brought her for somewhere else, a great gray ocean swelling with storm. She had squinted at the bottle of Stolichnaya, at the black dots drifting in what remained of its contents. Rick had done this? So she could be his consort? Given what she'd witnessed this night, it seemed silly to declare one detail of it more outrageous than the rest, but this . . . She could understand, well, imagine how an appearance by his father might have convinced her husband that eating the thing in the cooler was a good idea. But to leap from that to thinking that he needed to bring Connie along for the ride—that was something else.

The thing was, it was entirely typical of the way Rick acted, had acted, the length of their relationship. He plunged into decisions like a bungee-jumper abandoning the trestle of a bridge, confident that the cord to which he'd tethered himself, i.e. her, would pull him back from the rocks jagged below. He dropped out of grad school even though it meant he would lose the deferment for the sixty thousand dollars in student loans he had no job to help him repay. He registered for expensive training courses for professions in which he lost interest halfway through the class. He overdrew their joint account for take-out dinners when there was a refrigerator's worth of food waiting at home. And now, the same tendencies that had led to them having so much difficulty securing a mortgage—that had left the fucking cell phone's battery depleted—had caused him to . . . she wasn't even sure she knew the word for it.

The sky between the trees on the rise was filling with color, pale rose deepening to rich crimson, the trunks and branches against it an extravagant calligraphy she could not read. The light ruddied her skin, shone redly on the bottle, glowed hellishly on the frosted steps, deck. She stared through the trees at it, let it saturate her vision.

The photons cascaded against her leaves, stirring them to life.

(What?)

She convoluted, moving at right angles to herself, the sunlight fracturing.

(Oh)

Blackness.

(God.)

She lurched to her feet.

Roots tingled, blackness, unfolding, frost underfoot. Connie gripped the liquor bottle by the neck and swung it against the porch railing. Smashing it took three tries. The last of the vodka splashed onto the deck planks. She pictured hundreds of tiny black—what had Rick's father called them?—embryos shrieking, realized she was seeing them, hearing them.

Blackness her stalk inturning glass on skin. Connie inspected the bottle's jagged top. As improvised weapons went, she supposed it wasn't bad, but she had the feeling she was bringing a rock to a nuclear war.

The dawn air was full of the sound of flapping, of leathery wings snapping. She could almost see the things that were swirling around the house, could feel the spaces they were twisting. She released the blanket, let it slide to the deck. She crossed to the door to the laundry room, still unlocked. Had she thought it wouldn't be? Connie adjusted her grip on her glass knife, opened the door, and stepped into the house.

*. . . that last amorphous blight of nethermost confusion which blasphemes and bubbles at the centre of all infinity—the boundless daemon-sultan Azathoth, whose name no lips dare speak aloud, and who gnaws hungrily in inconceivable, unlighted chambers beyond time . . .*

"The Dream-Quest of Unknown Kadath" · H. P. Lovecraft (1943)

# • AT HOME WITH AZATHOTH •
## John Shirley

When Frederic DuSang saw the eye text from Filrod, he knew the bait had been taken. He knew it before he even read the eye-t. He had that tingle, like when code was about to become a program; that particular shiver of closure.

But it wasn't over yet. He still had to reel him in . . .

Walking down the Santa Cruz Beach boardwalk to the VR ride, on a wet September morning, Frederic tapped the tiny stud, under the skin beneath his right eye, the contact cursor in his fingernail telling the device to transcribe a subvocalization—he had learned to subvocalize his voice-recogs for security. And he subvocalized, "Text: 'Come over at seven tonight if you want it, FilRod. FdS.'"

The head chip heard and obeyed, sending the text to Filrod's palmer.

The guy's name was Rodney Filbern but everyone called him by his screen name, and Filrod replied almost immediately: *Not a good time for me. Just tranz it?*

Frederic responded: *Tough, sorry, leaving town. Not offering it any other way. Wouldn't work. Need you there in person.*

Filrod bit down harder on the hook. *OK Fred u dick, will be there.*

Frederic snorted. He hated being called Fred.

He reached the perpetual carnival on the boardwalk, waved to his manager, a bruise-eyed, rasta-haired old surfer, and went to work at the VR ride, putting pallid teenagers through full-body virtual experiences and cleaning up the stalls afterward . . . As always, as he mopped, thinking, *I need a new goddam job.* Vraiment, *yo.*

• • •

Frederic's thoughts were sometimes in French because his parents were French and they'd tried to make him bilingual. Never quite got there, but they left their mark.

His mom had left his father four years earlier, after Jackie killed himself. Jackie was . . . had been . . . Frederic's younger brother . . .

Frederic's *père* was a thin man with shoulder-length white hair and an eagle-beak nose. When Frederic came home that evening, he looked at Frederic over his glass of Bordeaux—with that familiar dull wince, that *dépression nerveuse* expression he got when he thought about his son.

*Okay,* Frederic thought, *so I'm almost twenty-six and still living with you, so what. I know what you don't know, you old* fils de pute.

He nodded to his dad, in honor of the free rent, and started for the basement door.

"Frederic," Dad said muzzily. "A moment, eef you please. We should talk about . . . Oh I don't know, somezing . . . "

Frederic paused and looked back at his dad. There was a little extra slurriness, a particular mush in his father's voice, and more French accent then usual, too much for a bottle of wine. Probably he was back on the Oxycontin. Supposedly he took it for a work-related injury. Right, Dad. Frederic's father had been a computer programmer in Silicon Valley. Made good money, too, till Jackie died and Mom left, and then Dad started sinking, slowly sinking, and now they were living mostly on his disability, since Frederic spent most of his money on AI and chip augs.

"Dad, I thought you weaned off that shit."

Dad opened his mouth to deny he was on it but Frederic looked at him evenly—and his *père* gave him the ol' Gallic shrug. He licked his lips and articulated more carefully, "Oh well, you know, zuh scan . . . the scan, it said the crack in the vertebrae was open again, so . . . "

"Whatever. Come on. You're just . . . it's about Mom and Jackie. So if you gotta self-medicate, whatever. You do that, go ahead. I've got my own thing. Okay?"

Frederic turned and went down into the basement, thinking he should probably get his old man to go to a therapist, but dad hated shrinks and Frederic just couldn't carry the weight of dealing with dad's stuff. He did, in fact, have his own thing.

He veered between storage boxes and went to his basement room.

Once his father's den, the room was now Frederic's own little sound-proofed warren of linked-up used hard drives, monitors, transervers, low-grade floating AI, a desk he used for extra shelf space, and in a corner—almost an afterthought—was an old futon with yellowed sheets reeking of mildew. *The Skuzz Den,* Frederic's mom had called it. Laughing, though, as she said it. That was something he loved about her, that she laughed at you in a way that meant she didn't care if you had failings, it was all good, no one's perfect. Now he hardly ever saw her.

Frederic sat on the futon, bunched up pillows behind his back, and reached over to the hardware to activate the tranz box. The virtual screen appeared in front of him—something only he could see, at the moment, thanks to his implants—and Frederic muttered the keywords that would activate the floating AI ovoid bobbing near his bed. The AI chirped and Frederic muttered the first password, got his menu, flicked a finger at the air to open *SpaceHole*, got the prompt screen, and . . .

And hesitated. It always made him nervous, kind of sick and giddy, to open this program. Buster Shecht was still missing. But Buster was a crazy fuck, could be missing for lots of reasons. The reason didn't have to be the Azathoth.

Anyway, Buster Shecht wasn't half the programmer Frederic was; couldn't hack his way out of a paper bag. Could be he'd screwed something up and got some kind of brainfry—maybe the yellowflash feedback effect in an implant? It wasn't unheard of. Frederic was not going to screw up.

He licked his lips and spoke the three entry words—words that Buster had found online, in the Necronomicon file.

The "screen" flickered in his mind's eye; shashed, pixel bits spinning like water going down a drain in the center . . . and then in the very center of the virtual screen they interacted, as cellular automata do, and formed a spreading organization—something ugly, jagged, but hinting darkly at life.

The whirling finished, and the image sucked away into the SpaceHole—and the Realm of Azathoth unfurled to fill the screen . . .

That's what Buster had called it . . . *Azathoth.* Claimed the thing living in Azathoth itself taught him the name. If it had, that must mean it was, in fact, the result of a program some brilliant game design engineer had worked up, the gamer having put that in somewhere, and not—as Frederic theorized—the result of a series of meta-program worms linking up in cyberspace, almost like the way the early forms of life had linked up to make more complex organisms, in that giant bowl of hot primordial soup the sea had been.

Of course there was Buster's explanation—or what he claimed to believe, that last time he'd been here in the skuzz den. Probably just playing Frederic for lulz:

*"Dude, I'm going to tell you this and you're gonna think I'm snagging but man, this is for real: the fractal set I worked up outta the Rucker formula, it opened a door into a real place, man. Check with Jacques Vallee: information is a form of energy. In fact everything's a form of information. And, deep down, information is the form of everything. So we can create real objective stuff with pure information long as it's the right information . . . And I'm telling you, Azathoth is a for-reals place."*

*"You do know I stopped smoking dope, right?"* Frederic had said. *"You think you're gonna get me all freaked and shit, but it's flat not happening man . . . "*

Frederic shook his head, remembering. What he was seeing couldn't be a real place. This place couldn't *really* exist . . . except in the mind of some lunatic. It was just a cellular automata model, tessellation automata, iterative arrays.

*Automata cellulare*, his dad would say.

They were fractal patterns generating templates of life forms in a three-dimensionally modeled artificial environment, purely digital, and he knew from looking at great special effects all his life how animation could seem crazy-real.

And of course he was seeing it in a virtual screen, the floating AI's work projected to his chip, his chip projecting to his mind, his mind projecting to his mind's eye, so that he saw a three-dimensional place, and the things in it, hanging in space just up above . . .

There was no clear-cut edge, unlike other virtual projections. It was squamous, wrigglingly ragged along the edges of the "tank" of image that floated over him. It just plain seemed *alive*. Amazing animation work, really, given the source of it—a couple of deep-web eccentrics, Buster figured, had worked it up, made it out of some bits and pieces of online gaming environments, movie clips copied and altered, someone's personal animation program, all mixed together.

That was the only acceptable explanation for what he was seeing: a *place* that was an *entity*; an entity that was a *place*. It was as if he were looking with X-ray eyes into something's body, but he was also looking into a world, an entire landscape. Those numerous writhing protracted pyramids of ichorous green were organs of perception, maybe; but at the same time they were a kind of forest and somehow he knew that if he were to go there (horrible thought), the growths would tower menacingly over him; yet for sure that thicket was some kind of living cilia; that jade and purulent sky was a high enclosure of living tissue—at the same time he was certain that if he were to reach it, himself, to ascend to it, he would penetrate *into* it, and it would go on and on and on, unending. And surely that iridescent, spiky compound tetrahedron in the foreground, slowly whirling, fulminating with bloody fury, was an angry thought crystallizing in a trapped mind.

He could almost . . . *almost* . . . hear it thinking. It thought in minatory buzzing sounds; its words became its form . . . its mind defined its world . . .

Frederic shivered. *C'est fou.* He was having some kind of weird psychological reaction to the program. And this was only the first mode; overdrive mode was faster, captivatingly visual, something you had to use big will power to look away from . . .

He stared into the mêlée of brutal abstract shapes, the slow-motion maelstrom of Azathoth, wondering about Buster . . .

And *Buster appeared* there, at that exactly moment, within Azathoth. Buster's chunky, acne-spackled bearded face materialized in the center of the translucent compound tetrahedron. Buster's mouth moved; after a moment Frederic heard the words, materializing in his mind.

*"Frederic, bro, I'm stuck, digesting in Azathoth, no hope for me, doesn't matter, ready to disintegrate, only way out, but your brother, nearby . . . "*

Frederic's stomach lurched. "Shut up about Jackie, Buster!" he blurted.

Then he snorted at himself. Buster wasn't really there. His mind had probably superimposed the image, made up some story about Buster, put it in the program. Ostensibly, the AI wasn't supposed to take anything from your mind but a literal interpretation of your words, subvocalized, and occasional motional directions, and certain very defined projections . . . but for a while ecog chippers had suspected that there was an unpredictable involuntary telepathic level to the connectivity.

Here it was—this *fantôme,* this digital ghost, was proof of espering chips. He'd have to tell DG and the torrent skaters about it.

The iridescent crystal entrapping "Buster" mutated into a solid icosahedron—and went opaque.

Buster vanished.

Had Buster been—digested?

*Cut it out, you're getting sucked into the fantasy. This program is some kinda lulz hoax and somewhere some programmer's laughing his fucking ass off right now.*

Didn't matter. It'd do for what he had in mind—it'd do for Filrod.

He had planned to insert Jackie into the images; to toss in the candid footage he had of Filrod jerking off over tranny porn, which he'd gotten when he'd hacked Filrod's webcam system, whirl it all together in this sick place, let it iterate, copy and paste it into every variant of YouTube there was. Make Filrod pay for what he'd done.

The plan was to get Filrod stuck in this place, long enough to really make him feel it—because when you went into overdrive mode on this program, that's what happened. It was hypnotic, was Azathoth, inexplicably hard to look away from, and you could mix in any image you projected so it looked like you were in Hell surrounded by . . . whatever the programmer inserted. If he wanted to put images of the new president's inauguration into it, you'd see the Prez and his backers splashed all over the Azathoth landscape. And you could feel weirdly trapped there . . .

Images of Filrod's shame, Filrod's guilt, could be wrapped around him in overdrive mode . . .

But now—he might have a more direct mode of attack on Filrod . . .

Filrod himself. He had an ecog chip, after all . . .

He glanced at his watch—and right then, as if on cue, the doorbell rang upstairs.

Filrod was a broad-shouldered college student with widely spaced front teeth, a dull, blunt face, and faux-hawked brown hair. Frederic had heard that Filrod was barely passing his classes; the jock was not exactly stupid but never far enough from his interchatter channels to focus on anything. He was a wide receiver on the football team and wore the school jersey with his number, 8, on it.

*Behind the eightball, you asshole*, Frederic thought, as Filrod hunkered on the futon beside him.

"You wanta hit some syntha?" Filrod said, when he came in, waving the e-pipe.

"Nah, I gave it up, you go ahead," Frederic said, distractedly, as he tinkered with the hardware by the futon, trying to get the best signal.

Filrod sucked on the e-pipe, blinking at the floating AIs, and asked as he blew out a stream of chemical-laden water vapor. His eyes glazed as the drug hit him. "Don't those things use up a lotta power, floating around?"

"They're made of super-light materials, man, and they tend to get less interference from the drives if I keep 'em floating. Do have to change batteries pretty often though." Frederic finished tinkering and waved smoke out of his face. "Enough with that shit, I don't want your secondhand smoke, dude."

"Whatever." Filrod switched the pipe off, tucked it away in a pants pocket. "So can you get me the stuff I need to see or not?"

"Yeah, *if* you transfer the money to my account." The money he never actually expected to get. This wasn't about money.

"You show me the stuff, I transfer, right here."

Frederic shrugged. "'Kay, fair enough." He prepared the virtual screen, gave Filrod the frequency, so he could see it too. Then he decided to prep Filrod himself a bit more. Set him up good. "Okay, you sent me the password, the ISP, all that—file names. You sure you sent me *everything*?"

"Everything! My mom's will's in there, man. I need to see it, I gotta know. She's pretty sick. But the mean ol' cow lingers on and on." He shook his head sadly. "I think I'm gonna get kicked outta school—won't have my school money, nothin' to live on. I need to know if money's coming."

Frederic looked at him. Something in Filrod's voice, a certain tightness, said *cover story*.

Christ. Was Filrod thinking of killing his moms, easing her off into the ether, since she was sick anyway. Was he going to do it if he had enough inheritance coming to justify the risk of a murder?

Wouldn't be surprising . . .

"Okay, Filrod, so . . . this isn't going to look like a conventional penetration program. This'll look—different. It's three-dimensional, it's cyberspace stuff, it's very . . . hard info-animation." He'd made up that last term to keep Filrod confused.

It worked. "Hard info . . . whatever. I just need to see her will and testament stuff and I know this fucking attorney has it on e-file."

"Sure, we'll get there. But see this technique is more . . . stealth. You know? Don't want 'em to know we did this, right?"

"Right, that's for fucking-A sure. Don't want nobody to know."

"Then—lock in. Stare right into that circle you see forming there. It's called SpaceHole. Look right into it, keep your eyes on it, and we'll see what we find . . ."

"That thing? It doesn't look like any kind of . . ."

"Trust me, dude, this is what you need to see."

Filrod blinked, and stared into the SpaceHole, and Frederic sent a message to the AI, moving into Mode One of Azathoth.

"What the *fuck* . . . !" Filrod blurted, staring into the changeworld, the shifting landscape that was a mind—that was an entity, Azathoth; that was a program, really—and what would be Filrod's Hell, if Frederic had anything to say about it.

Frederic sent the second signal—to overdrive Azathoth into full manifestation—and looked away from the floating three-dimensional screen as he did so . . .

Filrod gasped.

Frederic smiled grimly—then uploaded the first vid, of Filrod pleasuring himself as he gaped at some serious porn.

Filrod made a choking sound.

"Turn that shit off!" he managed, his voice hoarse, almost inaudible.

"Why, man?" Frederic asked calmly, looking at him. "It was you who found that video of my brother posing all sexy for an under-twenty gay dating service. My brother wasn't ready to come out to my folks yet—we got some old-fashioned grandparents he was worried about—and he was going to a private school because Dad was trying to get churchy. My *père* was raised Roman Catholic . . . and there's been big pushback from the religious types about gay marriage last few years. The school is like brainwashing these kids against gays and . . . well, my brother Jacques, little Jackie, he was full-on *gay*. I knew it, but we didn't really talk about it much, and he didn't tell anybody else, he wanted to do it all private until he could face the bullshit as an adult living on his own. But then you hacked him, Filrod, because he was talking to your girlfriend and *man* did you misread that shit, until you found out he wasn't hitting on your girl, you saw the dating service video he'd made for Gay Youth Meet-Up. And you told everyone, showed the jocks at his school and they beat him up and he lost feeling in some nerves in his arm, and his left hand wasn't working, and then a priest saw the dating video, when you guys put it up online, and brought Jackie into his office and gave him the hellfire talk and made him *thoroughly* miserable . . . "

"I didn't know that was going to—"

Frederic shook his head, and pressed on. "And *then* you posted some lies about him stalking some teenager, that Danny Zoski, which was *totally* not true, and so people said Jackie was a pedophile—he was all about real adult men, not *kids*—and then people stopped talking to him and he took some drugs over it they left him depressed and then they were going to kick him outta the school and . . . Lemme see, I leave anything out? Oh yeah. He killed himself. *He fucking hung himself.*"

"I . . . " Filrod made an *uck* sound.

Frederic could see Filrod was trying to look away from the hypnotic drain of Azathoth . . . and Frederic was careful not to look into it himself. "Yes, 'Filrod'?"

"I . . . I . . . "

"Spit it out, dude!"

" . . . didn't know he was your brother."

"Jackie didn't like the surname DuSang, 'cause it means 'of blood' and Jackie had hemophilia, and my folks said he could go by grandma's name, once he turned eighteen. So he changed it. Then you met him. Then he killed himself. Cause and effect: sensitive person runs afoul of an emotional cretin, and dies."

" . . . sorry."

"Oh, because he was my brother? But it's okay to hound a gay kid into suicide? Long as they're not related to someone you know?"

"Um . . . no."

"Yeah, well, *fuck* you—and your *sorry.* You *boasted* about what you did after he killed himself, I got the emails . . . see 'em there? They're going up around you too. Read 'em, asshole. You're in that world, in your mind now, and it's not easy to get out. *All* that stuff is there. Now I'm going to upload some . . . "

Then Frederic heard Jackie's voice. And for a moment he was struck dumb.

"Sorry to see you hurting dumb animals, Frederic." Jackie said, gently chiding.

"What?"

The voice had come from the floating screen. And Frederic had to look.

He saw his brother's face, in a wobbling globe of translucent emerald and gold, a *fantôme* floating over the Azathothian landscape.

His brother was looking right at him.

And Jackie said, "The idiot Filrod here is just a dumb animal. It's like poisoning a dog that bit you 'cause it went crazy being locked to a short chain all day. Not really the dog's fault it bit you. But I do hate Filrod, that's true. Even now. And it's hard to hate anyone where I am now."

"Where you are . . . ?"

"I'm in a kind of limbo sorta place kinda oblique to Azathoth. Where Azathoth is, that's where a lotta people get stuck. Poke their noses in the wrong place. Me, I'm in another world, and it's not bad. It's pretty awfin' awesome. I'll be here a thousand years or so, the guardians tell me, and I don't mind. But see, it's like it's a through-the-looking-glass inside-out upside-down mirror place in relation to Azathoth; they're opposites, you know? Symmetrical opposites. It ain't Heaven, where I am, and Azathoth ain't Hell—but close enough."

Frederic gawked at the apparition of his dead brother. It sounded exactly like him; sure *looked* like him, even down to that typical humorously rueful expression.

Frederic wondered if he were being pwned somehow. Was this some hoax? Had Filrod outsmarted him?

But he could see Filrod himself, a replicant of his mind inhabiting Azathoth—trapped in a crystalline world of self-loathing. The miniature Filrod in the floating screen image was a kind of Filrod avatar, matching the physical one who gasped and moaned and whimpered beside Frederic.

Frederic shook his head slowly. "Jackie . . . is it really . . . ?"

"Yes. It is. I'm not in Azathoth—but I heard you messing around in it, I heard your mind . . . and I'm able to talk to you *through* it, because I'm in its opposite, and they're *connected,* in a weird way. Like, you know, those old Yin Yang symbols, the white and black going around and around in one circle together. You know?"

"I guess . . . "

"So I'm able to talk to you from my world. See, dude, Azathoth is *real*. It's not a program. Azathoth is a real world. And a real creature—all at once. But you've got a kinda digital device for looking into it. You're not seeing into a program—you're seeing it *through* a program."

Frederic felt sick, hearing that. Somehow, it all came together in his mind with a click. *This is real.* "I'm going to get sucked into it!"

"I don't know if you are or not. I hope not, bro. Once you're there, I probably can't help you. Your body'll die and . . . well, let's see if I can head it off."

"Jackie . . . listen . . . I'm sorry I didn't help you . . . I should've *helped* you when you were so depressed. I was caught up in my own stuff . . . "

"I know. It's okay. I just wanted to say . . . don't worry about me. I'm in pretty good shape now. Like I said: I'm stuck in this place for a while, but it's not a bad place. It's just somewhere you go if you kill yourself. Killing yourself, you get *stuck* in the next world, and you have to work that off. So don't ever do that, Frederic. But one day I'll move on. And that's something I got an ache to do, to move on . . . " Jackie smiled. "To move on in the right way."

Frederic couldn't smile back. He felt a mounting terror, seeing the hideous, encroaching reality of Azathoth widening, stretched out from the floating screen, like a beast widening its jaws to swallow him . . .

Then Jackie's image seemed to expand—and seemed to rush at him, getting between him and Azathoth, Jackie's face coming like the grill of an onrushing car bearing down on him, Jackie grinning mischievously—

And then Frederic felt the shove. He heard Jackie shout, *"Go, bro!"*

And there was a tremendous pressure, physically throwing Frederic backwards, so that he crashed into some of his hardware. That was going to hurt, later.

But now all he felt was dazed, as he lay on the angular pile of electronic odds and ends, sparking smoke around him, staring at the ceiling.

Frederic was distantly aware that he'd been about to fall into Azathoth . . . and now he was free, staring at the AI bobbing near the ceiling, the light on it like a green eye glaring down at him . . .

Jackie had saved him—his brother had pushed him out of the jaws of Azathoth.

But what about Filrod?

*It's like poisoning a dog that bit you 'cause it went crazy being locked to a short chain all day.*

Filrod howled pitifully.

Wincing from his bruises, Frederic sat up—just in time to see Filrod's soul sucking out of his body; his naked form, translucent, turning in mid-air to try to claw its away back, struggling against the hungry vortex, face contorted with horror. Mouthing *Please help me!*

Then there was a nasty sucking sound . . . and Filrod's soul was gone, into the whirling SpaceHole.

In Frederic's room, Filrod's body slumped—lifeless.

Frederic looked at the Azathoth image, now in Mode One . . . saw Filrod's soul in there, mangled but recognizable, as jaws of crystal closed and crushed and chewed and chewed . . . and chewed harder.

Frederic looked away.

He called to the AI, floating overhead, to come to manual station—meaning into his hands.

It floated down to him, he grabbed it, switched off its flight power—and then threw it, hard as he could, at the wall.

And the AI smashed into crackling pieces.

The floating 3-D screen vanished—Frederic thought he heard a cry of despair from Filrod as it went . . .


Frederic sat for a while, trembling. The trembling seemed to metamorphose into sobbing. And once, loudly, he shouted, "Jackie!"

He glanced over at Filrod's body. He didn't want to touch it, but he had to.

He got up, grimacing, and knelt by the ungainly body, felt the still-warm wrists for a pulse.

No. Nothing. The guy was stone dead.

That wasn't something Frederic had planned for. But it was hard to feel bad about it. What was he going to tell the police?

The truth. *Hey, the guy was smoking that synth dope, just a lot of it, then he keeled over. Bad ticker I guess.*

Frederic turned away, stood up, looking for his cell phone. Sooner he called the cops, the better.

He heard the door open—turned to see his father looking at him, puzzled, concerned. The old dude had heard his yell about Jackie.

Frederic felt like he'd never seen his father's face clearly before . . .

The look on his father's face was so deep—had so many levels of pain. Like someone trapped in Hell.

Frederic wiped his eyes, and got up. He wended his way through all his gear, went to his dad, and put his arms around him, and together they wept—though Frederic knew his dad didn't understand any of it.

It didn't seem to matter.

*When these things had come to the earth they had . . . preyed horribly upon the beings they found. Thus it was when the minds of the Great Race sped across the void from that obscure trans-galactic world known in the disturbing and debatable Eltdown Shards as Yith. The newcomers, with the instruments they created, had found it easy to subdue the predatory entities and drive them down to those caverns of inner earth . . .*

*"The Shadow Out of Time" · H. P. Lovecraft (1936)*

## • THE LITANY OF EARTH •
## Ruthanna Emrys

After a year in San Francisco, my legs grew strong again. A hill and a half lay between the bookstore where I found work and the apartment I shared with the Kotos. Every morning and evening I walked, breathing mist and rain into my desert-scarred lungs, and every morning the walk was a little easier. Even at the beginning, when my feet ached all day from the unaccustomed strain, it was a hill and a half that I hadn't been permitted for seventeen years.

In the evenings, the radio told what I had missed: an earth-spanning war, and atrocities in Europe to match and even exceed what had been done to both our peoples. We did not ask, the Kotos and I, whether our captors too would eventually be called to justice. The Japanese American community, for the most part, was trying to put the camps behind them. And it was not the way of my folk—who had grown resigned to the camps long before the Kotos' people were sent to join us, and who no longer had a community on land—to dwell on impossibilities.

That morning, I had received a letter from my brother. Caleb didn't write often, and hearing from him was equal parts relief and uncomfortable reminder. His grammar was good, but his handwriting and spelling revealed the paucity of his lessons. He had written:

*The town is a ruin, but not near enouff of one. Houses still stand; even a few windos are whole. It has all been looked over most carefully long ago, but I think forgotten or ignored since.*

And:

*I looked through our library, and those of other houses, but there is not a book or torn page left on the shelves. I have saugt permisson to look throuh the collecton at Miskatonic, but they are putting me off. I very much fear that the most importent volumes were placed in some government warehouse to be forgotten—as we were.*

So, our family collections were still lost. I remembered the feel of the old pages, my father leaning over me, long fingers tracing a difficult passage as he explained its meaning—and my mother, breaking in with some simple suggestion that cut to the heart of it. Now, the only books I had to work with were the basic texts and single children's spellbook in the store's backroom collection. The texts, in fact, belonged to Charlie—my boss—and I bartered my half-remembered childhood Enochian and R'lyehn for access.

Charlie looked up and frowned as the bells announced my arrival. He had done that from the first time I came in to apply, and so far as I knew gave all his customers the same glare.

"Miss Marsh."

I closed my eyes and breathed in the paper-sweet dust. "I'm not late, Mr. Day."

"We need to finish the inventory this morning. You can start with the Westerns."

I stuck my purse behind the counter and headed back toward the piles of spine-creased Edgar Rice Burroughs and Zane Grey. "What I like about you," I said honestly, "is that you don't pretend to be civil."

"And dry off first." But no arguments, by now, that I ought to carry an umbrella or wear a jacket. No questions about why I liked the damp and chill, second only to the company of old books. Charlie wasn't unimaginative, but he kept his curiosity to himself.

I spent the rest of the morning shelving. Sometimes I would read a passage at random, drinking in the impossible luxury of ink organized into meaningful patterns. Very occasionally I would bring one forward and read a bit aloud to Charlie, who would harumph at me and continue with his work, or read me a paragraph of his own.

By mid-afternoon I was holding down the register while Charlie did something finicky and specific with the cookbooks. The bells jangled. A man poked his head in, sniffed cautiously, and made directly for me.

"Excuse me. I'm looking for books on the occult—for research." He smiled, a salesman's too-open expression, daring me to disapprove. I showed him to the shelf where we kept Crowley and other such nonsense, and returned to the counter frowning thoughtfully.

After a few minutes, he returned. "None of that is quite what I'm looking for. Do you keep anything more . . . esoteric?"

"I'm afraid not, sir. What you see is what we have."

He leaned across the counter. His scent, ordinary sweat and faint cologne, insinuated itself against me, and I stepped back out of reach. "Maybe something in a storage room? I'm sure you must have more than these turn-of-the-century fakers. Some Al-Hazred, say? Prinn's *Vermis*?"

I tried not to flinch. I knew the look of the old families, and he had none of it—tall and dark-haired and thin-faced, conventional attractiveness marred by nothing more than a somewhat square nose. Nor was he cautious in revealing his familiarity with the Aeonist canon, as Charlie had been. He was either stupid, or playing with me.

"I've never heard of either," I said. "We don't specialize in esoterica; I'm afraid you'd better try another store."

"I don't think that's necessary." He drew himself straighter, and I took another step back. He smiled again, in a way I thought was intended to be friendly, but seemed rather the bare-toothed threat of an ape. "Miss Aphra Marsh. I know you're familiar with these things, and I'm sure we can help each other."

I held my ground and gave my mother's best glare. "You have me mistaken, sir. If you are not in the store to purchase goods that we actually have, I strongly suggest that you look elsewhere."

He shrugged and held out his hands. "Perhaps later."

Charlie limped back to the counter as the door rang the man's departure. "Customer?"

"No." My hands were trembling, and I clasped them behind my back. "He wanted to know about your private shelf. Charlie, I don't like him. I don't trust him."

He frowned again and glanced toward the employees-only door. "Thief?"

That would have been best, certainly. My pulse fluttered in my throat. "Well informed, if so."

Charlie must have seen how hard I was holding myself. He found the metal thermos and offered it silently. I shook my head, and with a surge of dizziness found myself on the floor. I wrapped my arms around my knees and continued to shake my head at whatever else might be offered.

"He might be after the books," I forced out at last. "Or he might be after us."

He crouched next to me, moving slowly with his bad knee and the stiffness of joints beginning to admit mortality. "For having the books?"

I shook my head again. "Yes. Or for being the sort of people who would have them." I stared at my interlaced fingers, long and bony, as though they might be thinking about growing extra joints. There was no way to explain the idea I had, that the smiling man might come back with more men, and guns, and vans that locked in the back. And probably he was only a poorly spoken dabbler, harmless. "He knew my name."

Charlie pulled himself up and into a chair, settling with a grunt. "I don't suppose he could have been one of those Yith you told me about?"

I looked up, struck by the idea. I had always thought of the Great Race as solemn and wise, and meeting one was supposed to be very lucky. But they were also known to be arrogant and abrupt, when they wanted something. It was a nice thought. "I don't think so. They have phrases, secret ways of making themselves known to people who would recognize them. I'm afraid he was just a man."

"Well." Charlie got to his feet. "No help for it unless he comes back. Do you need to go home early?"

That was quite an offer, coming from Charlie, and I couldn't bear the thought that I looked like I needed it. I eased myself off the floor, the remaining edge of fear making me slow and clumsy. "Thank you. I'd rather stay here. Just warn me if you see him again."

The first change in my new life, also heralded by a customer . . .

It is not yet a month since my return to the world. I am still weak, my skin sallow from malnourishment and dehydration. After my first look in a good mirror, I have shaved my brittle locks to the quick, and the new are growing in ragged, but thick and rich and dark like my mother's. My hair as an adult woman, which I have never seen till now.

I am shelving when a familiar phrase stings my ears. Hope and danger, tingling together as I drift forward, straining to hear more.

The blond man is trying to sell Charlie a copy of the *Book of the Grey People*, but it soon becomes apparent that he knows little but the title. I should be more cautious than I am next, should think more carefully about what I reveal. But I like Charlie, his gruffness and his honesty and the endless difference between him and everything I have hated or loved. I don't like to see him taken in.

The blond man startles when I appear by his shoulder, but when I pull the tome over to flip the pages, he tries to regroup. "Now just a minute here, young lady. This book is valuable."

I cannot imagine that I truly look less than my thirty years. "This book is a fake. Is this supposed to be Enochian?"

"Of course it's Enochian. Let me—"

"Ab-kar-rak al-laz-kar-nef—" I sound out the paragraph in front of me. "This was written by someone who had heard Enochian once, and vaguely recalled the sound of it. It's gibberish. And in the wrong alphabet, besides. And the binding . . . " I run my hand over it and shudder. "The binding is real skin. Which makes this a very expensive fake for *someone*, but the price has already been paid. Take this abomination away."

Charlie looks at me as the blond man leaves. I draw myself up, determined to make the best of it. I can always work at the laundromat with Anna.

"You know Enochian?" he asks. I'm startled by the gentleness—and the hope. I can hardly lie about it now, but I don't give more than the bare truth.

"I learned it as a child."

His eyes sweep over my face; I hold myself impassive against his judgment. "I believe you keep secrets, and keep them well," he says at last. "I don't plan to pry. But I want to show you one of mine, if you can keep that too."

This isn't what I was expecting. But he might learn more about me, someday, as much as I try to hide. And when that happens, I'll need a reason to trust him. "I promise."

"Come on back." He turns the door sign before leading me to the storage room that has been locked all the weeks I've worked here.

I stayed as late as I could, until I realized that if someone was asking after me, the Kotos might be in danger as well. I didn't want to call, unsure if the phone lines would be safe. All the man had done was talk to me—I might never see him again. Even so, I would be twitching for weeks. You don't forget the things that can develop from other people's small suspicions.

The night air was brisk, chilly by most people's standards. The moon watched over the city, soft and gibbous, outlines blurred by San Francisco's ubiquitous mist. Sounds echoed closer than their objects. I might have been swimming, sensations carried effortlessly on ocean currents. I licked salt from my lips, and prayed. I wished I could break the habit, but I wished more, still, that just once it would work.

"Miss Marsh!" The words pierced the damp night. I breathed clean mist and kept walking. *Iä, Cthulhu* . . .

"Please, Miss Marsh, I just need a moment of your time." The words were polite enough, but the voice was too confident. I walked faster, and strained my ears for his approach. Soft soles would not tap, but a hissing squelch marked every step on the wet sidewalk. I could not look back; I could not run: either would be an admission of guilt. He would chase me, or put a bullet in my skull.

"You have me mistaken," I said loudly. The words came as a sort of croak.

I heard him speed up, and then he was in front of me, mist clinging to his tall form. Perforce, I stopped. I wanted to escape, or call for help, but I could not imagine either.

"What do you want, sir?" The stiff words came more easily this time. It occurred to me belatedly that if he did not know what I was, he might try to force himself on me, as the soldiers sometimes had with the Japanese girls in the camp. I couldn't bring myself to fear the possibility; he moved like a different kind of predator.

"I'm sorry," he said. "I'm afraid we may have gotten off to a bad start, earlier. I'm Ron Spector; I'm with the FBI—"

He started to offer a badge, but the confirmation of my worst fears released me from my paralysis. I lashed out with one newly strong leg and darted to the side. I had intended to race home and warn the Kotos, but instead he caught his balance and grabbed my arm. I turned and grappled, scratching and pulling, all the time aware that my papa had died fighting this way. I expected the deadly shot at any moment, and struggled while I could. But my arms were weaker than Papa's, and even my legs were not what they should have been.

Gradually, I realized that Spector was only trying to hold me off, not fighting for his life, nor even for mine. He kept repeating my name, and at last:

"Please, Miss Marsh! I'm not trained for this!" He pushed me back again, and grunted as my nails drew blood on his unprotected wrist. "Please! I don't mean you any harm; I just want to talk for five minutes. Five minutes, I promise, and then you can stay or go as you please!"

My panic could not sustain itself, and I stilled at last. Even then, I was afraid that given the chance, he would clap me in irons. But we held our tableau, locked hand to wrist. His mortal pulse flickered mouse-like against my fingertips, and I was sure he could feel mine roaring like the tide.

"If I let you go, will you listen?"

I breathed in strength from the salt fog. "Five minutes, you said."

"Yes." He released me, and rubbed the skin below his wristwatch. "I'm sorry, I should have been more circumspect. I know what you've been through."

"Do you." I controlled my shaking with effort. I was a Marsh; I would not show weakness to an enemy. They had drunk deep of it already.

He looked around and took a careful seat on one of the stones bordering a nearby yard. It was too short for him, so that his knees bent upward when he sat. He leaned forward: a praying mantis in a black suit.

"Most religions consist largely of good people trying to get by. No matter what names they worship, or what church they go to, or what language they pray in. Will you agree with me on this much?"

I folded my arms and waited.

"And every religion has its fanatics, who are willing to do terrible things in the name of their god. No one is immune." His lips quirked. "It's a failing of humanity, not of any particular sect."

"I'll grant you that. What of it?" I counted seconds in drips of water. I could almost imagine the dew clinging to my skin as a shield.

He shrugged and smiled. I didn't like how easy he could be, with his wrist still stinking of blood. "If you grant me that, you're already several steps ahead of the U.S. government, just after the first World War. In the twenties, they had run-ins with a couple of nasty Aeonist groups. There was one cult down in Louisiana that had probably never seen an original bit of the canon, but they had their ideas. Sacrificial corpses hanging from trees, the whole nine yards." He glanced at me, checking for some reaction. I did not grant it.

"Not exactly representative, but we got the idea that was normal. In '26, the whole religion were declared enemies of the state, and we started looking out for anyone who said the wrong names on Sunday night, or had the wrong statues in their churches. You know where it goes from there."

I did, and wondered how much he really knew. It was strange, nauseating, to hear the justifications, even as he tried to hold them at a distance.

"It won't shock you," he continued, "to know that Innsmouth wasn't the only place that suffered. Eventually, it occurred to the government that they might have over-generalized, but it took a long time for changes to go through. Now we're starting to have people like me, who actually study Aeonist culture and try to separate out the bad guys, but it's been a long time coming."

I held myself very still through his practiced speech. "If this is by way of an apology, Mister Spector, you can drown in it. What you did was beyond the power of any apology."

"Doubtless we owe you one anyway, if we can find a decent way of making it. But I'm afraid I've been sent to speak with you for practical reasons." He cleared his throat and shifted his knees. "As you may imagine, when the government went hunting Aeonists, it was much easier to find good people, minding their own business in small towns, than cultists well-practiced in conspiracy and murder. The bad guys tend to be better at hiding, after all. And at the same time, we weren't trying to recruit people who knew anything useful about the subject—after a while, few would have been willing even if we went looking. So now, as with the Japanese-American community, we find ourselves shorthanded, ignorant, and having angered the people least likely to be a danger to the country."

My eye sockets ached. "I cannot believe that you are trying to recruit me."

"I'm afraid that's exactly what I'm doing. I could offer—"

"Your five minutes are up, sir." I walked past him, biting back anything else I might say, or think. The anger worked its way into my shoulders, and my legs, and the rush of my blood.

"Miss Marsh!"

Against my better judgment, I stopped and turned back. I imagined what I must look like to him. Bulging eyes; wide mouth; long, bony legs and fingers. "The Innsmouth look," when there was an Innsmouth. Did it signal danger to him? Something more than human, or less? Perhaps he saw just an ugly woman, someone whose reactions he could dismiss until he heard what he wanted.

Then I would speak clearly.

"Mister Spector, I have no interest in being an enemy of the state. The state is larger than I. But nor will I be any part of it. And if you insist, you will listen to why. *The state* stole nearly two decades of my life. *The state* killed my father, and locked the rest of my family away from anything they thought might give us strength. Salt water. Books. Knowledge. One by one, they destroyed us. My mother began her metamorphosis. Allowed the ocean, she might have lived until the sun burned to ashes. They took her away. We know they studied us at such times, to better know the process. To better know how to hurt us. You must imagine the details, as I have. They never returned the bodies. Nothing has been given back to us.

"Now, ask me again."

He bent his head at last. Not in shame, I thought, but listening. Then he spoke softly. "The state is not one entity. It is *changing*. And when it changes, it's good for everyone. The people you could help us stop are truly hurting others. And the ones being hurt know nothing of what was done to your family. Will you hold the actions of a few against them? Should more families suffer because yours did?"

I reminded myself that, after humanity faded and died, a great insectoid civilization would live in these hills. After that, the Sareeav, with their pseudopods and strange sculptures. Therefore, I could show patience. "I will do what I can for suffering on my own."

More quietly: "If you helped us, even on one matter, I might be able to find out what really happened to your mother."

The guilt showed plainly on his face as soon as he said it, but I still had to turn away. "I cannot believe that even after her death, you would dare hold my mother hostage for my good behavior. You can keep her body, and your secrets." And in R'lyehn, because we had been punished for using it in the camps, I added, "And if they hang your corpse from a tree, I will kiss the ground beneath it." Then, fearful that he might do more, or say more, I ran.

I kicked off my shoes, desperate for speed. My feet slapped the wet ground. I could not hear whether Spector followed me. I was still too weak, as weak as I had been as a child, but I was taller, and faster, and the fog wrapped me and hid me and sped me on my flight.

Some minutes later I ducked into a side drive. Peering out, I saw no one following me. Then I let myself gasp: deep, shuddering breaths. I wanted him dead. I wanted them all dead, as I had for seventeen years. Probably some of them were: they were only ordinary humans, with creaking joints and rivulet veins. I could be patient.

I came in barefoot to the Kotos. Mama Rei was in the kitchen. She put down her chopping knife, and held me while I shook. Then Anna took my hand and drew me over to the table. The others hovered nearby, Neko looking concerned and Kevin sucking his thumb. He reminded me so very much of Caleb.

"What happened?" asked Anna, and I told them everything, trying to be calm and clear. They had to know.

Mama Rei tossed a handful of onions into the pan and started on the peppers. She didn't look at me, but she didn't need to. "Aphra-chan— Kappa-sama—what do you think he wants?"

I started to rub my face, then winced. Spector's blood, still on my nails, cut through the clean smell of frying onion. "I don't know. Perhaps only what he said, but his masters will certainly be angry when he fails to recruit me. He might seek ways to put pressure on me. It's not safe. I'm sorry."

"I don't want to leave," said Neko. "We just got here." I closed my eyes hard against the sting.

"We won't leave," said Mama Rei. "We are trying to build a decent life here, and I won't be scared away from it. Neither will you, Aphra-chan. This government man can only do so much to us, without a law to say he can lock us up."

"There was no law countenancing the things done to my family," I said.

"Times have changed," she said firmly. "People are watching, now."

"They took your whole town," said Anna, almost gently. "They can't take all of San Francisco, can they, Mama?"

"Of course not. We will live our lives, and you will all go to work and school tomorrow, and we will be careful. That is all."

There was no arguing with Mama Rei, and I didn't really want to. I loved the life I had, and if I lost it again, well . . . the sun would burn to ash soon enough, and then it would make little difference whether I had a few months of happiness here, or a few years. I fell asleep praying.

One expects the storage room of a bookstore to hold more books. And it does. Books in boxes, books on shelves, books piled on the floor and the birch table with uneven legs. And one bookshelf more solid than the others, leaves and vines carved into dark wood. The sort that one buys for too much money, to hold something that feels like it deserves the respect.

And on the shelves, my childhood mixed with dross. I hold up my hand, afraid to touch, to run it across the titles, a finger's breadth away. I fear that they too will change to gibberish. Some of them already are. Some are titles I know to have been written by charlatans, or fakes as obvious as the blond man's *Grey People*. And some are real.

"Where did you get these?"

"At auction. At estate sales. From people who come in offering to sell, or other stores that don't know what they have. To tell the truth, I don't entirely either, for some of them. You might have a better idea?"

I pull down a *Necronomicon* with shaking hands, the one of his three that looks real. The inside page is thankfully empty—no dedication, no list of family names. No chance of learning whether it ever belonged to someone I knew. I read the first page, enough to recognize the over-poetic Arabic, and put it back before my eyes can tear up. I take another, this one in true Enochian.

"Why buy them, if you can't read them?"

"Because I might be able to, someday. Because I might be able to learn something, even with a word or two. Because I want to learn magic, if you must know, and this is the closest I can come." His glare dares me to scoff.

I hold out the book I've been cradling. "You could learn from this one, you know. It's a child's introductory text. I learned a little from it, myself, before I . . . lost access to my library." My glare dares him to ask. He doesn't intrude on my privacy, no more than I laugh at what he's revealed. "I don't know enough to teach you properly. But if you let me share your books, I'll help you learn as best I can." He nods, and I turn my head aside so my tears don't fall on the text—or where he can see.

• • •

I returned to work the next day, wearing shoes borrowed from neighbors. My feet were far too big for anything the Kotos could lend me. Anna walked me partway before turning off for the laundromat—her company more comfort than I cared to admit.

I had hovered by the sink before breakfast, considering what to do about the faint smudge of Spector's blood. In the end, I washed it off. A government agent, familiar with the Aeonist canons, might well know how to detect the signs if I used it against him.

Despite my fears, that day was a quiet one, full of customers asking for Westerns and romances and textbooks. The next day was the same, and the day after that, and three weeks passed with the tension between my shoulder blades the only indication that something was amiss.

At the end of those three weeks, he came again. His body language had changed: a little hunched, a little less certain. I stiffened, but did not run. Charlie looked up from the stack of incoming books, and gave the requisite glare.

"That's him," I murmured.

"Ah." The glare deepened. "You're not welcome here. Get out of my store, and don't bother my employees again."

Spector straightened, recovering a bit of his old arrogance. "I have something for Miss Marsh. Then I'll go."

"Whatever you have to offer, I don't want it. You heard Mr. Day: you're trespassing."

He ducked his head. "I found your mother's records. I'm not offering them in exchange for anything. You were right, that wasn't . . . wasn't honorable. Once you've seen them—if you want to see them—I'll go."

I held out my hand. "Very well. I'll take them. And then you will leave."

He held on to the thick folder. "I'm sorry, Miss Marsh. I've got to stay with them. They aren't supposed to be out of the building, and I'm not supposed to have them right now. I'll be in serious trouble if I lose them."

I didn't care if he got in trouble, and I didn't want to see what was in the folder. But it was my mother's only grave. "Mr. Day," I said quietly. "I would like a few minutes of privacy, if you please."

Charlie took a box and headed away, but paused. "You just shout if this fellow gives you any trouble." He gave Spector another glare before heading into the stacks—I suspected not very far.

Spector handed me the folder. I opened it, cautiously, between the cash register and a short stack of Agatha Christie novels. For a moment I closed my eyes, fixing my mother's living image in my mind. I remembered her singing a sacred chanty in the kitchen, arguing with shopkeepers, kneeling in the wet sand at Solstice. I remembered one of our neighbors crying in our sitting room after her husband's boat was lost in a storm, telling her, "Your faith goes all the way to the depths. Some of us aren't so lucky."

"I'm sorry," Spector said quietly. "It's ugly."

They had taken her deeper into the desert, to an experimental station. They had caged her. They had given her weights to lift, testing her strength. They had starved her for days, testing her endurance. They had cut her, confusing their mythologies, with iron and silver, noting healing times. They had washed her once with seawater, then fresh, then scrubbed her with dry salt. After that, they had refused her all contact with water, save a minimum to drink. Then not even that. For the whole of sixty-seven days, they carefully recorded her pulse, her skin tone, and the distance between her eyes. Perhaps in some vague way also interested in our culture, they copied, faithfully, every word she spoke.

Not one sentence was a prayer.

There were photos, both from the experiments and the autopsy afterward. I did not cry. It seemed extravagant to waste salt water so freely.

"Thank you," I said quietly, closing the folder, bile burning the back of my throat. He bowed his head.

"My mother came to the states young." He spoke deliberately, neither rushing to share nor stumbling over his apparent honesty. Anything else, I would have felt justified interrupting. "Her sister stayed in Poland. She was a bit older, and she had a sweetheart. I have files on her, too. She survived. She's in a hospital in Israel, and sometimes she can feed herself." He stopped, took a deep breath, shook his head. "I can't think of anything that would convince me to work for the new German government—no matter how different it is from the old. I'm sorry I asked."

He took the folder and turned away.

"Wait." I should not have said it. He'd probably staged the whole thing. But it was a far more thoughtful manipulation than the threats I had expected—and I found myself afraid to go on ignoring my enemies. "I will not work for you. But tell me about these frightening new Aeonists."

Whatever—if anything—I eventually chose to pass on to Spector, I realized that I very much wanted to meet them. For all the Kotos' love and comfort, and for all Charlie's eager learning, I still missed Innsmouth. These mortals might be the closest I could come to home.

"Why do you want to learn this?" Though I doubt Charlie knows, it's a ritual question. There is no ritual answer.

"I don't . . . " He glares, a habit my father would have demanded he break before pursuing the ancient scholarship. "Some things don't go into words easily, all right? It's . . . it feels like what *should* be in books, I suppose. They should all be able to change the world. At least a little."

I nod. "That's a good answer. Some people think that 'power' is a good answer, and it isn't. The power that can be found in magic is less than what you get from a gun, or a badge, or a bomb." I pause. "I'm trying to remember all the things I need to tell you, now, at the beginning. What magic is *for* is understanding. Knowledge. And it won't work until you know how little that gets you.

"*Sharhlyda*—Aeonism—is a bit like a religion. But this isn't the Bible—most of the things I'm going to tell you are things we have records of: histories older than man, and sometimes the testimony of those who lived them. The gods you can take or leave, but the history is real.

"All of man's other religions place him at the center of creation. But man is nothing—a fraction of the life that will walk the Earth. Earth is nothing—a tiny world that will die with its sun. The sun is one of trillions where life flowers, and wants to live, and dies. And between the suns is an endless vast darkness that dwarfs them, through which life can travel only by giving up that wanting, by losing itself. Even that darkness will eventually die. In such a universe, knowledge is the stub of a candle at dusk."

"You make it all sound so cheerful."

"It's honest. What our religion tells us, the part that is a religion, is that the gods created life to try and make meaning. It's ultimately hopeless, and even gods die, but the effort is real. Will always have been real, even when everything is over and no one remembers."

Charlie looks dubious. I didn't believe it, either, when I first started learning. And I was too young then to find it either frightening or comforting.

. . .

I thought about what Mr. Spector had told me, and about what I might do with the information. Eventually I found myself, unofficially and entirely on my own recognizance, in a better part of the city, past sunset, at the door of a home rather nicer than the Kotos'. It was no mansion by any imagining, but it was long lived-in and well kept up: two stories of brick and Spanish tile roof, with juniper guarding the façade. The door was painted a cheerful yellow, but the knocker was a fantastical wrought-iron creature that reminded me painfully of home. I lifted the cold metal and rapped sharply. Then I waited, shivering.

The man who opened the door looked older than Charlie. His gray hair frizzed around the temples and ears, otherwise slick as a seal. Faint lines creased his cheeks. He frowned at me. I hoped I had the right address.

"My name is Aphra Marsh," I said. "Does that mean anything to you? I understand that some in this house still follow the old ways."

He started, enough to tell me that he recognized my family's name. He shuffled back a little, but then leaned forward. "Where did you hear such a thing?"

"My family have their ways. May I enter?"

He stepped aside to let me in, in too reluctant a fashion to be truly gallant. His pupils widened between narrowed eyelids, and he licked his lips.

"What do you want, my lady?"

Ignoring the question for the moment, I stepped inside. The foyer, and what I could see of the parlor, looked pedestrian but painfully familiar. Dark wood furniture, much of it bookshelves, contrasted with leaf-green walls. Yet it was all a bit shabby—not quite as recently dusted or mended as would have satisfied my mother's pride. A year ago, it might have been the front room of any of the better houses in Innsmouth. Now . . . I wondered what my family home had looked like, in the years after my mother was no longer there to take pride in it. I put the thought forcibly out of my mind.

" . . . in the basement," he was saying. "Would you like to see?"

I ran my memory back through the last seconds, and discovered that he was, in fact, offering to show me where they practiced "the old ways." "I would. But an introduction might be in order first?"

"My apologies, my lady. I am Oswin Wilder. High priest here, although probably not a very traditional one by your standards."

"I make no judgment." And I smiled at him in a way that suggested I might well do so later. It was strange. In Innsmouth, non-Sharhlyd outsiders had looked on us with fear and revulsion—even the Sharhlyd who were not of our kind, mostly the nervously misanthropic academics at Miskatonic, treated us with suspicion. Respect was usually subordinated to rivalries over the proper use of ancient texts. The few mortal humans who shared both our town and our faith had deferred openly, but without this taint of resentment.

He led me down solid wooden steps. I half expected a hidden sub-basement or a dungeon—I think he must have wanted one—but he had worked with the home he already had. Beyond the bare flagstone at the foot of the stairs, he had merely added a raised level of dark tile, painted with sigils and patterns. I recognized a few, but suspected more of being his own improvisations. At the far end of the room, candles flickered on a cloth-covered table. I approached, moving carefully around the simple stone altar in the center.

On the table sat a devotional statue of Cthulhu. I hardly noticed the quality of the carving or the material, although my childhood priest would have had something to say about both. But my childhood was long discarded, and the display struck my adult doubts with forgotten force. Heedless of the man behind me, I knelt. The flickering light gave a wet sheen to tentacles and limbs, and I could almost imagine again that they were reaching to draw me in and keep me safe. Where the statue in Innsmouth's church had depicted the god with eyes closed, to represent the mysteries of the deep, this one's eyes were open, black and fathomless. I returned the gaze, refusing to bow my head.

*Have you been waiting for us? Do you regret what happened? With all your aeons, did you even notice that Innsmouth was gone? Or did you just wonder why fewer people came to the water?*

*Are you listening, now? Were you ever there to listen?*

More tears, I realized too late—not something I would have chosen for the priest to see. But I flicked a drop of my salt water onto the statue, and whispered the appropriate prayer. I found it oddly comforting. My mother, old-fashioned, had kept a jar of seawater on the counter for washing tear-streaked faces, and brought it to temple once a month. But I had still given my tears to the god when I didn't want her fussing, or was trying to hide a fight with my brother.

We were near the ocean now. Perhaps the Kotos could spare a jar.

My musings were interrupted by the creak of the basement door and a tremulous alto.

"Oz? I knocked, but no one answered—are you down here?"

"Mildred, yes. Come on down; we have a guest."

Full skirts, garnet red, descended, and as she came closer I saw a woman bearing all my mother's remembered dignity. She had the air of magnificence that fortunate mortals gained with age; her wrinkles and gray-streaked hair only gave the impression of deliberate artistic choices. I stood and ducked my head politely. She looked me over, thin-lipped.

"Mil—Miss Marsh," said Wilder. "Allow me to introduce Mildred Bergman. Mildred, this is Miss Aphra Marsh." He paused dramatically, and her frown deepened.

"And what is she doing in our sanctum?"

"Miss *Marsh*," he repeated.

"Anyone can claim a name. Even such an illustrious one." I winced, then lifted my chin. There was no reason for me to feel hurt: her doubt should be no worse a barrier than Wilder's nervous pride.

Taking a candle from the altar for light—and with a whisper of thanks to Cthulhu for the loan—I stepped toward her. She stood her ground. "Look at me."

She looked me up and down, making a show of it. Her eyes stayed narrow, and if I had studied long enough to hear thoughts, and done the appropriate rites, I was sure I would have heard it. *Anyone can be ugly.*

Wilder moved to intervene. "This is silly. We have no reason to doubt her. And she found us on her own. She must have some knowledge of the old arts: we don't exactly put our address in the classifieds. Let it go and give her a chance to prove herself."

Bergman sniffed and shrugged. Moving faster than I would have expected, she plucked the candle from my hand and replaced it on the table. "As high priest, it is of course at your discretion what newcomers must do to join the elect. The others will be here soon; we'll see what they think of your guest."

I blinked at her. "I'll wait, then." I turned my back and knelt again at the god's table. I would not let her see my rage at her dismissal, or the fear that the gesture of defiance cost me.

· · ·

The first and most basic exercise in magic is looking at oneself. Truly looking, truly seeing—and I am afraid. I cannot quite persuade myself that the years in the camp haven't stolen something vital. After doing this simple thing, I will know.

I sit opposite Charlie on the plain wood floor of the storage room. He has dragged over a rag rug and the cushion from a chair for his knees, but I welcome the cool solidity. Around us I have drawn a first-level seal in red chalk, and between us placed two bowls of salt water and two knives. I have walked him through this in the book, told him what to expect, as well as I am able. I remember my father, steady and patient as he explained the rite. I may be more like my mother—impatient with beginners' mistakes, even my own.

I lead him through a grounding: tell him to imagine the sea in his veins, his body as a torrent of blood and breath. I simplify the imagery I learned as a child. He has no metamorphosis to imagine, no ancestors to tell him how those things feel under the weight of the depths. But he closes his eyes and breathes, and I imagine it as wind on a hot day. He is a man of the air, after all. I must tell him the Litany so he will know what that means, and perhaps he will make a new grounding that fits.

Bodies and minds settled, we begin the chant. His pronunciation is poor, but this is a child's exercise and designed for a leader and a stumbling apprentice. The words rise, bearing the rhythm of wind and wave and the slow movement of the earth. Still chanting, I lift the knife, and watch Charlie follow my lead. I wash the blade in salt water and prick my finger. The sting is familiar, welcome. I let a drop of my blood fall into the bowl, swirling and spreading and fading into clarity. I have just enough time to see that Charlie has done the same before the room too fades, and my inward perceptions turn clear.

I am inside myself, seeing with my blood rather than my eyes. I am exquisitely aware of my body, and its power. My blood *is* a torrent. It is a river emptying into the ocean; it thunders through me, a cacophony of rapids and white water. I travel with it, checking paths I have not trod for eighteen years. I find them surprisingly in order. I should have known, watching mortals age while my hard-used joints still moved easily—but that river still carries its healing force, still sweeps illnesses and aches from the banks where they try to cling. Still reshapes what it touches, patiently and steadily. Still carries all the markers of a healthy child who will someday, still, go into the water. I remember my mother telling me, smiling, that my blood knew already the form I would someday wear.

I am basking in the feel of myself, loving my body for the first time in years, when everything changes. Just for a moment, I am aware of my skin, and a touch on my arm.

"Miss Marsh, are you okay?"

And now I remember that one learns to stay inside longer with practice, and that I entirely neglected to warn Charlie against touching me. And then I am cast out of my river, and into another.

I've never tried this with anyone outside my own people. Charlie's river is terribly weak—more like a stream, in truth. It has little power, and detritus has made it narrow and shallow. Where my body is yearning toward the ocean, his has already begun to dry out. His blood, too, knows the form he will someday wear.

He must now be seeing me as intimately.

I force the connection closed, saying the words that end the rite as quickly as I dare. I come to, a little dizzy, swaying.

Charlie looks far more shaken. "That . . . that was real. That was magic."

And I can only feel relief. Of course, the strangeness of his first spell must overwhelm any suspicion over the differences in our blood. At least for now.

Wilder's congregation trickled in over the next hour. They were male and female, robed richly or simply, but all with an air of confidence that suggested old families used to mortal power. They murmured when Wilder introduced them to me; some whispered more with Bergman afterward.

It only seemed like an endless aeon until they at last gathered in a circle. Wilder stood before the table, facing the low altar, and raised his arms. The circle quieted, till only their breath and the rustling of skirts and robes moved the air.

"*Iä, iä, Cthulhu thtagn* . . ." His accent was beyond abominable, but the prayer was familiar. After the fourth smoothly spoken mispronunciation, I realized that he must have learned the language entirely from books. While I had been denied wisdom writ solid in ink, he had been denied a guiding voice. Knowing he would not appreciate it now, I kept my peace. Even the mangled words were sweet.

The congregants gave their responses at the appropriate points, though many of them stumbled, and a few muttered nonsense rather than the proper words. They had learned from Wilder, some more newly than others. Many leaned forward, pupils dilated and mouths gaping with pleasure. Bergman's shoulders held the tension of real fervor, but her lids were narrowed as she avidly watched the reactions she would not show herself. Her eyes met mine and her mouth twitched.

I remembered my mother, her self-contained faith a complement to my father's easy affections. Bergman had the start of such faith, though she still seemed too conscious of her self-control.

After several minutes of call and response, Wilder knelt and took a golden necklet from where it had been hidden under the folds of the tablecloth. It was none of the work of my people—only a simple set of linked squares, with some abstract tentacular pattern carved in each one. It was as like the ornate bas-relief and wirework necklace-crowns of the deep as the ritual was like my childhood church. Wilder lifted it so that all could see, and Bergman stood before him. He switched abruptly to English: no translation that I recognized, presumably his own invention.

"Lady, wilt thou accept the love of Shub-Nigaroth? Wilt thou shine forth the wonders of life eternal for our mortal eyes?"

Bergman lifted her chin. "I shall. I am her sworn daughter, and the beloved of the Gods: let all welcome and return their terrible and glorious love."

Wilder placed the chain around her neck. She turned to face the congregation, and he continued, now hidden behind her: "Behold the glory of the All-Mother!"

*"Iä Cthulhu! Iä Shub-Nigaroth!"*

"Behold the dance in darkness! Behold the life that knows not death!"

*"Iä! Iä!"*

"Behold the secret ever hidden from the sun! See it—breathe it—take it within you!"

At this the congregation fell silent, and I stumbled over a swallowed shout of joy. The words were half nonsense, but half closer to the spirit of my remembered services than anything Wilder had pulled from his books. Bergman took from the table a knife, and a chalice full of some dark liquid. As she turned to place it on the altar, the scent of plain red wine wafted to my nostrils. She pricked her finger and squeezed a drop of blood into the cup.

As we passed the chalice from hand to hand, the congregants each sipped reverently. They closed their eyes and sighed at private visions, or stared into the wine wondering before relinquishing it to the next. Yet when it came around to me, I tasted only wine. With time and space for my own art, I might have learned from it any secrets hidden in Bergman's blood—but there was no magic here, only its trappings.

They were awkward, and ignorant, yearning and desperate. Wilder sought power, and Bergman feared to lose it, and the others likely ran the same range of pleasant and obnoxious company that I remembered from my lost childhood congregation. But whatever else they might be, Spector had been wrong. The government had no more to fear from them than it had from Innsmouth eighteen years ago.

As Charlie shuts the door to the back room, I can see his hands trembling. Outside this room he wears a cynical elder's mask, but in truth he is in his late thirties—close enough to my age to make little difference, were we both common mortals. And life has been kind to him. What I now offer has been his greatest frustration, and his eagerness is palpable.

As he moves to clear the floor, I hold up my hand. "Later, we'll try the Inner Sea again"—his unaccustomed smile blossoms—"but first I need to read you something. It may help you to better understand what you're seeing, when you look into your own blood."

What I seek can be found in at least three books on his shelf, but I take down the children's text, flipping carefully until I come to the well-remembered illustration: Earth and her moon, with thirteen forms arrayed around them. I trace the circle with one too-long finger.

"I told you that you can take or leave the gods, but the history is real. This is that history. We have evidence, and eyewitnesses, even for the parts that haven't happened yet. The Great Race of Yith travel through space and through time, and they are brutally honest with those who recognize them. The Litany of Earth was distilled over thousands of years of encounters: conversations that together have told us all the civilizations that came before the human one, and all the civilizations that will come after we're gone."

I wait, watching his face. He doesn't believe, but he's willing to listen. He lowers himself slowly into a chair, and rubs his knee absently.

I skip over the poetry of the original Enochian, but its prompting is sufficient to give me the English translation from memory.

"This is the litany of the peoples of Earth. Before the first, there was blackness, and there was fire. The Earth cooled and life arose, struggling against the unremembering emptiness.

"First were the five-winged eldermost of Earth, faces of the Yith. In the time of the elders, the archives came from the stars. The Yith raised up the Shoggoth to serve them in the archives, and the work of that aeon was to restore and order the archives on Earth.

"Second were the Shoggoth, who rebelled against their makers. The Yith fled forward, and the Earth belonged to the Shoggoth for an aeon."

The words come easily, the familiar verses echoing back through my own short life. In times of hardship or joy, when a child sickened or a fisherman drowned too young for metamorphosis, at the new year and every solstice, the Litany gave us comfort and humility. The people of the air, our priest said, phrased its message more briefly: *This too shall pass.*

"Sixth are humans, the wildest of races, who share the world in three parts. The people of the rock, the K'n-yan, build first and most beautifully, but grow cruel and frightened and become the Mad Ones Under the Earth. The people of the air spread far and breed freely, and build the foundation for those who will supplant them. The people of the water are born in shadow on the land, but what they make beneath the waves will live in glory till the dying sun burns away their last shelter.

"Seventh will be the Ck'chk'ck, born from the least infestation of the houses of man, faces of the Yith." Here, at last, I see Charlie inhale sharply. "The work of that aeon will be to read the Earth's memories, to analyze and annotate, and to make poetry of the Yith's own understanding."

On I count, through races of artists and warriors and lovers and barbarians. Each gets a few sentences for all their thousands or millions of years. Each paragraph must obscure uncountable lives like mine, like Charlie's . . . like my mother's.

"Thirteenth will be the Evening People. The Yith will walk openly among them, raising them from their race's infancy with the best knowledge of all peoples. The work of that aeon will be copying the archives, stone to stone, and building the ships that will carry the archives, and the Evening, to distant stars. After they leave, the Earth will burn and the sun fade to ashes.

"After the last race leaves, there will be fire and unremembering emptiness. Where the stories of Earth will survive, none have told us."

We sit for a minute in silence.

"You ever meet one of these Yith?" Charlie asks at last. He speaks urgently, braced against the answer. Everything else I've told him, he's *wanted* to believe.

"I never have," I say. "But my mother did, when she was a girl. She was out playing in the swamp, and he was catching mosquitoes. Normally you find them in libraries, or talking to scholars, but she isn't the only person to encounter one taking samples of one sort or another. She asked him if mosquitoes would ever be people, and he told her a story about some Ck'chk'ck general, she thought the equivalent of Alexander the Great. She said that everyone asked her so many questions when she got home that she couldn't remember the details properly afterward." I shrug. "This goes with the magic, Mr. Day. Take them both, or turn your back."

The basement door creaked, and skirts whispered against the frame.

"Oz," came Bergman's voice. "I wanted to talk to you about . . . Ah. It's you." She completed her regal descent. "Oz, what is *she* doing here?"

I rose, matching her hard stare. If I was to learn—or perhaps even teach—anything here, I needed to put a stop to this. And I still had to play a role.

"What exactly is it that you hold against me? I've come here many times, now. The others can see easily enough—none of them doubt what I am."

She looked down at me. "You could be an imposter, I suppose. It would be easy enough. But it's hardly the only possible threat we should be concerned about. If you are truly of the Deep Ones' blood, why are you not with your noble kin? Why celebrate the rites here, among ordinary humans who want your secrets for themselves?"

*Why are you not with your kin?* I swallowed bitter answers. "My loneliness is no concern of yours."

"I think it is." She turned to Wilder, who had kept his place before the altar. "If she's *not* a charlatan . . . either she's a spy, sent to keep us from learning her people's powers, or she's in exile for crimes we cannot begin to imagine."

I hissed, and unthinkingly thrust myself into her space, breathing the stink of her sharply exhaled breath. "They. Are. Dead."

Bergman stepped back, pupils wide, breath coming too quickly. She drew herself up, straightened her skirts, and snorted. "Perhaps you are a charlatan after all. Everyone knows the Deep Ones cannot die."

Again without thinking, I lunged for her. She stumbled backward and I caught her collar, twisted, and pulled. She fell forward, and I held her weight easily as she scrabbled to push me away. I blinked (eyes too big, too tight in their sockets), anger almost washed away by surprise. It was the first time the strength had come upon me.

And I had used it on an old mortal woman whose only crimes were pride and suspicion. I released her and turned my back. The joints of my fingers ached where I had clenched them. "Never say that again. Or if you must, say it to the soldiers who shot my father. We do not age, no—not like you do." I could not resist the barb. "But there are many ways to die."

Oz finally spoke, and I turned to see him helping Bergman to her feet. "Peace, Mildred. She's no spy, and I think no criminal. She will not take your immortality from you."

I paused, anger not entirely overwhelmed, and searched her features carefully. She was slender, small-eyed, fine-fingered—and unquestionably aged. For all her dignity, it was impossible that she might share even a drop of blood with my family.

She caught my look and smiled. "Yes, we have that secret from the Deep Ones. Does it surprise you?"

"Exceedingly. I was not aware that there *was* a secret. Not one that could be shared, at least."

A broader, angrier smile. "Yes—you have tried to keep it from us. To keep us small and weak and dying. But we have it—and at the harvest moon, I will go into the water. I am beloved of the Elder Gods, and I will dwell in glory with Them under the waves forever."

"I see." I turned to Wilder. "Have you done this before?"

He nodded. "Mildred will be the third."

"Such a wonderful promise. Why don't you walk into the ocean yourself?"

"Oh, I shall—when I have trained a successor who can carry on in my place." And he looked at me with such confidence that I realized whom he must have chosen for that role.

Mildred Bergman—convinced that life could be hoarded like a fortune—would never believe me if I simply *told* her the truth. I held up my hand to forestall anything else the priest might have to say. "Wilder, get out of here. I'll speak with you later."

He went. If he had convinced himself I would be his priestess, I suppose he had to treat me as one.

I sat down, cross-legged, trying to clear the hissing tension that had grown between us. After a moment she also sat, cautiously and with wincing stiffness.

"I'm sorry," I said. "It doesn't work like that. We go into the water, and live long there, because we have the blood of the deep in us. The love of the gods is not so powerful. I wish I had more to offer you. There are magics that can heal, that can ease the pains of age, that can even extend life for a few decades. I will gladly teach them to you." And I would, too. She had been vile to me, but I could invite her to Charlie's back room to study with us, and learn the arts that would give her both time and acceptance. All but one spell, that I would not teach, and did not plan to ever learn.

"You're lying." Her voice was calm and even.

"I'm not. You're going to drown yourself—" I swallowed. "I'm trying to save your life. You haven't done a speck of real magic in this room, you don't know what it's like, how it's different."

She started to say something, and I raised a hand. "No. I know you won't listen to what I have to say. Please, let me show you."

"Show me." Not a demand—only an echo, full of doubt.

"Magic." I looked at her, with my bulging eyes and thick bones, willing her, if she couldn't yet believe, at least to look at me.

"What's involved in this . . . demonstration?" she finally asked, and I released a held breath.

"Not much. Chalk, a pair of bowls, and a drop of blood."

Between my purse and the altar, we managed to procure what was needed—fortunate, as I would have hated to go up and ask Wilder to borrow them. Having practiced this with Charlie, I still had the most basic of seals settled in my mind, at least clearly enough for this simple spell. I moved us away from the carefully laid tile to the raw flagstone behind the stairs. There was no reason to vandalize Wilder's stage.

Bergman did not know the Litany, nor the cosmic humility that was the core of Sharhlyda practice. And yet, in some ways, she was easier to work with than Charlie. I could tell her to feel her blood as a river, without worrying what she might guess of my nature.

As I guided her through the opening meditation, Bergman's expression relaxed into something calmer, more introspective. She had some potential for the art, I thought. More than Wilder, certainly, who was so focused on the theater of the thing, and on the idea of power. Bergman's shoulders loosened, and her breath evened, but she kept her eyes open, waiting.

I pricked my finger and let the blood fall into the bowl, holding myself back from the spell long enough to wipe the blade and pass it to Bergman. Then I let the current pull me down . . .

Submerging only briefly before forcing myself upward, out of the cool ocean and into the harsh dry air. I took a painful breath, and laid my hand on Bergman's arm.

A thin stream moved through a great ravine, slow and emaciated. Rivulets trickled past great sandy patches. And yet, where they ran, they ran sweet and cool. The lines they etched, the bars and branches, made a fine and delicate pattern. In it I saw not only the inevitable decay that she strove against, but the stronger shape that was once hers—and the subtler strength in the shape she wore now.

"You *are* one of them."

I returned, gasping, all my instincts clamoring for moisture. I wanted to race upstairs and throw the windows open to the evening fog. Instead I leaned forward.

"Then you must also see—"

She sniffed, half a laugh. "I see that at least some of the books Wilder found can be trusted. And none of them have claimed that the Deep Ones are a more honest race than we. They do claim that you know more of the ancient lore than most humans have access to. So no, I don't believe that your immortality is a mere accident of birth. It can be ours as well—if we don't let you frighten us away from it."

We argued long and late, and still I could not move her. That night I argued with myself, sleepless, over whether it was my place to do more.

Of course Charlie asks, inevitably.

I have been teaching him the first, simplest healing spells. Even a mortal, familiar with his own blood, can heal small wounds, speed the passage of trivial illnesses and slow the terrible ones.

"How long can I live, if I practice this?" He looks at me thoughtfully.

"Longer. Perhaps an extra decade or three. Our natures catch up with us all, in the end." I cringe inwardly, imagining his resentment if he knew. And I am beginning to see that he must know, eventually, if I continue with these lessons.

"Except for the Yith?"

"Yes." I hesitate. Even were I ready to share my nature, this would be an unpleasant conversation, full of temptation and old shame. "What the Yith do . . . there *are* spells for that, or something similar. No one else has ever found the trick of moving through time, but to take a young body for your own . . . You would not find it in any of these books, but it wouldn't be hard to track down. I haven't, and I won't. It's not difficult, from what I've heard, just wrong."

Charlie swallows and looks away. I let him think about it a moment.

"We forgive the Yith for what they do, though they leave whole races abandoned around fading stars. Because their presence means that Earth is remembered, and our memory and our stories will last for as long as they can find younger stars and younger bodies to carry them to. They're as selfish as an old scholar wanting eighty more years to study and love and breathe the air. But we honor the Yith for sacrificing billions, and track down and destroy those who steal one life to preserve themselves."

He narrows his eyes. "That's very . . . practical of you."

I nod, but look away. "Yes. We say that they do more to hold back darkness and chaos than any other race, and it is worth the cost. And of course, we know that we aren't the ones to pay it."

"I wonder if the . . . what were they called, the Ck'chk'ck . . . had a Nuremberg."

I start to say that it's not the same—the Yith hate nobody, torture nothing. But I cannot find it in me to claim it makes a difference. Oblivion, after all, is oblivion, however it is forced on you.

The day after my fourth meeting with Spector, I did not go to work. I walked, in the rain and the chill, in the open air, until my feet hurt, and then I kept walking, because I could. And eventually, because I could, I went home.

Mama Rei was mending, Kevin on the floor playing with fabric scraps. The *Chronicle* lay open on the table to page seven, where a single column reported the previous night's police raid on a few wealthy homes. No reason was given for the arrests, but I knew that if I read down far enough, there would be some tittering implication of debauchery. Mama Rei smiled at me sadly, and flicked her needle through a stocking. The seam would not look new, but would last a little longer with her careful stitching.

"You told him," she said. "And he listened."

"He promised me there would be no camps." Aloud, now, it sounded like a slender promise by which to decide a woman's fate.

Flick. "Does he seem like an honorable man?"

"I don't know. I think so. He says that the ones they can't just let go, they'll send to a sanitarium." Someplace clean, where their needs would be attended to, and where they would be well fed. "He says Wilder really does belong there. He believed what he was telling the others. What he was telling Bergman."

And she believed what he told her—but that faith would not have been enough to save her.

No one's faith ever was.

Flick. Flick. The needle did a little dance down and around, tying off one of her perfect tiny knots. Little copper scissors, a gift purchased with my earnings and Anna's, cut the dangling thread. "You should check on her."

"I don't think she'll want to see me."

Mama Rei looked at me. "Aphra-chan."

I ducked my head. "You're right. I'll make sure they're treating her well."

But they would, I knew. She would be confined in the best rooms and gardens that her money could pay for, all her physical needs attended to. Kind men would try to talk her back from the precipice where I had found her. And they would keep her from drowning herself until her blood, like that of all mortals, ran dry.

I wondered if, as she neared the end, she would still pray.

If she did, I would pray with her. If it was good for nothing else, at least the effort would be real.

*Yog-Sothoth knows the gate. Yog-Sothoth is the gate. Yog-Sothoth is the key and guardian of the gate. Past, present, future, all are one in Yog-Sothoth. He knows where the Old Ones broke through of old, and where They shall break through again. He knows where They have trod earth's fields, and where They still tread them, and why no one can behold Them as They tread.*

"The Dunwich Horror" · H. P. Lovecraft

## • NECROTIC COVE •
### Lois H. Gresh

The sun hangs low and drools lava across a sea the color of stillborn baby. A dead branch whisks my cheek as I step from the trail onto the beach, and blood trickles into my mouth. The air reminds me of cantaloupes left on the counter too long. Insect wings brush my neck, a sting, and my skin swells and itches. None of this bothers me. I'm here, at long last, I'm *here*.

I stand transfixed as the emptiness inside me fills with emotions I don't understand.

*Necrotic Cove, where we come to be cleansed and purified.*

Tatania says, "Can we leave now? You've seen it, isn't this enough?"

I mouth the word *no*, but I don't think I say it. It's as if I've always been locked outside of the universe, looking in but never fitting in until this very moment.

I gaze to my left and right, where cliffs reflect the sun. The sand spreads like a fan stained by cyanosis, and the water is comatose. This is a place of death, and yet I feel something flickering to life within me.

Tatania grasps my elbow. "Watch it, you're going to fall," she says, and yes, I find that I'm tottering, and I'm so weak that even an old woman's claws bruise me. I squint at her. My best friend since childhood, she'll do anything for me, won't she? Even leave the comforts of her widow's lair to follow me here. Anything to please pathetic Cassandra before my spine finally snaps and the cancer finally eats what's left of my ulcerated insides.

I clasp Tatania's waist and steady myself. I say, "My dying wish, and you granted it."

"You're not dead yet, Cassandra. Stop saying that." She drops to the sand beneath the brown entrails of a palm. Leans against the trunk, stretches her legs, flinches as the sand burns her thighs. "Sit beside me, dear," she says.

I do as she asks. I always do what Tatania wants.

"Four hours we hiked, and through a path so narrow a squirrel couldn't make it through." Tatania removes her hat and fans her face. Sweat glues her dyed black hair to her scalp. I have no idea why she bothers to dye her hair, it's so obviously fake at our age. She wipes her forehead with the back of a hand and scratches an insect bite. Her rings flash the sun into my eyes, and I shift my view back to the cliffs, their coppery sheen far more beautiful than her diamonds.

"I'm not surprised that nobody comes here." Her laugh breaks into a cough. "The beach smells like a sewer, and the insects are horrible."

I can't explain the allure of this place to someone like Tatania. She's never been empty and alone like me. She's always *belonged*. Married three times, always to wealthy men, she never had to work, never did much of anything other than make it to her tennis lessons on time, pamper herself with fine food and wine, subject herself to botox, and let the doctors carve her up with plastic surgery. Light blue contacts on her navy eyes. Tatania looks like a parody of her younger self, but she doesn't realize it. She's more comfortable at thousand-dollar-a-plate parties and vodka lunches at Chez Grande. But she's always up for a wild time, and I don't know why, but I needed her to come with me.

"Listen," I say, "I'll cool down in the water, and then we can head back, okay?"

Her face tightens into the mock-grimace of the surgically preserved. This is her way of issuing a slight smile of agreement. As she stretches onto a towel, I peel off my T-shirt and shorts, pull my gray hair into a ponytail, and slip off my sandals. My feet are tired from the long walk, my calves ache, but the sand scorches so I hurry to the water, and as only the chronically ill know how to do, I ignore the pain shooting down my legs.

The water quickly sucks me in and coats me with muck. I see nothing through the bruise of the surface, but I feel the fish, their silken gills fluttering like butterfly wings on my legs. I flip to my back and float. Amniotic water cradles me, and the whisper of a breeze, like an angel's touch, caresses my face. My heart surges as if to the other side of the air. And the pain leeches from my back and legs into the water.

My esophagus and stomach, my intestines: all such a mess, riddled with holes, I can hardly eat or even drink water without the pressure in my ribs and the squeezing of pain through my torso into my back. Constant falls have fragmented my back, the bones so thin they don't register on medical equipment, the bones like shrapnel on my nerves.

The peace here is beyond anything I've known. This must be what it's like when people find Jesus or whatever other gods they worship. Must be what it's like when men orgasm, when women feel beautiful, when cats catch mice.

Wide-winged birds float past, and my ears buzz as their notes fall into harmony with my breathing. I pant, and the notes intensify in pitch and go up an octave. I almost smile, I'm so content, but I don't know how to smile, not really. I hold my breath until my lungs hurt, and the birds stop singing.

*I'm one with the water and all it contains, one with the air and everything in it.*

The locals claim that boats never make it to this cove, that the sea rises and swallows them at the horizon. The locals fear this place and are happy enough to stay away. Me, an outsider, just an old woman with nothing to lose, well, what's left to fear when you don't care if you die?

Back on shore is Tatania, rolled to one side, belly protruding, eyes riveted to a paperback rather than the beautiful sea.

My breath spills into the heat of the noonday sun.

My heart pounds in rhythm to the wings of birds and to the gills of the fish.

I doggy-paddle toward the jagged rock towering over the right side of the cove. Peek again at Tatania, sleeping now, her body heaving up and down, and she must be snoring in her "feminine way," as she likes to put it.

The cliffs call to me through the harmonies of the birds and the fish. The rhythms form words I don't know,

*F'ai throdog uaaah*

and

*ogthrod ai-f geb'l-ee'h*

I'm not crazy, never been crazy. Even with all the medicine, I'm not the type to let my mind drift into the stupors of drugs or self-pity. I simply stopped caring long ago whether I was dead or alive, which in my case is a form of death anyway. And the stories of this place, the Necrotic Cove, I could not ignore. It is said, by the people who fear this place, that it can devour your soul and lay you to rest. And this is what I want. I don't want to die in a hospital, a nursing home. I want to die on a beach or in waters that tranquilize and numb me, I want to die beneath copper cliffs and a molten sun. Had I told this to Tatania, she would have found a way to prevent me from coming here.

I paddle toward shore, then drag myself to the beach and press my palms against the cliff. The rhythms pound—

*F'ai throdog uaaah*

*ogthrod ai-f geb'l-ee'h*

—over and over again.

I lift my hands and look at the palms, the dust of a thousand sunsets on them. I rest my cheek against the rock, let it flush my senses. Did Tatania feel this ecstasy, this merging of dizziness and excitement, when she married for the first time, when she had sex with all those men between the marriages, when she got drunk and snorted coke and popped pills, when she partied all night, when the most handsome men wanted her, when she caught the eyes of the bad boys? I've always been alone, not even one man wanted me, so I don't know how it feels to be loved with the type of passion that Tatania has always known. Always scorned, insulted, rejected, and only Tatania has stood by me as a friend. But this place and I, *this*, this is *intense*. This ecstasy, like my head's in the clouds and all I can do is ride the tidal waves crashing down my body. This place and I, we merge as lovers, or maybe as conjoined twins.

Eventually, I pull back, and the removal of flesh from rock jolts me, and sadness floods the space of me that only moments before brimmed with ecstasy. My fingertip grazes the rock, so soft now like velvet, and joy brightens the edges of my darkness. My cheek back upon the rock, and ecstasy thrums through my body again—and I gasp, all the pain vanishing, *for the first time in decades, there is no pain.*

I pull back again, testing, and blackness envelopes me as if I've left my first love. I must get Tatania, bring her to the cliff, press her against the rock, let her feel for herself why I had to come to Necrotic Cove. Then she'll understand the allure. My oldest and only friend, Tatania, who sheltered me when kids made fun of me in kindergarten and beat me up in third grade, who didn't waver in my teens when boys taunted me as uglier than any dude, who filched money from her husbands for me when I lost job after job as the illnesses took root and spread. Dearest Tatania, you must feel my ecstasy now, for if not for you, I would have died long ago.

And so I race to her. My arms and legs flash before me, skinny tubes of flesh bruised blue from the sea and streaked copper from the cliffs.

I crouch, ignore the burning sand, and I shake her. "Wake up, Tatania! You must wake up!"

"Have you lost your mind?" Her eyes slowly open and focus on me, then abruptly, she shoves me off. "Are you insane? Let me rest before we have to hike four hours back to that damn village." Mascara and eyeliner blotched by humidity and heat. Pancake makeup washed away by sweat, her face mottled by liver spots. The bristles of gray stubble on her chin, the lone hair curling from the middle of her neck.

*I love Tatania.*

Twins, she and I, joined almost since birth. Her husbands, and all the other men who came and went, mean nothing. They didn't last. Only Tatania and I lasted, only Tatania and I remain together,

*and isn't that so,*

*isn't it?*

She drifts back to sleep, as I notice the bumps popping up all over my skin. They're the size of goosebumps but not distributed in any pattern I recognize. Purple, each one, with a speck of glitter in the center. Perhaps bug bites or an irritation from the strange water?

The bumps are kind of pretty, I think, as if I'm laced in jewels.

Shadows ripple across the sand, and I look up to see black clouds scuttle like giant insects across the sun, streaming from one cliff to the other, then disappearing into the rock.

The breeze is no longer an angel's touch. It's rougher now, and the clouds coalesce, and the sky is a blood clot that rips open and weeps, the tears viscous and dark. Could it be that the angels cry for *me*, for *Cassandra*, who never believed in god and angels in the first place?

· · ·

"*Cassandra.*" My name slithered from his mouth, the monster in a jeans jacket with the cigarette dangling from his teeth. "*The Deformed,*" and a laugh when he shoved me against the cement wall. I cowered as he jabbed me with tobacco-stained fingers, and I whispered "*No no no*" over and over again in the most pathetic way, but he didn't listen to my pleas, they just made him bolder.

And suddenly, Tatania was there in prissy skirt and shirt with her latest boyfriend, Cole somebody-or-other, tall and muscular with angular cheekbones and the smug confidence of boys born with it all. I didn't like Cole. He always got in the way of me and Tat.

"Stop it!" she demanded of the monster, this jerk who picked on me because I was so weak. I was easy prey. He stepped back, cocky grin, smoke rushing from his mouth, stinging my eyes, making my throat clench. Coughing, I slid along the concrete toward Tat and Cole, thinking that their names together sounded like a brand of Dollar Store thread. Fancy name to hide something febrile and weak that I didn't think would last.

"Come here, Cassy dear," and Tat hugged me close, and I settled my cheek against her perfectly ironed shirt, pink and smelling like flowers. Her breasts swelled, her heart beat softly against me, and I held back tears and wrapped my arms around her waist and clutched her tight. I never cried. I never laughed. I never showed emotion. Except when I begged the monster not to beat me up.

Cole grabbed the monster's jacket and shook him, but all Cole got for his trouble was smoke in his face and a hard shove against cement. With all his football muscle, Cole was no match for the monster, street lean, mangy, the type who enjoyed a fight more than anything else.

Fast-forward three years, and I found myself at their wedding. Cole, her first husband fresh out of high school. His worshipping eyes, his adoration, "Oh Tatania, so kind, so sweet, the most wonderful girl in the world, how can I be so lucky?" he gushed.

"No, I'm the lucky one, dearest . . ."

*Ooze. Ooze.*

*Ooze ooze ooze ooze*

*Would they never shut up?*

I didn't see her for a while, he was so high on her due to her beauty and the constant kindness she'd shown to me all those years.

*Me.*

I was responsible for bringing Tat and Cole together.

When they divorced and she got half of his fortune, quite substantial, she came back to me.

As she always did.

Lightning flashes, blood clot sky, sun no longer molten. Thunder like 9/11 and the towers falling, a sand storm whisking grit into my eyes. Tatania jerks awake and shrieks, "What's going on, Cass?" She uses my pet name from long ago. "What's wrong with my skin? My god, what's wrong with *you*?"

Tatania's skin glitters with bumps just like mine, except they're sparse on her and littered across me. I hold up an arm, and the wind whips it back against my shoulder socket. Ninety-degree angle to my shoulder—in the wrong direction—but my arm doesn't break. The bumps have congealed into gelatinous mounds all over my arm. Mounds that are like muscles, glistening purple and twinkling dots. Mesmerizing twinkle. *Mesmerizing . . .*

She slaps my face. I feel no sting. "Snap out of it, Cass!" she screams. "We have to get out of here, and I mean *now*!" She jumps to her feet, and against what's now a stiff wind, forces her withered old body toward the jungle. Her hair stands on end, glued by purplish muck into spikes. Her skin strains against the bones of her face, the tightly stitched skin so smoothly applied by surgeons. Screaming, hands on her face, bloody hands now grabbing for the dead palms.

Lightning cracks the sky and illuminates the copper whorls blowing off the cliffs and dancing with the rain of angels' tears.

"The trail's not here anymore!" Tatania, hysterical.

Yes, I *see*. The trail's gone, the tropical growth burgeons, and coconuts smash to the sand. One hits Tatania's shoulder, and she falls, still screaming. I drag myself to her. The wind feels good in my lungs. The coconuts are hollow. Dead. They don't hurt me at all. But Tatania's shoulder is broken.

I lift her onto my body, and I slither toward the cliffs. They call to me, those cliffs, in an unknown language like the words of flowers.

*Y'ai 'ng'ngah Yog-Sothoth*

*F'ai throdog uaaah*

*ogthrod ai-f geb'l-ee'h*

Tatania's body has bumps now, too, and they pulse as they cling in perfect symmetry to bumps on my upper mounds. This is how I hold her, bumps fitting bumps, conjoined twins, glued together now for eternity. Each iridescent globe reflects us both, one beautiful and the other Deformed.

We're all One, purified and clean, no longer locked outside the very universe we inhabit. Hear the rhythms of the flowers, Old Ones. Hear the song, and feel the beauty.

*Y'ai 'ng'ngah Yog-Sothoth*
*F'ai throdog uaaah*
*ogthrod ai-f geb'l-ee'h*

I must bring Tatania with us. I won't leave her behind.

The rain coats me like oil, but it hits her like needles and pierces her skin. I feel the impact of those needles through her body. I feel the punctures. I feel her wince. I feel the strength drain from her.

I roll my mounds, huge purple slugs glistening with bumps and pricks of diamond, and I hold her fast, my bumps fitting hers as puzzle pieces fit together. I press her against the cliff, where the copper dust blows. She coughs, and I'm forced to detach her from the rock so she can get her breath. She gasps now, sees me, shrieks. And I see her, the face with shredded skin, the contacts long gone and the old lady's eyes dim and dark, one gouged.

*What have we done? Tatania, my only friend . . .*

My flesh suckers to the rock, and something pulls me closer, I can't detach, I don't want to detach. For a moment, I struggle against the power of the rock, but in the end, I submit to it and spikes of pleasure wash through me.

*Tidal waves of ecstasy, flame consuming my heart,* I can't *let go of this, I can't, and my soul transcends and surges into the rock, into the rain, into the clouds, everywhere at once, merging with the birds, the fish, the rock, and*

*Tatania! no no no no no*
*Tatania! ooze ooze ooze ooze*
and
*isn't it always like this,*
*and isn't it?*

Her skin, stretched so thin, bursts open, and she screams once, a flash of a scream, and she's no longer attached to me. My body is one with the rock. Iridescent bubbles on the cliff above me reflect her body as she falls to the sand. Everywhere, walls glow and cradle me in purple and bumps and the musk of rotting lopes and peaches. Pressed inside, wrapped in warmth, I *belong*.

Tatania isn't with us. She's beyond the rock, still on the beach. I'm inside now, where I *belong*, inside the cliff, where my bumps swell and cling to the bumps surrounding me. All of us, we belong, one with Yog-Sothoth, who dwells in the higher planes and comes to us in glistening wonder. Behold us, for we are the Old Ones.

We heave, our hearts one giant heart, together. We breathe, our lungs one giant lung, together. We whisper like angels, we sing like birds, we're softer than the gills of fish.

We are. It's as simple as that. We are.

Clasped in each other's arms, bracketed by life and death that no longer touch us.

*We are.* We give ourselves to the whole. *We are.*

*Y'ai 'ng'ngah Yog-Sothoth*
*Yog-Sothoth 'ngah'ng ai'y zhro*

I drift beyond the boundaries of time.

I float in the crevices of space.

I remember things I'd rather forget.

Tatania's second husband, Arnold, the type of man I thought I might finally attract. He weighed about a hundred forty pounds, tall and skinny as a scratch, bald with thick gray hair on his back and shoulders, a caved-in face with squashed nose and rosebud mouth: not a pretty man by anyone's standards. Except perhaps, mine.

But Tat wouldn't have it. She wanted Arnold for herself. He was rich, and she wanted more than Cole had given to her.

I wasn't jealous. I never got jealous. Tat deserved everything good. I was lucky to have her as a friend. She stole money from Arnold, filched it from his "accounts," whatever that meant, neither of us really knew. But I was already riddled with disease and broken bones, and nobody wanted to hire me to do anything, and Tat was all I had.

*Faithful friend.*

*Tatania.*

*I love you, Tatania.*

Over meatloaf one night, Arnold threw down his fork, *plate clatter skit across floor*, and fury in his little knot of a face, he accused his wife of stealing from the company.

Lump of meatloaf choking my throat, *grab for water*, one thumb and two fingers on my hand, my arm a bone encased in scabs. *Slash slash alone at night late at night I slash my arms yes I do and why I tell you why godammit I will tell you*
*if only you ask*
*but you never ask.*

"I give all the money to Cass." Tat's voice was honey smooth, her eyes soft and loving as she looked from her husband to me and back again. She lowered her head. "I give it all to Cass," she repeated. "What else can she do, if I don't help her?" As if I wasn't there with meat in my throat.

*But I don't mind, I never mind.*

"Oh, poor Cass," said Arnold, immediately relenting, "you are so dear to both of us, and Tatania, my sweet sweet wife—"

And so we replayed it.

"No, I'm the lucky one, dearest . . . "

Ooze. Ooze.

*Ooze ooze ooze ooze*

I didn't see her for a while, he was so high on her due to her beauty and the constant kindness she'd shown to me all those years.

*Me.*

I was responsible for bringing Tat and Arnold together.

When they divorced and she got half of his fortune, quite substantial, she came back to me.

Like she always did.

I need to belong.
Push
*I love you, Tatania.*
Push

Finally, I heave my bulk back through the rock and pop to the other side, the exposed cliff where the storm rages and Tatania is unconscious on the sand.

I roll her onto me again, my beloved Tatania, and her bumps grip mine, and together we roll toward the crashing surf.

*Wave high above, black lip, dog-rabid froth*, Tatania flickers in and out of consciousness, face almost gone, lips flapping in the wind, her mouth a giant hole, her teeth bigger than I remember.

Conjoined twins. I won't leave her here to die.

Glued to my upper mound by the bumps, she doesn't wobble or fall as we slide beneath the steel wave and bob on the turbulence.

*Waves cresting, crashing, slide beneath the muck and the foam,*
*float float here*
*where I belong*
*where we are*

My strength flows from my bumps to hers, *conjoined twins*, and I nourish her. Gummy strings, *umbilical cords*, form between her bumps and mine. We bob like this for I don't know how long, and then Tatania's breathing steadies and her heart picks up.

*Why have you always been so kind to me, Tatania?* I think it, and she answers, "I felt sorry for you. I liked having a faithful puppy. You made me look good. I got three husbands, the money. I came with you to a beautiful island and walked to a beach. I didn't realize it would be hell. You came on a lot of my vacations. Riviera, Rio, St. John."

*True, because we've always been friends.* I just want her to accept me as I am. Don't want her pity, don't want to be her faithful puppy, just want her affection. If only, after all these decades, Tatania would truly be one with me, nobody else, just me.

*There's no hell, Tatania, no life, no death, no angels, nothing. Only that which is elusive and humble. Give yourself to me. Here, drink and let me nourish you.*

"You're sick! Disgusting and sick!" she cries, but she lets my energy flow through the umbilical cords and bumps, and then a wave surges and slams us against the cliff. My bumps bolt us to the rock, and Tatania hangs off my outer side, glued securely to me but howling for release. Her fists beat me.

"*Cassandra,*" she spits my name, "you're not even The Deformed! You're a total *freak, a monster!*"

The wind pounds me against the cliff, it's a hurricane blasting into the cove, and I beg her,

*be one with me, nobody else, just me*
*admit it, that it's me and only me you love, Tatania.*

She's hysterical, calling me terrible names, even worse names than the bullies used all my life. She'd rather die than be anywhere near me. I'm grotesque. She's always known it. *I'm* the monster. *I'm* the reason she lost her husbands, me, all *my* fault, they couldn't stand being around me anymore, could they? Yes, all those years she took care of me, out of pity, yes, but why does it matter? She took care of me. *I'm* the monster. And she'd rather *die* . . .

We're held together by bumps. Only bumps. I realize there's nothing else between us. Not really. She never saw the real me, and she never appreciated what I gave to her. She always cast me aside for those men, time and time again, she just used me to make herself look good,

*and isn't that so,*

*isn't it?*

She was my friend when it suited her. Her affection, it comes and goes. Riviera, Rio, St. John: only when she was old and lonely.

She isn't real. She's false and phony. She's *human*.

"I got you shelter, gave you food. I was your friend, Cassandra, and you were nothing but a fucking ingrate monster pathetic whore spawn of shit should be beaten into a pulp you fucking ugly THING—"

If I could cry, I would, but I can't cry, so I do the only thing I know how to do. *All my umbilical cords snap like Dollar Store threads.*

Her body thumps down the cliff, tattered pieces snagged on rock, and then she shatters into a blast of wind. What's left of her fizzes into the muck below.

My bumps shudder from the release. If I still had lips, I'd smile. Maybe I'd even laugh, because I get it now. For the first time, I actually get it.

I *belong*. She's *never had anyone but me*. She's *alone*. She's *the monster*. She's *the fucking ingrate monster pathetic whore spawn of shit that should be beaten into a pulp fucking ugly* THING—

No longer skating through the higher dimensions of space and time and merely looking into the human world, the Old Ones are what matter. We're clean and pure, we're true beauty. We have no need for Botox and diamonds and plastic surgeries and prissy skirts and other human nonsense. The Old Ones *are* the diamonds, and the *humans* are The Deformed.

We are. It's as simple as that. We are.

Clasped in each other's arms, bracketed by life and death that no longer touch us.

*We are.* We give ourselves to the whole. *We are.*

And as the winds settle and the sun torches the blackness from the sky, Tatania's remains dissolve, and I slip back through the iridescence and into the cliff to join the others.

*I am forced into speech because men of science have refused to follow my advice without knowing why. It is altogether against my will that I tell my reasons for opposing this contemplated invasion of the Antarctic— with its vast fossil hunt and its wholesale boring and melting of the ancient ice caps. And I am the more reluctant because my warning may be in vain.*

*"At the Mountains of Madness"* · H. P. Lovecraft (1936)

# · ON ICE ·
## Simon Strantzas

The bearded Frenchman landed the plane on a narrow sheet of ice as expertly as anyone could. It wasn't smooth, and the four passengers were utterly silent as the hull shuddered and echoed and threatened to split along its riveted seams. Wendell closed his eyes so tight he saw stars, and clung to what was around him to keep from being thrown from his seat. When the plane finally slid to a stop, part of him wanted to leap up and hug not only the ground but the men around him. He didn't, because when he finally opened his eyelids the first thing he saw was the thuggish Dogan's disgusted smirk, and it quickly extinguished any lingering elation. Isaacs, for all his faults, was not so inhibited. Instead, he had his hands pressed together in supplication and whispered furiously under breath. It caught Dogan's eye, and the look he and Wendell shared might have been the first time they had agreed on anything.

"The oil companies have already done a survey of Melville Island, so there shouldn't be too many surprises ahead," Dr. Hanson said. "However, their priority has never been fossils—except, of course, the liquid kind—and it's unlikely they saw much while speeding across the ice on ATVs, doing damage to the strata. So we have ample exploring to do. We'll hike inland for a day and set up base camp. From there, we'll radiate our dig outward."

Gauthier unloaded the plane two bags at a time, and his four passengers moved the gear to the side. They packed light—only the most essential tools and equipment—so the hike would be manageable, but seeing the bags spread across the encrusted surface, Wendell wondered if he were up to the task. It took too long to load everything on his narrow shoulders, and when he was done he suspected the pack weighed more than thirty pounds. Dr. Hanson looked invigorated by his own burden, his face a smiling crimson flush. Isaacs was the opposite, however, and visibly uncomfortable. Wendell hoped the goggle-eyed boy wouldn't be a liability in the days ahead.

They walked across the frigid snow, and nearly an hour went by before Dr. Hanson turned and looked at the breathless entourage behind him.

"So, Wendell," he called out, barely containing his anticipation and glee. "Have you noticed anything peculiar so far?"

Wendell glanced at both Dogan and Isaacs, but neither showed any interest in Wendell's answer. Even Dr. Hanson seemed more concerned in hearing himself speak.

"For all the research the oil companies did here, it looks as though they made a major error in classifying the rock formations. It doesn't really surprise me—you said they weren't here looking for rocks. Still, they thought all these formations were the result of normal tectonic shifts—that these were normal terrestrial rocks."

There was a pause.

"And that's not the case?"

"No, these are aquatic rocks. The entire island is full of them."

"And how do you account for so many aquatic rocks on an island, Wendell?"

"Lowering water levels, increased volcanic activity. The normal shifts of planetary mass. It's unusual for something so large to be pushed up from the ocean, but the Arctic island clusters have always had some unique attributes."

Dr. Hanson nodded sagely before catching his breath to speak.

Wendell noticed that the dribble from Hanson's nose was opaque as it slowly froze.

"These islands have always had a sense of mystery about them. The Inuit don't come here, which is strange enough, but they have a name for these clusters: *alornerk*. It means 'the deep land.' I don't know where that term comes from, but some claim it has survived from the days when the island was still submerged."

"That would mean either Melville Island only surfaced sometime in the last ten thousand years, or—"

"Or there was intelligent life in the Arctic two hundred million years before it showed up anywhere else on the planet."

"But that's impossible!" Dogan interrupted, startling Wendell. He looked just as confused. Dr. Hanson merely laughed excitedly. "Yes, it's the worst kind of lazy science, isn't it? I wouldn't put too much stock in it."

They fell back into a single line quickly: Dr. Hanson leading the way, then Dogan, Wendell, Isaacs, and finally the pilot, Gauthier. Wendell made a concerted effort to keep close to the front so he might hear anything Dogan and Dr. Hanson discussed, but the sound of their footsteps on the snow had a deafening and delirious effect—at times he hallucinated more sounds than could be possible. The constant crunch made him lightheaded, a problem exacerbated by the cold that worked at his temples.

But it was Isaacs who suffered the worst. Periodically, Wendell checked to see how far behind his fellow student had fallen, and to ensure he hadn't vanished altogether. Yet Isaacs was always there, only a few feet back, fidgeting and scanning the landscape. Gauthier likely kept him in place. The two made quite a sight, and Wendell was amused by how little Gauthier did to conceal his contempt. Isaacs was a frightened rabbit in a cage. Gauthier, the snarling wolf beyond the lock.

"This feels wrong," Isaacs whined, and Wendell did his best to pretend he hadn't heard him. It did not dissuade Isaacs from continuing. "You can't tell me this feels right to you guys. You can't tell me you guys don't feel everything closing in."

Wendell glanced back. It was reassuring to see that even an expensive jacket couldn't prevent Isaacs from being ravaged by the weather—his eyes bulged, his color was pale.

"Isaacs, look around. There's not a wall or anything in sight. Nothing to box you in. The idea you feel confined—"

"I feel it, too."

Nothing about Gauthier's face betrayed that he'd spoken. Nevertheless, Wendell slowed to close the distance between them. Isaacs did the same, eyes wide and eager.

"What are you talking about?"

"Don't you feel it?" Isaacs said. "I feel it all over my body. I don't like being here alone."

"You aren't alone. There are five of us, plus a plane. And Gauthier has a satellite phone, just in case. The only thing boxing you in is all your protection. You're practically surrounded."

"Then why are we so alone? Where are all the animals?"

"They were probably on the shore. Gauthier, we saw some birds or something when we flew over, right?"

The pilot shook his head slowly. It spooked Wendell nearly as much as Isaacs had.

"Well, I'm sure there are animals around. They're probably hiding from us because they're afraid."

"I don't have a good feeling about this, Wendell," Isaacs said. "I don't have a good feeling about this at all. We should get back on the plane and go."

"Wait, did Dogan put you guys up to this?"

The look of surprise did not seem genuine, though it was hard to be certain. Wendell wanted to press further, but he heard Dr. Hanson's voice.

"Wendell! Isaacs! Come, you must see this!"

Wendell turned to the men before him. They looked confused. When the three reached Dr. Hanson and the visibly uncomfortable Dogan, Wendell didn't immediately understand what the concern was. Before them lay ice, just as it lay everywhere. Dr. Hanson smiled, but it held no warmth. It was thin and quivering and echoed his uneasy eyes.

"Do you see it? Right there. On the ground. Where my foot is." There was only ice. Wendell kneeled to get a better look, but a pair of iron hands grabbed him and yanked him back to his feet. He stumbled as Gauthier set him down.

"Don't," was all the pilot said.

"Are you really that much of an idiot?" Dogan asked, and Wendell felt once again the butt of some foul trick. Had it not been for Dr. Hanson's distinct lack of humor, Wendell might have stormed off into the snow. Instead, he tamped his irritation and looked again.

He wasn't certain how long it took, but slowly what the rest had seen resolved. Isaacs, too, spotted it before Wendell, serenading them with a litany of "oh, no," repeated over and over. Dr. Hanson tried to help by asking everyone to back away, while Wendell wondered why no one simply told him what he was missing.

Then he realized it wasn't him who was missing something but someone else, because trapped beneath the sheet of ice was what could only be a severed human finger.

The flesh was pale, verging on white, and beneath the clouded surface it was barely visible. Wendell inspected the hands of the party to be sure it hadn't come from any of them.

"I don't like this. I don't like this at all."

"It's not going to leap out and grab you, Isaacs. Get a grip on yourself."

"But where did it come from? Doctor Hanson, could it have come from Doctor Lansing's party? You said they were here for a few days. Why else would they have left after finding only those three small ichthyosaur bones?"

"I asked Doctor Lansing that very question, Wendell. He simply responded by asking me how many bones beyond three I thought would be necessary to collect to prove his point. Five? Ten? Fifty? He said all he felt necessary were three to prove ichthyosaurs traveled this far north. I'll grant you: that makes little sense, but that's Doctor Lansing for you. Even he, however, wouldn't be foolish enough to waste time poring over this discovery. More than likely, it was due to some accident involving the oil men here before us. There's nothing we can do for the fellow that lost it, and we have more important discoveries to dig up, discoveries beside which this will ultimately pale. Let's march on. We still have a journey ahead of us."

Dr. Hanson resumed walking, Dogan trotting after him. Isaacs looked as though he was going to be sick, but before he could Gauthier shoved him.

"Keep moving. Standing too long in the open like this isn't a good idea. You never know what's watching."

Wendell looked around, but all he saw were hills of ice in every direction. If anything was watching, he had no idea where it might be hiding.

Wendell couldn't stop thinking about the finger as they continued on. Maybe it was the sound of their footsteps, or the dark beneath his parka's hood, but he felt increasingly isolated from the group, and as they traveled he became further ensnared in thought. He'd never seen a severed body part before, and though it barely looked real beneath the ice, it still made him uncomfortable. Someone had come to Melville Island and not only lost a finger but decided to leave without it. How was that possible? Wendell shivered and tried to get his mind on other less morbid things. Like water.

Water is the world's greatest sculptor. It is patient, careful, persistent, and over countless years it is capable of carving the largest canyons out of the hardest rock. Who knew how long it took to carve the shapes that surrounded the five of them as they walked? It was like a bizarre art gallery, full of strange smooth sculptures that few had ever seen. Wendell reached into his pocket and fished out his digital camera. As he snapped numerous photos, he realized he was the only one doing so. Dr. Hanson barely slowed his pace to acknowledge the formations, and the sight of the towering rocks left Isaacs further terrorized.

"Do you have to take pictures? Can't we just keep going?"

"Dr. Hanson said to document everything."

"Then why didn't you take one of that finger?"

It was a fair point. Why hadn't he taken that photograph?

"It's not really part of the history of Melville Island, or the life that was here, is it?"

Isaacs shrugged, then spun around like an animal suddenly aware of a predator. Wendell stepped back.

"What is it?"

Isaacs took a deep breath, then exhaled slowly. "Nothing. I guess."

He wanted to say more, but despite Wendell's prodding Isaacs remained quiet.

They trudged along the ice, keeping their heads down as they followed Dr. Hanson. He had studied the maps for months and was certain that their best bet was to set up base camp about twenty-five miles in. From that point, they could radiate their survey outward and see what they might discover.

Wendell wondered, though, if it wouldn't have been better to remain nearer the shoreline where remnants of a water-dwelling dinosaur might be more evident. He kept his opinion private, not wanting to contradict a man capable of ending his career before it started. Which was why Wendell was both surprised and irritated when Dogan posed the same question. And even more so when he heard Dr. Hanson's response.

"Good question, Dogan. I like that you're thinking. It shows a real spark your fellow team could learn from. However, in this case you haven't thought things through. Don't forget that during the Mesozoic area we're most interested in the Earth had yet to fully cool. Melville Island was more tropical than it is now. The greatest concentration of vertebrates will likely be farther inland. It shouldn't take us more than a few more hours to get there."

The thought of traveling a few more hours made Wendell's body ache. The cold had already seeped through his insulated boots and the two layers of socks he wore inside them.

"Maybe we could stop and rest for a second? I don't know how much longer I can carry this gear." As Wendell spoke the words, his pack's weight doubled in tacit agreement.

"I suppose it couldn't hurt," Dr. Hanson said, and Wendell wasted no time slipping the burden off his shoulders. Immediately relieved, he then sat on the snow to give his tired feet a rest. Dr. Hanson, Isaacs, and Dogan all followed his lead. Only Gauthier remained standing, one hand on his belt, the other in his frozen beard. He looked across the horizon while the others used the moment to eat protein bars and contemplate what had led them to their seats at the top of the world.

It had been days, and over-familiarity combined with sheer exhaustion was enough to keep them quiet. No one spoke or glanced another's way. They simply kept their heads down and tried to recuperate before the next leg of the journey. Dr. Hanson's eyes were wide as he plotted their next steps. Isaacs experienced jitters, which continued to multiply as the group remained stationary. Dogan, however, was the opposite. With eyes closed and arms wrapped around his legs, he appeared to have fallen asleep. Until Gauthier delivered a swift kick to his ribs.

"What was—?"

The pilot shushed him quickly. Dogan, to Wendell's astonishment, complied.

"Did any of you see that?"

They all turned. Around them was the vast icy expanse, wind pushing clouds over the snow-encrusted tundra, eddies dancing across the rough terrain. But Wendell saw nothing different from what he'd already witnessed. A glance at the other men revealed the same confusion. Wendell looked at the towering Gauthier, waiting for the answer to the question before them, but the pilot was silent. He merely continued to stare. Isaacs could not bear it. "What? What do you see?"

"Shut up," Gauthier hissed, and Isaacs cowered, his breathing uneven. Dr. Hanson flashed an expression that was buried so quickly Wendell didn't have time to process it.

Gauthier raised his arm and pointed away from where they had been walking, off into the distant vastness that flanked them.

"I think something's been tracking us."

"What do you mean?"

"I mean I've been watching while you four were stumbling along, and I saw something—a shadow, keeping pace with us. It's been there ever since we left the runway."

"Where is it?"

"There. Do you see it? In the distance. It's not moving now. Just a shadow. Watching us."

Wendell squinted, but still saw nothing.

"It's likely a polar bear," Dr. Hanson said. "I've been warned they come to the island, looking for seal. No doubt he knows we're here."

"Should we be worried?" Isaacs asked.

"It's not going to come after us," Dogan said. Dr. Hanson was more hesitant.

"Well, I don't know if I'd go that far. But there's enough of us that it should keep its distance."

That failed to reassure Wendell. And if he wasn't reassured, then Isaacs—

"So you're saying a polar bear is following us, and we shouldn't be worried? Nothing to worry about at all?"

"It's okay, Isaacs. You'll be okay. Gauthier, tell them not to worry."

"Don't worry. It's moving now. It looks too small to be a polar bear anyway. Probably just a pack of wolves."

It wasn't long before they were moving again.

They successfully made it to the camp site without further report of being trailed. The lack did nothing to calm Isaac's nerves, but Dogan reverted to his old ways, insinuating himself between Dr. Hanson and Wendell any time they might have had a moment to speak. It was infuriating.

The five of them had been awake and traveling for well over twenty hours, and as far as Wendell could tell the sun had not moved an inch. The clouds, however, were not so bound, and he suspected their speed had as much to do with Hanson's decision to camp down as did the coordinates Dr. Lansing had provided him. The last thing Wendell wanted to do when they finally stopped walking was set up the tent, but Gauthier helped them all find the motivation through the promotion of fear.

"The way this wind is breaking? There are storms brewing ahead, somewhere beyond the ridges. The weather here is unpredictable. If we don't get cover and fast, we might not be around long enough for you four to start digging up bones. Get ready for what's coming."

"But what is coming?" Dogan asked. Gauthier laughed. "A storm, man. A storm."

In the time it took to tell them, thick smoke-like clouds had rolled across the clear sky, casting a long shadow across the top of the world. Somehow, from somewhere, the men found the energy to erect their shelter, and Wendell silently admitted it felt good to have Dogan as an ally for once.

The storm arrived as the last peg was hammered in place. The five of them huddled beneath the tarpaulin tent, one of the tall water-carved rocks acting as both anchor and partial shield from the winds. Inside the enclosed space their heat quickly escalated, but Gauthier warned them to keep their coats on in case the wind wrenched the tent from the ground.

Strangely, Isaacs was the most at peace during the ordeal. While Dogan and Wendell held down the edges of the tent, their knuckles white, Isaacs had his eyelids closed and head tilted back to rest on his shoulders. He sat cross-legged, his body moving with the slightest sway. Wendell thought he also heard him humming, but convinced himself it was only the wind bending around the sheltering rocks.

They stayed hunkered for hours, wind howling outside, pulling at the thin barrier of canvas standing between them. The sound of it rippling back and forth was a terrifying thunder, and even after hours enduring it, the noise did not become any less so. Each clap was an icy knife in Wendell's spine, and as he shook under the tremendous stress he used every ounce of will he had within him to maintain his rationality and tamp down his fear. Deep breaths, slow, long, continued until the knot inside his chest slackened. It was only when he felt he could look again at his fellow captives without screaming that he dared. Isaacs remained blissfully distant, his mind cracked, and he was simply gone from it to another place. Gauthier and Dr. Hanson spoke among themselves, planning and debating the next course of action, all at a volume that was drowned by the howls and ripples. Only Dogan noticed Wendell, and the scowl across his face suggested that whatever truce the circumstances had negotiated for them was fleeting at best. He stared directly at Wendell with a stubbly, twisted face and did not bother to look away when Wendell caught him, as though he wore his disgust with pride. Wendell took a breath to speak and tasted the most noxious air. Dogan shook his twisted face, but it was no use; the fetid odor filled their lungs. Wendell covered his nose and mouth with his gloved hand. Whatever it was, it was sickly and bitter and smelled not unlike dead fish.

Outside there was a long sorrowful howl that sounded so near their shelter that Wendell prayed desperately it was only the wind echoing between the stones.

Sleep did wonders for Wendell's demeanor, and when he emerged from the battered shelter a few hours later he stepped into a world canopied by a cloudless sky punctuated at the horizon by a single glowing orb. Gauthier was already awake, and Wendell found him prepping their equipment, beads of moisture frozen in his unkempt beard. He did not look pleased. Something was wrong.

It was only once outside the tent Wendell noticed it—something in the post-storm air, some excess of electricity, or maybe a remnant of the foul odor that stained his clothes. Whatever it was, it was troubling.

Dr. Hanson emerged a few minutes afterward with an eagerness to meet the glaciers head-on.

"You're up early. Good man! Why don't you hand me one of those coffees?"

Isaacs, too, joined them, and when the thick-set Dogan finally emerged from the tent, the look on his face upon seeing the rest of the team gathered made Wendell certain any ground gained the night before had been lost. Dogan was the same man he'd always been, and Wendell did his best to deal with it. He was frankly too tired to keep caring.

"After we've made our breakfast," Dr. Hanson said, blind to the turmoil of the students around him, "let's start our search for some ichthyosaur fossils. Right now, we are most concerned with locating those."

"Dr. Hanson?" Isaacs said.

"We should start at those ridges." Dogan pointed into the distance opposite, where a slightly elevated ring circled the land. "Water would have receded soonest from those areas, leaving the earliest and most complete fossils for us to find."

"Good thinking, Dogan. I applaud that."

"Doctor Hanson?" Isaacs repeated.

Dogan may have gotten the doctor's attention, but Wendell was not going to be outdone.

"Maybe, Doctor Hanson, we should use a grid pattern closer to where Doctor Lansing and his students made their discovery? I mean, from there."

Dogan shot Wendell a look, and Dr. Hanson laughed at them. "Both good ideas, men, but don't worry. I already have a plan. You see, based on my expectations, the fossil—"

"Doctor Hanson?" Hanson sighed.

"Please don't interrupt me, Isaacs."

"Doctor Hanson? Can you come look at this?" Isaacs was kneeling by the tent, staring into the ground.

Immediately, Wendell was certain it was another finger. Another pale white digit trapped beneath the ice. Or perhaps it was a whole hand. Something else lost for which there could be no reasonable explanation. Dogan approached, as did Gauthier, both alongside Dr. Hanson. Wendell remained where he was, worried about what they would find, though their faces suggested it wasn't anything as mortally frightening as a severed finger. But it was also clear no one knew if it was far worse. Wendell hesitated but approached Dr. Hanson, his heavy boots crunching the ice underfoot. When he reached the four men, any conversation between them had withered.

Something impossible was caught in the tangle of boot prints surrounding the tent: an additional set of tracks in the crushed and broken snow. They differed from the team's in size—they were smaller, hardly larger than a child's, and each long toe of the bare foot could clearly be traced.

"Is it possible some kind of animal made them?"

"No," Dr. Hanson said. "These are too close to hominid."

"They *can't* be, though. Can they?"

"I thought this island was deserted."

"More importantly, what was it doing standing here in front of our tent?"

"I don't like this," Isaacs said. For once, Wendell agreed with him. "Doctor Hanson, what's going on?"

"I wish I knew, Wendell. Gauthier, what do you think?" Gauthier looked at them over his thick beard. It was the first time Wendell had seen puzzlement in the pilot's eyes. Gauthier looked at each of them in turn as they waited for him to offer an explanation, but he had none to offer. Instead, he turned away with a furrowed brow.

"Where is everything?"

Wendell didn't initially understand what he meant, not until he walked into the center of the camp. He looked back and forth and into the distance, then pushed the insulated hood off his head.

"It's all gone. Everything."

It had happened while they slept. Someone or something had come into the camp and stolen all their food and most of their supplies.

Things became scrambled. The men spoke all at once, worried about what had happened and what it might mean. Wendell was no different, a manic desperation for answers taking hold. Dr. Hanson did his best to calm them all, but the red rims around his eyes made it clear he too was shaken.

"I don't understand it," he repeated. "There aren't supposed to be any visitors here beyond us."

"It looks as if you were wrong. There is someone here. Someone who's been following us."

It sounded crazy, and Wendell fought to keep from falling down that rabbit hole. Perversely, Dogan was the one Wendell looked to for strength, and only because he could imagine nothing worse than failing apart in front of him. Isaacs on the other hand suffered no such worries. He was nearly incapacitated by terror.

"We can't stay here. Didn't you guys hear it? Last night? That muffled creaking? And the crunch—I thought it was something else. I thought it had to be. It couldn't have been footsteps, but all I see on the ground are thousands of them, and all our stuff has vanished. We can't stay. We have to go. We have to go before it's too late."

"This expedition is a one-time event. It took all the grant money to send us here. If we don't bring back something, we will never return to Melville Island."

"Good," Isaacs said, his whole body shaking. "We shouldn't be here. There's something wrong."

Dr. Hanson scoffed, but Wendell wasn't certain he agreed. Dogan certainly seemed as though he didn't, but said nothing. After the journey they'd taken and what they'd seen, they had to trust Dr. Hanson knew what to do.

But what he did was turn to Gauthier for an answer, only to receive none. The pilot was more interested in sizing up Isaacs. When he finally spoke, it startled all of them. Isaacs almost screamed.

"The kid is right. We can't stay here. Even if we wanted to. Our supplies and rations are gone. We wouldn't last more than a few days."

Dr. Hanson shook his head. Wendell could see he was frustrated. Scared, tired, and frustrated.

"I told you: we can't go back. This is it. There's no time to spare, not even a few days. Not if we're to complete our tasks in the window. We have to stay here."

"Do we all need to be here, Doctor?" Dogan asked. His voice wavered with uncertainty.

Dr. Hanson hesitated a moment. "No," he said, "I expect not. At least, not all of us."

Dogan looked directly at Wendell. Wendell swallowed, outsmarted, and prepared himself for the inevitable. Instead, Dogan surprised him.

"Send Gauthier back to replenish our supplies while we stay here and work. It's only a few days. We can hold out that long, but we can't go on forever without food."

"Maybe Isaacs should join him," Wendell added, nodding when Dogan looked over. "He sounds on the verge of cracking, and for his sake as well as ours he should be off this rock if he does."

"Yes, we should go. Can we go? Can we?" Isaacs looked ready to swallow Gauthier. His bug-eyed face was slick and pallid, and Wendell wondered if Isaacs was too sick to travel. Then he wondered if it might be worse if he stayed.

Dr. Hanson did not seem entirely convinced. None of them did. None but Isaacs. Wendell had to admit, thinking about the strange footprints in the snow outside the tent, he wasn't sure if he'd rather be the one leaving.

"Maybe we should vote?" Dogan said.

"No point," Gauthier said. "I'm leaving. The kid can come if he wants."

Isaacs looked as if he were going to dance. Hanson nodded solemnly while Dogan said nothing. Wendell wasn't sure what he felt.

They split what little food they had left among them before Gauthier and

Isaacs loaded their packs and left. There were six energy bars, a bag of peanuts, and four flasks of water. The two men took only half a bar each—as little as they could to get them back to the landing strip while Wendell, Dogan, and Dr. Hanson kept the rest to help them last until the plane returned.

"I want you to get back here as soon as you can," Dr. Hanson said. "We can't afford to be down this many men for long."

"We'll be back as soon as we can," Gauthier said, then handed Dr. Hanson a small leather bag. "Take this. In case of emergency." Dr. Hanson looked in the bag and shook his head.

The two men waved at them as they started back—Isaacs nearly bouncing on the ice, while Gauthier's gait remained resolutely determined. They passed the tall, smooth rocks without trouble, and the crunch of their boots on the icy snow faded quickly once they were out of sight. The three remaining men stood in uncomfortable silence. Wendell worried they had made a grave mistake.

"I'm sure they'll be back before we know it." Dr. Hanson tried to sound upbeat and reassuring; Wendell wondered if he was as unconvinced as he sounded. "But in the interim, we have the equipment, and we're at the primary site. I know the situation is not as fortunate as we would have liked, but let's see how much we can get done before Gauthier gets back. We are here for another three days, so let's take the time to gather the information necessary to salvage this expedition."

The three of them trekked out from the base camp on Dr. Hanson's suggestion despite all they'd seen, right into the bleakness of Melville Island. Trapped, they needed something to occupy their minds, distract them from disturbing sights like the severed finger, like the worrying sea of bodies that had mysteriously surrounded them as they slept. The only thing the three could do was resume their search for the elusive evidence of ichthyosaurs in the Arctic Ocean. They spent what hours remained in the day scouting those locations Dr. Hanson highlighted, turning over rocks, chipping through ice and permafrost, doing their best without tools, a researcher, and a pilot. And with each hour that passed they discovered nothing, no sign of the ichthyosaurs they were certain had once swam there. Dr. Hanson grew increasingly quiet as he brimmed with frustration, and Wendell decided to stay out of his way until they finally retreated to the base camp. Dogan, however, was the braver man. Or more foolish.

"Doctor Hanson, I have to tell you, I'm concerned."

"Oh, are you? What could possibly concern you?" Dogan didn't hesitate.

"I'm concerned for our safety. I'm concerned our emergency transportation has left, that we're undermanned, and that neither Wendell nor I truly have any idea where we are. We're just following you blindly. I'm worried about our safety."

"Well, don't be, Dogan. Let us return to the base camp. We will reassess our plans there. Perhaps you and Wendell can help determine our next course of action. There is something on Melville Island worth finding no matter what the cost. I intend to stay until we do."

But when they finally reached the base camp they discovered what that cost was. It had vanished. Along with it, any trace of their presence, including their footprints. It was as though they had never been there.

"Are you sure this is the right place?"

"Of course I'm certain. Don't you recognize the shape of rocks? Or the nook we used for shelter? This is most certainly the right place."

The three stood watching the snow for a few minutes, as though the sheer force of their collective will would make the camp re-materialize, and when that too failed to yield results Dogan sat down on the snow, spent, a heavy-browed doll whose strings had been cut.

"Maybe we should go back to the landing strip," Wendell suggested. "Gauthier and Isaacs may not have left yet."

Dr. Hanson shook his head. "We've barely begun, we can't leave."

"But, Doctor Hanson, our camp—look around us. We can't stay here. Whatever it is that's—"

"Enough!" Dogan said, struggling to his feet with a concerning wobble. "I'm not waiting to be hunted by whatever is out there. At least at the landing strip, we'll be ready to leave once Gauthier gets back. I don't give a shit about ichthyosaurs or Mesozoic migration patterns or just when the hell Melville Island formed. All I want right now is to get off this iceberg and back to civilization where it's safe. And Wendell, I'm betting you feel exactly the same. So, are you coming or not?"

Wendell liked neither solution. Dogan was right: staying seemed like idiocy—something was watching them, stealing from them, and had left them for dead. And yet, his solution made no sense. How did he know whatever was following them wouldn't track them to the landing strip?

How did he know when or even if Gauthier would be back to rescue them? Wendell wasn't convinced, but to blindly ignore what he had seen so far and continue to explore Melville Island with the same willful ignorance as Dr. Hanson seemed ludicrous.

"All I know is that whatever we do, we can't stay here. We need to keep moving."

"I don't think the two of you understand the importance of what we are doing here, or the costs involved. This is not simply a trip to the shopping mall. This is not something easily aborted. We must stay and complete our expedition. We have found nothing so far to justify the cost, and without that we will never be granted the opportunity to return. My tenure at the university will shield me from losing my position, but likely I'll never complete my work. Isaacs, he'll get by on his father's wealth, but the two of you? Your careers will be irrevocably damaged. Your graduate studies will have become a waste. This is the moment. This is the place where you both have to decide your respective futures. I already know what needs to be done. I implore you both to stay with me and discover those secrets hidden long before man's eyes could witness them. Stay with me and discover the true history of the world."

But Dogan wouldn't. And Wendell reluctantly concurred.

The three men split what remained of the food and set a timeline for Dr. Hanson's research. They agreed that he would keep trying to contact Gauthier via the satellite phone the pilot had given him, and when he got through he would let Gauthier know that both Dogan and Wendell had returned to the landing strip, and what his own coordinates were so the party could return to meet him. If before then anything should occur that might suggest Dr. Hanson was still being followed, he would immediately set out for the landing strip and join the two men there. Wendell didn't like the idea of leaving him alone, especially with little more than a half an energy bar and overburdened with excavation equipment, but there was no choice. Hanson insisted on completing the expedition, no matter what the cost.

Dogan, on the other hand, was not so committed. He and Wendell took the rest of the food and began their long hike back. Clearly, it wasn't lost on Dogan that he had chosen to retreat with his worst enemy; Wendell certainly felt no better about it.

The trek across Melville Island was as quiet as it had been the first time, the two men walking single file over the uneven terrain. But Wendell's dread made the journey much worse. They had been numbered five before, not two, and they hadn't carried the suspicion they were being stalked by a predator. On the occasions the two men stopped to rest, they didn't speak, sharing an overwhelming fear of what was happening. Wendell hoped if they remained silent the entire trip would simply be a hazy dream, one from which he'd soon awake. But he didn't.

His stomach rumbled after the second hour of their journey, and the sourness on his tongue arrived after the fourth. His head ached dully, letting him know his body was winding down. Dogan, too, seemed to be having trouble concentrating on the direction they were supposed to go, and more than once he stopped to ask if Wendell wanted to take the lead while he plotted their next steps.

They took a rest after a few hours to eat a portion of their reserves. It seemed so little once Wendell saw it through the eyes of hunger, and it took immense willpower to keep from swallowing it all. He was exhausted, and Dogan looked no different, his eyes rimmed with dark circles against pale skin. His voice, too, was throated.

"Who would have thought it would be you and me, trying to keep it together?"

Wendell wanted to laugh, but just wheezed air.

"I don't think anyone would believe it if we told them."

"I'm not sure I believe it myself."

And like that, things had changed between them. Wendell didn't know how long it would last, or if it would survive their return to civilization, but at that moment they were bonded, and Wendell would have done anything to keep Dogan at his side. It was unclear how long they sat, silently building their strength for the journey ahead, but their stupor was broken by an unsettling howl. Dogan and Wendell straightened, eyes wide and searching the landscape in all directions for its source.

"There!" Dogan shouted, and went off running toward the sound, his feet sinking into snow as he dashed, his limbs flailing for balance. Wendell followed blindly in Dogan's footsteps, hand pressed against his pack to ensure nothing was spilled. When he finally caught up, both he and Dogan were panting, barely able speak.

"What did you see?" Dogan pointed.

There was nothing there, but that wasn't what caused Wendell to shiver uncontrollably. It was instead what had been there, and the evidence it left in the crusted snow—a flurry of footprints, none larger than a barefooted child's. They proceeded in a line, leading back in the same direction from which Wendell and Dogan had come, as though whoever or whatever had made them had been keeping a steady watch on the two students since they left Dr. Hanson. It was no longer possible to avoid the truth: something was following them, something that wasn't a wolf or polar bear or any other northern predator. It was something else, and they knew absolutely nothing about it.

"What are we going to do?" Wendell asked. Dogan's eyes teared from the cold.

"What else can we do? We get the hell out of here right now." They didn't stop until they reached the landing strip, both afraid of what might happen if they rested too long. By Wendell's watch it was well past midnight, though the frozen sunlight still shone, lighting their way. When they arrived, they found the strip vacant. No plane, no sign of life. Just a long stretch of iced snow and an ocean off in the distance. Wendell couldn't explain why the discovery was crushing—Gauthier and Isaacs had over a day's head start, and Wendell knew they wouldn't have waited. And yet it was devastating. He and Dogan had walked so far . . .

"On the bright side," Dogan said, "we know they found their way back. That means they'll be returning soon. It's better than finding them stranded like us."

"True, true."

Wendell looked back at the snow and ice they had walked across. There were shadows moving out in the nooks and recesses, but none that seemed unusual. Wendell wondered what an unusual shadow would even look like, and whether he was in any condition to find out.

"We need cover. Who knows how long we'll be waiting." There was a depression in an ice drift that shielded them from the brunt of the wind and snow. Their combined body heat warmed the air enough to diminish the chill under their jackets, and Wendell was able to peel back the farthest fringes of his hood so he might speak to Dogan without shouting. It had been so long since their last snack, simply raising his voice aggravated his headache.

"Do you think Doctor Hanson is okay?"

"If anyone would be, I'd bet on him. That old man is resilient."

"I'm not sure we should have left him, though."

"He wanted us to."

"I know, I know. I just feel it was a mistake."

Wendell closed his eyes to rest them. The brightness of the snow after being under a hood for so long was blinding. It would take some time to adjust.

"Did you get a good look at it?" Dogan asked.

"At what? The snow?"

"No, not the snow, you idiot. What was following us in the snow. What left those footprints."

"I don't want to talk about it." He didn't even want to *think* about it. Dogan wouldn't be dissuaded.

"I'm sure I was close to it, but I barely saw anything more than a blur."

"Maybe you were seeing things. Maybe your hunger—"

"Did you, or didn't you, see those footprints in the snow?"

"I—"

"Do you think I put them there?"

"No, I—"

"Did you put them there?"

"How would I—?"

"Well, they got there somehow. Just like they got inside our camp. It wasn't an accident. It was something, watching us."

Wendell took off his mitten glove and rubbed the side of his face. It made him feel better, and slightly more present. "I don't know, Dogan. It so hard to think. I'm tired and hungry and terrified of what's out there and of never getting back home. My brain feels like mush."

"How much food do you have?"

He opened his pockets and turned out what was left. An eighth of a power bar, a handful of nuts. His water supply was okay, but only because he and Dogan had been filling their flasks with snow to melt.

Dogan assessed the situation.

"Yeah, I don't have much more than that, either."

"Are you worried?"

"About being here?" He frowned. "No. I'm sure Gauthier will be back."

"How can you be so sure?"

He shrugged.

"What else do I have to do?"


Wendell eventually fell asleep. He and Dogan had huddled close to conserve heat, and when they both ran out of energy to talk Wendell's eyes flickered one too many times. There was the sound of the ocean, and the wind rushing past, and then nothing until Dogan shook him awake.

"Look."

The snow had accumulated since they took shelter, and the footprints they had made were buried, but Wendell could still see the wedge cut into the corridor down which they'd come, and in the distance a solitary figure staggering toward them.

"Is that Doctor Hanson?" Wendell worried he was suffering from a starved hallucination.

"I don't know."

"Is it what's been following us?"

Dogan didn't respond.

Whether from hunger or cold or exhaustion, Wendell's eyes teared as he watched the limping figure. His muscles ached, trying to tense in anticipation but too exhausted to do so. The approaching shape resolved itself first for Dogan, who made an audible noise a moment before Wendell realized what—or rather whom—he was seeing. Isaacs stumbled forward, and a few steps before meeting Dogan and Wendell he crumpled and dropped to his knees, then collapsed face-first into the frozen snow.

They scrambled to him as quickly as their tired bodies could manage. Isaacs was nearly lifeless, his left leg bent at an angle that suggested it was broken, but leaning close Wendell could hear his shallow breathing. They wasted no time dragging Isaacs back to their shielded depression, and while Wendell did his best to splint the leg, Dogan brushed the remaining snow from Isaacs's face and pulled up his hood to help protect him.

"What do you think happened?" Dogan quietly asked.

"What do you mean?"

"He looks strange. What's up with his *eyes*?"

Wendell shook his head.

"I'm more concerned about what he is doing on Melville Island at all."

Isaacs breathed heavily as he lay unconscious. They shook him and called his name, worried about what had happened, but neither Dogan nor Wendell understood what he mumbled. There was something about a plane, which did not ease Wendell's worry.

When they were finally able to rouse him, Isaacs screamed. The piercing sound overloaded Dogan's starved brain and he lashed out, striking Isaacs in the face. Then Wendell was between them, urging both to calm down. Isaacs shook, pulled the straps of his hood tighter, hid his face. All that was left were his large watery eyes.

"Isaacs, it's okay. You're okay. I'm sorry I hit you, but you're safe. Do you understand?"

He was a trapped animal, shivering uncontrollably.

"Do you understand?"

Isaacs nodded.

"What happened?" Wendell asked. "Why are you here? Where's Gauthier?"

Isaacs continued to rock, hiding behind his drawn hood.

"It's okay, Isaacs. Just tell us what happened."

"Gauthier and I made it back here to the plane," he said. Even in his semi-consciousness, he sounded terrified. "The wings were iced, he said, and we couldn't take off. He told me to go outside with a bottle of propylene glycol and spray them down after he started the plane. He said the heat and the solution would melt everything. While I was doing that the wind was blowing like crazy. I thought I heard yelling, but I wasn't sure. Then out of nowhere the plane was shaking. I lost my balance, and the plane jerked and started to move. I was falling and tried to grab hold of something, but the wing was slick and I was already rolling off it. I don't remember anything after that."

Wendell tried to make sense of Isaacs's story, but couldn't wrap his mind around it. He was exhausted, hunger and the elements taking their toll, and could barely think. He looked to Dogan, who appeared just as troubled.

"Did Gauthier say anything?" Dogan asked.

He was worsening, and there was nothing Dogan or Wendell could do. Already his lips had turned a bizarre shade of red, and his eyes could not focus. He coughed violently and spit pink into the snow. Then he lay his head down. "I can't. I—I don't want to die."

Wendell put his hand on Isaacs's shoulder.

"You aren't going to die here. We won't let you."

Isaacs coughed again.

Dogan and Wendell looked at each other. Dogan shook his head.

"We have to find Doctor Hanson. We need that satellite phone."

"We can't leave Isaacs," Wendell said. "He won't last without our help. And how are we supposed to find Doctor Hanson? We'll be dead before we do. We have no idea where he is. I think we're better off waiting right here."

They spent the next few hours trying to sleep in their makeshift shelter, the three men huddled to conserve warmth. While Dogan and Isaacs slept, the wind had become a gale, and it again brought with it the overpowering stench of fish and sea, so thick Wendell could hardly keep from gagging. He tucked his face into his coat as best he could to survive it.

The men did not sleep for long, but it was long enough that when they awoke they found Isaacs had crawled away from the safety of the depression and frozen to death. It made no sense, but nothing did any longer. The arctic cold of Melville Island had upended everything. Dogan was upset and wanted to drag Isaacs back, close enough to protect his body should anything come looking for it, but he didn't have the strength left. Neither of them did. It was then they agreed, for the sake of the fallen Isaacs, that their hunger had become too severe. But when they turned out their pockets, they found them empty. Isaacs, too, had been stripped of all food and supplies. There was nothing left to sustain them. Dogan cried, certain he'd eaten all their shares unwittingly in a somnambulistic frenzy, but Wendell wasn't convinced. It didn't explain the hazy footprints that encircled them.

Dogan and Wendell paced in the subzero weather, trudging out a trail while trying to keep themselves warm. Eventually, even the effort of pacing proved beyond Dogan, and he stumbled and toppled to the ground. Wendell knelt down but didn't have strength to help. All he could do was stay nearby.

"I can't keep going," Dogan said. "I can't."

"We have to," Wendell said.

But Wendell knew they would never make it. They started talking then to keep themselves awake and alert, to remind each other not to give up. They talked about how they came to be under Dr. Hanson. They talked about Isaacs, about whether he had crawled away on purpose, or if it was due to some horrible mistake. They talked about Gauthier and what had happened to him. But mostly they talked about themselves, their childhoods, their lives before meeting. They talked until they couldn't, until Dogan was delirious and stopped making sense. Wendell tried to rouse him, to keep him moving, but he couldn't. He didn't have the energy. So tired, he could barely keep his eyes open. They fluttered more and more until they stopped completely. Before they did, the last thing Wendell saw was something in the distance, crouching. Watching them. And then it moved.

A slap that tore off his face woke him from death. He opened his stinging eyes, and only his lethargic malnourishment prevented him from screaming. The shrunken man's face hung inches from his own. It was dark brown, as though deeply tanned, with lips gray to the point of blue. He did not tremble, though he was dressed in nothing more than a cloth that covered his sex, and he was perilously thin. What startled Wendell most, however, was his eyes. They were larger than any Wendell had ever seen, and spaced so far apart they threatened to slide off his skull. He couldn't have been more than four feet tall. Wendell was certain it wasn't a dream, but if it were it was the worst dream he'd ever suffered. He tried to moisten his mouth to get his tongue working, and when he did all he could hazily croak was, "Dogan?"

The half-man grunted, then hobbled away. Wendell wanted to pull himself up, but discovered he had been swaddled with furs. He could turn his head, but only with great difficulty, and only enough to see Dogan similarly wrapped a few meters away. Dogan had two more of the dark half-men at his head, and they were trying to feed him though he was still unconscious. Isaacs lay face down a few feet further in the snow, a fourth shrunken man holding his lifeless arm to his gray lips and sniffing. Wendell nodded at no one in particular, and as the world grew dark once more he felt he was being dragged. In his delirium, the dragging went on and on forever.

Something was wriggling in his mouth, trying to crawl down his throat. Wendell struggled awake, gagging, and managed to spit it out. A piece of unrecognizable yellow meat curled on the ice, while a short distance away those small dark half-men from his nightmare danced, their bare feet crunching on the snow. There was no longer anything binding his limbs but weakness, and he'd been left propped up next to Dogan. Both of them were awake and shaking.

Only unrecognizable pieces remained of poor Isaacs.

"I don't know what's going on, Wendell. I don't know where we are, but look." Dogan nodded his head across the ice and Wendell saw Dr. Hanson. He lay face down in the snow, unmoving, his pack beside him and torn open, equipment scattered. Wendell squinted to see if the satellite phone was still there, and in his concentration missed what Dogan was saying.

"Do you see it?" Dogan repeated.

"I think so. It's right by his hand."

"No, you idiot. Do you see *it*?"

Wendell looked up again, past Dr. Hanson and at the group of five near-naked men dancing before a shorn wall of ice. It stretched out further than the end of his sight in either direction; the break no doubt formed when tectonic plates shifted the glacier. What was uncovered was so impossible Wendell would have thought his mind had cracked had Dogan not witnessed it first.

There was a monstrous creature encased halfway in the solid ice. It had large unlidded eyes, milky white; its mouth wide and round, its scaled flesh reflecting light dully. Where its neck might have been was a ring of purplish pustules, circling the fusion of its ichthyic skull to its tendonous body. Chunked squid limbs lay outstretched, uncontrollable in its death. The air was again dominated by the overpowering odor of the sea. The shrunken men before it treated it as a god, and yet it was clear the five could not have been the ones to uncover it—with the sharpened rocks they used as tools it would have taken generations to carve that deep and that much. They peeled strips of its flesh away and ate them raw, and when they looked back at Dogan and Wendell it was suddenly evident why their features had transformed over time, their eyes grown wider, jaws shorter, skin rougher. Their fish faces stared at Wendell, expectantly. It was true he was hungry beyond imagination, but he was not so hungry that he might eat what they presented.

The sour taste and sensation of what they had previously tried to feed him returned, and he looked down. The morsel continued to writhe slowly in the snow.

"Did you—did they make you eat any?" Wendell asked, then realized

Dogan had turned the palest shade. They had. Wendell feared for his life, and his sanity.

"How do I look?" Dogan managed through his chattering teeth, and Wendell lied and told him he was fine. Was Wendell imagining the flesh had already changed him, already started prying his eyes apart? Was it even possible after so small a meal? But he realized with horror that he didn't know how much Dogan had willingly eaten, nor if either of them had been force-fed in their delirium.

"Can you move?" Wendell asked, fleetingly energized by his fear. "We need to get that phone. We need to call for help."

"How? Even if we manage to get it, we'll never escape with it. We have no idea where we are. We might not even be on Melville Island anymore."

"We have to try. Maybe Gauthier has already come back and is waiting for us at the landing strip. What else can we do? End up like Doctor Hanson and bleed out in the snow? Or worse, like Isaacs, torn to pieces?"

"We should escape."

"And what then?" Wendell whispered. "Die in the snow, waiting for them to find us?"

Dogan paled.

"Did you—did you see that?"

Wendell looked up. The five dark men sat mesmerized before their dead idol.

"It moved," Dogan said. "Did you see it move?"

"It can't move. Whatever that thing is, it's dead."

"It's not dead—look, it moved again."

Wendell looked closer at Dogan's face and saw the swelling and the subtle distortion. There was no longer time to gather strength. Whatever they fed him, Dogan had eaten more than he thought. It was transforming him. Wendell did not want to suffer the same fate.

"Stay here," he said, though when he looked over he wasn't certain he'd been heard. Dogan appeared fascinated by what was trapped in the ice.

Wendell lowered himself onto his stomach and crawled toward Dr. Hanson, keeping an eye on the gathering of disciples ahead. He moved elbow-to-knee as slowly as he dared, not willing to risk being seen. The half-men were feral, and as smart as they were, they were still animals, waiting to attack anything that moved. Wendell had only one chance to get the satellite phone and figure out a way of escaping from the nightmare he and Dogan found themselves in. His hunger had not abated, but enough strength had returned that he was able to make it to Dr. Hanson's body in under ten minutes.

The tribe of half-men had not moved from around their dead idol. They bounced on their haunches, made noises like wild animals, followed imaginary movement before them with precision. What was strange, however, was that each reacted differently to what it saw, as though they did not share the same sight. One stood while another howled, the rest looking in different directions. Wendell couldn't make sense of it, and reminded himself not to try. He had to focus on that satellite phone and getting back.

He searched the body, doing his best to forget who it had been. Dr. Hanson's face had been removed—the pale flesh frozen, tiny blood icicles reaching from the pulpy mess to the ground. Wendell turned to keep from panicking and checked the pockets of Hanson's coat and everywhere he could reach for the satellite phone. But it wasn't there. Wendell rolled on his side and tried unsuccessfully to flag Dogan for help. Dogan was staring straight ahead at the impossible giant embedded in the ice, eyes open wide and spread far apart.

Dr. Hanson's pack was ripped open in the blood-soaked snow, the items within trapped in sticky ice. Wendell heard a loud creak and froze. In his mind's eye he saw himself spotted, then swarmed by ugly bodies and ripped limb from limb. But when he raised his head he found nothing had changed. The five men remained bent in supplication. Almost by accident Wendell spotted the leather pouch Gauthier had given Dr. Hanson pinned beneath the doctor's torso. Wendell managed to pry it free of the ice, then put it into his own pocket and gently eased his way back the distance to Dogan. Or what was left of Dogan.

"Come on. Let's go," Wendell whispered, but Dogan didn't respond. Wendell grabbed his wrist and tried yanking, but Dogan had become a dead-weight, staring beatifically ahead, his face transformed. Mouth agape, eyes spread apart, staring at the dead thing as though it were alive, Dogan was unblinking as tears streamed down his sweating face. Dogan, Wendell's enemy, Wendell's friend, was gone.

There would be time for grief later. Wendell reached over and put his hand on Dogan's shoulder. "Stay strong. I'll be back as soon as I can with help." Then he attempted to stand and discovered he wasn't able to do so. His legs had given up for good, buckling as Wendell put weight on them. He tried again and again, desperate to escape before it was too late, but he couldn't get up. After a few minutes, Wendell felt the sensation in his hands going, too, his control slipping away. Everything he saw took on a hazy glow, the edges of his vision crystalizing. The sky jittered, as did the snow.

Dogan wasn't the only one who'd had his unconscious hunger overfed with flesh. It was no wonder they had been left unbound at the edge of the camp and ignored. The creatures had no worry. All the damage had long been done. They simply needed to wait.

Wendell scrambled the small leather bag he had taken from Dr. Hanson's body out of his pocket. He prayed the satellite phone would be unharmed, that Gauthier had already returned and was waiting for them. If Wendell could only call him, it might not be too late for rescue. He could still escape the horrible things he was witnessing. That creature in the ice—Wendell thought he saw it move, thought he saw one of its giant milky eyes blink, even though so much of its flesh had already been stripped. It blinked, and the coils that sprouted free from the ice twitched and rolled, and a scream built inside him. But when it escaped it wasn't a scream at all but laughter. Laughter and joy. That terrified Wendell further, the joy, because it finally turned the five beasts his way. They rolled onto their haunches, staring at Wendell and his catatonic friend.

Wendell took off his glove and reached into the bag slowly to remove the phone, but what he found there was nothing of the sort. It was another kind of escape, the one thing a man like Gauthier would hand over when he was suggesting that someone protect himself. From out of the leather bag Wendell withdrew a handgun, and even in the cold wind he could smell the oiled metal.

Those five men looking agitated and more bestial than ever before. They snarled, while behind them a giant that Wendell refused to believe was alive illuminated like the sun pinned above. It filled the horizon with streaks of light, tendrils dancing from the old one's gargantuan head. It looked at the five half-men radiating in the glow. It looked at Dogan, kneeling and waiting for it to speak to him. Then it looked at Wendell and all Wendell's hunger was satiated; he was at one with everything.

But he knew it was a lie. It was the end of things, no matter what the disembodied voices told him. The five shrunken men approaching him stealthily on all fours would not return him to civilization, would not return him to health. Dogan and he would be something more to them—sustenance in the cold harshness of the Arctic, pieces of flesh chewed and swallowed, digits shorn until they rained on the snow. These things were much like Wendell, in a way. Much like everyone. They struggled to unearth what they worshipped most, something from a world long ago gone, and if remembered, then only barely and as a fantasy. But it was far more real than Wendell had ever wished.

Those subhuman things were closing in, and there was little else Wendell could do but surrender to them, let them take him away.

Or he could use Gauthier's gun.

He lifted the weapon and squeezed the trigger. The half-men scattered, but not before he put two of them down. The alien's appendages flailed madly, and waves of emotion and nausea washed over Wendell. He couldn't stand, but was eventually able to hit the remaining three as they scrambled for cover. It took no time at all for him to be the last man alive, surrounded by the blood and gore of everyone he knew. Everyone but the mesmerized Dogan.

It was too late for either of them. Even with the half-men dead, Wendell could feel the draw of the flickering creature in the ice, and knew he would be unable to resist much longer. In an act of charity and compassion, he raised the gun to Dogan's temple and squeezed the trigger. There was a bright flash, and a report that continued to echo over the landscape longer than in his ears. Dogan crumpled, the side of his head vaporized, his misery tangible in the air.

But it was not enough. That thing in the ice, it needed him, needed somebody's worship on which to feed, and as long as Wendell was alive it would not die.

Wendell put the gun against his own head, the hot barrel searing his flesh, but he could do nothing else. His fingers would not move, locked into place from fear or exhaustion or self-preservation. Or whatever it was that had been fed to him, pulling the flesh on his face tighter. Somehow the handgun fell from his weakened grasp, dropping onto the icy snow and sinking. He reached to reclaim it and toppled forward, collapsing in a heap that left him staring into those giant old milky eyes.

Wendell didn't know how long he lay in the snow. He was no longer cold, was no longer hungry. He felt safe, as though he might sleep forever. The old one in the ice spoke to him, telling him things about the island's eonic history, and he listened and watched and waited. Existence moved so slowly Wendell saw the sun finally creep across the sky. No one came for him. No one came to interrupt his communion with the dead god. All he had was what was forever in its milky white stare, while it ate the flesh and muscle and sinew of his body, transforming him into the first of its new earthly congregation.

*This is no common case—it is a madness out of time and a horror from beyond the spheres which no police or lawyers or courts or alienists could ever fathom or grapple with.*

*The Case of Charles Dexter Ward · H. P. Lovecraft (1941)*

## • THE WRECK OF THE *CHARLES DEXTER WARD* •
### Elizabeth Bear & Sarah Monette

### Part One

Six weeks into her involuntary tenure on Faraday Station, Cynthia Feuerwerker needed a job. She could no longer afford to be choosy about it, either; her oxygen tax was due, and you didn't have to be a medical doctor to understand the difficulties inherent in trying to breathe vacuum.

You didn't have to be, but Cynthia was one. Or had been, until the allegations of malpractice and unlicensed experimentation began to catch up with her. As they had done, here at Faraday, six weeks ago. She supposed she was lucky that the crew of the boojum-ship *Richard Trevithick* had decided to put her off here, rather than just feeding her to their vessel— but she was having a hard time feeling the gratitude. For one thing, her medical skills had saved both the ship and several members of his crew in the wake of a pirate attack. For another, they'd confiscated her medical supplies before dumping her, and made sure the whole of the station knew the charges against her.

Which was a death sentence too, and a slower one than going down the throat of a boojum along with the rest of the trash.

So it was cold desperation that had driven Cynthia here, to the sharp side of this steel desk in a rented station office, staring into the face of a bald old Arkhamer whose jowls quivered with every word he spoke. His skin was so dark she could just about make out the patterns of tattoos against the pigment, black on black-brown.

"Your past doesn't bother me, Doctor Feuerwerker," he said. His sleeves were too short for his arms, so five centimeters of fleshy wrist protruded when he gestured. "I'll be very plain with you. We have need of your skills, and there is no guarantee any of us will be returning from the task we need them for."

Cynthia folded her hands over her knee. She had dropped a few credits on a public shower and a paper suit before the interview, but anybody could look at her haggard face and the bruises on her elbows and tell she'd been sleeping in maintenance corridors.

"You mentioned this was a salvage mission. I understand there may be competition. Pirates. Other dangers."

"No to mention the social danger of taking up with an Arkhamer vessel."

"If I stay here, I face the social danger of an airlock. I am a good doctor, Professor Wandrei. I wasn't stripped of my license for any harm to a patient."

"No-oo," he agreed, drawing it out. She knew he must have her C.V. in his heads-up display. "But rather for seeking after forbidden knowledge."

She shrugged and gestured around the rented office. "Galileo and Derleth and Chen sought forbidden knowledge, too. That got us this far." Onto a creaky, leaky, Saturn-orbit station that stank of ammonia despite exterminators working double shifts to keep the toves down. She watched his eyes and decided to take a risk. "An Arkhamer Professor ought to be sympathetic to that."

Wandrei's lips were probably lush once, but years and exposure to the radiation that pierced inadequately shielded steelships had left them lined and dry. Despite that, and the jowls, and the droop of his eyelids, his homely face could still rearrange itself beautifully around a smile.

Cynthia waited long enough to be sure he wouldn't speak before adding, "You know I don't have any equipment."

"We have some supplies. And the vessel we're going to salvage is an ambulance ship, the *Charles Dexter Ward*. You should be able to procure everything you need aboard it. In my position as a senior officer of the *Jarmulowicz Astronomica*, I am prepared to offer you a full share of the realizations from the salvage expedition, as well as first claim on any medical goods or technology."

Suspicion tickled Cynthia's neck. "What else do you expect to find aboard an ambulance, Professor?"

"Data," he said. "Research. The *Jarmulowicz Astronomica* is an archive ship."

Next dicey question: "What happened to your ship's surgeon?"

"Aneurysm," he said. "She was terribly young, but it took her so fast—there was nothing anyone could do. She'd just risen from apprentice, and hadn't yet taken one of her own. We'll get another from a sister ship eventually—but there's not another Arkhamer vessel at Faraday now, or within three days' travel, and we'll lose the salvage if we don't act immediately."

"How many shares in total?" A full share sounded good—until you found out the salvage rights were divided ten thousand ways.

"A full share is one percent," he said.

No self-discipline in space could have kept Cynthia from rocking back in her chair—and self-discipline had never been her strong point. It was too much. This was a trap.

Even just one percent of the scrap rights of a ship like that would be enough to live on frugally for the rest of her days. With her pick of drugs and equipment—

This was a trap.

And a chance to practice medicine again. A chance to read the medical files of an Arkhamer archive ship.

She had thirteen hours to find a better offer, by the letter of the law. Then it was the Big Nothing, the breathsucker, and her eyes freezing in their tears. And there wasn't a better offer, or she wouldn't have been here in the first place.

"I'll come."

Wandrei gave her another of his beatific smiles. He slid a tablet across the rented desk. Cynthia pressed her thumb against it. A prick and a buzz, and her blood and print sealed the contract. "Get your things. You can meet us at Dock Six in thirty minutes."

"I'll come now," she said.

"Oh," he said. "One more thing—"

That creak as he stood was the spring of the trap's jaw slamming shut. Cynthia had heard the like before. She sat and waited, prim and stiff.

"The *Charles Dexter Ward*?"

She nodded.

"It was a liveship." He might have interpreted her silence as misunderstanding. "A boojum, I mean."

"An ambulance ship *and* a liveship? We're all going to die," Cynthia said.

Wandrei smiled, standing, light on his feet in the partial gravity. "Everybody dies," he said. "Better to die in knowledge than in ignorance."

The sleek busy tug *Veronica Lodge* hauled the cumbersome, centuries-accreted monstrosity that was the *Jarmulowicz Astronomica* out of Saturn's gravity well. Cynthia stood at one of the Arkhamer ship's tiny fish-eye observation ports watching the vast misty curve of the pink-gray world beneath, hazy and serene, turning in the shadows of her moons and rings. Another steelship was putting off from Faraday Station simultaneously. She was much smaller and newer and cleaner than the *Jarmulowicz Astronomica,* which in turn was dwarfed by the boojums who flashed bioluminescent messages at each other around Saturn's moons. The steelship looked like it was headed in-system, and for a moment, Cynthia wished she were on board, even knowing what would be waiting for her. The *Richard Trevithick* had not been her first disaster.

She could not say, though, that she had been lured on board the *Jarmulowicz Astronomica* under false pretenses. The ship's crew of scholars and their families badly needed a doctor. Uncharitably, Cynthia suspected that they needed specifically a non-Arkhamer doctor, who would keep her mind on her patients.

The lost doctor—Martha Patterson Snead had been her name, for she had come to the *Jarmulowicz Astronomica* from the *Snead Mathematica*—might have been a genius, but as the *Jarmulowicz Astronomica* said goodbye to the *Veronica Lodge* and started on her stately way toward the *Charles Dexter Ward,* Cynthia found herself treating a great number of chronic vitamin deficiencies and other things that a non-genius but conscientious doctor should have been able to keep on top of.

Cynthia's patients were very polite and very grateful, but she couldn't help being aware that they would have preferred a genius who let them die of scurvy.

Other than nutritional deficiencies, the various cancers of space, and prenatal care, the most common reason for Cynthia to see patients were the minor emergencies and industrial accidents inevitably suffered in lives spent aboard a geriatric steelship requiring constant maintenance and repair. She treated smashed fingers, sprained wrists, and quite a few minor decompression injuries. She was splinting the ankle of a steamfitter's apprentice and undergraduate gas-giant meteorologist—many Arkhamers seemed to have two roles, one relating to ship's maintenance and one relating to academic research—when the young man frowned at her and said, "You aren't what I expected."

She'd forgotten his name. She glanced at the chart; he was Jaime MacReady Burlingame, traded from the *Burlingame Astrophysica Terce.* He had about twenty Terran years and a shock of orange hair that would not lie down, nor observe anything resembling a part. "Because I'm not an Arkhamer?" she asked, probing the wrist joint to be sure it really was a sprain and not a cracked bone.

"Everybody knows you're not one of us." He twitched slightly.

She held him steady, and noted the place. But when she glanced at his face, she realized his distress was over having said something more revealing than he intended. She said, "Some people aren't pleased about it?"

He looked away. She reached for the inflatable splint, hands gentle, and did not push. People told doctors things, if the doctors had the sense to keep quiet.

His pale, spotted fingers curled and uncurled. Finally, he answered, "Wandrei got in some trouble with the Faculty Senate, I hear. My advisor says Wandrei was high-handed, and he's lucky he has tenure."

Cynthia kept her head down, eyes on her work. Jaime sighed as she fitted the splint and its numbing, cooling agents began to take effect. "That should help bring the inflammation down," she told him. But as Jaime thanked her and left, she wondered if she ought to be grateful to Wandrei or if she ought to consider him her patron.

But she wasn't grateful—he had taken advantage of her desperation, which was not a matter for gratitude even if it had saved her life. And the Arkhamers didn't seem to think in terms of patronage and clients. They talked about apprentices and advisors, and nobody expected Cynthia to be Wandrei's apprentice.

She also noticed, as the days drew out into weeks, that nobody was approaching her about taking an apprentice of her own. She was just as glad, for she had no illusions about her own abilities as a teacher, and no idea how one person could go about imparting a medical school education from the ground up, but it made her feel acutely isolated—on a ship that was home to several hundred people—and she lay in her hammock during her sleep shift and worried about what would happen to the shy, solemn Arkhamer children when she was no longer on board. At other times, she reminded herself that the *Jarmulowicz Astronomica* was part of a network of Arkhamer ships, and—as Wandrei had said—they would acquire another doctor. They were probably in the middle of negotiating the swap or the lease or the marriage or whatever it was they did. But when she was supposed to be asleep, she worried.

They knew they were nearing the *Charles Dexter Ward* for days before he showed up on even the longest of the long-range scanners. The first sign was the cheshires, the tentacled creatures—so common on Arkhamer vessels—which patrolled the steelship's cabins and corridors, hunting toves and similar trans-dimensional nuisances that might slip through the interstices in reality and cause a potentially deadly infestation. One reason Arkhamer ships were tolerated at stations like Faraday was because the cheshires would hunt station vermin just as heartily. Boojums took care of their own pest control.

Normally, the cheshires—dozens or hundreds of them, Cynthia never did get a good count—slept and hunted seemingly at random. One might spend hours crouched before the angle of two intersecting bulkheads, tendrils all focused intently on one seemingly random point, its soft body slowly cycling through an array of colors that could mean anything or nothing at all . . . only to get up and slink away after a half-day of stalking as if nothing had happened. Cynthia often had to shoo two or three out of her hammock at bunk time, and like station cats they often returned to steal body heat once she was asleep. But as the *Jarmulowicz Astronomica* began encountering the spacetime distortions that inevitably accompanied the violent death of a boojum, the ship's cheshires became correspondingly agitated. They traveled in groups, and any time Cynthia encountered two sleeping, there was also one keeping watch . . . if a creature with sixteen eyes and no eyelids could be said to sleep. Cynthia tried not to speculate about their dreams.

The second sign was the knocking. Random, frantic banging, as if something outside the ship wanted to come in. It came at unpredictable intervals, and would sometimes be one jarring boom and sometimes go on for five minutes. It upset the cheshires even more; they couldn't hear the headache-inducing noise, being deaf, but they could feel the vibrations. Every time Cynthia was woken in her sleep shift by that terrible knocking, she'd find at least one and usually more like three cheshires under her blankets with her, trying to hide their wedge-shaped heads between her arms and her body. She'd learned from her child patients, who lost their shy formality in talking about their playmates, how to pet the cheshires, how to use her voice in ways they could feel, and she would lie there in the dim green glow of the one working safety light and pet the trembling cheshires until she fell asleep again.

The knocking was followed by what the Arkhamers called pseudoghosts—one of them explained the phenomenon in excruciating detail while Cynthia cleaned and stitched a six-inch long gash on her forearm: not the spirits of the dead, but microbursts of previous and future time. "Or, rather, future probabilities, since the future has yet to be determined."

"Of course," Cynthia said. The girl's name was Hester Ayabo Jarmulowicz; she was tall and skinny and iron-black, and she had laid her arm open trying to repair the damage done to an interior bulkhead by the percussive force of the knocking. "So the woman I almost ran into this morning before she vanished in a burst of static—was that Martha Patterson?"

"Probably," Hester said. "Not very tall, wiry, freckled skin?"

"Yes. Keep your arm still, please."

"That was Doctor Patterson. Before Doctor Patterson, we had Doctor Belafonte, so you may see him as well."

"And your future doctors, whoever they may be?"

"Very likely," Hester said.

Cynthia saw Dr. Patterson several times, and once an old man who had to be Dr. Belafonte, but the only future ghost she saw was herself—her hair longer, grayer, her clothes shabbier—standing beside the exam table with a scowl on her face that could have been used for spot-welding.

What frightened Cynthia most—aside from the nauseating, almost electric shock of walking into the medical bay and seeing *herself*—was the way that scowl had looked as if it had been carved into her face.

It made no sense. Why would she still be on the *Jarmulowicz Astronomica?* She didn't want to stay, and the Arkhamers clearly didn't want to keep her. But then she thought, in the middle of autoclaving her instruments, *Wandrei trapped me once.*

That was not a nice thought, and it brought others in its wake, about pitcher plants and the way they started digesting their prey before the unfortunate insects were dead, about the way her future self's face had looked as if it were eroding around that scowl.

She schooled herself for being morbid and tried to focus on her patients and on her reading in the ship's archives (Wandrei had at least kept his word about that), but she was very grateful, as well as surprised, when, a few days after their conversation about pseudoghosts, Hester Ayabo marched into the medical bay and announced, "Isolation is bad for human beings. I am going to eat lunch with you."

Cynthia toggled off the display on the patient file she had been updating. "You are? I mean, thank you, but—"

"You can tell me about your studies," Hester said, midway between an invitation and a command. She gave Cynthia a bright, uncertain, sidelong look—*like a falcon*, Cynthia thought, *trying to make friends with a plow horse*—and Cynthia laughed and got up and said, "Or you can tell me about yours."

Which Hester was glad to do, volubly and at length. She was an astrobiologist—the same specialty as Wandrei, and Wandrei was in fact a member of her committee, which seemed to be a little like being a parent and a little like being a boss. Hester studied creatures like boojums and cheshires and the dreadful bandersnatches, creatures that had evolved in the cold and airless dark between the stars—or the cold and airless interstices of space-time. She was very excited by the chance to study the *Charles Dexter Ward*, and on their third lunch, Cynthia found the nerve to ask her, "Do you know how the *Charles Dexter Ward* died?"

Hester stopped in the middle of bringing a slice of hydroponically cultivated tomato to her mouth. "It is something of a mystery. But I can tell you what we do know."

It was more than Wandrei had offered; Cynthia listened avidly.

As Wandrei had told her, the *Charles Dexter Ward* had been an ambulance ship—or, more accurately, a mobile hospital. He had been in service for more than ten solar, well known throughout the farther and darker reaches of the system. His captain was equally well known for disregarding evidence of pirate status when taking patients on board; though there was no formal recognition of neutrality once you got past the sovereignty of Mars, the *Charles Dexter Ward* was one boojum that no pirate would attack. "Even the Mi-Go," Hester said, "although no one knows why."

Cynthia tried to hide the reflexive curl of her fingers, even though there had been no hint of special meaning in Hester's tone. "What became of his crew?"

"Probably still aboard," Hester said. "Possibly some are even alive. Although you can't eat boojum. It's not what we'd consider meat."

"How did the *Jarmulowicz Astronomica* find out about him?"

"Another Arkhamer ship picked up a distress buoy. They couldn't stop for her"—and Hester's sly look told Cynthia that, friends or not (were they friends?) Hester would never tell an outsider why—"but they sent us a coded burst as closest relative. We may not beat other salvage attempts, even so. The beacon just said that the ship was moribund—no reason given. Possibly, the captain didn't know, or if something happened to him, it might have been junior crew who sent the probe. And nobody tells us students much anyway."

Cynthia nodded. She put her hand on her desk, about to lever herself to her feet, as Hester sucked down a length of tofu. "Huh," Cynthia said. "Do boojums die of natural causes?"

Lips shining with broth, Hester cocked her head at her. "They have to die of something, I suppose. But our records don't mention any that have."

By the time they were within a hundred kilometers of the dead boojum, the banging and the manifestations were close to constant. Cynthia dodged her own shadow in Sick Bay almost reflexively, as she might a surgical nurse with whom she had established a practiced partnership. It was a waste of mental and physical energy—*I could just walk through myself*—but she couldn't bring herself to stop.

Hester brought her cookies, dropping the plate between Cynthia and the work screen on which she was studying what schematics she could find of the *Charles Dexter Ward*—spotty—and his sister ships—wildly varying in architecture. Or growth patterns. Or whatever you called a boojum's internal design.

"We'll be there next watch," Hester said. "You ought to rest."

"It's my work watch," Cynthia said. The cookies were pale, crisp-soft, and fragrant with lemons and lavender. It was everything she could do to nibble one delicately, with evident pleasure, and save the others for later. Hester did not take one, though Cynthia offered.

She said, "I've another dozen in my locker. I like to bake on my rec watch. And you *should* rest: the President and the Faculty Senate have sent around a memo saying that everybody who is not on watch should be getting as much sleep as possible."

Cynthia glanced guiltily at her wristpiece. She had a bad habit of forgetting she'd turned notifications off. Something like a giant's fist thumped against the hull; she barely noticed. "I should be cramming boojum anatomy, is what I should be doing."

Hester smiled at her, but did not laugh. "You've been studying it since we left Faraday. You have something to prove?"

"You know what I have to prove." But she took a second cookie anyway, stared at it, and said, "Hester. If you only see one ghost . . . does that mean that there's only one future?"

"An interesting question," Hester said. "Temporal metadynamics aren't really my field. It may mean there are futures in which there are no people in that place. It may mean that that one particular future is locked in, I guess."

"Unavoidable?"

"Inescapable!" She grinned, plush lips a contrast to the wiry narrowness of her face and body. "I'm going to go take my mandated nap. If you have any sense you will too. You're on the away team, you know."

Cynthia's startle broke the cookie in half. "Read the memo," Hester advised, not unkindly. "And get some sleep while you can. There's unlikely to be much time to rest once we reach the *Charles Dexter Ward*."

## Part Two

The corpse of the *Charles Dexter Ward* hung ten degrees off the plane of the ecliptic, in a crevice of spacetime where it was very unlikely that anyone would just stumble across it. Cynthia had been called to the bridge for the first time in her tenure as ship's surgeon aboard the *Jarmulowicz*

*Astronomica.* She stood behind the President's chair, wishing Professor Wandrei were somewhere in sight. She'd been too nervous to ask after his current whereabouts, but an overheard comment suggested he was at his instruments below. She, on the other hand, was watching the approach to the ruined liveship with her own eyes, on screens and through the biggest expanse of transparent crystal anywhere on the ship.

She rather wished she wasn't.

The boojum was a streamlined shape tumbling gently in the midst of its own web of tentacles. Inertia twisted them in corkscrews as the boojum rotated grandly around its center of mass, drifting further and further from the solar system's common plane. It was dark, no bioluminescence revealing the details of its lines. Only the sun's rays gently cupping the curve of the hull gave it form and mass.

Around it, where Cynthia would expect to see the familiar patterns of stars burning in the icy void of the up-and-out, the Big Empty, the sky was shattered. A great mirrored lens, wrenched loose and broken into a thousand glittering shards, cast back crazy reflections of the *Jarmulowicz Astronomica,* the *Charles Dexter Ward,* and the steelship already moored to the dead boojum, a ship so scarred and dented that all that could be deciphered of its hull markings was the word CALICO. It was a small ship—it couldn't boast more than a two- or three-man crew—and didn't worry Cynthia. What did worry her were all those jagged bits of mirror, all those uncalculated angles of reflection. The very things a mirror like that was meant to blind would be drawn to this jostling chaos, and with the boojum dead, neither the *Jarmulowicz Astronomica* nor her competition had much in the way of defense—unless the stupid stories Cynthia had been hearing all her life were true and the Arkhamers had some sort of occult weaponry that nobody else knew about.

Unfortunately, she was pretty sure they didn't.

"All right," said the President, loudly enough to cut through the two or three muttered discussions taking place at various points on the bridge. "We have three immediate objectives. One, obviously, is the reason we're here"— and she nodded at the derelict before them—"the second is salvaging and neutralizing that reflecting lens, and the third is making contact with the *Calico* over there. We need to see if we can come to a mutually beneficial agreement. Please talk to your departments. By no later than the top of the next shift, I want a roster of volunteers for EVA. I know some departments badly need the practice." She glanced at an elderly Arkhamer Cynthia did not know; there was clearly a story there by the way the man blushed and stammered, but Cynthia doubted she'd ever hear it.

"What about the *Calico?*" a voice said from the doorway. It was Wandrei, and if he was in disgrace, he didn't seem to mind.

"Professor Wandrei," the President said coolly. "Are you volunteering?"

"Of course," Wandrei said, smiling at her affably. "And since I imagine they've docked at the most useful point of—ah—ingress, may I suggest that you send the planned away team with me?"

There was a fraught silence. Cynthia stared fixedly at the nearest of the *Charles Dexter Ward*'s blank, glazed eyes and cursed herself for thirty-nine kinds of fool. Finally, the President said, "Thomas, you're plotting something."

"I pursue knowledge, Madam President," said Wandrei, "as we all do. Or have you forgotten that I sat on your tenure committee?"

One of the junior scholars gasped. Cynthia did not look away from the boojum's dead eye, but she could hear the smile in the President's voice when she said, "Very well. Take Meredith and Hester and Doctor Feuerwerker, and go find out what the *Calico* is doing. And remember to report back!"

The *Jarmulowicz Astronomica* possessed two landing craft, a lumbering scow called the *T. H. White* and an incongruously sporty little skimmer called the *Caitlín R. Kiernan.* The skimmer seated four, if nobody was too fussy about his or her personal space, and Hester knew how to fly it—which meant, Wandrei said, herding his team toward the *Caitlín R. Kiernan,* that they didn't need to wait for one of the two people on board who could fly the *T. H. White.*

The President was right, Cynthia thought, as she strapped herself in next to Meredith. Wandrei was plotting something. He was almost bouncing with eagerness, and there was a gleam in his eye that she did not like. But she couldn't think of anything she could do about it from here.

Hester ran through her pre-flight checks without letting Wandrei hurry her. Meredith—a big blond Valkyrie whose specialty was what she called boojum mathematics—apologized for crowding Cynthia with her shoulders and said, "Could you see a cause of death, Doctor. Feuerwerker?"

"No," Cynthia said. "He just looked dead to me. But I don't know if I'd recognize a fatal wound on a boojum if I saw one."

"It probably didn't leave a visible mark," Wandrei said from where he was riding shotgun. "So far as our research has discovered, there are only two ways to kill a boojum. One is to cut it literally to pieces—a tactic which backfires disastrously far more often than it succeeds—the other, to deliver a systemic shock powerful enough to disrupt all of the creature's cardio and/or synaptic nodes at once."

"That's one mother of a shock," Cynthia said, feeling unease claw its way a little deeper beneath her skin.

"Yes," said Wandrei and did not elaborate.

Hester piloted the *Caitlín R. Kiernan* with more verve than Cynthia's stomach found comfortable; she gripped her safety harness and swallowed hard, and Meredith said kindly, "Hester is one of the best young pilots we have."

"When I was a child, I wanted to jump ship on Leng Station and become a mechanic," Hester said cheerfully. "I tried a couple of times, but they always brought me back." She piloted the *Caitlín R. Kiernan* in a low swooping arc across the *Charles Dexter Ward*'s forward tentacles, and they could see that Wandrei's guess had been correct; the *Calico* had succeeded in prying open one of the *Charles Dexter Ward*'s airlocks, and the ship was moored partly within the boojum.

Cynthia hoped the Arkhamers had a better way in than that.

As it turned out, they didn't. And Cynthia was unsettled to watch Meredith and Hester strap sidearms on over their pressure suits. Were they really expecting that much trouble from the crew of the *Calico?* And didn't salvage law give her first picking? Or would the Arkhamers' earlier intercept and beacon trump that?

Cynthia had never encountered a dead boojum before, and she had braced herself with the knowledge that there would be any number of things she wasn't expecting. But no amount of bracing or foreknowledge could ever have been sufficient for the stench of the *Charles Dexter Ward*—a fetor so intense Cynthia would have sworn she could pick up the scent through her helmet, and before the airlock cycled. What that said about the spaceworthiness of the *Caitlín R. Kiernan,* Cynthia did not care to consider.

What the cycling outer airlock door revealed was more of a shock than it might have been if she hadn't already been dragging her tongue across her teeth in a futile effort to scrape the stench of death away. The membranes between the struts were not glossy with health, appearing dull and tacky instead, but the amazing stink that left her lightheaded and pained even within the oxygenated confines of her helmet had led her to expect— well, what course *did* decay take, on a boojum? Writhing infestations? Deliquescence? Suppurating lesions?

There was none of that.

Just the ridged stretch of intact-seeming corridor disappearing into the curvature of the dead ship, and the reek of putrescence. *Don't throw up in your helmet,* Cynthia told herself. That would be one sure way of making things even less pleasant.

The *Charles Dexter Ward* retained good atmospheric pressure—though Cynthia couldn't have attested to the air quality—and she didn't need to tongue on her suit intercom for Wandrei and the others to hear her when she said, "Isn't anything we salvage from this mess going to be unusable due to contamination?"

Meredith said, "Anything sealed should be fine. And we wouldn't want unsealed medical supplies anyway."

"I can smell it through my suit."

Wandrei looked at her with curious intensity. "Really?" he said, brow wrinkling behind his faceplate. "I don't smell anything."

"Maybe your suit has a bad filter," Meredith said. "We do our best to check them, but, well." She shrugged—a clumsy gesture, but Cynthia understood. When everything the Arkhamers owned, from their clothes to their ship, was second-hand, salvaged, scavenged, there was only so much they could do.

"That's probably it," she said, although she wasn't sure—and from the look he gave her before he turned away, Wandrei wasn't sure, either.

"Let's see if we can't find the crew of the *Calico*," he said.

*I am walking in a dead body,* Cynthia said periodically to herself, but aside from the eye-blurring stench that no one else could smell, the only sign of death was the darkness. Every boojum Cynthia had ever traveled on had used its bioluminescence to illuminate any space its human crew and passengers were using. But the *Charles Dexter Ward* stayed dark.

They proceeded cautiously. Cynthia remembered Hester saying the crew of the *Charles Dexter Ward* might still be alive somewhere in their dead ship, and there was the nagging question of the *Calico*'s crew—a question that got naggier and naggier the farther they went without finding a single trace of them.

"We know they weren't on their ship," Hester muttered. "Corinne hailed them until she was hoarse."

"And they haven't been salvaging," Meredith said. "None of the doors since the airlock has been forced open."

"My question," Cynthia said, "is how long they've been here. And if they aren't salvaging, what are they doing?"

That was two questions, and actually she had a third: what did Wandrei know that she and Hester and Meredith didn't? He didn't seem worried, and she had noticed after a while that, although he wasn't in a hurry, he did seem to know where he was going. She didn't want to be the one to mention it, though. Not a good idea for the politely tolerated outsider.

"What else *can* you do on a dead boojum?" Hester demanded.

"Maybe," Cynthia said after a moment. "Maybe they weren't here for salvage in the first place. Maybe they needed a hospital. Not all doctors are as laissez-faire as Captain Diemschuller."

"The *Calico*'s too small for piracy," Meredith said, "but I agree with your general principle. If they aren't here for salvage—how do we find the operating theaters?"

Her question went unanswered as they came to a corridor junction and caught sight of another human being.

He was in shirtsleeves rather than a pressure suit, wearing the uniform of the Interplanetary Ambulance Corps, dark blue with red piping and *CDW* embroidered on his sleeve. Across his chest were blazoned a row of symbols including a caduceus, a red crescent, and the Chinese ideogram for "heart." Despite being distracted by the medical symbols, Cynthia knew there was something wrong with him several seconds before she was able to identify why she thought so. And the man—youngish and tall, his skin fishbelly pale in their floodlights—stood and stared at them, his face so perfectly blank that Cynthia finally realized that was the problem. No relief, no anger, no fear—not even curiosity.

"Hello!" she said, starting forwards and forcing brightness into her voice as if she could compensate for his nullity. "I'm Doctor Feuerwerker with the

*Jarmulowicz Astronomica.* Is your captain—" And then she was close enough to see him clearly, close enough to see that the shadow at his midsection was not a shadow but a hole, jagged-edged and gaping, where his stomach used to be, close enough to see the greenish tinge to his pale skin.

Her voice was thin and screechy in her own ears when she said, "He's dead."

"*What?*" said Hester.

"He's *dead.* He's been dead for weeks."

"But he's standing up. A dead body couldn't . . . " Hester's voice dried up with a faint click as the dead man turned, giving them a good view of his disemboweled torso, and started walking down the hall away from them. His locomotion wasn't perfect, but it was damn good for someone who'd probably been dead for three months.

Hester started to blaspheme, and Meredith ungently hushed her. This was not the place to be attracting that kind of attention.

"It might be a parasite," Cynthia said, having run frantically through her knowledge of what could animate a corpse. "Something that got through a gap in spacetime when the *Charles Dexter Ward* died. We have to tell the *Jarmulowicz Astronomica*"—surprised, Cynthia realized her concern was not for herself, stuck here in the belly of a dead boojum, but for Jaime and the shy children and the cheshires Cynthia couldn't count—"can we call them from here? How far back—"

"Calm yourself, Doctor Feuerwerker," said Wandrei. "What you see is not the work of a parasite. It is the pursuit of knowledge."

That brought her up short. She looked at him, calm and sweating behind the faceplate of his pressure suit, and swallowed against a curl of bright nausea. "You knew about this?"

The twitch at the corner of his lips was more disturbing than the dead man striding away from them. Hastily, Cynthia turned her attention forward again. There were medical-school stories of the horrors Arkhamer doctors got up to. Cynthia had never credited them, considering them part of the general anti-Arkhamer bigotry that permeated so many institutions of higher learning—and so many spacedock taverns.

Now she wondered if she had been too willing—in her conscientious open-mindedness—to assume there was no truth behind the slander. *Ooh, ethics now, Doctor Feuerwerker? That's a new look on you.*

She stepped forward, following the dead man. Wandrei and the other women jogged to catch up, their pressure suits rustling with the sudden movement. As Wandrei fell back into stride beside Cynthia, she said, "So when did the *Charles Dexter Ward* sign on an Arkhamer doctor?" Wandrei remained silent, though she waited after each sentence before adding the next. "That's what got the ship killed, isn't it? That's the real motive behind coming here."

"Reanimation isn't a topic we commonly pursue," Wandrei said. "But if . . . if someone has made it work—think of the advance to human understanding. To medicine."

"To shipping," Meredith said.

"There are a number of applications," Hester was beginning, when Cynthia almost-shouted, "Are you fucking *nuts?* Every scare story I've ever heard about raising the dead says that either dying or coming back drives people mad. Are you really suggesting—"

"Are you a scientist, Doctor Feuerwerker?" Wandrei asked. "Then I suggest you wait for the data."

The walking cadaver did not move particularly fast. When she caught up to him, he turned to her, jaw moving. If he was trying to say something, the lack of lungs and diaphragm impeded the process. Upon closer inspection, he was a major and a registered nurse. The name on his shirt pocket read *Ngao.* His eyes, dull and concave where the ship's environment had begun dehydrating them, fastened on Cynthia's face through the helmet.

His jaw worked again.

Was he conscious? she wondered, the chill running up her back so real that her head wrenched to one side. Did he know he was dead? Eviscerated? Did he ever try to touch his stomach and have his fingers brush his spine? She wanted to apologize, even though Major Ngao's fate was none of her doing. But she, too, had sought after forbidden knowledge—not reanimation, at least the irony wasn't that cruel. She'd muttered those same words about *science* and *the pursuit of knowledge* and told herself that Chen and Derleth would be pleased. That Galileo would be pleased.

Had it been a lie? She didn't know. Chen and Derleth and Galileo had been dead for centuries. She couldn't ask them—and even this lunatic on the *Charles Dexter Ward* couldn't bring them back. She remembered her burning certainty that the truth was there, attainable and valuable beyond any price—and she remembered Captain Nwapa's expression, too, that one flicker of horror before the captain got her game-face back. It took a lot to rattle a boojum captain, and Cynthia was not proud of the achievement.

Wandrei said crisply, "Take us to Doctor Fiorenzo," before Cynthia could find any words that weren't trite and false—*and probably pointless, really, Dr. Feuerwerker, the man's missing nine-tenths of his vital organs, do you think he has any attention to spare for you?* And if nothing else, Cynthia thought grimly, now at least she had a name to hang the nightmare on.

The corridors of the *Charles Dexter Ward* were dark and silent as Cynthia followed the Arkhamers following the dead man. From time spent on the *Richard Trevithick* and other boojums, she knew a little about their internal architecture, and she'd done her best to stay oriented, so she was fairly sure that they were heading away from the rending plates and tearing diamond teeth of the *Charles Dexter Ward*'s mouth (and she couldn't help wondering if his crew had called him Charlie, the same way the *Richard Trevithick*'s crew always referred to their boojum as Ricky—it was a stupid thought and wouldn't be banished). The anatomy of boojums adhered to no principle that Terran mammals abided by, including bilateral symmetry, but if you were headed away from the mouth, you were probably headed toward the cloaca. And most ships' systems were stuck as deep in the bulk of the boojum as the bioengineers could get them.

The *Charles Dexter Ward* being a hospital ship, there was not one specific area that Cynthia would have identified as the sickbay. Rather she and the others had passed corridor after corridor of clinical chambers and wards, rooms that Cynthia was sure would have reeked of disinfectant and that eternal powdery medicinal smell were it not for the eye-watering putrescence overwhelming everything. They found the operating theaters, which looked as if they'd been the scenes of intense guerilla fighting, and Cynthia's pace slowed automatically, trying to reconstruct what had happen, where the defenders had been, how the line of attack had run, whether that was all human blood in horrible sticky pools, or if some of it was other colors.

"Doctor Feuerwerker," Meredith said, pointing, and she saw that farther down the corridor, in the direction that Major Ngao was plodding, uninterested in what might have been the site of his own death, there was, for the first time in hours, a gleam of light that they hadn't brought with them from the *Caitlín R. Kiernan*.

And as they followed the dead man—he dripped, occasionally, an irregular trail of brownish fluid on the corridor floor—around the bend in the dead boojum's corridor, Cynthia saw an open pressure hatch, a slice of light spilled across the floor, and a glimpse of one of the medical labs.

Within it, she could just make out some white-coated movement.

She followed Wandrei, she thought, because she had so little idea what else to do. *This is how war crimes happen. People get overwhelmed and follow orders. If you were as brilliant as one of these Arkhamer doctors, you'd know what to do besides whatever Wandrei tells you.*

And then she bit her lip inside the helmet and thought, *If I were as brilliant as one of these Arkhamer doctors, the* Richard Trevithick *might be as dead as Charlie here.*

That thought chilled whatever part of her the quietly guiding dead man had missed.

Something brushed Cynthia's right glove, then grabbed it. Her throat closed with fright, and she turned as she tried to pull away, looking down to see what horrible thing had caught her. But it was a suit gauntlet, tight against her own, and when she looked up again, she met Hester's gaze dimly, through two helmet bubbles glazed with the reflected light of the lab up ahead. She'd stopped, lost in thought. The idea of being left out here in the dark with the stars knew what made her heart jump like a ship's rat in the claws of a cheshire.

She squeezed back and caught a flash of Hester's teeth, bright against the darkness of her face. They moved forward together, though any comfort from the other woman's presence was abrogated by a series of scraping sounds that Cynthia's medical ear easily identified as metal on bone.

Five more steps brought them into the lab. Cynthia found herself fascinated by the way the light—clip-on work lighting trailing to batteries, and not biolume—caught on the scratches on Meredith's and Wandrei's pressure suits as they stepped out of the shadows of the corridor. She was avoiding looking past them, at whatever the lab contained, and their broad shoulders mercifully blocked most of the view.

Then Wandrei stepped to one side, to make room for her and Hester, and raised both hands to open the catches on his helmet. As he lifted it off,

Cynthia had to fight the urge to reach out and slam it back into place—as if a standard, somewhat worn pressure suit was any protection in a situation like this.

Cynthia stayed on suit air anyway. It made her feel a little better, and she noticed Meredith and Hester were in no hurry to uncouple their helmets either.

"Doctor Fiorenzo," Wandrei said pleasantly. "Allow my to introduce my colleagues. I take it you've had some success?"

"Limited," Fiorenzo answered in a light contralto, turning from a dissection table upon which the twitching remains of something that couldn't possibly still be alive were pinned. She did not seem at all surprised to see them—and that Wandrei apparently did not need to introduce himself. "I'm pleased you're here. After the accident . . . Charlie dead and all the crew . . . "

Her face revealed grief, tension, relief. What would it be like, trapped alone parsecs off any shipping lane, inside an enormous dead creature slowly rotting around you?

The introductions were a scene of almost surreal cordiality. Fiorenzo was a narrow-shouldered, olive-skinned woman. Her face was smooth everywhere but at the corners of her eyes as she smiled, and she wasn't old enough to be going salt-and-pepper yet, though what few strands of gray there were stood out like silver embroidery on black velvet against the darkness of her hair. She wore it in a pixyish crop, like a lot of practical-minded spacers.

*I thought you'd be older,* Cynthia didn't say, in the hellish mundanity of pleasantries carried out while the relic of Major Ngao stood against the far bulkhead, arms folded across his chest, watching cloudy-eyed but seemingly intent, as if he were following the conversation. She was spared from having to shake hands because Fiorenzo was gloved, and she was spared from having come up with something else to say when Fiorenzo paused at her name, frowned, and said, "Feuerwerker. They threw you off the *Richard Trevithick* just before— Damned shame. That was good research. It's about time somebody found out what's in one of those biosuspension canisters!"

Cynthia managed not to step back, rocked by a peculiar combination of the warmth of a fellow scientist's regard and the horror of who, exactly, was praising her. Her jaw was still working on an answer when Fiorenzo continued, "Well, you're welcome here now. We'll find some things out, you and I! Maybe even a thing or two about the Mi-Go!"

"Thank you," Cynthia said weakly. She let Fiorenzo, Meredith, and Wandrei step away. Hester crowded close and leaned their helmets together in order to whisper: "What did you *do?*"

"I thought everybody knew already."

"Tell me anyway."

Cynthia couldn't quite figure out where to start. She was still fumbling when Hester broke and asked outright, "You were trying to reverse engineer a Mi-Go canister?"

"A vacant one," Cynthia said in weak protest. "Not one with somebody inside."

"Sweet breathsucker," Hester said. "Haven't you heard about what happened to the *Lavinia Whateley?*"

A boojum privateer. Vanished without a trace after pirating a cargo of the Mi-Go's canisters of disembodied brains. Rumor was that all hands and even the ship herself had wound up disassembled and carted off to the outer reaches of the solar system, living brains forever locked in metal tins, going immortally mad.

Cynthia nodded tersely, lips thin. "I didn't say it was a good idea."

Hester looked like she wanted to say something else, but Wandrei called her over. Cynthia stayed where she was, not wanting to intrude on an Arkhamer conversation.

Although . . . *was* Fiorenzo an Arkhamer? Cynthia'd learned enough to recognize the names of the Arkhamer ships—all of them named for one of the nine which originally set out from Earth—and *Fiorenzo* wasn't one of them. But Wandrei called her Doctor Fiorenzo, and she'd introduced herself the same way—Julia Filomela Fiorenzo. No "Jarmulowicz" or "Burlingame" or "Dubois." So either she wasn't a Arkhamer—whom the Arkhamers *treated* like an Arkhamer, and Cynthia wasn't buying that for a second—or she *was* an Arkhamer and her ship had disowned her.

*Well, gosh, Doctor Feuerwerker. I wonder why.*

Her ship had disowned her, but Wandrei hadn't—and Cynthia remembered the comments about Wandrei getting in trouble, remembered the President's suspicions, and knew that, yes, Wandrei had brought them out here, not on a mission of mercy, but to check in on Fiorenzo's experiments. Experiments which the rest of the *Jarmulowicz Astronomica* did not know about, or at least did not know were still on-going.

*Sweet merciful Buddha of the Breathsucker,* Cynthia thought and looked down to discover that she'd wandered over much closer than she'd meant to get to the dissection table where Fiorenzo had been working when they came in.

The creature on it had once been human. It should not still be alive.

Or possibly it wasn't. She twisted her head, forcing her gaze away from the wet holes where the thing's face had been, and found Major Ngao watching her. Watching? Staring at? Staring through? She had to squeeze her eyes shut and bite down hard on her lip to keep the bubble of hysteria from escaping, and when she opened her eyes again, she was staring down at the dead, twitching creature's chest.

Where, under the blood, the words *Free Ship Calico Jack* were still, just barely, legible on the scraps of its uniform.

Cynthia stepped back, a big over-dramatic step that caught everyone's attention, Fiorenzo's voice dying in the middle of a sentence: "the bodies just aren't fresh enough. I need—"

"Doctor Feuerwerker?" Wandrei said, with that nasty snide tone that every teacher in the universe used when they'd caught you not paying attention in class.

Cynthia opened her mouth, without the least idea what was going to come out—and more than half convinced it was going to be, *There's nothing to ensure freshness like harvesting them yourself, is there, Doctor Fiorenzo?* But some remnant of self-preservation interfered, and what she said was:

"How did the *Charles Dexter Ward* die?"

"What?" Fiorenzo said; Wandrei was frowning. Cynthia repeated the question.

"Oh. There was . . . the mirror broke," Fiorenzo said with a vague gesture. "And the doppelkinder came. They killed the crew and the ship."

"How did you escape?" Meredith asked, wide-eyed.

"Luck, I think," Fiorenzo said with a shrug that almost looked like a spasm, and a bitter laugh. "I was the pathologist, and I was in the morgue when it happened. I think they just couldn't smell me. And you know they don't last very long."

Yes, like homicidal mayflies. They rarely lasted more than a few hours after they'd killed their primary host. Cynthia nodded and did not—did *not*—look at the dissection table. "And you've been here ever since?"

Fiorenzo offered a sad, slanted little smile. "There's been nowhere I can go."

Fiorenzo wanted, she said, to transfer her most promising experiments to the *Jarmulowicz Astronomica*. As she and Wandrei and Meredith started a discussion of how that might be accomplished, Hester caught Cynthia by the arm and dragged her grimly out into the hallway, still within the light of Fiorenzo's rigged operating theater, but well out of earshot.

There Hester stopped and leaned into Cynthia's helmet again. "She's lying."

"About what?" Cynthia said, her mind still stuck blankly on that poor twitching thing strapped down on Fiorenzo's operating table.

"Doppelkinder can't kill a boojum. They won't even go after one. Boojums don't recognize their own reflections."

"Wait. What?"

"Doppelkinder hunt in mirrors," Hester began with exaggerated patience.

"Not that," Cynthia said. She'd been terrified of doppelkinder since her first Civil Defense class when she was five. "Boojums don't see themselves in mirrors?"

"Two-dimensional representations don't mean anything to them. Cheshires are the same way." Hester managed a smile, although it wasn't a very good one. "That's why there's that folk saying about how you can't fool a cheshire. The most cunning optical illusion ever created won't even make them twitch."

"And doppelkinder are dependent on optical illusions," Cynthia said, finally catching up to what Hester was trying to say.

"They don't eat people's eyes for the nutritional value."

"Right. But if the doppelkinder didn't kill the *Charles Dexter Ward,* what did?"

Hester folded her arms and gave Cynthia a flat obdurate stare. "I think *she* did."

"Fiorenzo?" Cynthia spluttered a little, then caught herself and regrouped. "Not that I don't believe she would do it in a heartbeat, but *why?* Why the boojum, I mean? And for the love of little fishy gods, *how?*"

Hester's gaze dropped. "You were supposed to talk me out of it. It's a crazy idea, and I know it's because I'm jealous."

"Jealous?"

"If Professor Wandrei had even *once* shown this kind of interest in my work . . . " She trailed off, her face twisting.

"I understand," Cynthia said and dared to offer Hester's shoulder a clumsy pat. "But, Hester, I don't think you're wrong. I'm pretty sure she killed the crew of that little scavenger ship." And she told Hester about the uniform.

"We have to tell Professor Wandrei," Hester said, taking a step back toward Fiorenzo's little island of lunatic light.

This time it was Cynthia who caught hold of Hester's arm. "Do you really think he doesn't know?"

She hated herself a little for the sick expression on Hester's face, the knowledge that she, Cynthia Feuerwerker, had just opened her mouth and killed something irreplaceable.

Hester said, barely whispering even though they were still helmet-to-helmet, "What should we do?"

Cynthia opened her mouth to say, *What CAN we do?* and all but physically choked on her own words. Because that was how war crimes happened. That was how you ended up a future-ghost on a Arkhamer ship with the lines of a scowl bitten so deep in your face you never really stopped frowning.

And Hester was watching her hopefully. Hester, knowing what she'd done, was still willing to believe that Cynthia would do the right thing.

Cynthia took a deep breath. "If she killed the *Charles Dexter Ward,* how did she do it? I mean, you and Wandrei said there were only two ways, and she clearly didn't cut him to pieces, so . . . ?"

"She must have rigged some kind of galvanic motor," Hester said. "If she hooked it up to the UPS—and a hospital ship would have to have one, even a liveship—that would take care of the power requirements . . . "

Cynthia got a good look at the wideness of Hester's eyes before she realized that here in the dark corridor, even with their helmets leaned up together, she shouldn't have been able to make out the details of her friend's expression. Hester stepped back slowly, her features revealed more plainly as Cynthia's shadow no longer fell across her face. Cynthia forced her gaze to the right.

All along the passageway, bioluminescent runners were crawling with unexpected brilliance. Fiorenzo had reanimated the *Charles Dexter Ward.*

"Aw, shitballs," Hester said.

. . .

## Part Three

Looking away from the light that showed the *Charles Dexter Ward* was no longer entirely dead was as hard as opening a rusted zipper. But Cynthia did it, and didn't let herself look back. She pulled Hester a little further down the corridor and said, "Now we *really* need to know how she killed him. And whether it'll work a second time."

"It should," Hester said. "Whatever force is animating him, a big enough shock should disrupt it. We just have to find her machine."

"I like your use of the word 'just.' Something like that—would it be portable or not?" The *Charles Dexter Ward*'s bioluminescence was continuing to ripple and pulse in an arrhythmic not-quite-pattern that was like nothing Cynthia had ever see a boojum do before. It was already giving her the mother of all headaches, and if it was a reflection of the *Charles Dexter Ward*'s state of mind, then she couldn't believe it was a good auspice.

"One that could kill a boojum? Definitely not."

"So wherever she built it, that's where it is. But how do we *find* it? It's a boojum—how do we even *look?*"

"Um," said Hester and tugged Cynthia another few steps away from Fiorenzo's lab. "The closed stacks have a schematic. Professor Wandrei said not to share it with—"

"Outsiders," Cynthia finished wearily, and Hester ducked her head like a reproved child. And of *course* the Arkhamers had a second, inner archive to which Cynthia had not been given access. It was their secrets that kept them alive and independent. "It's okay. You don't have to—"

"No, at this point it's only stupid and self-destructive," Hester said. "Here."

Cynthia's heads-up was filled with a spidery green constellation: the human-scale paths through the *Charles Dexter Ward*. She had only a moment to appreciate them before her pressure suit ballooned taut and a sudden sharp pressure in her ear canals distracted her. Reflexively, she opened her mouth and closed her eyes—every spacer knew and feared that sensation—but it was just a pressure fluctuation, not a hull breach. She closed her mouth again and blew until her ears popped.

When she opened her eyes, Hester was looking at her, head swaying in relief. "Good idea, staying suited."

Cynthia took a tentative breath and gagged. The reek of putrescence that had poisoned every breath since she stepped through Charlie's airlock was thick enough to taste now, and she wasted thirty seconds re-checking her perfectly functioning suit seals. "By Dodgson's blessed camera," she swore, then belatedly realized she didn't know how Hester felt about taking sacred names in vain. "I think that took a year off my life."

"So long as it's just one," Hester said. She ran a gloved hand up one of Charlie's dead interior bulkheads, tracing the rippling patterns of necroluminescence. Her fingers found an indentation, and Cynthia could see her face screw up with disgust through the bubble of the helmet. When she pushed in, her glove vanished to the knuckles. Charlie's flesh made a squelching sound.

Hester hooked and ripped; mucilaginous strings of meat stretched and rent. She tossed a panel to the deck; it rang like ceramic. Behind, a cavity lined with readouts and conduits lay revealed. Hester, wincing, reached for a small rack of what Cynthia recognized as wireless connectors. She tugged one loose, made a face, and—before Cynthia could decide that she really ought to stop her—slotted it into a jack on her suit.

"Hester—"

"Shush," Hester said. "I spend enough time researching the damned things. A dead one shouldn't bo—oh."

"What?"

"*Run.*"

They ran. Suits rustling and rasping, booted feet thudding dully on the decking. Off to the left, something scurried. Cynthia's head snapped around, but Hester put a hand on her arm and pulled.

"Tove," she said.

Normally, you would never see a tove on a boojum, but Charlie's death had strained the fabric of space-time, making inter-dimensional slippage easier, and a dead boojum could not eat its own parasites as was their usual habit. Cynthia thought about the shattered ward-mirror, intended to defend against nastier creatures than toves: doppelkinder, raths, and other predators. It worked because it reflected nothing but the Big Empty— even at dock, those warped enormous mirrors wouldn't reflect on a human scale and thus could not be exploited by doppelkinder, just as they blinded

254 · The Wreck of the *Charles Dexter Ward*

raths. Mirrors were not standard equipment on all ships, but for a hospital ship like Charlie they were an extra line of safety. *Charlie broke it dying,* she guessed. Fiorenzo had invented the doppelkinder—who didn't hunt boojums and who would never have left Major Ngao's eyes intact—as an alibi.

Then she heard something else, not the scuttling of a tove, but a wetter sound, a bigger sound. She didn't have the strength of will not to glance back, and there, barely illuminated by Charlie's twitchy necroluminescence, she saw human silhouettes, a reaching arm with the remains of an Ambulance Corps uniform, the glare of an eyeball in a half-skinned face.

Hester swung through a hatchway, pulling Cynthia with her, and slammed the emergency plate located behind glass on the other side. A blast door dropped with decapitating force. If the *Charles Dexter Ward* were to be hulled, it was in the interests of crew and ship that pressure doors should guillotine any unfortunate they caught. It was a case of one life for many, and spacers learned not to stand in doorways.

"That won't keep them for long," Hester panted. "But we can stop for a second."

Cynthia tried to slow her breathing, to get more use out of her canned air. "Where in the nine names of Hell did they come from?"

"Charlie opened a door," Hester said.

Cynthia squinted, but that didn't make what Hester was saying make any more sense. "I'm missing some context—"

Hester tapped Charlie's connector, plugged into her opposite forearm jack. "I've got access to his logs, and I think . . . I think he didn't like Fiorenzo killing his crew, because it's pretty clear from the logs that she *was.* I think that's why she electrocuted him. But the reanimated crew was killing the living crew, and she doesn't seem to be able to control what she makes. So she lured them into a vacuum bay and sealed the door—"

*But vacuum can't kill things that are already dead.*

"Charlie let his crew out," Cynthia said.

Hester nodded, the boojum's crawling green and violet necro-luminescence rippling across her corneas and the bubble of her suit. "He can open any door I override. And they're probably not very . . . safe. Anymore."

"No," Cynthia agreed. "Not safe." Her throat hurt. She made herself stop swallowing and worked enough spit into her mouth to say, "We'd better keep moving. We have to find Fiorenzo's device. Before her mistakes find us."

## Part Four

"She said she was in the morgue," Cynthia muttered.

"What?" Hester said, distracted by shooting the rotting hand off their lead pursuer.

"Doctor Fiorenzo. She said when it happened, she was in the morgue. And she was the pathologist. If she was going to hide something *anywhere,* she'd hide it there."

"I imagine you didn't get too many people dropping in for a friendly chat," Hester said. "So where's the morgue from here?"

By the time Cynthia had enough breath to reply—running in a pressure suit was no picnic, and although Fiorenzo's reanimated corpses weren't very fast, they were undistractable and relentless—Hester had found the answer herself. "One up and two over. Okay then."

Cynthia had spent time on a handful of boojums—as passenger, as crew, that last nasty week on the *Richard Trevithick* as a prisoner—and there was no standard system of orientation. Some boojums had no internal signposts at all; unless the captain gave you the schematic, you were dependent on a crew member to guide you around. The *Charles Dexter Ward* was probably the best and most thoughtfully labeled boojum Cynthia had ever seen, and even so it was essentially markers to help you plot your position on a gigantic imaginary three-dimensional graph, onto which Charlie only problematically mapped.

But it was better than nothing.

And it was better than being torn apart by these mindless, malevolent things that Fiorenzo had created out of what had once been men and women. And surely, Cynthia thought, remembering the row of symbols on Major Ngao's uniform, the men and women who deserved it *least.* She had been appalled by Fiorenzo and afraid of her and a little (*admit it, Cynthia*) envious, but now she began to be truly angry. Not at the pursuit of forbidden knowledge, but at the wanton destructiveness.

"Up is good," Hester panted beside her. "The ladder'll take them longer."

"I just wish it would stop them," Cynthia said. "Or that *anything* would." Thus far, though they'd kept ahead of the reanimated, they hadn't managed to lose them—certainly not to stop them.

"Here," Hester said. The ladder was stainless steel dulled with Charlie's slow decomposition; Hester had to override the hatch at the top with Cynthia crammed against her lower legs to avoid the frustrated grabs of the reanimated beneath them.

Hester helped Cynthia through the hatch and they slammed it closed again. Then they took off running—two shambling scientists pursued by more shambling corpses than they could stop to count.

The morgue, when they found it, was long and low and cold—and all too obviously the right place. It crawled with the same decayed-looking light as the rest of the *Charles Dexter Ward,* but here that light limned empty body bags and open lockers. Cynthia was careful to close and dog the door behind them before they proceeded down the length. Her skin crawled at the idea of locking herself in here, blocking her own route of escape . . . but what waited outside was worse. They'd managed to leave the reanimated behind, but Cynthia had no confidence that that would last.

They came around a corner to find Dr. Fiorenzo crouched behind an autopsy table, huddling with Professor Wandrei over a gaping hole in the decking. The ragged, ichorous edges framed something that looked like an exposed boojum neural cluster. The former Major Ngao was silently handing Fiorenzo tools. Fiorenzo had a veterinary syringe in her hand, a medieval-looking device with a needle easily four inches long. It was filled with some colorless fluid. Cynthia could make out two more empties on the floor.

Meredith . . . Cynthia didn't have to get close to see the lines of black stitchery holding the crushed edges of her neck together. Her head lolled to one side, tongue drooping from her slack mouth, and her eyes were half-lidded and beginning to glaze.

Cynthia wondered how Fiorenzo had arranged to have one of the pressure doors catch Meredith, and how long it would be before she got around to Wandrei. And how he could be so blind as not to see that he would be Fiorenzo's next experiment.

Hester raised and aimed her pistol. Wandrei must have glanced up just then, because he made a warning sound.

Fiorenzo rose to her feet and turned. Light shivered along the needle of the syringe as she lowered it to a non-threatening position beside her thigh.

The thing that had been Meredith took a shuffling step closer and Cynthia hid her cringe. For a moment, Cynthia waited, searching for words. Wondering why Hester hadn't pulled the trigger.

"Doctor Feuerwerker—" Wandrei began.

Somehow, Cynthia silenced him with a glance. It must have been scathing; even her eyes felt scorched by it.

Fiorenzo's eyes met Cynthia's. "You're a doctor. A researcher. You should understand!"

"I understand that you're a mass-murderer, and you're putting everyone in this sector of space at risk. Your monsters—your *victims*—aren't far behind us. What are you going to do when Charlie lets them in here?"

"I'm getting close!"

"No, you're *not*." Cynthia waved a little wildly at Major Ngao. "Maybe you've made him not-dead, but you haven't made him alive. You can't. You can't make Meredith alive and you can't make that poor bastard off the *Calico* alive. You can animate the meat, but that's not the same thing and you know it. This boojum isn't *alive*. What it is, is *wrong*."

The *Charles Dexter Ward* shuddered beneath their feet, as if in agreement. Cynthia lurched into Hester, Wandrei and the two dead people went down, and even Fiorenzo had to grab at a safety-bar to keep her feet. Cynthia was reaching for Hester's arm, to lift her sidearm back on target—

Fiorenzo slammed the syringe with which she had been about to inject the *Charles Dexter Ward* through lab coat and trousers and into her own thigh.

Cynthia stared, disbelieving. Fiorenzo straightened, smiling, and was starting to say something when she seized, crashing to the deck as stiff and solid as a bar of iron. Cynthia said over her to Wandrei, "We have to stop this."

"Science, Doctor Feuerwerker," Wandrei began, and Cynthia shouted, "Science schmience!" which startled him into shutting up.

Cynthia was a little startled herself, but she plunged on while she had the initiative, "Fiorenzo's leavings out there aren't science. They're walking nuclear waste. And what she did to Meredith is murder."

"That was an accident," Wandrei said.

Hester made a bitter noise that wasn't a laugh. "Do you really believe that?"

Wandrei didn't answer her. He said, "Doctor Fiorenzo has achieved a remarkable—" and that was when he made the mistake of letting Meredith get too close.

Cynthia and Hester had not stopped to ponder the intentions of their reanimated pursuers, not with Charlie's stuttering necroluminescence all around them and the carnage everywhere they looked. But if they *had* wondered, any last niggling doubt would have been unequivocally dispelled.

Meredith tore Wandrei to pieces, starting with his mandible.

Hester screamed; so did Wandrei, for a while. *By the Queen of Hearts, is that his endocardium?* Cynthia dragged Hester back, both of them sprayed with Wandrei's blood like stationer graffiti, and said, her voice low and frantic, "We have to find the machine. Now. While the door's still closed and Meredith is . . . distracted."

Hester's gulp might have been a sob or a hysterical laugh, but she nodded.

They looked around, trying to ignore the gory welter in the center of the room. There wasn't much there beyond dissection tables and refrigeration units. A microscope locked down on a stand, a centrifuge . . .

"Why would you have so many refrigeration units when the universe's biggest refrigerator is right outside your door?" Cynthia muttered. "One, sure, for samples and emergencies, but . . . "

They skirted the edges of the room, both keeping an uneasy eye on their roommate, but Meredith seemed to have forgotten about them, which was all to the good. The first refrigerator unit was just that, a nice Tohiro-Nikkonen that now needed very badly to be cleaned out. The second was a jury-rigged *something*—from the look on Hester's face, she had no more idea than Cynthia did. But next to that, back in the corner where it was awkward to reach, lower and bulkier—"That's it," Hester said. "Has to be."

"Can you figure out how to turn it on?" Cynthia said. She stole a glance at Fiorenzo—still seizing—and Meredith. Still . . . busy.

"Watch me," Hester said confidently and wiggled into the cramped space. "Or rather, don't watch me. Watch for company." And she passed Cynthia her pistol.

"You got it," Cynthia said, although it wasn't clear that the pistol would be any more use than a wedding bouquet if the reanimated found them and Charlie decided to open the doors.

Pursuant to that thought, she asked, "Can you communicate with him at all? Charlie, I mean?"

"I've tried," Hester said. "I don't know if it's just that I *can't* or that he doesn't recognize me as crew."

"Rats," Cynthia said. "Because it occurred to me that the best way to get rid of the reanimated would be for Charlie to eat them."

"Oh," said Hester. "Well. That would certainly be tidy. Although I'm not entirely sure that he *could.* It doesn't look to me as if Fiorenzo's reanimated can actually digest anything."

"Well, there goes that idea," Cynthia said. "But he could still chew on them, couldn't he?"

"If they went to his mouth. But he probably can't just . . . reabsorb them."

The *Charles Dexter Ward* shuddered again; Hester was knocked against the wall, and Cynthia ended up in a drunken sprawl against the galvanic motor.

"I think," Hester said dryly, "that something isn't quite right."

"Do you think that's what the second dose of serum was for?"

"Probably."

"Do you think without it, he'll die again?" Horrible, to sound so hopeful. Horrible, to be in a situation where that was the optimum outcome.

"Ngao hasn't," Hester said.

Cynthia was trying to think of an answer that was neither obscene nor dangerously blasphemous when motion caught her eye. She jerked around, but it wasn't Meredith or Ngao; it was a tove.

"There weren't any toves in here, were there?" They'd encountered a tove colony several corridors away from the morgue, thick on the ceiling and walls, and starting to creep across the floor. The smell cut through even the stench in Cynthia's nostrils, and she and Hester both had to fight not to gag at the crunch and lingering squish of toves under their boots.

"No," Hester said. "Why?"

Cynthia aimed carefully and shot the tove. "Just hurry up, okay?" All by themselves, toves weren't much more than a nuisance—at least, not to a healthy adult. But where toves went, raths were sure to follow, and raths were dangerous. And where raths went, would surely come bandersnatches, and while a bandersnatch could probably deal with Fiorenzo's mistakes, it would happily annihilate the rest of them as well.

"Fiorenzo's got it backwards, you know," Hester said in a would-be-casual voice, instead of calling Cynthia on the evasion.

"Oh?" Cynthia said warily. Hester was under tremendous pressure and had just watched one member of her family murder another at extremely close range. Cynthia wouldn't blame her in the slightest for falling apart, but they desperately needed it not to be right now.

"The fresher the body, the worse the results," Hester said. "Meredith being Exhibit A. She must have reanimated Meredith within *minutes*."

*Only as long as it takes to sew a head back on,* Cynthia thought. Aloud, she said, "I see what you mean."

"So she's wrong," Hester said fiercely. "I had to say it to someone. The odds of having the opportunity to refute her theories in print . . . "

Cynthia wanted to close her eyes, but she had to keep watch on Meredith, Fiorenzo, Ngao . . . and everything else. She said, "I understand."

"Okay," Hester said, scrambling back to Cynthia's side. "The machine is drawing power, and I've started it cycling. Now we just have to attach the leads to Charlie's nervous system." She brandished a thick double-handful of cables, and Cynthia followed her gaze to the hole Fiorenzo had dug in the deck of the morgue, with Wandrei's remains on one side and Fiorenzo's rigor-stiff figure on the other. Ngao was standing patiently where Fiorenzo had left him. Meredith had moved to the door, which she was pawing at with obvious confusion. But she wasn't Charlie's crew; he wasn't opening it for her.

"Can't we just, I don't know, rip him open ourselves?"

"It would take too long," Hester said with a crispness that betrayed her own reluctance. "Besides, I don't have the specialized diagnostic equipment we'd need to find a node, and Fiorenzo must have cannibalized hers—or maybe *left* it somewhere."

Cynthia swallowed her arguments. "Okay. Will the cables reach?"

"I suspect that node is where she attached them the first time," Hester said. "But let's find out."

Hester paid the cables out carefully; Cynthia kept pace, trying to keep her attention on far too many threats at once. A cheshire's sixteen eyes had never sounded so good. Cynthia and Hester's movement attracted Meredith's attention, and she started in their direction, not in the all-out berserker charge of the other reanimated, but in that slow-seeming sidle that had lethally fooled Wandrei.

Cynthia shot her, aiming as best she could for the knee. They had learned, by the good old scientific method of try-it-and-find-out, that the pistol could not damage a reanimated corpse enough to unanimate it. But it could cripple one. The trick was to make sure any bits you knocked off were too small to do any damage when they kept coming after you.

At this range, even Cynthia couldn't miss. Meredith didn't make a sound—she couldn't, with severed vocal cords—but the silent rictus of shock (*pain?* Cynthia wondered bleakly, *betrayal?*) was almost worse. She went down, and continued dragging herself forward—but her hands couldn't get much purchase on the deck plates protecting the *Charles Dexter Ward*'s tissue, especially slick as they were with Wandrei's fluids.

Hester had reached the dark and wetly shining hole. She knelt clumsily, then looked up, a brave if not very convincing effort at a smile on her face. "You'd better," she started; then voice and smile failed together, her face going slack with an emotion Cynthia couldn't identify—until a voice behind her, a grating, hollow snarl said, "*Stop.*"

And then she knew, because she could feel her own face mirroring Hester's: it was horror.

Cynthia turned. Dr. Fiorenzo was struggling to her feet. She stretched. She examined her hands. She took a carotid pulse.

She smiled. "All it took," she said calmly, "was a fresh enough specimen. Really, Doctor Feuerwerker, you of all people should appreciate my success."

Cynthia stepped backward. Once, twice. She worried about stepping into the pit, about tripping over Hester. About edging too close to Meredith and her undead strength. But she couldn't take her eyes away from Fiorenzo. And she couldn't—viscerally couldn't—let Fiorenzo close the gap between them. No matter how sweet and reasonable she sounded.

Something brushed Cynthia's ankle. She almost squeezed off a shot—the last in the pistol—before realizing that it was Hester, mutely offering up the power cables. They were too thick to manage one-handed. Cynthia would have to let go of the gun.

"Not live," she said.

Hester said, "I'll worry about that."

Carefully, watching Fiorenzo the whole time, Cynthia handed Hester the gun and took the cables. They were heavy. How had Hester handled them so easily?

"Doctor Fiorenzo," she said. "Stop."

Fiorenzo took another step, but she was eyeing the cables cautiously. Cynthia was at the limit of their length, and the pit was behind her. She could retreat no farther.

"I assure you, I'm no threat," Fiorenzo said. "This process will *save* lives."

Cynthia heard Hester scrambling. Did she intend to get past Fiorenzo somehow? No, she was edging to the side, still keeping Cynthia as her buffer. *Thanks a lot.* But if their positions were reversed, would Cynthia be doing any differently?

"It will save your life," Fiorenzo said.

And lunged.

Her strength was incredible. Cynthia swung the cables against her head, again and again, until Fiorenzo pinioned her arms. They rolled to the floor. Fiorenzo landed on top. Fiorenzo's teeth worried at the seam of Cynthia's pressure suit; Cynthia got a foot up and kicked, but couldn't knock her off.

"*Incoming!*" Hester yelled. Fiorenzo's head jerked up, and Cynthia thought, *What damned good is*—

The report of the pistol would have been deafening in the confined space of the morgue, if not for Cynthia's suit filters. Fiorenzo thrashed for a second, the left side of her skull blossoming into a cratered exit wound. Cynthia threw herself free and rolled across the decking.

"Cables!" Hester yelled.

Cynthia grabbed them from the middle and yanked. The ends came slithering toward her, sparking against the deck. Heavy yellow sparks. Cynthia grabbed them by the insulation and lifted.

Fiorenzo rolled to a crouch, then stood. She laughed, one eye bobbing gently on the end of its optic nerve against her cheek. She sprang forward like a racer—

Cynthia jabbed the cables into her chest.

Fiorenzo arched back as the current went through her, hands splayed and clawing. She didn't scream; there was no other sound to cover the crack of electricity, the hiss of cooking flesh.

She slumped. Cynthia jumped backward, but Fiorenzo's outflung hand still fell across her boot. She turned wildly; Meredith was still crawling toward her. Hester crouched by the controls, sliding the master switch back to *off.*

"Decomp tie-ins," Hester said. "You use the bolt nearest the panel." She stepped over Fiorenzo's corpse, her boot disturbing the gentle wisps of steam still rising, and dropped into the hole again. "And hand me the fucking cables again, would you please?"

Following orders was the easiest, most pleasant thing that Cynthia had ever done. She clipped and locked her safety line to the bolt. She slid the power control back to *full.*

"Do it!" she shouted to Hester.

And Hester must have done it, because the *Charles Dexter Ward* convulsed. Cynthia was jerked hard against her tether and then slammed back into the machine—and that was with only enough slack to attach the line. Everything unanchored went flying; she heard the crunch as Meredith hit a bulkhead, and then she was jerked forward again and blacked out.

She couldn't have been out for more than a minute, she reckoned later; she could hear things still cascading in thumps and crunches. But the ship himself was not moving, and more importantly, more tellingly, his necroluminescence was gone. The only light was Hester's suit lamp, and Cynthia fumbled her own on.

"Thank the ancient powers and the Buddha," Hester said in a thin fervent voice. "I thought you were dead."

Cynthia swallowed bright copper where she'd bitten the inside of her mouth. "Ow."

"Yes." Hester was undoing her safety line and dragging herself upright. Cynthia undid her own line with shaky fingers, and then her head cleared and she made it to her feet in one adrenaline-sour jerk. She twisted around, scanning, but Meredith was nowhere within the limited range of her light. She saw one of Ngao's legs and part of his spine; he had been torn apart by the force of Charlie's convulsions. As she watched, the foot twitched.

"Do you think we can make it back to the *Caitlín R. Kiernan* alive?" Hester said.

Cynthia squared her shoulders, wincing a little, and answered: "I think we can try."

## Epilogue

In his (second) death throes, the *Charles Dexter Ward* had taken a chunk out of the *Jarmulowicz Astronomica,* like a kid biting a chunk out of an apple. The casualties were five dead and thirteen injured, and they would have been worse except that everyone possible had been press-ganged into helping with the broken ward-mirror. The medical bay was gone, and now Cynthia knew why she'd only ever seen the one future-ghost, because there had only been one future path in which there was still a medical bay—the future path, she knew with cold uncomfortable certainty, in which she had not stood up to Wandrei and Fiorenzo, in which the *Charles Dexter Ward* had not died twice.

Cynthia patched up the crew as best she could with bandages made of cloth and splints repurposed from any number of functions, and the crew patched up the *Jarmulowicz Astronomica*. The mass funeral was devastating; Cynthia stood with Hester and let Hester's grip leave bruises on her hand.

She bunked in with Hester, which was tight but doable. On her first sleep shift, after she finished brushing what she hoped was the last of the *Charles Dexter Ward*'s death stench out of her mouth, she came into Hester's room and found two smug cheshires in the hammock slung crossways above Hester's bunk. She surprised herself by bursting into tears.

"I'm okay, I'm okay," she said, fending off Hester's concern. "I just didn't expect them to find me."

"They know you," Hester said, as if it were all that simple.

The *Jarmulowicz Astronomica* sent out a distress signal, and before leaving the *Charles Dexter Ward,* they set warning beacons around the boojum's carcass. The Universal Code didn't have an entry for *REANIMATED*; Hester told Cynthia that the Faculty Senate passed a motion to submit a proposal to add it before agreeing that the best they could do for now was *EPIDEMIC* alternating with *BANDERSNATCH,* and trust that it would be dire enough to warn people away.

And there was always the story, Cynthia thought, and that would do more good than a hundred beacons. Their distress call was answered, less than a week out, by a liveship, the *Judith Merrill,* and her crew lost nearly all their native distrust of Arkhamers in their desire for the details—Cynthia, as a non-Arkhamer, was pestered nearly to death. But she was willing to tell the story as often as necessary to make people believe it, and she knew perfectly well that half the reason she got so many questions was the *Judith Merrill*'s crew double-checking what the Arkhamers told them. Everyone knew Arkhamers lied.

She was amused, though, and also touched that their greatest concern was for what Fiorenzo had done to the *Charles Dexter Ward*. They were fiercely protective of their ship, and while they were horrified by the idea of Fiorenzo reanimating the dead, it was Charlie they wanted to lynch her for. It was the wreck of the *Charles Dexter Ward* that was going to make the story, and Fiorenzo would be merely its villain, not a scientist striving—however wrong-headedly—for knowledge.

With the *Jarmulowicz Astronomica* in a cargo bay, Cynthia and Hester (and a random assortment of cheshires) were sharing a dormitory cubicle somewhere under the *Judith Merrill*'s left front fin. The purser had offered to put her somewhere else, but Cynthia had turned him down. Until they reached Faraday Station, her contract bound her to the *Jarmulowicz Astronomica*. And even after that, friendship would bind her to Hester.

And, the bare truth was, she didn't want to try to sleep alone.

When Cynthia reached their cubicle at the start of her next sleep shift, she said, "What makes forbidden knowledge forbidden, anyway?"

Hester looked up with visible alarm.

"No, I haven't found another Mi-Go canister," Cynthia said, amazed to find that she was able to joke about it. "I was just thinking about Fiorenzo and, well, how do you figure out where to draw the line? Because apparently I don't know."

"You do know," Hester said. "You knew Fiorenzo was wrong before I did."

"I knew Fiorenzo was *suicidal*. That's not quite the same thing."

"No," Hester said. "You looked at Ngao and you knew it was wrong. You saw the person suffering first, not the scientific achievement."

Cynthia winced. She had looked up Major Ngao—Major Kirawat Ngao, RN, MSc—but had had to draw back from attempting to contact his next of kin. What could she say? *I'm sorry your loved one was murdered and reanimated by an unscrupulous scientist, and is still animate and possibly conscious—though in pieces—in the belly of a dead boojum.* That was rank cruelty.

It was Ngao and the rest of the *Charles Dexter Ward*'s crew that she still felt worst about; Charlie himself was at least peacefully dead—even the pseudoghosts had faded out before the *Jarmulowicz Astronomica* was picked up by the *Judith Merrill*, showing that the spacetime disruptions were healing. But the reanimated were trapped in their dead ship, and the best that could be hoped for was that Fiorenzo's serum might someday wear off.

"Someday," which might just be another word for "never."

"You said yourself," Hester continued, pursuing the argument and jarring Cynthia out of a sad and pointless spiral of thought, "that you wouldn't put anyone in a canister, and I suspect you wouldn't have experimented at all if it had still had a brain in it."

"No," Cynthia said, then muttered rebelliously, "I still think we could find really valuable applications for the knowledge."

"Which is exactly what we told you about Fiorenzo," Hester said.

"Ouch," Cynthia said. She swung into her hammock and rearranged the cheshires to give her space.

"Mostly, I've always thought 'forbidden knowledge' was another way of saying, 'don't do that or the bandersnatches will get you,'" Hester pursued thoughtfully. "Or, I suppose, the Mi-Go."

"Which is frequently true," Cynthia said.

"Yes, but it never stops us." Hester looked up at Cynthia, her eyes dark. "Maybe that's the worst part of human nature. Nothing *ever* stops us. Not for long."

"Not for long," Cynthia agreed and petted the tentacled horror on her lap until it cuddled close and began to purr.

*With him he bore the subject of his visit, a grotesque, repulsive, and apparently very ancient stone statuette whose origin he was at a loss to determine.*

"The Call of Cthulhu" · H. P. Lovecraft (1928)

### • ALL MY LOVE, A FISHHOOK •
### Helen Marshall

Listen.

It was not that I believe my father did not love me. He did. It is not that I fear I do not love my own son. I *do*. I do love him. It is a truth written in my blood and bones. Inescapable. As strong as faith and deep as ritual. But there is a thing that pulls inside me—it pulled inside my father, my babbas, this I know—and it is something like love and something like hate.

Do you know the feeling of being on a boat for the first time? It is a feeling of alternating weightlessness and great heaviness. Now your body is light—soaring even!—and now your knees are catching the great burden of you. Some men stagger about as if they are drunk. It makes others ill. Being a father is very much like that. There is great joy in the littlest thing. A smile. A skill freshly mastered. The way he walks on legs that have not learned to carry him. The shape his mouth makes when he begs for milk. But also a great blackness that descends. Your child will not be mastered. He grows at odds to you. Now he is your friend. Your comfort. Now he is your enemy. He will best you. He will live long after you have died, make his way in a world that no longer needs you or cares for you. Now he is your greatest luck. Now you wish you had drowned him at birth.

Stefanos was quiet as a boy. Prone to long silences, eyes fixed on the horizon, his little fingers dancing across his palm as if he were counting. He is quiet as a man. Dark-haired. His jaw has the same sharp line that mine does, that my babbas had once. But his eyes are the same tawny brown as his mother's: like the heartwood of an olive tree. They grow very round when he laughs, which is seldom. He smiles rarely, but he has a very beautiful smile.

Perhaps it is something hooked inside all the men of our line—the way my babbas would jam a fishhook in a piece of wood for luck and quick healing if he cut himself on it. I remember dark spells when I was a child. I would disappear to the cliff face around sunset some days when the wind was high enough to maybe send a young boy—small for my age—reeling off the edge and into the dark waters of the Aegean. I called these the knuckle cliffs. Their cracked ridges reminded me of my father's hands—callused hands, unyielding as granite. Yet in the evening the sun would catch hold of the edges of the gneiss and send up very beautiful sparks of light.

My mother worried for me during these spells, but when I returned, wind-chapped and shivering, she would brew strong coffee over the gas burner and sit with me as my body, wracked with shivers and nearly blue, quieted. Together we would listen to the wind scrabbling at the cliffs, whistling through the holes in the plaster and brick. Her voice was a plucked string humming out tunes of worry: "Kostas, what were you doing out there? The wind, you hear, boy? Aieee!"—a toothless whistle, a half-sucked breath—"Please don't go out again. Please. I could not stand for it."

My babbas would say little, but his eyes were flinty and cold. He would work me hard the next day, re-caulking the boat or checking the nets until my fingers bled from loosening and retying salt-hardened knots. He was impatient with me. A hard man, intolerant of weakness. He had survived two wars in his lifetime, buried his brothers, seen his home ravaged by looters and communists. Sometimes I hated him. Sometimes I think he hated me.

But I loved him too. Perhaps even more because of that hardness. We are like that as children—always chasing storms, running toward the wolf's teeth. And perhaps he did love me. He taught me a trade and made sure I never starved as he had, never suffered the ache of a stomach gnawing away at itself. But he grew to smile less and less for me. Eventually the love I had for him, at high tide when I was seven or so, began to recede. When it did, it left little behind but sharp rocks, broken shells and the gasping struggles of tiny fishes—ignorant of death until they were taken.

It is one such memory—a broken fragment whose shape I have never fully understood—that I hold closest to my heart. So close it cuts me, I know, but that is the way of memory.

Our family had lived on the island for many years. My babbas was a sailor and a fisherman. He kept a single caïque for long lining, which he made himself, from memory, without any plan. It was on my father's caïque I learned to navigate the waters around the island, to work the windlass if we were trawling. It was there I learned to obey.

Though Mama kept several crosses in the house and mass was a regular, solemn ritual for us, my babbas was not a particularly religious man. Like many of the older sailors he had his own private rituals, his own fears and superstitions, his own way of spitting in the nets before he cast them, or reading the clouds for signs of storms. He kept sacred objects. A medallion of Saint Christopher which Mama gave him when they married. A little pouch filled with the bones of a bat. But his most precious possession— and never mentioned in the house after the incident I will tell you, for Mama did not like to think of her husband as an old pagan—was a small statue. Babbas told me that it was shaped in the image of Poseidon who had once owned the island of Delos—the sacred island, a place of many gods once, where it was forbidden for any to be born and any to die. I have seen this island from the water. It is filled with broken columns and arches, a graveyard now.

The statue was very old, a stone lump, now the color of old teeth. There was a face, yes, but its features had been worn down to something of a skull: gaping eye sockets big enough to hold my thumbprint when I was an infant. A snake's nose—just two slits in a little mound. The upper arm had broken off, leaving a solid stump like a growth. The right arm, clenched against the body, had worn away into a ribbed mass.

The statue was very dear to my babbas, and it is perhaps this love for it that drew me to the thing when I was a child. I longed to hold it. Mama said I wept for it in the secret language of babes before any could understand me. Once, in my infancy, I remember knocking it from its position beneath Mama's portrait of Jesus above the table. Babbas was furious! I remember bursting into tears immediately at the sight of him, red-faced and grunting like a bull, his fists clenching and unclenching.

"Mama!" I cried, lunging for the safety of her arms. But Babbas was faster, terrible in his fury, like a storm overtaking me on the cliffs: hot air whistling from his nostrils, the sudden slick sweat of his hand pressing against my mouth. There was violence in him. I had known that always. Babbas was an ocean. His strength was irresistible. My arms were weak, my skin soft and ready to bruise.

He took a knife to my palm and cut a single red line. He would have severed my thumb if I struggled, but I did not. I was helpless. As brittle and breakable as the twig of bone he kept in his pouch. I could not see his face. His hair hung lank and damp as a curtain. It clung to his chin in a strange pattern. Mama was screaming at him, and this shocked me more than anything, how suddenly these people I loved had become like animals to one another. To me!

Babbas pressed my bleeding hand against the little statue—and in that moment it seemed like a great tooth. Oh, how I howled! I feared it would gobble me up! But the blood only smeared against the jagged line of that lumpish stone body, the little withered arm smashing against my palm.

Then it was over. Aieee. It was over.

Perhaps I am lucky. In another age Babbas might have drowned me in the sea. Or left me on a hill to be torn apart by animals. It is strange to look at one's own father and think he might have done such a thing, but I cannot say with any certainty that it would have been beyond him.

I loved him. He was a stranger to me. The scar still grins at me when I look for it.

When I was older, Mama told me that some piece of the statue had broken in the fall. I had not known, I was too young then, but the family's luck was not good for several years. Babbas's boat was loosed from the shore in a bad storm while all the other boats were safely harbored. No one knew how the ropes slipped or the knots failed. But they did. Much of our meager savings went to repairs. I know Babbas blamed me.

But that thing—whatever it was that had my clumsy infant fingers reaching and reaching and always reaching for it—it never left me. Babbas took the statue away and kept it in a secret place, but by the time I was ten I had discovered it again. I would sneak into his room and take hold of it from behind the loose brick where he kept it among his other sacred possessions. I would turn it over gently in the uncertain light and run my fingers along its grooves. I could see the rusted spots of my own blood, ancient then, or so it seemed to me. It could have been anyone's blood.

It was blood that bound me to Babbas. Our shared blood. Sometimes it made me smile to see my blood upon the statue. Sometimes it made me feel proud.

• • •

My babbas left Mama when I was fifteen.

It was a shock to me but by then I cannot say it was an unwelcome one. I had lived in the shadow of his temper for many years, and grown up stunted the way a tree does when it must cling to rocky soil. I knew he was unhappy. There are many forms of violence that one can do upon another when love is gone. Once blood bound us like a knot. Now blood made my mother and me weak to him, vulnerable, those first touched by the storms of his passions. There were ways he could hurt us for loving him when he did not love in return.

What we did not know was that he had found happiness with another woman. She was pregnant, Babbas told us. He had responsibilities to her. I was close enough to fully grown that Mama would not starve if I was a man. He delivered the words like kicks. Carefully. They were meant to cripple, perhaps; to wound, almost certainly. But to me they simply brought relief in the knowledge that, with another child, he would not return to us.

He took few things. A wool blanket. His favorite knife. A pot he had mended on several occasions. It heated unevenly, burnt whatever it touched or left it raw, but when it disappeared from its hook, Mama wept like a child and I wrapped her in my arms. Arms muscled from turning the winch on our boat, hauling nets from the sea. They were not weak arms. They were a man's arms. We would survive.

It was only some time later that memory struck me. I raced to Babbas's room—the room he had shared with Mama for all the years of my life. I went to the little hiding place. He had left the stub of a candle. A tin medallion of Saint Christopher. A satchel filled with bat bones—they were lucky, he had told me once. But the statue was gone. Of course it was gone. These other things were trinkets. These were the lesser lucks he had carried with him. He had taken his greater luck with him for that new child.

I hoped his seed would stunt and shrivel.

I hoped he would never have another son.

I hoped the baby would be weak.

I hoped its mouth would mewl for milk but no milk would sate it.

I hoped its lungs would howl and howl and howl as the wind howled in the winter but there would be no season for it, only the howling, forever and ever.

He was not coming back. He had abandoned us entirely.

• • •

Time passes. The sea goes out. It comes in again.

By the time my son was born my mother and Babbas had reconciled. The other woman moved to the mainland to work in a shop that sold jewellery to the foreigners. I never knew what happened to the child: if he had been real or simply a convenient fiction on my father's part. A reason for leaving we might understand.

I was twenty. A man as my father had demanded and my mother had required.

At first I was afraid of fatherhood.

I confess that when Marina—the beautiful dark-eyed girl I had married—told me of the child planted in her belly, I was tempted to demand she find us a way out of the mess. Such things were possible, I knew. There were things to be done to loose the thing from the womb, to let it unspool in blood like a badly wound ball of yarn.

I even spoke to Babbas of this. It was midday. The sun falling on the water looked, not like a mirror as some say, but like fine blankets of lace piled high upon one another, the kind of blanket under which an old man might sleep in the winter.

"Aieee, Kostas," my babbas said, making the same whistling noise my mother had made once. They were growing into the same person, these days. "Of course, you will have the child."

"What can you tell me of fatherhood?" I asked him.

"A child is a blessing," he said, and spat. The water shivered. The old man in the ocean was sick today.

I smiled at him, and tried to find love in the answer he gave me, but the old scar itched when I worked the winch. I watched my father in the stern with the tiller. His hair was a tangle more silver now than black, the skin of his face bruised into dark pouches beneath his eyes. His tongue, when it touched his teeth, was tobacco-stained, the color of a worm. I, who had been a small boy once and weak, towered over him now.

I wondered if I had been a blessing to my father.

I wondered at that other child he had left behind. Or had died. Or had never lived.

I knew Marina could not keep the baby.

But that night when I saw my wife, her face was shining with excitement. Excitement, yes, and maybe just a hint of fear that I would say to her exactly what first sprang into my head.

"Are you happy too, Kostas?" she asked me. She was curled against me in the bed we shared, her hands resting in the knotted wire of my hair, salted and damp. Her voice was soft, sweet. She sounded nothing like me.

She spoke her words the way they are spoken on the mainland. The way farmers speak them.

"A child is a blessing," I told her.

I could not bring myself to speak my heart.

I would be a father. I would help her bring a son into the world.

My son was a blessing.

At two he toddled about, his head barely higher than the table, eyes that saw spoons and jars of salt, the knees and ankles of our guests when he hid. His speech was slow to come. When it came, he did not speak like other boys.

I remember Marina gave him a set of toy soldiers. They were made of lead, heavy things, and clumsily crafted. The paint flaked off to expose the dull sheen of metal beneath. But the boy loved them.

One day I saw that Stefanos had separated out a single soldier. Not the poorest of the lot, by any stretch, but certainly no favorite. The figure— head tilted to the ground, helmet askew, caught in some badly rendered mimicry of motion—held a red rifle by the barrel as if he intended to use it as a club. The rest of the soldiers circled him at a distance, wary perhaps, or merely watching the shadow show in amusement.

"A firing squad?" I asked him playfully.

"No, Babbas."

"Then what?"

Stefanos shook his head. "The other soldiers do not like him."

"Why do they not like him, Stefanos?"

"God lives in this one," he said.

Marina did not like this very much. She shooed him from the house and placed the soldiers all in a box. Except the lone soldier in the center.

"Throw this in the sea," she begged me. One delicate hand clutched the lead soldier, the other, white knuckled, squeezed the folds of her skirt.

My wife asked little enough of me, and I could see the fear in her eyes, the rolling white edges of them, and so I did as she asked.

Stefanos never spoke of his missing soldier, but sometimes he would wear a strange look on his face: as if he had breathed all the silence in the room into his chest and held it there, his lungs a perfect prison. He became a quiet boy, but always obedient. I loved him.

I did not speak to Marina further concerning the little toy she had brought for Stefanos. I could not. I could not tell her about the way the metal seemed to glow like a coal in my hand when I touched it. Not hot, exactly. But something. The way I hated the feel of it in my hand. That raised red rifle pressing into the mound beneath my thumb. It was as if I had touched something unclean. It would have only frightened her further to hear these things. And, besides, Stefanos soon outgrew such toys. He did not dwell long in childhood.

Even now I look at Stefanos in admiration. At twenty, he is good at his work. Far better than I ever was. But I worry for his happiness. I worry he is not kind enough to the women who sometimes smile at him, that he will never find a wife and have a child of his own. There is too much quiet in him, too much solemnity. When I look at him I see so little of myself there, except, perhaps, in the shape of his jaw, the curve of his forehead. But perhaps he keeps much of himself hidden from me. Perhaps all sons do, as I hid myself from my father.

And he always obeys me. If I tell him to handle the boat in a certain fashion or to set it on a particular angle to the wind, he will always do so. He never speaks against me even if, privately, he may disagree. If anything, there might only be the briefest pause—barely a pause at all!—before he says, "Yes, Babbas."

I believe he respects me. I think that obedience comes from respect, does it not? But still I wonder if it would have been easier if we argued. If he had a streak of insolence in him. As it is, I have begun to listen for the pauses. To hate the feel of his eyes on me a moment too long before they flinch away.

Sometimes I change course. Sometimes I ask myself, "Kostas, have you checked the lines? Are you certain of the waters?"

Sometimes I stare at my son. "Stefanos knows something," I say to myself. "What does he know?"

More than once these questions have averted disaster, but would it not have been easier if he had simply told me straight off? Is he afraid of me? I have never once given him cause to be afraid. To doubt my affection. Have I? I have never laid a hand upon him. I have never cut a grinning red mouth into his hand. I have never spoken of my doubts.

This is the great fear of fatherhood. To know that love is a chancy thing. It has its tides, it has its seasons, and it can shatter a man's luck. I know the shape of the waves, the sound they make as they grind against the hull, as they drag pebbles on the beach. I know the constellations. I know the pattern of the clouds. But even now I do not know my own son.

My father—Old Babbas now—had always been a strong man, his muscles thick and corded underneath his loosening, wrinkled skin. The other sailors respected him. He had built the caïque himself, fitted the planks. Two wars he had fought in, and lived. No bullet found him. He laughed at storms. But the years were a burden upon him.

Now he could work the winch of the windlass. He could haul in the nets. Now he could not. His legs failed him. He gasped for breath. Then he died.

After his death it fell to me to tend to his effects. Stefanos and I went to the little house he had lived in, but there was little of value. Two copper pots, one dented and mended, the other new. Chipped crockery. A jug with a split lip. I recognized the wool sweater that hung on the chair. It stilled smelled of my father, the peculiar sweet smell of his sweat. I folded it gently.

"You should keep that," Stefanos said.

"The hem is unraveling."

"Mama can mend it," he told me. He rested a hand lightly on my shoulder, but I turned away, wiped at my eyes with the back of my hand. The unwashed salt of the sea stung.

His bed, when we found it, was unmade. The sheets were dirty and stank.

"Babbas," said Stefanos.

"We should burn these. They will be no good to anyone."

In the bedroom I found the old nook I had pillaged so often as a child. There it was. The little statue. I had not known I was looking for it, but having laid eyes on its familiar shape, my blood long since flaked away from the belly, the jagged, teething line of the arm, I felt a keen sort of tension go out of me like the slacking of a rope.

I picked it up slowly. Stefanos watched me. I could feel his eyes tracking my movements.

The statue was much how I remembered it. Ugly. Misshapen. Now I wanted to smash it to pieces. Now I wanted to clutch it to my breast.

"Babbas," said Stefanos.

Truthfully, I had forgotten he was there. But he was. I could see the shape of his shoulder in the dull light. His smoothly muscled arms. Even the black wiry hairs stood up, pricked to attention.

"That is mine. Old Babbas gave it to me."

"You are mistaken," I scoffed. The feel of the stone was cool in my hand. The weight was exactly the same. It should have felt lighter. My hands had been a boy's hands when I last held it. Or perhaps I had diminished. Perhaps I had lived through the better part of my life already.

"No, Babbas. It was for me to have. He told me so."

"Listen, boy," I said. "I have loved this statue since I was a boy."

"He said you broke it."

"I—" My tongue stumbled.

"You must give it to me," Stefanos said. His eyes were calm. Sad even. "He did not want you to have it."

He was normally such an obedient son! I turned away. Tried to make a jest of it.

"Surely you would not turn against me now," I teased. "You would not risk my love for such a little thing?"

"No, Babbas." It was like his body had been set ablaze. There was a heat to him. A furnace nestled inside. His teeth were set so that he smiled differently in the half-light. His lips twitched as if a ghost tugged at them. I shivered though the room was stiflingly hot now.

Still he was so quiet! My silent son! His tongue was a dead snake, why did it never stir? Except now. Except in disobedience. Could he not see the old man had been addled? Did he not know that a father's possessions were the fair due of the son? Ungrateful! Intolerable! Had that man not been my father? Had I not loved him as best I could, forgiven his abandonment, given him a grandson, comfort in his old age?

"It is mine." I howled the words at him. I had kept my own silences too long. He would hear me now. He *must* hear me. "It is my right!"

"No, Babbas," he said. "Please. Set it away."

I did not want to listen. I clenched my fist, made a great club of it. My nails pressed into the sick white scar my own father had given me. I wondered where he had left the knife. I thought of all the sons who had been left on hillsides for animals. The sons who had been torn apart by wolves. It was only as I raised my hand into the air—ready to knock his insolent teeth out!—that I was aware I had made any movement at all.

Stefanos, for his part, was still.

It was as if we were on the boat again. He did not speak, but there was the slightest pause in his breathing. That tiny silence I had learned to recognize. And then I knew—he would let me strike him. He was younger. His arms were tireless, his joints did not stiffen, did not slow. He was more than my match. But he would let me strike him.

There was only the pause. Only the waiting.

I have never felt such shame. It came sickening and sudden. What was this thing that had come between us?

I sat down heavily on the bed, appalled.

I did not want him to touch me, but he did. He rested a hand easily on my shoulder. A light touch, but strong.

"Let me tell you," Stefanos said, " how this statue came to him."

"How do you know this story?"

"He told me."

"He never told *me*."

"I shall tell you."


These were his words:

Once there was a time when Old Babbas had been a young man, twenty perhaps. The war had just claimed the first of his brothers. The family had little to eat. So Old Babbas took out the boat though the wind was high and it was not a good time to sail. Many had warned him against this, but he was young, full of anger and grief, and perhaps he wished the waves to claim him. I do not know. He did not tell me. Only that a storm overtook him and smashed his boat against the shore of the sacred island, Delos, which was once called the invisible island when the gods kept it beneath the waters.

He had never set foot on the shore because of the old law that no man should be born or should die there. But the storm broke him upon the beach and he found himself pierced badly by a spar. He who knew his own strength best could feel it pour out of him in a bright pool on the beach. He lay on the sand amongst the fish and the broken shells and the things that had crawled out of the ocean during the storm, and he knew he must not die. And so he prayed to the dark god of the ocean—not as my mother or my grandmother would have it—but to the one who watches us when we take to the waves, the one who blesses us with fish and curses us with salt.

You have seen the island from a distance. You have seen the temples there, the ruined pillars of marble. How they catch the sun and send off such a dizzying light. Perhaps Old Babbas found himself amongst one such temple. In any case, he discovered there this little statue, and the statue drank his tears and the statue drank his prayers and the statue drank his blood. And though the night was long and cold, and the storm was fierce, he did not die as he supposed. When daylight touched the marble and sent it blazing, his brothers found him.

Old Babbas had believed himself lucky, but, of course, this was not so: the war took his brothers one by one by one, and it took their sons and it took their daughters. Only you were spared. You alone. And now me. Of course, me.

Old Babbas never knew much of the statue. He called it his luck. He called it his curse. Perhaps it is Poseidon, as he believed. But perhaps it was not. Perhaps there is another god who lives within the ocean. Waiting.

There are things in the ocean, Babbas, that you cannot imagine. I have seen them. And this statue? All your life you have sought after the shadow of the thing instead of the thing itself. A rock is not a god, even if it is in the shape of one. You are clutching at moonlight on the water as if it were the water and not the light itself that was beautiful.

But I have seen more than moonlight. I have seen the shape of dark things in the night. You have given your blood to the rock, yes, but there is something of it lodged in me, like a fishhook, and I will not heal from it. Do you not see that? Do you not understand?

This, this is mine. My blessing and my curse. You will die one day. I have seen your death, Babbas, as I saw the death of Old Babbas before you. But I have not seen my own death, do you understand? For me there is something else and I do not know what it is, but I cannot turn away from it.

There are things you do not understand. The old man of the ocean slumbers beneath his blanket of salt but he shall not stay silent forever.

And I belong to him. This is what Old Babbas told me. You were spared. But one of us must go.

I cannot say if I believed what Stefanos told me. All I can say is that when he finished his tale, his hands were shaking, and I clutched at him as I had when he was a small child. In that moment, whatever else he was, I saw him as very young. And very afraid.

For the long years of my life there has always been a grief in me. It has a weight and it has a shape that I recognize. And perhaps all sons carry it. Perhaps all fathers carry it. He does not want this thing. He does not want it as I wanted it, my fingers always itching to claim it as my own. But something has hooked within him. He struggles like a fish on the line but it will not let him free.

I hold Stefanos in my arms—and he is burning, he is burning—and there is an awfulness, an uncleanness to him. Perhaps I ought to have strangled him at birth. Left him in the wilderness. But when I close my eyes I am struck by the sense that we two are aboard a very small caïque, and I know the ocean is beneath me, monstrous deep and very very wide, the waves rocking us both. Now light, now heavy, now joyful, now terribly sad.

It is every father's dream that his son should outlive him. No father wishes to see the death of his offspring.

And yet. And yet. I do not know my son. I do not know what shall come from him.

And so I hold him. And I pray Stefanos will be a good man. I pray he will care for his mother.

I pray he will have sons of his own in time, and that he will take some measure of comfort from them—if such a thing is allowed to him.

I pray—it is a failing on my part, perhaps, the curse of too-weak love that I cannot take this from him—but I pray that when I am dead, he will bury my bones far from the sea, where the earth makes a knuckle to beat back the waves.

*Who knows the end? What has risen may sink, and what has sunk may rise. Loathsomeness waits and dreams in the deep, and decay spreads over the tottering cities of men.*

"The Call of Cthulhu" · H. P. Lovecraft

# • THE DOOM THAT CAME TO DEVIL REEF •
## Don Webb

Among Lovecraft's papers at Brown University was a large manila envelope containing a school exercise notebook and a newspaper clipping. The notebook's owner, Miss Julia Phillips, had been mistakenly identified as a cousin of American horror writer Howard Phillips Lovecraft (1890-1937). Over four-fifths of the pen and pencil entries are rather commonplace detailing Miss Phillips' life as a seamstress in the Providence of the 1920s, her growing depression, and her commitment to Butler Hospital. As both of Lovecraft's parents had ended their years in the selfsame institution, Julia had been perceived as another branch of a less than mentally healthy tree. It wasn't until Lovecraft's biographer S. T. Joshi read the volume that it was seen as anything other than a rather dreary memento. It is in the last few pages of the book wherein Julia's dreams or waking fancies take an amazingly cosmic tone that the book became of interest to Lovecraftian scholars. The relationship of Julia and Howard is unknown. Lovecraft had little interest in psychiatry, rather than his occasional denunciation of Freud in his letters. No one has been able to discover how Lovecraft came into possession of the book.

What is clear is that Julia's fantasies became Lovecraft's inspiration for his 1931 novella "The Shadow Over Innsmouth." Lovecraft's notes in the volume are slight, but he occasionally erased Julia's words altogether and wrote in his fictional equivalents. For example, Julia records that she is writing about the real world Massachusetts town of Newburyport where Julia had spent her childhood. Lovecraft erased all but one instance of "Newburyport" and wrote in "Innsmouth." Likewise, certain demons or gods of Julia's delusions have been replaced with Cthulhu, Dagon, and Mother Hydra. It is tempting to speculate that Lovecraft had considered the diary as a sort of *objet trouvé* or "ready-made" to continue the mythic patterns he began in earlier work, especially "The Call of Cthulhu" (1926). Perhaps Julia's rather simple style, reflecting her fifth-grade education, was too limiting for Lovecraft, or perhaps the whole notion struck him as artistically dishonest. Given Lovecraft's penchant for recording even the smallest details of his moods and life in his letters it seems remarkable that Julia's diary was never mentioned.

Inevitably that class of literalist thinker that assumes all of Lovecraft's stories are some sort of mystic channelings, have claimed the diary of Julia Phillips is the work of a kindred soul—likewise expressing the "mysteries of the Aeon." Perhaps Lovecraft himself, who had played with the artistic notion of art and dream coming from some sort of Otherness, was attracted to and then repulsed by the contents of this diary for that seeming. Again, unless further documentation comes to light we shall never know.

Here is what we do know about Julia Phillips. She was the third of six children to be born to Rodger Allen and Susan Williams Phillips. Born in 1891, she was a year younger than Lovecraft. Her father was a green grocer and her mother supplemented the family's income with sewing, a skill young Julia excelled at. Her sickly youth kept her a homebody while her two brothers joined the merchant marine and her three better-adjusted (and apparently better-looking) sisters found husbands. When her parents died she went to live with her eldest sister, Velma, and alternated between manic periods of religiosity and depressed periods of terrible lethargy. At first she was the merely eccentric aunt, whose financial contribution was greatly valued. As time wore on, she became worrisome to her sister and brother-in-law. In 1924 Julia tried to kill herself with rat poison after months of the darkest depression. The family had her committed to Butler. She remained in Butler until 1927. For the majority of her stay she was a model patient. She repaired the garments of other patients, took part in the sing-alongs, and greeted her family in a sane and cheery tone during their infrequent visits. The entries prior to her commitment were made in pen, but the hospital only allowed a No. 1 pencil during Julia's stay.

The last dated entry in Julia's diary was August 7, the day the "Peace Bridge" was opened between Fort Erie, Ontario, and Buffalo, New York:

"Perhaps mankind has learned to live in Peace—God bless Prince Edward and Prince Albert and Governor Smith."

In late August 1927 Julia began obsessing on a hurricane that hit the Atlantic shore of Canada. She complained that authorities were unaware of the danger the sea stood for. She warned (somewhat prophetically) of an upcoming Pacific earthquake. In early September most of freedoms of movement in the hospital grounds were curtailed when she either shaved off or otherwise removed most of her hair. It was at this time Julia did involve herself in what limited art therapy the Butler offered. She painted five canvases of "disturbing maritime scenes." These seem to have been sold at the annual art show; sadly little is know of them save that she used the (at that time) radical technique of grattage, which had been introduced to the art world by Max Ernst. Exactly how an undereducated American woman could invent the same art technique that a German surrealist had created for his series of paintings of "enchantment and terror," is more than a bit of a mystery. Perhaps the art instructor had kept abreast of the European art scene. It is likely that during this time, the "channeled" portion of the diary was written.

On September 14, an underwater earthquake in Japan killed 108 people. The next day a "Mr. Kenneth S. Gilman" paid a visit to Julia. All of Julia's visitors had been either been family or former sewing clients, and it is assumed that he belonged in one of these categories. He paid three visits and, after winning the confidence of the staff, took Julia on a carriage ride. They never returned. The newspaper treated it as a major crisis—for two days.

A legal notice of her being declared dead appeared seven years later. Three years after that Lovecraft died of intestinal cancer. Mr. Joshi suggests that Lovecraft, having taken an interest in the case because of the two articles in the *Brown Daily Herald*, had contacted the director of the institution. Perhaps a lack of interest or sense of shame on the part of Julia's family had made them uninterested in the notebook. Perhaps the notebook had merely been lent to Lovecraft and he failed to return it

In addition to the change of narrative voice in the last section of the diary, the handwriting becomes bolder. Some of the margins are decorated with little glyphs of stylized fish reminiscent of the Rongorongo glyphs of Easter Island. The theology and cosmology of the piece seem to be a mixture of aboriginal Australian religion and a good deal of Lovecraftian musings. Since Julia's background would seem to suggest no clear method of knowing the former, and *Weird Tales* was an unlikely reading material for Butler Hospital—the passages are striking.

Here are the final words of Julia Phillips, where Lovecraft has erased her words and written in his own we will indicate with *italics:*

In the changeable world of land something dire is happening. The humans are learning to kill themselves, which is good I think, and learning to kill the seas, which would mean death to the world. The seas taste of their oil and trash. The beautiful mother of pearl walls of our new home, *Devil Reef,* is stained black. I hate this place, the waters are much too cold, and the fishing is poor. Our new home has no name, the Great *Cthulhu* has not dreamed of it yet. We had great hopes as He reached out to us and our weakened descendants, the humans, two orbits ago. He tries to bring Thought to all life here. That is why He came to this watery globe from the green star in my great-great grandmother's time. He is such a suffering god. The humans have recast Him as one of their own. They think He brings salvation instead of Thought. All will think here, even the plants and the fungi, if the humans do not hurt the water too much. He rose briefly two orbits ago. He will stir in a few days, but not rise. We have learned how he tosses and turns. I am not hopeful for the humans, they are too far degenerated from us. Even those we have crossbred with can live only a few hundred orbits. No wonder they kill this world; they do not stay here long enough to love it. It seems wrong to me to bring self-awareness to such a species.

The hope of Ra-natha-alene to save the human race by intermarrying with them is not held by many of us. It did not work in my youth and it does not work now. The humans are greedy for gold, so it was easy to make a deal with *Marsh* but they do not profit by our Teaching. In the spiral towers of their cells we help them find the way back, we make them more beautiful, but it is not enough. On the land they hide away when their Beauty starts to show. They wear our crowns, but they do not Think, or if they Think it is as something minor—an artist or a magician. No architects. No mathematicians. No biologists.

There was a storm recently, much cold water was disturbed to the north of our new home. We had not controlled it by Dreaming. It is not in the Dreamtime and the hateful aurora wind from space keeps Deep Thoughts from hatching in our brains. The storm affected me badly, scattering some of my mind into human bodies. I will have to gather myself together. I hate their world with its right angles that turn thinking into sleeping. There were deaths in Canada, a cold white land. Not enough deaths I think.

The humans of *Innsmouth* have learned a little about Dreaming in their Swirl, they spill blood and sexual fluids to *Father Dagon and Mother Hydra,* but they think in animal terms, they are too much of the life of this world. They have taken the animal needs and called them Sex and Money. Even when they become Beautiful, these two abstractions rule them. I am worried that they will subvert our goals. Some among them believe that warm-blooded animals are more evolved—more progressive than we. The humans worship themselves though a demon called Darwin. If their line of faith were right I would be greater than my grandmother, my grandmother would be greater than hers, and she would be greater than *Mother Hydra*. Yet a few of the humans have discovered entropy. A few know the cosmos is decaying.

Bad news has come from the *Esoteric Order of Dagon* the humans of North America have spread the bloodlines beyond Ra-natha-alene's plan. They know that when the Change comes upon humans they will seek us out. Therefore they reason that humans changing will move back to Newburyport and bring wealth and connections from their lives with them. They seek to intermarry with traveling salesmen in a ridiculous scheme to make their town more of a center of commerce. They don't care how this can spread out tendrils of our souls. Their belief that each being has a unique soul leads to the simple numerical argument of more of "Us" equals more power. In orbits of bad sunspot activity (such as this year) the changing humans will Dream of us, or will have parts of the Dreamtime of Great *Cthulhu* become parts of their foundational consciousness. They don't understand what a strain their Change places upon us. Each new hybrid pulls at our peace, especially in places not established by the Dreamtime. Soon such humans will come to *Innsmouth* and we will literally be pulled to the land to greet them, our nurturing instincts taking the place of our common sense. Worse still, humans, who have not heard the Dream cantrips when they eat their mother's slime, will know great fear. They will see their Change in terms of death, not rebirth. And as they are not conscious entities they cannot think directly of death. Death to a being that can not remember anything before its hatching is a terrible consciousness. In the myths of the humans they dimly know what they were, they were deathless. But they see this as some sort of garden. One of the hybrid offspring in Florida is trying to recreate the Dreamtime there just as the people of Nan Madol did a few hundred orbits ago. Ra-natha-alene thinks these stirrings of true Architecture might trigger some ancestral memories on the human's part, but I am dubious. Some of us are having glimpses of human minds during the daytime. I have seen myself trapped in a body with disgustingly scaleless skin and hair. I fear that I will Dream myself there, pushed by the aurora.

I will dance at the Council and try to persuade the mothers to leave this place and swim back to our second home. We must regroup where the Architecture is strong, and Dreams are caught and farmed and milked in the old way. We must prepare against the human onslaught. Once our race was mighty. Were we not the race that called the dolphins and whales back to the sea? Were we not the race that broke up the single large landmass and kept the ages of ice at bay? If only we had not experimented with the hairy ones, adding to their spirals. What arrogance seeking to bring self-awareness to this dying world. The humans inherited our arrogance but not our wisdom. They see us as their dry-land ancestors living in lands that have sunken—Atlantis, Lemuria, *R'lyeh*. As they degenerate their myths will say we lost our footing due to black magic. They can't even guess that our life cycle is hampered by their yellow sun's deadly radiation. If we last until that star is normal and the great bands of radiation leave this world, we will flourish again. Let us wait, I shall dance to the mothers, let us wait until the stars are right. Then we can Gift the creatures of this world with Dreamtime.

Ra-natha-alene and her sisters mock me. They say that humans cannot grow to be a threat. They ignore the vast expansion of human numbers in the time since Nan Madol. They argue that as Great *Cthulhu* makes human artists and mystics Dream, humans will give up their fixation with death. No race can kill a planet they say. I warn them, there is no race as vile as humans.

Worse news has come. The hybrids came to *Devil Reef* to swim and dance at the new moon. One of the wandering rogue offspring has come to *Innsmouth*. He does not know that he is of us. His instincts provoke him to actions and accidents that he sees as chance. He is at the hotel. The mothers grew excited, their gill slits flaring purple. They will rise and seek him out. I see that this will lead to disaster. They will seek to nurture and protect him. What will happen if he merely flees them? They cannot kill one of their children even if his blood is nauseatingly warm and his skin covered in hair. It could take only one revealing of our presence to harm us here. There is no Dreamtime in the walls of our new home. Humans have grown deadly, yet the mothers do not believe what the Spiral has told us of their war in Europe.

It has happened, as I feared. The nursery parade gathered in town last night and the human saw them and heard the croaking of the nursery songs. The sounds released the Change, but he had not been fed the Dreams as the *Innsmouth* children had been. Even though I loathe humans, I felt pity for this long-lost cousin. I can imagine the rapid beating of his heart. I can imagine the cooling of his blood, which to him would feel like fear of death. The great Priestesses had put on their tiaras and the hybrid Priestesses had put on the robes. They made their slow awkward way toward his room. It was easy for him to outrun them. Without the Dreamtime to guide him he would have seen this all as nightmare.

With luck his shock will silence him before he can tell others, and then when the Change comes upon him, he will seek us out. His skin will grow scaly and only the soothing feel of salt water will bring relief. His nascent gills will swell, and our thoughts will be drawn to his head like the bees of his world are drawn to blooming flowers. The Beauty will overcome terror. Tonight I will pray and Dance at the thrones of my ancestors *Father Dagon and Mother Hydra*. May they soothe his mind and still his lips! May his Change not bring fear!

There have been Navy ships over our reef the last two days. We try to send them Dreams, but the steel hulls of the ships reflect our wills back to us. It is as I feared. It is not like the old orbits, when we touched their minds and they saw mermaids calling each to each. The mothers said the words of light and made the wheels of bioluminescence appear in the water, vast whirling signs. But this did not soothe the humans. Once humans have weapons they are not willing to be soothed, so far have they degenerated from us.

Canisters began to fall from the sides of the ships, half our size. I began swimming. They were depth charges and they exploded with epic sound against our reef. The walls of our new home shattered, great panes of mother of pearl began wheeling through the water, reflecting the lights of the bioluminescent wheels and the explosions filling the sea with green and pink lightning. Shock wave after shockwave passed though the ocean—and dead and dying fish buffeted my body as I swam with all my might. Then some jagged pieces of the mother of pearl began to cut into me and my dark blood mixed crazily with the glowing waters. I felt the drums of my ears pop and the violent storm around me became strangely still. More of the fragments tore into me. I saw the arms of my mother floating by, leaving a wake of dark pupil blood and the smell of raw death. I prayed to *Mother Hydra* that she may Sleep and Dream until her next Cycle. I reached out for her soul and found nothing but the cold unforgiving water. Then a fragment of shell struck my face and I was cut free from my body. I tried to make my soul Sleep with the words that bring Sleep: Fhtagn nerzin kyron Meftmir!

I did not Sleep but was sucked into the mind of a human, the one I had glimpsed before. A female that has not made the slime of motherhood. She was confined in a place of the mad, where the smells are terrible and the light is harsh. She is made to listen to a horrible caterwauling called "hymns," and to eat dead food and be treated with metabolic poisons superstitiously thought to calm her mind. Fortunately her mind is strong, so strong that she had never been able to fit into their world. She was born in *Innsmouth* several orbits ago. She is one of the rogue lines, descendant from *Marsh* himself four generations ago. She was not brought up in our way, but as a human, and thinks that the divine would be found in her terrible form.

I hate the way the air does not support her ugly body as she walks about. I try to Remember who I am by writing and painting. I tried once to Dance, but the other humans restrained the body. For days they kept me from moving. I cannot believe that they could be so cruel. I wished to kill the body and try again to Sleep, but the humans worship bodies and will not let me do so.

In the past few days I have found ironic hope. I cannot send my soul far, so I know not what lies on the far side of the world. Yet I have no reason to presume that our Pacific home has fallen. Surely the strange angles of the Dreamtime have kept the Watery Abyss intact! But I found him. The one who brought the doom to *Devil Reef*. With the cruel irony of this planet, the Change came upon him the day of the depth charges. His body yearned for the sea just as our new home was pounded to flinders. I am nurturing him. As a true being I was not old enough to be a mother, but in this human body I can make the slime and feel the emotions. I enveloped him with the love of the mother.

We have made a plan. He will come to this place and free me. He understands the human world well. He has done certain things to his appearance to hide the Change. He will spirit my body away. He tells me that this will be easy because humans do not value females and mad females are of no use. He has enough money to buy us train tickets to the West Coast. He will take me to a place with the lovely name of Land's End and there we will shed both human clothes and form. I feel that I can awaken the sea form of this Julia. We will swim to our home and dwell there in glory.

Thus ends the words of Julia Phillips' diary. The only other item in Lovecraft's envelope was a clipping from the *Brown Daily Herald* describing the testing of a new depth charge on Ward's Reef near Newburyport. The bombing went on for three days . . .

*. . . a new abyss yawned indefinitely below the seat of the blast; an abyss so monstrous that no handy line might fathom it, nor any lamp illuminate it. . . . so far as they could ascertain, the void below was infinite.*

"The Transition of Juan Romero" · *H. P. Lovecraft (1944)*

# • MOMMA DURTT •
## Michael Shea

It was a little past ten o'clock on a Friday night. Kimberly Haas, expert and easy, was riding the 580 rapids, steering a Titan northbound on that mighty freeway. Her half of the river was all ruby tail-lights, and the oncoming stream was all diamonds. *What a rush!* thought Kimberly, like riding a dinosaur—one that could do *seventy.*

She was hauling twenty-K gallons along the star-spangled rim of the San Francisco Bay, and the Bay was a *galaxy* in a space movie, this huge array of blazing lights. Black void at its center studded with islands and ·necklaced with bridges. Kim Haas, starship trooper . . .

"Hey Alex," she said to her partner, "*Starship Troopers!*"

They laughed. This was their sixth run driving for Kleenco. Though the pickup-points varied, the kind of load they hauled never did. Tonight: a pharmaceutical company in Hayward, a pesticide manufacturer in Emeryville, and a plastics plant in Oakland: solvents, sludges, and still-bottoms. A witches' brew of industrial chemistry.

"Let's get a brewski," Kim said. "We're almost there."

"I dunno. We're almost late now, and Chip seemed *really* pissed."

"Yeah, but he's *always* pissed. And we're always gonna *be* late!" Kim, though in her early twenties, was already tired of men's pre-wired predictable hissy-fits. "We're always gonna be late, because he never gives us enough time, and because while we're pickin' up there's always some holdup or other in loading this shit at three or four different places every night!"

Alex nodded, staring at the highway, and feeling his own doubts about this easy money they'd been amazed to fall into these last few weeks.

Brooding on the river of lights he said, "True that. But he did make a *really* big point of it tonight, comin straight back."

Kim looked at him with his new Zapata 'stache—still a bit thin as yet— and thought that she still liked him just as she had in high school. Basically a nice guy, a bit touchy sometimes. She was a white country kid whose dad had driven big rigs for the vineyards, Alex a brown country kid whose several uncles *still* drove trucks back in Mexico. Since high school neither one of them had done anything even close to as cool as driving this tanker. Kim had clerked at the Circle K and Alex had rented out scaffolding and weed-whackers for Action Rents.

And look at them right now: piloting this beautiful beast over the colossal crooked frame of the Richmond Bridge, cruising like a star-liner above the red-and-white river of traffic, the whole Bay encircling them with galactic scenery out of some sci-fi flick.

Kim didn't *want* to have any reservations about this totally cool job. But there was a side to it that nagged at her.

"Toxics," she said, as if trying the word out. Then a little more forcefully, "That's why he's always so uptight. All this is illegal." She waited, uneasy, hanging that one out there. It had gone five nights unspoken but now she'd said it: their unseen passenger, the truth.

He tossed it back: "Well *duuuhhh*! But look. Hey. Lets *get* a brewski. What's a few minutes. If he wants us on time, he's gotta *give* us more time."

They were just south of Petaluma, and Kim eased the rig down an off ramp, steering the big tanker rocking and squeaking through dark streets to where a liquor store was the only thing alive for blocks around. They left the truck idling, and jumped down from the cab.

The store's neon shed a sick greenish light on the pavement. The sidewalks were eerily empty.

No. There was someone sitting on the dark curb just beyond the store. Someone *big* struggling to his feet . . . *her* feet? Yes. A bulky bag-lady in multi-layered shabby clothes.

Odd, how slowly she rose up, like a gradually inflating balloon of dirty rags. The two of them found themselves turning towards her, watching her rise. Then, just as they caught themselves and began to turn away from her, she moved with sudden energy, shambling crabwise—surprisingly quick for her great size—and intercepted them before they reached the store's entry.

Her face was swollen and crusted with dirt; her breath gusted cold and vile from her wide, loose mouth. They shifted to steer around her, but her bigness seemed somehow to slow down their movements, as if she exerted a kind of gravitational pull.

"Drink up, kids!" she hissed, and thrust a bottle at them. Kim received it, and felt its cold in her palm. The huge derelict winked at them. A dizzying chemical whiff, like a still-bottom, came off of her.

Then she pulled her own bottle from her rags, winked again, hoisted it, and drank. She drank obscenely. Her flabby throat working up and down, her dirty jowls quivering, her scabby eyes squeezed shut in the bliss of guzzling.

Kim, flustered, stammered some thanks for the beer as they retreated, and hustled away from the hulk. When she looked at the bottle in the light of the store's entry, she was surprised to it was perfectly clean and new looking. *Great Old Ones Ale*, in gold gothic lettering, arched across its label.

"What was that all about?" muttered Alex as they hustled into the store. At the counter, a wino was puzzling out his pennies and dimes but when they got to the register with the sixer, the huge eerie lurker was gone.

They got back in the cab and back on the freeway, both silent until Alex said "Man! She smelled like . . . "

They both tried to think of the precise word, groping for it until Kim said, "She smelled like the kinda shit we truck."

"That's it," said Alex. And they shared a moment of strange self-consciousness about this grand rig they were so jazzed about piloting. Here was their tanker, huge, towering above the traffic, rolling down the public highway, heavy with high-caliber toxins. High, wide and handsome their tanker cruised up the 101.

Alex cracked a beer.

Kim looked doubtfully at the bottle of *Great Old Ones Ale* in the cupholder. "These micro-breweries and their weird-ass names. No way I'm drinkin' it," and took one of theirs instead.

Kim swung them off 101. They rolled down a narrower highway through darker countryside. Sleeping orchards, a few vineyards, some country houses slid past them under the silver moon.

She geared their rig up through the switchbacks of the hills, the oaks gestured in the sweep of their lights. The big truck's headlights set all those crooked trees slow-dancing with their crooked shadows. Gaps here and there showed the young truckers fragments of the jeweled Santa Marta plain below and behind them.

"You gotta meet my Auntie some day," Alex said, scanning that view. "She's like half Miwok or something. Anyway she told me this mountain Chip's mine is in was like a Spirit Place—like where you go to fast and have visions? Go to like, face your demons and stuff."

"Spirits! Rad. I wish there *was* something cool like that about it. That would be something, but I think what these guys are doing up here is just plain old creepy and criminal."

"Yeah, but we don't really know that, not for sure. Anyway, we're definitely good and late now. Maybe he's just gonna fire us. When Chip said get back on time, he put a lot into it."

"I think he sounded scared," Kim said hauling on the wheel. "He just doesn't wanna stay late."

"Whaddya mean *late*? He sleeps up there at the mine! What does he care?"

"He just doesn't like to wait up for us. He wants to go to *bed*."

Alex turned his face away, irritated. "Maybe, but *I* got the feeling he's got company coming that he doesn't want us to meet."

"Where the hell do you get that idea?" She mimicked Chip's scoldings, " 'I wancha here, downloaded, an *outta* here by eleven-thirty! For once! Can'ya manage it?' Why else would he be so pissed? He's scared."

Three quarters up the hill, the road mounted a broad shoulder of the mountain, and halfway out across that shoulder was the gated compound of the Quicksilver Mine. Through gaps in the treeline, fragments of Santa Marta's jeweled plain glittered here and there below and behind them.

Chip was already rolling the cyclone gate back. Their headlights latticed his scrawny little body in the chain-links' shadows as the gate slid aside. He had his rubber boots and rubber apron on, and his respirator was hanging by its straps from his skinny old neck. They pulled in and he stomped over, mounted the step-up and thrust his head in Kim's window.

"You goddam kids think you signed on for a day at the beach?"

*Very* pissed. His back-sloped forehead suggested some browless animal, maybe a possum. "I can't believe you come a half hour late after what I told you! You two swing your ass up there, you *squirt*, an' you *leave*!"

At the hill's crest was the mouth of the Quicksilver's shaft, breathing out the white light of arc-lamps at the stars. Down near the gate was the office trailer, and beyond that was a sizeable pyramid of disposal drums five tiers high, with just enough moonlight on them to sketch their rims and bulges. It had been explained to both young drivers that these were filled inside the shaft from the holding tank, and then conveyed down the tracks in the ore carts left over from the mercury mining days. Much farther below, they were told, the drums were stacked securely in passages carved in the mine's walls.

The only part of this process that Kim and Alex had ever seen was the offload hose snaking from their tanker up through the mouth of the shaft, as they sat idling and running their offload pump.

Initially they'd thought "Great, an environmentally correct operation!" But somewhere in the course of delivering a hundred thousand gallons, they'd noted that the great pyramid of drums had never altered its outline. It suggested to Kim one of those old jungle ruins the Maya or Inca left— moonlit and with an aura of ancient evil—erected for strange gods and human sacrifice.

Chip, radiating anger and impatience, clung to the door of the cab as Kim backed the tanker up to within thirty yards of the mine's mouth. There, Chip jumped down and hurried into the shaft, pulling his mask on, to re-emerge a moment later dragging the fill-hose.

Was there any possibility this hose did fill a holding tank inside . . . ? Naw. They were just squirting all this black poison straight into the shaft, to soak into the naked earth. Chip's gnomish fury, and his expression of disgust, proved that if nothing else did.

" . . . just can't *believe* you kids! Unship your out-take!"

Chip helped them couple the fill-hose to the tanker's offload spout, and switch the pump on. "I got *people* comin'," he told them. "You squirt your goddam load, you uncouple, an' you drive the fuck outta here. Can'ya do that? Can'ya manage it?"

He stomped back down to the office trailer. They sat in the cab, a couple of scolded kids. "Just tell me straight," Kim said grimly. "Do you think Chip's just a really grouchy old man, or do you think he's afraid?"

"Okay. How I heard about this job was my cousin Nolo, who was drivin' for these guys. He left real sudden down to L.A., but I got him to give me

294 • Momma Durtt

their number before he went, couldn't believe he was dumping a gig like this. Now maybe I'm thinking Nolo got it right."

Over the sound of their offload pump they heard a vehicle coming up the highway. Headlights swung in through the gate. A big dark van stood idling there.

Chip hustled out of the office and stood by the van's driver's side. He was talking to the driver, a slight cringe in his posture. He made a gesture toward the tanker, seeming to dismiss it, to be explaining something.

The tanker's offload pump cut off. Kim and Alex got out quickly, eager to be gone before they met whoever had just driven that van in. They uncoupled their offload spout, coiled it onto its rack, and got back into the cab. They were hurrying to the max, while at the same time trying to seem casual.

Before Kim could slip the tanker into gear, the dark van rolled forward, driving right up into their headlights. It seemed to intend coming bumper-to-bumper with them, but just a few yards away from them it swung right, showing them its glossy black flank, and idled there, its driver's head profiled in the tanker's lights.

The driver turned his head and faced them directly, deliberately showing them his face, faintly smiling. A startling face, its features finely chiseled. For several slow beats he blocked them there, staring. Then he slipped his brake, and eased his van slowly up to the shaft-mouth.

Kim steered the tanker down the slope and into its slot beside the office. They jumped out and hustled down to Alex's old Chevy pickup. Usually Kim felt the contrast, felt diminished switching the big rig for her or Alex's four-wheeler. But tonight, the pickup felt light and frisky, a godsend—like an escape pod from a big spaceship that was blowing up.

Alex took the curves fast, and that was fine with Kim.

"What was that look?" he said. "Like he was showing us his face."

"No," Kim replied, her eyes fiercely fixed on the road. "He was looking through our headlights, trying to see our faces."

"How could he see anything?" Alex asked.

"You see his eyes? I almost think he could see us *through* our headlights. That was one spooky guy. You know what? Money or no money, maybe I don't wanna keep working here, much as I love driving this rig."

"Me either."

She glanced at him gratefully. "The thing is, I'm seriously broke."

Alex gave her his hey-girl smile. "Check this out. I gotta friend I can move in with practically for free, an you could come too."

"Wow, thanks, but just friends, okay?"

"C'mon, gimme some credit. But hey, you wanna go out tonight? The Red Elvises are at the Phoenix."

"No shit?" They cracked two beers, from their after-work sixer they kept in whichever ride had brought them up to work at the mine. The old pickup dove down toward the lamp-starred Santa Marta plain as they talked music.

Sol Lazarian parked his van well downslope of the shaft-mouth, so his soldiers would have to climb a bit with their burdens before carrying them down into the shaft. It was tricky footing down there, and he wanted them warmed up for the work.

Lazarian smilingly thought of tonight's task as "compounding the assets" of his employer, Lou Bonifacio of New Jersey: they were putting two of Bonifacio's dead enemies inside one of Bonifacio's toxic dumps in California.

Rather than hide his face, Lazarian had given the drivers of that tanker a good look at it. A couple of kids—a girl and a young man. They'd brought, like him, their offering to this place. Had they felt its aura?

Sol thought it unlikely. He himself had frightened them, as he'd meant to do, but they, being young, had probably not sensed the terrible magic of this ground.

The driver before them, an older Latino, had perhaps sensed it and quit. The driver before *him* was still here—down in the shaft where Sol had put him. He hadn't sensed anything. He had just been running his mouth off one evening in the tavern he favored.

Sol shouldered the heavier of the two bodybags and led briskly upslope with it. His two helpers were slower. Big, bearded Junior Lee carried the two satchels of weights. Sonny Beasely—almost as big as Junior Lee, but an edgier guy with acne-scarred cheeks—had the lighter bodybag.

"Look at 'im," muttered Junior, impressed. "That sumbitch musta gone two-forty at least," referring to the corpse Lazarian toted so lightly. Trudging up after, the pair watched the big man—so light of foot—leave them farther and farther behind.

Sonny grunted, low voiced, "Don't it seem strange doin' this? Fuckin *ocean's* just five miles west."

"Said we're goin' way down in."

"So someone *else* could just walk way down in, and *find* these stiffs there!"

"Maybe we're gonna *bury* 'em down there."

"If we're gonna *bury* 'em, we could bury 'em just as deep up in these hills, without goin' *down* a fuckin' mineshaft."

They saved their breath for the rest of the climb. Waiting above them, Lazarian stood backlit by the shaft. His dreamy smile was invisible to them as he watched them come. Their faces were a quarter-turned to each other as they climbed, trading doubts perhaps, showing brief profiles of effort and unease.

Did these two simpletons feel the power here? Yes, rudimentary though their spirits were, Lazarian read in their eyes that they felt it as they came up and faced the shaft-mouth. Uneasily they registered the aura of that big, dark gullet.

*Click.* The image of them in this instant strobed in his mind's eye, the way they looked right now in their moment of uneasy conference, repeating, repeating as if his visual cortex was a projector whose sprocket gear was slipping. When younger, these little epiphanies had unnerved him. Now he knew them to be a kind of signature radiation which his prey emitted as they neared death—like that given off by particles that were swallowed in a Black Hole.

"You need a breather?" Sol asked when they joined him up in the lip of the shaft-mouth.

"No! (*gasp*) Good to go!"

"No way, Sol!"

"Okay. So let's pop on the masks, Guys!" said genial Sol. They all three set down their burdens and put on their masks, respirators with complex double filters that looked like the mouth-parts of insects. Even before entering, just standing here in the shaft's mouth the air was awesome. Sonny and Junior gaped at each other as they struggled with their straps. The vapors were a waft of pure uncanniness, moving through their braincells like the creepy fore-tremors of a major acid high.

Sol Lazarian was no less awed than they were. It was a reek so potent it became deafening, a pandemonium of stenches impacting the mind like a chorus of shrieking angels, a mob of divine sopranos gone mad.

His soldiers, watching Lazarian put his mask on, felt an identical little chill.

The big man's beauty was always a little unbelievable seen up close: the carven features, the rosebud mouth, the heavy-lidded eyes two pools of luminous candor. Shocking, though, when half that face was holstered in the mask, and you felt no mismatch between those lovely eyes, and what looked like the jaws of a huge bug.

"Man this air is messin' me up, Sol," Sonny croaked through the crude amplifier. "You could sell it to junkies."

"Relax." Lazarian's voice came out mellow, almost unmangled by the mask. "Breathe through your filters, you'll be fine. And listen: count your steps going down. We think the guy running this place for us is ripping us off, taking other deliveries on the side. So count your steps down so we can check the fill-level."

He doubted his laborers could show the concentration for a count. His real aim was to create a pretext for leaving them down there while he went back up for the weights and bags he was going to use on them in their turn. They took up their burdens and lanterns again, and he led them down into the shaft of the old Quicksilver Mine. Here in the well-lit shaft-mouth they were in a stage set. There was a holding tank for delivered toxins, and a little stack of empty drums to be filled from that tank. There was a donkey engine mounted on the track, and some carts linked to it by cable—everything needed for lowering sealed drums of toxins carefully into the shaft for clean storage.

But sixty yards down, the rails gave out, recycled long ago for their steel. Below that point, as they pushed their bubble of light down the steepening pitch, there was only the black, six-inch fill-hose running along down the shaft floor beside a crude staircase of rail-less cross-ties. And as they descended, their lanterns' light made the hose's shadow twitch and shift, like a giant house snake, the resident genius of this place dancing down shaft beside them.

Ever deeper they sank down through a strange, ethereal inferno. Down here it wasn't the men who sweated out into the air, but the air that sweated itself into the men, air like dragon's breath, a micro-blizzard of molecular razors, and the brew that exhaled it was perhaps the perfect human solvent.

At this thought Lazarian's smile bloomed within his mask, a secret flower.

Even sooner than Lazarian had expected, they reached the black pool. It was always a shock encountering it. Its stillness seemed to mask a secret aggression, as if this slug of earth-socketed poison—more than a mile in depth—had stealthily been hastening up to meet them, and had, just an instant ago, paused, pretending immobility, its flat black eye dazzling their lights back at them, its cold breath licking the skin of their faces like a demon's caustic tongue.

Oh, there was great power here. He had not been wrong to cross a continent with these corpses expressly to offer them here. This pool was Death's most absolute orifice, the threshold of a perfect annihilation. He watched his soldiers awkwardly crouching, unlimbering wire, cutters, and weights from the satchels. Their dazed unease was understandable, entering this place for the first time. Even these morons sensed what was here.

"So what was your count, guys?" he asked them. Smiled again within his mask to see their eyes' identical looks of guilty alarm.

It made him wonder: were such crude life-forms as these an *insult* if offered in sacrifice? To the Power that he had from the first felt to be hidden in this shaft, were two such primitive souls worse than no sacrifice at all? Come to that, were even the slightly more intelligent, slightly more dangerous men inside the body bags also too crude, too worthless an offering?

How could he know? On the threshold of such a Mystery as Lazarian sensed down here, who *did* know the rules? In the end, his own instinctive sense of a presence, his Awe—that was the real offering. His soul's readiness was the incense he burnt on the altar. The sacrifices themselves must always be guesswork, mere gesture. They displayed his devotion, whether or not the god here valued them.

Granting all this, it was Lazarian's intuition that told him he did right. Every life, however simple, in passing through Death's membrane, forced open a seam between the space-time of this world and the unknowable Outside. Every death created a brief aperture through which something might be glimpsed.

"Never mind, guys," Lazarian said. "I kept count. They're overfilled." He pulled two fat packets of hundred-dollar bills from his pocket, and waggled them. "I know how neat and tight your wiring's going to be, so I want you to take your bonuses now." Their eyes crinkled above their masks—so pleased, pocketing the cash!

And Lazarian *would* send them into the pool with their money still in pocket. Like grave goods in the ancient world's funerals, it was a ceremonial responsibility. Death would reveal nothing to those who tried to get revelation for a bargain price.

He told the men, "I'm going up to talk to the gate-man. Weight them heavy. I'll be back down before you get both of them wired."

Long minutes later, though they could no longer see Lazarian's ascending light, Sonny's voice was still cautiously low:

"You believe this stench?"

Junior—slightly dazed, his eyes goggled—shook his head. He was looping wire around the middle of the smaller of the two bodies, and threading the wire through a ten-pound weight-disc. "Fuckin *smell* feels like it's leakin' in through my skin!"

Their mask-muted voices rang strange to them, like buried men speaking from their graves. "Lift 'im a little higher," Junior said, as he threaded the wire through another weight.

The gaseous air lay like a lubricant mist on everything. The weight slipped from his grip. It rolled, bounced off a lower tie, and jumped into the pool. The pair recoiled to either side from the tongue of black slop thrown back from the splash.

"You dipstick!"

"It slipped! Shoot me!"

"*Don't* slip!"

The booming of their angry voices suddenly subdued them. The after-splash of the weight into the pool made the pond gently vibrate, and its rim kiss the walls of the shaft:

*slap*-suck, *slap*-suck . . .

The echoes took forever to die down. It seemed to Sonny a long time that they crouched there, listening. He wondered if the air was stoning him, messing with his time sense. He was crouched there, meaning to get back to work, but not doing it.

It was Junior who got them moving. "Tilt 'im up again."

They got back into it. Sonny manipulated the corpse while Junior paid off the wire.

"They were so *stiff* when we loaded 'em," Junior said. "They're a bitch to handle all floppy like this!"

They'd crossed the country in a little under forty-eight hours. The corpses were stiff to start with, but now that rigor would have been useful, it was long gone. The slack stiff slumped, resisting their work. Now that they had the third wire loop pinching into its bagged length, it had begun to look segmented, like a caterpillar.

Sonny remembered a book about Houdini he'd read in slam, and thought of something funny. He weighed his words. You had to be careful, if you wanted Junior to understand something.

"Hey Joon. You know that when you tie a guy in a buncha short lengths like this? Instead of tyin' him in one long piece? You tie him in short lengths like this, and it's harder for him to get out of. You know—free himself, *escape*."

Bug-muzzled Junior sat goggle-eyed, staring at him. With just his eyes showing like this he looked . . . shocked at what Sonny had said. Wasn't getting the joke at all.

Sonny pulled down his mask a little to show Junior he was smiling, making a joke. "You know—get himself untied?"

Junior's brow corrugated. Really concentrating now, and still not getting it. With his forehead corrugated like that, he looked almost terrified, like these stiffs might suddenly try to untie themselves.

"You fuckin idiot," Sonny said, and then couldn't help laughing at that face of Junior's. "It's a *joke*! How're they gonna escape? They're fuckin *dead*!"

And then both of them looked for a moment at the bagged stiffs—as if they hadn't quite fully grasped that fact before.

They worked on. They said nothing more, but their least movements wove fine webs of echo around them.

The last weight was wired. Stiff Number One was now a black caterpillar of seven unequal segments, with the discs attached to it like the eggs of some parasitic wasp.

Sonny thumbed out the razor tip of a utility knife, and cut the "window" Sol had prescribed—a big, square flap out of the bag over the stiff's face, to let the solvents in to work on the nude corpse. As he cut, he felt the blade meet doughy resistance, and when he unmasked the face found a deep, unbleeding slice beside the nose.

"Sorry about that, wise guy."

"Who do ya think he was?" asked Junior.

"An East-coast greaseball like the other one. Who cares?" He and Junior had staged a hold-up in an Italian restaurant; the distraction had covered Lazarian's abduction of this guy from a back table.

Corpse Number Two had required the pair to enter the lobby of a plush high-rise, and kick up a drunken fuss about being admitted to the elevators up to "Lulu's" condo. Four really big guys, armed, had poured from the elevator a moment later. Though the two tried to prolong the distraction, they were thrown out on their ass PDQ, but Lazarian still had the big stiff in the van by the time they returned to it. Guy was wearing sweat-stained exercise togs, apparently had been having a workout in his home gym.

"You come a long way, Bo-seephus," Sonny told Stiff One. To Junior he said, "Why the hell did he take us all the way out *there* to get these guys, then bring them all the way back *here* to get rid of 'em?"

Junior shrugged mountainously. "Who knows? He's a goon, got his goon reasons. I mean, this is a pretty good hidin' place."

"Yeah, but between here an' *Jersey* there's three thousand miles of—"

"What's that?"

*Slap*-suck, *slap*-suck, *slap*-suck . . . The pool was quaking again, still gently, but just a little stronger than before. Both men were lifelong Californians, but now they were discovering that a casual attitude about earthquakes decreased radically as the depth of your body under the earth increased.

"The stuff probably just keeps settling," said Sonny. "Down into cracks an' holes down there."

"I don't see no bubbles." The cogency of this remark, coming from his slow-witted friend irritated Sonny.

"Okay, okay. So whaddya say we just quit fuckin' the dog, Joon? You get that end, I'll get this end."

They stood up with the corpse hammocked between them. "One . . . two . . . "—they had a fair swing going—"three!" The dead goon was launched. He lay face-up on the air for a moment. Framed in the "window" they'd cut, his eyes and mouth were pools of shadow in the oblique light from the lanterns. The shadows made the face live in that instant—it seemed to grimace as it fell.

It had to be this druggy air that made them both so late in jumping back—the splash was *big* and it wet their boots and spattered the lanterns.

Cursing, they wiped their boots on their jeans and set the lanterns higher up. Would the pond never settle? Jittering and splashing and slopping . . . They stood watching that turbulence, and imagining the wise guy's journey down the steep shaft, a long slo-mo tumble down through the most perfect blackness there ever was.

"How far down you think he'll go?" rumbled Junior.

Sonny understood exactly what Junior was picturing: the weighted mummy sinking, striking the shaft-floor a little farther down, jouncing up off the ties, tumbling slowly farther down, jouncing again.

They both looked up behind them at the tunnel's steep pitch. Sonny rumbled, "If the slope don't change he'll just keep bouncin' down."

"So how far down's this tunnel go?"

"It's called a shaft, Joon. Tunnels you can come out the other end of."

"So how far down's this *shaft* go?"

"Well . . . " Sonny's mind kept jouncing down deeper and deeper with the corpse, and saw no end to it. "How should *I* know?" It was funny how they kept freezing up and *listening* down here. And now they'd done it again, just crouching there, the silence deepening around them.

"Know what I think, Sonny?" Junior's eyes had a look in them that Sonny had never seen before. It was like . . . *amazement.* "I think that this is some strange shit for us to be doin' down here."

This declaration flashed Sonny on some of the other strange things they had done as "soldiers." He considered these, and then he nodded. "I think this *is* the strangest shit we've done yet."

"And the hardest work too." They roused themselves, and started wiring Stiff Two. Heavier though it was, they were working more smoothly now—suddenly almost deft. Perhaps it was that they both felt a new tension in the shaft, felt the presence of something that seemed to applaud their work, to will it forward.

"Jesus!" Junior yelped, dropping a weight and his pliers. A roiling sound, a silken fizzing filled the shaft. The pool was foaming, bulging upwards at its center, mounting in a dome of turbulence, rising as if lifted by some powerful under-pressure.

Had the respirators melted from their faces? It felt like the poisoned air had suddenly soaked through their skulls, and was licking the brain-meat out of them. The pressure-dome mushroomed to the ceiling, and came surging at them.

They turned to launch themselves up-shaft, and tripped over the half-wired second body. Got up and scrambled past it, a voice in Sonny's skull saying: *One heartbeat too late.* They were just getting their stride on the ties, the lighter Sonny taking the lead, as the gust of the black wave's air pressure touched their napes.

The wave punched Sonny's legs out from under him, gripped his waist like a cold, melting hand, and dragged him back down. He rammed desperate knees against the stone, felt bone crack and his fingernails torn off, but held on against the terrible back-drag of caustics draining off of him.

Looking back over his shoulder, he saw that Junior Lee had been dragged all the way down, and now was up to his neck in the pool, his arms scrabbling for the shaft floor just out of reach. And there, just beyond Junior, Sonny saw what *stood up* from the pool, saw its hugeness and the wild night-black glare of its eyes. Awed, Sonny watched it seize Junior by the back of the neck and lift him up like a kitten, and with its free hand, hugely fisted, smite the pool, to send a second, mightier wave booming up the shaft straight at Sonny.

Again Sonny scrambled up-shaft, his knee broken but fighting himself up one tie higher, another tie, another . . . while a voice in his head was saying: *just one heartbeat too late.*

A tongue of waste shot past him along the shaft wall, and as he reached the lanterns, the wave curved around just beyond them, and came sweeping back down towards him like a gathering arm. For an instant, the lanterns made a black mirror of the oncoming liquid wall, and in it Sonny saw himself: a bug-mouthed being on its belly and reaching for a lantern, its eyes bulging at its oncoming end.

The descending wave's satin mass wrapped him in blindness, flipped him on his back and snatched him down, the stepped earth under him beating him, braining him, blotting him out. A perfect blackness was the aftermath. The echoes of uproar and choked-off shouts collided again and again with the stone walls, subsiding at long last to a faint liquid chuckle.

Shortly after, there came down the sound of a heavy tread descending the shaft from the far, faint circle of moonlit sky high above.

Sol Lazarian stopped at the limit of the drenched zone, which now extended fifteen yards up-shaft of the pool itself. Not a sign of his soldiers remained, nor any sign of the two bagged dead they'd carried.

Fear, in Lazarian, was a darker shade of joy, it was the same radiation at a different frequency. When he broke a man's life in his arms, his prey's shock was his joy's fuel. And, when any horror laid its hand on him, he felt not crushed, but light, combustible, packed like dynamite with a savage sympathy for that larger joy, that joy more monstrous than his own, that might be about to consume him.

Already at thirty-eight, young for a real master, he had consumed a dozen other first-rate killers. Real samurai like himself, not moronic buttons—of those he kept no count. And all these gifted men had learned that to endanger Lazarian was to inspire and ignite him. His startling face got eerily prettier, his manner even more serene. You had him distracted. You watched him fail to spot your trap. You sprang it on him, and suddenly, there was Sol Lazarian's forearm across your throat and Sol Lazarian's mellow baritone crooning unspeakablities in your ear . . . and there was your neck breaking.

He stood thoughtful for a moment, ears straining. *Ta*-da-dum *Ta*-da *Ta*-dum, *da* . . .

In the spectrum of things audible there is a doubtful zone shared by that which is imagined and that which is faintly *heard*.

If real, this voice was beautiful and sad. A velvet-and-molasses gospel voice. It gave him a delicate attack of the creeps, a horripilation of the fine black lanugo that covered the back and shoulders of the pale giant, and that no living man had ever seen.

*Ta*-da-dum *Ta*-da *Ta*-dum, da . . . Sol thrust his light further forward seeking some purchase on what he'd heard, and the movement of his light revealed that the blackness under his feet was a shape, not a blot. Something distinctly outlined in the stone and timber. His hair stirred. Its outline was precisely that of a huge, outreached hand.

Lazarian stood squarely in the palm of that hand. *You are mine*, it said. *Give me more,* it said . . . Yes, it demanded more, as plain as printed speech. Demanded more.

Not many nights later Sol Lazarian had fetched another body from New Jersey, this one still living, though snugly bound: Lou Bonifacio.

Accomplishing this had been no slight feat.

Lazarian had had to kill no fewer than four buttons in swift succession—and quite good samurai they had been—two of them, anyway, so good Sol had for some moments considered bringing one—or even both of their bodies—back as additional offerings to the shaft.

But after all, the capture and sacrifice of his Capo must rightly claim his sole attention. To kill one whom he had served was an act of great spiritual weight.

Coming west, the securely bound Bonifacio had dozed for a long stretch of hours—an aging body, perhaps subconsciously fleeing its dire predicament. But he came awake again as their van climbed the switchbacks toward the Quicksilver Mine.

He was gagged. Lazarian had been driven to gag him not long after their journey's outset. Lou's abusive raging had quickly exhausted Lazarian's intention to be courteous and sociable on the long drive. Now, even after so long at the wheel, Lazarian had never felt more awake. His heart rose in him while his van, turn by turn, ascended the switchbacks.

He drove rapt, so clearly recalling it—the black hand perfectly articulated, telling him whose Hand he stood in.

But *whose*?

Who but the one he'd lived and worked to meet? It was the hand of Annihilation itself, standing up and reaching out. The whole world had altered in answer to his sacrifice of those two goons! The spirit in the shaft had seized both his kills and his hirelings, obliterated the four of them, and left for Lazarian an urgent sign, the extended hand that said *GIVE MORE*.

Very soon now he was going to learn what he would purchase with this more powerful offering. A full-fledged Capo plucked right from his fortress.

In that moment of his first offering's acceptance, his spirit had been enlarged, as if he had fed *himself* those lesser lives.

The odd thing was, that it was to Bonifacio himself that Lazarian wanted to talk about it, his Capo, a man who had himself offered human sacrifices. Who better able to provide a judgment of the eerie rightness of this shaft, the Dantean poetry of its deeps? It was to Lou he longed to confide that he found dread here too. For he did not know how much this black hand offered, and how much more it might *demand*.

If only they could toss it back and forth, as they had on other, no less homicidal excursions during their long shared past. He smiled wistfully. *Honestly, whaddya think, Lou? I think you have to agree: apart from it being a really secure site, your life will unlock something big down here. Down here your life will buy me some kind of real power. Doncha think?*

Lazarian steered through the last switchback, and out onto the mountain's broad shoulder. A fragmentary moon showed them Chip sliding open the gate of the compound a moment before Lazarian's headlights splashed across him. Chip had been informed that his assistance tonight was required. He brought out a sturdy dolly. Lazarian stood the shackled Bonifacio in the dolly and bound him to it, and then hauled him up to the shaft. The shaft-mouth was wreathed in the mist of artificial light that it breathed out at the stars.

His tone gentle, Lazarian told the dollied Capo: "In plain, unvarnished English, Lou, I'm giving you to a god down in there. I don't exactly understand Her, and I don't know what She'll do with you. I sincerely hope it won't involve doing you any harm. I only want to say that in spite of my handing you over, *I* have never wished you anything but the best, Lou. And for all I really know, maybe She won't either."

As he spoke he was clipping lights to the dolly, and to the bonds that bound Lou to it. Lazarian knew his little speech was disingenuous—was a false mercy of delayed revelation. Bonifacio was almost certainly going to end up in the pool.

He said, "Excuse me putting my mask on, Lou. The air down there's really intense . . . Can you hear me okay? These speakers aren't so great."

Lazarian began to ease the dolly smoothly down the ties. This kind of descent was almost dance-like. Very soon they were below the lighted zone, and carrying their own bubble of light downshaft, utter darkness both behind and ahead of them. Softly they jolted deeper and deeper.

"I'm sorry about this dolly arrangement, Lou, but I think you'll agree it's the least painful way I can keep you both comfortable and secure."

Bonifacio was an older brute, beginning to melt down at the corners and angles of his great frame, but as Lazarian jolted him softly, steadily down the shaft, he lay rigid in his bonds, and his gagged glare never ceased to blaze at his captor. Lazarian had to smile.

"Lou, you're old-school in the best sense. If I hadn't gotten the drop on you, I'm sure you'd be grinding my bones to powder right now with your teeth! It's always a pleasure to be dealing with a professional."

Lazarian's great strength managed to ease down his massive cargo with a rolling smoothness, always iron-muscled in resistance to the earth's black yawn of gravity he stepped down into.

The steadiness of his descent gave an hypnotic regularity to the shaft's support beams, little timber stonehenges holding the earth apart, rising to swallow them at regular intervals as he stepped down, stepped down, stepped down . . .

*Momma Durtt get you by de-greees jus' take hold an' squeeze an' squeeze . . .*

All doubt gone now, she was speaking to him.

Just to him, Lou didn't seem to hear it. Ever so faint it sounded, far down in that darkness beyond his bubble of light. Echoey now . . . *was* he hearing it? Or was it the low commotion of his own masked breathing?

*Momma Durtt get you, by degrees . . .*

To Lazarian's eyes, a faint aura was beginning to glow from Bonifacio's body. There was a kind of Egyptian pomp in Lou's big mummified mass as he floated half-recumbent down the shaft on his dolly, his eyes blazing above his bound mouth . . .

And justly so, Lazarian thought, for in Lou he was sacrificing a kind of deity, one of those furious Elementals like Hades or the Midgard Serpent, brought to heel by gods in tales . . . he was imbued with infernal majesty.

Then, far down below their light-bubble, from the perfect dark they descended to, something stirred . . .

A liquid sound? A soft, wet impact?

Lazarian stayed their descent, and leaned near Bonifacio's ear to say, "We've conjured a god here, Lou, I'm sure of it. With my own eyes I've seen . . . unbelievable evidence. We've conjured a *goddess*, more precisely. I've heard her voice, heard her *sing*."

The bound man's eyes flared with a new shade of fear—the fear of lunacy in his captor—which Sol Lazarian saw, and had to laugh. "No! I'm not crazy, old friend. I know how that sounds, but I *have* heard her sing!

"And I'm afraid I have to be honest with you, Lou. I've *procured* you, you might say, *for* the goddess here." He paused in their descent, resting briefly. "But the goddess, unfortunately, lives *in* the toxics, and that seems to be where her offerings must be placed."

Silence then between them, stepping down through the last long steepness, the burdened dolly's wheels groaning.

The ether-reek swelled thicker, swallowing them like a cold reptile mouth. And here was the pool . . . Lazarian said, "I'm *offering* you, Lou—not *giving* you. Here, I will stand you up." He propped the dolly upright on the lowest crosstie above the black tarn that breathed its sharp, glacial breath in their faces. "I'm not putting you in—just putting you where she can take you. If she is as real as I think, I suppose she . . . *consumes* you—I don't really know. But I hope that you know how truly I regret what's going to happen here."

Lazarian bent and locked the dolly's wheels. He gave Bonifacio's shoulder a pat, and retreated four ties upshaft of him. Crouched there, uncramping his leg muscles.

Lou was standing very carefully balanced. He was snugly bound and bandaged to the dolly, but his rage and horror made the little lights he was decorated with tremble on the black pool, which seemed to be almost as still as stone.

But no, not absolutely still. The subtlest of tremors now and then, here and there, skimmed its blackness.

Here in this grotto, this *chapel* of annihilation, Lazarian groped for the proper gesture. What did the black gulf want of him? What gesture of his must call forth the thing that hid here? Should he show his awe? His gratitude? All he could think to do was to declare his reverence. He addressed the pool.

"I give you the one who conjured you. The one who fed you the poisons that your Nullity grew from. He is your food now, a token of my reverence. In return, grant me *vision*! Grant me power in your service!"

Bonifacio was an earthy man, of strong simple appetites. Teetering on this narrow footing at the rim of nothingness, he had as firm a grip on himself as a man thus situated can have. Hearing Lazarian imploring the pool of poison like a god, the Capo knew himself to be in the hands of Lunacy incarnate, and with a wordless prayer he commended his soul to the abyss.

At which instant a huge black hand rose dripping from the pool and seized him. Its mighty grip was more than half his height, but enough of the Capo's head and shoulders protruded to show that his features were as much convulsed with fury as with fear.

The great black knuckles liquesced as they gripped him, the huge fist melting as it lofted and seemed to heft him, as if assaying value.

And then, in sudden shock, it seemed to Lazarian that he himself melted, that he hung unbodied in the lethal air, because what was happening? The pool behind the huge hand began to bulge, and dome up as an immense face surfaced, her wet black eyeballs (big as human heads) glaring from a thorny thicket of hair, her jeering mouth a big whirlpool slowly spreading on her face.

The goddess thrust Bonifacio into the melting cavern of her mouth, wherein the Capo's wordless roar was echoed and then drowned out as he plunged—dolly and all—from sight.

She faced Lazarian, this face of hers as big as his whole body, a melting face unendingly reborn, her eyes mockingly, merrily glaring in his.

And Lazarian's soul spoke within him: *I've done it! I've broken through! Into the world of miracles!*

"You will not die," her hissing lips of poison told him, each word a wet adhesion to his flesh. "You will serve me while this world lasts, and you will sow plague and poison upon it.

"I am the miracle you have lived and labored for. Of the Great Old Ones, I am the youngest, no older than this venomed globe itself, but until Dark claims us all again, you'll till my earth and feed my monsters up to strength to work this world's destruction."

Gleeful now, her seething face, she lofted her great melting fist, and brandished it upshaft, and—far, far up the reverberating tube—an engine growled to life, avalanching echoes down upon them.

Lazarian found his voice hoarse with grateful joy. "I will serve you, Great One! I will serve you to the end of our time!"

The black giant grinned from her tarn. "Then let us make some *room* for your labor! Let us give scope to your service, and give you the *power* to serve!"

A mighty din of fractured stone filled the shaft, as a huge convulsion shook the earth they stood in. Raining dust and gravel, the mine's walls and ceiling heaved, shuddering away from Lazarian.

And when it stilled, the shaft's diameter had tripled, the crude-hewn stone ceiling was thrice his height above him, and the pool of poison was now a wide pond. The engine's noise, still high and far, rang down more hollowly now.

"In power and style you will serve me," the giantess leered at him. "Behold!" The distant engine's roar *descended*, and its guttural howl came snarling down before it. Rapt, Lazarian gazed up at the lofty walls of stone that contained him—now high and shrine-like.

Here came the tanker's headlights blazing down from on high, its echoes a ghostly landslide that broke against him. The shaft tremored like a waking dragon around him. He stood enraptured, unavoiding. The deep tarn was at his back, yet he stood serene as the headlights came down like comets.

Outside, far above him, under the silent sky, only a few deep dinosaur sounds welled up at the moon—some dim commotion far under the earth, but peace up here. Chip was gone—he'd taken off the moment the earth had shaken. A long and unmarred silence followed in the compound then, peace beneath the pale moon.

Until at length, a growling began to *rise* from the Quicksilver's throat, rose quickly to crescendo, and out of the earth the tanker erupted.

It launched its hugeness arcing through the air, surged airborne twenty yards or so, until it colossally *whumped* down, ponderously tap-danced on its heavy tires, then leveled off, and hit the highway.

You could tell she was full by the sway of her, but even so she ate up the switchbacks, tires smoking down the mountain, zig and zag. And impossibly soon, she hit the cross-country straightaway toward the mighty 101—a linear glow past shadowy hills and groves.

As she rolled through the fields her looks improved. The moonlight seemed to wipe her bulky mass clean. Her tank turned a bright polished silver, and her cab grew glossy black with silver trim.

As she surged up onto the 101, she was gorgeous, all scoured steel and glossy black enamel. She rode high in the river of southbound headlights, a star-cruiser cargoed with Death for the Cities of Light that rimmed the great bay to the south. And high in her cab, commanding the wheel sat Lazarian, his eyes rapt on the cities of light as he hurtled towards them. He drank with gusto from the bottle of ale which he gripped in one hand.

A week later, Alex and Kim had a window seat in a roadside diner. An onramp onto 101 climbed right past their window, up through a Friday night blaze of neon colors. As they gazed out the glass, a gorgeous tanker truck slid to the ramp and surged up it.

"Whoa," said Kim, "isn't that . . . ?"

"Damn. It is." The pair watched with awe as the great machine roared onto the freeway and geared up for points south.

*When a traveller in north central Massachusetts takes the wrong fork at
the junction of the Aylesbury Pike just beyond Dean's Corners, he comes
upon a lonely and curious country. . . . It is always a relief to get clear
of the place, and to follow the narrow road around the base of the hills
and across the level country beyond till it rejoins the Aylesbury pike.
Afterwards one sometimes learns that one has been through Dunwich.*

"The Dunwich Horror" · H. P. Lovecraft (1929)

## • THEY SMELL OF THUNDER •
### W. H. Pugmire

### I.

Enoch Coffin drove his truck along the rutted road, past the stone wall of
what might once have been a habitation, although no house stood within
sight. There was just a wide dry field that reached to where the lush forest
took over on the rising slopes, with here and there growths of high weeds
mingled with the tall yellow grass. The sky was overcast and the weather
cool, but Enoch liked the window down when he drove and didn't mind
the chill. "Lonesome country," he mumbled as his pickup bumped over the
road's furrows, and he cast a backward glance to make certain the artistic
gear in the rear cargo bed had remained secure. Further on, the road inclined
and he could see the mountains above the dense woodland, and something
in the primeval aura of the sight excited him—he felt very far from Boston.
As his truck crossed over the bridges that spanned ravines and narrow rocky
vales, he studied the curious manner in which some of those ancient bridges
had been constructed, how various combined portions of timber seemed
emblematic in the signs and signals they suggested. The domed hills were
close now, and he stopped the truck in order to step out and piss; and as he
relieved himself he marveled at the stillness all around as his eyes scanned
the shimmering line of the Miskatonic River that passed below the wooded
hills. As he stood there a ratty jalopy passed him on the road, and he smiled
at the way the suspicious eyes of its driver studied him. Whistling, Enoch

raised a hand and made the Elder Sign, which the other driver hesitantly returned.

He drove onward and came to a bumpy riverside road and then drove slowly across an ancient bridge that crossed the Miskatonic, experiencing a sense of nervous expectancy concerning the soundness of the bridge. The structure's hoary age affected Enoch's senses and filled him with foreboding—such things should not be, should not exist in this modern age. The artist was delighted that it did exist so as to spin its macabre spell. But the tenebrous bridge was merely prelude. As the pickup truck slowly crossed it, Enoch sensed a change in the air that wafted through his vehicle's window. The shadowed atmosphere felt, somehow, heavier, and it carried an extremely unpleasant smell such as he had never experienced. Reaching, finally, the other end of the bridge, his truck drove again across a rough road and Enoch laughed out loud at the sight of Dunwich Village before him, huddled beneath what he knew from his yellowed map was Round Mountain. His fingers itched for pen and pad so that he could capture the uncanny sight with his craft. How could such squalid, disintegrating buildings still be standing? In what era had they been raised? Enoch then began to notice some few lethargic citizens who shuffled in and out of one ridiculously old broken-steepled church that now served as general store, and the artist was amazed at how the inhabitants of the village were so in tune with its aura of strange decay. He had entered an alien realm. The foetid stench of the air breathed in was almost intolerable, even to one such as Enoch who relished decayed necromancy.

He drove for another three miles, checking with his 1920's map that his correspondent had sent him, and stopped at the pile of ruins that had once been a farmhouse just below the slope of Sentinel Hill. He sat for a while in his stilled vehicle and watched the three persons who worked at a curious construction of wood, a kind of symbolic design that reminded Enoch of the patterns he had seen on the bridges he had crossed on his way to Dunwich. Finally, he pushed open his door and stepped onto the dusty road, holding out his hand to the frantic beast that rushed to him and licked his palm.

"Spider," a man called to the dog, which moved from Enoch and trotted to his master. The artist approached the stranger and they exchanged smiles. "Mr. Coffin, I recognize you from the newspaper photos. I'm Xavier Aboth."

Enoch reached for and clasped the young man's extended hand. "You found your way easily?"

"Oh yeah, your grandpappy's map served me well. I took very good care of it, it's so delicate." He looked to the top of the high hill and could just see some of the standing stones with which it was crowned. "The infamous Sentinel Hill. And this must once have been the Whateley farmstead."

"Aye, that it is. We're just sturdyin' up the sign here. Hey—Alma, Joseph." The lad motioned for his friends to join them. "This is the artist who was hired to illustrate my book of prose-poems. Enoch Coffin, Alma Bishop and Joseph Hulver, Jr."

Enoch shook their hands as the woman studied him. "Clever of our Xavier, writin' his own book. Course, he's been to Harvard and Miskatonic. Mostly them as gone to university never return. We're glad this one did." She smiled slyly at the poet.

"I'll let you two finish up. The powder is in that plastic bag there. It needs to be sprinkled exactly as ye're sayin' the Words." He turned to Enoch. "My place is up a mile and a half yonder. No, Spider can chase after us on the road, he loves that. Yeah, I walked over, it's a nice stroll. I like to stop and bury things in Devil's Hop Yard, over there. You know, things that help enhance the alchemy of the bleak soil."

The two men entered the pickup, and Xavier whistled to his canine, which barked joyously and ran beside the truck as Enoch drove. As he drove, Enoch glanced nonchalantly at his companion's dirty clothes and soiled hands. Xavier was extremely unkempt, living up to the image of Dunwich folk that had been related to Enoch by some who learned that he was journeying there. The word about Dunwich and its denizens was that they were little more than ignorant hill-folk who rejected modernity and lived primitive and solitary lives. Rumors of inbreeding were prevalent, and Enoch's one friend who had visited Dunwich Village complained of the hostility he encountered there from people who mistrusted those who were not kindred.

Enoch drove for a while and then the road turned and passed near another high hill, below which stretched an infertile hillside that was naught but rocks and corroding soil. The young man leaned out his window and called to the dog. "It's okay, Spider, jest run." Then he turned and smiled at Enoch, shrugging. "He gets nervous near the Hop Yard." The truck continued to follow the road until coming to a small plot of land on which a shack that was little more than a cottage leaned beneath the dark sky. "Go ahead and park next to my old jalopy there." The artist did so and climbed out of the vehicle, offering his hand once more to the friendly canine. He joined Xavier in taking out some of the gear from the cargo bed.

"Smells like a storm is brewing," Enoch said, looking up at the sky.

"Aye, we'd best get this lot inside."

The young man's language gave Enoch pause: was this the poet who had crafted such beautiful and compelling prose-poems? The lad's spoken language was simple and at times uncouth. Perhaps returning to this forsaken homeland after spending years away at university had killed any elegance of tongue and returned him to the local patois. He followed Xavier to the door of the house and inside, and was relieved that the place was bigger on the inside than it looked on the outside.

"I'm givin' you the upstairs with the bed. I often just sleep down here on the sofa. The light's real good up there cos I put in a winder in the roof above the library, to help with readin'. I like lots of light when I read. Come on up. Oh, them steps are firm, don't worry, you just need to balance yourself cos there's no handrails."

They walked up what was a combination of ladder and steps, through a rectangle in the living room roof and into a cozy bedroom. Xavier tossed the equipment he was holding onto the bed and stretched as he sauntered into the next room, which proved to be a spacious study filled with books, two tables and three sturdy chairs. The ceiling was very low, just an inch from Enoch's crown when he stood at full height. He set his gear on the bed next to Xavier's pile and nodded with approval.

"This is nice. You're certain you want to surrender your bed?"

"Rarely use it. And I suspect you'll want to work up here. It's real quiet, not another neighbor for half a mile."

As if on cue, a faint sound of rumbling came from someplace outside. Xavier nodded.

"What was that?" Enoch asked.

"Oh, that's just the hills. They get talkative just before a storm." He raised his face and shut his eyes; he inhaled deeply. "Can you smell the thunder?"

Enoch's nostrils gulped the air, as from above the ceiling window electricity flashed. The sky boomed as the deluge broke.

• • •

## II.

Once alone, Enoch sat on the bed for a little while and listened to the storm. He found his host an enigma. Xavier was much younger than expected, and when Enoch reached into his knapsack for his own copy of the boy's privately printed chapbook of macabre prose-poems and vignettes he saw that there was no personal information concerning the lad except that he resided on a family homestead in the town of Dunwich—no age or other biographical tidbits were offered. How could such a simple-minded fellow write such strange and mature work? The artist rose and walked into the other room, the "library," and sat at the larger of the two tables, the surface of which was littered was piles of books and holograph manuscripts. Nearest him was a tea tin filled with pens and pencils, and next to it were old hardcover editions of the prose-poems of Charles Baudelaire and Clark Ashton Smith. Atop one pile of manuscripts was a chapbook edition of the prose-poems of Oscar Wilde, the cover of which was smudged with dirty fingerprints. Moving that, he reached for the topmost sheet of paper and squinted his eyes in an attempt to read its minute handwriting. The sheet was covered with crossed out words and eliminated lines, but with effort Enoch could make out a cohesive text, which he recited in his soft low voice.

"I am the voice of wind and rain through leaves that move beneath one black abyss. The limbs of trees bend to my song and shape themselves with new design, forming sigils to the haunted sky in which I originate. I taste the husks of mutant trees that are rooted in the tainted soil, and I whisper within the sigils that have been etched into that shell of wood, the Logos that awakened me as mortal pleas. I am the voice of tempest spilled from depths of black abyss. Awakened, I sing so as to arouse that which is Elder than my immortal self."

Outside the small house, the rain stopped and all was still except for an occasional chattering of night birds. Enoch stepped down the ladder stairs so as to bid his host goodnight, but the lower regions of the abode were vacant of inhabitant. Shrugging to himself, the artist climbed back up the steps and undressed. The bed was comfortable and its blankets kept him warm in the cool room. He was almost asleep when he thought he heard movement within the room and imagined warm breath on his handsome face. Strangely, Enoch did not dream as was his wont, and it seemed that

316 · They Smell of Thunder

very little time had passed before he awakened to the smells of breakfast food from below. Slipping into shirt and trousers, he stepped barefoot to the lower room and saw movement in the small kitchenette at back. Xavier smiled as Enoch entered the room and skillfully placed eggs, sunny-side up, onto two slices of soda bread that sat on a plate next to sausage and bacon.

"Mother got used to soda bread durin' her months in Ireland, when she went back to attend some family burial. I've changed the recipe a wee bit by usin' buttermilk instead of stout. Help yourself to fresh coffee and we'll eat in the front there."

Enoch poured himself a cup of coffee, which he drank black with heaps of sugar, and accepted the plate of food offered him. Walking into the main room, he fell into a comfortable chair and placed his plate on the small stand beside it, then cursed when he saw that he had forgotten eating utensils. Xavier joined him in the room and set a fork onto the artist's plate, and then he sat at a small table, moving away a bunch of books to make room for his dish. The dog lay before the hearth, its paws next to a food bowl.

"It's kind of incredible."

Enoch looked at the poet. "What's that?"

"That Rick would send you here to—what?—get a handle on me and have me collaborate with your illustrations for the book. You don't find it insultin'?"

"Not at all."

The boy shrugged. "Art is personal, right? Individual. My things come from these weird places inside me. But your stuff will be your interpretation of my stuff, you know, triggered by the pictures it puts inside your noggin. I don't want to explain my stuff to you—I want you to find the parts of it that I don't see so clearly. When I write, it's like I go into a trance and become somethin' . . . someone else. Sometimes I'll read over a thing and say, 'Where the hell did *that* come from?' It's like seein' a photo of yourself for the first time, when before all you knew was your reflection in the mirror. You're all different and you don't even recognize yourself."

Enoch laughed. "Well, Richard wants your first hardcover edition to be rather special, limited though the edition will be. He produces beautiful books. I have those weird places inside me, too, and thus I know their feeling and can reproduce them with my art. The outré is my forte, Mr. Aboth."

The poet cringed. "I hate being called that. Xavier, please. Well, I don't really know what you and Rick are expectin' of me, cos I don't know fuck-all about art technique and all of that. How is this gonna work?"

"All right, here's what's expected. We have been brought together because we are alchemists, as is our publisher. Our art is predicated . . . " The poet frowned. "It's established on a foundation of love for arcane things and our knack for evoking mysteries beyond corporeal time and space."

"I'm gonna let you down if that's what you think. I'm not ashamed of my witch-blood and all, but it doesn't guide the way I live."

Enoch finished the food and set his plate down roughly. "How can you say that when you've written the prose you have? Your language is skilled and gorgeous, and it sings of alchemy."

"But that ain't me—or, it's a part of me and a part of somethin' else, my Muse. It's the thing I conjure when I put my mind to workin'."

"And where does it come from, this something else, if not from a place inside you?"

"Nah, it's the part of me that leaves and joins the others in that secret place, and they dance with me and make me dream, and then I'm still kinda dreamin' when I sit up there and scratch my words out. It's ritual, sure."

"And where do you go, when you 'leave' and mingle with these others?"

Xavier turned to gaze out the window. "To the hills, and under them, to the secret places that we know in Dunwich." Enoch watched as the boy's eyes began to darken. "And they sing to us, as our mamas sang when we were babes. We hear them there, beneath the hills and in the clouds. We smell them atop the rounded summits among the standing stones and skulls. The storm is their kiss, with which they claim us." The poet sat dead still for some few moments, and then he blinked and smiled. "I can show you, if you like. You'll need to draw the hills for the book, they're important. Bishop Mountain is real close."

Without finishing his breakfast, the boy stood up and snatched a shoulder bag from a peg on the wall by the front door, and then he opened the door and vacated the house as Spider trotted behind him. Cursing, Enoch rushed up the stepway and got into socks and shoes, and then he joined the poet outside. The boy led Enoch toward a hill that rose behind the house, and as they walked toward the back area Enoch noticed three low mounds in the ground, two of which were topped by boulders on which curious symbols had been etched.

"That's Mother, and that's Grandpa," Xavier said as he pointed to the two graves.

"And the other?"

The lad shrugged. "Just some body we found atop Sentinel Hill. Didn't feel right to leave him up there, with his hide all melted onto his bones and all, so I brought him down here and gave him ceremony. Felt right. People go up there to open the Gate without really knowin' what the hell they're aimin' it. Usually they just get scared and scat, but this un had a bit of success. That was a noisy night," he concluded, laughing. He pointed to the hill. "It's a bit of a trek, but it feels good climbin' up there, and the view is mighty nice. Let's go. You comin', Spider? He doesn't always like to join. Dogs are super sensitive." Enoch watched the beast tilt its head at them and watch as they moved toward the hill, and then he walked in a circle and settled on the ground, his head on his paws.

They walked toward the hill and began to ascend it, wandering into its growth of woodland. Xavier's stride was steady and rather jaunty, and this walk was obviously a favorite activity. Enoch glanced at his wristwatch now and then, and after a forty-minute hike they were out of the woods and approaching the round flat apex of the hill. They followed a footpath that led them to the place where a circle of rough standing stones formed a circle.

"Come on to the other side, you can see better there. Watch your step, there's a bunch of stones that's easy to stumble over, and some of their edges are kinda sharp. There, that's the Devil's Hop Yard that we passed, and there's my place. It used to be where the Seth Bishop house stood, that was destroyed during the Horror, and Grandpa was able to buy the land and build our stead. Farm never was much and I hated that kind of work anyway, so I've found work in the Village. Won't never make much livelihood writin' my stuff, but that's more a hobby anyways. Nice clear mornin' after last night. Did the storm keep you awake?"

"No."

"I can't never sleep during a storm. I like to listen to it talk, all soothin' like. We get plenty of storms in Dunwich. That's Sentinel Hill to our right."

"Where you found the stranger's corpse."

"Yeah. He was probably some kid from Miskatonic who got in good with the librarian and read the old books and had ideas. Tried to open the Gate, most like, not understandin' it needs to be done durin' the Festivals and all. I can't be bothered with none of that. Grandpa knew a lot about it and tried to get me interested. Dunwich heritage and all of that. You were wrong, Mr. Coffin—okay, Enoch; I'm not really an alchemist, not the sort you probably think me to be. I know enough about the signs and callin' to the hills, and I tend the Hop Yard and a few other sites cos I'm part of the land and its people. But I use my weird skill for my writin'. I conjure words, language. Whoa, words are powerful little devils. Poetry is just as potent as some passage outta the *Necronomicon*. And not so lethal to them as don't know what the hell they're doin'. Bad poetry just makes you look like a damn fool. Bad raisin' up can leave you a dead fool." He turned to stare at Enoch. "Is your art your alchemy, Enoch?"

"Not really—it is my *art*, and therein lays its potency. But I paint the esoteric things without explicating them."

"There you go again—big words. But I think I know what you mean. You peel back the shroud without explainin' the rotten mess beneath it. Do you always understand your vision?"

The artist laughed. "Almost never. I allow the secret things to keep their mysteries, few of which I fully comprehend. I don't want to kill mystique—I want to suggest the secret things that may be found within fabulous darkness and let them have their aesthetic effect. I want to conjure art as it seduces my brain and enhances vision. Do you understand that?"

"Hell yeah. That's what I do. I hear the others in my head and let them fuck my brain, and then I write the visions they leave beneath my eyes. That's what it is—*vision*, seeing somethin' old and secret, and tryin' to explain how it feels inside your soul, where it plants all kind of roots. Hell yeah."

Enoch walked away from his new friend and went to touch a hand to one of the standing stones. "Were these erected by aborigines of the land?"

"What, by Indians? Nope, they wouldn't never climb up the hills of Dunwich. These stones were probably here afore any of them squeezed outta their mammas. Too bad there ain't no wind, it sounds awesome when it dances around these stones."

"Wind is easily conjured." Enoch smiled slyly at the lad.

"I know. Grandpa used to call it when he was feeling lonely for his kindred." Xavier's face grew slightly sad. "Mama used to call the wind now and then, when she couldn't sleep. I think that's what she was doing, singin' real low and weird, and then outside you'd hear the wind arisin'."

"Something like this?" Enoch placed his other hand onto the pillar and began to whisper to it, and then he rested his ear against the surface of stone and shut his eyes. When he heard the song beneath the stone, he pressed his mouth against the pillar and repeated the ancient cry. Xavier shuddered as an element entered into the air around them, and then the tears began to blur his vision as Enoch sang the ancient song that the boy remembered from childhood when it was murmured by his dam. He tried to speak the arcane words but found that his voice choked with sudden sobbing. Reaching for him, Enoch brought the young man into his embrace and pressed their moist lips together with what was almost a kiss. He raised his mouth to Xavier's eyes and warbled the primordial melody onto them, and he smiled as the boy panted onto his own face, a sensation that he remembered from the previous night, when someone watched him closely as he sank toward slumber. Enoch moved his face away and peered into the boy's eyes, and then he smiled and kissed the fellow's streaming tears as, around them, an alien wind began to hum between the spaces of the standing stones. Enoch raised his eyes skyward and watched the shapes that formed as sigils of shadow far above them. He then took Xavier fully into his arms and sang the song of tempest at the youth's ear, clasping the lad's quivering form in his strong unyielding arms.

### III.

The men sat in silence and lamp light in the main room of the small house. Enoch had just read aloud some few pieces from the manuscript of Xavier's forthcoming collection, and the young man was curiously moved by the sound of his work read by another. The artist sipped at his cup of coffee and gazed at the fellow near him. How old was the poet? Was he even twenty? He looked, in the soft light, like a little lost boy as he scanned the sheets that Enoch had read out loud.

"Your prose is beautiful, Xavier. The prose-poem is, I think, the perfect form for the macabre. One can express anything and everything, concisely yet with force. These are finer than those in your chapbook, your language is more mature."

The boy laughed. "The instructors at school were always tryin' to correct my speech. 'Stop talkin' like a Dunwich farmer,' they'd yell. Like I was supposed to be ashamed of where I come from. They've had a thing against Dunwich at Miskatonic for ages, and I was glad to leave early cos of Mother's illness. Didn't want to go to damn University anyway, but she wanted it and it made her happy. She thought they could learn me how to write 'with more distinction' was how she'd phrase it. But I didn't want to be molded by their ways. My talent is mine own, a gift from them outside. Don't need no mollycoddlin' old fool in spectacles fussin' over me and tellin' me how to write and pretendin' to care so much about my 'gift,' their eyes all shinin' and stupid." His laughter had a bitter ring. "Anyway, had to come home and tend Mother as was dyin'. She went a little witless near the end and used to sing with the whippoorwills. But she'd get all quiet when I conjured the others and spoke to her all elegant-like; and she'd put her soft hands on my face and call me her lovely boy."

Not knowing what to say, Enoch glanced around the room and let his eyes settle on a round wall hanging that was composed of connected sticks. "I saw those totemic sigils on some of the bridges that I crossed. You were attending one when I first saw you."

"Oh, the river signs are different from the Whateley charm."

"No one has cleared the Whateley wreckage and claimed their land."

"Nope. The memory of the Horror runs deep with some. Grandpa was thought crazy for buildin' on this spot, but ain't nothin' wrong with it."

"And the Whateley land?"

"Best left undisturbed. There's just a few of us visit it and tend the charm and the lair and all. Ah, I see that look in your eye. Ain't too late yet. We'll take my jalopy. Nah, Spider don't venture out after dark. Good boy, Spider," he said, patting the beast's head. "No, you won't need a jacket, it's a warm night." Exiting the house, they boarded the lad's old car and drove through darkness. "You remind me of Grandpa, the way your eyes shine when there's magick brewin'. I've never felt the thrill, and Mother was kind of blasé about it all. I think the Horror scared most folk more than they'd ever admit, cos it weren't never figured out what the Whateley's were up to. We just know it was somethin' awesome, somethin' for a special season. But the season has passed, and now there's just what was left behind."

"An aftermath of Horror?"

The boy chuckled. "You're kinda a poet yourself, when you speak sometimes."

The rough road took them to the Whateley ruins, and Xavier turned to reach down behind the driver seat and pulled out what looked like an antique oil lantern. Stepping out of the car, the boy motioned for Enoch to follow him as he pulled a lighter from his pocket and lit the lantern's wick. Silently, they walked to the ruins, and the artist was aware of an alteration in atmosphere, and of a peculiar smell that permeated the place. Something untoward had had its origin here, of that there was no doubt. He stopped to gaze to the flat apex of Sentinel Hill and felt a thrill of horror course through his flesh. What else had trod this unholy ground, on what grotesque gargantuan hoofs? It had left its aftermath absolutely, an eidolon that tried to spill its shapelessness into one's skull and teach one's lips to shriek its name. Finally, Xavier stopped and bent to move some planks away that covered double doors built into the ground. The lad pulled open one door and descended, his shadow playing weirdly on the stone steps and walls of dirt as he stopped to flick his lighter to a torch that protruded from one surface. The underground chamber was revealed. Enoch noticed that the hideous stench was not so strong in this lair beneath the house. He breathed quietly as his anxious eyes scanned the entered realm, and when he passed a small antique chest filled with ancient gold coins he let his hand bury itself therein.

"Wizard's booty," Xavier whispered. "Best left alone."

The artist raised his hand out of the pile and surreptitiously pocketed one gold coin, and then he moseyed toward the unearthly lattice structures that hung on one wall. What they were he could not fathom. They seemed composed of bleached sticks from trees and thin lengths of board that had been fastened together in weird display, although he couldn't tell in the poor light with what they had been conjoined. He couldn't bring himself to touch them, for something in their outré nature confused him. He backed away and was amazed at how bizarre the sticks seemed, more phantom-like than physical, like the fossils of spectral things.

"I've never seen their like," he whispered.

"Nope, Wizard Whateley was unique. Some old journals of folk that had visited this place before his death said that these things were fastened on some sealed doors in the house and on the old clapboarded tool-house.

If you look at them too steadily they find you in dreamin'. Had a shared dream with those folks you met t'other day, and from it we built the one afore the house. Keeping somethin' out, or somethin' in, I guess. The hill noises get loud here on the Sabaoths. It's Roodmas on Tuesday. If you're interested we can light a fire on Sentinel Hill and such." The young man looked around and frowned. "Kinda grim in here, ain't it? Let's get."

Without waiting the lad walked to the wall torch and snuffed it out on the dirt floor, and then held his lantern before him as he ascended the stone steps. Enoch waited for a moment in rich darkness, the one illumination in which came from the lattice designs on the wall. Enoch studied them in fascination, and it came to him that they resembled doors on a fence. He wondered what he would find, should he push one open and peer onto the other side. Then the artist cautiously found his way to the steps and climbed toward outer aether.

## IV.

Enoch, alone in his rooms, sat at the smaller table and sketched onto a pad, trying to recreate the lattice designs that he had seen in the Whateley underground lair. He found it curious how his vision blurred as his mind tried to recall the exact shapes of the designs he had beheld, and how cold his brain felt when he concentrated too fully on remembering. Finally, he gave up and, rising, stretched his arms until his palms touched the low ceiling. Glancing through the ceiling window, he saw many points of light in the black sky. He was restless and a little bored, and so he slipped into his jacket and quietly walked down the steps to the lower room, where Xavier was sleeping soundly on the sofa with one lowered hand resting on his dog's head. The animal did not move as it watched Enoch go to the door and step outside. His truck sounded loud when he switched on the ignition and drove slowly down the rutted road to Devil's Hop Yard. The artist stopped his vehicle and stepped onto the road, sneering at the odorous Dunwich air as it crept into his nostrils and tainted the taste in his mouth. The desolate field was acres long and absolutely barren, and he hesitated for some few moments before finding the nerve to step onto its precinct. Bishop Mountain loomed above him, beneath moving clouds that were lit up by soft moonlight. Yes, this was cursed sod, and Enoch muttered protective spells as he trod its wasted demesne. Finally, he knelt and placed his hands on the surface, flatly, trying to sense what, if anything, was held beneath the ground.

"Perhaps a drop of witch blood will awaken you," he whispered as he took his switchblade out of his pocket and opened it. Holding the steel blade to moonlight, he made signals to the sphere's dead light, and then he quickly sliced the blade through an index finger and watched the dark liquid spill onto the dirt. A sound arose from beneath him, a faint rumbling that grew into a kind of cracking or quaking; and then a current of chilly air poured down the great round hill, to him, air that babbled senselessly at his ears. The earth below him trembled as from other distant hills came a response of other rumblings. "Gawd, what visions would you plant if I slumbered on your sod?" He then reached into another pocket and brought forth the ancient golden coin that he had pilfered from the Whateley warren, the metal of which felt weirdly hot in his hand. He raised the coin to his mouth and kissed it, and then he used one side of it to etch a diagram into the dirt. Chanting, he dug into the earth with the hand that held the coin, burying it as deep as he could burrow. All around him, the noises silenced. Enoch spat into the small dark area of his bloodstain and then staggered to his feet. How heavy were his limbs, as if some force below were trying to coax him underground. Like a clumsy drunk, he lurched from the Hop Yard to the road and his truck. He frowned as the blurriness of his vision and drove extremely slowly to the Aboth homestead. Entering the house, he found the living room vacant of man and beast. Heavily, he climbed up the steps and sat on his bed.

Dunwich was dead silent, and he was sleepy. He reached down so as to remove his shoes, and as he held the heel of one his hand was littered with the debris that clung to it—the particles of soil from Devil's Hop Yard that he had carried with him. Mumbling incoherently, he removed the other shoe with his other hand, onto which other particles of dirt adhered. Enoch clapped his hands but the soil would not fall from them, and so he cursed and ran his fingers through his hair and over his face. Granular fragments fell onto his eyes, which he rubbed wearily, thus pushing the substance into the choroid. Something beneath his face tickled him, and the artist laughed as he pulled off his shirt and reclined on the bed.

The artist raised his face to eerie amber moonlight as he danced upon a gravesite. Below him, the rumbling from some deep place underground kept rhythm to his movement, and when he bent his head so as to watch his happy feet, he saw that he was frolicking upon the grave of the stranger whose dissolved corpse had been found atop Sentinel Hill. What a lonely little grave, the artist thought, and how wretched must be the solitude within the pit of death. He knelt and moved his hands into soft earth, and when his hands found the flimsy object he pulled it up and out of earth. The skeletal mouth was open, and some dried fleshy substance still covered one eye socket. The artist reached into his pocket for the golden coin, with which he would cover the other socket, and he was mystified to find the coin missing. No matter, he could still entertain his captive; and so he lifted the thing in moonlight and wondered at the way some of the bones had been deformed with melting, as if kissed by acidic lips. He brought the creature's skull close to his face and tried to imagine the countenance that had once covered it. They pirouetted among the other gravesites until he heard the baying of a winged thing that sallied to him through the mist of moonlight. The hound-like thing was familiar, for he had seen its likeness in the *Necronomicon*. He did not like the way the beast leered at his partner's skull as heavy liquid slipped from bestial tongue, and so the artist placed his hand protectively over the cranium. Yet the beast was not to be deprived, and it bayed again as it stretched its liquid tongue to the artist's hand and licked it; and as the rough member lapped at his flesh, the artist saw that skin slip from his appendage and cover the skull, which took on fleshy form in which boiling black liquid, churning inside sockets, formed new orbs that blinked and laughed, and new mouth that breathed upon him.

Enoch groaned in slumber and pushed away the canine head that nuzzled his hand as the young human mouth so near to his breathed language onto his eyelids.

## V.

He awakened to find Spider reclined on the floor next to the bed and studying him with poignant eyes. Smiling, Enoch called to the dog and clapped his hands, to which the animal responded by leaping onto the bed and licking one hand happily. "Your tongue is smooth, not rough like the feline variety," the artist said, to which the beast tilted its head as if attempting to contemplate the spoken sound. Now fully awake, Enoch pushed out of bed, slipped into clothes, and then he was preceded by Spider

326 · They Smell of Thunder

down the steps to the living room where Xavier and the girl Alma Bishop smiled at him. Enoch thought he could detect the tang of new-shed orgasm in the air, but it may have been mere fancy. Smiling at the couple, he sat at a small table at which Xavier had been working and on which sat two piles of paper. In the shorter pile, the paper was filled with the poet's minute handwriting, and in the other pile the paper was blank. Unable to resist, Enoch slipped a blank sheet near him and picked up a pen, and then he began to sketch. The youngsters did not move as they watched the artist work, aware that they were posing. After twenty minutes, Enoch smiled and stood, handing the sheet to Alma, who murmured appreciatively as she saw the drawing in which she and Xavier were expertly portrayed.

Outside, Enoch raised his face to the sun and felt its welcome warmth as he ran his hands through his hair, in which he still felt particles of Hop Yard grime. He moseyed to the small well and, yanking it rope, raised a sunken wooden bucket out of semi-clear water; then he set the bucket on the well's stone ridge, cupped his hands into the liquid and raised those expressive hands so that the water spilled over his hair. He dipped his hands into the bucket again and lowered his face into the cupped water. Wiping his eyes, he caught sight of his battered pickup truck, which he had seldom seen in daylight. The pickup had belonged to an artist chum who had committed suicide, and it was usually kept hidden in a rented garage—Enoch preferred the keen pleasure of riding on trains to that of driving the vehicle. Yet he confessed to himself that he had enjoyed driving it around Dunwich, had enjoyed a sense of freedom of movement that it had given him.

The young couple came outside and the girl kissed Xavier goodbye, then turned to smile at Enoch. She held the sketch in her hand as she wandered from them down the road. Xavier strolled to where Enoch stood, dipped one hand into the bucket and brought water to his mouth.

"You did a strange thing last night."

"No I didn't. Your work is about the land, the land I need to become intimate with. I need to eat it with my eyes and taste it with my hands, get the feel of it underneath my skin and in my blood. Such a rich mythic land, darkly fertile." He stepped nearer to the boy. "I appreciate it. I like its inhabitants. I'm going to start working on your portrait tonight, per your request that an illustration portray you rather than a photograph." His hands lifted so as to explore the young man's visage. "I like your face, with its length of nose and compressed lips. You keep your mouth so tightly clamped, as if afraid of spilling secrets."

"We'll have to do that project before nightfall. It's Roodmas. I've got somethin' to do atop Sentinel Hill."

"I can sketch ye up thar."

The boy laughed. "Nah, I don't think so. Your hands will be occupied with—other things."

They parted, and Enoch, feeling restless, took his sketchpad as he walked for hours to investigate some bridges. He enjoyed drawing the ancient structures, which were becoming rarer in New England as they were replaced with modern structures. On one bridge he found a particularly enticing lattice diagram that had been worked into the structure with newer wood than that with which the bridge had been constructed, yet as the artist tried to draw the graph he experienced an aching behind the eyes. He rubbed his eyes with his fingers, and then worked those fingers in an attempt to ape the diagram on the bridge; but as he did this his hands became sharply chilled, kissed with occult frigidity, his witch-blood advised him to desist.

The sun was sinking behind the hills by the time he returned to the house, and he was surprised to find Alma there again, sitting at the hearth with her arms around Spider's neck.

"Ah, good," the poet told him. "I thought you'd miss it. Do you want to drive? Okay, hang on a tic." Xavier went into the kitchen and opened a cupboard, from which he took a small jar that was filled with pale powder. He signaled with his eyes that he was ready, and together the men walked out and into the pickup. They drove through the decadent Massachusetts countryside as sunset deepened into dusk, and the silent boy scanned heaven in search of birth of starlight. Enoch parked his truck just in front of the large lattice diagram that had been erected before the ruins of the Whateley farmhouse, and getting out of the truck the artist went to handle the joined sticks.

"This is a bit different from the others on the bridges, a bit simpler in motif. Is this your work?"

"Hell no. We learned it from that worn by Wizard Whateley. The others are inspired by dreams and all, and they're true as far as they go; but they're mostly for water and what it calls with flowin'. This one is more—cosmic." The lad smiled at the use of what he considered a sophisticated word.

"And where is Wizard Whateley, Xavier?"

Coyly, the lad smiled and nudged his head toward Sentinel Hill. "Up thar." Holding tightly to the jar of powder, he moved toward the incline, and Enoch followed silently. Strangely, as they walked over stones and high grass that led into woodland, the boy began to sing

*"An' un day soon ye day'll come*
*When heav'n an' airth'll drone as un,*
*An' chillen o' Dunnich hear ye cry*
*O' eld Father Whateley from all sky."*

They tramped through the woodland, and out of it, toward a twilit sky, toward the round apex of Sentinel Hill and its rough-hewn stone columns, its large table-like altar, its tumuli of human bone. Enoch knelt beside one pile of reeking remains and noted how some of them were oddly deformed, seemingly melted at places—and this reminded him of something he could not quite recall, a dream perhaps. As he was hunkered by the bones, Xavier stepped to a brazier and took a box of wooden matches from an inner coat pocket. One struck match was tossed into the brazier, which exploded into soaring flame. Enoch arose.

"Over here," the boy called as he moved over the coarse ground to a place where a length of oblong stone lay flatly on the earth. Had it been composed of wood the object might have served as lid for a small coffin. Enoch looked over the symbols that had been etched into it, most of which he recognized from having studied them in tomes of antique lore. "Help me shove it a bit," the boy instructed. "I could do it alone, but it's best to have an assembly. Just this top part here, yeah, there ya go. Phew, you never get used to the stink. Funny that he should smell still, havin' been gone so long; although, of course, it ain't all him that's reekin'."

The huddled skeletal remains were of a small lean fellow, and although most of the flesh had long erased, one patch of dry hide clung to the skull and formed a kind of face to which a growth of beard still clung. The thing was naked of clothing except for a thick robe of purple thread. What really captured Enoch's attention was the design of latticed wood attached to a cord that wound around the throat. This small item was far more similar to the designs in the underground Whateley lair than any of the others Enoch had seen. He stared at it as the boy next to him sprinkled a little of the powder from the jar over the dead thing's face and uttered whispered words. Below them, sounds issued from the beneath the hill, and the flames in the brazier soared as if they had found new fuel. Enoch stood and sniffed the dark air.

"Storm's brewing," he informed the lad.

Xavier rose to a standing position and stared at stars. "Nah, it's them."

"Them?"

"The others—them old ones. They smell o' thunder. They loom among the stars, and between them." His eyes grew odd and shadowed. "They sing of deceased glory and show the silhouette of what has gone before, as they bubble between dimensions and weep the antique cry. Let us sing with them now, my brother, as they split the veil and show the thing that was, the thing that is, the thing that will be. They walk supernal among the smoldering sparks above us, craving the scent of mortal blood, which nourishes them weirdly. They form themselves with blood and debris of starlight so as to gibber in the mortal plane. Cthulhu is their kindred, yet Cthulhu sees them dimly. They pulse between the planets and kiss the palms of the Strange Dark One, Avatar of Chaos. We sing for them to unlatch the Gate, so as to usher forth the time of Yog-Sothoth. We see it there, the Gate and Threshold, between dimensions. We call it with our tongues, our hands."

The poet raised his hands and latched his fingers together, his digits impossibly aping the design of the dead wizard's icon. The hill noises escalated, and with each new pulse of sound the brazier flames expanded. Enoch watched what looked like smoke coil among the stars, which extinguished one by one. Xavier stood upright, an elect messenger who held his fleshy signal to the flowing obscurity of the sky. He bleated arcane language to the dark cosmic abyss, and in answer to his cry a pale form began to reveal itself. It was the esoteric lattice design, perfectly formed, fluid and sentient. It was the awesome Gate of Yog-Sothoth, a thing that trembled as it sensually divided itself so as to reveal the eidolons beyond it, the ghosts of they who lived brief mortal lives. There was the frail white-haired woman of fearsome and foolish countenance, and there was one offspring of her loins, a dark and goatish beast. And there—there was the awesome one, the one of such abbreviated promise, with its gigantic face that stretched across the sky, that face of which one half replicated the suggested visage of the interred wizard.

Enoch watched this display of lost glory and future promise, and knew that he was naught. Shaking uncontrollably, he flung himself before the Messenger with pleading in his liquid eyes. But the Messenger merely glanced for one moment at the frail and puny freak before him; and then in contempt he struck the artist's head.

*This was that cult . . . it had always existed and always would exist, hidden in distant wastes and dark places all over the world until the time when the great priest Cthulhu, from his dark house in the mighty city of R'lyeh under the waters, should rise and bring the earth again beneath his sway. Some day he would call, when the stars were ready . . .*

*"The Call of Cthulhu" · H. P. Lovecraft (1928)*

# · THE SONG OF SIGHS ·
## Angela Slatter

### I

*February 12th*

> *The song of Sighs, which is his.*
> *Let him kiss me with his mouths:*
> *for his love is better than ichor.*

The translation is coming along, but ponderously.

It takes so long to get the languages to agree, the tongues to collude. But it is close. Some days, though, I wonder why I don't adopt an easier hobby, like knitting or understanding string theory. I tap on the thick folio with nails marred by chipped polish. I remind myself this is for fun and stare at the creamy slab of bound pages, let my eyes lose focus so all the notations of my pen look like so many chicken scratches. So they all cease to make sense. If I stare long enough, perhaps I might see through time, see the one who wrote *this* and ask, perhaps, for its greater meaning.

A polite cough interrupts my reverie. I look up and find twenty pairs of eyes fixed upon me. I realize that I heard the buzzer a full minute ago, that my class has quietly packed up their texts and pads, pens, and pencils.

"Doctor Croftmarsh?" says one of them, a handsome manly boy, tall for his age, dreamy blue eyes. I cannot remember his name. "Doctor, may we go? Only, Master Thackeray gets annoyed when we're late."

I nod, pick his name from the air. "Yes, Stephen, sorry. Offer my apologies to the Master and tell him I will make amends. Read chapter seven of the Roux, we will discuss what he says about Gilgamesh tomorrow."

Thackeray will expect expensive whisky in recompense; he does not miss an opportunity to drink on another's tab. His forgiveness is dearly bought, but it is easier to keep him sweet than make an enemy of him. There is the scrape and squawk of chair legs dragged across wooden floorboards, and desk lids clatter as students check they've not forgotten anything.

As they file out, I offer an afterthought, "Those of you wishing to do some extra study for next week's exams, don't forget your translations. The usual time."

"Yes, Doctor Croftmarsh," comes the chorus. There will be at least six of them, the brightest, the most ambitious, those desiring ever so ardently to get ahead. This is what the academy specialises in, propelling orphans *upward*. Idly, I make a bet with myself: Tilly Sanderson will be the first to knock at 6:30.

The door closes softly behind the last of the students and the space is silent, properly silent for the first time today, no *whoosh* of breath in and out, no nasal snorts or adenoidal whistles, no sneezes, no sighs, no surreptitious farts, no whispered conversations they think I cannot hear simply because they don't want me to. Dust specks cartwheel in the shafts of light coming through the windows. I close my eyes, enjoying the sensation of not being scrutinised for however brief a time. A band of tension is tightening across my forehead. Beneath my fingers, the substantial cushion of journal pages is strangely warm.

II

*February 13th*

> *Because of thy savour*
> *thy name is as fear poured forth,*
> *And thus do virgins fear thee.*

The refectory is awash with polite noise, the clatter of cutlery against crockery, the *ting* of glasses and water jugs meeting. Students and teachers, all at their allotted tables, talk quietly to one another, all in their own class groups.

The academy is a large place, a great building in the Gothic style, four long wings joined to make a square, with a broad green quadrangle in the middle. Two sides of structure face the sea, looking out over the epic cliff drop; the other two are embraced by the woods and the well-tended grounds. The nearest town is ten miles distant. There is a teaching staff of twenty, three cooks, four cleaners, two gardeners and a cadre of two hundred-odd students.

As a child, I was occasionally sent to stay with an acquaintance of my parents, here in this very house, before its owners' dipping fortunes made a change of hands essential, and it became a school for exceptional orphans. I recollect very little about those visits, having but dim impressions of many rooms, large and dust-filled, corridors long and portrait-lined, and bed chambers stuffed with canopied beds, elaborate dressers and wardrobes that loomed towards one in the night like trolls creeping from beneath bridges. I remember waking from nightmares of the place, begging my mother and father not to be sent there again.

It was only after they were gone, when I was grown and qualified, seeking employment and a quiet retreat after the accident, that I saw an advertisement for a history teacher. It seemed like the perfect opportunity. I have been here for a year.

This is what I'm told I remember.

I'm assured it's one of those things, this kind of amnesia that takes away some recollections and leaves others—I retain everything I must know in order to teach. I keep every bit of study I ever undertook tucked under my intellectual belt. I memorized the things that have happened since I came here. I may even recall the car accident—or at least, I have a sense of an explosion, of flying through the air, of terrible, intense pain—but I'm never quite sure what I can actually *invoke* of that time.

I suppose I am fortunate to be alive when my parents are not. I've been promised that many people I once knew are dead, but I'm uncertain whether I actually *feel* a loss. There are no remnants of that old life, no photos of my parents and I. No holiday snaps, no foolish playing-around in the backyard photos. I have no box of mementoes, no inherited jewelry, no ancient teddy bear with its fur loved off. Nothing that might provide proof of my growing up, of my youth, of my *being*.

I fear I have no true memory of who I am.

In the same notebook where I make my translations, in the very back pages are the scribbles I write to remind myself of who I am supposed to be. I read them over and again: I am Vivienne Croftmarsh. I have a PhD.

I teach at the academy. I am an only child and now an orphan. I translate ancient poetry as a pastime.

This is who I am.

This is what I tell myself.

But I cannot shake the feeling that something is working loose, that the world around me is softening, developing cracks, threatening to crumble. I can't say why. I cannot deny a sense of formless dread. My hands are beginning to ache; I rub at the slight webbing between the fingers, massaging the tenderness there.

"Wake up, dreamy-drawers." Fenella Burrows is the closest thing I have to a friend here; she plants herself and her lunch tray across from me at the deserted end of the table I've chosen. Most of the faculty take the hint and stay away, but not her and I don't mind. She tells me we went to school together, but isn't offended when I am unable to reminisce. She jerks her head towards the journal and my ink-stained fingers. "How's it going?"

"Getting there. Second verse."

"Second verse, same as the first," she snorts. Fenella throws back her head when she laughs, all the mouse-brown curls tumbling down her back like a waterfall. She leans in close and says, "Don't look now, but Thackeray is watching you."

I pull a face, don't turn my head. "Thackeray's always watching."

"Oh, don't tell me you don't think he's attractive."

Yes, he is attractive, but he stares too much, seems to see too much, seems to dig beneath my skin with his gaze and pull out secrets I didn't know were there. That's the sense I get anyway, but I don't tell Fenella because it sounds stupid and *she* clearly finds him appealing. Her smile is limned with the pale green of jealousy. "He's all yours," I say.

She sighs. "If only. No one wants the plain bridesmaid."

"How were your classes this morning?" I ask.

"Tilly Sanderson out-Frenched me."

"That sounds appalling and punishable by a jail term."

"Grammar-wise, you fool." She adds more salt to the unidentifiable vegetarian mush on her plate. I can't really bear to look at it. Fenella insists it's an essential tool in her diet plan. I see no evidence: her face is still as round as a pudding and so is she.

"Well, she's very smart."

"Yes, but I hate it when the little beasts are smarter than us." She shovels the mess from her plate to her mouth and seems to chew for a long time.

"Honestly, don't you think eating is meant to be, if not fun, then at least easy? How much mastication does that require?"

"It's good for you; it's just a bit . . . fibrous."

"It looks like the wrong end of the digestion process."

"You're an unpleasant creature. Don't know why I talk to you." She steals a chip off my plate.

I stare up at the head table, frown. "Have you seen the Principal lately?"

"A day or so ago," she says. "Why?"

"Just feel like they haven't been around for ages."

"That'd be your dodgy memory. Old trout will be here somewhere," she says dismissively. "You can always talk to Candide, if it's urgent."

"No, nothing really. Just curious. Also, I don't want to get trapped by the Deputy Head—last time I ended up listening to him recounting his thesis from 1972 on the evils of the Paris student uprisings of '68." Candide's about sixty, but he seems older and dustier than he should. Fenella hooks her thumbs under the front facing of her academic gown, tucks her chin into her neck and looks down her nose at me, adopting a sonorous intonation.

" 'Bloody peasants, disrespecting their betters. It's all one can expect from a nation that murdered its own royalty and has far too many varieties of cheese.' "

"Don't make the mistake of mentioning Charles I and the thud his head made on the scaffolding. I learned that the hard way."

We laugh until we're gasping, and the older teachers are looking at us disapprovingly. We'll be spoken to later about the dangers of hilarity in front of the students and letting our dignity visibly slip. Causes the natives to become restless if they think we're human and we lose our grip on the moral high ground.

## III

*February 14th*

> *Lead me, I will wait for thee:*
> *the King once summoned me into his chambers:*
> *and I was glad and rejoiced,*
> *I remember thy love more than life:*
> *All tremble before thee.*

There are two kinds of people in this world: those who, when faced with a window two floors up, will immediately accept the limitations it places upon them; and those who instantly look for a way to subvert both the height and the threatened effects of gravity. This room is full of the latter. It's one of the reasons I love teaching: the opportunity to find those who would chance a fall in the attempt to fly, rather than stay safely within bounds.

The buzz of conversation in my oak-paneled rooms washes over me. Stephen and Tilly are arguing about whether Ishtar is more or less powerful as a profligate prostitute goddess, or is simply a male wish-fulfillment fantasy; the other five watch the back and forth of a teen intellectual tennis match. The tipple of port has made them aggressive and I imagine sex will be the result at some point. Time to nip that in the bud. I give a slow blink, to moisten my dried eyeballs, and clap my hands.

"Enough, enough. You're not talking history anymore, you've slid into pop culture, which is Doctor Burrows' area not mine," I say. "Look at the time. Off you all go."

"Goodnight, Doctor Croftmarsh," they say. The closing of the door and then the one student left, the one who always waits behind; the one who stands out, and frequently apart from, her fellows. Tilly, who thinks herself special, and is, I suppose. So much talent, so clever; she will do well when she goes out into the world.

"How are you?" she asks and I am a bit taken aback. She steps close, takes my hands in hers, begins stroking the palms, an intimate, invasive gesture. I don't think she knows she's doing it. "Do you feel it yet? Has it begun?"

"Do I feel *what*, Tilly?"

Her face changes, the avid expression painted over by one of uncertainty, perhaps fear. What does the child mean?

"Tilly." Thackeray's voice is low but seems to affect the girl like the crack of a whip. She starts and looks guilty. I didn't even hear the door open. "Tilly, don't bother Doctor Croftmarsh. It's late and time for you to be getting back to your room."

Tilly drops my hands, and dips her head, blond curls covering her blush-red face. She makes for the exit, then looks back over her shoulder before she leaves, smiling a sunburst at me and then throwing an odd glance at Thackeray, which I cannot interpret.

"Sleep well. Don't forget to read the Roux," I say after her as the door closes and Thackeray leans his back against it.

He grins, his thick lips smug, then he moves into the room without invitation and helps himself to the whisky waiting on the shelf, knocking one of the heavy crystal glasses against the other. He raises the bottle at me, and I nod. Beneath his black woolen academic robe he is still a rugby player, but slowly going soft and bloating in parts. His pale cheeks are shadowed with ebony stubble; the ruffian's posture hides an acute, albeit lazy intelligence; sometimes I wonder how he came to teach at a place as exclusive as this.

"So, young Tilly Sanderson," he begins, handing me one of the tumblers. His own measure is far more generous. He slumps into the chair I recently vacated, drapes himself across it, long legs stretched forward, one arm hanging down almost to the carpet, the other hand clutching his drink. His voice is low, trying for levity, but there's a dark edge that tells me to tread carefully. "Not teaching her something new, are you?'

"Don't be ridiculous." I sip at the whisky, feel it burn down my throat then take up residence in my belly, heating me surely as a fire. From a chest at the foot of my writing desk, I pull an unopened bottle and hold it out to him.

"What? Can't want me gone so soon, surely." But he gets to his feet and reaches out. He wraps his large hand around not just the neck, but my hand as well, trapping me unless I want to sacrifice forty-year-old Scotch. His breath is hot and malt-rich on my face; I can feel the warmth radiating off his body, and my cheeks flame with a dim memory of drunken fumbling. I'm not sure how far it went. "Surely we could indulge ourselves once again . . . Who's to know?"

I would know. And so would he. And it would give him something else to use against me in a school where fraternization of any kind is reason for dismissal. I know how the world works; he would receive a slap on the wrist and I would be gone without references. "Good night, Thackeray."

I pull away and he has to juggle to save his prize. He gives a slow smile, takes his defeat well, throws back the amber in his glass and returns the empty to the shelf.

He leaves and I feel as if I can breathe for the first time in an age. From the corridor, I hear the whisper and scuffle of boots. My heart clenches at the idea that any of the other teachers might have seen him coming out of my room. I creep over and crack the door, putting my eye to the sliver.

Thackeray and Tilly stand close, oh so close. His free hand is roaming up one thigh, over her hip, then cupping her backside roughly. Her face is hidden from me, pressed into his chest.

I step back. The headache that's been with me all day worsens; I feel as if the bones of my skull are pushing against each other. I rub my palms across my face, hoping to hold the pieces in place, to press the pain back.

IV

*February 15th*

> *I am hidden, but lovely, O ye daughters of darkness,*
> *as the dreams of Great Old Ones,*
> *as the drowned houses of R'lyeh.*

The office door, with its frosted glass panel reading simply PRINCIPAL, is unlocked, and there is no sign of the watchdog, Mrs. Kilkivan. The Tilly-Thackeray situation gave me a restless night and I thought I might approach the Head before class.

Inside, the floor is covered with an enormous rug that stretches almost to the boundaries of the enormous office. The walls are covered by bookshelves, neatly stacked with hardbacks, decorative spines showing off silver lettering. Three display cases take up one corner, each with a series of ancient gold jewelry, marked with carefully hand-written labels and histories: this one found in ancient Babylon, this one from a well in Kish, yet another dug up from the depths of Nineveh, this from Ashur, these from Ur and Ebla. Artifacts excavated from the cradle of civilization; I seem to recall the Head had been active in archaeological digs in early life, and that father and mother, uncles and aunts, had all spent time in the Middle East.

Beneath the broad tall window is a desk roughly the width of the office, with just enough space to walk around, if you've slim hips. The desk is neat and tidy, a notepad on the blotter which is perfectly aligned with the edge of the mahogany edifice, the bases of the two banker's lamps also carefully placed, one on the left corner, the other one the right. The pens, fine things, are in individual cases on the polished surface; a sturdy pewter letter opener lies next to them, protected in a bronze enameled sheath.

Some of the shelves are bereft of books, but stand instead as habitations for busts of Greek and Roman philosophers, statuettes of gods and demons, strange twisted things that would not be out of place in a museum.

Unable to resist the impulse, I step around the desk, plant myself in the ample leather seat and try one of the drawers. Locked. All of them. I rub at my forearms; the skin is dry, thickening, irritated. The grandfather clock strikes the hour and I will be late for class. I snatch a piece of paper from the notebook and scribble a message to the Principal that I need a word. I place it in the centre of the blotter, where it cannot be missed. I carefully put the pen back in its case, only after trying to wipe off any finger marks.

Here is my problem: Tilly seemed willing. She is almost eighteen—yes, we keep them here longer, if they wish. Eighteen, nineteen, twenty. Some stay on and become staff, studying, learning from the teachers here, which gives them a far better training than they would find elsewhere. Here is my other problem: the possibility of Thackeray revealing what may have happened between us, but which I am unsure even took place. And Tilly, she is a child, easily influenced.

Who do I protect? Myself or the child?

I don't know what I will tell the Head. Candide will be useless; he will simply give me a slow blink and ask *whatever do you mean*? The Principal is the key. When we meet I will know what to say.

V

*February 16th*
> *Look not upon me, because I am disguised,*
> *because the sun hath burned me:*
> *Earth's children were angry with me;*
> *they stole what was mine;*
> *They kept him from me.*

The west wing houses the library; it's stacked with shelving and desks overrun by computer terminals and printers. A wooden set of card index drawers stands lonely and lost in the middle of the room—the young librarian doesn't know quite what to do with it and is too afraid of the ghosts of librarians past to throw it out. Curiosities abound: a giraffe's skeleton, a giant cephalopod, spears and shields and helmets of disappeared empires, bronze horse statuettes, elephant tusks and rhinoceros horns, all take up space on walls, shelves, nooks and alcoves. There are portraits, too: long-dead educators staring down with what might be disapproval or hauteur or both.

The only wall unencumbered by shelves or display items is covered by a tapestry. A woman sits enthroned on a stone seat, a staff in one hand, a snake in the other. Her eyes are wide, almost too much so: icthyoid and protuberant; her lips pouting, her nose somewhat flat; hair a mess of black; yet there is a kind of beauty to her, a compelling strangeness that draws the observer in. She wears a simple green robe, something that seems almost armored, perhaps scaled, and at her slippered feet, a field of blossoms: black, silver, red, yellow, and richest chestnut petals on stalks of green. She sits most closely to the left of the tapestry—or rather, to the right—and to the right, or rather her left, nothing more than a verdant tangle of forest. Branches and trunks, undergrowth and vines, all twist together to form a dense curtain, seemingly without uniformity or plan, utterly wild and overgrown, curled around the stony ruins of a building crushed by the foliage.

In a quiet corner of the room sits Fenella, surrounded and almost concealed by a fortress of books built on the desk in front of her. At one of the tables are Tilly and Stephen and their various acolytes; I note the blond curly head turn towards me, offering a smile, but I pretend not to see her, keep myself aimed directly at my friend.

"Have you seen the Head?" I ask, *sotto voce*, as I scratch at the sides of my throat, trying to get rid of the terrible itching there. She jumps, pulled from her concentration by my question, both hands thumping on the tabletop in fright.

"Don't you knock?" One of the book towers wobbles and begins a slow slide. She tries to stop it, then gives up and lets the tomes fan out, domino-like, until the final one teeters on the edge and falls. It marks the end of its descent with a noise like a shot that stops the library for a few moments.

Fenella folds her arms and looks at me.

I ask again, "Have you seen the Head?"

"This morning," she says. "What is *wrong* with you?"

And she's right, I'm jumpy, sweating, twitching at the slightest noise, the tiniest hints of something moving in the corner of my eye. There's still the headache: as if someone is trying to crack my skull open. And I cannot shake the accompanying sense that success will result in a dark river, a black tide flowing out of me. I blink, hard, eyes dry.

"I don't feel well," I say. "And . . . "

She puts a hand on my forehead—the cool flesh is a shock against my hot skin. "Go and lie down. You don't have any classes this afternoon."

"Thackeray," I say, the words becoming harder to force out, the hurt pressing in on my head. "Thackeray and Tilly, were . . . "

She tilts; the whole room tilts and I can't figure out why. I wonder that the books aren't falling from the shelves; then I realize I'm the one who's on an angle. I'm the one who's falling. I hit the floor, head bouncing against the polished parquetry.

There's a burble of noise around me; I see figures looming above, blurring. Beneath my head, I feel a beat. A thudding, ever so gentle, a mere echo of a vibration, a rhythm, a pulse, a song, but it will grow stronger, of that I have no doubt. It travels up me like a tremor, a whisper of motion. It moves me and shakes me and lulls me all at once. I close my eyes, for I have no choice, and everything is blocked out.

The last thing I hear is Fenella swearing at the crowd to stand back and let me have some air. I try to smile, but cannot feel my face.

VI

*February 17th*

> *Tell me, O thou whom my soul loveth, where thou waitest,*
> *where thou sleepest:*
> *for I shall not be as one turned aside*
> *by the rise and fall of aeons.*

Sound, unclear, as if heard through water. I swim up, slowly, ignoring the yearning pain in my bones. Voices. It's voices: male and female.

All I can feel beneath me now are the soft crisp linens of my bed; no more subtle rhythm, no more gentle beat. Clear-headed at last, but I keep my eyes closed, for they still retain an echo of the ache. And I listen.

"How is she?" Thackeray, subdued.

"The same as she always is at this point." Fenella, cool. They've been arguing.

"No. It seems different—she's never struggled like this."

Fenella is silent.

"What if she's—?"

"You're an idiot." Fenella, angry. "*She* saw you. You can't just fuck about for the better part of a year. You put us all in danger. We're not completely invisible here."

"We've been over this already. What does it matter? She'll be gone soon."

"We go to all the trouble of choosing, of making each one think they're special."

"So? I just made her feel a little bit extra special."

"Everyone else here is *careful*. Goes out of their way to keep us all secret and safe." Her voice drops. "I will tell her, when this one is gone and *she's* back."

"You worry too much, Burrows. Her time is short," he sneers.

"She won't need long."

That shuts him up, then there is a shuffling, his heavy steps moving away, the door opening and closing. I crack an eyelid and see Fenella, hands over her face, shoulders slumped. I know my vision is still wrong because she seems to have only three fingers. She sighs, throws back her shoulders, takes a deep breath. I focus.

She leans over me without really looking at me, touches my face. Five digits, of course; stupidity. I do not react, keep my breathing steady, slow. She steps away and leaves the room.

I wait, counting down seconds, counting down until I feel safe. I sit up, throw back the covers, swing my legs out of bed. Through the window I can see the sky, blue-black, dotted with stars, buttoned-down with a full moon; 11:30 says the bedside clock. I have slept long.

My legs tremble, I straighten. My hands spasm, the base of my skull feels . . . stretched. I shake my head, leave the room, uncaring that my pink flannel pyjamas are not the best attire for sneaking through corridors.

The dust and darkness are heavy in the Principal's office. The moonlight streams in and on the broad expanse of the desk I can see a piece of paper. My note. Untouched, unmoved, unread.

Once again, I pull at the drawers, knowing they'll still be locked. I take the letter opener from its place and jam it into the keyhole, then into the thin space between the bottom of one drawer and the top of another, jiggle it, jimmy it and to my surprise the bottom one grinds open with a protest. The fine dark wood splinters, exposing its pale naked inside. The drawer slides on reluctant runners.

In the bottom is a sewing-box, a padded embroidered thing, quite large, a silver toggle slid through the loop on the front to keep it closed. I unclasp it and flip it open. Inside, threads. So many threads, all twisted into figures of eight, their middles cinched in by the end of the very same thread. Tens, twenties, fifties, hundreds? So many: black, silver, red, yellow, richest chestnut. On the padded silk inside the lid, an array of needles, sentinels pinned through the fabric, all fine and golden, some thicker than others, fit for all manner of work, for varying thicknesses of material, canvas, skin, hide, what-have-you. I reach in, prick my index finger, watch the blood well and drip onto the pale blue silk, clotting bundles of thread.

I suck on the injured digit and notice, behind the casket, a creamy wad of pages. I draw them forth. Each one has a ragged edge as if torn from a journal. Each one is filled with scribbles, ancient cuneiforms of text, amateurish translations beside those obtuse scratchings:

*I am hidden, but lovely, O ye daughters of darkness. They kept him from me. I remember thy love more than life. Let him kiss me with his mouths. Thy name is as fear poured forth. Lead me, I will wait for thee.*

Each page dated; I can see a series of different years. How many? Oh, god, how many?

The grandfather clock interrupts me as I kneel there on the floor. It chimes the quarter-hour and I watch the hands move. The office door opens and Tilly's soft voice, rich with anticipation, a little fear, calls "Doctor Croftmarsh? It's time."

"Tilly. Tilly, you have to get away from here." I scramble up off my knees, try to move towards her at the same time, stumble twice before I stand and manage to get a hand on her arm. The touch is as much to steady me as to underline my point to her. "There's something going on. We have to go—we'll go out through the kitchens, no one will see us—"

"Doctor Croftmarsh, don't be ridiculous," she says, barely concealing disdain. I tighten my fingers around her wrist. She jerks her arm away.

"No, Tilly, I'm not being silly. Something is happening and you're in danger."

"No," she says, smiling, but I can't quite fathom the demeanor. "I'm not in danger—*He* has called my name and I will heed him. He will know me and choose me for I am *new*."

And all at once I know that inimitable combination of tone and expression: triumph and malice, jealousy and hope. The child thinks she is part of a greater mystery. She thinks Thackeray will—will what? Despair and desperation well up inside me as rhythmic pulses of pain.

We stare at each other, time seemingly marching in place until, at last, there is the sound of the final *flick* of the clock hands shifting into place. Mechanisms begin to sing *midnight* and all of my agonies fall away. I smile at the girl and offer my hand in conciliation.

VII

*February 18th*

> *If thou know not, O thou greatest among beasts,*
> *Send me dreams so I might guess,*
> *and kill the flock by the shepherds' tents.*

With my free hand I hook the edge of the tapestry and pull. The right half of it hangs from a rail separate to that for the left, so, when drawn across, the picture changes, the forest folded back upon itself becomes a creature, muscular, tentacled, winged; the broken stones become a second throne and the lord's limbs, now seen true, caress his bride in lewd love.

More importantly, this redecoration shows a door in the wall behind the arras, a door which leads down to the academy's rarely used chapel; to the undercroft more precisely. I wrench it open and a whiff of dust puffs out. Dust and something else, like long-dead fish.

"Come, Tilly," I say. There is no answer. I turn to look at her; she is staring at the hanging. I take her face in my hands, run my fingers through her hair, tender as a mother. I kiss her on the forehead, a chaste embrace, and say, "You were right: you have been called, Tilly, and you are needed. You are anointed, the *coming one*. And *He* will know your name and I shall see you covered in the throes of glory before this night is out."

In the darkness, I can see with the unerring gaze of a creature from the deep. In her gaze is my reflection, my features rewritten by my memories, my *true* memories: eyes set wide and angled up, icthyoid and protuberant, pouting lips, flattened nose. And the hair, a waving tangle of green-black tentacles, a-shiver with a life of their own. I stretch, my bones cracking. I am taller.

The girl's expression is stunned. "Doctor Croftmarsh?"

I nod and smile, my teeth sharp and liberally spaced. The girl shudders. Some panic at this moment, the imminence of death shaking them from the enchantment of being chosen; some go quietly. Tilly, I suspect, is beginning to realize that she did not take note of the fine print in the deal that was struck. I lock a webbed hand around her wrist and pull her towards her destiny.

My head is full of things long forgotten, long set aside so that I—we— might hide and survive. Today, this anniversary of the Fall of Innsmouth, of my Lord's terrible injuries and afflictions, of his ever-dying, this day the memories are whole. They do not *afflict* me. They are *mine* and they rest easy in the pan of my skull.

"Never fear, Tilly." The language feels strange in my mouth, the words seemingly square, not sibilant, not long and serpentine, but blocky. I persist, dragging the girl behind me, down into the darkness of the cold stone staircase and the crushing blackness of the undercroft and the tomb. The space is just large enough to fit the rest of the staff, teaching and domestic, all changed, all re-made like me; all clustered in a tenebrous group at the far end of the crypt. "Know that you are a part of something great."

Here she will breathe her last, her soul, her blood given so that my lord may heal. A process oh-so-slow, but only on this one day is the barrier between his death and my life thin enough for this service.

In my haste I am clumsy.

In her terror she is strong.

When she kicks at me, I loosen my grip and she pulls away, races in the shadows, back towards the stairs, towards freedom. All the trouble gone to, to cut her from the herd, to groom her, to make her feel special—and she runs. There is the sound of a slap, a grunt.

"Careless," says Thackeray. "You are not what you were." He holds the girl still, carries her as a child does a reluctant cat, her back against his chest, her limbs splayed, belly exposed. She no longer struggles. Thackeray offers her to me. I stare into her moon-wide eyes and whisper, "All will be well."

The talons of my right hand open up her chest, the nightgown then the skin. A silver mist bursts from the hole, followed by a gush of blood, and both are drawn down to the stone of the tomb, then immediately begin to seep through the porous surface.

I hear, as her life pours out, the great booming rhythm of my lord's heart, strengthened across aeons, across life and death and the space in-between. Such a slow healing.

From the gloom steps Fenella, a broad smile on her plain face. "We must talk, before you grow forgetful again," she says.

I don't answer, merely look at the shell of Tilly Sanderson sprawled across my husband's resting place where Thackeray discarded her. The rhythm of his renewal is loud and I think: *If one can do this, then surely a legion . . .*

"You will lose yourself once more," Fenella continues. "We must discuss matters for the coming year."

"Tomorrow's forgetting will be but a dream," I say, skittering my nails across the top of my lord's tomb, finding not a skerrick of blood left there.

I am so tired of waiting.

How many years between Innsmouth and now? How many times have I taken filaments from young heads and selected a fine needle so I may embroider a new flower into the weave of the tapestry, its border growing with each passing sacrifice? How many years have I sat beside a *rock* and told my lord, my liege, my love the same tale, of the patient queen who hides away, protecting her beloved from his enemies? The tale of a wife who loses herself for his very sake, who folds the cloak of Vivienne Croftmarsh around her recollections, her histories, and suppresses everything she is so hunters may not track him through the power of her memory. A woman who sings him his song, his hymn, his dirge, and waits and waits and waits.

A woman who is weary of waiting.

From beneath, from across, I hear him sigh.

"Bring them," I say to Burrows and Thackeray, who give me blank stares. My voice is thunder when next I speak, and they cringe with the power of my rage. "Bring them all!"

"But—" begins Thackeray and I grab the front of his shirt and lift him off his feet, reveling in the strength of my arm, myself; and knowing, at last, that I am unwilling to once again give up this self. I shake him for good measure.

"Bring them, by twos and threes. Bring them here and we shall see my lord awake before too many more cycles have passed. I am tired of waiting."

A new tomorrow is about to dawn on The Esoteric Order's Orphans Academy. And then, when my lord shall finally rise again, I shall take my proper place at *His* side . . .

*The material seemed to be predominantly gold, though a weird lighter lustrousness hinted at some strange alloy with an equally beautiful and scarcely identifiable metal . . . one could have spent hours in studying the striking and puzzlingly untraditional designs—some simply geometrical, and some plainly marine—chased or moulded in high relief on its surface with a craftsmanship of incredible skill and grace.*

"The Shadow Over Innsmouth" · H. P. Lovecraft (1936)

## • FISHWIFE •
### Carrie Vaughn

The men went out in boats to fish the cold waters of the bay because their fathers had, because men in this village always had. The women waited to gather in the catch, gut and clean and carry the fish to market because they always had, mothers and grandmothers and so on, back and back.

Every day for years she waited, she and the other wives, for their husbands to return from the iron-gray sea. When they did, dragging their worn wooden boats onto the beach, hauling out nets, she and the other wives tried not show their disappointment when the nets were empty. A few limp, dull fish might be tangled in the fibers. Hardly worth cleaning and trying to sell. None of them were surprised, ever. None of them could remember a time when piles of fish fell out of the nets in cascades of silver. She could imagine it: a horde of fish pouring onto the sand, scales glittering like precious metals. She could run her hands across them, as if they were coins, as if she were rich. Her hands were chapped, calloused from mending nets and washing threadbare clothing. Rougher than the scale that encrusted the hulls of the boats.

Her husband had been young once, as had she. Some days she woke up, and in the moment before she opened her eyes, she believed they were still young. His arms were still strong, and she would guide them around herself, until he was holding her tightly against him. A fire burned in her gut, and she felt as she had the night after their wedding, both sated and still hungry, arrogantly proud that he belonged to her forever. She always knew which boat was his, of the dozen silhouetted against the horizon on the far end of the bay.

Then she opened her eyes, saw the creases of worry in his face, the streaks of gray in her own once-dark hair, and remembered that years had passed, and nothing had gotten better. She clung to the pride she once felt. She remembered what it had been like, and on those days she wanted so badly to seduce him. But he was too tired to be seduced, and she was too tired to keep trying. The best she could do was take a small geranium from her flowerbox to stick in his buttonhole or behind his ear. Sometimes when she did, he smiled.

Every day, the fishermen returned empty-handed, and they bowed their heads, ashamed, as if they really had thought today, this day of all days, their fortunes might change. Once a week they went to the village's small church, where the ancient priest assured them, in the same words he'd used every week for decades, that their faith would be rewarded. Someday.

Basket in hand, she would pick a path through the sand to his boat. He would greet her silently, frowning. The shame, apology, in his eyes had faded over time. Now, there was only defeat, and habit. He goes out in the boat because he always has, because he has nothing else to do, because she is always standing on the beach with her basket, waiting for him and a catch that never quite materializes.

She was always too tired to touch his face, to offer a smile of comfort. Dutifully, silently, she gathered up the day's catch from where it flopped on the wet sand. A few dull creatures, sickly whitefish no bigger than her hand. Not enough to cover the bottom of her basket, but she would scale them, gut them, clean them, and take them to the square to sell.

Their village did not have a market of its own. Instead, a buyer in a rickety truck, its sides built up with wooden slats, came to buy what they offered. The only reason the man came at all was because he could pay less here than anywhere else. They should ask for more money, she always told herself, they deserved more money. But when she stepped forward, shoulders set and chin raised to stand up for herself, the other women held her back. They couldn't afford to drive him away. Sometimes, though, she recalled the pride she once felt and made her demand.

He simply turned his back, threatening to get in the truck and drive away. She had to beg him to stay, and when he offered less than he ever had before, she had to accept. He fed on their desperation with a smug smile. They did not have a choice; no one else would ever come to make an offer.

Now, she was the one to feel shame peeling back her face. She'd take the few coins in exchange for the scant catch, and think of the impossibility of even wishing for something better. She kept on, for no other reason than her husband made the effort to take out the boat at dawn. Going through the motions was the least she could do. So the circle played out, and would play out for all the days to come. To do anything else would upend the order of the universe. At least they didn't have children, as if the village's population had thinned as thoroughly as the bay's.

The last thing she did each day, after their dinner of soup and hard bread, as the sun went down, was water the box of flowers in the single window of their one room clapboard home. The red geraniums usually flowered and granted some color to her tired, washed-out world. They even smelled a little, a faint perfume cutting through the stink of fish. As long as she had fresh water for the flowers, as long as the flowers sparked green and red against the salt-scoured drabness of her house, she could continue to wake each morning and imagine that she was young, imagine that today was the day her husband would return to shore with a boatful of fish, and their fortune.

One day she woke up, opened her eyes, got herself and her husband out of bed. Fed him and sent him off to the boats, but he returned a short hour later, and asked her to come with him to the beach. They'd found something.

On the sand, the fishermen and their wives gathered, standing in a semicircle around a figure: a man, shoeless, in torn and weathered clothing, lying face up at the tideline, unconscious. The waves lapped at his feet, and there were grooves in the sand that hinted that he must have clawed up from the surf. A castaway perhaps, but no other debris littered the beach, no broken spars or ripped sails, no other bodies or survivors. No storm raged last night, to account for a body washed up on their shore.

Disbelief at the oddness, the disruption in the eternal routine, kept anyone from moving closer. So she was the one who went to the man, brushed his tangled black hair from his pale face and touched his neck, feeling for his pulse. When he opened his eyes, she flinched. Not a drowned body, but a man, alive. His eyes were the gray of slate.

He smiled at her.

Seeming hale and strong now, he sat up and smiled at them all, not at all like a man who'd been found on the beach, baking under the morning sun after freezing in the night air. She stared at her hand; he'd been cold, where she touched him.

When he spoke, his voice wasn't at all parched like it should have been, washed up from the sea as he was. Instead, it was clear, deep, beautiful, and he made them an offer. He promised them bounty, all the treasure they'd wished for for so many years, all that they'd prayed for and never received. To prove he could make good on his vast assertions, he asked to borrow one of the fishermen's nets. Her husband gave him his. Taking the net, the stranger waded into the water, until the waves met his knees, and he cast. The net settled, sank, and, skillfully, as if he'd fished all his life, as if he'd come from a place where men had fished for hundreds of years, perhaps even a small poor village like this one, he held on to the net, dragged it, gathered it in, hauled it to shore. He leaned against the weight of it, because the net was full.

A hundred fish thrashed against the net's fibers. But more than fish, there was gold: he reached in among the flopping bodies and drew out a cup, a plate, and a circlet—a band of twisted gold that might fit around a woman's arm. The bend of it spiraled one way and another, resembling the infinite curl of a seashell. The shape drew the gaze, which fell into it, spiraling down until you believed you might fall in truth, and then you looked up into the sky, and realized the sky too went on forever. She stopped thinking at all, lest she become ill.

The castaway reached out, offering her the band of gold. She took it; it was cold, burned her hand with its chill, but she held it tightly, drawn close to her breast. This was all the riches she had ever dreamed of.

The god of the village's old priest had never given such glittering proof of his good faith.

The price they had to pay was blood. It didn't even have to be their own. Just blood, shed in sacrifice, which, when she thought of it, made a certain kind of sense, as much sense as the wealth the castaway drew forth with his net—a concrete wealth that she could feel and taste, not a wish and hope for something that might never come. What else did they have to trade but blood? Never mind all the blood she and her husband had already shed, stabs from fishhooks, burns from rough nets, bruises, broken bones, blisters, a slip of a knife, chapped hands from so much washing, washing, washing, until the water she rinsed in ran red.

Accidental blood didn't count. The bargain needed fresh blood, clean and intentional.

She knew exactly where to find the blood they needed.

While the others glanced between them, uncertain, she rounded her shoulders and caught her husband's gaze. Convinced him she knew what to do, took his hand, and marched to the village square.

Everyone followed her, except for the old priest in his faded gray robes. The cloth might have been white once, before she was born. The old man was afraid and begged her, all of them, to stop. He could barely look at the castaway and made the sign against evil at him. For his part, the castaway laughed, and that was all it took to drive the priest into his church. She saw the priest one more time trying to light a candle in the window, but his matches were damp, and the wick was moldy. He stood there, striking over and over, his motions sharp and desperate, his face pursed in concentration. She looked away, didn't look again. He'd never helped them, in all her years of praying for fish, for health, for salvation. How wonderful now, to be doing something more than praying.

At the same time she always did, she went to the square, her basket in hand, waiting for the man in the rickety truck. She looked like she did any other morning, waiting for what their buyer thought of as charity, what the wives knew was shame. The air seemed very quiet, not even the gulls crying over the water.

The buyer arrived in a puff of stinking exhaust, climbed from the rusted cab of his truck like he always did, his smile broad as if he had just finished laughing at a joke. Faced her, arms spread, as if to say good morning and what fine weather. She didn't give him time to look surprised as she dropped her basket and slashed his throat with the hooked gutting knife she'd kept hidden at her side.

It was a cut she'd made a thousand times, designed to part flesh instantly and spill the guts cleanly. His throat opened, shining red like the inside of a fish's gills. His eyes bulged, round and unblinking. The man fell soundlessly, and his blood spilled. A much darker red than her geraniums.

How nice, to see some color in their faded world.

She showed them all how easy it was to make a strike for a better future.

The next day, every boat was filled with fish and gold.

The new god provided. She spent hours studying the gold band around her arm, tracing her fingers along its arcs and spirals, sighing at its color, an inspiring glow, what she imagined the sun must look like in a fairy-tale kingdom, so perfect and warm. Along a certain curve, she could imagine that the metal caressed her back.

The second sacrifice was even easier.

The village had one inn, a decayed plankboard house, two stories, with a cupola that looked over the bay. It might have been elegant, once, and was still the most stately building in the village, with its overgrown yard and peeling façade. In summer months, a handful of tourists might decide the village was quaint and choose to spend a night here. They never stayed more than one.

But this was winter, and no one had passed through for months—until today, which must have been a sign. She spied on the man, a sickly young thing with an ill-fitting suit and scuffed hand-me-down briefcase. The innkeeper said he was a scholar studying the region's history, and had asked many outlandish questions about economic depression and whether it might be brought on by curses. Depended on how you defined curses, she thought.

Approaching midnight, a whole crowd of them went to the inn to do the deed. Again, she held the weapon and made the cut. The rest stayed behind to ensure the sacrifice could not flee.

He didn't escape. He hardly made a sound when she struck. She stood over his bed as he gaped, and he didn't even seem surprised as he bled out.

Her husband brings her trinkets of gold that he draws up in his nets, along with fish, though she cares less and less about the fish. Now, when she pulls herself to him and guides his hands to her hips, he digs in his fingers greedily, clutching her to him so that her breasts are flattened by his chest. His eyes are bright enough to match the flashing of jewels in sunlight as he kisses her, and she is warm as fire, no matter how clammy the winter air outside grows.

The flowers have died. Their scent has long ago faded, and for a time, she continues to water the dried out, blackened stems, the broken petals lying shattered on the cracked soil of the planter box. It's out of habit rather than hope. One day she forgets, distracted by the twisted gold band around her wrist. Its light draws her like a sun, if she could remember what the sun looks like. She follows the pattern of its spirals, the depth of its whorls, and she can almost hear the chanting of the beings who made it. They must be beautiful.

The fisher folk gather in the square in front of the old priest's church. The old priest hasn't been seen in some time. She hardly wonders what has happened to him, and can't remember what he looked like or what he preached. She forgets the old life, because what of it is worth remembering? Though she notices the splash of red across the church door. It reminds her of her geraniums, and she always liked flowers.

These days, her husband comes home smiling and rushes at her, arms outstretched to grab her up, to feel every inch of her, carry her to their cot and pin her there. She burns, answering him. It's no longer work to seduce each other, and they rut like eels, writhing around one another. After wearing each other out, they fall asleep smiling, wake smiling, and they kiss deeply, wetly, before she sends him off to the boats. The ocean has become a joy instead of the torment it was. She can smell nothing now but salt and slime.

She bathes sometimes in the old tub that has stood behind their shack for years, gathering debris. She cleaned it out, scrubbed it, filled it with water from the sea, and now soaks in it for hours. Her graying hair coils and snakes around her like the limbs of some leviathan. When she pulls at the strands, they come out, and she stares, studying them. Wraps them around her fingers and wrists, twining them with the twisted gold she wears. She'll fall asleep like this, floating, suspended, dreaming of deep places and distant voices; then wake submerged, staring up through the distorted lens at a wavering world, gray and dimly lit, and hardly notice that she has not drowned.

Once, she looks up through the warped glass of the water and sees the castaway above her, looking back, seeming to study her, taking in every inch of her naked body, curled up in the tub. She recalls that she should be embarrassed at the very least, mortified and blushing. She should hide herself. Ought to be angry and cry out for her husband. But she doesn't. Though her skin is cool, her mouth clammy, her gratitude for him burns, and she would take his hand and draw him down with her, to show him how deep her faith runs. But he touches her face, strokes back what's left of her hair, smiles like a father showing affection for a favorite daughter.

And she thinks, he does love me, he loves us all.

They perform the rituals, make the sacrifices. They watch the little-used roads for signs of travelers, whom the innkeeper invites into his decrepit building with a hungry gaze and grasping hands. So eager, most guests are suspicious. Some listen to their instincts and leave, in which case they'll be taken on the road leading out of the village. Some stay, though soon the keeper won't have a room to offer that isn't stained with blood.

Her husband loses his thick brown hair, leaving a scalp like a whale's hide. She still loves to rub her scaled hands over it, stroking him to a frenzy as he lays his now-toothless mouth against her neck for sucking kisses. His boneless arms fit so tightly around her, and her legs cling to him with a sinuous determination, like an octopus gripping its rocky mount. They lie in the salty bathtub together, and it feels like home.

Their new priest preaches of a time when they will go to the sea. This is their reward, eternal life in the holy depths. No longer slaves to the sea, but masters of it. So he says. They gather, chanting, and the rituals make her feel like that first glimpse of gold did: overwhelmed, soaring over an abyss, the infinite spirals, so much greater and terrific than anything she had ever seen before. She has kept that gold band around her wrist, where it remains locked, her peeling gray flesh swelling in folds around it.

There comes a time when they are gathered, chanting and writhing, performing their sacred rites of blood, when she isn't sure anymore which of the gray-skinned, eel-headed men is her husband. If she calls out his name, none of them will answer, but she doesn't call, because she doesn't remember. They seem like such small things, names and husbands. Now, she only dreams of the time which must come soon—always, must come soon—when they will go to their reward, to dwell in the eternal kingdom in the darkest places under the ocean.

She remembers one thing. Tiny, so small and inconsequential she has forgotten to forget. A day, a moment in a day, in her young and newly married life, before the future stretched unbreaking. She found a wooden box which she filled with dirt and mulch. She planted flowers, watered them, kept them alive for years, until she didn't. Reds and greens and yellows, a memory of color that stings her mind like the cut of a knife. She flinches at the sting, hardly knows why. Instead, she turns again to the sound of chanting, which by now has become the sound of resolve.

When she slips under the waves and lives forever more in a world of gray, she wonders if her resolve will break. Because even then, she'll remember the warmth of the sun on her face, and the scent of the flowers.

*Especially was it unwise to rave of the living things that might haunt such a place, of creatures half of the jungle and half of the impiously aged city . . .*
*"The Facts Concerning the Late Arthur Jermyn and His Family"*
*· H. P. Lovecraft (1929)*

## · IN THE HOUSE OF THE HUMMINGBIRDS ·
### Silvia Moreno-Garcia

Is the recorder on? Yes, I see the blinking light. Sorry, I've never been interviewed before. Oh . . . oh yes.

War is a flower. It's a line in a book that belonged to Don Fermin.

If you think about it, it makes sense. After all, Huitzilopochtli, the Aztec god of War and patron of the city of Tenochtitlan, was the Hummingbird of the Left. The souls of dead warriors return to our world in the shape of hummingbirds. Why shouldn't war be a flower?

No sir, I have never seen a ghost. I've worked the night shift in downtown Mexico City for most of my life, spent time in centuries-old houses, convents and shops, and I never bumped into a spook. Nevertheless, the House of the Hummingbirds was haunted.

No, sir. There is a difference between a haunting and a ghost. The well in the house was haunted.

The house? It was at the end of the Alley of General Manuel Mier y Terán. Every street in the downtown core once had a different, far more interesting name. Sometimes you can see the faded plaques on the corners of some streets revealing their lost histories, like smudged fingerprints. The Street of the Burned Woman is the 5a. Calle de Jesús María and the Alley of the Dead Man is now a section of Calle República Dominicana, probably because government officials think is best to name streets and buildings and bridges after notable figures instead of referring to half-forgotten suicides, criminals, and lunatics.

The house at Mier y Terán was known as the House of the Hummingbirds after the tin-glazed, ceramic tiles decorating a thin strip on the uppermost part of its façade. Thanks to these tiles the whole street had once been known as the Street of the Hummingbirds.

Spooky? No. It was a typical colonial house, just like many in downtown Mexico City, with the only difference that it was in good shape compared to some of the other old buildings in the area. Because, I must say, this was in the seventies, when the whole downtown core was falling to pieces and palaces were turned into slums and garbage-strewn monstrosities. Street vendors would be bullied out in the nineties, but at that point they owned the streets and you had to club your way home through certain areas because the merchants of *chaquiras* and cigarettes blocked doors and windows when they sold their wares. Pickpockets stole with abandon. The streets were uneven, cracked, with outdated drainage systems. Windows which had been bricked during the reign of Santa Anna—to avoid paying certain taxes—were still blind more than a century later. It was a sad sight.

But the House of the Hummingbirds remained in its spot looking whole, dirty tiles and all, even though the viceroys and the viscounts had long departed from its street. Like all large colonial houses it had a tall, great wooden double-door which opened into a large interior patio chock full with massive potted ferns. When I worked in the house the building had been converted into the headquarters of a political magazine. After crossing the patio one reached the house proper, its rooms now turned into offices. There was a central hallway which led all the way to the back of the house and to a smaller patio—this one without ferns—and what had once been the stables, now serving as a space for the photography department.

It was here that you would find the well.

Mexico City was built on a lake and a well is not such an unusual sight. One time, when I was working as a guard at a construction site, the crew digging new foundations was shocked to discover water bubbling to the surface. They thought they had struck a pipe. It turned out there was a spring beneath the building site, long forgotten, and they had to bring in special machinery to drain the soil dry.

When you think about it, it was all this digging of wells and the extraction of water which has caused the city to sink. I once read in the papers that the Metropolitan Cathedral has sunk twelve meters since it was built three centuries ago. We are, literally, slowly descending into the muck from which the city was born.

So yes, a well, and so what? Nothing, really. It was made of stone and someone had taken the trouble of carving it with lots of birds and wings and feathers. Whoever had done the job was a poor artist because the birds looked very ugly and some didn't look very much like birds at all. Maybe people who know about paintings and such might disagree, but I only made it to the first year of high school and I'll say it looked like an ugly mess. The well was covered with a heavy stone slab and this also had more hummingbirds—or whatever type of bird it was supposed to be—carved on its surface.

Don Fermin, more educated in these matters than I was, told me the Aztecs did not have an alphabet and used pictograms to tell their stories. The well, I thought, might be narrating a story without words.

I didn't like the well. When I was doing my rounds I used to walk by it very fast, crossing the courtyard with a determined strut. When you work nights as a security guard the dark ain't scaring you. But there was something about the shape of the well as I emerged from the hallway and onto the courtyard; something that made me press my lips together and hold my flashlight very tight.

I'd walk by and I'd remember that I had no gun, not even a club; only my keys and my flashlight. It seemed damn close to being naked.

I also had some funny thoughts when I went by the well. Like once I thought it seemed so dark . . . like ink. I thought somebody had painted it with a marker; that it wasn't really there. It was a black doodle on a piece of acetate. Then another time I got thinking about my history class and a morning when I was half-asleep, my head resting on top of the books, and the teacher started talking about the Mayan cenotes, the sacred waterholes where they used to fling young men as sacrifices to the gods.

I also had the idea that the air near the well was colder than the air around other parts of the house and Doña Adela, the owner of the guest house where I lodged, told me this was a sure sign of ghosts.

I didn't like the well but in the end it was a minor annoyance. The job paid steady and paid well, and it was far less work than patrolling the department store where I was also employed part-time. Plus, Don Fermin had never seen no ghost in the house.

Don Fermin was a half-deaf man who worked through the weekdays while I took the weekend shift. Pushing seventy, he was the son of an *escribano*—a letter writer—and quite educated in all sorts of books and histories, the kind of stuff I never got to reading because I had to leave school and start working. It was he who told me Santa Anna levied a tax on doors and windows, and that people bricked most of these to evade it. He also said the house had once belonged to a guy named Fray Bartolomeo de Rivera, who'd ended up before the Spanish Inquisition for some thing or another.

I liked talking to Don Fermin and on my night off I'd often go to see him, catching him lolling in front of the little black-and-white TV set we kept in the night guard's office. I'd bring him sweet bread from the bakery three blocks away and he'd talk about the city in the times when men carried swords at the hip and ladies rode in carriages.

Ah, Don Fermin. When he retired they gave me the weekday shift with five days of full-time work and I had to find and train my replacement for the weekends.

That's when the trouble began.

If it had been up to me, I wouldn't have hired Salvador Machado. He was a student at the UNAM, working on his bachelor's degree and looking for extra cash. I think his aunt in accounting got him the job, probably guessing it was easy work and he'd have plenty of time to read.

I don't think he cared one bit about the job, about the house; his swagger and his indifference struck a sour note with me. Everything I showed him: the paperwork, the nightly tasks we had to complete, was met with indifference or a condescending smile.

I suppose most people think my job is easy, though them people wouldn't last two weeks in my shoes. The mere shift in schedules, having to sleep with the day and get up at dusk, is enough to upset most folks. Then there's walking in the dark, making the rounds in the hot summer nights or the chilly winter. The shit that happens at nights: homeless men sneaking into a construction site and having to chase 'em off, people trying to dump garbage onto your lot, a prostitute deciding she's found a perfect site to service her clients. One time when I was working in a building that had an old neon sign hanging outside, a group of kids tried to steal it. I swear to God. These six or seven punks with their screwdrivers and hammers trying to run off with a six-foot sign. Night duty takes a certain personality type and Salvador didn't have it.

The first night, when I was showing him the layout of the building and taking him through the house, he smoked a cigarette and walked with one hand in his pocket, an eyebrow quirked like he owned the joint.

"Now we go to check the photographer's studio," I said, leading him across the small courtyard.

He stopped all of a sudden. "What's that?" he asked.

"What's what?"

"That," he said.

"The well," I said.

There was enough moonlight to half-sketch its shape so that it didn't look like ink on acetate, but it also didn't look too pleasant to me in the silence of the courtyard.

Crickets never nestled in this courtyard and maybe that's part of why I didn't like the well: it seemed to hush everything in its vicinity.

"Can I take a better look at it?"

I didn't want to arch the flashlight in the well's direction, feeling that wouldn't be right. I shook my head. "We're doing the rounds."

He took out his lighter and stepped forward, a little flame blooming and offering a dim halo of light.

"Look, have the flashlight," I said because it seemed even worse to be looking at it by the light of a flame.

He took the flashlight and stepped closer to the well, leaning down to run his hands over the carved birds, something which I had never done or had a desire to ever do. I shivered and tugged at the cuffs of my shirt.

"Hey kid—"

"I didn't know there was a well in this house. It's not mentioned in any chronicles."

"In a what?"

"I'm doing my thesis on Mexican legends of the downtown core of the city. I think I would have heard if there was such a well."

"There's lots of old stuff 'round these streets," I said.

"I know that," the young man said petulantly. "I've picked half a dozen different sites for my studies. This house is one of them and I had never read of this. Do you know how old it is?"

"No. We have to do the rounds."

"Yes, the rounds," Salvador said sounding irritated.

It didn't look like he wanted to move but then he simply shrugged. He handed me back my flashlight and we continued walking.

The second night of our training Salvador brought a camera with a big flash bulb and some very heavy books. He wanted to take pictures of the well. I thought it was a terrible idea and told him so.

"It ain't your house for you to be taking pictures of it," I said.

"What, like I need permission to take a few crummy snapshots?" he asked sounding offended.

"I don't want to get in trouble."

"They're not going to fire you because I took photographs of the house."

I wasn't thinking about getting fired. I shook my head and grabbed my clipboard, glancing at it and then up at the grainy image on the television set. Tin Tan was playing a caveman, complete with a loincloth and a big club.

"Look, the Aztecs called Huitzilopochtli the left-handed hummingbird and they thought warriors who died in battle reincarnated as hummingbirds. The carvings on that well seem Prehispanic to me. They might have been taken from an older site."

"I don't understand," I said, though I remembered Don Fermin had told me the Spaniards had used the stones from Aztec temples to build their houses and churches. Was Salvador talking about something like that?

"Of course not," Salvador said with a huff. "Listen, I'm going to take photos of the well."

"You do that and you'll end up with a bloody nose," I said.

One time Don Fermin told me about filth-death. It was the concept of sin among the Aztecs, sin which would not only affect the person who committed the sin, but which could rub onto others. Like a disease.

I've always gone by the numbers. I do right. Follow the rules. I suppose part of it is because I believe some of this filth-death thing. That if we are not careful, we stain our souls and the souls of others.

I always thought we ought to respect the well. Otherwise we risked staining our hands.

Of course, Salvador did not understand. But he shook his head and raised his hands in a pacifying gesture.

"Fine," he said.

"Let's do them rounds," I said.

Salvador seemed rather irritated but I didn't care much what he thought. When we walked by the well he flicked his cigarette away, like a child trying to get back at me. I looked at it as it burned like a single yellow eye upon the ground and frowned.

"Pick it up," I ordered him. "We're not paid to litter."

"Oh, bullcrap," he said.

He picked it up all the same.

Salvador Machado smoked like a train and did as he pleased. That I learned quickly. During the first two weeks on the job I stopped by to check on him and found him with his feet on the table, his papers all spread out, puffing happily away. The radio was at full volume. The music made the walls shiver.

"Hey," I said, "what's the idea?"

He turned around and didn't even attempt to look worried, simply lowering the volume and frowning at me.

"Just some entertainment, that's all."

"You can watch the TV on mute," I said. "That's the rules."

"The rules," he muttered tossing his cigarettes into the dregs of his coffee cup. "The TV doesn't work."

"Of course it does," I said.

He went towards the set and turned it on, flipping the dial. There was a lot of snow. He moved the rabbit ears trying to get a signal and quickly gave up, returning to his seat.

"It doesn't work."

I approached the television set and tried my hand at the rabbit ears. A black and white picture emerged. Pedro Infante on a motorcycle.

"There," I said.

Salvador did not seem convinced. I looked down at his papers and saw that he'd made some drawings of the well. There were other things as well.

"What's this?" I asked, lifting a piece of paper.

"A rubbing. It's normally used for gravestones. You rub charcoal across a clean sheet of paper and it leaves an impression."

His choice of words disturbed me. I thought of the rubbing as a piece skin or a nail that has been stripped from a corpse. I dropped the paper.

"I didn't say—"

"You said I couldn't take *photographs*," he replied.

"That I did," I said.

Nothing much happened after that. Salvador was working the weekends while I worked the weekdays. It was December and the nights got chillier so I started wearing my blue sweater. On Saturday evenings I went to visit Don Fermin's and we drank coffee while he told me about Tenochtitlan, its ancient web of canals, the arteries of the city on which floated thousands of barges; canals which had been paved by the Spaniards.

Don Fermin took out the dominoes, his wrinkled hands slowly shuffling the tiles round and round. Sometimes I thought about the well while we played. The black spots on the white tiles seemed like little holes in the night sky, yawning and oozing darkness.

I thought about asking him about the well. I thought he might know more about it, like its age or who'd carved it. Our conversations about the well had always been . . . well, I don't want to say we *avoided* talking about it, but we circled around the topic. He might show me his history books or mention something about the Aztecs, but we did not directly speak about it.

I never did ask Don Fermin anything about the well. I don't think I really wanted to know.

One Saturday, shortly after I had stepped into my room, the phone rang. I thought maybe it was Don Fermin. Maybe I had forgotten something at his apartment. Instead, it was Salvador.

"Hi," I said. "How you doing? Are you having trouble with the antenna again?"

"It's got nothing to do with the damn television," he said, his voice clipped. "Listen, I need you to take the rest of my shift for the night."

"You feeling sick?"

"Yeah. Maybe. There's something. . . How fast can you come?"

"An hour or so."

"Hurry up."

He hung up. I decided to let the brat sweat it and spent a good amount of time parting my hair and shining my shoes. I packed my lunch and filled my thermos with coffee and off I went to catch the bus.

Salvador wasn't in the office when I arrived, though his books and papers were spread over the table. I figured he was doing the rounds and sat down to wait for him, switching on the TV set. I waited for thirty minutes for him to come back before I decided to look for him.

I started thinking maybe the guy had gone out to drink before coming to work and had passed out in a hallway. The poor bastard might have stumbled down the stairs and hurt himself. Unfortunately, there was only one flashlight and Salvador had taken it with him.

I made quick work of the lower floor and then went upstairs, poking my head into the empty offices, calling for him.

Eventually it became obvious I'd have to look in the stables.

I'd have to cross the small courtyard.

I decided to be quick and direct about this. However, once I stepped into the courtyard I felt my courage fading. There was no moon that night. No stars. The sky was smooth as velvet black.

I felt a great desire to return to my room and spend the rest of the night watching old movies on the television set.

But I knew the way. I must walk the path. I edged close to the wall, fixing my eyes on the old stables, avoiding the sight of the well.

I was halfway there when I heard it.

It was a whisper. It trailed up my back and reached my ears, the voice buzzing like an insect. Then there was a soft scratching and the shuffle of a foot upon stone.

The buzzing increased and I thought maybe it wasn't an insect. Maybe it was the flapping of wings.

There came another footstep upon the floor. The sound echoed and bounced around me. I lowered my head and pressed my hands against the wall.

I thought about a poem Don Fermin had read to me one time.

*All the earth is a grave and nothing escapes it, nothing is so perfect that it does not descend to its tomb.*

I whispered that line half a dozen times, with my hands glued to the wall.

A loud boom caused me to turn. I saw the flashlight rolling towards me across the floor. Instinct made me scoop it up and I held it, aiming the beam in the direction of the well.

Salvador was on the floor next to it, staring at the sky.

I rushed towards him and stared at his face, which was streaked with blood. His eyes seemed glassy and unfocused. He was breathing very slowly, his chest hardly rising. I stepped back and bumped my foot against something. I looked down: it was the well's stone cover.

The courtyard grew quiet.

There was a great deal of fuss about Salvador Machado after that. His family hired a lawyer and started arguing it was the magazine's fault that this had happened. The accident only took place because the premises were so poorly maintained. They claimed that Salvador had tripped or fallen, hitting his head. The magazine talked about a nervous breakdown brought on by an excessive consumption of drugs and alcohol, typical of the circle in which Salvador moved. Others said Salvador Machado had been trying to commit suicide by jumping into the well. An eager cop even looked at me with suspicion, perhaps thinking I had attempted to murder the student, but they dropped that theory pretty quick. I mean, Salvador hadn't really been physically hurt. He'd just gone a bit loopy.

The well's stone cover caused a smaller amount of concern, though it also came with its own set of problems. The thing was very heavy and it took three men to lift it back in its place, but that was only after two other men simply quit and refused to do the job.

Several years ago I took my son to the Museum of Anthropology to do some research for a paper. We walked by the exhibits, he took notes and every now and then I leaned down to read the little white placards explaining what I was looking at.

There was one typed card that said Aztec instruments for ritual bloodletting were often in the shape of hummingbirds, their needle-sharp beaks piercing the skin.

When we left the museum I stood under the shadow of the tall statue of the rain-god Tlaloc. Don Fermin once told me about the night in 1964 when they dragged the statue to its current place outside the museum. It rode on a gigantic wheeled platform, in a steel harness, from its home by the town of Coatlinchan where it had been carved. It rained that night, as though a storm followed the statue.

We are shocked when we think about the Aztecs sacrificing captives at the foot of their temples, consecrating their buildings with blood. But I've known of more than one man injured, maimed or killed at the construction sites where I've worked.

The foundations of buildings are drawn with blood.

Once you accept that, you know certain places must be haunted. Our City of Palaces, by its nature, must have more than its share of hauntings.

As I said at the beginning, I can't speak of ghosts but there was something in the House of Hummingbirds. What exactly, I cannot say. I think Don Fermin knew but never told. I think I've been close to understanding it but I will never speak it out loud.

Oh, you need something more concrete than that? Well, I'll tell you this: Look around carefully when you walk these old city streets at night. Whatever was in the House of the Hummingbirds, I've felt similar things brush by in *other* places.

You can turn your recorder off now.

*. . . a blasphemous abnormality from hell's nethermost craters; a nameless, shapeless abomination which no mind could fully grasp and no pen even partly describe.*

"The Lurking Fear" · H. P. Lovecraft (1923)

## • WHO LOOKS BACK? •
### Kyla Ward

Who looks back on the Waimangu track?

Not Kelsie Munroe, running light over gravel, the slope gentle but the surface potentially foul. The track's made for walking, not running or driving. There is a road proper for that, for ferrying tired tourists back from Lake Rotomahana. You're meant to walk one way down the length of the valley, taking in all its steams and smokes, and weirdly colored sinter. But Kelsie never walks where she can run and Lewis jumps.

Lewis Zabri keeps her pace for now: brown skin abreast of freckles, black stubble beside red hair. They dress much the same; singlets, shorts and runners, packs strapped into the small of the back. Kelsie is taller and can beat him over short sprints but this is four kilometers of up and down, winding and in places rough. Lewis keeps himself loose and breathing easy. He knows she's planning something.

The valley of Waimangu, New Zealand, is the youngest landscape on earth. Nothing here, not the trees, not the streams, nor the cliffs themselves, existed before the eruption of 1886. The ground split, swallowing everything, then spewing it out again as boiling mud. Forest and farmstead, whole villages died. For kilometers around, there was not a single living thing. On the walls of the Visitors Center, blurry black and white photos show weirdly peaked hills and plains of ash. It's gone green now: first the extremophile algae, then lichen and ferns, then melaleuca spilling down the slopes in a long, slow race, the reclamation marathon. The algae was first to reach the bank of Frying Pan Spring. But Kelsie, or maybe Lewis, will catch up soon.

You're not meant to run and definitely not to leave the track, risking a scalding, broken limbs or damaging the unique terrain. But Lewis and Kelsie leap, climb, and throw themselves off things as a matter of course and the terms of this race have been agreed: first to the lake via the Mount Haszard lookout. Ahead of them, and still a serious drop below, is where the track and creek first cross. The climb to the lookout begins there, but Lewis sees no reason to wait. Running straight at the guardrail, he extends hands and flips himself over the cliff in a perfect *saut de chat*. He doesn't so much as glance over his shoulder.

Kelsie is not impressed. She trains in parkour herself but this isn't the terrain. Lewis can say what he likes about the zone and the flow, but terrain is king. She knows this and that's why she'll win. He's risking a spill for a gain she'll more than make up at the lookout, if the map approximates reality. Worse yet, this close to the Visitors Center he's risking the rangers seeing him.

Three meters below her now, Lewis adjusts automatically to the crunch and mealy slide beneath his feet. So long as he stays off the algae, he'll reach the start of the climb seconds ahead of Kelsie and that gain he'll keep. Ribbons of color unwind beside him, pink rock and water a startling green. Steam sifts across his field of vision and there is frantic noise around him, an all-encompassing bubble and hiss. One part of his mind feels the heat and moisture and yes, some fear; the other only registers angles, surfaces, opportunities. He is in the zone, feeling the flow. The goal of all his training is to clear his mind of the artificial clutter of modern life and here, now, he is almost free. That's why he'll win.

Kelsie burns on down the track. Despite his pretensions to this or that philosophy, Lewis never really thinks, or else thinks that everywhere is just like London, where no one gives a damn. But sometimes people do care. They care about traveling together. They care about sleeping together. By God, a whole lot of them care when someone tic-tacs on the shrine at Tanukitanisan Temple and what was the point of that? They had to leave Japan overnight and it didn't even make the blog. Then again, nor will the stunt she's banking on today, for which she's carrying an extra kilo. Twenty meters, ten: Lewis vanishes ahead of her into the steam. She can hear the creek: is that the creek? It sounds like voices. It's like from out of the ground, from the weeping black ferns and deliquescent rocks there rises a deep and liquid dissension. The warmth envelops her, damp upon her arms and face, sulphurous in her eyes and nose. For a moment she runs blind.

Lewis rejoins the track and not a moment too soon: Kelsie is coming up fast. Here, the valley narrows sharply and the banks seem to be rotting, a foul, yellowish slough choking the creek bed. He peers ahead for the turn-off and sees only the wildly swirling fog. Is he motion then, with nothing to mark his passage? Can there be motion in a void? Yes, there can: so long as Kelsie comes behind. Grinning just a little, he eases, anticipating her sight of his back. She takes all their games so seriously, even in bed. Then something shifts beneath his feet. The gravel is suddenly live as well as warm. The fog billows and the noise of the creek rises sharply around him: is that the creek roaring? He does not stop, cannot, as directly in front of him, something forms from the white.

Kelsie knows that sound isn't the creek. Its voices have not vanished, merely retreated behind the encroaching rumble of a truck on gravel: she has Australian ears, accustomed to country sounds. A bank of wind hits her face, clearing the steam and she sees Lewis running slow and beyond him a large, white utility bearing the park logo. Coming straight at him, at her. Behind the cab she glimpses ridiculous things, white and shapeless with reflective face plates and Lewis is—oh no, he's not! Not slowing or swerving, Lewis guns straight into the path of the moving vehicle and vaults. Hands and foot on the bonnet, next step against the windscreen. Even though the truck is jerking, skewing to a stop, he executes the move with perverse bloody brilliance. Straight over the top he goes and through the white shapes, revealed by their reaction as men in thermal suits. In the instant of their shock, before they even imagine her presence, she shifts balance and angle, and leaps out across the water.

Lewis sees angles, shapes, the moving flat of the truck bed. His pulse sings as he leaps to the ground and keeps running, unfaltering. Yes, yes; that was perfect! Did those guys even see him? By those shouts and grinding, clunking gears, oh yes they did. A grin splits his face as he rounds the bend and sights the turn-off.

Kelsie grinds uphill through ferns and bushes, wincing as she pushes on her right ankle. Her leap covered the distance as she saw it, but seeing isn't believing down here. Solid is slurry, ferns anchor foam. Her ankle stings and she's not sure if it's burn or graze. Either way, she's committed: their rules don't compensate for accident, pursuit, or even biohazard. It's win or lose and she is not losing today, there's too much at stake. So she climbs a bad climb. Exposed rock to fallen log: it's an obstreperous sign of her progress that the plants get bigger. The pink and yellow cools into gray; spindly trunks and spiking tussocks block her view of the stream, but she can still hear voices. And not shouting scientists and squealing rangers; the old voices, that the Maori tribesmen must have heard to mark this place as the realm of monsters. While Lewis was psyching himself up, she read the placards in the Visitors Center. Then suddenly, startlingly she is out of the bush with hard-pressed earth beneath her feet. Before her the path to the look-out swerves up a steep defile. But she is alone and whether Lewis is ahead or behind, she has no idea.

Lewis would say he was ahead: ahead of the utility and its shrouded occupants. What the Hell were they doing, dressed up like that? The cluttered part of his mind noticed machines in the back of the ute, the monitors and probes. It made sense they'd check the valley regularly, though he would have thought they'd use the access road for that. But here he turns up the hill and here the Klu Klux Rangers cannot follow him, if that's what they're shouting about. It's true they could reverse all the way back to where the climb rejoins the main track and wait for him there, but surely they're got somewhere to be! Another blast of air strikes him from down the valley. He hears a new note in the creek, a warbling, high-pitched sound.

Kelsie plows up the path but she's spent her best. If by some miracle Lewis is behind her now, she'll abandon her plan and take the track down to the lake. But how to tell? The vegetation here is thick. Strange flowers rise aside of the path: purple trumpets on stems like giant foxgloves. Huge tree ferns, the biggest she has ever seen lip over her head and reach for her feet with long, black tendrils. Branches bristle with inch-long thorns. Still, a faint whispering rises from the earth, punctuated by the rasp of her feet and controlled breath. Then suddenly by screams.

Lewis looks up to see the white utility, with its doors swinging and machines falling as the vehicle flies through the steaming sky. Rangers fall too: foolish, flailing space men, mission aborted. One remains braced in the drivers seat: Lewis sees him clearly as the truck rotates. That's a whole truck up there, spinning slowly as though something wraps it, carries it amidst shifting coils. And as the nacreous mist thickens, something does.

372 · Who Looks Back?

Kelsie all but stumbles towards the lookout. She's made it: there's a bench concreted firm into the ground and there's the cliff. Ferns, flowers fall away: the valley lies before her, a snaking, smoking rift down to the metallic sheet of the lake. Nothing in that view suggests a source for the dreadful sounds, the mash of flesh and branches. It was behind her then, the accident. *Lewis, oh my God*. And she turns. She begins to turn back, as branches crack and wind flattens, and something huge and whistling like a train churns up the hill. Into her view drops a white utility. It drops from the sky right before her eyes, crashing, sliding away down the cliff as something in the air loosens and billows, shooting away with a furl resembling the feeding fringe of a coral polyp as much as steam or clouds or a weather balloon: what the Hell is she *seeing*?

Lewis hasn't stopped moving down the main track. This was where both truck and terror came from, but they aren't there now and he can really put on some speed. His is the discipline of pure motion, but maybe there's something in this headlong rush of a small, brown boy being hunted through the London alleys. The track bends and bends again; on his left Mount Haszard and on his right the creek, bubbling with increased vigor. And his cluttered mind suggests that if what he saw was an explosion, the freakish herald of a volcanic event, then in all likelihood he's running right into it. Where is Kelsie? If he was so far ahead that she didn't see the horror, then she might well have continued on up to the look-out. He's closer now to the exit than the entrance: when he reaches that he'll head up and meet her. They're bound to be safe on the mountain.

Kelsie had the rope and carabineers in her pack. This was her plan: an assisted fall from the look-out, ten meters down onto what they called the Terrace, then a straight though possibly scalding sprint to the shore. She'd take risks when it counted. Confined to the remainder of the path, Lewis would have lost minutes and been lost in wide, white-grinning admiration of a stunt so worthy of himself. Then she could have told him she was through.

Now she goes through the same motions to deadly purpose: there are people down there, she can hear them. Anchor on the bench and on the largest tree, though that wouldn't be worth much: quickly, quickly pull the sleeve in place so the cliff doesn't cut the cord as she goes over. Climbing was her first love, in the erosion gullies around the farm: her first attempt to escape. Her second took her to London and where hasn't she been since then? Stepping off into air, she looks down.

Lewis hears another rumble. A thrashing, boiling, torrential sound: in the direction of the lake, pure white striates the sky. There's been no geysers in Waimangu since just after the eruption, when they claimed it held the largest in the world. What's this then, what is this? It's *incredible*! In all his travels, running round and round the world in search of its edges, he's never seen the like! The entire lake must be rising and even as he runs, as the track beneath him starts to shake and the outrunners of the wind hits, there's as much delight in his whoop as fear. Until he realizes that the wind and the whistling is coming from behind him.

Kelsie drops into ruin. The valley floor is made up of smashed sinter, broken rocks, raw scars scraped through the undergrowth, and white wreckage steaming—all of it steaming. A white figure flails, caught half in metal, half in water the same unearthly green as the spring. Rumbling, roaring, human screams a tenuous thread of sound. Kelsie is shaking, everything is shaking and as she lands, nice and light and square, she's nearly flung off her feet. Not even unhooked she is turning, stumbling, drawing the rope across the heaving pink and yellow ground. Inhaling an overwhelming smell, like eggs boiling in a rusted kettle, she reaches down and hauls on wet fabric.

Lewis slithers in blood-warm water, popping and stinging against his skin. There was nowhere else to go as something that wasn't a trick of the light, nor a current of superheated water or anything else but a creature came hunting. His entire body knew it and that wracks him beyond the heat and acid. He keeps himself loose and floating: going with the flow, but he isn't alone. Slick like rubber and obscenely buoyant, white corpses follow the current, floating swiftly towards white Hell.

The ranger's name is Ahere, her skin darker than Lewis where it isn't burned, her eyes a brimming brown. Crying and hugging Kelsie, she tells her things: a seismological blip, a bloom on the thermal map, an early morning expedition in full heat-wear down to check the lake. A new vent had opened, yes, but there had been nothing to suggest more until the thing emerged. *Hīanga*, she says, we put the lines down and it comes, we put the lines down and it catches us! She points frantically to a strange, circular mark in the sinter, a circle at least a meter across with five deep indents that

Kelsie assumes was caused by some part of the utility. All she really gets from Ahere's story is that the lake is dangerous. But there's no going back the way she came: the whole cliff looks unstable and she doubts Ahere could make it in the best circumstances. Whatever Ahere saw, whatever she saw, they have no choice and apparently there's a reason. Ahere is saying they'll be safe.

When Lewis was a little boy, he loved dinosaurs (raptors, hunting him through the alleys). Ruins too, the temples and tombs of all the ancient civilizations, but keep digging and you reach dinosaurs, their big, stone bones tomb and temple both. To go back further takes more than science or even imagination, but clawing at foam and slurry, Lewis realizes that this isn't the youngest landscape on earth: it's the oldest. Go back further and it was all like this or near enough, a fury of earth and water. Near enough for that thing, maybe; that primal, elemental thing. Maybe life on earth did not begin with cells, but with fire and air. The cluttered part of his mind runs on like this, the other is crawling in the sludge, out of the creek but keeping low. It wants to find a hole and crawl inside: the other is telling him he needs to find the widest open space, where the rocks won't fall on him. That's what they said in Japan. He can only hope Kelsie is safe.

Kelsie was going home. From the North Island of New Zealand, Sydney is a hop across a puddle. She was going home and not like she swore to her father she never, ever would. She got the news two days ago in Wellington: her grant had come through and she had a whole new life of work and study waiting. But how to tell Lewis she's sick of living in hostels, tired of waitressing in shitholes to fund the next leg of the trip, while he blogs and preaches parkour. She knows he wants to climb Machu Picchu, has tagged Easter Island and Antarctica as stations in his quest for who knows what, and perhaps he will. But she's going to die in New Zealand with a stranger staggering on her arm, as the earth shakes beneath their feet and through the steam, the whistling rises once again.

Lewis runs. On the path but hunching, nearly on all fours. The hunter is still out there: he hears its whistling, its rush. He pushes, burning all his last and, miraculously, there is Kelsie paralleling him through the steam. All this, and neither has gained so much as a step! He lopes along the gravel, she jogs across the world famous Warbrick Terrace, deep crimson flashing under her feet. Her hair flashes: she is magnificent, she would be flying were she not hampered by a pale and lumbering thing. A monstrous form, a homunculus or golem with gleaming white skin. And fly she must, for through the clouds the hunter is coming: he feels its wind, sees the mist clear. And as it comes, his shrieking, cluttered mind sheers clean away. He sees angles and surfaces. Instinctively he understands that little warm-blooded things scuttling through ferns don't interest this hunter. How could they threaten it? How could they even feed it? It's the monster it seeks, with its unnatural contours: he yelps and changes course.

Kelsie hears Ahere shriek and feels her suddenly sag against her: thinking she's stumbled, she yanks her up and then sees her face plate is shattered. Her nose and eyes have vanished behind a web of cracks and there is blood. Are there stones in the air now? She grabs Ahere, reaching into her core for one last effort and oh my God there's Lewis sprinting toward her, Lewis with his stubbled head, arms and legs pumping crazy. She lets go of Ahere's arm and sees Lewis raise his, a sharp, black rock in his hand. It freezes her brain. She can't comprehend what she's seeing, match cause and effect. Only when the second flint strikes the helpless woman, opening a gash in her thermal skin, does she leap to intercept him, grabbing his arm, hauling at him, her height and weight costing both their footing and bringing them down.

She's in his arms now, rolling and thrashing; he laughs and rolls with her, all heat and sweat and hair. Slipping, sliding, seeping crimson; he's hard as a rock, licking permanganate from her skin.

He's below her and she strikes him hard, no longer thinking of Ahere but rather of his grasping hands, his grinning mouth, of being dragged and used, and assumed. Of needing to win so she can finally, finally not need him.

Something passes over them, the two little mammals rolling in the mud. Something screams in agony and the crimson drenching them is at blood heat.

Kelsie stares down at Lewis and things click back into perspective. He's still grinning but he's shivering and what comes out of his mouth isn't words. She could leave him here, she really could. In light of what he did and the trouble she'll have, perhaps she should. But she can't. Somehow, she has to get them all to the lake. Looking around, she can no longer see Ahere so presumably she's followed her own advice. Aching weary but somehow no longer terrified, she staggers up and then offers Lewis her hand.

He had rather lie here, wet and happy, but everything is shaking and they had better find shelter. Somewhere quiet and dark where the water makes no sound. He stays close to his mate, gaze darting through the undergrowth and ears peeled for the hunting cry of the things below, that strike from above. Their voices are everywhere, but only the whistling counts.

Up ahead, Kelsie sees black and white. Black the fringe of unbelievably stubborn vegetation: white the boiling lake. There's no escaping there. Then part of the black resolves into a roof and windows, wheels, and she realizes what Ahere must have meant. Running off from the dock, directly ahead of her and Lewis lies a road, and parked upon it is a small bus. The access road and the bus that takes tourists out of the valley! A broad and stable slope, solid walls and engine: this is their way out and always was. Where is Ahere? There's no sign of her here. Oh please, let her not still be back there . . .

He knows the artificial hollow is a trap. They can't go in there: he takes hold of his mate to pull her away. She resists him, chattering shrilly as though it's he who doesn't understand. He does understand, the hunters are waiting for more white monsters! Now she is grabbing him, dragging him towards the unnatural planes and sharp angles, and what is that dark substance streaming across the ground like water, yet solid? He twists out of her grasp, makes a blow of it, a stunning blow to the side of her head—and misses. She has jumped clear of him, landing on the black.

Kelsie screams as the bus explodes upwards in a geyser that holds a shadow, a writhing, tubular shadow that crushes windows and seats. Shrapnel scatters but she is already running, uphill again but she will not give in to what she saw and will not die in the grip of a nightmare. Lewis pursues her; she hears him plowing through the bush at the side of the road, chuckling in his madness. She veers away from him, though it costs her speed, and now she is shrinking from the whistling in the air, from the steam-shadow hurtling, coalescing into solidity right above her.

He gathers up all his strength, all his superbly honed muscle, and makes his leap. Although he no longer considers it as such, this is the pinnacle of parkour: a *passe muraille* such as hearsay finds impossible to believe, that makes the witness gasp and the practitioner sigh. Not to scale a wall, but to interpose himself between his mate and the thing with the whiplash body, the grasping tendrils, the five-pointed sting. It is not fully material, not at its full strength when he hits, so the impact sends that sting plunging into the tar. But it solidifies around him, lifts him up with a billow and swarm, and does not fade as it carries him out, over the edge of the world.

At his yell, his triumphant scream, Kelsie glances over her shoulder. Who looks back on the Waimangu track? Anyone who does will never really leave. When the rescue team finds Kelsie, she has painted herself with sulphur and antimony, and is using her pitons to punch the five points into the road, again and again.

*"Ever Their praises, and abundance to the Black Goat of the Woods. Iä! Shub-Niggurath! The Goat with a Thousand Young!"*
*"The Whisperer in the Darkness" · H. P. Lovecraft (1931)*

# · EQUOID ·
## Charles Stross

"Bob! Are you busy right now? I'd like a moment of your time."

Those thirteen words never bode well—although coming from my new manager, Iris, they're less doom-laden than if they were falling from the lips of some others I could name. In the two months I've been working for her Iris has turned out to be the sanest and most sensible manager I've had in the past five years. Which is saying quite a lot, really, and I'm eager to keep her happy while I've got her.

"Be with you in ten minutes," I call through the open door of my office; "got a query from HR to answer first." Human Resources have teeth, here in the secretive branch of the British government known to its inmates as the Laundry; so when HR ask you to do their homework—ahem, provide one's opinion of an applicant's suitability for a job opening—you give them priority over your regular work load. Even when it's pretty obvious that they're taking the piss.

*I am certain that Mr. Lee would make an extremely able addition to the Office Equipment Procurement Team,* I type, *if he was not already*—according to your own goddamn database, if you'd bothered to check it—*a lieutenant in the Chinese Peoples Liberation Army Jiangshi Brigade.* Who presumably filled out the shouldn't-have-been-published-on-the-internet job application on a drunken dare, or to test our vetting procedures, or something. *Consequently I suspect that he would fail our mandatory security background check at the first hurdle.* (As long as the vetting officer isn't *also* a PLA mole.)

I hit "send" and wander out into the neon tube overcast where Iris is tapping her toes. "Your place or mine?"

"Mine," says Iris, beckoning me into her cramped corner office. "Have a chair, Bob. Something's come up, and I think it's right up your street." She plants herself behind her desk, leans back in her chair, and preps her pitch. "It'll get you out of the office for a bit, and if HR are using you to stomp all over the dreams of upwardly-mobile Chinese intelligence operatives it means you're—"

"Underutilized. Yeah, whatever." I wave it off. But it's true: since I sorted out the funny stuff in the basement at St. Hilda's I've been *bored*. The day-to-day occupation of the average secret agent mostly consists of hurry up and wait. In my case, that means filling in on annoying bits of administrative scutwork and handling upgrades to the departmental network—when I'm not being called upon to slay multi-tentacled horrors from beyond spacetime. (Which doesn't happen very often, actually, for which I am profoundly grateful.) "You said it's out of the office?"

"Yes." She smiles; she knows she's planted the hook. "A bit of fresh country air, Bob—you're too pallid. But tell me—" she leans forward— "what do you know about horses?"

The equine excursion takes me by surprise. "Uh?" I shake my head. "Four legs, hooves, and a bad attitude?" Iris shakes her head, so I try again: "Go with a carriage like, er, love and marriage?"

"No, Bob, I was wondering—did you ever learn to ride?"

"What, you mean—wait, we're not talking about bicycles here, right?" From her reaction I don't think that's the answer she was looking for. "I'm a city boy. As the photographer said, you should never work with animals or small children if you can avoid it. What's come up, a dressage emergency?"

"Not exactly." Her smile fades. "It's a shame, it would have made this easier."

"Made *what* easier?"

"I could have sworn HR said you could ride." She stares at me pensively. "Never mind. Too late to worry about has-beens now. Hmm. Anyway, it probably doesn't matter—you're married, so I don't suppose you're a virgin, either. Are you?"

"Get away!" *Virgins*? That particular myth is associated with unicorns, which don't exist, any more than vampires, dragons, or mummies— although I suppose if you wrapped a zombie in bandages you'd get a—*stop that*. In my head, confused stories about Lady Godiva battle with media images of tweed-suited shotgun-wielding farmers. "Do you need someone who can ride? Because I don't think I can learn in—"

"No, Bob, I need *you*. Or rather, the Department for Environment, Food and Rural Affairs needs a liaison officer who just happens to have your background and proven track record in—" she waves her left hand— "putting down infestations."

"Do they?" I do a double-take at *putting down infestations*. "Are they *sure* that's what they need?"

"Yes, they are. Or rather, they know that when they spot certain signs, they call us." She pulls open a desk drawer and removes a slim folder, its cover bearing the Crowned Portcullis emblem beneath an elder sign. "Take this back to your office and read it," she tells me. "Return it to the stacks when you're done. Then you can spend the rest of the afternoon thinking of ways to politely tell HR to piss up a rope, because tomorrow morning you're getting on a train to Hove in order to lend a DEFRA inspector a helping hand."

"You're serious?" I boggle at her. "You're sending me to do what? Inspect a farm?"

"I don't want to prejudice your investigation. There's a livery stable. Just hook up with the man from *The Archers*, take a look around, and phone home if anything catches your attention."

She slides the file across my desk and I open the flyleaf. It starts with TOP SECRET and a date round about the battle of the Somme, crossed out and replaced with successively lower classifications until fifteen years ago it was marked down to MILDLY EMBARRASSING NO TABLOIDS. Then I flip the page and spot the title. "Hang on—"

"Shoo," she says, a wicked glint in her eyes. "Have fun!"

I shoo, smarting. I know a set-up when I see one—and I've been conned.

To understand why I knew I'd been tricked, you need to know who I am and what I do. Assuming you've read this far without your eyeballs boiling in your skull, it's probably safe to tell you that my name's Bob Howard—at least, for operational purposes; true names have power, and we don't like to give extradimensional identity thieves the keys to our souls—and I work for a secret government agency known to its inmates as the Laundry. It morphed into its present form during the Second World War, ran the occult side of the conflict with the Thousand Year Reich, and survives to this day as an annoying blob somewhere off to the left on the org chart of the British intelligence services, funded out of the House of Lords black budget.

Magic is a branch of applied mathematics, and I started out studying computer science (which is no more about computers than astronomy is about building really big telescopes). These days I specialize in applied computational demonology and general dogsbody work around my department. The secret service has never really worked out how to deal with people like me, who aren't admin personnel but didn't come up through the Oxbridge civil service fast-track route. In fact, I got into this line of work entirely by accident: if your dissertation topic leads you in the wrong direction you'd better hope that the Laundry finds you and makes you a job offer you can't refuse before the things you've unintentionally summoned up get bored talking to you and terminate your *viva voce* with prejudice.

After a couple of years of death by bureaucratic snu-snu (too many committee meetings, too many tedious IT admin jobs) I volunteered for active duty, without any clear understanding that it would mean *more* years of death by boredom (too many committee meetings, too many tedious IT jobs) along with a side-order of mortal terror courtesy of tentacle monsters from beyond spacetime.

As I am now older and wiser, not to mention married and still in possession of my sanity, I prefer my work life to be boringly predictable these days. Which it is, as a rule, but then along come the nuisance jobs— the Laundry equivalent of the way the US Secret Service always has to drop round for coffee, a cake, and a brisk interrogation with idiots who boast about shooting the president on Yahoo! Chat.

In my experience, your typical scenario is that some trespassing teenagers get stoned on 'shrooms, hallucinate flying saucers piloted by alien colorectal surgeons looking to field-test their new alien endoscope technology, and shit themselves copiously all over Farmer Giles' back paddock. A report is generated by the police, and as happens with reports of unknown origin, it accretes additional bureaucratic investigatory mojo until by various pathways it lands on the desk of one of our overworked analysts. They then bump it up the management chain and/or play cubicle ping-pong with it, because they're too busy working to keep tabs on the Bloody Skull Cult or cases of bovine demonic possession in Norfolk or something equally important. Finally, in an attempt to make the blessed thing *go away*, a manager finds a spare human resource and details the poor bastard to wade through the reports, interview the culprits, and then tread in cow shit while probing the farm cesspool for the spoor of alien pre-endoscopy laxatives. Nineteen times out of twenty it's an annoying paper chase followed by a day spent typing up a report that nobody will read. One time in twenty the affair is enlivened by you falling head-first into the cesspit. And the worst part of it is knowing that while you're off on a wild goose chase so you can close the books on the report, your everyday workload is quietly piling up in your in-tray and overflowing onto your desk . . .

Which is why, as I get back to my office, close the door, light up the DO NOT DISTURB sign, and open the folder Iris gave me, I start to swear quietly.

What the hell do the love letters of that old fraud H. P. Lovecraft have to do with the Department for Environment, Food and Rural Affairs?

Dear Robert,

I received your letter with, I must confess, some trepidation, not to mention mixed feelings of hope & despair tempered by the forlorn hope that the uncanny and unpleasant history of my own investigations & their regrettable outcome will serve to dampen the ardor with which you pursue your studies. I know full well to my great & abiding dismay the compulsive fascination that the eldritch & uncanny may exert upon the imagination of an introspective & sensitive scholar. I cannot help but be aware that you are already cognizant of the horrible risks to which your sanity will be exposed. What you may not be aware of is the *physical* damage that may fall upon you pursuant to these studies. It took my grandfather's life; it drove my father to seek redress by means of such vile & unmentionable acts that I cannot bring myself to record their nature for posterity—but suffice to say that his life was shortened thereby—and it has been grievously injurious to my own health & fitness for marriage. There, I say it baldly; but for the blessed Sonia I might have been a mortal wreck for my entire life. It was only by her grace & infinite patience that I regained some modicum of that which is the birthright of all the sons of Adam, and though we are parted she bears my guilty secret discreetly.

I confess that I was not always thus. My childhood was far from unhappy. I grew up an accident-prone but happy youth, living with my mother & my aunts in reduced but nevertheless genteel circumstances in Providence town. At first I studied the classics: Greek & Roman & Egyptian were my mother tongues, & all the rhapsodies of the poetic calling were mine! My grandfather's library was the orchid whose nectar I sipped, sweeter by far than any wine. He had amassed a considerable archive over the course of many years of travel inflicted on him by the base necessity of trade—I must interject at this juncture that I cannot stress too highly the need to shun such distractions as commerce if one is to reach one's full potential as a scholar by traversal of the path you propose to embark upon—and the fruits of his sorrows fermented into a heady vintage in time for my youthful excursions into his cellar to broach the casks of wisdom. However, I came to recognize a bitter truth as I assayed the dregs of his collection: my kindred souls are as the dust of the church-yard. As with Poe so am I one with the dead, for we persons of rarefied spirit & talent tread but seldom upon the boards of earth & are summoned all too soon to the exit eternal.

Now, as to the qualities of the MS submitted with your latest missive for my opinion, I must thank you most kindly for granting me the opportunity to review the work at this early stage—

I go home nursing a headache and a not inconsiderable sense of resentment at, variously: Iris for tricking me into this job; DEFRA for asking for back-up in the first place; and Howard Phillips Lovecraft of Providence, Rhode Island, for cultivating a florid and overblown prose style that covered the entire spectrum from purple to ultraviolet and took sixteen volumes of interminable epistles to get to the point—whatever point it was that constituted the meat of the EQUESTRIAN RED SIRLOIN dossier, which point I had not yet ascertained despite asymptotically approaching it in the course of reading what felt like reams & volumes of the aforementioned purple prose—*which is infectious.*

To cap it all, my fragrant wife Mo is away on some sort of assignment she can't talk about. All I know is that something's come up in Blackpool that requires her particular cross-section of very expensive talents, so I'm on my own tonight. (Combat epistemologists and violin soloists both are underpaid, but take many years and no little innate talent to train. Consequently, the demands on her time are many.) So I kick back with a bottle of passable cabernet sauvignon and a DVD—in this case, plucked at random from the watch-this-later shelf. It turns out to be a Channel Four production of *Equus*, by Peter Shaffer. Which I am hitherto unfamiliar with (don't laugh: my background veers towards the distaff side of the Two Cultures) and which *really* doesn't mix well with a bottle of red wine and H. P. Lovecraft's ghastly prose. So I spend half the night tossing and turning to visions of melting spindly-legged Dali horses with gouged eye sockets— I've got to stop the eyeballs rolling away, for some reason—with the skin-crawling sense that something unspeakable is watching me from the back of the stables. This is bad enough that I then spend the second half of the night sitting at the kitchen table in my pajamas, brute-forcing my way through my half of my annual ideological self-criticism session—that is, the self-assessed goals and objectives portion of my performance appraisal—because the crawling horrors of human resources are far less scary than the gory movie playing out behind my eyeballs.

(This is why many of my co-workers eventually start taking work home— at least, the non-classified bits. Bureaucracy is a bulwark of comforting routine in the face of the things you really don't want to think about too hard by dead of night. Not to mention being a safer tranquilizer than drink or drugs.)

In my experience it's best to go on-site and nail these bullshit jobs immediately, rather than wasting too much time on over-planning. This one is, when all is said and done, what our trans-Atlantic cousins call "a snipe hunt." I'm hoping to nail it shut—probably a little girl with a strap-on plastic horn for her pony—and be home in time for tea. So the next morning I leave home and head straight for London Bridge station rather than going in to the office. I fight my way upstream through the onrushing stream of suits and catch the commuter train that carried them into London on its return journey, rattling and mostly empty on its run out to the dormitory towns of East Sussex. It's just me and the early birds taking the cheapskate stopping service to Crapwick to avoid the hordes of holiday-makers (and pickpockets) at Thiefrow. And that's the way I like it.

I have a name and destination in the Request for Support memo Iris gave me: we're to investigate one G. Edgebaston, of Edgebaston Farm Livery Stables, near Hove. But first I'm supposed to meet a Mr. Scullery at a local DEFRA office in East Grinstead. Which is on the London to Brighton line, but it'll take me a good hour of start-stop commuter rail and then a taxi ride of indeterminate length to get there. So I take a deep breath and dive back into the regrettably deathless prose of the Prophet of Providence.

Listen, I know what you're thinking.

You're probably thinking WHAT THE HELL, H. P. LOVECRAFT? And wondering why I'm reading his private letters (most certainly not found in any of the collections so lovingly curated by Lovecraft scholars over the years, from August Derleth to S. T. Joshi), in a file so mind-numbingly trivial that its leakage on the front page of a major tabloid newspaper would be greeted with snores.

This is the Laundry, after all, and we write memos and file expense reports every day that deal with gibbering horrors, things that go bump in the night, the lunatical followers of N'yar lath-Hotep, the worshippers of the Sleeper in the Pyramid, alien undersea and lithospheric colonies of BLUE HADES and DEEP SIX, and Old Bat Wings himself.

You probably think HPL was one of ours, or that maybe one of our predecessor agencies bumped him off, or that these letters contain Great & Terrible Mysteries, Secrets, & Eldritch Wisdom of the Ancients and must be handled with asbestos tongs while reading them through welders' goggles. Right?

Well, you would be wrong. Although it's not your fault. You'd be wrong for the same reason as the folks who think modern fly-by-wire airliners can fly themselves from takeoff to landing (who needs pilots?), that Saddam really *did* have weapons of mass destruction (we just didn't search hard enough), and that the Filler of Stockings who brings presents down the chimney every Newtonmas-eve is a benign and cheery fellow. You've been listening to the self-aggrandizing exaggerations of self-promotion artists: respectively, the PR might of the airliner manufacturers, dodgy politicians, and the greeting card industry.

And so it is with old HPL: the very model of an eighteenth century hipster, born decades too late to be one of the original louche laudanum-addicted romantic poets, and utterly unafraid to bore us by droning on and on about the essential crapness of culture since Edgar Allan Poe, the degeneracy of the modern age, &c. &c. &c.

His reputation has been vastly inflated—out of all proportion—by his followers, who think he is the one true wellspring of wisdom concerning the Elder Gods, the Stars Coming Right, and various hideous horrors with implausible names like Shub-Niggurath, the goat of a thousand young, who spawns mindlessly on the darkest depths of the forest . . .

. . . Whereas, in actual fact, his writings are the occult equivalent of *The Anarchist Cookbook*.

It's absolutely true that Lovecraft *knew* stuff. Somewhere in grandpa's library he got his hands on the confused rambling inner doctrines of a dozen cults and secret societies. Most of these secrets were arrant nonsense on stilts—admixed with just enough knowledge to be deadly dangerous. Occultists of old, like the alchemists who poisoned themselves with mercury in their enthusiasm to transform lead into gold (meanwhile missing the opportunity to invent the modern discipline of chemistry as we understand it), didn't know much. What they *did* know was mostly just enough to guarantee a slow, lingering death from Krantzberg Syndrome (if the Eaters in the Night didn't get them first). Not to mention the fact that the vain exhibitionists who compiled these tomes and grimoires, strung out between the narcissistic urge to self-exposure and their occupational addiction to secrecy, littered their scribbled recipes with booby traps on purpose, just to fuck with unauthorized imitators and prove how 'leet they were for being able to actually make this junk work without melting their own faces.

But the young idiot savant HPL was unaware of the social context of eighteenth century occultist fandom. So he naively distilled their methanol-contaminated moonshine and nonsense into a heady brew that makes you go blind and then causes your extremities to rot if you actually try to drink it. It's almost as if he mistook his grandfather's library for a harmless source of material for fiction, rather than the demented and dangerous documentation of our superstitious forerunners.

*The Anarchist Cookbook*, with its dangerously flawed bomb formulae, hasn't maimed half so many hands as HPL's mythos. His writings look more like fiction than allegorically-described recipes to most people, which is a good thing; but every so often a reader of his more recondite works becomes unhealthily obsessed with the idea of the starry wisdom behind it, starts thinking of it as something real, and then tries to reverse-engineer the design of the pipe bomb he's describing, not realizing that Quality Control was *not* his strong point.

There are bits of the True Knowledge scattered throughout HPL's oeuvre like corn kernels in a turd. But he left stuff out, and he added stuff in, and he embellished and added baroque twiddles and stylistic curlicues as only H. P. Lovecraft could, until it's pretty much the safest course to discount everything he talks about—like Old Bat-Wings himself, Dread Cthulhu, who dead but dreaming sleeps in Drowned R'lyeh beneath the southern ocean.

Watch my lips: Cthulhu does *not* exist! And there is no tooth fairy.

(Santa Claus is another matter; but that, as they say, is a file with a different code word . . .

East Grinstead is buried deep in the heart of the Sussex commuter belt: this is Ruralshire, nor are we out of it. It's an overgrown village or a stunted town, depending on how you look at it, complete with picturesque mediaeval timbered buildings, although these days it's mostly known for its weirdly large array of fringe churches. I stumble blinking from the railway station (which is deathly quiet at this time of day, but clearly rebuilt to accommodate rush hour throngs), narrowly avoid being run down by a pair of mounted police officers who are exercising their gigantic cavalry chargers outside the station in preparation for crowd control at the next sudden-death derby (Brighton Wanderers v. Bexhill United, or some such), and hail a taxi. A minute's muttered negotiation with the driver ensues, then I'm off to the office.

When we arrive, I'm half-convinced I've got the wrong address. It's way the hell up the A22, so far out of town that at first I'm wondering why I got off the train in East Grinstead—but no, that's what Google said. (Not for the first time I wish I had a car, though as I live in London on a civil service salary it's not a terribly practical wish.) The taxi drops me in the middle of nowhere, next to a driveway fronted by a thick hedgerow. There are no obvious offices here, much less the sort of slightly flyblown agricultural veterinary premises you'd expect the Animal Health Executive Agency to maintain. So I look around, at a loss for a minute until I notice the discreet sign pointing up the drive to the Equine Veterinary Practice.

I amble into the yard of what looks like a former farmhouse. It's been inexpertly fronted with a conservatory that houses a rather dingy reception area, complete with a bored-looking middle-aged lady tapping away on her computer while wearing an expression that says if it's MySpace, she's just been unfriended by the universe.

"Hello," I ask her. She ignores me, intently tapping away at whatever so preoccupies her on her computer. "Hello?" I repeat again. "I'm here to meet Mr. Scullery? Is he around?"

Finally she deigns to notice me. "He's on a job for the Department," she says. "He won't be available until Thursday—"

I let her see my teeth: "Perhaps you can tell him that Mr. Howard is here to see him? From the office in London. I assume it's the same job we're talking about."

"He's on a job for the—" Finally what I just said worms its way through her ears and into her brain—"I'm sorry, who did you say you were?"

"I'm Mr. Howard. I've come all the way down from London. About the Edgebaston brief." I bounce up and down on my toes. "He asked for me, so if you'd just like to—"

She is already reaching for the phone. "Hello? Mr. Scullery? I have a Mr. Howarth from London, he says you asked for someone from London to help with Edgebaston Farm? Is that right? Yes—right you are, I'll just tell him." She puts the phone down and smiles at me in that very precise, slightly self-deprecating way farm-bred ladies of a certain class use to let you know that there's nothing personal about the knee cap they're about to deliver to your left nut: "Mr. Scullery says he's running half an hour late and he'll be with you as soon as he can. So if you'd like to take a seat in the waiting area? I'm sure he won't be long." She turns back to her computer as if I'm invisible. I hover indecisively for a moment, but I know when I've been dismissed; and so I go and find a waiting room seat to occupy (sub-type: wooden, elderly, not designed with human buttocks in mind) and mooch listlessly through the stack of magazines for space aliens that they keep on hand to distract the terminally bored.

Dear Robert,

I must confess that, pursuant to my reply to your last missive, I experienced no small degree of self-doubt as to the perspicacity

& pertinence of my critique. If you will permit me to attempt to justify my equivocation, I would like to enter in my defense a plea of temporary insanity. Your confabulation, while a most excellent evocation of a legendary monster, bears special & most unpleasant personal resonances from my regrettable youth. It is not your fault that the heraldic beast you chose to depict in this form is a marvelous horror in my eyes; indeed, you must be somewhat puzzled by my reaction.

I regret to inform you that your description of the unicorn, while vivid in its adhesion to the classical description of same & sharply piquant in depicting his pursuit of the gamine subject of the narrative, is fundamentally inaccurate in both broad outline & fine detail. Explorers might once have sketched fanciful depictions of the Chinese Panda, but today we are fettered by the dour tyranny of camera & zoo; to diverge so drastically from the established order of nature is to risk the gentle reader's willing suspension of disbelief. Regrettably, the horrid creature you caricature is all too real; it will in due course be a matter of the most mundane familiarity to readers, & familiarity inevitably brings such enthusiastic flights of fancy as your missive to grief on the cold stone flags of reality.

Please extend me your trust on this matter. Unicorns are not a suitable topic for romance or fantasy. On the contrary, the adult unicorn is a thing of dire & eldritch horror & I would advise you to pray to your creator that you live to a ripe old age without once encountering such a monstrous creature.

I, alas, was not so lucky & the experience has blighted my entire adult life . . .

I kill time waiting for the Man from Ag and Fish by working my way through a stack of glossy magazines for aliens. Passing over the princess-shiny pinkness of *Unicorn School™: The Sparkling* with a shudder, I work my way through a thought-provoking if slightly breathless memoir of "Police Cavalry v. Pinko Commie Striking Miners in the 1980s"—the thoughts it provokes focus on the urgent need to commit the author to an asylum for the violently insane—and am partway through reading a feature about modern trends in castration techniques (and how to care for your gelding) in *Stallion World* when the door slams open and a gigantic beard wearing a loud tweed suit explodes into the reception area: "*Lissa!* Melissa! I'm back! Can you tell Bert to hose out the back of the Landy? And fetch out the two sacks of oats behind the passenger seat! Where's this man from the ministry? Ah, there you are! You must be Mr. Helmuth! I'm Greg Scullery. Pleased to meet you!"

He bounds across the reception area before I can put the magazine down and grabs my right hand, pumping it like a windlass while I'm still coming to my feet. Mr. Scullery is wiry and of indeterminate middle age. He could probably pass for a farmer with bizarre (albeit dated) sartorial taste—ghastly green tweed suit, check shirt, a tie that appears to be knitted from the intestines of long-dead badgers—but his beard is about thirty centimeters long, grizzled and salted and bifurcated. It has so much character that it's probably being hunted by a posse of typographers. "Um, the name's Howard. Bob Howard." I try not to wince at the sensation in my hand, which feels as if it has been sucked into some kind of machine for extracting oil from walnuts. "I believe you requested backup? For some sort of infestation?"

"*Yes!* Yes indeed!" I remember my other hand and use it to make a grab for my warrant card, because I have not yet had an opportunity to authenticate him.

"Seen one of these before?" I ask, flicking it open in front of him.

The walnut-crusher shifts gear into a final grind-into-mush setting: "Capital Laundry Services? Oh yes indeedy! I was in the Rifles, you know. Back in my misspent childhood, haha." The walnut slurry is ejected: my right hand dangles limply and I try not to wince conspicuously. "Jolly good, Mr. Howard. So. Have you been briefed?"

I shake my head, just as the bell above the reception area door jangles. A young filly is leading her mater in. They're both wearing green wellies, and there's something so indefinably horsey about them that I have to pinch myself and remember that were-ponies do not exist outside the pages of a certain bestselling kid-lit series. "Is there somewhere we can talk about this in private?" I ask Greg. "My manager said she didn't want to prejudice me by actually telling me what this is about."

His beard twitches indignantly while it sorts out an answer. "One of those, eh? We'll see about that!" He turns towards reception, where Jocasta or Penelope is trying to evince a metabolic reaction from Melissa the receptionist, who is still deep in MySpace meltdown. "Lissa! Belay all that, I'm going out on a job with Mr. Howard here! If Fiona calls, tell her I'll be back by five! Follow me." And with that, he strides back out into the farmyard. I swirl along in the undertow, wondering what I've let myself in for.

Greg leads me across the yard to a Land Rover. I don't know a lot about cars, but this one is pretty spartan, from the bare metal floor pan punctured by drain holes, to the snorkel-shaped exhaust bolted to one side of the windscreen. It's drab green, there's a gigantic spare tire clamped on the bonnet, and I wouldn't be surprised to hear it has an army service record longer than Greg's. That worthy clambers into the driver's seat and motions me towards the passenger door. "Yes, we have seat belts! And other modern fittings like air conditioning" (he points at a slotted metal grille under the windscreen), "and radio" (he gestures at a military-looking shortwave set bolted to the cab roof), "even though it's a pre-1983 Mark III model. Just hang on, eh?" He fires up the engine, which grumbles and mutters to itself as if chewing on lumps of coal, before it emits a villainous blue smoke ring as a prelude to turning over under its own power. Then he rams it into gear with a jolt, and we lurch towards the main road. I'm certain that the rubber band this thing uses in lieu of a leaf spring profoundly regrets how very, very wicked it was in an earlier life. And shortly thereafter, so do my buttocks.

Dear Robert,

Many thanks for your kind enquiry after my health. I am, as is usually the case, in somewhat precarious straits but no better or worse than is to be expected of a gentleman of refined & delicate breeding in this coarsened & debased age. My digestion is troubling me greatly, but I fear there is nothing to be done about that. I have the comfort of my memories, & that is both necessary & sufficient to the day, however questionable such comfort might be. I am in any event weighed down by an apprehension of my own mortality. The sands of my hourglass are running fast & I have no great expectation of a lengthy future stretching before me; so I hope you will indulge this old raconteur's discursive perambulations & allow me to tell you what I know of unicorns.

I should preface my remarks by cautioning you that I am no

longer the young man whose memories I commit to paper. In the summer of 1904 I was a callow & untempered fourteen-year-old, with a head full of poetry & a muse at either shoulder, attending Hope High School & keenly absorbing the wisdom of my elders. That younger Howard was a sickly lad, but curious & keen, & took a most serious interest in matters astronomical & chymical. He was at heart an optimist, despite the death of his father from nervous exhaustion some years previously, & was gifted with the love of his mother & aunts & grandfather. Oh! The heart sickens with the dreadful knowledge of the horrid fate which came to blight my life & prospects thereafter. The death of my grandfather in that summer cast a pall across my life, for our circumstances were much reduced, & my mother & aunts were obliged to move to the house on Angell Street. I continued my studies & became particularly obsessed with the sky & stars, for it seemed to me that in the vastness of the cosmos lay the truest & purest object of study. It was my ambition to become an astronomer & to that end I bent my will.

There were distractions, of course. Of these, one of the most charming lived in a house on Waterman Street with her family & was by them named Hester, or Hetty. She attended Hope High, & I confess she was the brightest star in my firmament by 1908. Not that I found it easy then or now to speak of this to her, or to her shade, for she is as long dead as the first flush of a young man's love by middle age, & the apprehension of the creeping chill of the open grave that waits for me is all that can drive me to set my hand to write of my feelings in this manner. Far too many of the things I should have said to her (had I been mature enough to apprehend how serious an undertaking courtship must be) I whispered instead to my journal, disguised in the raiments of metaphor & verse.

Let me then speak plainly, as befits these chilly January days of 1937. Hetty was, Hetty was, like myself, the only child of an old Dutch lineage. A year younger than I, she brought a luminous self-confidence to all that she did, from piano to poetry. I watched from a distance, smitten with admiration for this delicate & clever creature. I imagined a life in literature, with her Virginia playing the muse to my Edgar & fancifully imagined that she might see in me some echoing spark of recognition of our shared destiny together. In hindsight my obsession was jejune & juvenile, the youthful obsession of a young man in whose sinews and fibers the sap is rising for the first time; but it was sincerely felt & as passionate as anything I had experienced at that time.

That was a simpler, more innocent age and there were scant opportunities for a youth such as I to directly address his muse, much less to plight his troth before the altar of providence & announce the depth of his ardor. It was simply not done. You may therefore imagine my surprise when, one stifling August Saturday afternoon, whilst engaged in my perambulations about the paths and churchyards of Providence, I encountered the object of my fascination crouching behind a gravestone, to all appearances preoccupied by an abnormally large & singular snail . . .

My tailbone is aching by the time Greg screeches to a halt outside a rustic-looking pub. "Lunch time!" He declares, with considerable lip-smacking; "I assume you haven't been swallowing the swill the railway trolley service sells? They serve a passable pint of Greene King IPA here, and there's a beer garden." The beard twitches skywards, as if reading the clouds for auguries of rain: "We'll probably be alone outside, which is good."

Mr. Scullery strides into the public bar (which is as countrified as I expected: blackened timber beams held together by a collection of mirror-polished horse brasses, a truly vile carpet, and chairs at tables set for food rather than serious drinking). "Brenda? Brenda! Ah, capital! That'll be two IPAs, the sausages and cheddar mash for me, and whatever Mr. Howard here is eating—"

I scan the menu hastily. "I'll have the cheeseburger, please," I say.

"We'll be in the garden," the beard announces, its points quivering in anticipation. And then he's off again, launching himself like a cannonball through a side door (half-glazed with tiny panes of warped glass thick enough to screen a public toilet), into a grassy back yard studded with outdoor tables, their wooden surfaces weathered silver-gray from long exposure. "Jolly good!" he declares, parking his backside on a bench seat with a good view of both the parking lot and the back door (and anyone else who ventures out this way). "Brenda will have our drinks along in a minute, and then we shall have a bite of lunch. So tell me, Mr. Howard. What *did* your boss tell you?"

"That you work for DEFRA and you know about us and you're cleared to request backup from my department." I shrug. "When I said she doesn't believe in prejudicing her staff I meant it. All I know is that I'm supposed to meet you and we're going to go and investigate a livery stable called, um, G. Edgebaston Ltd. What's your job, normally? I mean, to have clearance—"

"I work for DEFRA in—" He pauses as a middle-aged lady bustles up to us with a tray supporting two nearly full beer glasses and some slops. "Thank you, Brenda!"

"Your food will be along in ten minutes, Mr. Scullery," she says with an oddly proprietorial tone; "don't you be overdoing it now!" Then she retreats, leaving us alone once more.

"Ah, where was I? Ah yes. I work for the Animal Health Agency." The beard twitches over its beer for a moment, dowsing for drowned wasps. "I'm a veterinary surgeon. I specialize in horses, but I do other stuff. It's a hobby, if you like, but it's official enough that I'm on the books as AHA's in-house cryptozoologist. What about *you*, Mr. Howard? What exactly do you do for the Laundry?"

I am too busy trying not to choke on my beer to answer for a moment. "I don't think I'm allowed to talk about that," I finally manage. (My oath of office doesn't zap me for this admission.)

"Yes, but *really*, I say. What do you know about cryptozoology?"

"Well." I think for a moment. "I used to subscribe to *Fortean Times*, but then I developed an allergy to things with too many tentacles . . . "

"Bah." Greg couldn't telegraph his disdain more clearly if he manifested a tiny thundercloud over his head, complete with lightning bolts. "Rank amateurs, conspiracy theorists and *journalists*." He takes a mouthful of the Greene King, filtering it on its way down his throat. "No, Mr. Howard, I don't deal with nonsense like Bigfoot or little gray aliens with rectal thermometers or chupacabra: I deal with *real* organisms, which simply happen to be rare."

"Unicorns?" I guess wildly.

Greg peers at me over the rim of his pint glass, one eye open wide. "Don't *say* that," he hisses. "Do you have *any* idea what we'd have to do if there was a unicorn outbreak in England? It'd make the last foot and mouth epidemic look like a storm in a tea-cup . . . "

"But I thought—" I pause. "Hang on, you're telling me that unicorns are real?"

He pauses for a few seconds, then wets his whistle before he speaks. "I've never seen one" he says quietly, "for which I am profoundly grateful because, being male, if I *did* see one it'd probably be the last thing I ever set eyes on. But I do assure you, young feller me lad, that unicorns are very real indeed, just like great white sharks and Ebola Zaire—and they're just as much of a joking matter. Napalm, Mr. Howard, napalm and scorched earth: that's the only language they understand. Sterilize it with fire and nerve gas, then station armed guards." Another mouthful of beer vanishes, clearly destined to fuel the growth of further facial foliage and calm Mr. Scullery's shaky nerves.

I shake my head. The EQUESTRIAN RED SIRLOIN dossier was suggestive, but it's always hard to tell where HPL's starry wisdom ends and his barking fantasy starts. "Okay, so you want backup when you go to run a spot check on Edgebaston's stable. Why me? Why not a full team of door-breakers, and a flame thrower for good luck?"

"They've got *connections*, Mr. Howard. Bob, isn't it? The Edgebastons have run Edgebaston Farm out at Howling ever since Harry Edgebaston married Dick and Elfine's daughter Sandra Hawk-Monitor, and renamed the old farm after his own line—and wasn't that a scandal, most of a century ago!—but in this generation they're pillars of the local community, not to mention the Conservative Club. Suppliers of horses to Sussex Constabulary, first cousins of our MP, Barry Starkadder. You do *not* want to mess with the squirearchy, even in this day and age of Euro-regulation and what-not. They'll call down fire and brimstone! And not just from the Church in Beershorn, I'm telling you. Questions will be asked *in Parliament* if I go banging on their front door without good reason, you mark my words!"

"But—" I stop and rewind, rephrasing: "something must have raised your suspicions, Mr. Scullery. Isn't that right? What makes you think there's an outbreak down at Edgebaston Farm?"

"I have a pricking in my thumbs and an itching in my nostril." The beard twitches grimly. "Oh yes indeed. But you asked the right question! It's the butcher bills, Mr. Howard, that got my attention this past month. See, old George has been buying in bulk from old Murther's butcher, lots of honeycomb and giblets and offal. Pigs' knuckles. That sort of thing. Wanda's happy enough to tell me what the Edgebastons are buying—without me leaning too hard, anyway—and it turns out they're taking about forty kilos a day."

"So they're buying lots of meat? Is that all?" I think for a moment. "Are they selling pies to Poland or something?"

"It's not food-grade for people, Mr. Howard. Or livestock for that matter, not since our little problem with BSE twenty years ago." Greg raises his glass and empties it down his throat. "And it's a blessed lot of meat. Enough to feed a tiger, or a pack of hounds, 'cept Georgie doesn't ride with the Howling Hounds any more. Had a falling-out with Debbie Checkbottom six years ago and that was the end of that—it's the talk of the village, that and Gareth Grissom wearing a dress and saying he wants a sex change, then taking off to Brighton." He says it with relish, and I try not to roll my eyes or pass comment on his parochial lack of savoir faire. This is rural England, after all; please set your watch back thirty years . . .

"Okay, so: meat. And a livery stable. Is that *all* you've got?" I push.

"No," Greg says tightly, and reaches into his pocket, pulls something out, and puts it on the table in front of me. It's the shell of a cone snail, fluted and spiraled, about ten centimeters long and two centimeters in diameter at its open end, gorgeously marbled in cream and brown. It's clearly dead. Which is a very good thing, because if it were a live cone snail and Greg had picked it up like that it would have stung him, and those bastards are nearly as lethal as a king cobra.

"Very nice," I say faintly. "Where did you find it?"

"On the verge of the road, under the fence at the side of the back field under Mockuncle Hill." The beard clenches, wrapping itself around a nasty grin. "It was alive at the time. Eating what was left of a lamb. Took a lot of killin'."

"But it's a—" I stop. I swallow, then realize I've got a pint of beer, and my dry throat really needs some lubrication. "It *could* be a coincidence," I say, trying to convince myself and failing.

"Do you really think that?" Greg knots his fingers through his beard and tugs, combing it crudely.

"Fuck, no." I somehow manage to make half a pint of beer disappear between sentences. "You're going to have to check it out. No question. In case there are females."

"No, Mr. Howard." He's abruptly as serious as a heart-attack. "*We* are going to have to check it out. Because if there's a live female, much less a mated pair, two of us stand a better chance of living long enough to sound the alarm than one . . . "

(cont'd.)

Having for so long been tongue-tied in her presence, I was finally shocked out of my diffidence when I saw the object of Hetty's interest. "I say, what is *that*?" I ejaculated.

My rosy-cheeked Dawn turned her face towards me & smiled like a goddess out of legend: "It is a daddy-snail!" she exclaimed. She reached towards a funerary urn wherein languished a bouquet of wilted lilies & plucked a browning stem from the funereal decoration—she was in truth poetry in motion. "Watch this," she commanded. My eyes turned to follow her gesture as she gracefully prodded the lichen-crusted rock before the snail's face. The shell of the snail was a fluted cone, perhaps eight inches long & two inches in diameter at the open end. Its color was that of antique ivory, piebald with attractive glossy brown spots. I could see nothing of the occupant & indeed it could have been a dead sea-shell of considerable size, but when the lily-stem brushed the gravestone an inch or two in front of it there was an excitement of motion: the cone rocked back on its heel & spat a pair of slippery iridescent tongues forth at the stem. With some disbelief I confess to recognizing these as *tentacles*, as unlike the foot of the common mollusk as can be (although our friends the marine biologists assert that the cephalopodia, the octopi & squid & chambered nautilus, are themselves but the highest form of invertebrate mollusk, so perhaps attributing ownership of tentacles to a land-snail is not such an incongruous stretch of imagination as one might at first consider); but while I was trying to make sense of my own eyes' vision, the demonic cone grabbed hold of the parched stem of the flower and *broke it in two*!

"Do you see?" Hetty beamed at me. "It is a daddy-snail!" Then her dear face fell. "But he is on his own, too far from home. There are no missy-horses here, & so he will surely starve & die unfulfilled."

"How do you know this?" I asked stupidly, confounded by her vivacity & veneer of wisdom in the matter of this desperate gastropod.

"I have a mummy-horse quartered in our stables," she told me, as matter-of-fact as can be, with an impatient toss of her golden locks. "Would you help me carry Peter back to the yard? I would be ever so grateful, & he would love to be among his kindred."

"Why don't you do it yourself?" I asked rudely, then kicked myself. Her speech and direct manner had quite confounded me, being as it was so utterly at odds with my imaginings of her lilting voice & ladylike gentility. (I was a young and dreamy boy in those days & so ill-acquainted with females as to picture them from afar as abstractions of femininity. It was a gentler & more innocent age &c., & I was a creature of that time.)

"I would, but I'm afraid he'd sting me," she said. "The sting of a daddy-snail is mortal harsh, so 'tis said."

"Really?" I leaned closer to see this prodigy for myself. "Who says?"

"Those families as raise the virgin missy-horses to ride or hunt," she replied. "Will you help me?" She asked with imploring eyes & prayerful hands, to such effect as only a thirteen-year-old girl can have on the heart-strings of a pigeon-chested boy of fourteen who has been watching her from afar and is eager to impress.

"Certainly I shall help!" I agreed, nodding violently. "But because it stings, I must take precautions. Would you wait here and stand vigilant watch over our escaped prisoner? I shall have to fetch suitable tools with which to fetter the suspect while we escort him back to jail."

She nodded her leave & I departed in haste, rushing up the lane towards home to borrow certain appurtenances from our own out-building. I fetched heavy gloves & fireplace tongs, the better with which to grasp a snake-tongued tentacular horror; and looking-glass, paper, & pencils with which to record it. Then I rushed back to the graveyard & arrived quite out of breath to find Hetty waiting complaisantly near our target, who had moved perhaps a foot in the intervening quarter-hour.

I wasted no time at all in plucking the blasphemous mollusk from its stony plinth with tongs and gloves. As I lifted it, the creature stabbed out with a sharp red spike which protruded from the point of its shell: I was heartily glad for my foresight. "Where do you want me to take it?" I asked my muse. I gave the cone a sharp shake & the red spike retracted, sullen at being foiled.

Hetty clapped delightedly. "Follow me!" she sang, & skipped away between the gravestones.

Of course I knew the front of her parents' house on Waterman Street, but I felt it unwise to show any sign of this. I allowed Hetty to lead me through the boneyard & along a grassy path between ancient drystone walls to the alley abutting the back of her family home. There was a tall wooden gate, and beyond it a yard and stables. I was preoccupied with carrying the cone-shell at arm's length, for its homicidal rage had not escaped my attention. Periodically it shivered & shuddered, like a pot close to boiling over. Being thus distracted I perhaps paid insufficient attention to the warning signs: the flies, the evident lack of labour applied to cleaning the back stoop, & above all the sickly-sweet smell of rotting meat. "Come inside," Hetty said coyly, producing a key to the padlock that secured the gate. "Bring Peter with you!"

She opened the gate & nipped inside the yard. I followed, barely noticing as she secured the portal behind me with hasp & cunning padlock. "Come to the stable," she sang, dancing across the cobbles despite the pervasive miasma of decay that hung heavy over the yard like the fetid caul of loathsome exudate that hovers above the body of a week-dead whale bloating in Nantucket sound during the summer months. "Let me show you my darling, my one true love!" As she said it, the cone in my tongs gave a quiver, as of rage—or mortal terror. As it did so I gagged at the stench inside the yard, & my grip loosened inadvertently. The snail-thing gave another ferocious jerk, then slipped free! It caught the end of my tongs with one sucker-tipped tentacle, uncoiled to lower itself to the decaying straw-strewn cobbles below, then let go before I could respond. Hetty gave a little shriek of dismay: "Oh, the poor little man! Now the others will eat him alive!"

For what happened next I can only cite my callow youth & inexperience in exculpation. I panicked a little, tightening my grip on my tool as the deadly giant snail turned around as if assessing the arena in which it found itself. I took a step backwards. "What is going on?" I demanded.

The singular snail reared, point uppermost, as if tasting the sour & dreadful air. A host of small tentacles appeared around its open end, and it began to haul itself on suckers across the decay-slicked stones, proceeding in the direction of the stable doors & the darkness that I could even then sense lurking within.

Hetty smiled—a horrid, knowing expression, unfit to grace the visage of a member of the fairer sex. "The daddy-snails and the missy-horses dance together & dine, and those that survive join in matrimonial union to become a mummy-horse," she intoned in a sing-song way, as if reciting a nursery rhyme plucked from the cradles of hell. "*My* mummy-horse rests yonder," she said, gesturing at the decaying stable doors, slicked with nameless dark fluids that had been allowed to dry, staining the wood. "Would you like to see my mummy?"

I felt faint, for I knew even then that something terrible born of an unfathomable madness had happened here. Heartbroken—for there is no heartbreak like that of a fourteen-year-old lad whose muse reveals feet not of clay but of excrement—I nevertheless gathered my courage and stood my ground. "Your mummy," I said. "You do not speak of Mrs. van t'Hooft, in this case?"

She shook her head. "My *mother*—" she pronounced the word strangely—"is sleeping in the stable with mummy-horse. Would you like to see her?" A horrid glow of anticipation crept into her cheeks, as if she could barely conceal her eagerness to cozen me within.

I wound up the reins of my bravery to the breaking-point & tightened my grip on the fire-tongs. They felt flimsy & intangible in my grasp: oh for the shield and sword of a Knight of the Round Table! My kingdom for a charger & a lance, or even the cleansing flare of a dragon's hot breath! "Show me to your mummy-horse," I told Hetty, thinking myself brave & manly & willing to face down monsters for a young man's apprehension of love: thinking that whatever this monster was, I should have the better of it.

More fool I!

They do things differently in East Sussex, or so I gather. My informant in this matter is Greg Scullery, and the nature of the difference is a leisurely lunch at a country pub in place of a hasty sandwich break snatched at one's office desk in Central London.

I am initially worried about Greg's willingness to down a pint before lunch, but by the time our food arrives and we've cleaned our plates my worries evaporate—assisted by Greg's smooth transition onto lemonade and soda, albeit replaced by new worries about what we're going to find down on Edgebaston farm. Because Greg has got that disturbing snail-shell, and with the fresh context provided by the Lovecraftian confessional in the EQUESTRIAN RED SIRLOIN dossier, I'm going to have a hard time sleeping tonight unless I successfully lay that particular ghost to rest.

"It's not a horse, let's get that straight," Greg explains between bites of a disturbingly phallic sausage. "It's not *Equus ferus caballus*. It might *look* like one at certain points in its life cycle, but that's simple mimicry. Not Batesian mimicry, where a harmless organism imitates a toxic or venomous one to deter predators, much as hoverflies mimic the thoracic coloration of wasps, but rather the kind of mimicry a bolas spider uses to lure its prey—using pheromonal lures and appearance to make itself attractive to its next meal. It's an equoid not an equus, in other words."

I suppress a shudder. "How do you tell a female unic—equoid—from a real horse?" I ask.

"Come along to Edgebaston Farm and I'm sure I'll be able to show you," he says, setting aside the plate holding what's left of his bangers and mash as he rises to his feet. "Have you read the backgrounder I sent your people? Or the infestation control protocol?"

"All I've read is H. P. Lovecraft's deathbed confession," I admit.

"His—" Greg stops dead in his tracks—"*really?*"

"His first flame, Hetty van t'Hooft, introduced him to, well, he called it a unicorn. That was right before his nervous breakdown." I shake my head. "Although how much stock to place in his account . . . "

"Fascinating," Greg hisses between his teeth. "I bet he didn't mention napalm, did he?" I shake my head. "Typical of your effete word-pusher, then, *not practical*. But we can't just call in an air strike either, these days, can we? And it'll take rather a lot of pull to convince the police to take this seriously. So let's go and beard Georgina in her den and see what she's hiding."

I follow Greg through the pub and back to his Land Rover. "Are we just going to go in there and talk to her?" I ask. "Because I thought uni— equoids—are a bit on the dangerous side? In terms of how they co-opt their host, I mean. If she's got a shotgun . . . "

"Don't you worry about Georgina, young feller me lad," Greg reassures me. "*Of course* she's got a shotgun! But she won't use it on us. The trick is to not look like we're a threat to her Precious, if she is indeed playing host to a fertile equoid. If we're lucky and she isn't under its spell things will go much more smoothly. So we're not going to mention the blessed thing at first. Remember she runs a farm? I'm just dropping in to check her hounds' vaccination records are up to date. While I'm doing that, you go and take a peek behind the stable doors with that phone camera of yours: then we'll put our heads together. Piece of cake!" he adds confidently, as he pushes the ignition button and his chariot belches blue smoke.

"Right." *You have got to be kidding*, I think, clinging to the grab bar for dear life as Greg shoves the Landy into gear and we bounce across ruts and into the road. "Do you have any idea of the layout of Edgebaston Farm? Because I don't!"

"It's jolly simple, Mr. Howard *sir*." (Oh great, now he's reverting to grizzled-veteran-sergeant-briefing-the-young-lieutenant mode.) "Edgebaston Farm covers two hundred acres on a hillside overlooking Howling, but the farm itself—the stables and outhouses—are in the shape of an octangle surrounding the farmhouse, which is a long triangle two stories high. The left point of the triangle, the kitchen, intersects the cowsheds which lie parallel to the barn, which is your target. They're all built from rough-hewn stone and thatched: no new-fangled solar panels here. It started out as a shed where Edward the Sixth housed his swineherds . . . "

"Yes, Greg, but what do I do if there's a fucking unicorn in the barn?"

"You run away very quickly, Bob. Or you die." He glances at me pityingly in the rearview mirror. (The Landy is sufficiently spartan that the reflector is an after-market bolt-on, with that imported American warning: *objects in mirror are closer than they appear.*) "Isn't that part of your job description? Screaming and running away?"

I am extremely dubious about my ability to outrun an equoid. "Uh-huh. The only kind of running I generally do is batch jobs on a mainframe." I clutch my briefcase protectively. "What we really need is a pretext to see what they're keeping in the stables, one that won't get us killed if you're right about what's lurking in the background." I pause for a moment. "They're a livery stable, aren't they? Do they do riding lessons?"

Greg nearly drives off the road. "Of course they do!" His beard emits an erratic hissing noise like a pressure cooker that's gearing up for a stove-top meltdown. After a moment I recognize it as something not unlike laughter. Eventually the snickering stops. "And if they're harboring equoids they won't be able to offer you a horse. But won't that take too long?"

"It had better not." I take a deep breath. "Okay, Greg. Here's our story: you're checking the dogs, and I'm your nephew from London. I'm working in Hastings for a month and while I'm there I want to learn to ride . . . "

How to describe the smell, the foulness, the louring portents of ominous doom that sent shivers of fear crawling up & down my spine? At the remove of a third of a century, that scene still retains the power to strike terror into my craven heart. I am no adventurer or chevalier; I am an aesthete & man of letters, ill-suited to the execution of such deeds. And though at fourteen I was in the flush of youth, and fancied myself as prepared for deeds of manly heroism as any other lad, I yet held a shadowy apprehension of that future self whom I was fated to become. I, Howard Phillips Lovecraft Esq., a man of contemplative & refined sensibilities born into a decadent latter age of feral brutes menaced by the unspeakable stormclouds of Bolshevism & Jew-Fascist Negro Barbarism sweeping the old countries of Europe, fear that I am nothing more than a commentator, doomed to write the epitaph to Western civilization that will, engraved upon its stony headstone, inform the scholars of a future age—should any eventually emerge from the imminent darkness—of the cause of its fate.

People like my Hetty. People who with the best will in the world would take in & nurture at their rosy breasts the suckling horror that in my fictions I have named Shub-Niggurath, the spawning goat of a thousand young, a shuddering pile of protoplasmic horror that mindlessly copulates with itself and, spurting, squirting, licking its own engorged & swollen *membrum* & *vulvae*, inseminates with sucker-adorned tentacles (each cup enfolding the horror of a barbed, venomous hook with which to tear the flesh to which it adhered) the inflamed orifices & lubricious, pulsing cysts from which the abnormal spawn gushes in ropy streams of hideous liquor—

Ia! How to describe the foul smell, the vile purulent exudate of eldritch emulsion bearing gelatinous bubbles of toadspawn from its body, did toadspawn only contain minuscule conical snail-bodies & horse-like bodies—not sea-horses yet, for no sea-horse has legs, but bodies *of the size of* sea-horses—Ia! The language of the English lacks a sufficiency of obscenity to encompass the monstrous presence of Hetty's "mummy-horse." It looked at me with liquid brown eyes as deep as any mare's, long-lashed & contemplative: some of them embedded within it, others extruded atop stalks like those of a vile unclean slug. It had mouths, too, and other organs, some of them equine, others bizarrely, inappropriately human. I am reduced to the muttered imprecations of the subhuman & deranged; unmanned & maddened by the apprehension of the limits of sanity imposed by witnessing the ghastly immanence of an Elder Thing come to spawn in a family stable in Providence.

Imagine, if you will, a huge pile of gelatinous protoplasm ten feet in diameter & six feet high! It bears the charnel stink of the abattoir about it, a miasma composed of the concentrated fear & faecal vileness of every animal it has consumed to reach its present size. *Their* bones & skulls lie all around, & it is evident from a swift perusal of the scene that though it started on its equine stable-mates, the "mummy-horse," gracile & pallid, with the calcified body of a spiral coned snail fused to the bone between its eyes, has absorbed its own legs, & head, & indeed every portion of its anatomy not dedicated to its adult functions of eating & spawning. There are *human bones* scattered around the festering midden in which it nests, for its virginal bellwether has with girlish laughter & coy blandishments tempted first the human members of the household & then every adult she can reach to enter the den of the monster. It is the way of this horror that when she finally ceases to provide it with a banquet of men & women, boys, girls, & babies, it will take her for its final repast, & subsequently it too will succumb, for its cannibal kind feed their spawn not with milk but with their own suppurating, foul flesh.

I know not from which hadean pit of horrors the spawn of the unicorn hail, but through subsequent years of research I have learned this much: that the cone-snails are the male offspring & the "horses" are female, and they tear & bite & eat anything that approaches them except a member of the distaff sex. They mate not by insemination but by fusion, the male adhering to the forehead of the female. Their circulatory systems fuse & the male is presently absorbed, leaving behind a spiral-fluted horn containing only the reproductive gonads, which presently discharge via the shared venous circulation. Once mated, the tiny "unicorns" tear into the maternal corpus, bloating their stomachs & growing rapidly; they squabble over the remains & spear one another & cannibalize their weaker siblings, until in the end the survivors—barely two or three in each litter of thousands—leave their charnel nursery behind & set out in search of a new virgin hostess who will take them in & groom & feed them. And so the wheel of death rolls ever on . . .

There is cold comfort to be drawn from the sure and certain knowledge that the correct way to deal with the problem you're facing in your job involves napalm, if you find yourself confronting a dragon and you aren't even carrying a cigarette lighter.

(Thumps self upside the head: Dammit, HPL's style is infectious! Let me try again . . . )

With Greg driving me—if not mad, then at least in the direction of a neck brace—I barely notice either the time or the road layout as we hurtle towards Edgebaston Farm. We arrive all too soon at a desolate drystone wall overlooking a blasted heath, judder across a cattle grid set between the whitewashed gate posts, and embark on a hair-raising hillside descent along a poorly-maintained driveway that ends in a yard surrounded by mostly-windowless outbuildings that look like the mediaeval predecessors of World

War II bunkers. It is not remotely like any of my preconceptions of what livery stables should look like—but then, what do I know?

Greg pulls up sharply and parks between a Subaru Forester covered in mud to the door sills and a white BMW. I do a double-take when I spot the concealed light-bar of an unmarked Police car on the BMW's rear parcel shelf. I remember what Greg said about the Edgebastons supplying the local cops with horses for their mounted police. Back home in London they're more interested in flying squirrels—Twin Squirrel helicopters, that is—but I guess here in Ruralshire they still believe in a cavalry charge with drawn batons and added eau de pepper spray. Or maybe the Chief Constable rides with the local Hunt. Either way, though, it's a warning to me to be careful what I say. In theory my warrant card is supposed to compel and command the full cooperation of any of HMG's servants. In practice, however, it's best to beware of local entanglements . . .

Greg marches up to the farmhouse door and is about to whack it with the knurled knob-end of his ash walking stick when it opens abruptly. The matronly lady holding the door handle stares at him, then suddenly smiles. "Greg!" she cries, not noticing me. I take stock: she's fortyish, about one-sixty high and perhaps seventy kilos, and wears jeans tucked into green wellies with a check shirt and a quilted body-warmer, as if she's just stepped in from the stables. Curly black hair, piercing blue eyes, and the kind of vaguely familiar facial bone structure that makes me wonder how many generations back it diverged from the royal family. "How remarkable! We were just talking about you. Who's this, are you taking on work-experience trainees?"

I emulate lockjaw in her general direction, it being less likely to give offense than my instinctive first response.

"Georgina," says Greg, "allow me to introduce my colleague—"

"Bob," I interrupt. Georgina darts forward, grabs my hand, and pumps it up and down while peering at my face as if she's wondering why water isn't gushing from my mouth. "From London." It's best to keep introductions like this as vague as possible.

"Bob," she echoes. To Greg: "Won't you come in? Inspector Dudley is here. We were discussing retirement planning for the mounted unit's horses."

"Jack Dudley's here, is he?" Greg mutters under his breath. "Capital! Come on, young feller me lad." And with that, he follows Georgina

Edgebaston as she retreats into the cavernous farm kitchen. "And how is your mother, Georgie?" Greg booms.

"Oh, much the same—"

"—And where's young Lady Octavia?" Greg adds.

"Oh, she's back at school this week. Jolly hockey sticks and algebra, that kind of thing. Won't be back until half-term." The lady of the manse calls across the kitchen: "Inspector! We have visitors, I hope you don't mind?"

"Oh, not at all." A big guy with the build and nose of a sometime rugby player rises from the far end of the table, where he's been nursing a chipped mug. He's not in uniform, but there's something odd about his clothing that takes me a moment to recognize: boots and tight trousers with oddly placed seams, that's what it is. He's kitted out for riding, minus the hard hat. He nods at Greg, then scans me with the professional eyeball of one who spent years carrying a notepad. "Who's this?"

"Bob Howard." I smile vacuously and try not to show any sign of recognizing what he is. There's another guy at the far end of the kitchen, bent over a pile of dishes beside the sink. I get an indistinct impression of long, lank hair, a beard, and a miasma of depression hanging over him. "Greg's showing me around today. It's all a bit different, I must say!"

"Bob's a city boy," Greg explains, as if apologizing in advance for my cognitive impairment. "He's working in town for a month, so I thought I'd show him round. He's my sister's eldest. Does something funny with computers."

That's getting uncomfortably close to the truth, so I decide to embellish the cake before Greg puts his foot in it: "I'm in web design," I say artlessly. "Is that your car outside?" I ask Dudley.

The inspector eyeballs me again. "Company wheels," he says. To Georgina, he adds, "Well, I really should be going. Meanwhile, if you can think of anyone who has room to take in our retirees I'd be very grateful. It's a problem nobody mentioned in the original scope briefing—"

"A problem?" Greg asks brightly.

"Jack's looking for a new retirement farm for the Section's old mounts," Georgina explains. "We used to take them in here, but that's no longer possible."

"Old mounts?" I ask.

My obvious puzzlement gives them a clear target for a patronizing display of insider knowledge. "Police horses don't come cheap," Greg explains. "You can't put any old nag up against a bunch of rioters." (The inspector nods approvingly, as if Bexhill-upon-Sea might at any time to supply a rioter whose average age is a day under seventy! Horses v. wheelchairs . . . ) "They have to use larger breeds, and they have special training. And they don't stay in service forever—in at six, retired by sixteen. But that's relatively young to retire a horse, so the number of stables who can handle an ex-police mount is relatively small."

"We used to take them in until suitable new owners could be found," Georgina explains, "but that's out of the question now—we're at full occupancy. So I was just explaining to the inspector that while I can help him find a fallback, I can't take Rose and Oak when they reach retirement next month." She smiles politely. "Would you care for a cup of tea?"

"Don't mind if I do!" Greg chortles. I nod vigorously, and refrain from paying obvious attention as the inspector makes his apologies and slithers out of the kitchen. I'm a good boy; I pretend I don't even notice him eyeballing the back of my neck thoughtfully from the doorway. Ten to one he'll be asking questions about me over Airwave before he gets back to the local nick. Let him: he won't learn anything.

"So why can't you take the police horses?" I ask as disingenuously as possible, while Georgina fusses over kettle and teapot. "Are you full or something?"

Greg spots my line of enquiry and provides distracting cover: "Yes, Georgina, what's changed?" he asks.

She sighs noisily. "We're out of room," she says. "Leastwise until we can empty the old woodshed out and get it ready to take livestock instead." She turns to the guy at the sink: "Adam, would you mind taking your clettering outside, there's a good lad? Mr. Scullery and I need a word in private."

Mr. Miasma rises and, wordlessly but with misshapen stick in hand, heads for the door. "I came to check the hounds' vaccination log book was up to date," Greg begins, "but if there's something else you'd like me to take a look at—"

"Well, actually there is," says Georgina. "it's about the stables." She's wringing her hands unconsciously, which immediately attracts my attention. "And those damned land snails! They're getting everywhere and I really can't be doing with them. Ghastly things! But it's mostly the new police mares.

Jack convinced me to take them in for early training and breaking to saddle, but they've been an utter headache so far. "

"New mares," echoes Greg. I'm all agog, but as long as Greg is doing the digging I see no reason to interrupt. "What new mares would these be?"

Georgina sighs noisily again as she picks up the kettle and fills the teapot. "Sussex Police Authority's Mounted Police Unit, operating out of the stables in St. Leonards, is in the throes of phasing out all their medium-weight mounts and replacing them with what they call Enhanced-Mobility Operational Capability Upgrade Mounts, or EMOCUM—god-awful genetically engineered monstrosities, if you ask me, but what do I know about how the police work out their operational requirements?" She puts the kettle down, then dips a spoon in the teapot and gives it a vigorous stir. "So it's goodbye to Ash and Blossom and Buttercup, and hello to EMOCUM Units One and Two, and if it *looks* like a horse and *acts* like a horse—most of the time—then it's a horse, so it needs stabling and currying and worming and training, stands to reason; but if you'll pardon my French, this is *bullshit*. Unit Two tried to eat Arsenic, so I have to move him out of the stable—"

"What? When was that? Why didn't you call me?" demands Greg. His beard is quivering with indignation.

Georgina rolls her eyes, then opens a cabinet and hauls out a double handful of chipped ceramic mugs. "You were attending to a breech delivery, one of old Godmanchester's Frisians as I recall. Melissa sent Babs instead and she patched him up—"

"Why would you leave arsenic lying around in a stable?" I ask, finally unable to contain myself. "Isn't that a bit risky?"

Two heads swivel as one to regard the alien interloper. "Arsenic is Octavia's horse," Georgina explains, her voice slow and patient. "A seventeen-year-old bay gelding. He used to belong to Jack's mounted unit but they put him out to pasture two years ago. Sixteen-and-a-half hands, police-trained, perfect for an ambitious thirteen-year-old."

I'm blinking at this point. I recognize "police," but the rest of the words might as well be rocket science or motorbike internals for all I can tell. All I can work out is the context. "So he's a horse, and he was attacked by one of these EMOCUM things?" I ask. "Was that serious?"

"It tried to *eat* him!" Georgina snaps. I recoil involuntarily. "It has *canines!* You can't tell me that's natural! It's messing with the natural order of things, that's what it is. Amos was right." She gives the tea another violent stir, then sloshes a stream of orange-brown liquor into the mugs—one of those breakfast blends with more caffeine than espresso and a worrying tendency to corrode stainless steel—and shoves them at Greg and myself. (Americans think we Brits drink tea because we're polite and genteel or something, whereas we really drink it because it's a stimulant and it's hot enough to sterilize cholera bacteria.) I accept the mug with some trepidation, but it doesn't smell of sheep-dip and my protective ward doesn't sting me, so it's probably not a lethal dose. "Babs stitched him up, but we can't get him to go anywhere near the stable now—he panics and tries to bolt."

"Where are you keeping him for the time being?" Greg asks, with the kindly but direct tone of a magistrate enquiring after the fate of a mugger's victim.

"He's in the south paddock while I sort out getting the woodshed refitted as a temporary stable, but there's damp rot in the roof beams. And we had to move Travail and Jug-Jug, too. Not to mention Graceless, Pointless, Feckless, and Aimless, who are all under-producing and their milk is sour and they won't go anywhere near the yard. It's a disaster, except for the cost-plus contract to look after the new Units. An absolute disaster! For two shillings I'd sell them to a traveling knacker just to get rid of them. But that'd leave Jack in the lurch, and the police with nowhere to put the other six they've got coming, and we can't be having that, so think of England, say I."

Greg takes a swig of rust-colored caffeine delivery fluid: the beard clenches briefly around it, then swallows. "Well, I suppose we'd better take a look at these EMOCUM beasties. What do you think, young feller?"

"I think that'd be a very good idea," I say cautiously. My head's spinning: Georgina has swapped out the game board from underneath our original plan—and what the *hell* are the police playing at? "Then I think we'd better go and have a word with Inspector Dudley. I have some questions for him, starting with where he got the idea of re-equipping the mounted unit with equoids . . ."

To paraphrase the stern & terrible Oliver, I beseech you, Robert, in the bowels of Christ, think it possible that you may be mistaken about unicorns. They are an antique horror that surpasses human understanding, a nightmarish reminder that we are but swimmers in the sunlit upper waters of an abyss & beneath us in the inky darkness there move monsters that, though outwardly of fair visage, harbor appetites less wholesome than Sawney Bean's. As Professor Watts reminds us, fully three-quarters of life's great & bounteous cornucopia consists of parasites, battening furtively on the flesh of the few productive species that grace creation. It is true that some of these parasites are marvelously attuned to the blind spots of their hosts; consider the humble cuckoo & the way its eggs, so different in shape & color from those that surround them, are nevertheless invisible to the host that raises the changeling in the nest. Just so too do unicorns exploit our beliefs, our mythology, our affection for our loyal equine servants! But their fair visage is merely a hollow mask that conceals a nightmare's skull.

I knew none of that as I stood in that terrible courtyard, feet braced uncertainly on slime-trailed cobblestones slick with the mucilaginous secretions of the flesh-eating snails, facing the darkness within the gaping jaws of the stable with only a pair of steel tongs in my hand—and the looking-glass I had fetched with some vague, childish idea of sketching the details of the snail's shell to compare with the encyclopedia in my grandfather's library. Standing there in that revelatory moment of which I have dreamed ever since, I knew only Hetty's blasphemous grin, the slithering horror of the tentacular mollusk as it fled towards the stables, and an apprehension of the greater nightmare that lurked beyond that shadow'd threshold.

But I was not unarmed! A stack of chopped lumber lay beneath a roof at one side of the barn, & the yard was strewn with moldering hay. I strode across, trying not to look within those horrid doors, & seized a slender branch that had been left intact, presumably as kindling.

"What are you doing?" demanded Hetty: "Won't you go inside right away? Mummy-horse needs help!"

"It's all right," I consoled her; "but I need to see what I'm doing if I am to help her." And with that facile reassurance I scooped up a handful of straw & used my handkerchief to bind it around the stick. Then I strode to the sunlit corner of the yard & pulled out my glass, bringing it to a focus on the straw.

Hetty stared at me oddly, then retreated to the barn door, her hips swaying lasciviously as she beckoned. There was, I recall, a sultry smile on her lips & a glazed & lustful expression that I, in my juvenile naïveté, barely apprehended was contrived to be seductive. As she stepped backwards into the shadows she raised her petticoats, revealing far more leg than common decency normally allowed in those days. I shuddered. "Won't you come with me?" she sang.

The tip of my wand erupted with a pale glow. I breathed on the straw until it caught. I found myself wishing I had some tar or paraffin; with barely a minute until it burned down, I knew I had scant opportunity. I stepped toward her, a steely resolve in my chest propelling me forward even though my knees nearly knocked together & my teeth clattered in my head. "I'm coming, dear," I said as Hetty retreated further into darkness, lifting her dress over her hips. She wore—pardon me for the nature of this confession—nothing beneath it, but was naked as the day she was born. Livid bruises studded her pale thighs, some of them circular, with puncture marks at their centers, scabbed-over wounds that hinted at unholy practices. No dance of the seven veils was this, but rather the puppet-show of a diseased and depraved imagination, seeking to corrupt & abuse the feeble-minded & weak-willed & lure them to a fate of unspeakable moral degeneracy.

The choking air within the barn reeked of overpowering decay, tempered by a musky odor that set my loins aflame despite my terror. I saw a lamp hanging from a nail just inside the door. Seizing it, I hastily applied the torch (fading to embers even then) to the wick, and just in time: for it caught. I raised the lamp & wound the wick up until it flared, & forced myself to look past Hetty— shamefully naked now, thrusting her hips towards me & supporting her uncorseted bosom with both hands in a manner transparently calculated to attract my attention—to behold the benthic horror of the angler fish lurking half-unseen in the twilight, dangling its shapely lure before me—its chosen prey!

This abomination stared at me with those glistening, liquid horse-eyes & woman-eyes: and it repeatedly coiled & recoiled tentacles like those of the Pacific octopus. Mouths opened & closed as those muscular ropes twitched & slithered around Hetty's feet. "Do you want me?" her sweet soprano offered, even as a pink-skinned tentacle with fewer suckers than most spiraled around her left leg, questing & climbing. "Mummy-horse says don't be afraid!" The pink & blindly questing *membrum* passed the level of her knees. "Mummy says she would like to speak with you, in a minute, through my mouth—" The tentacle's blind head (the *hectocotylus*, as I later identified it) reached between her buttocks from behind. Pulses shivered up it from stem to tip as she opened her cloacal passage to receive it with a sigh. Her knees flexed towards me, baring her naked womanhood, as her weight collapsed onto that vile and corrupt pillar of muscle. It supported her fully: her eyes rolled back in her head as she fainted. "*Howard*," said another's voice, speaking through her throat. "*Come to me & join in precious union with this mating body, for your arrival has been prophesied by the ancients of our kind & you will be a fitting adornment to my reign.*"

"Wh-what are you?" I asked, mesmerized—I was, as I have said, but a youth: I had never seen a woman's secret parts before, & even in the midst of this terrible *wrongness* I was excited as well as afraid—for it did not occur to me then that my very soul was in immediate danger.

"*We are Shub-Niggurath*," said the cyclopean nightmare that spoke through Hetty's vocal cords; "*we come from your future & it is prophesied that you will become one with our flesh.*"

Hetty's body now began to rise, legs straightening. Her arms rose too, outstretched and imploring towards me. Her neck righted itself & her eyes opened. "Howard?" she said in her normal voice. Then in the voice of Shub-Niggurath: "*Mate with us & give us the gift of your seed.*" Then again: "Howard? Something is wrong! I'm afraid . . . "

I stepped closer, mesmerized. Then another step. By the light of my raised oil lamp I beheld tears of blood weeping from her eyes. By my every inhalation I could perceive (from among the overwhelming, choking midden-stink of the stables) a peculiar stench emanating from her skin in place of the normal fragrance of the fairer sex. "Isn't this your mummy-horse?" I asked, driven by a cruel impulse: I wanted to touch her, I wanted to open myself to experiences I as yet had no understanding of: powerful emotions drove me on, no longer pure and holy terror but now tempered with an admixture of feral lust. "Isn't *this* what you want?"

"She hasn't done this to me before—" Shub-Niggurath: "*Take the gift we place before you, boy. Lose yourself in the flesh of Hetty van t'Hooft & revel in the pleasure & ecstasy of the union of bodies & souls! Join us, join us, join us!*" I saw the thick column of cephalopodian flesh pulsing behind & within her, operating her skin like a hellish glove puppet, & I slowly realized: this thing, this hideous monster that spawned endlessly in the filthy darkness of the family stable, was *hollowing her out from the inside*! It meant to use her as a lure, just as the angler mercilessly impales a fly on a barbed hook—& I was the juicy trout in its sights! The musky scent hanging all around made my heart beat faster & brought premature life to my youthful manhood, but *even then* I recognized that to succumb to such an unholy lust was a mistake I could ill afford to make.

Even so, I took another step forward. It was to nearly prove my undoing, for I had paid scant attention to the spawn that surrounded us, lurking in the far corners of the barn. But the spawn had begun to close in, ready to resume tearing at the flesh of their progenitor, and now by pure mischance I brought my shod foot down on an over-eager unicorn. It was a perfect miniature pony perhaps a hand high at the hock, sporting a viciously sharp horn an inch long. It screamed in a high-pitched voice & I slipped, falling to one knee. I looked up, straight at Hetty's female parts, & saw then what had been hidden in waiting for me: a livid appendage, either vastly expanded from her natural organ (like the *clitoris* of the spotted hyena) or worse, an extrusion of Shub-Niggurath itself, capped with the concentric circular jaws of a lamprey, alternately gaping open to bite & snapping closed with vile frustration, streaked with blood & mucus, pulsing as it quested blindly from its vulval nest to seek my face—

I screamed & threw the oil lamp. Then I pushed myself to my feet & fled. Fiery stabbing pain lanced through my hand; I glanced down & saw that I had been stung by the lance of a small snail-cone. The agony was pure & excruciating, & as breathtaking as a hornet sting. I caught my breath & screamed again, then stumbled backwards. Hetty was still upright, but quivered from head to toe in a quite inhuman manner, which I now know to be death spasms, like those that are seen when a felon is being hanged. Blood trickled from the sides of her mouth & from her ears now, as well as from the sides of her twitching eyes. The vileness that supported her skin now ate at her innards with its concealed radulae. But even as it consumed her & tried to extend its tentacles towards me, the spreading pool of oil from the lamp reached a half-collapsed bale of hay that lay beside a bloody exposed rib cage (whether of man or beast I could not tell, in the depths of my torment).

"*We will be back*," the horror gurgled through her dying larynx: "*and we will have you in the end!*"

The flames caught as I stumbled away, cradling my burning, wounded hand. I remember naught of the next two weeks but nightmares, but I was later told I lay febrile & unconscious & shuddering on the edge of death's dark cliff. Thereafter, whenever I was introduced to a member of the fairer sex who might flirt with me or whisper sweet nothings, all I could see was the husk of my Hetty, impaled and half-eaten on the tentacle of a nightmare from the far future, even as she whispered chilling blandishments to me; and all I could think of was the thing that lay in wait for me, & what the Beast had said at the end.

Not until I met the blessed Sonia was I was even partially healed of the wound in my soul that the *unicorn* inflicted. Even today I am only half the man that I might have been had I not met the abomination in the stable. And this is why I urge you not to write lightly of the four-legged parasite that preys upon our instinct to protect & cherish the fairer sex. They are a thing of unclean & blasphemous appetites that preys upon the weak & foolish & our own intrinsic tendency towards degeneracy & self-abuse. Worse still, they harbor a feral intellect *and they plan ahead*. They *must* be destroyed on sight! Otherwise the madness & horror will breed, until only darkness remains.

· · ·

After we drain our mugs of tea, Georgina shepherds us out into the farmyard to show us Lovecraft's Nightmares: Police Rapid Pursuit Edition.

I am actually quite apprehensive at this point, you understand. I've read enough of old purple-prose's deathbed confessions to Robert Bloch to be aware that unicorns are very unpleasant indeed. Even making allowances for Hipster Lovecraft's tendency towards grisly gynophobic ranting, Freudian fever-fantasies, and florid exaggeration, we're clearly about to meet something deeply creepy. Greg, for his part, is suitably subdued: even his beard hangs heavy, as if it senses a thunderstorm-drenching in the offing.

Only Georgina carries on as if everything is normal, and she at least has had time to get accustomed to the idea that there might be something nasty in one of the outbuildings. (Or standing next to the woodshed in a blanket with police high-visibility markings and a baton slung from the saddle. Whatever.) Also, Georgina has an ace up her sleeve—or maybe a baronetcy. She's clearly of such rarefied breeding that she feels no need to take shit from anyone. If you live in Ruralshire, England, you meet people like this from time to time. Their blood runs blue with self-confidence. Where ordinary folks enjoy messing around with flower beds, these folks open their garden to the Queen one weekend a year. The garden in question is probably one that their sixteen-times-great grandfather received as grace and favor after unhorsing an uppity duke during some battle everyone except mediaeval historians have forgotten about. If you catch them ranting about immigrants, chances are they're talking about those nouveaux-arrivistes, the Windsors. They dress in patched jeans, cable-knit sweaters, and green wellington boots; drive muddy Subarus or Land Rovers; own entire counties; and reduce police superintendents and MPs to helpless displays of forelock-tugging obeisance via some kind of weird reality distortion field.

Which probably makes Georgina the ideal person to look after a couple of fractious, under-trained, EMOCUM Units: because she takes no shit from anyone or anything, parasitic alien horrors from beyond spacetime included.

"I say! You there! EMOCUM Unit One! Stop trying to eat the vet at once! It's rude!"

A stable is a stable is a stable, except when, instead of regular horses, it contains carnivorous Furies with glowing blue eyes—in which case, the wooden partitions are reinforced with welded steel tubes, the brightwork on the bridles is made of machined titanium, and it stinks like the carnivore enclosure at a zoo where they've been feeding the lions and tigers rotten offal laced with laxatives. The stench when Georgina opens the side door makes my stomach heave, and I have to stand outside and take a few deep breaths before I can dive into the miasma. Suddenly the legend of the labors of Hercules—and the cleaning of the Augean stables—makes perfect sense to me.

When I manage to get my rebellious gastrointestinal tract under control, I step into a scene worthy of a Hieronymus Bosch triptych. It's like a stable, only reinforced, and equipped with devices that might in any other context be taken as instruments of torture, or at least evidence for the prosecution in a really serious animal abuse case: heavy shackles chained to concrete pillars, buckets of bloody intestines surrounded by clouds of buzzing flies, the omnipresent stench, humming fans and fluorescent lights. There are two horses present, one of whom appears to be leaning over the side of his stall and nibbling on Greg's beard with intent to be over-familiar, if Greg's indignant whimpering is taken into account. But then they notice my arrival. Both heads turn to focus on me. And I freeze, because they're not horses.

Being the object of attention of a pair of equoids—pardon me, Police EMOCUM Units—is a chilling experience. Have you ever been to a zoo or wildlife sanctuary and attracted the attention of a lion, tiger, or other big cat? You'll know what I'm talking about. Except equoids are horse-sized: two or three times as heavy as a (thankfully extinct) saber-toothed Smilodon, four times the weight of a modern Bengal tiger. They aren't quite in maximum-size Tyrannosaur territory, but they're not far off, and they're hot-blooded carnivores. When they focus on you, you simply know that they're wondering how you'll taste. It's a shuddery sensation deep in your gut that makes your balls try to climb up into your belly and hide (if you're male), and your ringpiece contract (regardless of sex). As they look at me I freeze and break out in a cold fear-sweat. They freeze too, heads pointing at me like gun muzzles.

Lots of details come into focus: they have no horns. Their eyes are slightly too close together, moved frontally to give them better binocular vision than any normal horse. Their nostrils and mouths look normal at first, but then one of them wrinkles its lips and I see fangs, and the edges of the lips retract much further than is natural for a grass-eater, revealing dentition more like something out of a nightmare concocted by H. R. Giger than anything a horse doctor might recognize. Oh, and the eyes? I mentioned that they're blue, and they pulse, but did I remember to say that they glow?

Resting on a stand next to one of the stalls is what passes for a saddle— one with a steel roll cage with wire mesh front and sides, and a police light bar on the roof. Obviously, riding an EMOCUM Unit is not a happy-fun experience. In point of fact, they exude danger so strongly that I'm wondering why the police didn't ask the saddlery to add machine gun mounts to the rider's safety cage—it couldn't be any less subtle.

"Who the fuck are they planning on deploying these things against?" I ask hoarsely; "An invading Panzer division?" Visions of the carnage after Dudley deploys his EMOCUMs for crowd control at a friendly away match overload even my normally-overactive sense of humor. These beasts are no laughing matter: you don't mock a main battle tank, either.

"Grrrrr . . . " rumbles equoid number one, inquisitively sizing me up for elevenses.

"I can't be sure," Georgina says thoughtfully, "but if I had to guess, I'd say they'll come in right handy when the illegal immigrants and bloody hippies in Brighton rise up to burn all us right-thinking people down. But in the meantime, they manufacture a hundred pounds of shit every day, and I can't even compost it!"

"Bastards," Greg mumbles indistinctly, clutching his chin.

"Do pay attention, I told you not to stand too close!" Georgina shakes her head. "They were a lot smaller when Jack dropped them off," she adds. She bends down, indicating knee height. "Still vicious as a bear-baiting dog, but at least they were manageable then."

"How long ago was that?" I ask, getting an even worse sinking feeling.

"About three weeks ago. They grow fast."

**MINISTRY OF DEFENCE**
**SECRET**
**Procurement Specification: M/CW/20954**
Date of Issue: July 1st, 1940
<u>Requirement for:</u>
Charger, Heavy Cavalry Mounted:

Must replace existing mounts for Horse Guards and other remaining Army Cavalry operational units.

Mounts should be between 13 and 17 hands high, weight 650–900 lbs, broken to saddle.

*Desirable characteristics:*

Mounts should exhibit three or more of the following traits:

• Endurance in excess of 6 hours at 30 miles/hour over rough terrain (when ridden with standard issue saddle, rider, and kit)

• Endurance in excess of 30 minutes at 50 miles/hour on metaled road surfaces (when ridden with standard issue saddle, rider, and kit)

• Ability to see in the dark

• Ability to recognize and obey a controlled vocabulary of at least 20 distinct commands

• Invisible

• Bulletproof

• Carnivorous

• Flight (when ridden with standard issue saddle, rider, and kit)

State of requirement:
Unfilled

**CANCELLED April 2nd, 1945**

Reasons for cancellation:

(1) Impending replacement of horse-mounted cavalry in all future operational roles,

(2) Procurement and initial delivery of AEC Centurion Mk 1 Universal Battle Tank supersedes requirement M/CW/20954.

Sitting back in the passenger seat of Greg's Landy, I massage my head as if I can somehow squeeze the aching contents into a semblance of order. "That was not what I was expecting."

"I've known Georgina since she was a wee thing, competing in dressage." Greg huffs for a moment, then produces a pencil case from the pile of debris under the driver's seat. He extracts what I initially mistake for a gigantic brown spliff. Then he produces a weird multitool, with which he amputates one end, and sets fire to the stump of the reeking roll-up.

"Careful with that spliff, Eugene," I start before I realize that it's actually a cigar, so old and foul that I cough up half a lung before I get the door open and scramble out. "Jesus, Greg!"

"Sorry, young feller." He's clearly unrepentant, but I notice that he's sucking on it like it's an asthma inhaler, and his other hand—the one grasping his walking stick—is shaking slightly. "I needs my weed after witnessing a scene like that."

"I am going to report this," I say heavily. "The EMOCUMs, I mean. This is way above my pay grade."

"Oh, really? I have never in all my days seen one of you people back down from a red-eyed abomination with too many tentacles—"

"You've never seen us pick a fight with the police, either, have you?" I snap at him, then walk it back: "Sorry, but we work with the boys in blue, they're not normally the subject of our investigations." I cough, trying to clear my lungs. They've been taking a battering today, between the fetid aroma of carnivore shit in the stables and Greg's diesel-smoked stogie. "Let me think. Okay, the EMOCUMs aren't going anywhere right now. They can wait for backup." (Assuming they're not actually one of our projects—one that Iris and I don't know about because we're not cleared for it. Crazier things have happened. In which case double-checking everything discreetly is the order of the day.) "But, hmm. What do you know about Inspector Dudley? Because he's the next link in the chain back to wherever they came from . . . "

The beard shakes like a bush in a hail-storm. "Sorry, lad, I can't help you. I deal with the likes of Georgina, or Sergeant Irving who runs the station stables in East Grinstead, not the organ grinder hisself."

"Who was conveniently present when we came to visit, and then slipped out. Oh shit."

"What's the matter?" Greg takes another epic lungful of vaporized bunker fuel, then his eyes wrinkle up. "You don't think—"

"When you sent a memo requesting a liaison visit from Capital Laundry Services, how exactly did you go about it?" I ask. "Did you by any chance ask someone else to send us an email? Someone like—"

"Gosh, now that you mention it—" He jabs his fingers knuckle-deep into his beard and tugs—"I'd ha' asked the fragrant Melissa to write to you! But I don't see—"

I roll my eyes. "Does Melissa have a boyfriend, by any chance?" I ask. "Who might happen to be a member of the local constabulary? Or a father or mother or sister or best pal from her school days, or something? Someone who might know about the EMOCUM procurement program?"

"Ooh, I see where you're going." Greg sighs, then reaches down and stubs out his vile cigar on the underside of his boot. He bags up the remains: I shudder slightly and climb back into the Land Rover's passenger seat. My stunned nasal passages can't make any sense out of their environment, but my pupils dilate and my pulse slows thanks to all the nicotine hanging in the air. "You're wondering where it all came from?"

"That's the key question," I agree, fastening my seat belt and pulling the door closed. "Where did Jack Dudley procure a handful of juvenile unfertilized female unicorns? And who put the idea into his head? Come to think of it, where are those bloody snails coming from? There's got to be a fertilized female in the sessile spawning phase of its life cycle somewhere hereabouts. It's one thing for some idiot mounted police officers to think that Baba Yaga's herd will be good for crowd control duty, but if there's any leakage—"

"I've got an inkling, but you're not going to like it. This could be the start of a large-scale outbreak," Greg says heavily. "A full infestation. Equoids are r-strategy spawners—" he catches my blank look and backs up. "Most organisms follow one of two types of reproductive strategy, young feller. K-selection—few offspring, lots of energy devoted to keeping them alive: that'd be us shaved apes, heh. And then there's r-selection: spew out thousands or millions of tiny spawn and hope some of them survive. Equoids do that, they spawn like pollen, or flies, or frogs . . . but they're also parasites that co-opt a host species and use it to nurture their brood. Anyway, the things in the barn, the adult sterile females, they're unusual. And that's a warning flag. If I had ter guess what's going on I'd figure there's a breeding queen out there who's worked out a low-cost way to help her spawn make it to adulthood. Something new, not just a single hypnotized girlie. Not sure what, but if we don't find the queen in time we're going to be neck deep in unicorns in these parts." He trails off into a grim and thoughtful silence.

"I'm going to phone home for support," I say. "Then while they're getting the circus loaded, I'll go pay the inspector a visit. I want to establish the facts on the ground, find out where he's getting the horses from."

"And what then? If you can't figure it out?"

"Whatever I find, I'm going to boot it upstairs then take a back seat. Like I said, this is well above my pay grade . . . "

I'm fairly sure that by this point in my report, you, gentle reader, will doubtless be raising a metaphorical hand, because the questions have been piling up thick and fast and you are reaching the end of your patience. So let me try to set your mind at ease with a quick run through the list of Frequently Asked Questions:

**Q**: Unicorns? Are they really this bad?

**A**: Yes. I wish I was making this up. Unfortunately old HPL's experience in his childhood sweetheart's back yard is about par for the course where those creatures are concerned. We are not in Unicorn School™: The Sparkling territory here. Or even My Little Pony. (Well, except for the Magic bit.)

**Q**: But what about the unfertilized ones?

**A**: It's the parasitic life cycle in a nutshell. Parasites, especially those with complex gender dimorphism and hypercastrating behavior (that diverts a host species' reproductive energies in service to their own goals) generally have some interesting failure modes. Among unicorns, if they don't mate young they tend not to mate at all—it's kind of hard for a foot-long cone snail to climb onto the forehead of something that resembles a carnivorous horse, isn't it? Especially without getting eaten. So the female grows to adult stature but is infertile. What you get is an equoid: an obligate meat-eater the size and shape of a horse, with the appetite of three Bengal tigers and the table manners of a hungry great white shark.

**Q**: Why haven't I heard about these already?

**A**: You probably have. There are plenty of legends about them—the mares of Diomedes, the Karkadann of Al-Biruni, the herd of Baba Yaga—but they don't show up very often in the historic record. This is because people who try to domesticate mature equoids usually end up as equoid droppings.

**Q**: But what if you get them young?

**A:** Good thinking! If you get them young you can semi-domesticate them. But to get them young, one has to locate a fertile adult in the sessile, spawning phase. (And survive the experience.)

**Q:** What are we supposed to do about them?

**A:** The sterile adult equoids themselves aren't necessarily a problem: they're basically dangerous but dumb. Georgina Edgebaston has been training two of them as EMOCUM Units, but they're under control. As long as she doesn't do anything stupid, like hitting one on the forehead with a giant venomous land snail, she's probably got them contained. I'm much more worried about where they're coming from. Equoids don't generally gambol freely on the Southern downs, because the trail of half-eaten children and screaming parents tends to attract attention. This means that there's probably a nest not too far away. And it is absolutely essential that Greg and I locate the nest so that it can be dealt with appropriately.

**Q:** The nest—what does "appropriate" mean in this context?

**A:** Let me give you a clue: I start by making some phone calls which, by way of a liaison officer or two, induce the police to evacuate the surrounding area. Then what appears to be a Fire Brigade Major Incident Mobile Command HQ vehicle arrives, followed by a couple of pumps which are equipped to spray something rather more toxic and inflammable than water. Finally, the insurance loss adjusters turn up.

That's what is supposed to happen, anyway. If it doesn't, Plan B calls for the Army to loan us a couple of Apache Longbow helicopter gunships. But we try not to go there; it's difficult and expensive to cover up an air strike, and embarrassing to have to admit that Plan A didn't work properly.

**Q:** You said equoids aren't intelligent. But what was all that Yog-Sothoth stuff HPL was gibbering about at the end? What about the mummy-thing—

**A:** Don't you worry your little head about that, it's above your security clearance. Just take it from me that everything is under control!

. . .

After I phone Iris, to deliver the unwelcome news that this smoke appears to be associated with an ignition source, I continue my investigation by going in search of the inspector.

There is an old Victorian police station in East Grinstead, complete with the antique blue gas lamp over the main entrance and a transom window (no longer used) just inside the lobby door. It also has a pair of tall gates that open into a courtyard. It currently does duty as a car park for the uniform cars and snatch vans, but one wall of the courtyard is still lined with stalls for the horses, and they're in good repair.

I am a civilian, casually dressed. I do not enter the courtyard, but instead walk up to the public entrance, past the information posters (COPPER THEFT: ARE YOU TAKING YOUR LIFE IN YOUR HANDS?), and in to the reception area.

I stand in front of the desk for almost a minute as, sitting behind it, PC McGarry (number 452) explains the correct protocol for helping scallies fall downstairs in a single-story nick to Constable Savage, a high flyer who has been transferred from Birmingham to expand out his résumé and help bring policing in Ruralshire into the twentieth century. From his shifty, impatient posture it's obvious that he'd much rather be out on the street monstering chavs. Finally I grow impatient and clear my throat. PC McGarry continues to drone on, obviously enjoying his pulpit far too much to stop, so I pull out my warrant card.

" 'Ere, Fred, don't you want to ask this gentleman what he's—" Savage's eyes are drawn to focus on my card wallet and his voice slows to a stop. "What?"

"Bob Howard, Capital Laundry Services. I'd like to speak to Inspector Dudley." I smile assertively. Cops are trained to de-prioritize the unassertive. "If I can have a minute of your attention?"

PC McGarry glances at me, clearly irritated by the interruption. "We don't need any dry-cleaning—"

I focus on him, borrowing the full weight of my ID card's glamor: "Never said you did, mate. I need to see Inspector Dudley. As soon as possible, about a matter of some considerable importance. He won't thank you for delaying me."

McGarry doesn't want to yield, but my warrant card isn't going to let him ignore me. "What's it about?" He demands.

"DEFRA want all the vaccination records for the new rides he's commissioning for the mounted unit," I deadpan. "I just missed him at Edgebaston Farm, but the long arm of the livestock law has a way of catching up."

McGarry eyeballs me dubiously, then picks up the phone. "Inspector? There's a Mr. Hobson from DEFRA down here in reception, says he needs to talk to you—something about Edgehill Farm? No sir, I don't. Yes, sir." He puts the phone down. "You. The inspector will be down in a minute." He points at a chair. "Have a seat."

"Don't mind if I do." I ignore the chair and walk over to the noticeboard, to read the public information posters while I wait. (STRANGER DANGER! and REMEMBER TO LOCK YOUR DOORS AND WINDOWS: RURALSHIRE REGULARLY GETS VISITED BY TOWNIE SCUM vie for pride of place with IS YOUR NEIGHBOR EMPLOYING ILLEGAL IMMIGRANTS? It's like their public relations office moonlights from the BNP.)

I don't have to wait long. I hear footsteps, and as I turn, I hear a familiar voice. "You. What do you want?" Inspector Dudley looks somewhat more intimidating in uniform, and he was plenty intimidating before. He stares down at me coldly from behind the crooked bridge of his nose. Luckily I don't intimidate quite as easily as I used to.

"Perhaps we should talk in your office?" I suggest. "It's about the EMOCUM Units you've requisitioned." I'm still holding my warrant card, and I spot his eyes flickering towards it, then away, as if he's deliberately pretending he hasn't noticed it.

"Come with me," he says. I follow the inspector past the reception area and into the administrative guts of the station: whitewashed partition walls, doors with numbers and frosted glass panels. The cells are presumably downstairs. He heads through a fire door and up a narrow staircase, then into an office with a single desk, a couple of reception chairs, and a window with a nice view of the Victorian railway station frontage. "Who are you, and what are you doing with that old fraud Scullery?" He demands.

"I'm from a department you probably haven't heard of before and mustn't speak about in public." I shove my card right under his nose, where he can't miss it. "The, ah, EMOCUM Units were not authorized by my department. As we have licensing and oversight responsibility for all such assets, I want to know where you heard about them, where you got them from, and how you're planning on deploying them." I smile to defuse the sting of my words. "All the paperwork and oversight reports you were making an end-run around have just caught up with you, I'm afraid."

"But the—" He sits down behind the desk, and something in his expression changes. A moment of openness passes, like the shadow of a cloud drifting across a hillside. His expression is closed to me. "What are you doing here? Everything is under control. There's no problem at all."

"I'm afraid I disagree." I keep my warrant card in plain sight. "Tell me: where did you source the EMOCUM Units? And who came up with the proposal in the first place?"

"It seemed like a goodoodood . . . " His eyes are drawn to the card, even as he stutters: "It was my idea! I'm sure it was. It seemed like such a good idea, so it must have been mine, mustn't it?"

"Really?"

"I thought-ought—" he's fighting the geas on the warrant card as hard as I've ever seen from anyone—"we-e should have a major capability upgrade! Yes, that's it! The Air Support Unit get all the attention these days, them bleeding flyboys! Their choppers can't manage more than four hours' airborne patrol time in twenty-four hours, and you can't use 'em to make arrests or for crowd control, but they suck the money out of my budget. It's us or them! Do you have any idea how much it costs to operate a mounted patrol? To put eight officers on saddles at a match I need twelve mounts because horses aren't like cars, oh no they're not—cars don't suffer from poll evil or grass sickness—and I need at least as many officers as rides. We need civilian auxiliaries because stables don't muck themselves out, on-call vets, and six bales of hay a day. Not to mention the ongoing maintenance bill and depreciation on our motorized horse box and the two trailers, plus the two pickups to tow them."

He begins to foam at the mouth as he winds up to a fine rant about the operational costs of maintaining a mounted unit: "In the last financial year my unit cost nearly six hundred thousand pounds, in order to provide three thousand six hundred mounted officer-shifts of six hours' duration each! The fly-boys cost eight hundred and twenty in return for which we get eleven hundred airborne hours a year and they are weaseling to have my unit decommissioned and our entire budget diverted to running a second

Twin Squirrel. I ask you, is that a good use of public funds? Or, I ask you this in all sincerity, would it be better spent on equipping our mounted officers with the best steeds for getting the job done?"

The inspector slams his open palm down on his desk, making the wilting begonias jump. He glares at me, the whites of his eyes showing. His pupils are dilated and his cheeks are flushed. He gasps for breath before continuing. I watch, somewhere midway between concern and fascination. This is not business as usual. What I'm witnessing is symptomatic of an extremely powerful occult compulsion that has been applied to the inspector. His words are powerful: I feel my ward vibrating on its chain, warming up painfully where it lies close to the skin of my chest.

"It is our duty to protect the public and enforce the Law of the Land! Duty, honor, courage in the service of Queen and Country! The Queen! I swore an oath to uphold the Law and I will uphold it to the best of my ability! That means enhancing our capabilities wherever possible, striving for maximum efficiency in the delivery of mounted police capabilities! We're barely keeping our heads above water in the face of a deluge of filth coming up from the big cities, darkies and gippos and yids and hippies and, and—Law and Order! We must maintain Law and Order! The Queen is coming! The Queen is coming! Equipping my division with EMOCUM Units will result in a great increase in our speed, mobility, and availability to enforce the Law of the Land in the coming strugg-ugg-uggle against-against the forces of darknesssss—"

His left cheek begins to twitch, and he starts to slur his words. I hastily flip my warrant card upside-down, then pull it back. The pressure from the ward pushing against my sternum subsides as inspector Dudley slumps sideways, gasping for breath. For a few horrified seconds I'm afraid he's having a stroke: but the twitching subsides and he straightens slowly, leaning against the back of his chair.

"What was I saying?" He asks, looking around hesitantly, as if puzzled to find himself in his own office. "Who are you?"

I take a gamble and hold up my warrant card: "Bob Howard. Who I am is unimportant. You don't need to know. But—" I lean forward—"where did you get the EMOCUM Units from?"

"I, I asked around." He sounds vague and disoriented. "They were just there when I needed them." His eyes roll back momentarily: "Sent by the

Q-Queen," he adds conversationally, in a tone that makes my skin crawl. He abruptly blinks back to full consciousness: "I don't know where they came from. Why?"

I try again. "Where did the requirements document for the EMOCUM Units come from?"

"I, uh, I've got it somewhere. There." He points a shaky finger at the grubby PC on one side of his desk. "It took ages to write—"

"Would you mind opening the file for me?" I ask. "In Word." I tense up, then haul out my phone as he reaches for the keyboard. It's a flashy new Palm Treo, and I've got some rather special software on it that can scan for certain types of occult hazard (in conjunction with the special-issue box of bluetooth-connected sensors in my jacket pocket). I punch up a utility (icon: this is your brain on drugs, superimposed over a red inverted pentacle) and aim my phone's camera at his monitor as he pokes unsteadily at the keyboard.

The inspector is so oblivious to my presence that I might as well not be here—except when he's forced to pay attention to me by my warrant card. This is, in itself, a serious warning sign: he's meant to be one of ours, dammit, and a Laundry warrant card is enchanted with a geas that compels subjects to recognize the lawful bearer as a superior officer in their own department. (Except within the Laundry itself, obviously—otherwise we could get into horrifying recursive loops of incrementally ascending seniority: imagine the consequences if this affected Accounting and Payroll!) Anyway, if Jack Dudley's mind is shying away from me, then someone has probably tried to install countermeasures against other adepts' glamours. Which is really bad news, because unicorns don't do subtle like that.

So I'm paying more attention to my phone—which is scanning for threat patterns—than to the screen the inspector is squinting at, when the familiar logo of Microsoft Office flashes up for a few seconds, followed in rapid succession by a window onto hell.

**MINISTRY OF DEFENCE**
**SECRET**
**Procurement Specification: R/NBC/6401**
Date of Issue: April 2nd, 1970
<u>Requirement for:</u>

Proposal for Strategic Deterrent (class: alternative, non-nuclear)
Type: Anthropic Eschatological Weapons System, Air-Dropped

In view of the increase in popular support for the Campaign for Nuclear Disarmament, it might at some future date be deemed politically expedient for the UK to decommission its strategic nuclear capability in the form of the Resolution-class submarines and their associated Polaris A3 SLBMs. However, the UK's strategic deterrent posture must be maintained at all costs in the face of the Soviet threat.

Chemical weapons are not fit for purpose in this role due to difficulty in ensuring delivery in adequate quantity. Conventional biological weapons (weaponized smallpox, plague, etc.) are not fit for purpose in this role due to the impossibility of immunizing the entire UK population and also of guaranteeing efficacy in the face of an enemy biowar vaccination defense program.

This requirement is for proposals for unconventional macrobiological weapons that are suitable for delivery by manned bomber/stand-off bomb (e.g. Blue Steel), which must undergo post-delivery amplification and inflict strategic-level damage on the enemy, which are not susceptible to pharmaceutical or medical defense, and which are self-limiting (unlikely to give rise to pandemics).

Desirable characteristics:
AEWS-AD must be storable, long-term (temperature/humidity constraints: see schedule A) without maintenance for up to 5 years.

Must be containerized in suitable form for mounting and delivery via WE.177 bomb casing or alternative equivalent structural unit compatible with bomb bay and wing hardpoints on all current operational strike aircraft and the forthcoming Panavia Tornado IDS.

Must be sterile/non-self-replicating or must replicate once, giving rise to infertile spawn.

A strike delivering a single AEWS-AD must be capable of depopulating a first-rank capital city (population ablation coefficient: at least 25%) in less than 24 hours.

AEWS-AD should additionally have three or more of the following traits: carnivorous, venomous, mind-controlling, invisible, pyrogenic, flying, basilisk gaze, bullet-resistant, radiation-tolerant for up to 20,000 REM (single pulse) or 1000 rads/hr (fallout), invulnerable to class 6 or lower occult induction algorithms.

State of Requirement:
Null and void.

**CANCELLED April 3$^{rd}$, 1970**
by Order of Cabinet Office in accordance with recommendation of SOE (X Division) Operational Oversight Audit Committee

Reasons for cancellation order:
The risk of unintentional containment violation or accidental release during the life of such a weapons system is low but nevertheless unacceptably high.

Deployment of AEWS-AD, whether in accordance with legal national command authority or otherwise, would constitute a violation of Section IV.B of the Benthic Treaty. This would deliver a guaranteed casus belli to BLUE HADES.

The probability of BLUE HADES retaliation for a violation of S.IV.B leading to the total extinction of the population of the British Isles is 100%, within the limits of error. This applies to the Republic of Ireland, the Isle of Man, the Channel Isles, and Great Britain and Northern Ireland. But this is not the limit of the extent of casualties from such a strike.

The probability of a BLUE HADES strike resulting in the total extinction of the entire human species exceeds 50%.

It is considered that attempting to develop a weapons system in the same category as AEWS-AD is so inherently destabilizing that such activities may be seen as justifying a pre-emptive strike by other human governments. Far from securing the realm against the threat of Soviet nuclear aggression, this project might actually provoke it.

(Addendum: SOE (X Division) OOAC recommends that it would be in the nation's best interests if all the members of the committee that drafted R/NBC/6401 could be induced to take early retirement; thereafter they should be denied access to sharp instruments. We are serious about this. Not since RARDE's BLUE PEACOCK project of 1954 to 1958 has this oversight body been asked to evaluate such an unedifying, if not actually insane, proposal.)

While I'm glancing down at my smartphone's two-inch screen, inspector Dudley is helping me with my enquiries by opening up the Microsoft Word file containing the requirements document he remembers drafting for replacing the Sussex constabulary's remaining horses with unicorn spawn—sorry, EMOCUM Units. What could possibly go wrong with that?

Well, I find out as the file opens. Because Jack Dudley may remember writing it, but unless he's a skilled battle magus as well as a police inspector, he sure as hell didn't write the Visual BASIC macro that fires up the instant the text appears on screen.

It all gets very messy, very fast.

Because I'm staring at my Treo instead of the PC, I feel it vibrate in my hand as the screen flashes red: THAUM OVERFLOW. I hear a loud whining buzz from the desktop, like a mosquito the size of a Boeing 737, then the unmistakable screech and click of a hard disk shredding its platters: funny, I didn't know you could do that in software any more, I just have time to register, as my ward heats up painfully. A second later, Inspector Dudley moans. It's a familiar, extremely unwelcome kind of moan, and it sends shivers up my spine because I hear it late at night when I've been working overtime, on a regular basis. It's the inhuman sound of a soul-sucked husk that hungers for brains, just like the Residual Human Resources on the Night Watch.

This isn't the first time I've seen this happen. You wouldn't believe the scope for mischief that the Beast of Redmond unintentionally builds into its Office software by letting it execute macros that have unlimited access to the hardware. I remember a particular post-prandial PowerPoint presentation where I was one of only two survivors (and the other wasn't entirely human). However, this is the first time I've seen a Word document eat a man's soul.

I straighten up and take two steps backwards. The doorknob grinds against my left buttock: dammit, why couldn't the door open outwards? I raise my phone and hastily stroke the D-pad, tracking down the app I need . . . and the fucking thing crashes on me. Oh joy. PalmOS: always there right when you least need it.

The inspector is rising from his seat, clumsily pushing himself away from his desk. His movements are jerky if not tetanic. He moans softly, continuously, and as he turns his head towards me I register the faint greenish glow in his eyes. I grasp the doorknob and freeze, a train-wreck of thoughts piling into each other in my mind's eye.

The CrossRail commuter train leaving Platform One is scared shitless because it's trapped in an office with a genuine no-shit mind-eating zombie, and the law of skin-to-skin contagion means that if the thing touches me I stand to literally lose my mind. This is mitigated slightly by the Sprinter to Crewe on Platform Two, which reminds me that I'm wearing a ward, so I might actually survive, if the zombie doesn't simply double down on my throat or drag me in front of the PC monitor, which is presumably still displaying the same summoning grid that ate Inspector Dudley's mind. The Gatwick Express steaming along the track between Platforms Four and Five at a non-stop ninety miles per hour sounds its air-horn to remind me that if I cut and run I will be leaving the aforementioned zombie unrestrained in a target-rich environment, namely a Ruralshire cop shop where their policy on undead uprisings is to order out for beer and pizza while watching *Shaun of the Dead* in the station house lounge once a month. And the train speeding out of Trumpton with a cargo of cocaine (thank you, Half Man Half Biscuit) is merely there to remind me that I still don't know where the spawn of the unicorn are coming from . . .

"Raaarrrrh." Inspector Dudley clears his throat and takes an experimental lurch towards me. I dodge sideways behind his desk, pocketing my phone in order to free up a hand, and simultaneously yank the power cord out of the back of his PC. (Rule 1: preserve the evidence, even if the hard disk has self-destructed and the file you want is loaded with a lethally contagious mind-virus.) "Raaargh?" The inspector calls.

I pick up the heavy old tube monitor and heft it in both arms. "Catch," I say, and throw it at the zombie.

I wince at the crunch as twenty kilos of lead-glass CRT impacts the already-broken nose. Dudley staggers and topples backwards: zombies, possessed as they are by a minimally-sentient and rather corporeally challenged Eater, tend not to be fast on their feet. Then the door opens.

"Inspector?" chirps Constable Savage. Then he spots me. I see the ten-watt bulb flicker fitfully to life above his head as he instantly jumps to the wrong conclusion. "Oi! You! Get on the floor! You're nicked!"

He begins to draw his baton as I back away, around the desk, closer to the window. I reach for my warrant card: "You're making a mist—"

"GRAAAAH!" Roars the inspector, rising from the floor, CRT clutched to his chest. Oh look, he appears to have a nose-bleed, gibbers the shunting engine in Siding Three. You're in for it now.

"Inspector?" Asks Constable Savage, "are you all right?"

There's a chime from my pocket, the beautiful sound of a Treo announcing that it has rebooted successfully. "He's a zombie!" I yell. "Don't let him touch you! His touch is death—"

Ignoring me, Savage reaches out towards the inspector: "'Ere, let me look at the no-o-o—"

Great. Now I'm facing two of them.

If my boss Angleton was here this wouldn't be a problem: one glance from him is sufficient to quell zombie brain-eater and union convenor alike. But I'm not some kind of superpowered necromancer, I'm just a jobbing sysadmin and applied computational demonologist. About the only card I'm holding is—

Well, it's worth a try.

I raise my warrant card and rehearse my rusty Old Enochian: "Guys! I am your lawful source of authority! Obey me! Obey me!" (Or words to that effect.) It's a horrible language, sounds like gargling TCP around razor blades. But it gets their attention. Two heads turn to face me. Their eyes glow even in daylight, the luminous worms of light twirling inside them. "Proceed to the stable block! Enter the first empty stall! Await your queen! Await your queen! Your queen is coming and she must find you there!" Then in English I add, "Law and Order! Law and Order!"

The last bit comes out like "lawn order," but repeating the catchphrase deeply embedded in what's left of the inspector's brain by the geas that had him in its grip seems to do the trick.

"Graah?" He says, with a curious rising interrogative note. Then he turns to face the door. "Ssss . . ." Clumsy fingers scrabble with the smooth surface of the old doorknob. The door inches open. I hope to hell nobody else is

of the old doorknob. The door inches open. I hope to hell nobody else is about to stumble into them on their way to the field-expedient cells. I really don't want this spreading any further. The fear-sweat in the small of my back is cold and slimy, and I feel faint and nauseous.

Constable Savage lost interest in his baton the moment he touched the inspector: I pick it up and follow them as they lurch and stumble down the staircase and out past the vacant front desk. As we pass the gents' toilet I hear a musical tinkling: Phew. Presumably that's McGarry on his break, in which case there may be survivors. With the odd moan, hiss, and growl, the two zombies cross the courtyard, lurching off the side of a parked riot van, and head towards an empty horse stall. I nip in front of them to unbolt the gate and open it wide. There's nothing inside but a scattering of hay, and the shamblers keep on going until they bounce off the crumbling brick wall at the back—by which time I have the gate shut and bolted behind them.

I pull out my Treo and speed-dial the Duty Officer's desk back at the New Annexe. "Bob Howard speaking," I say, "I'm in the Central Police Station in East Grinstead and I'm declaring a Code Amber, repeat, Code Amber. We have an outbreak, outbreak, outbreak. Code words are EQUESTRIAN RED SIRLOIN. I have two Romeo Hotel Romeo, outbreak contained, and a hot box on the second floor. I need plumbers, stat."

Then I head back up the stairs to the ex-inspector's office to secure the PC with the lethally corrupt file system, and await the arrival of the Seventh Cavalry, all the while sweating bullets.

Because I may have taken two pawns, but the queen is still lurking in the darkness at the edge of the chess-board . . .

**MINISTRY OF DEFENCE**
**SECRET**
**Procurement Specification: N/SBS/007**
Date of Issue: September 31st, 2002

Requirement for:
Proposal for system to support Special Boat Service underwater operations in the Arabian Gulf during Operation Telic.

S Squadron SBS, in accordance with orders from the Director Special Forces, is tasked with securing [REDACTED] on the coastline of Umm Quasr and Hajjam Island, and suppressing the operational capability of the Sixth Republican Guard Fast Motor Boat and Martyrdom Brigade to sortie through the Shatt Al-Basra and the Khawr az-Zubayr Waterway to threaten Coalition naval forces in Kuwaiti waters.

This requirement is for proposals for unconventional macrobiological weapons that operate analogously to the Ceffyl Dwr, Capaill Uisce and Kelpie of mythology. These organisms are amphibious but preferentially aquatic, carnivorous, aggressive, intelligent, and reputed to drag sailors under water and drown them. It is believed that with suitable operant conditioning and control by S Squadron troopers such organisms can provide a useful stand-off capability to augment the capabilities of underwater special forces operating in a dangerous high-intensity littoral combat environment . . .

State of Requirement:
Null and void.

**CANCELLED October 13th, 2002**
by Order of Cabinet Office in accordance with recommendation of SOE (X Division) Operational Oversight Audit Committee

Reasons for cancellation order:
1. Baby-eating aquatic faerie equines do not exist.
2. Even if they did exist, it is worth noting that Arab folklore and mythology does not emphasize fear of death by drowning; consequently the psywar potential of this proposal is approximately zero.
3. Operational requirement can be met through already-existing conventional means.
(Addendum: Going forward, SOE (X Division) OOAC recommends a blanket ban on all procurement specifications that involve supernatural equine entities (SEEs). For reference, see EQUESTRIAN RED SIRLOIN. This keeps coming up like a bad penny at least once every couple of decades, and it's got to stop.)

• • •

Forty minutes pass. I while away the time by making panicky phone calls to our INFOSEC desk—how the hell did that macro virus get into the file on the inspector's PC? I love the smell of an enquiry in the morning—while I wait in Inspector Dudley's office, sweating bullets. Finally I hear the heart-warming song of two-tone sirens coming down the high street. It's not the warbling war-cry of police blues and twos, but the regular rise and fall of a fire engine—which means my prayers have been answered, and the Plumbers are coming, in the shape of an OCULUS truck.

From the outside it looks like a bright red Fire Service Major Incident Command vehicle, but it's not crewed by Pugh, Pugh, Barney McGrew, Cuthbert, Dibble, and Grub—this one's occupants are the away team of twenty-one Territorial SAS, and they're more likely to start fires than extinguish them. I watch as it drives nose-first into the police station car park and stops. Doors open and half a dozen wiry-looking guys dressed head to foot in black leap out. They're armed to the teeth. One of them looks up at me and I wave. While I've been waiting I filled in the Duty Officer back at HQ with as much as I knew. Now Sergeant Howe and his men fan out and move through the nearly-empty police station. Two of them dash for the stall where I stashed the shamblers, carrying a field exorcism kit in a duffle bag. The others . . . I hear doors banging and much shouting as they go through the station like a tide of Ex-Lax.

I move to the desk and sit down behind it facing the door, making sure to keep my hands in view, and hold up my warrant card. I sit like this for approximately thirty seconds before it crashes open and I find myself staring up the business end of an MP5K. "Oops, sorry sir. Be right back." The MP5K and its owner disappear as I try to get my heart rate back down to normal.

Finally, after another minute, the door opens again—this time more sedately. "Hello, Bob!" It's Alan Barnes, chipper and skinny, with slightly hyperthyroidal eyes. He bounces into the room, head swiveling. "Nice pair of shamblers you've penned up down there. What do I need to know?"

Alan is a captain in that corner of the Army that we work with when this sort of situation comes up: namely one particular squadron of the Territorial SAS, a peculiar special forces unit composed of reservist veterans who have seen more and stranger things than most of their colleagues would credit with existing. His crew of merry pranksters are securing the premises as we speak. "There's a file on this computer," I say, patting the box on the desk. "You heard about the business in Darmstadt with the infected PowerPoint presentation?" He nods. "Well, there's a Word document with an infected startup macro on this thing's hard disk. Which it attempted to scribble on when the inspector—in the stables right now—tried to open it for me." He nods again, looking thoughtful. "This needs Forensics to go over it. We're looking for a requirements document which seems to have come out of nowhere, and which persuaded Inspector Dudley that it was all his own idea to replace the horses in his mounted unit with, ah, EMOCUM Units. Otherwise known as the subjects of EQUESTRIAN RED SIRLOIN."

Alan has a notepad. "How do you spell that?" He murmurs politely.

I fill him in as fast as possible. "DEFRA spotted it, there's an emergent cuckoo's nest down on Edgebaston Farm but the farm owner doesn't seem to be infected—" yet "—so I suggest once we've secured the station we rendezvous with Greg Scullery and proceed to the farm to conduct a full suppression. What remains after that is to—" my shoulders slump "—work out where the hell the brood-Queen's spawning-nest is, and take her out." I swallow, then continue: "Which is bound to be harder than it was in Lovecraft's day, if only because the thing has concealed its tracks well, and appears to be pulling the puppet strings of local Renfields like the Inspector. If it figures out we're coming it may be able to organize a defense. In the worst case scenario, East Grinstead is going up in flames. And that's before we get to the thorny question of where that demon-haunted requirements document came from."

Alan sits down on the wobbly swivel chair with no armrests. "I'm not familiar with, ah, EQUESTRIAN RED SIRLOIN," he admits. "I'll need to get clearance and then—"

We don't have time. On the other hand, ERS is barely classified at all. I pull out my briefing papers: "On my cognizance, and in view of the severity of the situation, with a class two Eater outbreak in train, I take full responsibility for disclosing EQUESTRIAN RED SIRLOIN. Or, at least, what I know about it," I add hastily. (Because if it is an inside job, (a.) I don't know enough to blow its cover, and (b.) it's just very publicly shat the bed, and whoever is running it is probably in for the high jump whatever I do. In other words, my and Alan's attempts at mopping up are unlikely to make the mess any worse.)

Alan raises an eyebrow. "Are you sure?"

I shrug. "It's classified MILDLY EMBARRASSING NO TABLOIDS. I'm sure they'll offer me a cigarette and a blindfold at the firing squad."

Alan nods and takes the papers. "Right," he drawls. What I'm doing is technically unauthorized, but my Oath of Office lets me get away with it without even a warning tingle. I'm pretty sure Iris will sign off on it when I file my report. And if not, I can't see the Auditors yelling at me for briefing my field support team. Then his eyes focus on the first page, and the list of decreasing classification levels, and the index of documents attached, and his eyebrows climb so high they nearly merge with his hairline. "Unicorns? Bob, what have you gotten us into this time?"

"I wish I knew, Alan. But they're not sparkly . . . "

*Ring-ring.* "Yes, who is that?"

"Greg? It's Bob here. Where are you?"

"I'm back at the office, sorting out some paperwork. Has something come up?"

"You could say that. Listen, can you meet me at the old police station? As soon as possible; it's urgent. There are some gentlemen I'd like to introduce you to. We want your input on operational planning."

"I—yes, I daresay I could do that, young feller. Is five o'clock too late?"

I glance at Alan. He nods, minutely controlled. "Five o'clock but no later," I say. We exchange pleasantries: "See you. Bye." I glance at my phone: it's ten past four. Back at Alan: "In my opinion, we're not ready to go public," I explain. "No point frightening the bystanders."

"Hmm." Alan gives in to toe-tapping and thumb-twiddling, impatient tics that seem to vanish whenever an actual operation starts. "Let's go over the map again, shall we?"

We've got an Ordnance Survey 1:12,500 spread out across the table in the antique briefing room. A couple of constables have shown up for shift change, and we've taken pains to explain the situation to them in words of one syllable: a chief inspector from a mega-city like Hove or Brighton is on her way in to take control of the policing side of the operation, but I gather she's caught up in traffic, so for now we're relying on Sergeant Colon to keep everything looking vaguely like business as usual. Alan's driver finally un-wedged the OCULUS truck from the cobblestoned yard, and it's parked outside. The contingency story for the reporter from the Bexhill Babble is that we're conducting a joint major incident containment exercise simulating an outbreak of anthrax on a local farm. Which is close enough to the truth to make what we're really doing look plausibly routine if not actually boring, so that when we get the officers of the law to cordon off Edgebaston Farm nobody will so much as blink.

The map is accurate enough to let Alan's merry headbangers lay down a barrage of covering fire if that's what it takes. I point out the various elements of the farm. "The barn: there are two or more EMOCUM Units stationed there. Carnivorous, fast, hopefully hobbled. The woodshed: has damp rot in the roof beams. Currently full of lumber, they're planning on putting the cows in it when they get round to emptying it. South field: two horses, four cows (one of them with a wooden leg). Basically harmless. The EMOCUM Units are distinctive—the eyes are too close together and glow blue, and their fur is white—"

"Don't you mean they're cremelo? Or at least perlino?" Alan raises an eyebrow at me.

"Whatever." I shrug. "They look like horses, walk like horses, have breath like a leopard. Oh, there'll also be saddles with roll cages stashed in the barn—"

"Roll cages?" His eyebrows are really getting a workout today.

"With wire mesh reinforcement, yes, to stop the nice horsies eating their riders. Seriously, if any of your men see a horse-shaped object that can't instantly be confirmed safe, they should shoot to kill. We're dealing with the Hannibal Lecters of the riding world here."

"Moving swiftly on—" Alan points at the farm house itself. "What can you tell me about this structure?"

"Oh, that. Farmhouse, repeatedly built, razed, re-built, extended, and re-razed ever since the twelfth century. A.D., not B.C., though you might be hard put to tell. Main entrance opens into a porch with boot racks, closet to the left, huge farm kitchen to the right, passage leading into house at the back, and no, before you ask, I didn't get a good look inside. Why do you—"

"People," Alan interrupts conversationally. "Who am I dealing with here?"

"Apart from Georgina Edgebaston herself, who is apparently as well-connected as a System X exchange, I have no idea. Farm hand called Adam, daughter called Octavia who's at boarding school, I gather. We'll really need to pick Greg's brain. And the—no, police records'll be no use." I shrug. (The Edgebastons are the sort of people the police work for, not against. And you don't keep files on your boss if you know what's good for you.) "If we can get anything useful out of Inspector Dudley—"

Alan shakes his head. "Sandy confirms the exorcism worked, but both victims are in bad shape. The ambulance should be arriving at St. Hilda's any time now." He glances at his wristwatch. "Okay, so it's a centuries-old farmhouse. Which means any floor plan on file with the County planning office will be years or decades out of date, if they even bothered filing one in the first place."

"Why are you focusing on the farmhouse?" I ask, feigning casual interest.

He flashes me a smile. "Because if there's one thing all the unicorn legends are clear about, it's the little girl! The, ah, brood-queen's primary host. Do you know what boarding school Mrs. Edgebaston's daughter attends?"

I suddenly realize where he's going with this line of enquiry. "Let's find out, and confirm that she's really there." My phone's really getting a workout. I call the Duty Officer back at head office and pass the buck. (Let someone else fight their way through social services and school phone switchboards this afternoon.) "And let's hope there's no brood-queen to mop up. Ahem. So where are we going with this?"

"Here." Alan points at the various gates leading into the fields around Edgebaston farm. "First: I'm going to station police officers on all the B-roads leading past the fields. Cover Story Alpha applies and will justify the operation. The south field gate will also have two of my people, armed, in case of attempted equine excursions. I take your point about friend/foe discrimination. Secondly: OCULUS units one and two, accompanied by your tame veterinary inspector, will move in on the farmyard. Brick two will secure the exterior of the barn, brick three will take the other outbuildings, while the rest of us serve a search warrant on the farmhouse itself and conduct a room-to-room inspection." The SAS doesn't deal in fire teams and squads and platoons, it divvies up into bricks (more formally patrols) and troops and squadrons.

"Wait, you're pulling in a second OCULUS?"

Alan's cheek twitches. "After reading that file, I'd be happier to simply call in an air strike."

The office door opens and a familiar face appears: "Scary" Spice, whom I have worked with before, and who has a penchant for blowing stuff up. "Sir? The XM-1060s have arrived. Sergeant Howe has detailed Norton and Simms to load and fuse them, he wanted you to know they'll be safed but ready when you need them." He spots me. "Hi, Bob!" Then he ducks out again.

"What are they?" I ask.

Alan twitches again: "Thermobaric grenade launchers. Just in case."

Now my cheek twitches. It's a sympathy thing, triggered by my involuntary ringpiece clenching. "Is that really necessary?"

"I hope not, Bob. I hope not . . . "

Which is why, at a whisker after six o'clock in the evening, I come to be sitting in the front passenger seat of Mr. Scullery's Land Rover, which is bumping and jouncing across a pasture that clings precariously to the side of Mockuncle Hill. I am holding Greg's rifle for him because he is gesticulating wildly with both hands while trying to steer with his beard. The steering wheel, unaccustomed to such treatment, squeals and tries to escape every time we bump across a post hole. "Never heard anything like it!" He expostulates wildly: "Young Barnes is overreacting wildly."

"In case you hadn't noticed, he's running this show."

"In my day he was a wet-behind-the-ears cornet, young feller—"

I roll my eyes as the beard describes Alan's prehistoric sins, from back when dinosaurs roamed the earth and Greg was in the service. "Listen," I interrupt between tooth-rattling jolts, "let's just stick to business, okay?" I scan the field for alien life forms such as cows, three-legged or otherwise, and the retired police horses we've been told to expect here.

The sun is setting, behind the bulk of the hill. There's still light in the sky, but the shadows have become indistinct and hazy, and a golden glow washes out all contrast as it slowly dims towards full dark. The lights will be flickering to life on the streets in town. This is a really stupid time of day for us to be doing this, but Alan wants to get it underway ASAP, and will be turning up at the farmhouse door in another five minutes. Behind us, a jam sandwich has parked up across the lane, light bar flickering as the constables tape off the entrance to the field. Our job is to round up the local legal livestock and neutralize them safely so that Alan's merry men don't mistake them for equoids. Hence the tranquilizer gun and the vet.

(I also half-suspect that Alan has sent Greg and me on this wild horse chase to keep us out of his hair during the somewhat more fraught process of storming a farmhouse without killing the human occupants.)

I'm just checking the near-side wing mirror when my Treo rings. I glance at it: it's the Duty Officer back at HQ. My stomach flip-flops. "Howard here," I say.

"We have the information you requested about Octavia Edgebaston, sir. Sorry it's taken so long; we had to contact Social Services in East Grinstead out-of-hours to get the contact details for her school, then get the headmistress out of her dinner. Yes, we've confirmed that Octavia Edgebaston is boarding as St. Ninian's School this week and is currently at prep in room 207—" I breathe a sigh of relief "—but her younger sister—"

"What?" I yelp involuntarily. "Greg! You didn't tell me Georgina had another daughter!"

"—Is truant, she didn't show up for register this afternoon and they're extremely worried—"

"What other daughter?" The beard sounds puzzled, almost dreamy. "There's no other—"

"—Lucinda Edgebaston, class 2E at St. Ninian's, aged twelve. She hasn't signed out of the school, and they're re-running the CCTV over the gate now just to check, but she missed all her afternoon classes—"

"How far away is St. Ninian's from Edgebaston Farm?" I ask.

"Ten or eleven miles," says the DO. "To continue: they've notified the police in Hove and they're keeping an eye out for her. One-forty centimeters, long chestnut hair, about fifty kilos, probably wearing Saint Ninian's school uniform. She won't have gotten far—"

My heart is pounding and the skin on the back of my neck is crawling. I have a very bad feeling about this. "Please hold," I tell my phone. "Greg: stop. Stop." I thump the middle of the dash. Greg slams on the anchors so suddenly I nearly go through the split windscreen. As it is, the barrel of the rifle bashes my forehead. I'm doubly glad I made sure it was unloaded and safe when he gave it to me to hold. (No, really; there's a luminous pipecleaner going in through the barrel and out of the open breech, because self-inflicted head shots are so not one of my favorite things. Actually, I'm not sure how to load it in the first place—it can fire tranquilizer darts as well as bullets—but it's the thought that counts.)

The Landy squeals and slithers to a muddy standstill in the middle of the south field. "What is it, young feller?" Greg asks me.

"Greg, does Georgina have a husband?" I ask. It's an odd question, and as it slides around the back of my skull like a ping-pong ball I feel my ward warm against my collar-bone.

The beard looks puzzled. "I don't rightly—" he pauses "—no, no, that's not right." Another pause. "That would be Jerry, Gerald, I forget his name. Haven't seen him in ages; I suppose they divorced. And then there's Octavia and the other and young Ada."

"Ada? How old is Ada, Greg? Concentrate!"

"Ada's just a toddler, Bob. I think she's four—" The beard scrunches up in violent concentration. "What!"

The explosion is so sudden I nearly jump out of my seat. "What?" I echo.

"How could I forget them! Georgina is married to Harry and they have three daughters, Octavia and Lucinda and Ada! Named after her great grand-nan," he adds conversationally. "But, but—"

I'm on the phone to the DO. "Update: I'm seeing signs of a geas here. Localized amnesia, level four or higher. Locals have no or restricted memory of adult Harry Edgebaston and minor Ada Edgebaston. There may be other drop-outs." I glance in the wing mirror again: "Lucinda is out of the picture, but—fuck me, Greg, drive!"

OBJECTS IN MIRROR ARE CLOSER THAN THEY SEEM, and the pallid ghost of Death's own horse is cantering behind us with sapphire-glowing eyes that pulse hypnotically in the twilight. On its back there sits a saddle with roll bars and steel mesh grilles, the rider a small but indistinct figure standing in the stirrups within. The Landy's rear lights flicker red highlights off the point of the lowered lance that's coming towards us as the horse-thing screams a heart-stopping wail of despair and rage.

I drop the phone in my front pocket as Greg floors the throttle and the Landy roars in response, belching a column of smoke that would do justice to a First World War dreadnought. We rock and roll uphill, and the point of the lance rips through the canvas cover over the load bed, then tears away into the night with a snort and huff of equoid heavy breathing.

For an instant, the dash of the Land Rover glows blue-green with a ghastly imitation of St. Elmo's Fire. My skin crawls and the ward heats up painfully. Greg grunts with pain and the steering wheel spins. For a moment the

Landy teeters on two wheels, nearly toppling, but then he grabs the wheel with both hands and brings us back down on all fours with a crash.

I fumble with the rifle, yanking the safety cord through the barrel and barking my fingers painfully on the breech. "Ammo, Greg," I gasp.

"In the center cubby, young feller, between the seats. Don't bother with darts." I yank the lid of the compartment between our seats open and rummage around until I feel the oily-smooth metallic weight of an unboxed stripper clip—what kind of bloody idiot keeps loose rifle rounds rolling around his car?—and I somehow manage to reverse the gun over my right shoulder and get the open breech into a position where I can start feeding rounds in. They're the real thing, I hope, but unfortunately there are only five of them. And I can just glimpse a gray-white blur in the twilight at the other end of the field, getting itself turned round to take another run at us—this time a full-tilt charge.

You might think that a mounted cavalry horse charging with lance is a wee bit dated, and less than a match for a bolt-action rifle and a Land Rover. However, you would be very wrong. The thing at the far end weighs over a ton, and it's about to take a run at us at over fifty kilometers per hour. The field is small enough that it's less than a minute away, and when it hits all that momentum is going to be focused behind a tempered steel point. That's about as much energy as a shell from a Second World War tank gun carries: more than enough force to shatter the engine block of an unarmored Landy, and once we're immobilized it can dance around until we're out of bullets, then bite and trample us to death at its leisure.

I close the breech and work the bolt to chamber a round. "Park up and drop the windows. Gun's loaded."

"Easy, young feller." We judder to a halt again. Greg yanks the hand brake, then slides a bolt and the entire windshield assembly flops forwards across the bonnet. "Give me that."

I hand the rifle over. He takes it in both arms and leans forward, barrel pointing across the spare tire. The spectre in front of us turns to face us. The eyes flare, alternating hypnotically. I feel a wave of malevolent intent spill across us. Hocks contract and unwind like spring steel as the equoid launches itself towards us. The spearhead glitters in our headlights, seemingly aimed right in my face. "Think you can hit the rider?" I ask anxiously.

"Piece of piss—" Greg freezes. "Oh no," he breathes.

It takes me another second or two to register what he's seen—his eyesight is better than mine—and I do a double-take because the rider, hunched beneath that odd steel canopy, lance cradled under one elbow like a knight of old . . . the rider is too small. Dwarfed by her mount, in fact. Greg is paralyzed because he's just realized he's drawing a bead on Lucinda Edgebaston, age twelve-and-a-half, who should be in the school dormitory doing her prep rather than galloping across a muddy field on top of a carnivorous horror that is using her as a human shield—

A heartbeat passes.

"Give me that." I grab the gun barrel. Greg lets it go without resistance, and that in itself is terribly wrong. I shoulder the thing, unaccustomed to its weight and heft. I've done a basic long-arms familiarization course out at the Village, but for the actual range time we used SA80s. It's only by sheer chance that I once asked Harry the Horse to show me how to load one of these antiques. The equoid is expanding in front of me like an oncoming train wreck. I don't have time to check the sights.

I let my breath out slowly and squeeze the trigger, hoping I'll hit something. There's a crash and a bang, and a fully laden freight train slams into my right shoulder. Through the ringing in my ears I hear a wavering inhuman scream, too long-drawn-out for human lungs. Then another freight train slams into the side of the Land Rover, and there's a screaming of torn and twisted metal as the thrashing equoid crashes down on us and the Landy topples sideways onto the hillside.

What happens next is a confusing mess. I nearly lose the rifle. I find myself lying on the passenger door, still strapped in, with Greg lying across me. There's blood, blood everywhere, and animal screaming from outside the Land Rover's cabin. "Greg, move," I say, and elbow him. More blood: he head-butts my shoulder, and I have a horrible feeling that a human neck shouldn't, can't, bend that way. He is, at the very least, unconscious, and possibly in spinal injury territory. Shit. More hoarse screaming. A clanging double-thud that sends a shock through the chassis of the vehicle. I find the seat belt button and try to worm my way forward, through the gap between the open windshield and the roofline, bashing myself in the face yet again with a rifle barrel.

Getting out of a toppled all-terrain vehicle in the dark while a pain-crazed monster bucks and runs around you, occasionally lashing out with its hooves at the felled Land Rover that hurt it, is easier said than done—especially when you're covered in someone else's blood, in need of a change of underwear, and trying to keep control of an unfamiliar weapon. It's so much easier said than done, in fact, that I don't succeed. Or rather, I get my head and shoulders out, along with the rifle, whose bolt I am frantically working when My Little Pony finally notices I'm still alive. It gives a larynx-shattering howl of pure rage, bares a mouthful of spikes that would give a megalodon pause, and closes in for the coup de grace.

I mentioned the rifle, didn't I? And I mentioned that EMOCUM Units aren't the sharpest knife in the toolbox, too? Well, what happens next is about what you'd expect: it's messy, and extremely loud, and I nearly shoot my right ear off as Buttercup bends toward me and opens wide in an attempt to bite my skull in half. Then I have to duck backwards sharpish to avoid being crushed by a ton of falling burger meat.

(Moral of story: if you are a flesh-eating monster, do not let the chattering monkey insert a bang-stick in your mouth while you're trying to snack down on its brains. Seriously, no good will come of this.)


More confused impressions:

I'm out of the Landy, standing in the field, frantically looking around. (Two rounds left in the magazine and one up the spout.)

The EMOCUM has collapsed in front of the toppled Land Rover. Brains and other matter show through the back of its shattered skull. I dodge fangs like daggers, and inhale a fecal smell so rich and intense I have to pause to control my stomach. I glance in the roll cage. There is moaning, audible through the ringing in my ears, and I feel dizzy. I look closer. Movement. "Lucinda?" I call. "Lucy?"

She looks up at me, one arm bent back unnaturally, still gripping the shaft of the shattered lance: I can see bone. The expression on her face is no more human than her mount's: "Hssss . . . "

"Be right back," I say hastily, stepping away. I fumble for my phone, then speed-dial the last number—the Duty Officer. "Howard here." I briskly explain the situation. "Need medical support with exorcism kit, south field—minor with broken arm and possible demonic possession. Scratch that: probable. Oh, and it'll take the jaws of life to get her out of the saddle." I look around. "One probable adult fatality, cervical fracture, lots of blood."

As I feared, when Lucy hit the Landy with her pig-sticker, the impact had had the force of a light artillery shell. "One dead sterile adult Echo Romeo Sierra, one unaccounted for. I'm proceeding afoot and armed."

I look around in the dusk. I see an indistinct hump in the field about thirty meters uphill. A buzz of flies surrounds it, but it's no cow pat; it's the whole damn animal, disemboweled and half-eaten. I bite back a hysterical giggle. This operation has officially fallen apart.

See, the whole idea was to discreetly secure the barn and then search the premises, on the assumption that the EMOCUM Units would be at home. But it now looks as if there's a subtle and nasty amnesia glamor covering parts of the farm, nudging everybody to forget the existence of certain people who have softly and silently been stolen away, presumably because they have seen the boojum.

And now that I think about it, there weren't anything like enough officers hanging around the police station, were there? Not for a mounted unit that needs eighteen riders and a bunch of civilian auxiliaries, never mind the everyday foot and car patrols. There weren't enough folks around the farm, either, and come to think of it Greg's veterinary practice looked half-empty . . .

My skin crawls. Somewhere out in the gathering twilight an EMOCUM Unit is stalking human prey. And somewhere else—if only I could work out where!—the Queen is brooding.

I'm halfway up the south field, working my way towards the farm itself, when the sky above me flashes orange, reflecting a dazzling glare from ground level. A second later there's a hollow *whump* like a gas range igniting, and a hot blast of wind across my face. I go to my knees in a controlled fall, land on a cow pat, skid, swear, and faceplant. The explosion rolls up into an ascending fireball that lights up the grass in front of my nose before it dissipates.

I realize what's happening: Alan's men have made hard contact. There's a rattle of small-arms fire, then another of those gas flares followed by a gut-liquefying explosion. They must be the XM-1060s Scary was talking about, I figure. I stay down, but pull my phone up and speak: "Bob here. I'm still in the south field, and the balloon's gone up about three hundred meters north of my current location. Can you let OCULUS Control know

I'm out here?" I do not want to be a blue-on-blue casualty. I'm shivering as I speak, and feeling shaky and cold. I work my jaws and spit, trying to get the metallic taste of blood out of my mouth. I'm pretty sure it's Greg's blood. I feel awful about getting him into this, and about leaving him in the Landy.

"Patching you through right away," says the DO, and there's a click.

"Bob? Sitrep!" It's Alan, sounding sharp as a button.

"I'm lying low in the south field about three hundred meters short of the yard. Greg's down, the Landy is down, we nailed one target, there is an injured little girl in the wreckage." I lick my lips, then spit: "Suspect EMOCUM Two is on the loose with a rider, either adult male or juvenile female. There's a stealth glamor on the entire farm; you may not spot the Queen until you step on her." A horrible thought hits me. "The woodshed."

I put it together all at once. No sniggering now: Georgina was planning to clear the woodshed, but there's damp rot in the roof beams. And it hasn't been cleared. And the four-year-old is forgotten. And there's "—Something narsty in the woodshed," I hear myself saying aloud into the phone. "Wait for me before you go in!" I add hastily. Ada. Named for her great-great. Why should that resonate so—"Alan. Brick three. You sent them to search the outbuildings. Have you heard from them recently?"

"Yes, Bob," he sounds almost bored. "They report all's clear."

"There's a glamor!" I realize I'm shouting. "Are they in the woodshed?"

"I'll just . . . shit."

"I'm on my way," I hear myself saying. "Let your people know I'm coming from the south field on foot." It takes all my willpower to force myself to push upright onto my knees, then to raise one leg, and then the other until I'm standing. I am deathly afraid of what I'm going to find in the farmyard. One foot goes in front of the other. Clump, clump, squish, clump. The small-arms fire has stopped, but something ahead is on fire and the flames are playing hell with my night vision. A smell of woodsmoke drifts on the evening breeze, making my nose itch but partly masking the uncanny stink of the field.

I stumble towards the skeletal outline of a gate. It takes me a while to cover the distance because I keep stopping to peer around in the murk, rifle raised. If EMOCUM Unit 2 was in the field with me I expect I'd know about it by now, but you can never be sure. How do feral unicorns stalk their prey, anyway? Do they run in packs, like wolves, or are they ambush hunters?

Beside the gate I stumble across the disemboweled corpse of another cow; Graceless, I think, going by the prosthetic leg. It's upsetting. (You can tell I'm English by the way pointless cruelty to animals dismays me.) The gate itself is hanging open, the chain and padlock neatly fastened around its post. EMOCUM Units don't have hands, so that tears it—we're definitely dealing with ensorcelled human servitors here. And that implies a controlling intelligence, which in turn implies—

The upper story of the west wing of the farmhouse is on fire. The thatching on the roof is smoldering, and the bright light of active combustion is rippling out behind a row of windows. I see the silhouettes of men crouching in the shadows around the barn. A fire engine hulks in the entrance to the yard, around the side of the house. I stand up. My phone rings. "Yes?"

"Get down, idiot." Alan is tense. I drop to my haunches, keeping the rifle barrel vertical. "It's the shed."

"Yeah." There's something narsty in the woodshed. "Brick three?"

"Not responding, presumed down." His voice is flat. "I'm behind the barn. Get yourself over here but stay low."

I scurry over to the barn, where I find Alan and Sergeant Howe and a couple of troopers. They're all in body armor and face paint, armed to the incisors with big scary guns. And they look very, very, pissed-off.

"There's probably a little girl in there, Alan. Four years old, and all alone in the nest of, of a spawning unicorn Queen." I'm light-headed and feeling careless, otherwise I wouldn't dare speak like that under the circumstances.

"Yes. Also Lance Davies and Troopers Chen, Irving, and Duckworth," he adds. "Do you have anything useful to contribute?"

"Lovecraft's monster implied that a spawning Queen becomes part of a group mind or a swarm intelligence, or somehow becomes conscious, shortly before its offspring eat it. We're now seeing signs of ritual magic—possession, concealment glamor. Let's put that down to the sidereal age—" CASE NIGHTMARE GREEN, when the stars are coming right and all things esoteric become dangerously accessible—"and speculate that the thing H. P. Lovecraft called Shub-Niggurath is using the thing in that woodshed as a vector." I swallow. "And it's in this farm. What I'm wondering is, what's it going to do now? We've got it encircled, but unlike the sterile females, it's not stupid. And it knows it's going to die. Its whole raison d'etre is to maximize the number of its spawn who mate and survive . . . "

I trail off.

A little girl, a toddler really, who is under the power of the thing in the woodshed. Her elder sister should be at St. Ninian's girl's boarding school, but has instead gone AWOL and turned up on the family farm, riding an EMOCUM, in the middle of term-time, just as we began to investigate. I shudder. "Someone needs to go over—" I stop. "Shit!"

"Bob! Explain."

"Lucinda is down on EMOCUM One in the South Field. Octavia was in prep an hour ago, but EMOCUM Two is missing. You know about schools and cross-infection? How if a kid goes to school with an infection, all their classmates and then everyone else catches it? If you wanted to massively amplify a unicorn infestation, about the best way to go about it would be to dump a ton of fertilized unicorn spawn on the doorstep of a girls' boarding school. Especially with the TV series and movies and magazine spin-offs doing the rounds right now." I spit again. "But the teachers and staff wouldn't let a girl bring a live pet into a boarding school. She'd have to smuggle them in some time after the start of term, hide them in the saddle bags, or send for a magic steed and go collect them in person."

Sergeant Howe stares at me like I've grown a second head, but Alan just nods. "You should double-check on that," he says. "Be rather awkward if we had to firebomb a boarding school." He taps his throat mike: "Alpha to all, flash, incoming hostile on horseback. Shoot the horse on contact, assume rider possessed. Over."

I'm on my phone to the DO again. "Howard here. Please can you double-check that Octavia Edgebaston is still doing her prep in her dorm? This is an emergency. If she's missing we need to know immediately. Also: any reports of white horses with glowing blue eyes riding cross-country—"

"Will do! Anything else I can help you with?"

I sigh. "That's all for now." I hang up, then look at Alan. "Why haven't you burned the nest already?"

"Well, now." Alan looks at Howe. "Sergeant, if you'd care to explain the little problem to Mr. Howard?"

Howe sucks his teeth and looks pained. "It's like this, Bob me old mate: it's a woodshed. Wood: made of cellulose, right? Burns if you ignite it?" I nod like a bobble-head. "Well, they also stored other things in there. Inadvisable things. This is a farm, and for fertilizer they use—"

"Oh no," I say, as he continues—

"Ammonium nitrate. About a ton of it. Harry Edgebaston moved it into the woodshed a month ago, last thing anyone remembers seeing him do." Howe bares his teeth. "It'll make a bit of a mess if it brews up."

Alan grins humorlessly. "Your theory that the thing in the woodshed is growing more intelligent and more powerful just got a boost, Bob. What do you propose to do about it?"

I'm about to swither and prevaricate for a bit when my phone rings again. It's the DO. I listen to what he has to say, then thank him and look at Alan. "A riderless stray horse jumped the gates at St. Ninian's about fifteen minutes ago. When it left, it had a bareback rider. So I reckon, let's see, ten miles . . . you've got maybe five to ten minutes to get ready for Octavia and EMOCUM Unit Two. They'll be trying to get to the barn." I bare my teeth. "I want a sample retrieval kit, and some extras. Then I'm going to go and talk to the monster while you guys neutralize Octavia and her ride. If I stop transmitting, pull back to a safe distance and use the woodshed for target practice. Any questions?"

Five minutes later, I'm ready. At Alan's sign, two of his troopers pull the woodshed door open in front of me. I step forward, into the stygian darkness within.

This is a pretty dumb thing to do, on the face of it; if you've read this report and the EQUESTRIAN RED SIRLOIN dossier you might well be asking, "What the fuck, Bob? Why not send in a bomb-disposal robot instead?" And I will happily agree that if we had a freaking bomb-disposal robot to hand we'd do exactly that. Alas, they're all vacationing in Afghanistan this month—either that, or they're in storage in a barracks in Hereford, which does us precisely no good whatsoever. And we're clearly dealing with a many-tentacled occult incursion from the dungeon dimensions here, and those things eat electronics for breakfast. Much better to send in a warded-up human being: faster, more flexible, and I've got a couple of field-expedient surprises up my sleeves to boot.

For one thing, I'm wearing a borrowed helmet with a very expensive monocular bolted to it—an AN/PVS-14 night vision camera. Everything's grainy and green and a bit washed-out, and I can only see through one eye, but: in the kingdom of the blind, and all that. For another thing, I'm wired up with a radio mike and carry a crush-proof olive drab box under my arm. We're pretty sure there are no survivors in the building, which makes my mission all the more important.

For another thing—hey, don't worry, I've nearly finished reading my laundry list—I may not be a hero, but I'm not the fourteen-year-old H. P. Lovecraft either. Dealing with eldritch horrors is part of my day job. It's not even as bad as the paperwork, for the most part. True, the "moments of mortal terror" shtick really sucks, but on the other hand there's the rush I get from knowing that I'm saving the world.

And finally?

I'm more than a little bit angry.

So I walk into the booby-trapped woodshed full of explosives. Two guys with guns are waiting behind the door as it scrapes shut behind me. All I have to do is yell and they'll do a quick open-and-close, then cover my retreat. I plant the horrifyingly expensive mil-spec shockproof LED lantern on the floor. Right now, it's a brilliant flare of light in my night vision field, quite bright even to my unaugmented eye. Showing me precisely where to jump if, if, if it's necessary.

I take another step forward, stop, and call out: "Hey, Shub-face! I'm here to talk!"

The silence eats my words, but I can feel a presence waiting.

The air in the woodshed tastes damp and smells of mold. I take a deep breath, then sneeze as my sinuses swell closed. Oh great, I think: I'm mildly allergic to elder gods. (Only it's not a god. It's just an adult unicorn in the sessile, spawning phase of the life cycle. A very naughty unicorn indeed.)

"We've got you surrounded," I add, in a more conversational tone. "Broke your glamor, rounded up all your Renfields. Took down most of your sterile female workers."

(Because I have worked out this much: the thing I'm dealing with isn't just a sexually dimorphic r-strategy hyperparasite; it's a eusocial hive organism that can co-opt other species the way some types of ant domesticate aphids. And I've got another theory about the intelligence that Lovecraft called Shub-Niggurath—although I'm not sure he wasn't pulling it out of his arse, as far as the name-calling is concerned—and where it comes from.)

I take another step forward and nearly trip over something hard that's the size of a football. I catch myself and look down. It's a human skull.

Fragments of flesh and the twisted remains of a radio headset cling to it. Shit. Well, now I know for sure where Alan's troopers ended up. I glance up.

The beams above my head support a layer of crude planks. It looks uneven and rough in my night scope. Odd trailing wisps of rotten straw dangle from it, as if a plant is growing on the floor above, pushing its roots between the cracks. Something moves. I stare, then look down as I hear a tiny *clonk*. A conical snail-shell as long as my little fingernail has fallen to the rough floor near the—ick, I glance rapidly away from the decapitated remains of the soldier. Then I force myself to look back. Wart-like, the snails rasp across the pitted and grooved body armor and fatigues, migrating towards the bloody darkness within.

"Shub-Shub-Shub," rumbles the huge and gloopy presence resting on the floorboards above my head. I jump halfway out of my skin, then step back smartly. There's a high-pitched squeal of rage and pain as my foot lands on something that skitters out across the floor: a tiny, gracile horse-shaped thing as long as my outstretched hand.

"Talk to me in human, Shub," I call, pointing my face at the darkness above. "I'm here to negotiate." Here to hear your last confession, I hope. Actually, I've overrun my safety point by a couple of paces—I should be standing on, or within three meters of, the door. But I need to find out if any of the troopers—or the little girl, Ada—are still alive. And I urgently need to find out just how intelligent this particular spawning unicorn Queen has become, to be laying gnarly plans to plant hundreds of fertile daughters on the population of a girls' boarding school, rather than allowing nature to take its course and seed a half-handful of survivors at random around East Grinstead.

"Shub-Shub-Shub," says the thing.

Then, in a heartbreakingly high voice with just a trace of a toddler's lisp: "Daddy, why is it dark in here?"

My stomach lurches. The voice is coming from the attic.

"Daddy? Turn on the lights, Daddy, please?"

Lights?

I take a step back, closer to my safety zone, then swing my head round slowly. With the night vision monocular it's like having a searchlight, able to pick out details only in a very small area. Close beside the door, there—I see a mains switch and a trail of wire tacked to the wall.

"Daddy? I'm afraid . . . "

I skid across the unspeakable slime on the floor and push the switch, screwing shut the eye behind the night vision glass as I do so. The blackness vanishes, replaced by a twilight nightmare out of Bosch, illuminated by a ten-watt bulb screwed to the underside of a beam.

Yes, there are logs in the woodshed. They're piled neatly against the far wall, beyond the rickety stepladder leading up to a hole in the ceiling. There are also the partially skeletonized bodies of two—no, three—soldiers—

"Daddy! Heeelp!"

A little girl's voice screams from the staircase opening, and I realize I'm much too late to help her. Even so, I almost take a step forward. I manage to stop in time. I know exactly why those three troopers died: they died trying to be heroes, trying to rescue the little girl. I close my eyes briefly, take a deep breath of the mold-laden sickly-sweet air. Take a step backwards, to stand in front of the exit from the charnel house.

(There are two skulls on the floor—one of the bodies still has a helmet. They're on either side of the ladder. Part of me wonders how the thing in the attic decapitated them. Most of me wants to close my eyes, stick my fingers in my ears, and scream I can't hear you.)

"Talk to me, Shub," I call. "You want to talk, don't you? It's the only way you or any of your brood are going to get out of here alive."

The roof beams creak, as if something vast is adjusting its weight distribution. "Shub. Shub. Glurp. Daddy, it wants me to talk to you. Daddy? Will you come up here?"

I swallow bile and tense my leg muscles to flee. "No," I say.

"Shub! Shub! Shub!" The thing with Ada in the attic, the thing working her vocal cords, booms at me, a menacing rumble. Obviously, it's not happy about its latest self-propelled snack refusing to follow the lure upstairs. I use the rumbling as my cue to unhook the sample jars and look around. Her spawn crawls over the woodpile, near the dead and half-eaten troopers. Tiny horses and cone snails, swarming and chewing. I swallow again. Look sideways: near the door, a handful of snail shells crushed by boots. Survivors inch across the floor around them. I crouch down and use my forceps to take living samples, one per glass-walled tube. Snail, horse, snail, horse. They go back into the crush-resistant fiberglass box and I lock it and sling it over my shoulder.

That's what I'm really here for, you know. It was pretty clear that this was a zero-survivor situation once Alan confirmed that brick three was missing. But anything I can learn from the Queen . . .

"We have met before," the Queen says through Ada's childish larynx.

"Have we?" I ask.

"You remember me. I was your Hetty. I said we would meet again. Isn't that right?"

My skin crawls. I begin to frame a reply, then stop. I was going to say something human, but: do not disclose operational intelligence to happy fun serial group mind horror. I try again: "You wake up each time: reincarnation, isn't it? You find yourself fat and sleepy and spawning in a warm, food-rich place. And you remember who you were—who you are. Is that right?"

"I knew you would understand! Come close and you can join me."

Bingo. "And you keep trying to do better each time, don't you? What was the idea, this time?"

"Will you join me if I tell you? I will make you immortal and we will thrive and feed and dance joyous through the aeons—"

"Yes," I lie.

"It has been so long since I have mated with another mind . . . Yes, you must join me! My idiot offspring eat their mother's flesh and then their siblings, before they mate and grow sleek and strong and seek out a nest and settle down, and I awaken behind their eyes. One or two in each brood prosper that way. But I have worked out a way for more to survive to maturity. Join me, help me, and we will be fruitful and amplify and become myriad."

"I don't think so." I can't hold it back any more.

"Why won't you—"

"Your last worker is on its way home to visit, carrying your last Renfield. But it's not going to be allowed to get here, Shubby. We're not going to let you distribute your spawn via the girls at Saint Ninian's. The school's on lock-down, and they know what to search for. Acid baths, Shubby. Anything that looks like My Little Pony is going to take a one-way trip through an acid bath and a furnace on sight. Snails, too."

A snarling animal scream cuts through the air behind me, from beyond the closed doors. It's cut short by a harsh chatter of automatic gunfire.

The thing above me roars in existential pain and heaves its bulk up, then brings it smashing down on the ceiling. Paint dust and splinters fall and the light bulb shakes, the shadows flickering across the room. "My children! My beautiful future flesh! My babies! Traitor! I would have loved and cherished your memories forever!" The snails and tiny horses swarm on the skeletonizing remains of the dead soldiers. Another voice cuts through the cacophony: "Dadd-ee! Help me!"

I step back towards the door. I tap my throat mike and speak quietly: "Got samples. No—" I glance at the ladder "—survivors. Over."

"Roger," Alan says calmly. "Target neutralized in yard behind you. Come on out. We're falling back now. Over."

I throw myself backwards at the woodshed doors. The ceiling creaks and screeches and then begins to buckle, giving way and drooping from the edges of the loft stairwell opening. Something huge is pushing through from above, something like the rasp of a slug the size of a bus, iridescent and putrefying and bubbling with feculent slime. It vents a warbling roar, "ShubShubShub." The door gives way behind me as I topple, getting a vague impression of writhing tentacles, a huge nodding eyeless horse-head, something like a broken doll impaled on a wooden stick—

Someone catches me and then I'm sprawling across a back as they pick me up and run across a farmyard, dodging around the fallen bulk of another of the horses from hell. I can see stars and a high overcast of cirrus whirling overhead as my rescuer pounds across the packed earth. Wall to one side, reflecting the livid glare of a burning building. "Get down!" someone shouts in my ear as he drops me on the ground in the lee of a drystone wall.

"Got it—" I scramble for cover as the incendiary fireworks surge overhead and the woodshed lights off with a *whump* I can feel in my bladder.

And then I lie there until Sergeant Howe gives everyone the all clear and sends a medic to look me over for triage, clutching the sample box like grim death and telling myself that it was all over for Ada Doom Edgebaston long before I walked through the woodshed door.

Because reincarnation only works for alien group mind horrors, doesn't it?

Keep telling yourself that, Bob. Take your sample tubes back to R&D in London, leave the burning wreckage of the farm behind. Take your cold comfort where you can, and keep telling yourself that the nasty thing old HPL saw behind the woodshed was lying or mistaken, and that you'll never meet it again.

Who knows? You might even be right . . .

· · ·

**HOME OFFICE**
**CONFIDENTIAL**
**Procurement Specification: HO/MPMU/46701**
Date of Issue: May 3rd, 2006

Requirement for:
Enhanced-Mobility Operational Capability Upgrade Mounts for Police Mounted Units

It is becoming increasingly clear that in the 21st century mounted police are seen as an anachronism by the public. Despite their clear advantages for crowd control and supervision of demonstrations and public sporting events, mounted operations are expensive to conduct, require extensive stabling and support infrastructure, and compete for resources with other specialist units (e.g. airborne, tactical firearms, scene of crime investigation).

This document contains the operational requirements for upgraded genetically engineered mounts that will enhance the capabilities and availability of our mounted officers . . .

Desirable characteristics:
Mounts should exhibit three or more of the following traits:
• Endurance in excess of 6 hours at 30 miles/hour over rough terrain (when ridden with standard issue saddle, rider, and kit)
• Endurance in excess of 30 minutes at 50 miles/hour on metaled road surfaces (when ridden with standard issue saddle, rider, and kit)
• Ability to see in the dark
• Ability to recognize and obey a controlled vocabulary of at least 20 distinct commands
• Invisible
• Bulletproof
• Carnivorous
• Flight (when ridden with standard issue saddle, rider, and kit)

State of Requirement

**CANCELLED September 5th, 2006**

by Order of Cabinet Office in accordance with recommendation of SOE (X Division) Operational Oversight Audit Committee

Reason for cancellation order:

• Sussex mounted constabulary has no conceivable operational requirement for sentient weapons of mass destruction.

• This requirement document has no identifiable origin within the Home Office.

• It echoes historic attempts to induce adoption of Equoid-friendly facilities within the armed services via requirements raised within the MoD. All of these have been successfully resisted.

• It is speculated that someone is trying to pull a fast one on us: does Shub-Niggurath have a posse in Whitehall? This matter warrants further enquiry, and has therefore been referred to External Assets for investigation and permanent closure.

*Unhappy is he to whom the memories of childhood bring only fear and sadness.*

"The Outsider" · H. P. Lovecraft (1926)

## · THE BOY WHO FOLLOWED LOVECRAFT ·
### Marc Laidlaw

Douglas sits alone at the side of the house, waiting for the Aunts to call him in, alert to the slightest creak of the front door or to one of their hard-toed shoes sounding upon the porch. They cannot see him from inside the house, so he always has time to hide the magazine, shoving it into the crawlspace along with the rest of his collection. There is a trace of autumn in the Sunday evening air, and the summer-blanched leaves of the old sycamores send a rustling shade over the crumbling pages he turns so slowly and savoringly. The paper feels soft and rough as a kind of leafy bark, not dissimilar to the earth where he crouches and thumbs through his issues of *Weird Tales* again and again.

The date on the magazine is April 1929. This is only September, yet he has read the copy cover to cover so many times that the magazine appears as worn as one twenty years old, its bright reds faded to vermilion, the fearsome masked priest now a colorful faceless smudge. The other issues are in worse shape, what's left of them. Hard to imagine that once they had been bright and crisp—as bright as the quarters or the stacks of pennies he'd shoved across the newsstand counter. Some, found in downtown secondhand shops, were old when he'd bought them for a fraction of their cover price. But they are no less precious for it. His only regret is that the oldest ones suffer more from his constant rereading, and he has been forced to stop carrying them around with him, away from the house and the watchful Aunts, to the parks and libraries and quiet private places where a boy might hide and read in peace, and seek the strange thrills these stories provide.

Douglas hides the magazines from the Aunts because they have already shown they do not understand. They have forbidden him to spend his allowance on such things; forbidden them in the house; forbidden him from reading such horrors. "Nightmares, trash, and madness," they had called the tales; and that word alone had ensured his disobedience, for it was madness he sought to understand. Madness was the reason he lived here, after all; it was the reason the old women had brought him in as a foster child: "A kind of madness took them," was all they ever said when he asked about his parents. More than that, and the nature of madness, he was left to investigate on his own; and it came to him in these tales which spoke openly of unreason, of madness caused by fear. And as he read, he became enwrapped in a kind of beauty, borne by the words. Madness became a key, opening the door to new worlds where he could lose himself while feeling that he could go beyond himself . . .

Hinges squeal. "Douglas? Douglas, child, where are you?" Aunt Melissa steps onto the porch and comes quickly toward the corner. Douglas shoves the magazine into the dark opening and slips back around the side of the house until he stands in the back yard. He makes her call again, louder, and then responds. "I'm back here, ma'am!"

She cranes around the side of the porch, looking exasperated. He strides toward her, passing the crawlspace, and hurries up the front steps to stand at her side.

"Well, I promise you, I looked back there and didn't see a thing. Come in now and have your supper. Aunt Opal and I have things to do—we can't be waiting past dark while you dig your holes or arrange your soldiers, or whatever it is you get up to back there. School tomorrow, so early to bed tonight."

"Yes, ma'am."

"That's a good child. Come and eat then. Oh, and before I forget."

She produces from one deep pocket a bright silver quarter. His heart leaps at the thought of what it will buy him. He hides not his smile but only its meaning. "Thank you, Aunt."

"Remember now, it's more than many have these days. Spend it wisely, as I'm sure you will. God bless you, child, you're a good boy."

The school day drags. Douglas sits alone, as ever, in the back of the sweltering classroom, writing slowly, scarcely seeing the columns of numbers he must add and manipulate, the dull rote words he must read. At recess he remains inside with his treasured April issue, gazing at the jumbled, nightmarish illustration that accompanies "The Dunwich Horror." Miss Marsh leaves him to his solitude. She has long since stopped trying to convince him to go out with the other children. She frowns, he thinks, whenever he produces one of his magazines; but she has never tried to confiscate one, never questioned what he reads. In this sense, the classroom is safe—perhaps the safest place he knows. Certainly safer than the schoolyard.

Today, a shadow falls over his desk. Miss Marsh hovers over him. "Douglas?"

Feeling his cheeks flush, he looks up at her, closing the magazine, pushing it under the desk.

"That's all right, dear. I was just wondering . . . I believe you might have just enough time to make it to the newsstand and back before lunch is over. Unless I'm very much mistaken about what day it is."

Her smile is knowing. He starts to speak, but whatever he might blurt, as he rises from his desk, banging his knees, nearly knocking his papers to the floor, remains unsaid.

"Don't be long now, Douglas."

He runs.

Out the schoolhouse, out the gate, and down the busy street. A streetcar jangles past; as he waits on the curb, he digs into his pocket, fails to find the quarter, and experiences a moment's terror—until his fingers brush the warm disk, and he pinches it, brings it out to reassure himself of its presence. He rubs it like a good luck charm. The streetcar passes and he darts across the street to the row of shops across the way, the newsstand at the corner.

For a moment the racks confuse him, and he seizes up with dread. What if it isn't here yet? There are piles of periodicals wrapped in twine, still to be unpacked and set out. Another thrill of disappointment, as when he thought his quarter lost, grips him. Then he spies the bright lettering, in an unaccustomed spot, peering out above the top of a mystery magazine: *Weird Tales, The Unique Magazine.*

He pulls it from the rack, slaps his quarter on the counter, cutting off the newsdealer's nasty snarl, and rushes away with hardly a glimpse at the cover: An enormous ape carries off a woman in a gauzy pink slip. More than that, he won't allow himself to see until he has time to truly savor it.

He slips back into the classroom with a few minutes of recess remaining.

Miss Marsh gives him a smile, and as he lays the issue reverently on the desk, she comes a few steps closer. For the first time, he refrains from hiding the magazine. Although it pains him to hold still, he looks up and sees her gazing at the cover. Her eyebrows arch; she laughs. "Oh, my," she says. "That looks like a very exciting story. Who wrote that one, do you think? Are these the authors?" She reads down the names listed on the cover: "Sophie Wenzel Ellis. Seabury Quinn. H. P. Lovecraft . . . "

His heart leaps at the name. Lovecraft! A new story! Douglas almost opens the issue right then, but Miss Marsh's expression gives him pause.

"H. P.," she says again. "I wonder if that could be the same . . . Howard Phillips . . . of Providence itself. Do you know his stories, Douglas? You do? I believe he is a local man. In fact, I think he lives not far from you on College Hill. Perhaps he'd like to know he has a bright young reader right here in Providence."

Miss Marsh suddenly catches sight of the clock, and gives a little gasp. Rushing to the door, she leans outside and bangs the triangle. The clanging blends into the shouts of children, and the room fills up again with the greater noise of students. Miss Marsh catches and holds his gaze through the crowd, but what she has promised seems too great to acknowledge. He looks away, rolling up the magazine and shoving it under his desk. What else does she know about him, he wonders? Does she understand how madness haunts him? Would the writer, H. P. Lovecraft, understand? It all seems too secret, too personal, to discuss with anyone. But if anyone might understand, it would be a man like the one who writes such stories.

He hardly notices the passage of the afternoon, wondering if what she said could be true. At home, the Aunts have gone off on some errand, leaving him free to surround himself with his collection. He sorts through the magazines and pulls out everything by Lovecraft.

Combing through the issues, he sees how many of these stories are by one man—by this same Lovecraft of Providence. He had not recognized the pattern until Miss Marsh pointed it out. The thought that a living person could have written these stories had never occurred to him. He had not required that of them. They existed, that was enough. They carried him away to other lands, other places exotic and faraway—with names like Celephaïs and Sarnath, Ulthar and Ilek-Vad—all so different from the names he saw around him: College Hill and Federal Hill, worlds, he saw now, which were locked away in the stories of Lovecraft. From one mind, then, so many of Douglas's own dreams had sprung. The knowledge is a key turning in a lock, revealing a new dimension to what he had already known. Indeed, Lovecraft had written "The Silver Key," in which Randolph Carter found a secret path into a land of dream; he had written "The White Ship" and "The Cats of Ulthar," and other tales of dream. But he had also written "The Rats in the Walls," a tale of madness that had chilled and fascinated Douglas in equal measure; "The Festival," "The Call of Cthulhu," "The Outsider," "Pickman's Model" . . . and these truly are tales of madness. They hold secrets dark as the ones that haunt Douglas, the nightmares that torment him when he tries to think beyond his own memories, to a time before the Aunts had taken him in, a muddled dream which tells him nothing, a dream which remains impenetrable, approachable only, perhaps, through a deeper understanding of what madness itself might mean.

He crouches by the house in the deepening gloom, reading and rereading, searching for clues. The latest issue holds a story of Lovecraft's called "The Hound," a tale of grave robbers who pilfer a cursed amulet and are pursued relentlessly by its winged guardian. Douglas has read the story before, in one of his older issues of Weird Tales, but it takes him some time to recognize it. Everything seems altered by the fact that it was written here in Providence. He pictures the story taking place somewhere nearby—the graveyard might be Swan Point; the baying hound pursues the robbers through familiar neighborhoods rendered strange and mysterious, filtered through the light of Lovecraft's words. His whole world feels changed in much the same way as the story. Providence itself has acquired a twilight tinge, a mysterious beauty he had never noticed until now. It took Lovecraft to make him see it.

Lovecraft . . .

His Aunts would know how to find the man. They have lived here all their lives; they know everyone, from the oldest families to the newest residents of the neighborhood. They had grown up in Providence when it was a much smaller town, and they still treat it as their own village. But how is he to question their knowledge without letting them know what he's asking? For Douglas is quite certain they would not approve.

He decides on a sacrifice. He will pose a riddle and watch them attempt to answer it, and in the attempt learn much.

Douglas sorts his tattered magazines, looking for a cover that features Lovecraft's name in suitably large letters. There are few appearances, and most are in small characters, rubbed illegible by constant use. Cringing inwardly, he returns to the latest, September, issue. With a pair of Aunt Opal's sewing scissors, he slices into the brand-new cover, painstakingly cutting around Lovecraft's name, removing the block of bright text. The wounded magazine he carefully replaces in the crawlspace, then slips onto the porch and puts the slip of colorful writing under the brass knocker, just at eye level. Then he lets himself into the house and busies himself with homework until he hears a clatter at the door: the Aunts are home. Muffled exclamations. They enter the house in a state of heightened excitement, their voices high chirps of curiosity.

"That's Lillian Clark's nephew, isn't it?"

"I know who it is, and I certainly don't intend to encourage him."

"Missy, whatever do you mean? He's no harm, that one. The poor fellow."

"He's not right and never has been. The hours he keeps. I hear he is an atheist, did you know that?"

"Let's be charitable, now."

"The fact remains . . . whatever does he mean by this? Leaving it as some sort of calling card. Keep your distance from that one."

"I was only thinking I might ask Miss Lillian."

"No!"

"Come now, it's only a short walk, what could it hurt? If her nephew is becoming more erratic, she should know. Before he harms himself, the poor man. You remember that time he collapsed on the street during a cold spell?"

"The only reason to speak to Lillian Clark is to ensure that she keeps her nephew away from us. If you wish to speak to her on that account, then I will accompany you."

"I will do no such thing. Let's just keep this to ourselves for now. If there's another event, then . . . then we'll discuss further steps. Now where is that boy?"

As Douglas listens, he cannot help but feel a kinship growing—affinity for a stranger. If the Aunts knew his secrets, would they speak of him in similar tones? Doesn't muttering follow him about—on the schoolyard, in the streets, haunting him, setting him apart? In this he feels a kinship to all outcasts. It sharpens his resolve.

He finds Lillian Clark's house the very next day, simply by greeting the postman on the walk to the Aunts' front door. The postman is happy to provide the street number and even a description. Douglas stops short of asking if he knows the name of Lovecraft. He does not want the great, the wonderful man to be warned of his existence. Douglas's admiration, his hopes, are too sensitive and secret. The deep sense of kinship he feels dare not name itself. It must be nourished in darkness. But he knows that if he can get close, he can touch the man directly—let him know that he understands, that they are kindred, that they share the same visions. But caution is engrained in his nature. Douglas prepares slowly.

In the shortening days, he devotes a measure of each afternoon before dusk to walking repetitively past the Clark residence, which proves to be not a house at all but an apartment building. Eyes glower at him from houses all around, and once he crosses the street to avoid a neighbor who clearly means to apprehend him. Of course he must return home before dark each night, and take great care not to arouse the Aunts' suspicions. Once he creeps out long after bedtime, down the dark streets, and takes up a post only to find a light burning still at this hour in one window of the apartment building. He imagines H. P. Lovecraft at work even now, hunched above a writing desk, pouring out his visions of otherworldly places. Imagine, setting pen to paper, and the paper carrying one away like a magic carpet, an enchanted scroll, to the River Skai . . . the wilds of Arkham . . . imagine . . .

Within a week, his pilgrimages acquire an air of desperation. On Saturday, he finds an excuse to tell the Aunts he will be out all day—he suggests he's hunting for a job in town, perhaps at the newsstand, or delivering papers. They remark on his initiative, pack him a lunch and watch him go. But it is straight to Lovecraft's building he heads, and although he cannot stay in one spot or cross the same path too many times without attracting suspicion, he manages to cover enough adjacent streets that he can keep the house in view every few minutes without himself being viewed by the neighbors. He consumes his lunch during the course of the day—crackers and cheese and wedges of bread spread with butter and sugar. He despairs. Eventually he tells himself that he will make one more circuit, and then return to pretend to the Aunts that his attempts to find work have all ended in discouragement.

From the side of Lovecraft's house, a man appears. It could be any one of the building's tenants, or even a visitor, but Douglas has a feeling about this man. There is an air of solitude about him. He stops in front of the building, tall and gaunt and wearing a dark suit that makes him hard to see against the lengthening shadows. Douglas slows his pace and tries not to show any interest. From half a block away there is little chance of drawing attention to himself, except by staring too hard. The man's face—it must be Mr. Lovecraft!—is partly hidden, in shadow itself, beneath the brim of his hat. He hesitates at the end of the drive and turns back to the house, then suddenly stoops and puts out his hand as if summoning with a magical gesture . . . what?

A cat appears, as if out of nowhere, a speckled calico that sniffs his fingers then rubs itself against his cuffs. Here comes a second, and a third, and now Douglas sees that they have emerged from under a hedge. A black cat walking stiffly, as if crippled by age; and a small kitten that bites the elder's tail, then throws itself against Mr. Lovecraft's foot and meows until he picks it up caressingly. Even in the shadow of the hat, Mr. Lovecraft's smile is clear. He whispers to the creatures, then sets the kitten down and sends it running back toward the hedge. Bidding them a soft farewell, he turns and heads off down the sidewalk, toward town. The calico follows him a short way, then rounds back toward the house, encountering Douglas following in Mr. Lovecraft's path. Douglas looks for the kitten but it has hidden itself. He would like to pet the creature that his idol has just touched.

The spires of Providence show themselves through the trees as the street tips downhill toward the town. Douglas keeps the dark-suited man in his sight at all times, never letting the gap between them grow too narrow, lest he be spotted. And Mr. Lovecraft stops repeatedly—at first constantly accosted by cats that seem to know him and anticipate his passing. To each one that will let him he gives an affectionate stroking. Douglas feels a pang; such kindness!

Then the houses with their sun-touched lawns fall away, and the city lies ahead. The absence of constant feline interruption should quicken Mr. Lovecraft's pace, but it seems to have the opposite effect. He walks with his eyes to the sky now, taking in the buildings, the sky, the sights of Providence. For Douglas, it is almost like having a silent guide, opening his eyes to beauties he had taken for granted.

On Thomas Street, heading west into the city, Mr. Lovecraft stands for several minutes staring up at an old colonial church—one Douglas knows from the Aunts to be a Baptist institution. Mr. Lovecraft adjusts his hat as if tipping it to the tall white steeple, and moves on. Where his eyes catch, where he pauses to take in the sights, Douglas also pauses. A visible shudder passes through Mr. Lovecraft as he passes the weirdly paneled Fleur-de-Lys Studio, a building that has always amused Douglas but today seems somehow repulsive. Is this something he has absorbed from Mr. Lovecraft's fascination? Certainly the building does not seem to belong among the others. Mr. Lovecraft turns left, heading south again on North Main, now barely glancing at the bulk of the Cheapside Block; then slowing again as he nears Market Square and the brick Market House. In the crowds here, Douglas knows he can come nearer without being seen. As Mr. Lovecraft heads west toward Westminster, Douglas darts nearer so as not to lose him. He comes so close that for a moment he can almost reach out and touch the object of his pursuit—and sees at this close range something that surprises him.

The suit, this close, looks shabby and worn. It reminds Douglas of clothes worn by some children at his school: the grubby ones, the ones his Aunts might speak of as "unfortunates." In these difficult times, Mr. Lovecraft's suit is not so different from many others in the crowd, but it sets Douglas back for a moment. He had assumed that writing stories would have made his hero rich. There is no evidence of that. Even the hat's brim is frayed. He hangs back a bit, not wanting more details to intrude on his vision of the man, preferring the slightly distant, somewhat blurry version—but knowing there can be no reclaiming it. For better or worse, this is H. P. Lovecraft the man.

Past the grimy granite pillars and portico of the darkening Arcade, Mr. Lovecraft turns abruptly into a shop. Douglas approaches slowly, staring into a brightly lit interior. Dusk is deepening in the street, but inside the shop it's all shining brilliant tile and glass cases, and Mr. Lovecraft looks like a spectral silhouette leaning forward. A uniformed attendant greets him with great familiarity, and then extends a small wooden paddle heaped with a creamy brown blob. Ice cream! Douglas realizes how long it's been since he finished his lunch. His mouth waters. Mr. Lovecraft scrapes the ice cream from the spoon against his teeth, then nods. A minute later he emerges from the shop with a hugely scooped cone, forced to tilt his head to one side lest it smear his hat brim. Douglas recognizes the scoop. The Aunts never let him so much as sample the flavor, stating it unsuitable for children, but he has bought himself a cone or two surreptitiously. Coffee ice cream is a Providence specialty.

His pace becomes more leisurely in the throng. The streets are full of citizens seeking an evening's entertainment, a meal, a stroll. Mr. Lovecraft savors his ice cream, and vicariously Douglas takes enjoyment from the older man's pleasure. All these sights and flavors, yes, they are part of Mr. Lovecraft's world—somehow they feed his fantasies, they stoke the visions that he then crafts into stories and passes on to Douglas. Douglas feels an almost unbearable pang of affection—for the shabby gentleman, clearly impoverished, spending his spare dimes on sweets, petting cats, strolling in the colonial byways like one in a dream. This—yes, this! Douglas feels the beginnings of a deep kinship, but really it is not the beginning—it is the culmination. It had begun with the stories . . . it had begun in Kadath and Sarnath, in Dunwich and in Celephais. Douglas understands him perfectly, the lonely man walking alone, so apart from and indifferent to the crowds that swarm around him. In this they are the same. In so many ways the same. Past banks and churches, the clanging of streetcars, the lights coming on around them, neon signs garish and alluring. At Mathewson Street, an immense church (another of the Aunts' landmarks, Episcopalian, said with faint dismissal), Douglas sees like a glowing shrine the marquee of the Loew's State Theatre. For a moment Mr. Lovecraft stares at it almost wistfully, he thinks; but then he turns and walks down another avenue, down streets less grand, darker. It's easy to remain unseen here. Mr. Lovecraft finishes the last of his cone, stops before a small alcove, brushes his hands together fastidiously, then steps in off the street, out of sight.

Douglas slowly approaches the alcove himself, and sees a small glass booth before double doors—a theatre, far less majestic than the Loew's, and almost unattended. In fact there is no one in the booth to sell tickets—until a figure swims up inside the glass, and Douglas stumbles away before he can be spotted.

Mr. Lovecraft!

He removes his suit jacket and hangs it from a hook at the back of the booth, then settles himself in a chair at the ticket window. There he waits, staring out at the night, while Douglas sinks back into shadow to watch.

To see a movie is a rare event for Douglas; he saves his quarters for his magazines and the Aunts have no use for films, much less now that they have begun to talk. Thus there is little meaning for Douglas in the titles that appear on the booth's placard: *Hallelujah!* sounds like something his Aunts might approve, but *The Mysterious Island* very much does not. The thought of such an island, wrapped in mystery, with Mr. Lovecraft presiding as keeper of the gateway, fills him with excitement and anticipation. He digs into his pockets in case some coins might have miraculously appeared.

Of Mr. Lovecraft he can see nothing now but his head and shoulders, with a harsh light thrown down onto him from above. A few patrons close around the booth, and Mr. Lovecraft dispenses tickets in a perfunctory manner, as if anxious for the customers to be gone. As the flurry of purchases subsides, Mr. Lovecraft turns to the coat on its hook and from an inner pocket removes a cylinder of paper. He uncurls it, flattens it on the counter, and produces from some hidden place a bottle of ink and a pen.

Is he . . . writing? In the lull between customers, composing? Is it possible that H. P. Lovecraft's miraculous tales are penned here, under such circumstances?

Douglas cannot contain himself. He wants to see the words trailing from the tip of the pen. He carefully creeps from the shadows, drawing closer to the glass, trying to see if he recognizes any especially magical syllables. He stays close to the doors, where the darkness is dense and he can stay hidden—but suddenly the doors fly open, and out comes a small group of women, laughing and chattering. Their appearance jostles Douglas close to the booth, and Mr. Lovecraft looks up. Their eyes lock. Douglas feels his eyes go wide, a shock almost physical in its intensity. Mr. Lovecraft's jaw is set. As he straightens in the chair, he drops his pen and the papers curl up instantly. He is about to say something but Douglas cannot bear it. It's too much all at once. In a panic, he bolts past the booth and into the street, and throws himself around a corner.

Breathless, he runs along the side of the building until another door nearly opens in his face, another explosion of laughter and voices, and he finds himself caught in a stream of filmgoers leaving the theatre. He holds the door for several ladies, out of habit, as the Aunts have taught him; and as they pour past, he finds himself gazing into the dark interior of the theatre. Thinking of the Mysterious Island, which might easily be an image out of Lovecraft's stories, he seizes an edge of the curtains that drape the exit; he rushes through the velvety portico and finds himself inside.

Most of the seats are empty, though a tide of newcomers continues to trickle in from the top of the aisles. Trying to calm himself, hoping not to attract notice, he sinks into the front row seat and tips his face toward the vast curtained screen, and closes his eyes to take stock of his thoughts.

He wonders how to make his way back to Mr. Lovecraft. He has accepted the challenge he felt the man offered, but he must prove himself worthy. Once the movie has started, if he can return to the booth, he might find both the courage and the words to explain that he too has dreamt of R'lyeh, that he has heard the hound that chases the bearer of the talisman, that he has felt the evil wind that blows through the hidden chambers of the Nameless City. But as the lights of the theatre dim, as the curtains draw back from the screen and the first newsreel begins to play, he wonders if perhaps there is something else he is meant to see. Surely there is a deeper reason H. P. Lovecraft himself sits and sells tickets to this particular house. Perhaps what awaits are not ordinary serials and newsreels, staid dramas and inane musicals. The projectionist could be an emissary of Lovecraft, the projector a beam straight from that burning imagination, the magic lantern of his feverish mind.

As the screen begins to quiver with light, Douglas chants the names beneath his breath: Nyarlathotep! Azathoth! The names ring him in the darkness.

And then the darkness is no more. An explosion of light in his eyes.

Blinded, he gapes and hears a high nasal voice. He gapes and sees Mr. Lovecraft glaring at him, holding him fast in the beam of an electric torch, trained on Douglas like a searchlight. The man's sharp pale features, caught in the beam for a moment, loom out of the theatrical dark, dwarfing the screen, and he says, "You!"

The word an uncontainable portent.

And then he leans closer, thrusting the torch like the barrel of a gun into Douglas's face, and says the words that send the boy reeling out into the night, as bereft as the blind worlds that spin in the void to the tune of a mindless idiot god.

Douglas flees, pitching down the dark Providence streets, his mind in shards, his dreams tattered, shedding magic and mystery as if they are coins in a pocket full of holes. Innsmouth, R'lyeh, Ulthar, all crumbling into ruins. Fast he plunges from the halls of dream, never to know Y'hanthlei, never to be carried on black wings. The streets of Providence hateful again, no solace in their antiquity, the churchyards simply full of bones, the hounds nothing more or less than the hounds that always hunted men. And as he flees toward the rest of his life, the words still ring and circle as they always will when he casts his mind back to this night, this theatre of despair. They will echo every day and far into the night, far into the years; they will echo even after Howard Phillips Lovecraft's death, an occasion of obscure satisfaction only capped by the unmarked grave that Douglas never bothers to seek out.

Echoing, yes, but never more terribly than that first night of horror, when he realized he could never escape into a weird dream of eldritch magic and mystery, from a truth too plain and too insistent.

Lovecraft's final words, ringing sharp and cutting, the words that send him flying, feeling faceless as a night gaunt, into the dark:

"Get out before I call the police, *you dirty little nigger!*"

# • About the Authors •

**Laird Barron** was born and raised in Alaska, did time in the wilderness, and raced in several Iditarods. Later, he migrated to Washington State where he devoted himself to American Combato and reading authors like Robert B. Parker, James Ellroy, and Cormac McCarthy. At night he wrote tales that combined noir, crime, and horror. He was a 2007 and 2010 Shirley Jackson Award winner for his collections *The Imago Sequence and Other Stories* and *Occultation and Other Stories* and a 2009 nominee for his novelette "Catch Hell." His most recent collection, *The Beautiful Thing That Awaits Us All*, won the Bram Stoker Award and was nominated for the World Fantasy Award. Other award nominations include the Crawford Award, Sturgeon Award, International Horror Guild Award, and the Locus Award. His first novel, *The Croning*, was published in 2012. He guest-edited *The Year's Best Weird Fiction, Volume 1* (2014). Barron currently resides in Upstate New York.

**Elizabeth Bear** was born on the same day as Frodo and Bilbo Baggins, but in a different year. When coupled with a childhood tendency to read the dictionary for fun, this led her inevitably to penury, intransigence, and the writing of speculative fiction. She is the Hugo, Sturgeon, Locus, and Campbell Award winning author of twenty-seven novels (including the acclaimed Eternal Sky series and her latest novel, *Karen Memory*,) and around a hundred short stories. Her dog lives in Massachusetts; her partner, writer Scott Lynch, lives in Wisconsin. She spends a lot of time on planes.

**Ruthanna Emrys** lives in a mysterious manor house on the outskirts of Washington, DC, with her wife and their large, strange family. She makes homemade vanilla, obsesses about game design, gives unsolicited advice, occasionally attempts to save the world, and blogs sporadically about these things at her Livejournal. Her stories have appeared in a number of venues, including *Strange Horizons*, *Tor.com*, and *Analog*.

**Lois H. Gresh** is the *New York Times* bestselling author (six times), *Publishers Weekly* bestselling paperback author, *Publishers Weekly* bestselling paperback children's author, and *USA Today* bestselling author of twenty-eight books and sixty short stories. Current books are anthology *Dark Fusions: Where Monsters Lurk!* (editor), story collection *Eldritch Evolutions*, *The Divergent Companion*, *Innsmouth Nightmares* (editor), and *Cult of the Dead and Other Weird and Lovecraftian Tales*. Look for recent stories in anthologies *The Mammoth Book of Cthulhu*, *Black Wings III*, *Gothic Lovecraft*, *Madness of Cthulhu*, *Searchers After Horror*, *That Is Not Dead*, *Expiration Date*, *Dark Phantastique*, *Black Wings IV*, *Mark of the Beast*, *Summer of Lovecraft*, *Mountain Walked*, *Eldritch Chrome* and *Jews Versus Aliens*.

**Brian Hodge** is one of those people who always has to be making something. So far, he's made ten novels spanning horror, crime, and historical fiction, and is working on number eleven, as well as nearly 120 shorter works and five collections. He lives in Colorado, where he also likes to make music and photographs; loves everything about organic gardening except the thieving squirrels; and trains in Krav Maga and kickboxing, which are of no use at all against the squirrels. Recent and forthcoming works include *Whom the Gods Would Destroy* and *The Weight of the Dead*, both standalone novellas; *Worlds of Hurt*, an omnibus edition of the first four works in his Misbegotten mythos; an updated hardcover edition of *Dark Advent*, his early post-apocalyptic epic; *Who We Are In the Dark*, his next collection; and his next novel, *Leaves of Sherwood*.

The *New York Times* recently hailed **Caitlín R. Kiernan** as "one of our essential writers of dark fiction." Her novels include *The Red Tree* (nominated for the Shirley Jackson and World Fantasy awards) and *The Drowning Girl: A Memoir* (winner of the James Tiptree, Jr. Award and the Bram Stoker Award, nominated for the Nebula, Locus, Shirley Jackson, World Fantasy, British Fantasy, and Mythopoeic awards). In 2014 she was honored with the Locus Award for short fiction ("The Road of Needles"), the World Fantasy Award for Best Short Story ("The Prayer of Ninety Cats"), and a second World Fantasy Award for Best Collection (*The Ape's Wife and Other Stories*). To date, her short fiction has been collected in thirteen volumes. Currently, she's writing the graphic novel series Alabaster for Dark Horse.

Before he became one of the creators and lead writer on the Half-Life videogame series, **Marc Laidlaw** was an acclaimed writer of short stories and novels. His novel *The 37th Mandala* won the International Horror Guild Award for Best Novel. A writer at Valve since 1997, his short fiction continues to appear in various magazines and anthologies.

**John Langan** is the author of two collections, *Mr. Gaunt and Other Uneasy Encounters* (Prime, 2008) and *The Wide, Carnivorous Sky and Other Monstrous Geographies* (Hippocampus, 2013), and a novel, *House of Windows* (Night Shade, 2009). With Paul Tremblay, he has co-edited *Creatures: Thirty Years of Monsters* (Prime, 2011). He lives in New York's Hudson Valley with his wife, younger son, and an ark's worth of animals.

**Helen Marshall** is an award-winning Canadian author, editor, and doctor of medieval studies. Her poetry and fiction have been published in *Chiaroscuro, Abyss & Apex, Lady Churchill's Rosebud Wristlet*, and *Tor.com* and have been reprinted in several year's best anthologies. Her debut collection of short stories *Hair Side, Flesh Side* (ChiZine Publications) was named one of the top ten books of 2012 by *January Magazine*. It won the 2013 British Fantasy Award for Best Newcomer and was short-listed for an 2013 Aurora Award by the Canadian Society of Science Fiction and Fantasy. Her most recent book is collection *Gifts for the One Who Comes After*, also from ChiZine Publications.

**Sarah Monette** grew up in Oak Ridge, Tennessee, one of the three secret cities of the Manhattan Project, and now lives in a 108-year-old house in the Upper Midwest with a great many books, two cats, one grand piano, and one husband. Her PhD diploma (English Literature) hangs in the kitchen. She has published more than fifty short stories and has two short story collections *The Bone Key* and *Somewhere Beneath Those Waves*. She has written two novels (*A Companion to Wolves* and *The Tempering of Men*) and four short stories with Elizabeth Bear, and hopes to write more. Her first four novels (*Melusine, The Virtu, The Mirador, Corambis*) were published by Ace. Her latest novel, *The Goblin Emperor*, published under the pen name Katherine Addison, came out from Tor in 2014. Visit her online at sarahmonette.com and katherineaddison.com.

Mexican by birth, Canadian by inclination. **Silvia Moreno-Garcia**'s debut novel, *Signal to Noise*, about sorcery, music, and Mexico City, was released this year by Solaris. Her first collection, *This Strange Way of Dying*, was a finalist for The Sunburst Award for Excellence in Canadian Literature of the Fantastic. She is the editor of *Fractured, Tales of the Canadian Post-Apocalypse*, and other strange works. She blogs at www.silviamoreno-garcia.com.

**Wilum H. Pugmire** has been writing like crazy ever since S. T. Joshi moved to his home town and became Pugmire's hypnotic mentor. Two new collections, *Spectres of Lovecraftian Horror* and *Monstrous Aftermath*, will be published this year. Pugmire is now busy assembling his second collection for Centipede Press, and is writing a second collection of Enoch Coffin stories with Jeffrey Thomas.

Specializing in dark fantasy and horror, **Angela Slatter** is the author of the Aurealis Award-winning *The Girl with No Hands and Other Tales*, the World Fantasy Award finalist *Sourdough and Other Stories*, Aurealis finalist *Midnight and Moonshine* (with Lisa L. Hannett), as well as *Black-Winged Angels*, *The Bitterwood Bible and Other Recountings*, and T*he Female Factory* (again with Lisa L. Hannett). Her short stories have appeared in *Fantasy, Nightmare, Lightspeed, Lady Churchill's Rosebud Wristlet, Fearie Tales, A Book of Horrors*, and Australian, UK and U.S. "best of" anthologies. She is the first Australian to win a British Fantasy Award, holds an MA and a PhD in Creative Writing, is a graduate of Clarion South and the Tin House Summer Writers Workshop, and was an inaugural Queensland Writers Fellow. She blogs at angelaslatter.com about shiny things that catch her eye.

**Michael Shea** learned to love the "genres" from the great Jack Vance's *Eyes of the Overworld*, chance-discovered in a flophouse in Juneau when Shea was twenty-one. He tilled the field of sword-and-sorcery for more than a decade (*Quest for Simbilis; In Yana, the Touch of Undying, Nifft the Lean*). Concurrently he wallowed in the delights of supernatural/extraterrestrial horror, primarily in the novella form (as can be seen in the collections *Polyphemus* and *The Autopsy and Other Tales*). In the last decade or so he added homages to H. P. Lovecraft to his novella work (as in collection *Copping Squid*.) His novel *Nifft the Lean* won a World Fantasy Award, as did novella "The Growlimb." His most recent novels are dark, satirical thrillers *The Extra* and *Assault on Sunrise*. Shea passed away on 16 February 2014.

Emmy-nominated **John Shirley** is a prolific writer of novels, short fiction, TV scripts, and screenplays who has published over three dozen novels and eight collections. His latest novels are *Doyle After Death* and his first historical novel, *Wyatt in Wichita*, which was published last year. As a musician Shirley has fronted his own bands and written lyrics for Blue Öyster Cult and others. In 2013 Black October Records released a two-CD compilation of Shirley's own recordings, *Broken Mirror Glass: The John Shirley Anthology*. See john-shirley.com for more information.

**Simon Strantzas** is the author of four collections of short fiction, including *Burnt Black Suns* from Hippocampus Press (2014), as well as the editor of *Shadows Edge* (Gray Friar Press, 2013) and *Aickman's Heirs* (Undertow Publications, 2015). His writing has been reprinted in *The Mammoth Book of Best New Horror*, *The Best Horror of the Year*, *The Year's Best Weird Fiction*, and *The Year's Best Dark Fantasy & Horror*; has been translated into other languages; and has been nominated for the British Fantasy Award. He lives in Toronto, Canada, with his wife and an unyielding hunger for the flesh of the living.

**Charles Stross** is a British SF writer, born in Leeds, England, and living in Edinburgh, Scotland. He has worked as a tech writer, a programmer, a journalist, and a pharmacist; he holds degrees in Pharmacy and in Computer Science. He has won three Hugo Awards for his fiction—including one for the novella reprinted in this volume—and his work has been extensively praised by, among others, Nobel Prize-winning economist Paul Krugman. Among Stross's more recent novels are *The Revolution Business* and *The Trade of Queens* (in his Merchant Princes series), *The Apocalypse Codex* (part of the Laundry series of novels and stories), *Rule 34,* and, with Cory Doctorow, *The Rapture of the Nerds*.

**Carrie Vaughn** is the author of the *New York Times* bestselling series of novels about a werewolf named Kitty, the fourteenth and final installment of which—*Kitty Saves the World*—will be published this summer. She's written several other contemporary fantasy and young adult novels, as well as upwards of seventy short stories. She's a contributor to the Wild Cards series of shared world superhero books edited by George R. R. Martin. An

Air Force brat, she survived her nomadic childhood and managed to put down roots in Boulder, Colorado. Visit her at www.carrievaughn.com.

**Kyla Ward** is a Sydney-based creative who works in many modes. Her latest release is *The Land of Bad Dreams*, a collection of dark poetry. Her novel *Prismatic* (co-authored as Edwina Grey) won an Aurealis Award. Her short fiction has appeared on *Gothic.net* and in the Schemers and Macabre anthologies, amongst others. Roleplaying games, short films, and plays—if you can scare people by doing it she probably has, to the extent of programming the horror stream for the 2010 Worldcon. A practicing occultist, she likes raptors, swordplay, and the Hellfire Club. To see some very strange things, try tabula-rasa.info.

**Don Webb**'s most recent book is collection *Through Dark Angles: Works Inspired by H. P. Lovecraft* (Hippocampus Press). Webb has had sixteen books and more than four hundred short stories published. He lives in Austin, Texas and teaches creative writing for UCLA Extension,

# • Acknowledgments•

"Mysterium Tremendum" © 2010 Laird Barron. First publication: *Occultation and Other Stories* (Night Shade Books, 2010).

"The Wreck of the *Charles Dexter Ward*" © 2012 Elizabeth Bear & Sarah Monette. First appearance: *The Drabblecast* #254 & #255, August/September 2012.

"The Litany of Earth" © 2014 Ruthanna Emrys. First publication: *Tor.com*, 14 May, 2014.

"Necrotic Cove" © 2013 Lois Gresh. First publication: *Black Wings III*, ed. S. T. Joshi (PS Publishing, 2013).

"The Same Deep Waters As You" © 2013 Brian Hodge. First publication: *Weirder Shadows Over Innsmouth*, ed. Stephen Jones (Fedogan & Bremer, 2013).

"The Transition of Elizabeth Haskings" © 2012 Caitlín R. Kiernan. First publication: *Sirenia Digest* #74, January 2012.

"The Boy Who Followed Lovecraft" © 2011 Marc Laidlaw. First publication: *Subterrranean Press Magazine*, Winter 2011.

"Bloom" © 2012 John Langan. First publication: *Black Wings II*, ed. S. T. Joshi (PS Publishing, 2012).

"All My Love, A Fishhook" © 2014 Helen Marshall. First publication: *Gifts for the One Who Comes After* (ChiZine Publications, 2014).

"In the House of the Hummingbirds" © 2012 Silvia Moreno-Garcia. First publication: *Lovecraft eZine*, Issue #19, November 2012.